# TOLL OF HONOR

# TOLL OF
# HONOR

## DAVID WEBER

A Baen Books Original

Baen Publishing Enterprises
P.O. Box 1403
Riverdale, NY 10471
www.baen.com

ISBN: 978-1-9821-9331-7

Cover art by David Mattingly

First printing, April 2024

Distributed by Simon & Schuster
1230 Avenue of the Americas
New York, NY 10020

Library of Congress Cataloging-in-Publication Data

Names: Weber, David, 1952- author.
Title: Toll of honor / David Weber.
Description: Riverdale, NY : Baen Publishing Enterprises, 2024. | Series: Expanded honor ; 1
Identifiers: LCCN 2023055257 (print) | LCCN 2023055258 (ebook) | ISBN 9781982193317 (hardcover) | ISBN 9781625799548 (e-book)
Subjects: LCSH: Harrington, Honor (Fictitious character)—Fiction. | Women soldiers—Fiction. | Space warfare—Fiction. | LCGFT: Science fiction. | Novels.
Classification: LCC PS3573.E217 T65 2024 (print) | LCC PS3573.E217 (ebook) | DDC 813/.54—dc23/eng/20231204
LC record available at https://lccn.loc.gov/2023055257
LC ebook record available at https://lccn.loc.gov/2023055258

Printed in the United States of America

10 9 8 7 6 5 4 3 2 1

# TOLL OF HONOR

# Book One

**HMS *Pasteur***
**Manticore Planetary Orbit**
**Manticore Binary System**
**March 17, 1905 PD**

"HOW YOU DOING THERE, Lieutenant?"

Brandy Bolgeo turned her head on the pillow and smiled. It was a worn, crooked smile, and she raised the cast on her right hand and forearm.

"I've been better, actually," she told the sick berth attendant.

"I hear that."

The petty officer tapped the display on the end of Brandy's bunk to check her chart, then nodded in satisfaction.

"I expect you're tired of hearing this, Ma'am," he said, "but you really are going to be fine. It'll take a while, but they do good work at Bassingford."

"I know." Brandy nodded. "They put my dad back together after that explosion on *Vulcan* in '97. Of course, he still had most of his original parts, except for one hand. They were busted up, but he still had them."

She looked down at the flat sheet covering the space her right leg should have occupied and grimaced.

"Hey, your chart says regen will work fine in your case!" the SBA said.

"But I'm going to be down with this for *months*." Brandy's grimace turned bitter. "This isn't the best time for any of us to take a vacation, PO!"

"Getting yourself put back together is *not* a 'vacation,' Ma'am." The SBA's tone was sterner. "It's called doing your job. And you and your people damn well earned the right to take however long it takes."

Brandy's mouth tightened as memories of all the shipmates who'd

3

never have the chance to put themselves "back together" flowed through her. HMS *Cassandra* had been brutally hit in what the newsies had dubbed the Battle of Hancock Station. Not that its name mattered a single solitary damn to anyone—like Brandy—who'd survived it. Almost a third of her crewmates aboard *Cassandra* hadn't. In fact, it was a miracle the battlecruiser herself had escaped destruction, and a quarter of her survivors—like Brandy herself— had been badly wounded. If Admiral Danislav had arrived with Battle Squadron 18's dreadnoughts even twenty minutes later than he actually had...

"You're probably right," she said after a moment. "I wish it wasn't going to take so long, but you're probably right."

"I *am* right," the SBA corrected her firmly, then smiled. "But once they get you back up on your feet—plural—do me one favor, Ma'am."

"And what would that be, PO?"

"Well, I think we do pretty good work here aboard the *Louie*, and we're always glad to be there when you need us, but we do try to discourage repeat customers. So try real hard not to end up in the body shop again, okay?"

"I think you can safely assume that's on my list of priorities." Brandy smiled back, more naturally. "This is probably something somebody should only do once."

"Actually, even if it would leave me with nothing to do, I'd prefer that people *never* did it." The SBA patted her gently on her good shoulder. "If I don't see you again before they transfer you, it's been an honor taking care of you and everyone else from Hancock. We're proud of you, Ma'am."

Brandy nodded, although she felt uncomfortable every time someone told her that. She supposed they had a point, and she knew they were sincere, but it still felt...wrong. Like she was stealing somehow from the men and women who would never come home from the Hancock System. Logically, she knew that was stupid—or at least irrational. But logic wasn't a lot of help just now.

The SBA headed on along the ward, and Brandy heard him checking in with his other patients. The enormous hospital ship had gathered in all of the Fifth Battlecruiser Squadron's wounded— including Admiral Sarnow, its commanding officer—immediately after the engagement, and they were damned lucky she'd been attached to Danislav's command. Under normal circumstances, she wouldn't have been, but given the level of tension with the People's Republic and Hancock Station's exposed position, the Admiralty had realized the odds that Danislav's squadron was sailing straight into battle were high, and Hancock's medical facilities were rudimentary, at best.

At that, though, the station's facilities had been better than the ones on *Cassandra*. After the battle, at least. Brandy's memories of the final stages of the engagement and its immediate aftermath were thankfully vague, but she remembered the battlecruiser's skinsuited sick berth attendants desperately sealing her into the emergency life-support pod as sick bay lost pressure. And she vaguely recalled the way the ship had lurched as laserhead after laserhead pounded her even as Brandy slithered down the slope into unconsciousness and wondered if she'd ever wake up again.

It was hard to believe that had happened barely ten days ago, but *Pasteur* had headed back to the Manticore Binary System within forty-six hours of the battle. Some of the damaged warships had left even before that. *Pasteur* had been delayed until search and rescue operations were officially completed, but the cripples like *Cassandra*—far too badly shot up to be combat effective but still capable of movement under their own power—had been sent directly home. Some of them were probably beyond repair, but those which *could* be repaired would be needed—desperately—as quickly as they could be returned to service.

*Too bad battlecruisers don't regenerate*, she thought. *The yard dogs on* Hephaestus *and* Vulcan *are good, but they're not miracle workers.* Cassie *snuck off before I could get a good look at her, but just from the damage she'd taken before I got clipped, she's going to be down for months. Probably almost as many as me.*

She closed her eyes, remembering her own terror amidst the roaring inferno in the ship's environmental spaces. Remembering how the ship lurched again and again as she fought her way back through the passages to her duty station in Damage Control Central. The lurid schematics, blazing bloodred with battle damage, when she got there at last. Remembering the chatter over the com. The staccato damage reports. The high-pitched stress in those voices. The voices that chopped off in mid-syllable as they took still more hits.

And then the moment the blackness fell and everything just . . . stopped.

*They try to get us ready for it. They really do. That's what the Last View is all about. But Commandant Vickers was right. They can't really prepare us.* Nobody *could.*

But at least she'd survived, she told herself. And the SBA was right. Bassingford Medical Center *did* do good work.

Maybe by the time they got done with her, she'd actually be ready to return to duty.

At the moment, she doubted it.

"I don't want you wearing him out, Sir."

The stern voice penetrated Mark Sarnow's semi-doze, and he opened his eyes. He also found himself trying not to smile, despite all the drugs floating through his system, as he saw the barrel-chested man trying to tiptoe into the compartment.

Sir Thomas Caparelli hadn't been designed by nature to tiptoe *anywhere*, Sarnow thought. As a midshipman, he'd collected at least three broken noses, two concussions, a broken shoulder, and an awesome total of yellow—and red—cards on the soccer pitches of Saganami Island, and in some ways, he'd changed very little over the ensuing decades. His weight lifter's torso and sprinter's legs were an only too accurate reflection of his preference for going through obstacles, rather than around them, and he looked ridiculous trying to sneak into an invalid's sickroom.

He was also the Royal Manticoran Navy's First Space Lord, however, and Sarnow reached for the controls to raise his bed into a sitting position.

Caparelli opened his mouth, probably to tell him to stay right where he was, but then the First Space Lord shook his head.

"I didn't mean to wake you," he said instead as the powered bed brought Sarnow upright. "And I don't think you're supposed to be sitting up yet."

"Probably not, Sir," Sarnow agreed, but he made no effort to lie back flat again, and Caparelli snorted.

Sarnow's tenor was weaker and hoarser than it ought to have been, the First Space Lord reflected. But for a man who'd lost both legs below the knee, broken all but one of his ribs, and had somewhere around a quarter kilo of splinters from his command chair's armored shell removed from his back, the admiral actually sounded far better than he'd anticipated.

"I'm not going to stay long," he said. "For one thing, your doctors would murder me if I did! For another, they're moving you dirtside in a couple of hours, so they'll need me out of your hair by then. I wanted a few words before they haul you off to Bassingford, though."

"Of course, Sir. What can I do for you?"

"The first thing you can do is not wear yourself out trying to do anything for me. Just listen."

Sarnow nodded, and Caparelli flashed a brief smile. Then his expression sobered.

"First, you and your people did magnificently," he said. "I know right now what you're feeling most is how badly you got hammered and how many of those people of yours you lost, but what you—and they—did to the Peeps was—Well, it was damned *amazing*, is what it was. We never expected them to hit you that quickly, and given Admiral Parks' dispositions—"

He shrugged, and Sarnow nodded in understanding. There were limits to how severely the First Space Lord would permit himself to criticize a station's official commander, especially before the full reports on something like Hancock were in and analyzed. Sarnow suspected a lot of *other* flag officers would be less reticent, yet the truth was that in his own opinion, the wisdom of Sir Yancey Parks' response to the Admiralty war warning could have been argued either way. It wasn't the one *he* would have chosen. In fact, it wasn't the one for which he'd argued. But given what Parks had known at the time, it hadn't been totally unreasonable. And in the aftermath, Parks had moved with commendable speed to counterattack and crush the Peeps' forward base in the Seaford System from which the attack had come.

It was unlikely that would absolve him in the Navy's eyes for what had almost happened—hell, what *had* happened—in Hancock, but at least he'd moved swiftly to claim the prize for which Sarnow's squadron had paid.

"What you may not have heard yet," Caparelli continued, "is that White Haven hammered Parnell in Yeltsin even harder than the Peeps hammered you in Seaford. They got out with almost half their fleet, but White Haven shot hell out of them before Parnell could disengage. From the tac data, it looks like at least a third of his survivors will be in the yards for months, if not longer. Between the two of you, you gave us a pair of overwhelming victories in the opening engagements. With a little luck, we'll be able to ride that while they're still off balance. At the moment, White Haven's moving from Yeltsin against Mendoza. Hopefully, he'll be able to take out Chelsea before they can redeploy, as well."

"That's good, Milord." Sarnow nodded. His voice was still weak, but satisfaction flickered in his green eyes.

"Well, I'm afraid we don't have an official declaration of war yet." Caparelli shrugged. "We should—Parliament should've given it to us the day word of Hancock hit Landing—but apparently politics are still politics." He grimaced with the sour disgust of someone whose position forced him to spend far too much time dealing with the realities of the Star Kingdom's political establishment. "I think we'll probably get it before much longer, though. Assuming the Liberals get their thumbs out, anyway." The First Space Lord's nostrils flared. "You may not believe it, but some of them are still arguing for 'the path of sanity' and 'not leaping to any hasty conclusions until we have all the information we need before we make any irrevocable decisions' despite the fact that the Peeps obviously shot first!"

From his tone, the First Space Lord was quoting someone exactly. In fact, Sarnow was pretty sure he could have guessed which of Countess New Kiev's Liberal Party peers had made the remarks. That second one, about "hasty conclusions," *had* to have come from the Earl of Dabney. The man was a pompous, sanctimonious, overprivileged windbag whose invincible confidence in his own opinions made him dangerous, in Sarnow's opinion. His dogged, unremitting opposition to every single year's Naval Estimates for the past fifteen T-years, despite the looming menace of the People's Republic of Haven, was a case in point.

On the other hand, unlike some other members of the House of Lords, like Baron High Ridge, say . . .

"Fair's fair, Sir," he said. "Don't say I agree with them, but I think a lot of them—the Liberals, I mean—are sincere."

"I'm prepared to admit *most* of them are sincere," Caparelli replied. "Not all of them, though. Especially not in the Lords. Given the company they keep there, *honesty* isn't all that high on their list. And even granting they really believe what they're spouting on the House floor, that just means they've put their heads very *sincerely* up their asses."

Sarnow chuckled, then winced, and Caparelli shook his head apologetically.

"Sorry! I don't imagine laughing does your gizzards a lot of good just now, Mark. Anyway, it won't hurt anything if they burn another couple of weeks before they vote out the formal declaration." He shrugged. "Given message transit times and deployment speeds, it'll be a while before we're ready for anything beyond the immediate counterstrikes. I've already authorized Riposte Gamma, and that's really about as far as we can go until we have better intel on what the hell the Peeps are going to do, now that their initial offensives got shot to hell."

Sarnow nodded again. The Royal Manticoran Navy believed in being both prepared and thorough when it came to defending the Star Kingdom's home star system and commerce from attack. As part of its thoroughness, it had dutifully considered the possibility of an attack by any hypothetical star nation, but it had always recognized that the only logical "hypothetical aggressor" was the People's Republic of Haven, and it had planned accordingly. The RMN had long recognized that the People's Republic would almost inevitably fire the first shot in the war against which both star nations had prepared for the last twenty T-years or so. Longer than that from Manticore's perspective; the RMN's buildup had actually begun well over half a T-century earlier, under Samantha II, ten T-years before Roger III came to the throne in 1857 PD, and it had only accelerated after Roger's death in 1883. Sixty T-years was a long time to think about something, so even though the Admiralty had always anticipated that the Peeps would shoot first, they'd given quite a lot of attention to considering just what the Star Kingdom might do in the event that Manticore—unlike any of the People's Navy's previous targets—survived that opening shot and got to shoot back.

The result was Case Riposte, a war plan whose options covered every imaginable set of circumstances. Riposte Gamma was, in fact, a far more optimistic variant than most Navy analysts had ever believed would be possible. If Caparelli had authorized Gamma,

Admiral White Haven must have inflicted truly catastrophic damage on the People's Navy when he ambushed it at Yeltsin's Star.

"All right, I should get the hell out of here so they can prep you for transport," the First Space Lord said now. "The real reason I came is that I know that if I were the one in that bed after how brilliantly my people had performed, *I'd* want to know what was happening. Especially"—Caparelli smiled warmly—"because the way they performed—the way *all* of you performed—is what's put us in a position to take the war to the enemy and kick the ever-loving shit out of him. Thank you. You did us all proud."

He held Sarnow's eyes until the admiral nodded in acknowledgment. Then he nodded back, waved one hand, and stepped back out of the compartment.

**Bassingford Medical Center**
**City of Landing**
**Planet Manticore**
**Manticore Binary System**
**March 20, 1905**

"GOT A VISITOR, Lieutenant!"

Brandy Bolgeo looked up from her book reader as Chief Petty Officer Jason Bates poked his head in through her hospital room's open door.

"It wouldn't happen to be a surly, disreputable-looking, overweight fellow going bald on top, who was once a guest in your establishment himself, would it?" she asked the senior floor nurse in a suspicious tone, and Bates chuckled.

"Actually, it is. But he's got a really nice lady with him. She *might* be able to make him behave."

"Not if it's who I'm pretty sure it is," Brandy said mournfully, setting the reader on her bedside table. "Still, I'm braced now, so I guess you'd better let him come in."

"You really are brave, Lieutenant," Bates said in suitably awed tones, then stepped aside.

"'Disreputable,' is it?" the round-faced, bearded man demanded as he walked into the room. "*Disreputable*. That's the best you could come up with after I spent an entire lifetime racking up black marks?"

"You did not spend 'an entire lifetime' racking up black marks," the dark-haired woman beside him said severely. "You didn't even join the Navy until you were twenty-three, Timmy! I realize you spent most of those years getting into trouble as a *civilian*, but the *Navy* didn't get a chance to whack you until you put the uniform on."

"I started as soon as I could," Senior Chief Petty Officer (retired) Timothy Bolgeo pointed out in an affronted tone. "And I certainly

11

did my best to make up for all that lost civilian time! I think I collected close enough to a lifetime's worth to be entitled to a little poetic license!"

"Ha! That's about the *only* poetic thing about you," Linda Bolgeo shot back. "Although," she added with a judicious air, "*they* seemed to feel obligated to make up for all that lost time, too, once they did get a chance to start whacking you."

"I rest my case," Tim said triumphantly as they crossed to the bed. Then he leaned in to hug Brandy, and she opened her arms wide. His own arms squeezed tight—tightly enough to belie the humor in his voice—and he held her close for several seconds before he inhaled deeply and stood back. He stood there, still looking down at her, until Linda gave him a pointed, none-too-gentle elbow jab. Then he twitched and moved aside with an apologetic chuckle. Linda snorted and leaned over to hug their daughter, as well, and Brandy's eyes burned as they embraced tightly.

"Sit. Sit!" she commanded then, waving at the hospital room's chairs with the lightweight splint which had replaced the cast on her right hand while her left hand swiped as unobtrusively as possible (which wasn't very) at her tears.

"So bossy!" her father replied, smiling at her as he took his wife's hand and the two of them settled obediently.

"How are you feeling, honey?" Linda asked, her expression serious, and Brandy shrugged.

"Honestly, I don't feel all that bad, Mom. I'd a lot rather not be here, of course, but aside from a little discomfort in the wrist from the quick-heal"—she waved her splint again—"nothing's actively hurting at the moment. My leg stump's starting to itch from the prep treatments, but I knew that was going to happen. *Somebody*"—she looked pointedly at her father—"spent an awful lot of time complaining about itching when he was checked in here."

"I have no idea who you could possibly be talking about," Tim said.

"You could try to look at least a *little* sincere when you lie, Timmy," Linda said.

"Ah, but that's part of my devious plan," he told her. "If I lie badly *most* of the time, it's a lot easier to sneak a lie through by lying *well* when I really need to."

"Yeah, sure." Brandy smiled at her father, and he smiled back, but she recognized the pain behind that smile. It didn't matter that she was almost thirty T-years old. What mattered was that he saw his little girl in that hospital bed.

"So, the docs all told us you really are doing well," Linda said now. "But you know you're going to be sidelined for quite a while, don't you?"

"Yes," Brandy sighed. "The quick-heal's already taken care of most of the soft tissue injuries, except for the cut in my side. Even that's a *lot* better than it was, though. Of course, it's slower on bone repairs. Which is why I'm still stuck with this." She tapped the splint with her left index finger. "Which wouldn't be such a pain if I weren't so right-handed." She rolled her eyes. "And they only started regen prep a couple of days ago. They say my profile's good, but it looks like I'm not going to respond quite as well as you did, Dad. And there's the minor fact that they have to grow me almost an entire new leg instead of just a hand I left lying around somewhere. They're talking about two months here in Bassingford—maybe even three. And then probably out-patient regen for at least another couple of months. So I'm afraid it looks like 'sidelined quite a while' is putting it mildly."

"You got that right, baby girl," Tim told her, seriously. "And when they do let you out, you're coming straight home to Liberty Crossing."

"They want me to rehab here in Bassingford's PT center, Dad, and—"

"'They' can want whatever they want," he said flatly. "What matters is what your mother and I want. We did all that work on the house while *I* rehabbed; Doc Whalen got all trained up working with me; and on top of that, your survivor's leave doesn't officially start until they certify your recovery *and* rehab." He raised his eyebrows. "I hope you weren't thinking you'd spend all that time anywhere except back home?"

Brandy looked at him, then shook her head.

"You do remember, Daddy, that I'm a commissioned Queen's officer? Which means I get to make at least a few decisions?"

"You can make all the decisions you want in the Service," he said. "But I'm not in the Service anymore, am I?" He grinned wickedly.

"No. No, you're not," Brandy acknowledged with a smile of her own. But it was a bittersweet smile, because she fully recognized the regret hiding behind her father's grin. Just as she knew exactly why he felt it . . . and why he'd left the Navy, anyway.

Senior Chief Bolgeo's twenty-seven-T-year Navy career had been a thing of legend, at least among his fellow noncoms. His extraordinary competence had been matched only by the occasionally epic occasions upon which he'd irritated officers who didn't measure up to his own standards. Those had made his career . . . interesting. Well, those and the ample collection of black marks, reprimands, and occasional demotions produced by his proclivity for hosting and participating in games of chance, especially those which revolved around playing cards. His passion was for Spades, but as long as cards were involved somewhere . . .

He'd been the sort of noncom any engineering officer would have killed to get, and his demotions had never lasted long. They had not, alas, been quite as infrequent as they might have been, however, because he'd also possessed an unequaled talent for pissing off supply officers, members of the shore patrol, and anyone else unfortunate enough to get in his way when he was locked in on a given project. But he'd loved his job, he'd loved the Navy, and as a little girl she'd known he would be a lifer.

That had been before the explosion aboard Her Majesty's Space Station *Vulcan* almost ten T-years ago, though. Brandy had been in her final year of high school when that happened, and she still remembered her mother's face when Tim's CO screened personally to tell her what had happened. And how bad it was.

Only two other members of SCPO Bolgeo's fifteen-man work party had survived, and although the disaster hadn't been his fault—the propellant explosion in the boat bay fueling system hadn't had a single thing to do with the power system his people were working on—he'd taken it hard. Hard enough that he'd sent in his papers when they finally let him out of the hospital after they finished regenerating the left hand he'd lost dragging one of those survivors out of the wreckage.

He hadn't actually left the Navy, though. As he was fond of pointing out, Bolgeos had served the Royal Manticoran Navy, one way or another, for over three hundred T-years, and he'd become a civilian—and far better paid—"double-dipper" with the Hauptman Cartel. He was currently a senior project manager for Hauptman's

Naval Services Division, and while Brandy knew he missed his own Navy career (although he would have died before admitting it), she also knew he took intense satisfaction from his current employment.

And the Navy had let him put the uniform back on long enough to give his new-minted ensign daughter her first hand salute when she graduated from Saganami Island.

"So," he said now, "since I am no longer a slave of the Service, bound to abject obedience to every petty commissioned tyrant, you can't give me orders, even if you were to be so drunk with power you made the attempt."

"I'm not so sure *you* can give *me* orders anymore, either, Daddy."

"Oh, I won't have to. I will shamelessly enlist your mother in my cause. And then you're toast."

"Dirty pool, Daddy!"

"That's because I was a sneaky, devious old senior chief rather than a guileless and innocent junior officer such as yourself."

"Oh, is *that* what it is? I always wondered."

"And now you don't have to."

"Would you two please stop it?" Linda Bolgeo asked. Brandy looked at her, and she shook her head. "They won't let us stay forever. In fact, they told us you have a regen treatment scheduled in less than an hour, Brandy. So could you two stop teasing each other long enough for us to have an actual visit?"

"Oh, I imagine we could," Brandy agreed.

"You're right, Linda."

Tim patted his wife on the knee. Then he looked back at his daughter, and his expression turned more serious.

"You wouldn't know this yet, Brandy, but Hauptman Navy's been clearing repair slips to handle some of the damaged units coming in. *Cassandra's* one of them."

Brandy's eyes darkened, and he nodded.

"I've got the seniority, now, honey. I put in for supervision on her repairs, and they gave her to me."

"I'm—" Brandy had to pause and clear her throat. "I'm glad she's in such good hands."

"Well, what kind of father doesn't look after his daughter's ride?" Tim flashed her a smile. It was brief. "I've walked the ship," he continued then. "I've seen what happened to Damage Control." For just a moment, his face might have been sculpted from iron. "Baby girl, I don't know how in God's name you got out of there alive. I really, truly don't. But I've spent so much time on my knees since I saw that compartment—"

His voice cracked, broke, and the iron crumbled. Brandy felt her own eyes burn and opened her arms once more. He crossed to the bed in a single stride, and she wrapped her left arm around him while she held her right out to Linda. An instant later, her mother was burrowed into the same embrace, and she pressed her face into their shoulders.

"It's okay, Daddy," she whispered. "It's *okay*. I'm gonna be fine!"

"I know that," he said. He straightened and cleared his throat. "Really, I do. But I'm a dad and your mom's a mom, and you're our daughter, and we came way too close to losing you. And that's why you're damned well coming home to Liberty Crossing when they let you out of this healing palace! You're not going back out to be shot at again before we have a chance to love on you properly."

"Okay," she said with a wavery smile. "Okay, you win."

"Always knew you took after your mom where the smarts were concerned."

"Mom, I'm not *positive* that's a compliment to either of us."

"The heck it isn't!" Tim looked at her quizzically. "Why do you think I've always called her 'She Who Must Be Obeyed in Liberty Crossing'?"

"Because you're smarter than you look?" Brandy suggested with a more natural smile.

"And just how hard would *that* be?" her mother asked with a laugh, reaching out to lay one palm against the side of Tim's face.

"Hey, I'm a Bolgeo, and Bolgeo males always face a . . . somewhat steeper intellectual challenge than other people. But we almost always rise to it. Why, the very first Manticoran Bolgeo was proof of that!"

"Oh, God!" Linda rolled her eyes. "You're not going to trot that out again, Timmy?"

"It's a critical piece of our family history!" Tim raised his nose with a sniff. Then he cocked his head. "And, actually, considering BatCruRon Five's flag captain, it's almost part of the same tradition!"

Brandy shook her head, but this time, she had to admit her father might have a point. Maybe only a tiny one, but a point.

The Bolgeo Clan was one of the Star Kingdom's larger yeoman

families. It boasted thriving branches on both Gryphon and Sphinx, it had contributed solidly, in its own modest way, to building the Star Kingdom's prosperity, and—counting her—there were currently over a dozen Bolgeos, commissioned and enlisted, on active duty in Her Majesty's Navy. But her very first Manticoran ancestor had come with what might have been conservatively described as a checkered past. When Dr. Tennessee Bolgeo immigrated to the Star Kingdom in 1521, almost four T-centuries ago, he hadn't meant to stay at all. In fact, he'd come for the express purpose of capturing specimens of the newly discovered Sphinx treecats and then smuggling them off-planet for off-world exotic animal dealers when he left.

Like many who'd come after him, he'd discovered there were safer things to attempt to trap, and he'd very nearly ended up dead when the treecat clan whose members he'd been stalking goaded a hexapuma into attacking him. In fact, he *would* have been killed, if a fourteen-year-old girl hadn't just happened to be present to shoot and kill the hexapuma, instead.

After which she'd held him at gunpoint until the Sphinx Forestry Service arrived to take him into custody.

That moment had been something of an epiphany for Dr Bolgeo, and when the Crown indicted him for poaching and conspiracy to smuggle exotic animals off-planet (the 'cats' sentience hadn't yet been acknowledged, so at least they hadn't charged him with kidnapping), he pled guilty without a whimper and asked for community service. They'd still given him a couple of T-years of jail time, but then he'd had another eight T-years of supervised probation during which he had, indeed, done community service. In fact, he'd put his genuine, not inconsiderable skills as a xenobiologist to good use and become a consultant to the Sphinx Forestry Service, working specifically (at his own request) with treecats. The 'cats had forgiven him. In fact, he'd become a frequent visitor with Bright Water Clan, and an elderly Tennessee Bolgeo had emerged from his well-earned retirement as one of the expert witnesses who'd testified in support of the Ninth Amendment when it was finally drafted forty T-years later.

And he'd also become a close personal friend of that fourteen-year-old girl . . . whose name had been Stephanie Harrington.

Brandy hadn't really thought about that when *Cassandra* was assigned to BatCruRon 5, but she'd thought about it since. And she'd come to the conclusion that the near-pine-cone didn't fall far from the tree where Harringtons were concerned.

*Which might just be true where* Bolgeos *are concerned, too, now that I think about it,* she reflected, gazing at her father. He even *looked* like the handful of old-style holopics of Tennessee Bolgeo.

"You know, I have to say I think Dame Stephanie would've been pretty darned proud of Dame *Honor*," she said, speaking her thoughts out loud.

"Damn straight." Tim Bolgeo's expression was sober and he nodded sharply. "You wouldn't believe some of the stuff I'm hearing about that battle."

"What kind of stuff?"

Brandy looked at him intently. Her father might have retired from the Navy, but he'd been a member in good standing of the senior chiefs' mess, and he still had better sources in the Service than anyone else she knew.

"Well, the official report's not out yet," he said. "Won't be for a while. But if a couple of people who screened me when they heard about how hard you'd been hit at Hancock are right, it's gonna be a shitstorm when it hits the 'faxes."

"Language, Tim," Linda said. But she said it in a resigned I-know-it's-futile-but-I-won't-give-up-the-fight sort of tone, and Brandy's lips twitched despite her father's expression.

"Why?" she asked. "We did exactly what we were there to do. Oh, we were supposed to scatter and run for it if the Peeps kept coming, but Captain Quinlan briefed all of his officers on the ops plan. The main thing was to draw them away from the station and over the minefield, not give them a stand-up fight, of course. No way we could've gone toe-to-toe with wallers! And I'll admit I expected the order to go ahead and scatter when the mines didn't stop them. But as soon as Captain Quinlan came up on the com to tell us Admiral Danislav had dropped out of hyper, I knew Admiral Sarnow wouldn't give it. *All* of us knew he wouldn't. Not when he realized he could lead them into a trap if he *didn't* scatter!"

"Really?" Tim looked at her. "You know *Nike* got hit? That Sarnow's two floors up from your room?"

"Yeah." Brandy nodded. "That happened . . . maybe a minute or two before the *Cassie* got clobbered."

"It also happened before you reached the scatter point."

"Wait." Brandy's eyes narrowed. "You're saying Admiral Sarnow *didn't* make the call for us to stay concentrated? Keep sucking the Peeps in?"

"That's exactly what I'm saying, honey." Tim nodded. "And according to my sources, neither did Captain Rubenstein, the only battlecruiser division CO still on his feet. It was Harrington."

"Dame Honor?" Brandy's eyebrows rose.

"Yep. The most junior battlecruiser captain left. *She's* the one who decided not to break and run. And I have to say I've got mixed feelings about that. She's the reason the battle was such a disaster for the Peeps, but she's also the one who kept you guys concentrated until my one and only daughter damned near got herself killed. On balance, I approve. I'm not so sure everybody else will. In fact, from what I'm hearing, some people are already bitching that she should've passed command to Rubenstein when Sarnow went down. That it wasn't her job to make that decision."

"But she was his flag captain," Brandy said. "If anybody in the entire task group knew what the Admiral was thinking, it was her!"

"I didn't say she was wrong," Tim said, cocking his head at her as he heard the sharp edge in her voice.

"Sorry, Dad." Brandy shook her head quickly. "It's just—I didn't get to actually *meet* her, but Janet did," she said, and Tim nodded in understanding. Lieutenant Janet Briscoe had been one of her closest friends since Saganami Island, and she'd also been HMS *Cassandra's* assistant tactical officer during the battle. "You know Janet's not the kind to impress easily, but Dame Honor pulled it off!"

"Can't say that surprises me, given Harrington's reputation. I served on Basilisk Station before she moved in and straightened out that rolling cluster—"

He glanced at his wife from the corner of one eye.

"Before she restored order, there, I mean," he said instead, after only the briefest pause. "And Petros Gianakis was an electronics tech in *Fearless* when she went up against a battlecruiser with a *heavy* cruiser at Yeltsin. Far as he's concerned, the only reason she doesn't walk across the Tannerman Ocean for light exercise is that she doesn't like wet feet!"

Brandy chuckled at her father's expression, but she also nodded.

"I'd say that sums up Janet's opinion of her, too."

"Well, there'll still be hell to pay, if what I'm hearing is accurate," Tim said much more seriously. "You know the real reason you got hit so hard? The real reason your mother and I damned near lost you?"

"Dad, it could've happened to anybody, and—"

"The reason it happened to *you*, sweetheart, is because a fucking coward panicked and ran."

Brandy stiffened in astonishment. But then she realized her mother hadn't even tried to correct her father's language this time. In fact, Linda Bolgeo's expression was a mirror of her husband's.

"What are you talking about?" she asked slowly.

"Your primary screening unit was CruRon Seventeen, right?" Tim raised an eyebrow, and Brandy nodded. "Well, Commodore Van Slyke was already dead by the time Danislav arrived. So command devolved on Captain Young. Captain *Lord* Pavel Young. And his ship took a hit—*one* fucking hit. And he ordered his squadron to scatter without orders from the Flag. They pulled out, Brandy. They pulled out; they opened a hole for the missiles that damned near killed your entire ship. And when Captain Harrington ordered him back into formation, the worthless piece of shit went right on running. The *rest* of his ships returned, which is probably the only reason *Cassandra* wasn't destroyed outright, but he and *Warlock* just kept running. And the Peeps' fire ignored him, because one heavy cruiser with a coward for a captain was worth a whole lot less than the rest of your task group."

Brandy's good hand rose to her lips, covering her mouth, and her tears blurred her vision as her parents looked unflinchingly back at her.

"Like I say," Tim continued after a moment, "the official after-action report hasn't been issued yet, and I doubt it will be for a while. Given what I'm hearing, Admiral Parks is going to have to convene a formal board of inquiry into what happened before he can issue one, and he won't be able to do that till he gets back to Hancock from Seaford and gets a chance to assemble all the witnesses. That's gonna take a lot longer than anybody likes, and even after he can, they are for *damned* sure gonna take the time to dot all the i's and cross all the t's on this one, because I know the Navy. If they don't hammer that worthless SOB for this, the Service will *never* forgive the Admiralty. And if they don't have an airtight case, with every single thing nailed down, there's gonna be a *lot* of pressure for a whitewash instead."

"What?!" Brandy looked at him incredulously, and he snorted harshly.

"Young's the son—and heir—of an earl, Brandy. You're from Gryphon. What do *you* think'll happen if his 'noble' father finds out the JAG intends to file charges?"

"A 'shitstorm,' I think you said," Brandy replied after a moment. "And you're right; they'll pull out *all* the stops to save him. But if that *is* what happened, they have to try him. I don't care whose son he is. And if they convict him, they damned well have to shoot him!"

She heard the raw fury in her own voice, and her father nodded again.

**Admiralty House**
**Office of the First Space Lord**
**City of Landing**
**Planet Manticore**
**Manticore Binary System**
**July 11, 1905 PD**

"SO THAT'S CONFIRMED?"

Sir Thomas Caparelli leaned back in the comfortable chair behind his enormous, immaculately organized desk.

"As close to it as it can be at this point," Admiral Patricia Givens replied. Givens was the Second Space Lord, the second-ranking uniformed member of the Star Kingdom's military. She was also the commanding officer of the Office of Naval Intelligence. Now she shrugged.

"The 'news organs' in the People's Republic have always been at least as much official mouthpieces as anything coming out of the Solarian League. Maybe even more. Some of the Solly newsies at least *try* to pretend they're part of an independent press; the Peep 'news services' have always just said whatever they're told to say, and all indications are that the one doing the telling right now is this lunatic Ransom. To be honest, we don't have much on her over at ONI. Hell, we don't have much on *any* of this new 'Committee of Public Safety's' members. We were too busy keeping track of Legislaturalists and the officers in their navy to even try to keep an eye on the various revolutionaries. Especially the ones hiding from the Peeps' own cops! All we really know—or think we do, at least—is that she came out of the Citizens Rights movement and up to the coup, she was almost at the very top of InSec's most-wanted terrorist list. We happen to have considerably more info on Pierre himself, though, because he was one of the biggest—if not simply *the* biggest—of the Dolist managers. That gave him a lot of clout under the old regime, and personally, I

23

think that supports the theory some of my analysts have put forward that he was the prime mover all along."

"So these analysts of yours don't think it was Parnell and the Peoples Navy?"

"If it was, they have to have been the most inept naval planners in history," Givens said grimly. "Which, judging by their track record over the last half T-century or so, they weren't."

She had a point, Caparelli reflected. Oh, the Peep Navy had always been a blunt instrument that eschewed anything like the scalpel of finesse when the chainsaw of brute force would work. What had happened to it in Hancock and Yeltsin, when its planners *had* tried for finesse, would probably have confirmed it in that institutional mindset. Assuming that any of those planners would ever have had the opportunity to analyze what had happened to them, at least.

Which, assuming Givens' sources were correct, they wouldn't.

"Whoever it really was," Givens continued now, "they took out President Harris and his entire government in the initial airstrike. If the Navy had been behind it, there would have been a follow-through, and there wasn't. Unless, of course, there *was* a follow-through and its name was Robert Stanton Pierre. I think he was behind the entire thing. And I think Internal Security had to be in on it with him, especially since InSec's been credited with taking down the assassins' shuttles—which just happened to eliminate anyone who could have testified about what really went down—and Oscar Saint-Just happens to be the only member of the Harris Cabinet who wasn't at the birthday party to get killed in the attack. Oh, and then there's the minor fact of how immediately Saint-Just threw his own support behind Pierre and this committee of his 'for the duration of the emergency.' But there's not a doubt in my mind that Pierre's the one who organized it. I think he knew about their navy's preoccupation with the impending offensive against us and took advantage of it when he and Saint-Just set it up. And then the two of them blew the crap out of the Harris government—except for Saint-Just, of course—and *pinned* it on the uniforms."

"To give him a pretext to purge the Navy, because it was the only organized force he didn't control that might have opposed him," Caparelli said thoughtfully.

"Oh, not just the Navy." Givens' eyes were grimmer than ever. "I mean, I think you're absolutely right, but the Navy's not all he's purging. Our network in the People's Republic's taken a real hit out of all of this, mostly because of how focused we'd been on the Navy and—on the political side—the Legislaturalists, but we're still getting some agent reports. They've always taken a while to get to us just because of the distances involved, and the delay in transit's even greater since we started actually shooting at each other. But all the ones I'm seeing emphasize that Pierre's going after all of the Legislaturalist families. He's taking them *all* down, Tom, and indications are that he's being one hell of a lot more ruthless about *how* he takes them down than they ever were about getting rid of their own opponents. I think we're going to see a lot fewer 'reeducation orders' and a lot more death sentences. And a lot more anonymous 'disappearances,' too."

"You think he's going after them just to free his own hand? Or because he's a genuine revolutionary reformer, like our good friend Countess New Kiev thinks?"

"I'm not sure 'New Kiev' and the verb 'thinks' belong in the same sentence," Givens said bitterly. "In answer to your question, though, I know Pierre's issuing statements in every direction—well, Ransom's issuing them in his name, anyway—about how dedicated his new Committee is to 'reforming the old system's abuses' and 'putting an end to the militarism which has burdened the People for far too long.' And, no, I can't *prove* it, but just between you, me, and these four walls"—she raised both hands, gesturing at the spacious office's walls—"he's lying out his ass."

"Really? Why?" Caparelli asked. Her eyes widened with what might have been disbelief, and he waved his hands. "Didn't say I disagreed. Just wondering if your logic matches mine, because New Kiev does have a point that he's saying all the right things for a 'true voice of reform.'"

"He is," Givens acknowledged in a slightly grudging tone. "And, in fairness, I suppose what I should have said is that he's lying his ass off if he truly thinks he can get away with that. Mind you, I don't believe he *is* a true reformer, but that could be my biases speaking. I'm sort of programmed to distrust *any* official policy statement from a Peep. Having said that, though, I think, first, that he's too much a captive of the old system because of his position in it. Second, from the sound of things, the only 'reforms' he's going to be able to put in place with a hope in hell of their standing will have to be pretty damned draconian, which means the People's Republic will only get more ruthless and despotic, not less. But third—and the one I think trumps every other consideration—is that pretty damned soon the Nouveau Paris mob is going to turn on *him*, now that it's tasted blood, unless he can point it at someone else. Preferably an *external* someone else. Like us." She shook her head, her eyes dark. "No matter how benign his motives may have been to start—mind, I don't think they were, but let's admit the possibility—sooner or later he's going to need what every dictator needs: a foreign enemy."

"That's my own impression." Caparelli pursed his lips. "On the other hand, there are those who might question my judgment in a case like this. One thing I'm *not* is a political analyst."

"That's not my strongest suit, either," Givens acknowledged, "but that's all some of my people over in ONI do. And while I personally long to someday once again become an honest naval officer, I've spent too many years looking at how politics and the Peep Navy's military posture interface, myself, since they made me a spook. So, yeah, I've had to develop at least some feel for them. And I'm telling you that Pierre and his frigging Committee will say whatever they think they need to say to keep us from shooting them all dead while they reorganize their military. They need one they can count on to shore them up domestically, and they'll need one for that 'foreign enemy' when the time comes to point the mob outward.

"In some ways, that's good, from our perspective. No matter what they do, these purges of theirs will bite their military efficiency right on the ass, because it's costing them so many experienced senior officers. But if he manages to make this new regime of his stand up, then eventually he'll start building up a stable of new commodores and admirals. And if he demonstrates that he's totally prepared to shoot anybody who fails to perform adequately, they'll be motivated as hell." She shook her head again. "We've got a window—the time it'll take him to do that—in which their Navy's in disarray, during which their efficiency will go straight into the crapper. It's not going to last, but it's starting to open even wider right now."

"And if *we* can see the writing on the wall, their senior officers certainly can, too," Caparelli mused. "I'm sure the ones he hasn't already gotten around to shooting or arresting have to be looking over their shoulders."

"You might say that."

Something about Givens' tone raised Caparelli's eyebrows, and she snorted harshly.

"We're starting to pick up what are probably feelers from some of the Peep system picket commanders," she said. "They're being cautious and circuitous as hell, but I think where some of them are headed is an offer to surrender their command areas to us if we promise *we* won't shoot them."

"Seriously? And if so, why is this the first I'm hearing about it?"

"This is the first you're hearing about it because yesterday afternoon was the first time *I* heard about it. And I have to point out that even if that's really what's happening, I doubt the offers will come from any of the truly critical systems. The ones farther inside the frontier, closer to Nouveau Paris, for example. Partly that's because the COs in those systems have much larger covering forces, which means they'd have to figure out how to convince a lot more officers and enlisted to go along with them. But there are also indications that when Pierre and his Committee sent dispatches to people outside the home system to tell them what had happened to Harris they sent orders to arrest as many senior officers as possible right along with them. And they made sure those dispatches—and orders—went to the most critical systems—like Barnett and Trevor's Star—first. If they'd given somebody like Parnell a couple of weeks—hell, just a few days!—to really think about what happened in Nouveau Paris, he'd have organized the Navy to shoot every one of the bastards dead. In fact, I think the . . . expeditious way he and his senior officers were taken into custody is one more straw in the wind pointing to how carefully somebody—somebody named 'Pierre'—planned and orchestrated this entire thing."

"Damn." Caparelli shook his head. "I wouldn't have shed a single tear if White Haven had blown Amos Parnell straight to hell in Yeltsin. But he never deserved this, if you're right about what's going on."

"I know." Givens nodded. "And then there's the minor fact that revolutionary regimes—especially those who need to prop up their authority at home—tend to be one hell of a lot more ruthless and extreme than regimes which are simply venal and corrupt. They may not be doing it right this instant, because they *really* want to buy as much time as they can before we amp up to full naval operations against them, but I guarantee you they'll go the full press 'foreign threat' route as soon as they think they can. And the fact that the Legislaturalists' propaganda's painted us as the enemy for so long will only make that even easier for them."

"Oh, thank you for pointing that out!"

"Unfortunately, it comes with my job description."

"I know—I know!" Caparelli shook his head. "But hearing what you've just said doesn't make me one bit happier with the political equation right here in Landing."

"I haven't been paying as much attention to our politics as I have to the Peeps', but from what I *have* seen, I'd have to agree with you. What does Baroness Morncreek think is happening with the declaration?"

Lady Francine Maurier, Baroness Morncreek, was First Lord of the Admiralty, although, technically, in her case it was First *Lady* of the Admiralty. Regardless of the finely parsed nuances of her title, she was the civilian head of the Royal Navy. Under another constitution, she would have been the Minister of the Navy, which, given the Navy's status as the Star Kingdom's senior service, made her the equivalent of most other star nations' ministers of war.

She was also a very smart woman who happened to be extremely unhappy at the moment.

"Given what you said a few minutes ago about those statements Pierre's issuing, it's probably not surprising the Liberals are dug in to delay any formal declaration of war," Caparelli said. "And without one, of course, I can't authorize any offensive operations outside Riposte Gamma's immediate moves. Those were already in the pipeline under our prewar standing orders and authorizations; anything more really requires a declaration of hostilities. Oh, I can take some additional steps, make a few more moves, close in on some of the forward bases we know the Peeps've been staging strikes through, but we'd be getting into a *really* iffy situation if we violated their prewar territory instead of just sparring between our borders. And let's not forget the minor inconvenience that our peacetime budget couldn't sustain actual combat operations for more than a couple of months, so without additional funding..."

He shrugged, and Givens nodded gloomily. It wasn't as if he was telling her anything she didn't already know.

"Duke Cromarty, Chancellor Alexander—and the Crown—are leaning on New Kiev and her idiots for all they're worth, but it looks to me like the idiots in question are too busy posturing for their political base to get on with the minor matter of actually fighting a war. To be fair—which, mind you, is the *last* thing I want to be—part of that's because they're stupid enough, or at least sufficiently ill-informed about us Neanderthal militarists and how wars work—that they think there's plenty of time. They think the Peeps self-inflicted wounds are doing so much damage that we'll be able to kick their asses without breaking a sweat whenever they finally get around to letting us. And as far as I can tell, they don't think there's any expiration date on that credit chip."

"Oh . . . my . . . God."

"Exactly," Caparelli said harshly. "Even worse, as far as I can tell, at least some of them—like that idiot Reginald Houseman and his merry band of 'military experts'—genuinely believe that if we only 'give peace a chance' Pierre will realize he's done so much damage to his own military that the only smart thing for him to do is to stand down. Which is even stupider of them, in a lot of ways, even leaving aside that bit about his needing an external enemy. Exactly how they expect him to sustain the People's Republic's economy after the way it's been run into the ground for the last T-century or so *without* conquering new revenue sources is beyond me, but, then, I'm only an ignorant knuckle-dragging naval officer."

"How long does the Baroness think this is going to drag out?" Givens' tone betrayed her anxiety, and Caparelli snorted.

"Not a whole lot longer." He allowed his chair to come upright. "The Duke still commands a working majority in the Lords. It's not sufficient to prevent the Liberals' filibustering, and he doesn't have enough votes to invoke cloture, but once they finally stop gassing away, he's got enough peers behind him to carry the declaration. His Centrists have an absolute majority in the Commons, too, and whatever people like Dabney and Winstainley may think, New Kiev realizes it would be suicidal for their lower house representation if their peers don't eventually at least stop delaying the declaration vote. They don't have to vote *for* it and alienate their hardcore base, but they're going to piss off enough swing voters and independents to get killed in the next general election if they delay things much longer. Especially"—his expression hardened—"when the fighting *does* go full bore, the casualty totals start coming back, and anyone with a functional brain realizes how much lower they would've been if we'd been able to begin full-scale offensive operations now, before Pierre has a chance to consolidate." He shrugged. "Lady Morncreek's best guess is that it'll probably be another week to ten days."

"Well, we've already lost enough opportunities that another couple of weeks probably won't hurt us a lot worse," Givens said. "I'd hate to see it get stretched out any farther than that, though!"

"Me, too." Caparelli nodded. "In fact I—"

His desktop com chimed, and he broke off to glance at his chrono. Then he grimaced and tapped to accept the call.

"I'm sorry, Sir," his flag secretary said from the com, "but Admiral Cortez is here for his thirteen hundred meeting."

"Thank you, Chris. Ask him to come on in, please."

"Yes, Sir."

Caparelli stood and extended his hand to Givens.

"As always, concise and to the point," he said. "I won't pretend I enjoyed hearing most of that, but that's hardly your fault."

"Fair's fair, Sir." Givens smiled crookedly. "I didn't much like hearing Baroness Morncreek's take on the declaration."

"Then we're even," Caparelli told her. "And"—the First Space Lord turned his head to smile a greeting at Admiral Sir Lucien Cortez, the *Fifth* Space Lord—"I don't expect I'll much like hearing what Lucien has to say, either." He grimaced. "There's a lot of that going around right now."

Givens' smile got a little more crooked, but then it faded as she saw Cortez's expression. The one thing the Fifth Space Lord didn't look even remotely amused by was Caparelli's quip.

"Lucien?" she said.

"Pat." Cortez nodded to her, but his eyes were on Caparelli. "I'm afraid you're *really* not going to like this, Sir," he said.

"Why?" Caparelli asked.

"Excuse me," Givens interrupted before Cortez could reply. "Is this something the two of you need to discuss privately? I mean, personnel isn't really my bailiwick, and if you'll forgive me, Lucien, you look like a man who's about to drop a tactical nuke."

"I see what makes you such a keenly observant intelligence analyst, Pat," Cortez said. "But it's not like what I'm about to say won't be public knowledge entirely too soon. And I'm thinking the Admiral can probably use all the input he can get before he takes it to Baroness Morncreek . . . and she takes it to the Prime Minister."

Caparelli's eyes widened. So did Givens', and the two of them looked at one another for a moment. Then Caparelli inhaled and pointed at the chairs facing his desk.

"Sit back down, Pat. It sounds like something new has been added."

"Yes, Sir."

She sank back into her chair, and the diminutive Fifth Space Lord settled into the one beside hers. Actually, he perched on the edge of the cushion and leaned forward, his expression intent.

"All right, Lucien," Caparelli said, and made a beckoning, go-ahead gesture with his right hand.

"Yancey Parks' official report is finally in." Cortez's voice was flat, harsh. "I've just come from Long Hall. Alyce Cordwainer and I used the ATTC's holotank to view his inquiry's findings and the accompanying sensor records."

Caparelli's expression congealed into a mask. The Fifth Space Lord commanded the Bureau of Personnel, which made him responsible for the management and administration of the Navy's manpower. Just as Naval Intelligence came under the Second Space Lord's oversight, the office of the Judge Advocate came under the umbrella of BuPers. And Vice Admiral The Honorable Alyce Cordwainer happened to be the Royal Manticoran Navy's Judge Advocate General, its highest ranking jurist.

Given the preliminary reports Caparelli had already viewed . . .

"How bad is it?" he asked after a moment.

"I don't think it gets any worse," Cortez said grimly. "It's taken too damned long—mostly because the combination of the operational tempo and transit times kept him from freeing up the number of captains Regs required to seat a board on Young's actions. But now that it's been seated and had a chance to look at the testimony and the records, it's confirmed everything we'd heard about Young. The miserable bastard panicked. He pulled out—he *ran*. Hell, he not only ran, he ignored a direct order from the task group flagship to return to formation. One his *exec* clearly heard because we have him on record trying his damnedest to shame Young into getting back on station! Which, of course, Young *also* ignored so he could keep on running. And the fact that he did contributed directly to the loss of at least three more ships and almost all of the damage *Cassandra* suffered. God only knows how many of our people got killed because of it, but Parks' minimum estimate is that it cost us *at least* seven hundred KIA."

"Shit," Caparelli said flatly.

"Oh, yeah." Cortez nodded. "You know Alyce isn't the sort to go off half-cocked, but I don't think I've ever seen her as pissed as she was after we finished reviewing the statements, testimony, and, especially, the tac data and com traffic. As she sees it, we have no choice but to charge Young under Articles Fourteen, Fifteen, Nineteen, Twenty-Three, *and* Twenty-Six."

Cortez winced.

The Twenty-Third and Twenty-Sixth Articles "only" defined the crimes of breaking off action with the enemy without orders . . . and disobedience to the direct orders of a superior. An officer *could* be shot for either offense, although the Navy would probably settle for simply cashiering him. But the Fourteenth, Fifteenth, and Nineteenth Articles of War defined "desertion in the face of the enemy" and formally categorized it as high treason.

And the penalty for *that* crime happened to be death, without provision for "or such lesser penalty as the Court shall decree."

"Well, isn't that lovely," Givens murmured.

"It's a sack of snakes, is what it is," Cortez said. "North Hollow will pull out all the stops to save his worthless scum of a son. And Janacek and that entire crowd will line up to help him. It's going to be a three-ring circus. Or maybe a *Roman* circus, complete with gladiators!"

"I know." Caparelli pinched the bridge of his nose, then lowered his hand. "I know. But we've got it to do, assuming Parks' report is as conclusive as you seem to be saying, Lucien."

"It doesn't get much more conclusive, Sir."

"Great."

Caparelli laid his hands flat on his desk with an expression of disgust. And of self-recrimination.

"This is our fault," he said bitterly. "Yes, it's going to be a mess, but we should have put Young on half-pay years ago. There was plenty of evidence that he was a waste of oxygen, and we should have acted on it long before we ever got to this point. Right after that business in Basilisk, at the very latest! If there's ever been a better example of an overbred cretin using his family connections to cover his incompetence, I've never seen it."

"With all due respect, Sir, you weren't sitting in that chair when Young did his damnedest to put a knife in Captain Harrington's back," Cortez pointed out.

"No, but I've been sitting in it for a while since then. And I should have—for that matter, *Jim Webster* should have—sent him dirtside and kept him there to rot instead of just shuttling him off to places where we figured he couldn't do much harm. We'd never've gotten away with it when Janacek was First Lord, but Morncreek would've backed us. And don't bother telling me we had bigger fish to fry than worrying about one incompetent, self-serving senior-grade captain. I seem to recall that you actually recommended putting him on half-pay, Lucien. And I let it drop, because trying to get the Navy back onto a war-fighting footing and keep it there once we got rid of Janacek was more important than the dogfight I knew North Hollow would organize if we decided we couldn't find a ship for his precious baby boy."

Cortez had started to interrupt, but he closed his mouth and sat back after Caparelli's last two sentences.

"You know, I agree with everything you just said, Tom," Givens said, "but the really ironic—in the most bitter possible sense of the word I can imagine—aspect of this whole thing is that it's Harrington he tried to shaft both times."

"It's personal for him," Cortez said. "For both of them, by now, although I've never seen Harrington deviate one centimeter from her duty to do anything about it. But Basilisk wasn't the first time he tried to ruin her career, Pat. It goes all the way back to the Academy."

"Really?"

"Yeah. It's pretty common knowledge in certain circles that there's bad blood between them, but it goes a lot deeper than just 'bad blood.' I don't think most people know how it all started, but the records over at BuPers are pretty clear for anyone who knows how to read between the lines. He and his family have been trying to derail her career ever since Saganami Island, and I got curious enough to go back and try to figure out why." His grimace was heavy with disgust. "Let's just say it's pretty clear she kicked his ass—literally—in the *women's* showers one night."

Givens' eyes widened, then narrowed, and he nodded grimly.

"She never filed official charges against him. Probably because she figured no one would take her word—or admit they did—if she accused the son of someone like North Hollow of attempted rape. She was wrong about that. I hope she realizes that now, and I wish to hell she *had* filed charges, but she was only eighteen at the time." Cortez grimaced again, this time angrily. "But even if she didn't report him, she definitely sent him to the infirmary that night, unless we want to believe the official story that he fell down a flight of stairs. Two or three tunes, judging by the damages."

Givens snorted in obvious satisfaction, and Cortez shrugged.

"I'm pretty sure you can imagine how someone like a Young took that. Worse, every time he's gone up against her directly since, he's gotten his ass kicked all over again, if with a little less...ah, direct physical contact. And all three of us know how her career's taken off since Basilisk, while his went straight into the crapper, where it belonged. All of which only makes someone like him even more determined to 'get even.'

"It doesn't look to me like that was his sole motivation—probably not even his *primary* motivation—in this case. I think it's abundantly clear—and I'm pretty damned sure both of you will agree with me on that, once you've had a chance to view the com traffic—that what was really driving him was cowardice. Terror. To be crude about it, he ran for his fucking life." Cortez's eyes were arsenic-bitter. "That's the reason I think we don't have any choice but to shoot the son-of-a-bitch this time. But having said that, I'm pretty sure that how deeply he hates Harrington was right up there with his cowardice. And you can add in the fact that *she* was the one ordering him back into formation."

He shrugged again, this time with more than an edge of angry resignation.

"You're probably right," Caparelli said heavily, after a moment. "And calling it a sack of snakes is probably the worst case of understatement I've heard in a long time. But it doesn't sound like we've got much choice."

"I don't see one, anyway," Cortez agreed. He drew a data chip folio from his pocket and laid it on Caparelli's desk. "Alyce is keeping all of this as closely held as possible. There's got to be some distribution in her own shop, but nothing's going out of it any way except by hand transmission. That's your copy of the report and her recommendations, Sir, and they aren't going to get any better when you actually view them."

"How long do we have to do the prep work?" the First Space Lord asked, and tapped his desk blotter smart screen to bring up his official calendar.

"Parks is being reinforced with another dreadnought division. As soon as they arrive, he'll be releasing the last of the units damaged at Hancock for repairs," Cortez said, and Caparelli nodded. Several of Parks' units —well, *Sarnow's*, actually—had damage that would require extensive yard time but hadn't been bad enough to render them combat ineffective under the current circumstances. Until there'd been time to reinforce Parks, he'd had no choice but to hold onto them out at the sharp end.

"According to our best current estimates, they should be arriving back here in the home system in another three weeks or so," Cortez continued.

"So around the first of the month," Caparelli murmured, gazing down at his calendar.

"About then, yes, Sir."

"Great." Caparelli sighed and tapped the calendar again, updating it with the estimated arrival date for his yeoman, then grimaced. "Hell of a way to start a new month," he said.

"I hope we *get* to next month before it hits the fan, Sir," Givens said somberly. Caparelli glanced up at her, and she shrugged unhappily, eyes bitter. "Vice Admiral Cordwainer's absolutely right about the need to keep this as tightly held as possible, but all three of us know there are still too many Janacek loyalists hidden away in one

Admiralty cubbyhole or another. Hell, I could probably name half a dozen of them right off the cuff, and I know damned well we haven't ID'ed *all* of them. And Janacek and North Hollow have been friends—well, allies—for decades. So it's not a question of *if* Cordwainer's recommendation's going to leak; it's only a question of *when*."

"And of how ugly it gets when it does," Caparelli agreed with an unhappy nod. "Oh, thank you *so* much for pointing that out to us, Pat!"

"One of my jobs," she said. "And, frankly, Sir, there are times I'm a lot happier to have *my* job instead of yours."

**Bolgeo Homestead**
**Liberty Crossing**
**Henderson Highlands**
**Planet Gryphon**
**Manticore Binary System**
**July 15, 1905 PD**

"THAT'S MUCH BETTER, BRANDY!" Ariella Brady said.

"Easy for you to say," Brandy replied, clinging to the parallel bars for support while her right leg quivered from the stretching exercises. "If they can regenerate an entire leg for me, then why do I have to work so hard after I get it back?"

"Bones and nerves and muscle tissue—*those* we can regenerate," Ariella told her cheerfully. "But regeneration's only the first step. If you were to push those brand-new tendons of yours too hard, for example, it would be way too easy to end up with something like an ACL tear. At which point we'd have to start over again with quick-heal, wouldn't we? And even after we get the tendons up to speed and that cartilage conditioned so you can actually start some impact workouts, you've got pretty close to zero muscle *mass*. Trust me, building that up again will be a lot more work than this is. It'll go faster, probably, but you'll burn a lot more calories in the process. And while I know you'd really prefer to get started on that right now, we can't, because until your leg is *fully* regenerated, they won't let me unleash my inherent sadism on you."

Brandy glowered at her.

She and Ariella had known one another for a long time, because Brady was the senior nurse therapist for Dr. Allen Whalen's practice, and Whalen had become the Bolgeo family physician while overseeing Senior Chief Bolgeo's physical rehab after the *Vulcan* explosion. Tim Bolgeo's rehab had been both less and more extreme than his daughter's was going to be. Because while he'd "only" had to regenerate a hand, as opposed to Brandy's entire leg, reconditioning—or, really, *initially* conditioning—a leg was a lot less complicated. A hand was far more...complex, with more tendons, ligaments, joints, and muscles, than a leg, and regaining hand strength and—especially—manual dexterity took time. In some ways, reconditioning the larger, more powerful muscles of the human leg was harder work, but it could be done much more quickly.

Once she was allowed to start on it, anyway.

She'd been released from Bassingford over a T-month ago, but regen took time. She'd continued the treatments on an out-patient basis since, and it still wasn't *quite* completed. But at least Ariella had finally allowed her to begin stretching exercises this week, although that was something of a mixed blessing at the moment. She was appalled by how much work would be needed, if just stretching exercises were *this* hard. As Ariella has just pointed out, her leg had no muscle strength at all, and she couldn't even begin working on *that* problem until Doc Whalen signed off on it structural integrity. Which, at this rate, was going to take *forever*, and she couldn't even start asking BuPers for a new assignment until she got *that* done, which meant—

*Oh, stop complaining!* she told herself as she wiped sweat from her forehead. *At least you're not one of those people who can't regenerate at all! Think how much "fun" this would be if you had to master a complete prosthesis like someone like Lady Harrington, instead.*

She grimaced at the thought. She'd never known, until her father told her, that Captain Harrington had lost an eye in Yeltsin. Like everyone else, at least in the Navy, Brandy knew Countess Harrington had been seriously wounded in her defense of the Mayhew family, but she hadn't realized she'd actually lost her left eye as a result. Nor had she realized Countess Harrington was one of the people who couldn't regenerate. That meant the docs had been forced to replace it with a prosthesis, instead, and rehabbing an artificial eye was a copper-plated bitch, from everything Brandy had heard. And while it was possible to provide an artificial eye with capabilities nature had never provided, some people never managed to adapt to one of them at all. In fact, a sizable percentage of recipients experienced some loss of function even *with* the "upgrades." Brandy had never seen any sign of that in Lady Harrington, though. Not that she'd spent any time hobnobbing one-on-one with the squadron's flag captain! But she'd been an anonymous, astronomically junior fly on the wall at more than one officers' video conference, which meant she'd actually had a fair amount of facetime, of the electronic variety at least, with her.

"Are you going to just stand there a while longer? Or can we move on?" Ariella inquired sweetly, and Brandy glared at the therapist.

"At the moment, I can't decide which of my legs is less happy with you," she said. "The new one is really pissed off, but its buddy on the other side seems equally ticked because it's having to work so much harder."

"And you haven't spent a lot of time on *either* of them for the last three T-months," Ariella pointed out. "So your left leg lost a lot of its muscle tone while you waited for the right one to finish regrowing."

"I did all my stationary exercises, just like they told me to. I was good! So why is this so hard?" Brandy complained.

"Because stationary exercises can help with flexibility but it's not the same as when there's actual weight on the leg, and they wouldn't let you put any weight on the leg until the regen specialists signed off on it. Especially on the bone density. Besides, it doesn't make a lot of sense for you to start walking until Bassingford's regenicists—and Dr. Whalen, of course—decide they're done, even if anyone was willing to let you. Remember, your right leg was still a good centimeter shorter than the left just a couple of weeks ago. Lot better idea to make sure they're both the same length before you start working on balance."

"I suppose," Brandy groused.

"My God, I thought your *Dad* was my crankiest patient!" Ariella shook her head with a grin.

"I am not 'cranky.' I'm only...impatient. You do realize my survivor's leave doesn't even start until you sign off that I've completed therapy?"

"And this is a problem?" Ariella cocked her head.

"Yeah, it is." Ariella frowned as Brandy's tone turned more serious, and Brandy waved one hand. "It's just...it's just that I feel like I should already be back aboard ship somewhere. I don't want to go out and get shot at again any more than the next woman, but I don't want to be sitting on my posterior while people I know and care about are getting shot at, either."

"I suppose I can understand that." Ariella nodded. "It's more than a little illogical, but I can understand it. At the same time, though, as fast as we can go is as fast as we're *going* to go. And I know it doesn't seem to you like we're making any progress just at the moment, but, believe me, that'll change. The entire structure of your right leg's muscles and—especially—its tendons are at what we might inelegantly call the 'wearing in' stage, right now. We're very carefully stretching and conditioning those tendons before we let you work them any harder, and until your bone density numbers are in the green, that's *all* we're letting you do. And the reason just stretching seems like so much work is that your leg muscles have very little—as in the next best thing to zero—strength. That's the bad news. The good news is that if the bone density curve holds up, Dr. Whalen should be able to sign off on it in just another week or so, at which point I *will* let you start doing strength conditioning, as well. And once we reach that point, you'll make progress a lot faster than you probably think you will right now. Trust me. I know it seems like it's taking forever, but when you turn that corner, you'll be astonished at how quickly it goes."

"If you say so," Brandy sighed, but she also smiled. After all, she remembered how her father had complained when it had been his turn. Which was why she'd been very, very careful to never voice a single "poor me" plaint in his hearing.

"Oh, I do. And now—" Ariella smiled at her. "About those stretching exercises, Lieutenant Bolgeo?"

✦   ✦   ✦

"So, how's it going, honey?" Tim Bolgeo asked across the dinner table, and Brandy puffed her lips.

"Ariella swears I'm doing great," she said. "And I guess I am. I wish it could go a little faster, though."

She reached under the table and tapped a knuckle on the exoskeletal "splint" which encased her new leg. Until Ariella signed off on her bone density for the regen sadists back at Bassingford, she was allowed out of the splint only when she was off her feet and planned to remain there, unless she was actively exercising under the therapist's eagle eye.

Brandy understood how important that had been while her leg was still growing, but the way it took all of her weight off the aforesaid leg was also the reason she'd built up no muscle mass at all while still hospitalized. It was ironic, really. If her leg had "only" been shattered and put back together surgically or with quick-heal, they'd have had her up on it for PT months ago. But because they were growing new tissue—and, especially, new bone—and because, according to the regen specialists, the bone in her leg remained dangerously fragile until it *finished* growing, she still hadn't been able to start true PT at all.

"Be patient," her father said sympathetically. "I know *I* wasn't the most patient man in the Star Kingdom when it was my turn, but—"

He paused as something remarkably like a snort came from Linda Bolgeo's direction in response to his chosen adverb. She gave him a very direct look, and he grinned back at her.

"As I was saying, while I was, of course, a model patient and a paragon of virtue while I convalesced, I did experience the occasional moment of impatience. And"—his expression sobered—"I wasn't feeling like I was shirking my duty while I did it."

"Daddy, I don't feel—"

"Oh, nonsense!" Tim shook his head. "Are you forgetting who raised you? Your mom and I know exactly what you're thinking, and you're wrong. In fact, I'm pretty sure that intellectually, you *know* you're wrong. You're not 'letting anyone down' by taking the time to heal, Brandy."

"I don't—" Brandy began.

"Yes, you do, sweetheart," Linda weighed in. "And I knew before we ever got you home that you'd feel that way. But your dad's right. You've already paid a lot more 'dues' than most anyone else in the Star Kingdom. Or in the *Navy*, for that matter. I understand that's not the way it works inside your head, but it happens to be the truth. So just accept that no one's letting you go back until Ariella *and* Dr. Whalen are satisfied and you pass your post-therapy physical at Bassingford. And that it's not *your* fault we're all going to be so unreasonable about it."

"Am *I* really being unreasonable, Mom?"

"In a word? Yes."

"And there you have it," Tim said in the tone of a man who recognized the sound of victory when he heard it. Brandy wiggled her nose at him—it was something she'd learned to do in grammar school—and he laughed.

"In the meantime, I have two items that might interest you, Lieutenant," he said then, and she arched an eyebrow.

"What sort of 'items'?"

"Well, the first and unofficial one of them is that a little birdie at Admiralty House tells me the JAG has formally recommended charges against Young."

"She has?" Her eyes narrowed. "And just how does it happen your little birdie knows that? JAG recommendations are supposed to be confidential until they're formally announced, and I don't remember any formal announcements from Vice Admiral Cordwainer. So if somebody in the Judge Advocate's office is telling you tales out of school—"

"It would be a violation of the Official Secrets Act and Article Nine," Tim completed, and nodded. "But the birdie in question isn't in the JAG's office. Nobody officially told him a thing about it, and no one officially told him it was confidential or classified, either. Which is sort of my point, honey." He shook his head soberly. "*Somebody*'s already leaked her recommendation, and I'd feel a lot better if I thought it was just some big-mouthed yeoman clerk. I don't think it was, though. Not given what else my little birdie's been picking up. It sounds a lot more to me like someone—and I would strongly suspect it was a *commissioned* someone, to be honest— deliberately made sure this got out before any of the Space Lords wanted it made public."

"You think somebody wanted it out so they could start spinning it to protect him?"

"That's what I'm *afraid* of, anyway." Tim nodded again, his expression grim. "It's the way those people's brains work."

Tim Bolgeo—like his wife and daughter—was a Gryphon. He was not only a Gryphon, he was a Gryphon Highlander. And when a Gryphon Highlander used the words "those people" to describe members of the Star Kingdom's aristocracy, it was not a term of approval.

Brandy was a little less steeped in Gryphon's traditional contempt for the nobly born, but she shared every iota of her father's refusal to kowtow to someone simply because they were entitled to put "lord" or "lady" in front of their names. And she also shared every bit of his contempt for the way in which some members of the aristocracy—

not *all* of them, because there were also aristocrats like Earl White Haven and Countess Harrington—rallied to the defense of their own, no matter how despicable someone's actions might have been.

"I hope you're wrong," she said somberly. "At the same time, I have to admit, I've been sort of waiting for exactly that to happen ever since you told me about how he ran for it."

"I hope I'm wrong, too," he said. "But the way he ran for it sort of brings me to my second item—the one that's official."

"What?" Brandy looked at him. "Are you *deliberately* not making sense, Dad?"

"Disrespectful young hellion," Tim said with a grin. "No, actually, what I'm thinking about is the contrast between his actions and those of certain other people. Like"—his eyes were suddenly very level— "you."

"And what are you talking about now?" she asked warily.

"I'm talking about that little thing you didn't mention to your mom and me," he said.

"What little thing?"

"The fact that Lieutenant Commander McBain sent you to sort out that situation in Enviro Three before the squadron ever sucked the Peeps over that minefield."

It was very quiet in the dining room, and Brandy looked back and forth between her mother and father.

"He had to send somebody," she said, after a moment, "and I was available. Heck, I was the most junior available warm body."

"And also the one who walked into that compartment to manually activate the fire suppression system, which explains why your skinsuit was already badly damaged before DC Central ever got hit. Which *probably* explains how the blast from that hit managed to do so much damage to your leg. And which overlooks the fact that you hauled two ratings out of that compartment with you. Two ratings who would definitely have died if you hadn't gotten them out."

"It was my *job*, Daddy," she said quietly, and behind her eyes she once again remembered the roaring inferno which haunted too many of her dreams. Remembered the damaged duct system and the warped blast doors, twisted and jammed by *Cassandra's* second or third hit, which had prevented her from simply sealing the compartment and venting its atmosphere. Her horror when she realized two of the life-support techs were still trapped in the compartment.

"Yes, it was your job," he agreed, and she knew he truly understood that, in a way too many people wouldn't have, because he'd been there and done that aboard a space station named *Vulcan*. "But I still wish you'd told us about it."

"I try not to think about it very much," she admitted.

"I'm afraid you'll find that just a little more difficult going forward," he said. "Because I was contacted at work today by one of Admiral Cortez's aides. The Admiral thought I might like to be the one to tell you."

"Tell me what?"

"That you're being awarded the Conspicuous Gallantry Medal."

"What?!"

Brandy came halfway out of her chair, then made herself sit back down.

"That's wonderful, Brandy!" Linda said.

"It's *wrong*!" Brandy protested.

Her mother looked at her with a confused expression, but, again, her father understood.

"No, it's not," he said. "This isn't a fortune cookie or a prize you found in a box of candy, Brandy. And they don't hand out CGMs on a whim. It's not something you 'win,' either. It's something you *earn*, and you damned well earned it aboard the *Cassie*."

"But—"

"But the people who didn't make it out are the ones who really deserve it, right? You don't deserve it because, just like you said, all you did was your 'job.' You're not the one who paid the price your dead shipmates paid."

Brandy nodded slowly as he put her roiling emotions into words with devastating accuracy, and he reached across the table to take her hand.

"Navies award medals for a lot of reasons. I'm sure they taught you about this at the Academy. But in case you were asleep in class that day, medals are the way the Navy expresses its approval for people who go above and beyond when they 'do their jobs.' And the Navy doesn't express that approval lightly, or just because the people in question deserve it—they *do* deserve it, but that's not the only reason they get the ribbons. It's because the people who rise to the occasion are the models, the *examples*. They're who we're supposed to look up to, the level *we're* supposed to rise to. And for better or worse, baby girl, that's who *you* are. Your mom and I have always known you're something special. Now the Navy knows it, and you're not allowed to disagree with them."

**Admiralty House**
**Office of the First Lord**
**City of Landing**
**Planet Manticore**
**Manticore Binary System**
**July 17, 1905 PD**

"EXCUSE ME, MILADY."

Lady Francine Maurier looked up from her paperwork as Nouzar Abbasi, her executive secretary, appeared in her open office doorway.

"Yes, Nouzar?"

"Lord Alexander is on the com."

The Baroness of Morncreek was a small, slender woman, well over twenty centimeters shorter than the sandy-haired Abbasi. She was also very attractive in a dark, feline sort of way, and the quality most people associated with her most strongly was composure. Like a treecat, her balance, physical and mental, was always sure, and she resolutely refused to let anything knock her off stride.

This time, though, she raised an eyebrow . . . which was her equivalent of a shouted exclamation of surprise.

The hour was quite late—Morncreek was a night bird by preference, but she had even more reason than usual to be up late tonight—and she'd spoken to William Alexander, the Chancellor of the Exchequer, less than two hours ago. The fact that he was contacting her in the office again so soon and this close to midnight was . . . unusual, to say the least. And given the debate scheduled for the next day, both of them should already have been at home getting a good night's rest, since they'd been chosen to present the Government's case before the vote was called.

*I know why* I'm *not sound asleep at home,* she thought wryly, looking down at the notes upon which she'd been working. *But why isn't* Willie? *And why do I think I won't like the answer when I find out?*

47

If she hadn't silenced her com, she'd probably already have the answer to that, of course, since Alexander could have screened straight through.

"All right," she said after a moment. "Thank you."

"You're welcome, Milady."

Abbasi gave her a slight bow and withdrew, and she turned to her com and tapped the acceptance key.

The Honorable William Alexander, the heir to the Earldom of White Haven, appeared on the display. He had the same dark hair and blue eyes as his older brother Hamish, and Morncreek knew both of them well. She actually knew Hamish better, since he was one of the Royal Manticoran Navy's most senior officers, but she knew William more than well enough to recognize the storm signals flying behind those blue eyes.

"Francine," he said.

"Willie," she acknowledged, and cocked her head. "Why do I think I'm not going to be happy to see you?"

"Because you're a highly intelligent woman," he said. "I doubt, however, that you can even begin to suspect just how *un*happy you'll be in the next, oh, sixty seconds."

"Why?" she asked, dark eyes narrowing.

"Because Allen and I just met with Michael Janvier."

Morncreek came upright in her chair, and the eyes which had narrowed widened.

"Allen," she knew, was Allen Summervale, Duke of Cromarty and Prime Minister to Queen Elizabeth III of Manticore. William Alexander was the Chancellor of the Exchequer, which made him the second-ranking member of the Cromarty Government. And Michael Janvier was the Baron of High Ridge, leader of the Conservative Association. He was also one of the most loathsome, bigoted, self-serving, intellectually and morally corrupt cretins to ever disgrace the Manticoran peerage.

And those were his *good* points.

"I'm already unhappy," she said, after a moment. "I can't think of a single thing he'd have to say to the two of you that *wouldn't* make me unhappy."

"Well, buckle up," Alexander growled, "because this one's going to land right squarely in *your* lap."

"What are you talking about?"

"We just found out why whoever leaked Cordwainer's recommendation leaked it," Alexander said grimly. "High Ridge demanded a meeting with Allen tonight, and at that meeting he told us he'd 'heard rumors' we intend to court-martial Young."

"Oh, *crap*," Morncreek muttered.

"Exactly. And I don't think it's even remotely coincidental that he wanted to meet with us tonight, before tomorrow's session."

Morncreek's lips tightened. The fact that Young's father—and High Ridge—would pull out all the stops to save him if they could was as inevitable as sunrise, which was the true reason that decision had been so closely held. Legally, the charges couldn't be formally filed until Young himself returned to the Manticore System to face them, but both the Government and the Admiralty *really* wanted to have the declaration voted out before word that he *would* be charged could get out and muddy the political waters.

The interval between the Battle of Hancock and the receipt of the Parks board of inquiry's report was part of the problem, of course. But much as she wanted to, Morncreek couldn't really fault Parks for that. Regulations had required that the board's members all be currently serving commanding officers of "appropriate rank and seniority," which in this case had meant senior grade captains. There *was* provision for relaxing those requirements if operational constraints made it "impracticable" to assemble the "appropriate" officers in a timely fashion. But they applied only "in a time of war," and the Star Kingdom still wasn't *formally* at war with anyone, because there'd been no declaration. Parks might have tried to fudge his way around that technicality, but he'd been too focused on his operational needs at Seaford and the surrounding systems. Even if he'd been tempted to, his staff JAG officer would probably have pointed out how Young's protectors could—and undoubtedly would—fasten on the least technical reason to have the board's report excluded from the inevitable court-martial. For that matter, Parks was almost certainly sufficiently astute to recognize the sort of political dogfight this had to turn into, so he might well have wanted it to arrive only *after* the declaration . . . which only a terminally pessimistic clairvoyant could have believed wouldn't have been voted out by now. And even if all of that hadn't been true, he probably couldn't have shaved more than two or three weeks off the delivery time, given travel distances, whatever he'd done.

Morncreek understood all of that. Unfortunately . . .

"He tried to strong-arm you into quashing the court-martial," she said. It was a statement, not a question, and Alexander nodded curtly.

"Of course he tried to shut it down," Alexander said now. "He called it 'only one more step in the Admiralty's unwarranted persecution of Lord Young.' One that 'no one with a decent respect for justice could allow to pass unchallenged.'"

For a handful of seconds, Morncreek could only stare at him, temporarily unable to believe that even High Ridge could have said something like that with a straight face. Then she shook herself.

"My God, Willie! '*Unwarranted persecution*'? The man should've been cashiered after Basilisk! Hell, he should never have been on a command deck in the first place! And we'll be looking at something a lot like a damned mutiny if we don't prosecute him after what he did in Hancock!"

"I know. I know!" Alexander looked like a man who wanted to chew iron and spit nails. "You do remember who my brother is? Who my *father* was? Trust me, I know!"

"I know you do. It's just—just that I can't believe even *High Ridge* could defend a piece of garbage like Pavel Young. I mean, I know the man's a diseased moral pygmy, himself, but *this*—! Even he has to recognize arrant cowardice when he sees it!"

"Oh, I'm sure he does," Alexander said affably. "After all, he looks in the mirror every morning, doesn't he?"

Morncreek winced slightly. Not that Alexander didn't have a point. High Ridge was absolutely fearless as he negotiated the corridors of power, but that was only because he literally couldn't conceive of a situation in which birth and position wouldn't protect him from the consequences of his own actions. And as she came back on balance mentally, she realized that was exactly how he could try to protect Young. As far as he was concerned, it was simply the system working the way it was supposed to.

"Did you or Allen confirm that the decision's been made?" she asked.

"Of course not. It didn't matter, though." Alexander shrugged angrily. "He knows. In fact, from the way he was talking I'm inclined to think someone slipped him an actual copy of Cordwainer's memo."

Morncreek frowned unhappily, but she also nodded.

"You're probably right. I wish you weren't, but there are enough Janacek loyalists still tucked away for somebody to have done exactly that." She rubbed an eyebrow for a moment. "So I assume you told him you could neither confirm nor deny?"

"Allen did, yes. And High Ridge took it—correctly—as confirmation. Which was when he dropped his little bombshell and *demanded* that Allen quash the court. And when Allen pointed out to him that the decision of whether or not to court-martial Young was a matter for the Navy and the Judge Advocate's Office, in which the civilian government had no voice, High Ridge suggested that while a mere prime minister might not be able to intervene, the Queen certainly could."

"You're serious? He actually *said* that?"

"In so many words."

"He's a lunatic! Her Majesty would *eviscerate* him if he suggested that to her!"

"Which is why he wanted Allen to do it for him. And when Allen declined, he dropped the other shoe."

"I hesitate to ask this, because I don't really want to find out how much worse it gets, but which other shoe?"

"That was why he wanted to meet with us before the vote tomorrow. It was to tell us that the Conservative Association 'will have no choice but to go into opposition as a matter of principle.'"

Morncreek stared at him, her brain unable—or, more probably, *unwilling*—to process the information. Silence hung for a long, still moment before she shook herself.

"He can't do this, Willie. Not even *he* can do this just to save a piece of garbage like Young!"

"He can. He *has*. And if I had to guess, it's at least partly because North Hollow really does have something in his files to hold over High Ridge's head. And it must be something big and nasty, too, because I don't think even Michael Janvier would risk crossing Allen—and Her Majesty—over something like this without someone putting the equivalent of a pulser to his head. But however we got here, that's where we are. And if the Association goes into opposition and joins the Liberals, Allen loses his majority in the Lords. Which means—"

"Which means," Morncreek interrupted, "that unless we cave and drop the charges against Young, which we can't possibly do, Allen doesn't have the votes to move the declaration."

"Actually, it could be even worse if he went ahead and called the vote and High Ridge managed to hold the Association for the Opposition. It's not certain that he could hold all of the Conservative peers, but it's damned likely. And he could almost certainly hold enough of them, especially with North Hollow's files looming in the background, which is why Allen can't risk it. Because if he forces the issue and High Ridge does hold enough of the Association, we could end up with a formal vote *against* a declaration of war, which would mean you'd have to call your people completely off. We couldn't justify continuing even limited operations in the expectation of a declaration if there'd been a formal vote to deny one."

"This has all the necessary ingredients for a total disaster, Willie," Morncreek said flatly.

"Oh, don't I know it?" Alexander shook his head in disgust. "And starting tomorrow, you and I and Allen will have to figure out how the hell we prevent one. Better get a good night's sleep, Francine. We're all going to need our rest."

**Bolgeo Homestead**
**Liberty Crossing**
**Henderson Highlands**
**Planet Gryphon**
**Manticore Binary System**
**August 24, 1905**

"WELL, LOOK AT YOU!" The dark-haired, muscular lieutenant commander with the small golden ring in her right nostril put her hands on her hips and grinned infectiously at Brandy Bolgeo. "Looking a lot better than the last time I saw you in person!"

"With all due respect, Commander Briscoe, Ma'am, that's a pretty low bar," Brandy said. She crossed the room with the swinging stride enforced by her right leg's grav splint and held out her hand with a matching grin. "And, if memory doesn't fail me, the last time I laid eyes on you in the flesh, as it were, you were a mere senior-grade lieutenant, such as myself, toiling in the trenches and far from the exalted heights of departmental command."

"True, true," Janet Briscoe conceded with becoming modesty. "I wouldn't want to say anything about water finding its own level, or cream rising to the top, or anything like that, of course."

"Oh, of course not! 'Cause if you did, I'd have to point out that cream isn't the only thing that floats, wouldn't I?" Brandy held out her hand for a handshake, then shrugged and threw her arms around the other woman to hug her firmly. Given her visitor's musculature, it was a longish reach. "It's good to see you, Janet. Really!" she said, standing back with her hands still on Briscoe's upper arms.

"Good to see you up and about, too," Briscoe replied in a more serious tone. "Truth is, you weren't looking that good the last time I saw you."

"Bassingford does good work," Brandy told her with an off-center smile. "Takes a while, but they do do good work."

"So does your dad." Briscoe grinned, but then her expression sobered. "Truth to tell, I wasn't all sure for a while that they were going to repair *Cassie* at all, Brandy." She shook her head. "The detailed survey once they had her back here in the yard . . . it was *bad*. Even worse than we thought it was when we were getting her home."

"I know. Dad's kept me updated."

Brandy twitched her head, then led the way back out onto the enclosed sun porch that ran the full width of the sizable Bolgeo home. It was winter on Gryphon, and Gryphon winters tended to be extreme, which meant the air-gapped crystoplast walls gave them an excellent view of snow devils dancing across knife-edged drifts on the breathlessly cold wind. It was a brilliantly lit icy vista, gilded with sun sparkle off the snow that only made it look still colder. But that vista also made the porch feel even toastier, and the two of them settled into comfortable loungers on either side of a table which bore a coffeemaker, a two-liter carafe of cocoa, and a towering pile of ham and cheese sandwiches.

"As you can see, I made preparations," Brandy said, and Briscoe snorted.

The lieutenant commander's dark, coppery complexion and powerful, although thoroughly feminine, physique was the gift of her immigrant ancestors, who'd moved to the Star Kingdom of Manticore—and, specifically, to the planet Sphinx—a century and a half earlier from Quelhollow in the Rindahl System. Quelhollow, one of old Earth's more ancient daughter colonies, boasted a gravity even heavier than Sphinx's, and Briscoe's great-great-great-whatever grandparents had been genetically modified to thrive in it. After four hundred T-years of immigration and intermarriage, virtually every established Sphinxian family incorporated at least some genetic modification, but the Quelhollow mods remained much more readily apparent to the casual observer than some others, like the Meyerdahl mods. And like most people who'd been genengineered for heavy-grav environments, Briscoe had a ferociously demanding metabolism.

"I'll have you know that I could go at least another . . . oh, ninety minutes before I'd need to eat," she said now.

"Sure you could." Brandy nodded with a serious expression. "I *believe* you. And I also believe in Santa Claus, the Easter Bunny, and every single word I read on the Infonet."

Briscoe laughed, then poured herself a mug of cocoa and reached for one of the thick sandwiches. This was far from her first visit to the Bolgeo Homestead, and she closed her eyes in bliss as she took the first bite. Linda Bolgeo knew exactly how to feed a Sphinxian, she thought, with slabs of ham, lots of mayonnaise, Swiss *and* provolone cheese, spicy brown mustard, banana peppers, and thick-cut onion rings.

"Are you sure we couldn't convince your mom to join *Cassie's* galley crew?" she asked after a moment.

"Hey! You've already got my daddy putting your ship back together again, Commander! And, by the way, in case I didn't mention it, congratulations. You deserved the slot."

"I dunno about that," Briscoe said a bit more somberly. "Commander Cartwright wrote me a lot better efficiency report than I deserved after the battle."

"No, he didn't." Brandy looked at her very levelly.

"Brandy, I was responsible for *missile defense*." Briscoe's bright green eyes went dark. "We got the shit pounded out of us, and I was the one who was supposed to stop it."

"No, you were the one who was supposed to stop what got past the screen. If I recall correctly, there was supposed to be an entire integrated missile defense net. You know, the one that kind of disappeared at the critical moment?" Brandy's own eyes were hard. "You did *damned* well after Young ran for it, and you damned well ought to know it. *I* do, anyway, and not just because I know *you*. Admiral Winston let me view the tactical records after they pinned the stupid medal on me. Believe me, I know exactly what you and your people were up against, Janet, and no one could've done better after Young bugged out on us!"

Briscoe looked back at her for a long moment, then bobbed her head in an abbreviated nod—more in acknowledgment than in agreement—and took another bite of her sandwich.

"Maybe you've got a point," she said. "Everybody keeps telling me that, anyway. And *most* of the time, I pretty much believe 'em. Gets bad sometimes in my dreams, though." She met Brandy's eyes as she admitted that. It wasn't something she would have confessed to just anyone, but Brandy only nodded back. After all, she had her own nightmares, didn't she?

"And for that matter," Briscoe continued more cheerfully, "I guess they wouldn't have given me the slot if they didn't figure I could fill it."

"I think you could probably say that," Brandy agreed. Her friend's promotion to lieutenant commander had coincided with her appointment as HMS *Cassandra*'s tactical officer when Commander Jason Cartwright, *Cassandra*'s previous TO, was promoted out of the ship. That was almost always at least a *full* commander's billet in a battlecruiser, which made her assignment a fairly emphatic statement of the Navy's opinion of the job she'd done in Hancock.

"Actually, in a lot of ways, it's probably a good thing it'll take so long to put *Cassie* back into commission, even with your dad in charge," Briscoe continued. "What with the casualties we took and how thoroughly we've been raided for experienced personnel since we went into the yard, I'm rebuilding the Tactical Department almost from scratch. I got to hang onto Chief Tillis and Senior Chief Langenbucher, but almost everybody else will be so new they squeak."

"Then you'll get to build it *your* way." Brandy shrugged. "You'll do just fine, Janet!"

"Probably. That's what Langenbucher keeps telling me, anyway. In his delightfully tactful fashion, of course!"

Brandy snorted as she poured herself a cup of coffee. Senior Chief Finnian Langenbucher had been Lieutenant Briscoe's senior noncom—which had also made him her keeper and mentor—when she first reported aboard *Cassandra* nineteen T-months before Hancock. "Delightfully tactful" was not the exact descriptor Brandy would have applied to him.

"You know, seriously, I'm sorry it's taken me this long to get out here to visit with you. I promise it wasn't just because of the weather." Briscoe waved at the ice and snow around them. "Mind you, only a Gryphon or a lunatic—but I repeat myself—would live someplace with weather like this, you understand."

"This from someone who was raised on *Sphinx*? Where, if I recall, winter lasts about a year and a half?"

"But it's so much nicer a winter," Briscoe said earnestly.

"And it lasts *three times* as long."

"Maybe. But *spring and summer* last three times as long, too!"

"Point," Brandy conceded. "Definitely a point."

Briscoe chuckled and leaned back, stretching her legs in front of her and crossing them at the ankle while she nursed her cocoa.

"You dad going to make it home for dinner tonight?" she asked after a moment.

"He's supposed to." Brandy shrugged. "Mom's still planning on it, and I was pretty confident he would, too. Up till a couple of hours ago, anyway."

"Oh?" Briscoe arched an eyebrow.

"Yeah, they grabbed him for a consult on *Nike*. Turns out getting to some of her damage's going to be tougher than anyone thought. And Dad was one of the project managers when they built her, so they want his input."

"And they only figured that out today, did they?" Briscoe shook her head. HMS *Nike* had returned to the Manticore Binary System just over three T-weeks ago.

"Fair's fair." Brandy shrugged again. "The initial report from Hancock Station missed some of the problems, and *Hephaestus* only got her docked where they could get a good hands-on look at her a couple of days ago. The yard *should* have had her at least a month earlier, but they couldn't pull her off of active operations for a detailed survey, you know."

"I guess." Briscoe nodded, then made a face.

"What?" Brandy asked.

"I was just thinking. If I'd been Dame Honor and they'd sent Young home aboard *my* ship, I think life support might just have had a minor accident in his case. It would have been a pity to waste the potential failures resulting from all that damage he let through. Especially if he was breathing *my* ship's air! Can you imagine what it must've been like to have him aboard *Nike*?"

"Yeah. I wouldn't have much enjoyed that, either. But as Dad pointed out, it meant she got to personally hand him over to the JAG when she arrived, too. She was standing right there when they took him into custody. There had to be some satisfaction in that!"

"Probably be more if his frigging daddy doesn't manage to stall things," Briscoe growled.

The lieutenant commander had her own very personal bone to pick with Pavel Young. As a fellow Sphinxian who'd deeply admired her battlecruiser squadron's flag captain, her tribal loyalty to Honor Harrington ran deep. As a tactical specialist, she knew exactly what Pavel Young had done to Mark Sarnow's task group when he'd cut and ran for it in Hancock. And as one of HMS *Cassandra*'s surviving officers, she knew with even more precise, painful exactitude what his cowardice had cost her ship . . . and people like Brandy Bolgeo.

It would be a cold day in hell before Janet Briscoe was interested in cutting Young a single millimeter of slack.

"There's no proof anyone's managing to 'stall' anything," Brandy pointed out.

"Say that with a straight face," Briscoe challenged.

"I didn't say no one was; I just said there's no proof of it, and there isn't. So far, at least. For that matter, he's only been back in-system for three weeks. There's a lot of i's to dot and t's to cross if the Navy's planning to try an earl's son on capital charges."

"And his daddy will make sure it takes as long as possible. Hopefully forever!"

"You sound more like a Highlander than a Sphinxian!" Brandy pointed out with a sour chuckle.

"Where Young is concerned? Hell, yes! I'll volunteer for the firing squad myself . . . if they ever get around to court-martialing the bastard."

"Not even North Hollow can spin things out forever," Brandy said philosophically.

"You sure about that?" Briscoe gave her a skeptical look. "According to what I'm hearing, he's the whole reason the Conservatives went into Opposition. He's got them lining up to hold the declaration of war hostage until the Navy promises not to shoot his precious baby boy!"

"That probably is what he's trying to do," Brandy acknowledged. "Oh, nobody's likely to admit it—not even the Prime Minister could afford to make that part of it public—but anybody who's ever paid attention to High Ridge knows that any time *he* talks about 'a matter of principle' it's really a steaming pile of crap. But be honest. The Conservatives wouldn't have a hope of pulling it off if the Liberals and Progressives weren't already providing covering fire by fighting the declaration tooth and nail for their own reasons."

"You mean reasons like 'because they're fucking idiots'?" Briscoe asked caustically, and Brandy snorted.

"I don't think I'd have chosen that exact ... pithy phrase, but yeah." She shrugged. "Daddy's still pretty tapped-in to the Navy grapevine, though. From what he's hearing, it won't be a lot longer before Young has to face the music. And God knows we need to get it behind us! We've *got* to be able to begin full-scale offensive operations!"

"Preaching to the choir, girl." Briscoe drank more cocoa, then took a rather moody bite out of a second sandwich.

"Yeah, and I need to get my sorry butt back up and running again," Brandy said sourly, and Briscoe frowned.

"You do realize that *ships* aren't the only things that need repairs, don't you? And that it takes as long as it takes? As I believe we were just discussing about *Cassie* and *Nike*?"

"Yeah, but—"

"But me no buts, Brandy Bolgeo!" Briscoe said sternly. "I believe we were also just discussing the fact that we don't even have a declaration of war yet, so keep your shirt on. Trust me, this thing'll last plenty long enough for you to get back aboard ship and get shot at some more. And," she added, looking at her friend shrewdly, "why do I sort of suspect your mom and dad aren't what you might call brokenhearted over having you home a little longer?"

"You do know us pretty well, don't you?" Brandy chuckled. "And, yeah. Mom's a little more willing to show that, but Dad's a lot worse at *hiding* it."

"Probably because he knows what's involved even better than she does." Briscoe reached across and patted Brandy on her good leg. "But listen to the docs, girlfriend. Don't push too hard, cause if you do, all you'll manage is to lose ground. Got me?"

"Got you," Brandy sighed.

"Good. And now that we've got that out of the way, let me tell you what the Navy wants to do to my perfectly good sensor arrays." Briscoe rolled her eyes. "They *say* it'll make things more efficient, give us more reach. Personally, I think they're lying out their asses, which was something I was looking forward to discussing with your male parental unit over dinner. I want to know what the heck he thinks he's doing letting them mess up my perfectly good ship this way. Man's got some explaining to do!"

"I wonder if that's another reason he commed to say he might be delayed?" Brandy mused.

"It's certainly possible!" Briscoe laughed. "I've been kinda...forthright in my evaluation of the proposed changes. Mostly, to be honest, because they're going to add another two weeks minimum to the overhaul. But still, would you believe that—"

**Dempsey's Bar**
**HMSS _Hephaestus_**
**Manticore Planetary Orbit**
**Manticore Binary System**
**September 22, 1905 PD**

"LET ME GUESS. You're looking for a certain lieutenant who just came up from Bassingford," the smiling hostess said.

"You really know me that well, Frederica?" Tim Bolgeo asked with an answering smile, and she shook her head.

"Well enough I probably could have guessed, if I'd had to. I didn't, though. Come on, she's waiting for you!"

Bolgeo chuckled and followed her through the crowded restaurant's cheerful conversation rumble and the clink of cutlery and flatware. Delicious smells teased his nostrils, and the man on the bar waved an equally cheerful greeting as he passed.

The hostess led the way to one of the smaller dining rooms off the main floor, and Brandy looked up with a sparkling grin as he entered. She came to her feet plural and held out her arms.

"So, you finally made it, Daddy!" she said. "It's a good thing I wasn't waiting to tell you anything _important_."

"Don't you go giving me a hard time, little girl," he replied as he hugged her firmly. "Just remember who's in charge of putting your ship back together."

"You mean my ex-ship." Brandy squeezed him tightly. "As it happens, I've got a new one."

"You do?" Bolgeo stood back and looked at her.

"Yep! I aced my physical, which means I'm cleared for duty again. And there was an email waiting in my inbox until Bassingford signed off. You are looking at the new chief engineer of Her Majesty's destroyer _Timberwolf_."

"I am? Outstanding! Of course, there's that little survivor's leave of yours, first."

61

"There is, and the clock starts ticking on it now. But that's okay. *Timberwolf*'s currently deployed with Commodore McIlhenny's squadron out at Grendelsbane. She's not due to rotate home for another couple of months. Then she'll be in yard hands for a while. She was three months overdue for a three-year overhaul before it all hit the fan at Hancock." Brandy shrugged, her expression slightly less cheerful. "She won't get that overhaul, not the way things are looking right now, but according to Commander Seseri—he's her CO—she's going to need at least a few months to deal with her most pressing issues. Assuming we can find the yard space and the budget to get them done."

"Yeah, there *is* that," Bolgeo sighed. "And I gotta tell you, Brandy, I don't think it's getting better anytime soon."

"Well, what can you expect when you leave the *Navy* in charge of something important?" a voice said from behind him, and he turned quickly to see the red-haired woman who'd just walked into the dining room.

"Iris!" He beamed. "What are you doing here?"

"Your daughter ran into me on her way from Bassingford," Sergeant Major Iris Babcock said, crossing the room and holding out her hand. "She said something about having lunch with a lowlife deadbeat and needing someone stalwart—like myself—along for moral support."

"Somehow, I don't think that's exactly the way she phrased it," Bolgeo replied with a grin, and Babcock shrugged.

"Close enough. Especially when I knew she was talking about *you*." She shook her head. "I cannot believe that you're still not in jail!"

"That's because you consistently underestimate my ability to evade arrest." Bolgeo squeezed her hand. "Not too surprising, I suppose, given the poor Marine brain you have to use to do the estimating."

"Stop that, both of you!" Brandy shook her head and did her best to bestow a stern glower on both of them. "There's nobody here but us three, so why don't the two of you stop pretending you aren't really good friends so we can sit down and eat."

"Give up the opportunity to tweak your dad's tail? Brandy!" Babcock shook her head. "Surely you know both of us better than that!"

"You're right." Brandy nodded. "Which is why I'm standing here trying to remember why I thought inviting you to join this convivial little gathering was a good idea."

"Touché!" Babcock said with a laugh, and looked back at her father. "It really is good to see you, Timmy. It's been too long."

"Same here...although, I'll deny it in front of witnesses, you understand."

"Of course."

Brandy shook her head with a resigned expression and waved at the table where she'd been waiting.

"That's probably the best I'm going to get out of you two, so why don't we go ahead and sit down and order. How much time do you have, Dad?"

"I've got to be back at the office in about two hours," he replied. "Iris?"

"I've got until eighteen hundred." Babcock shrugged. "It's not like there's any big rush to get back aboard. They're not going to let us *do* anything, anyway."

"Yeah," Bolgeo said sourly. Then he shook himself and turned back to Brandy as he and Babcock settled into a pair of waiting chairs.

"So, *Timberwolf*! One of the *Noblesses*, isn't she?" he continued in a more cheerful tone while Babcock punched up the menu on the tabletop.

"Yeah, she's no spring chicken." Brandy nodded. "Of course, she's from near the end of the production run, and she got all the final-phase upgrades. If the Peeps hadn't decided to go for broke, she'd still be in Silesia suppressing piracy. One of the things that was supposed to happen in that general overhaul was an upgrade to the Mod 6 launchers. Not gonna happen, so we won't be able to handle the latest generations of missile." She grimaced. "Probably means we'll be riding herd on the fleet train."

"I know you'd prefer something more...energetic," Bolgeo said, "but I hope you won't take it wrongly if I say your mom and I would be just as happy if you could avoid any more 'energetic' experiences. At least for a while."

"At the moment, it looks like the entire *Navy*'ll be avoiding them," Brandy replied. "I dropped by Admiralty House while I was dirtside and had a word with Calvin McAbee. You remember him, Dad?"

"Sure." Bolgeo nodded.

"Well, he's over at BuShips now, so finding out what my new billet is gave me an excuse to bend his ear a little. And he told me we're headed toward something an awful lot like a stand-down." Brandy's expression was worried now. "From what he's saying, we've pretty much accomplished most of Riposte Gamma's stipulated objectives. That means there's not a lot more we can do—officially, anyway—without a declaration. Coupled with all the maintenance funds we've diverted to operations, Admiral Caparelli'll have to pretty much revert to a defensive stance sometime real soon now."

"I know." Bolgeo's expression wasn't worried; it was disgusted.

"I know I'm just a Marine, and that Marines don't understand the finer, more complex aspects of the political process," Babcock said, looking up from the menu. "Having said that, I could venture an opinion on why that is, if anyone's interested in hearing it."

"I think Dempsey's throws people out when they talk that way," Bolgeo said, and the sergeant major snorted.

"Not that she isn't right, Dad," Brandy observed, and he nodded.

, "I told you what North Hollow was going to do, didn't I?" It was her turn to nod, and he shrugged. "Well, some things are easier to predict than others, and *those people* are about as easy as it comes."

"I hear you, Timmy," Babcock said. "I've got to say, though, that I didn't expect even High Ridge to be quite this blatant about it."

"He's not—not for public consumption, anyway," Bolgeo replied. "This is all a matter of high moral principle . . . for public consumption. And Cromarty can't call him on it—for that 'public consumption,' again—without washing an awful lot of dirty linen in public at a really bad time."

"I wish they'd just go ahead and get this over with." Brandy's tone was harsh. "They filed charges *three weeks* ago, Dad! Why haven't they seated the court yet?"

"Because North Hollow's brought in an entire gang of high-priced civilian lawyers," Bolgeo said. "And they've been filing delaying motions from the moment he put them on payroll. First, they asked for an extension to examine the charges and the relevant portions of the Articles of War, since, after all, they're *civilians*. What do they know about military law? And the JAG has to bend over backward, given the way the Conservative Association's just looking for something it can use to sandbag the Government. So they got their extension. And now they're filing every other delaying motion they can think of. Hell, they're probably going to ask to subpoena Yuri Rollins as a character witness for the defense!"

Babcock snorted. Admiral Yuri Rollins had commanded the Havenite fleet that attacked Hancock, and he'd become a POW after Sir Yancey Parks took the Seaford System away from him.

"I'd actually pay good money to see that, Timmy," the Marine said. "Especially when he agreed with the prosecution about what a miserable shit Young is!"

"But ultimately, they're not going to accomplish anything by all this," Brandy pointed out. "Either the evidence is there—and I'm pretty darn sure it is—or it's not, and this is a *military* court. It's not like they've got a jury full of civilians they can bamboozle or dazzle with their footwork."

"They don't think so either," Bolgeo said, tapping the tabletop to scroll through the menu.

"Then why?" she asked.

"Because they're playing for time." Her father looked up from the menu. "You just said it yourself. Until we get a declaration, we can't take the war to the Peeps. We're burning time—*lots* of time, when we could be rolling them up like a rug. When we finally do resume operations, the price tag'll be a lot steeper than it would be if we could go after them full-bore *now*, while they're so screwed up. They know that as well as you and I do; and what they're hoping is that the Admiralty—and Cromarty—will get desperate enough to cave and downgrade the charges in return for a declaration."

"Not gonna happen in a million years," Babcock said grimly. "Not this time. Too many people know what happened, and too many people are *pissed*, Timmy!"

"Of course it's not going to happen. But they'll get their money's worth out of North Hollow before they admit it. And they don't give any more of a damn what happens to the rest of the Star Kingdom while they're doing it than *he* does."

Bolgeo scowled, then shook himself.

"And that's enough about that sorry SOB," he declared. "My daughter's just been cleared for duty again, she's going to get her very own engineering department to run, and her mom and I have her home for another solid month of leave before we have to turn her loose. That being the case, I'm sure we can find something a lot more interesting and productive to talk about!"

**Prime Minister's Residence**
**City of Landing**
**Planet Manticore**
**Manticore Binary System**
**October 26, 1905 PD**

"COULD WE MAYBE FIND SOMETHING a little more enjoyable to watch?"

William Alexander's tone was plaintive as he glared at the smart wall at the end of the Prime Minister's dining room. At the moment, it showed live imagery of the current demonstrations outside Admiralty House. By the standards of a counter-grav civilization, the tower which housed the Admiralty was a mere nothing, little more than a hundred stories tall. That was still enough to turn the demonstrators into ants, clustered around its foot, as far as anyone looking down at them from Admiralty House's windows was concerned, however. Unfortunately, the scene *Alexander* was looking at came from camera drones hovering little more than a hundred feet up, which brought it into entirely too clear a focus for his digestion.

"Not watching it won't keep it from happening," Allen Summervale pointed out.

"No," Alexander agreed sourly. "But if I'm not watching it, then I can at least pretend there's a modicum of sanity *somewhere* out there."

He scowled as he watched the demonstrators hurl screaming abuse at one another. They were hurling a few other things, as well, although the cordon of Landing City Police keeping the irate mobs separated seemed to be keeping the projectiles in question nonlethal, at least. Not that someone who caught a balloon filled with bright red paint square in the face was likely to be very happy about it, anyway.

Alexander had no doubt the police drones sharing airspace with the newsies' cameras were keeping tabs on who'd thrown what. That was probably the reason no one was stupid enough to throw anything more dangerous than balloons and tennis balls. It was certainly the reason the badly overburdened Landing City courts would shortly receive a fresh influx of citations for disorderly behavior, vandalism, and possibly simple assault. The capitol city cops took that sort of behavior seriously.

Still, unless he missed his guess, things were building to the nightly climax, at which point the LCPD would deploy teargas to convince the "demonstrators" to go home. Many of them, he was sure, had brought along breath masks to protect themselves, but modern "teargas" was considerably more sophisticated than its crude, pre-diaspora ancestor. Anyone who exposed skin to it would find himself *highly* motivated to get himself home and into a shower ASAP.

Which didn't mean the same idiots wouldn't be back again *tomorrow* night.

He glared at the holo-posters floating above the demonstrators. Improbably—indeed, considering their subject, he was tempted to say "obscenely"—noble-looking, three-meter-tall portraits of Pavel Young glared valiantly at equally towering holos of Honor Harrington. Some of the idiots were actually chanting Young's name, as if he were some heroic paladin. Despite decades of political experience, Alexander couldn't—literally, *could not*—understand how *anyone* could buy into that interpretation of Pavel Young, although he supposed it was at least remotely possible that people who'd never had the misfortune to meet him truly could convince themselves of his victimhood. But in addition to *that* sort of idiocy, eye-tearing holographic banners, some of them as much as twenty meters in length, floated alongside Young's face, denouncing the "warmongers" trying to force a formal declaration of war. And, of course, equally spectacular banners soared above their opponents. denouncing the "corrupt politicians," "traitors," and—his own favorite—"gutless cowards" *opposing* that declaration.

There must be nine or ten thousand men and women out there, he thought. No doubt the LCPD could give him an exact count, if he really wanted one. Not that he did.

"You know, I sort of thought that once the verdict was in, this would start to taper off," he said.

"In a lot of ways, it has." The Duke of Cromarty shrugged. "The demonstrations are smaller now, and according to the police, more and more of them are what they call 'professional rowdies.' Quite a few of those just love a good riot, and they don't give much of a damn what it's over as long as they get to play in the street and throw smoke grenades, paint bombs, and the occasional brick. All in the name of free expression, of course." The Prime Minister looked as sour as Alexander felt. "As far as we can tell, the majority of the pro-declaration crowd are genuinely motivated, and the same thing's true for at least half of the Opposition demonstrators. Mostly Liberals, with a scattering of Progressives for ballast. But a lot, maybe the bulk, of the rest are hired guns. High Ridge and his crowd are flying them in and some of the Association's more deep-pocketed peers are picking up the tab for their housing and meals."

"That's *stupid*!" Alexander glared at Cromarty, mostly because there was no one else to glare at. "The court-martial's over! What the hell does High Ridge want now?!"

"In one way it's not over yet," Cromarty pointed out. "He's been convicted and sentenced, but the sentence hasn't been carried out yet."

"And they think they can get it *changed*?" Alexander's glare deepened. "They think they can arm twist Elizabeth into granting him some kind of *pardon*?"

"Hardly," Cromarty said dryly.

"Then what's this in aid of?"

"Oh, I expect High Ridge hopes to hit several birds with this particular stone. First, he's cementing his status as a loyal member of the Opposition, backing up New Kiev and her crowd and buying himself a stack of favors he can call in down the road. And don't think for a moment he's not thinking about that, Willie! Second, you know the Association's always decried our 'confrontational foreign-policy' where Haven was concerned. They figured—or said they did, anyway—that it would lead to exactly what we have now: a war. And they had no interest in fighting one. So from that perspective, High Ridge isn't actually lying about his party's position this time, even if his lips *are* moving. Third, now that Young's inherited his father's title, he's probably got his hands on the North Hollow files, which means he's got both those hands wrapped around the Conservative Association's throat. Believe me, High Ridge and most of his cronies would a lot rather face you, me, and Her Majesty than the consequences if Young makes some of the tidbits in those files public! And, fourth, the fact that we're not going to shoot the son of a bitch gives them an opening to scream that we obviously didn't have a good case against him in the first place."

"That's bullshit."

"Been hanging around with Hamish again, I see." Cromarty twitched a smile.

"Well, it is! They didn't find him *innocent* of the capital charges, Allen. They only announced a hung verdict on them when they convicted him of everything else!"

"Which High Ridge is now proclaiming was a put-up job." Cromarty's smile disappeared and he sighed. "He won't be able to keep it up, especially after Young—well, I guess North Hollow, now—is formally cashiered. Not for the Star Kingdom at large, although I don't expect him and his cronies to ever admit anything of the sort. But for now he's arguing that if North Hollow had *really* done the things he was accused of, we *would've* shot him. So, obviously, he didn't do them, whatever that 'corrupt, preordained' verdict might say." The Prime Minister shook his head. "I really wish Hamish had been able to bring in a guilty verdict on all specifications."

"I'm pretty sure he does, too," Alexander said. "We didn't do him any favors sticking him with the presidency of the court, though."

"We didn't. The computers' random, scrupulously fair selection process did that, remember? A completely blind process, with no human input, that assured everyone involved that no one had exercised any undue influence to 'shape' the selections."

"And if Hamish could have gotten to the programming, the computers would for damned sure have picked someone—*anyone*—else!"

"I don't doubt that," Cromarty said, and they looked at one another in matching disgust.

As the Prime Minister had said, the selection of officers for Pavel Young's court-martial had been scrupulously fair. BuPers' computers had chosen them completely randomly from the pool of available senior officers. Which, in this case, had selected anything but a neutral court.

"He certainly expressed himself . . . frankly to *us* when he found out who was on it," Cromarty continued. "I have to wonder what went on when they sat down to deliberate the charges, though. God, I wish I could've been a fly on the wall!"

"Well, don't expect Hamish to give you the gory details. I love my brother—I really, truly do—but there are times I'd like to strangle him. And this is one of them, because there's no way in hell he's going to violate the court's confidentiality to tell us who engineered the final verdict."

"'Engineered'?" Cromarty looked at him. "That's such a *sordid* verb, Willie! One entirely too close to what High Ridge is saying happened." Alexander looked back skeptically, and the Prime Minister shrugged. "Oh, I agree with you that that has to be what happened, and to be honest, it was probably the best outcome we could realistically hope for. But it sticks in my craw, Willie. It really does."

"I know." Alexander sighed. "And it sticks in Hamish's, too, I'm pretty sure. But I think it's obvious at least some members of the court went in determined to acquit rather than convict."

"Jurgens and Lemaitre, you mean?"

Rear Admiral of the Green Rexford Jurgens was a card-carrying Conservative and a Janacek loyalist from way back. Commodore Antoinette Lemaitre was his political antithesis, an equally rabid Liberal, but her antipathy for Honor Harrington had scarcely been a secret after the way Harrington had smacked down her friend and colleague Reginald Houseman. In this instance, despite their own cordial dislike for one another, she and Jurgens had undoubtedly gone into the trial with a matching determination to protect "the true execution of justice" from the "politically motivated kangaroo court" upon which they had found themselves serving.

And unlike Hamish Alexander, neither of them would have hesitated for an instant to put personal bias and ideology ahead of the discharge of their duty to the Navy and to the Crown.

"Of course I do! Who else could it've been? I'm damned sure Theodosia Kuzak and Thor Simengaard wouldn't have objected to shooting him, anyway!" Alexander snorted. "I don't think either of them would have convicted if they'd thought the evidence wasn't there, but what Young did must have stuck in *their* craws, too. They wouldn't have hesitated for a moment about the death sentence if they'd believed the evidence *was* there . . . and the fact that the verdict on all of the other specifications was unanimous suggests they thought it was."

"Which only leaves Sonja," Cromarty mused, and Alexander nodded.

The professional clashes between Hamish Alexander and Admiral of the Red Lady Sonja Hemphill, the acknowledged leader of the material-based strategists of the *jeune ecole*, were the stuff of legend. They'd known one another almost since childhood, and their... differences of opinion were epic. More than that, Hemphill was both heir to the Barony of Low Delhi and one of Sir Edward Janacek's cousins, and, like Jurgens, the Conservative Association had always been her ancestral home. At the same time, for all of her zealotry where strategy and weapons policies were concerned, Hemphill had also always been a realist about the Havenite threat. And unlike Jurgens, she possessed something approaching a moral spine. She couldn't have been happy with the Opposition's unyielding refusal to vote out a declaration of war.

"So you think she's the one who came up with the final verdict, too?" the Prime Minister asked after a moment.

"It wasn't Theodosia, it wasn't Simengaard, and it sure as *hell* wasn't my beloved older brother." Alexander shrugged. "Like you said, that only leaves Sonja."

"I'm actually a little surprised she was willing to break ranks on this one," Cromarty said.

"Sonja's never lacked for guts. I'm not all that surprised she'd tell High Ridge and North Hollow to pound sand if she thought that was the right thing to do, but *how* I wish she could have brought herself to break the deadlock and vote to shoot him the way he deserved." Alexander's voice was harsh, and his eyes were back on the smart wall's images of the demonstrators. "I thought she had enough integrity to do that, too."

"I agree entirely," Cromarty said. "On the other hand, she may actually have done us a favor. We're still getting the bastard out of uniform, in a way that makes it *damned* sure he'll never put it on again. And the guilty verdicts—and the sentence—handed down should come as close to kneecapping the new Earl North Hollow politically as we're likely to get. But we didn't turn him into a 'martyr' for the Opposition, either."

Alexander made a rude, incredulous sound and jerked his head at the smart wall, and Cromarty snorted.

"I meant 'martyr' as in 'a *dead* son of a bitch,'" he said. "Nothing we might do could have kept the Opposition from screaming about how 'unjustly' we've 'victimized' him. That's a given, Willie. But I honestly don't know what his father would've done if we'd gone ahead and shot him, and anyone with those files could do a *lot* of damage."

"Files *Young* now has, I might point out," Alexander said. "And, unless memory fails me, his father dropped dead in the courtroom, which would have made it a little difficult for him to take vengeance on us after we shot his son!"

"No, but no one knew he was going to do that until he actually did. And Pavel's got brothers, remember? They're no prizes, either, and they're going to take this not just as their brother's conviction, but as a slur on the family name. A blot on the North Hollow escutcheon."

"*Please!*" Alexander grimaced. "There are so many 'blots' on the North Hollow escutcheon that I'm astonished anyone can even *see* it!"

"But they aren't going to admit that. Even assuming they agreed with you and me, they'd never acknowledge it. And they studied at their father's knee just as much as he did. This way at least they don't have a dead brother to avenge, though. And to be totally honest, I think Stefan is probably even dumber than Pavel. God only knows what he'd do if he ever became earl!"

"Could it really be worse than what we've already got?"

"I don't know, and I don't want to find out," Cromarty said frankly. "And to be honest, I have no idea where Young—North Hollow—is going to go next. But I'm pretty sure this is about the closest to a 'soft landing' we could've engineered. Don't get me wrong! In a lot of ways, I absolutely *hate* it, and the Queen is even more pissed off about it than you and I are. But the important thing is to keep our eyes on the prize and get the damned declaration voted out as soon as we can. If *not* shooting North Hollow gets us there even a week sooner, then much as you and I may hate it, it's probably a bargain."

"I know. I know!" Alexander sighed, glaring at the smart wall. "I just can't help feeling like we blew it, though, Allen. We left the unmitigated bastard alive. Vengeance for vengeance's sake is pretty stupid, but there *is* such a thing as justice, and this wasn't it. Not for all the people he helped the Peeps kill in Hancock, and especially not for Lady Harrington."

Cromarty nodded, his own eyes on the smart wall.

"It's an imperfect universe, Willie," the Prime Minister of Manticore said sadly. "And some days, I hate it even more than usual."

**Steadholder's Palace**
**City of Harrington**
**Harrington Steading**
**Planet Grayson**
**Yeltsin System**
**November 5 1905 PD**
**[November 5, 4009 CE]**

IT WAS COMING ALONG NICELY, Howard Clinkscales thought, gazing through the crystoplast wall at the landscaped grounds. The gardens wouldn't *quite* be finished by the time she arrived, but all of the plantings and water features would be in, at least. And—he raised his eyes—the dome *was* complete. She'd be able to walk the grounds of her own palace without a breath mask. And it was a considerably larger dome than it might have been in years gone by, thanks to the crystoplast.

The planet Grayson hadn't had crystoplast all that long. It was yet another of the bewildering stream of new technologies pouring into the Yeltsin System from the Star Kingdom of Manticore.

That stream was more bewildering for some than for others, he acknowledged with a snort of dry amusement. People like Adam Gerrick, the steading's youthful chief engineer, were utterly delighted by it. For them, that stream was an unending toy chest of new opportunities and new possibilities. Of course, not everyone was an engineer, and among the ones who weren't, too many of the true dinosaurs—like himself, upon all too numerous occasions, Clinkscales acknowledged—were more than simply bewildered by it. They were confused, bereft of the certainties they'd counted upon all their lives, and all too many of them bitterly resented that jarring rearrangement of the Way Things Ought to Be. But Clinkscales had come to realize that the only choices for even the most deeply conservative were to adapt or go the way of every other dinosaur.

75

Well, to adapt but also to do their best to minimize the potential religious and social catastrophes lurking behind that tidal wave of technology, which was a nontrivial challenge, to say the least.

*Scylla and Charybdis*, he thought, and chuckled harshly. *I wonder if Benjamin would believe that particular ancient, pagan example would occur to an old fossil like me? Although, actually, he might. He always was an overly clever young jackanapes!*

That might not, he conceded, be the most respectful possible way to think about the Protector of Grayson, but he'd known Benjamin Mayhew literally since the day of his birth. He'd never really approved of Benjamin's father's decision to send his son and heir off to decadent Old Terra for his college education, and the boy who'd departed had come home as a young man with dangerously "progressive" ideas. Not that there'd ever been much chance he'd have the opportunity to put them into practice, given the figurehead status to which the Protectorship had been reduced.

Until the Yeltsin System and its fratricidal sister Endicott had been drawn into the vortex of the confrontation between the People's Republic of Haven and the Manticoran Alliance. The rest of the galaxy had ignored Yeltsin for over nine centuries. For seven of those centuries, as far as anyone in Yeltsin knew, no one had even remembered the system had been colonized in the first place. And even after the planet Grayson had been rediscovered by the occasional—*very* occasional—tramp freighter, there'd been no conceivable reason for anyone other than those same occasional tramp freighters to visit. And, to be honest, Howard Clinkscales had neither blamed the galaxy at large for that nor truly regretted it.

Unfortunately—or fortunately, depending upon one's perspective—Yeltsin was ideally located as a forward base for the alliance the Star Kingdom of Manticore had built against the People's Republic of Haven. Manticore had needed that base; Haven had been determined to deny the Star Kingdom that base; and that had placed Clinkscales' homeworld squarely in the sights of two competing and deplorably secular interstellar powers. Which was ultimately what had brought him to this office, gazing out through that crystoplast wall, thinking deep and profound thoughts.

He snorted in self-amusement.

*I've always known the Tester has a sense of humor*, he thought. *He wouldn't put up with human beings, if He didn't! But this is a particularly pointed joke, even for Him!*

If there had been a single man on the planet of Grayson who'd been more conflicted than he about involving his home star system in a great power rivalry that he'd been almost certain had to turn into a shooting war eventually, Clinkscales had never met him. Of course, there had been *Jared* Mayhew . . . who'd never had the least doubt where Grayson's and his own best interests lay.

The old man's eyes darkened with remembered betrayal, grief, and more than a trace of guilt. He'd loved Jared Mayhew. Like Jared's younger cousin, Benjamin, he'd watched Jared grow from boyhood into a man who stood strong in his faith, strong for the people of Grayson. A man who shared Clinkscales' own deep religious roots and determination to protect Grayson's people from the corruption of a Godless galaxy's licentiousness.

And a man who'd betrayed every oath he'd ever sworn under the eyes of God and Man. Who'd planned and organized the murder of his own cousin and his cousin's entire family in the service of the religious fanatics of Endicott. A man who'd used his friendship with Howard Clinkscales, the commanding general of Planetary Security, to further his traitorous plans. Oh, he'd known better than to give Clinkscales any inkling of what he had in mind. They'd known each other far too long for that. Clinkscales might have agreed with his fears, shared his desperation, yet that could never have induced him to violate his own oaths. But the fact that Jared knew that hadn't prevented him from using their friendship to access information he needed, not to mention using his contacts in the Navy and his own position as Yeltsin's Minister of Industry, to prepare for the Faithful's conquest—*reconquest*, in Jared's eyes—of Grayson. He'd known exactly how to avoid Security's procedures and protocols and the Navy's patrol patterns, and he'd actually used his control of the system's deep space industry, especially its asteroid-mining infrastructure, as cover to help Masada secretly build an advanced, fully equipped military base on Blackbird, one of the gas giant Uriel's moons.

And Howard Clinkscales, the man who'd been charged to protect both his planet and his Protector's family, had let him do it.

He was scarcely the only person Jared had deceived. Jared had never attempted to conceal his own religious conservatism, but no one—including his cousin, Benjamin—had ever suspected that his conservatism was actually fanaticism.

*And I should have. Tester! I would have . . . if I hadn't been so cursed close to my own brand of his madness.*

In his fairer moments, Clinkscales knew he was being unfair to himself when he thought that, but that made his blindness no less culpable. Nor did it change the fact, that the only reason Jared had failed in the end was—

"Excuse me, My Lord."

Clinkscales turned from the windows and raised an eyebrow at the young man standing in his open office doorway.

"Yes, Arthur?"

"Major LaFollet is here, My Lord," Arthur Freyd replied.

"Ah! And early, I see." Clinkscales smiled and walked across to his desk. "Send him in, please."

"Of course, My Lord."

The secretary, although his title really should have been executive officer, Clinkscales often thought, bowed slightly and disappeared. He was back a moment later with a man in the green-on-green uniform of the Harrington Steadholder's Guard.

Andrew LaFollet was tall for a Grayson, very close to Clinkscales' own hundred and eighty centimeters, with dark auburn hair and remarkably steady gray eyes. He was also dauntingly fit, with a solid, well-muscled physique and a perpetually centered balance. He owed the polished edges of that physique to the fact that he'd moved his always arduous exercise regimen into a gym with gravity plates set at 1.35 standard gravities, thirty-eight percent higher than Grayson's, more than two years ago. The balance and those steady eyes had come naturally, and Clinkscales felt a fresh sense of satisfaction as he surveyed him.

"My Lord." LaFollet braced to attention. With his peaked cap clasped under his left arm, he couldn't properly salute.

"Major." Clinkscales nodded and pointed at the chair in front of his desk. "Have a seat."

"Thank you, My Lord," LaFollet replied. But he also waited until Clinkscales had taken his own seat before he actually sat.

"Will there be anything else, My Lord?" Freyd asked.

"No, I think we're good for now. But I expect you and I will have a few more logistic details to hammer out when the major and I are done."

"Of course, My Lord."

Freyd bowed rather more deeply than before and quietly closed the door behind him.

Clinkscales tipped back in his chair, regarding LaFollet thoughtfully while he wondered if the major had a clue as to why he'd been summoned. It was impossible to tell from LaFollet's politely attentive expression as he sat neatly, his cap in his lap. On the one hand, no one outside this office was *supposed* to know. On the other hand, there was more than one reason he'd snatched LaFollet away from Palace Security to serve as the Harrington Guard's second-ranking officer.

"I wonder if you have any idea why I sent for you this morning?" he asked.

"Not officially, no, My Lord."

"An interesting adverb, 'officially,'" Clinkscales observed. "Should I assume from its use that you're sufficiently tapped in to have a pretty fair *unofficial* notion of why you're here?"

"I believe I may," LaFollet acknowledged with a slight smile. "And, if you'll permit me to say so, My Lord, this is a visit that's been long overdue."

In the wrong tone, that might have been construed as a criticism, Clinkscales reflected. And he supposed that it was a criticism, really. But not of the visitor in question.

"You're right," he said with a nod of agreement. "But we're about to fix that, finally." His tone was deeply satisfied, yet then he sighed. "On the other hand, I don't think she really understands everything that's about to change for her. Tester knows I've *told* her often enough, but—" He shook his head. "She's an incredibly smart woman, Major, but she absolutely refuses to think of herself as extraordinary in any way."

"Even incredibly smart people can have blind spots, My Lord."

"I know. But it's possible— No, it's not 'possible'; it's *probable* that this is going to make things a little . . . difficult for you." Clinkscales snorted. "After all, no reason you should be any different from the rest of us!"

LaFollet's smile broadened. He'd served in Palace Security for just over five years, and as Planetary Security's commanding officer, Clinkscales had been *Palace* Security's CO, as well. More to the point, the LaFollet clan had a long tradition of military service and Captain Kerwin LaFollet had been Brigadier Clinkscales' senior aide. They remained close, and Lieutenant General Clinkscales had stood sponsor to both of Kerwin's older sons when they applied for admission to the Grayson's Army's Isaiah McKenzie Academy. The major and Harrington Steading's lord regent had known one another for a very long time. Long enough that some might have wondered if his selection for his present duties had been influenced by that relationship.

No one who knew either of them would have entertained that suspicion.

But that relationship was also the reason LaFollet knew how incredibly difficult Clinkscales must have found it when so many things he'd held to be fundamental truths turned out to be less immutable than he'd always believed. Unlike others, Clinkscales had never believed that if Yeltsin just ignored Manticore and Haven they'd go away, leave Grayson in peace. And he'd always recognized that of the two, Manticore was far less likely to eventually simply ingest Yeltsin. But that had made him no happier about the corrupting foreign influence which must inevitably accompany any alliance with such a secular society. And every deeply conservative bone in his body had been offended when the commanding officer of the Manticoran diplomatic delegation's military escort turned out to be a woman.

Grayson women had always been better treated than their unfortunate sisters among Masada's fanatical Faithful. In many ways, they'd enjoyed highly privileged and protected positions. But that protection and those privileges had come at the expense of their *rights*. They'd been denied the vote, property ownership (except under very special circumstances), jury duty, and—especially!— *military* duty. Every right-thinking Grayson male had known women were too precious, too delicate, and too weak to bear the rigors of military discipline or be exposed to the dangers of military service.

Until they met Honor Harrington, at any rate.

The really remarkable thing about Clinkscales, LaFollet thought fondly, was that his stubborn, invincible, bone-deep integrity had refused to let him remain in that right-thinking majority. And that same integrity was the true reason Protector Benjamin had nominated Howard Clinkscales as the regent of Harrington Steading when it was created after Lady Harrington's desperate defense of Grayson. Benjamin had known Clinkscales would discharge his responsibilities as regent with that same unyielding integrity, even though he must inevitably find himself officiating over— *encouraging*—many of the very changes he once would have fought to the death to prevent. LaFollet had understood that part of Benjamin's thinking from the beginning. What he'd been slower to recognize was that the Protector had also known that the *rest* of Grayson knew about that integrity and the sincerity with which Clinkscales had always held his beliefs. So if *he* could adjust to— could *embrace*—the changes which must inevitably transform Grayson, then perhaps they could, as well.

And there were times, LaFollet knew, when Clinkscales had found his new responsibilities just as uncomfortable as he must have known he would when he accepted them.

"We have her arrival date now," the Regent continued. "She'll be here on the twenty-fifth. The Protector plans to give her a few days to get her feet under her here in Harrington, but he'll be sending out the writs of summons for her confirmation in a week or so, after he and Reverend Hanks have had time to confer. At the moment, it looks like either the twenty-ninth or the thirtieth. And once that happens, she's going to find out we really meant some of the things I've been telling her about. Including you."

"It's not like I haven't known this was coming, My Lord."

"No, but you're about to become the first man in Grayson history who's ever been responsible for a *female* steadholder's personal security, and she's foreign-born, on top of everything else. That's bound to create more than enough . . . delicate moments for you, let's say. And the fact that so far as I can tell she still hasn't fully digested what the letter of the law means for her won't make it one bit easier."

LaFollet nodded. Clinkscales regarded him steadily for several seconds, then let his chair come fully upright and folded his hands on the desktop in front of him.

"All right. I've notified Colonel Hill that you'll be officially transferring from the Steading Guard to the Stead*holder's* Guard as soon as the Conclave witnesses her oath. I'll leave it to you to notify the rest of your detail. And remind them that she'll be leaving Grayson again in no more than a month or two."

LaFollet opened his mouth, but Clinkscales raised a hand before he could speak.

"I know every one of them knew that would happen when they volunteered, Andrew. But there's a difference between knowing that's waiting somewhere up ahead and realizing it's right around the corner. There's no shame in someone's changing his mind before he's sworn his oath to her. Especially since some of them—like you—have waited over three years for this. A lot of things can change in that much time, including obligations to wives and children. All of them deserve the opportunity to tell us if any of those things have changed for them."

"I'll tell them that, of course, My Lord," LaFollet said after a moment. "I've kept tabs on what's happened in their lives, though. And we've been training as a detail for almost two years now. You're right that they deserve the opportunity, but I can tell you now that none of them are about to change their minds."

"I'm sure you're right." Clinkscales smiled a bit crookedly. "That doesn't change our obligation to give them the opportunity. And"— his smile disappeared—"there has been one change that might have affected some of their thinking."

"Captain Tankersley, you mean, My Lord?"

That steady LaFollet gaze never wavered, Clinkscales noted. Not that he'd expected it to. The major's devotion to Lady Harrington went to the bone, even if she didn't know it yet, and the Regent's observation wasn't a surprise to him. The communication between Harrington Steading and Manticore flowed both ways, and Lady Harrington had been scrupulous about staying on top of all of her official correspondence, yet Clinkscales had realized very early on that his Steadholder saw no reason to keep him informed of every little change in her life. Not that an unmarried woman's taking a lover would be regarded as a "little change" by far too many Graysons, he reflected dryly. But because he'd realized the potential consequences of being blindsided by something like that, he'd taken steps to create secondary channels through the Grayson Embassy in Landing that assured that he—and, through him, Major LaFollet—stayed up to date on those minor details she might not have seen any reason to mention. And in this case...

"That's exactly what I mean," he acknowledged. "In all honesty, I wasn't delighted when I first heard about the Captain. But one of the things this job has done is to bring me face-to-face with a lot of things that wouldn't have delighted me once upon a time. And the truth is that you and I both know how many steadholders have violated the Sixth Commandment over the years. Tester! I don't think I could begin to count how many times a steading's passed to an illegitimate heir! There may even have been an excuse for that, back in the old days, given the need to secure the succession, but I haven't noticed the practice slowing down among the current crop."

LaFollet was scarcely surprised by Clinkscales' disgusted tone. Infidelity to an oath of any sort was anathema to the Lord Regent, and adultery, the violation of his wedding vows to his wives, would have been unthinkable.

"I expect some of the boys will be unhappy when I brief them on the Steadholder and Captain Tankersley," the major said after a moment. "I haven't done that yet, of course, since there was no immediate prospect of giving our formal oaths. But I don't expect it to cause any of them to change their minds."

"No?" Clinkscales tipped his head. "Why not?" LaFollet's eyebrows lowered ever so slightly, and the Regent shook his head quickly. "I don't doubt you, Andrew, but I'm genuinely curious about your logic. Frankly, I'm wondering if the reason you don't expect them to change their minds is the same reason I've decided *I'm* nowhere near as uncomfortable about it as I thought I'd be."

LaFollet looked down at the cap in his lap for a moment, then back up at Clinkscales.

"My Lord, you know there's not a single man in the detail who didn't have his own deeply personal reasons for volunteering. I know you do, because you helped me screen them. And we didn't accept anyone we thought was so conservative that he'd be unable to adjust to the differences between Grayson and Manticore. This is one of those differences. And, with all due respect, your reference to the Sixth Commandment doesn't really apply here, does it? Neither the Steadholder nor Captain Tankersley are married, far less married to someone *else*, so there's no question about anyone's committing adultery. Even under our own laws, neither the Sword nor Father Church has the right to dictate to the consciences of two unmarried, consenting adults. *Society* may frown upon it, and the law is pretty strict—and explicit—about a father's obligations to his child, whether or not he's married to that child's mother. But there's no legal or religious bar to the Steadholder's taking an unmarried lover if that's what she chooses to do."

"I agree entirely, and that's the same conclusion I worked my own way to," Clinkscales said. "Somewhat to my shame, it took me longer to get there than it ought to have, however. You're absolutely right about both secular law and Father Church's teachings on this matter, but I'm afraid you put your finger on the heart of the matter when you mentioned society. And custom. The notion of unmarried lovers isn't one our culture as a whole is comfortable with."

"If you'll allow me to say so, My Lord, that's because the self-appointed keepers of public morality always think they know better than the Tester or Father Church when it comes to how everyone *else* ought to behave," LaFollet said tartly, and Clinkscales snorted in harsh amusement.

"The fact that you see that is one of the many reasons I wanted you to command her detail, Andrew. And if you're confident the other men will react the same way when you brief them in, then I'm satisfied."

LaFollet nodded, and Clinkscales turned to his chair to look back out into that landscaped garden.

"The fact that you and I—and the detail—feel that way doesn't mean everyone else will, though. We both know how people like Burdette and Mackenzie feel about Manticore's 'corrupting influence,' and I'm very much afraid the true bigots among them will decide her relationship with Captain Tankersley only confirms their worst fears. Worse, they'll see it as a weapon they can use against her. Given Lady Harrington's stature after the way she defended our entire planet, I expect them to be . . . circumspect, at least initially, about any public criticism or condemnation. But you and I both know it's going to come eventually. And it's going to be ugly when it does."

He turned his head to look at LaFollet once more.

"The truth is, it's easier to protect someone against bullets and bombs than against bigotry, Andrew. I've seen enough evidence of that in my own soul. I'm very much afraid the Steadholder doesn't truly understand yet how some of the genuine scum among the reactionaries will inveigh against her as soon as this becomes public knowledge. I don't expect much of that here, in Harrington, because every single Harrington is a voluntary immigrant. But it *will* happen."

"We'll just have to cross that bridge when we come to it, My Lord."

Andrew LaFollet's tone was calm, almost reflective, and Clinkscales looked back out the windowed wall to hide a thin smile as he reflected upon how unwise anyone would be to do anything of the sort in the major's vicinity. He might not be able to do anything about it legally, given Grayson's traditions of freedom of speech, but LaFollet was a resourceful man. There was no doubt in the Regent's mind that he'd find a way to make his displeasure evident.

Which suited Howard Clinkscales just fine.

**HMS *Nike***
**Manticore Planetary Orbit**
**Manticore Binary System**
**November 19, 1905 PD**

"More tea, Captain?" Chief Steward James MacGuiness murmured.

"Yes, please," Captain Alistair McKeon replied, and watched as MacGuiness refilled his glass. McKeon had never been exposed to the concept of iced, sweetened tea before his first visit to Grayson, but he'd become sadly addicted to it in the years since. And MacGuiness not only knew about his addiction but, evil man that he was, had learned exactly how to cater to it.

"This, as always, was delicious, Mac," the tall, brown-haired woman seated at the head of the table said, as if echoing McKeon's thoughts.

"I'll pass that along to the galley, Ma'am," MacGuiness replied, smiling at Captain Honor Harrington.

"I thought the tangerine duck was done particularly well, Mac," Doctor Allison Harrington said.

"Which is a high compliment from Mom," Honor pointed out. "We all know what those gourmands from Beowulf are like!"

The cream-and-gray treecat in the highchair to her left bleeked a laugh as Honor smiled teasingly at her mother.

"Is it my fault your father didn't even know how to steam rice properly before we met?"

"Hey!" Doctor Alfred Harrington—who was, in fact, an excellent cook in his own right—looked at his wife sternly. "That's a base libel! I knew exactly how to boil rice. I can't help it if effete, overcivilized people prefer separate grains. You boil it long enough to get rid of the air spaces, and you can fit a lot more of it on your plate!"

"How such a barbarian ever won my heart and hand is one of life's mysteries, Mac," Allison told the steward in a tone of sorrowful bemusement.

"I can see that, Doctor," MacGuiness replied gravely, then returned his attention to Honor. "Coffee and cocoa, Ma'am?" he asked.

"I think that would probably be a good idea," she approved.

"And the chocolate cake, Ma'am?" He smiled. "I believe it's double fudge . . . and I just happen to have come into possession of a small quantity of mocha chocolate ice cream as a side, should you be interested."

"Alas, you know me too well." Honor smiled back at him, then looked across the table at her father. "And what about you?"

"I think—solely because you and I are both descended from the Meyerdahl First Wave, you understand—that that would be an excellent idea," he replied gravely, and his undutiful wife gave a rather unladylike hoot of amusement. He looked at her with an affronted expression, and she shook her head.

"Do you have any idea how often over the last half-T-century I've heard that as an excuse to feed someone's sweet tooth? Oh, I know all about that metabolism of yours. God knows keeping Honor fed as a teenager was a challenge! But Mac knows as well as I do about you and double-fudge chocolate cake, Alfred Harrington!"

"I have no idea what you're talking about." He elevated his nose with an audible sniff. "Personally, I think your verbal abuse stems solely from the fact that certain individuals with less active metabolisms resent the fashion in which those of us blessed with *more* active metabolisms are free to indulge in the finer things in life without fear of unfortunate consequences."

"I've noticed the same thing, Daddy." Honor nodded soberly. "Mike was always that way at the Island, too. Every time I took an extra serving of blackberry cobbler and asked for the whipped cream, she looked at me like I was cheating or something. Sad." She shook her head. "So sad."

"Wait a minute!" Captain Michelle Henke protested. "I'm just an innocent bystander in this food fight!"

"Bystander, maybe," Honor said. "Innocent?" She extended one hand, palm down, and wiggled it from side to side.

Henke shook her head with a chuckle and looked at the short, powerfully built captain seated across the table from her.

"You see what I've been putting up with ever since the Academy,

Paul?" she said. "You sure you want to get involved with someone with her abusive personality?"

"Too late," Captain Tankersley replied. "Besides, I haven't noticed her being abusive to anyone who didn't *deserve* it."

"*Et tu*, Brute?"

"You know I don't speak Spanish." Tankersley's tone was so aggrieved, his expression so perplexed, that Honor giggled. She hated it when she giggled, and the twinkle in Tankersley's eye said he knew it.

"That was *Latin*, buffoon!" Henke's voice was unsteady as she fought her own laughter.

"Latin, Spanish, German—" Tankersley shrugged. "What's the difference?"

"Oh my God." Honor shook her head. "I happen to know you speak three languages in addition to Standard English, Paul!"

"Four, actually. Not that I'm keeping count, of course," Tankersley replied complacently.

"I think, Mac," Honor said, "that it would probably be a good idea to get dessert served before someone at this table comes by his *just* deserts. And"—she reached out to caress the treecat's ears—"I think Nimitz would probably appreciate a celery chaser for *his* duck."

The 'cat bleeked enthusiastic agreement, and Honor looked back at MacGuiness.

"You see?"

"Of course, Ma'am."

MacGuiness bowed with commendable gravity, and Honor shook her head as he disappeared through her dining cabin's hatch.

"Mac puts up with entirely too much out of all of you," she said severely.

"Well, after looking after *you* for five T-years, he should be all trained up by now," Henke replied. "I wouldn't want to say anything about pots and kettles, you understand, but—"

She shrugged, and Tankersley laughed.

"Are you going to just sit there and listen to them abuse me, Alistair?" Honor asked, looking at him across the table.

"You seem to be doing just fine to me," he said, and sipped iced tea.

"Yeah, sure!"

Honor shook her head again, and McKeon chuckled, but the truth was that he was deeply relieved to see the smile in her eyes as she looked around the table. She'd had precious little to laugh about in the eight T-months since the Battle of Hancock, and especially not in the last two T-months since the slowing operational tempo had finally allowed her to bring her own wounded ship home to Manticore.

He watched her profile as she turned to say something else to Tankersley, and his own eyes softened as Tankersley smiled back at her. That was one of the best things that could possibly have happened to her, not that McKeon would ever have expected it, given the circumstances under which she and Tankersley had first met. On the other hand, he wouldn't have expected his own deep friendship with her, either, given the circumstances under which *he'd* first met her.

His own smile faded just a bit as he recalled the day in HMS *Fearless'* briefing room when he'd finally confronted—admitted— how deeply he'd resented seeing her in the captain's chair he'd wanted so badly. Recalled admitting, not just to himself, but to *her*, how completely he'd failed her as her executive officer.

And recalled the way she'd acknowledged his failure and stepped past it, put it behind them as they built a rock-solid professional partnership . . . and what was probably the deepest friendship of his life.

Lady Dame Honor Harrington, Countess and—of particular significance, given this evening's dinner—*Steadholder* Harrington, had that effect on people, he thought, and she seemed to be the only person who never even realized she did. He suspected her parents explained a lot of that, and so did her adoption bond with Nimitz. A woman didn't grow up with those parents and that deep bond without becoming an exceptional person, but that indefinable . . . *something* about her, the effortless authority and charisma that made her not simply one of the Royal Manticoran Navy's most brilliant commanders but one of its best mentors and teachers of *future* brilliant commanders. . . . That came from somewhere else, from a gift, a spark, that touched only the truly great captains.

It was one she managed to pass along to others, too, and he doubted that she ever realized that, either. He himself would never possess that spark the way she did. He knew that. *No one* would ever possess it the way she did. But he knew he was a far better starship captain than he would ever have been if they'd never met.

Which made the reason for this convivial dinner bittersweet, to say the least. His mood darkened, and Honor looked across the table at him again as if she'd tasted the change in his emotions.

"Why do I suspect you're thinking less than happy thoughts, Alistair?" she asked almost gently.

"Who, me?" He gazed back at her with his most innocent expression, and she waved an admonishing forefinger at him.

"You," she replied, and then moved around the table, starting with her mother and working her way to Henke, "and you, and you, and you. In fact, the only person at this table—aside from Nimitz, who's too busy contemplating the celery about to arrive on his plate—who isn't thinking less than happy thoughts, is Paul."

"Don't leave *me* out," Tankersley protested. "I'll have you know I'm capable of thinking thoughts which are just as unhappy as those of anyone else around this table. Although," he added in the tone of one acknowledging a fair point, "mine *are* probably less ... cerebral than the others. But then, I'm a low and vulgar fellow."

"What *you* are is a jerk," Honor told him, touching the side of his face gently, but then she looked back at McKeon.

"Seriously, Alistair. Cheer up! I'll only be gone for a few months, and *Nike* will be in the yard dogs' hands the entire time. She may still have been combat capable, but in addition to finishing the flag deck rebuild, she's got a *lot* of other, littler stuff that needs attention, and just getting to some of it's going to be an incredible pain. So it's not like there's a lot I could be doing here that Eve Chandler and Rafe Cardones can't handle just fine."

"I know." McKeon nodded. "It's just that it's so damned unfair that *you're* the one being run out of the star system."

"First," she said firmly, "I'm not being run out of Manticore. And, second, the fact that I'm ... taking a brief vacation isn't *unfair.*"

"Forgive me, sweetheart, but it damned well *is* unfair," her mother said.

Honor looked at her, and Allison shrugged.

"In a 'fair' universe they would have *shot* the motherless bastard," she said, and her expression had turned as grim as her voice.

"Mother—"

"I have no intention of raining all over the dessert when Mac brings it in, Honor, but since this has come up, I'll just take this opportunity to say that ever since Pavel Young crossed your path at the Academy, I've been waiting for the day the mills of the gods finally caught up with him. And I wasn't a bit surprised when the sort of scum who'd tried to rape a fellow middy turned out to be a coward, as well. If there were any true justice in the universe, the Navy *would* have shot him, and you know it."

"Well, that's a downer," Honor observed wryly.

"It's also true!" Allison shot back. "In fact, I'm having a little trouble forgiving the Navy for just cashiering him."

"That wasn't really the Admiralty's choice," Alfred said, reaching to take Allison's hand. "Trust me, they *wanted* to shoot him."

"Really?" Allison turned her head, and the anger her earlier humor had masked looked out of her eyes at him. "Obviously not everybody in the Navy did. Or they would have."

"All right. That's fair," Honor conceded. "If he'd been convicted on all of the specifications, they would have. So the fact that he wasn't *would* seem to indicate that at least someone on the court-martial board who knew he was guilty cast a political vote when it came to the capital charges. And I won't pretend that knowing he walked away from the firing squad when whoever it was knew perfectly well that he was guilty doesn't make me angrier than hell, Mom."

Honor Harrington seldom used even the mildest of profanity, and the huge, almond eyes she shared with her mother were just as hard as Allison's own. But then she inhaled deeply.

"Knowing that makes me angry, it makes me sick at heart, and it makes me incredibly bitter when I think about all the people in Hancock he helped the Peeps kill when he ran for it," she continued. "But that doesn't mean it was the wrong decision."

"What?" Allison stared at her, and even her father seemed to twitch in surprise. In fact, the only person who didn't seem surprised by her last sentence was Tankersley.

"I said that doesn't mean it was the wrong decision." Honor shrugged. "Understand me, I don't like it one bit, I don't think it was the one the facts supported, and I know as well as anyone else in this compartment that the Navy's failure to shoot him happened only because of corruption and the raw, naked abuse of political power."

Her eyes were still hard, but her voice was level, almost conversational. "All of that may be true, but what's also true is that there *wasn't* any 'right' decision in this case. There couldn't be, given the politics in play." She grimaced. "I don't like politics. I don't understand politics, and I don't really *want* to understand them, but sometimes we all have to do things we don't want to do. So, I've been forced to try to understand this."

McKeon watched her expression, remembering the Honor Harrington he'd first met as she came aboard HMS *Fearless* as the light cruiser's newest commanding officer. She hadn't "understood politics" then, either, which might have explained why she'd ignored all the reasons she shouldn't step on all those wrong, politically powerful toes to do her duty. It might have...but it didn't. The explanation was far simpler than that: she'd known what her duty *was*, and she was constitutionally incapable of doing a single centimeter less.

And that was what he was seeing in those brown eyes of hers now, he realized. That same woman, five years later, with enormously more experience, still refusing to do a single centimeter less than her duty to her Star Kingdom demanded.

"We *need* that declaration of war," she said now, laying her folded forearms on the table leaning slightly forward over them. "Right now, Admiral Caparelli and the Admiralty are fighting a 'non-war' on a shoestring. Alistair, you and Mike both know Caparelli's already operating well beyond the theoretical limitations of Riposte Gamma trying to keep *any* momentum on our side. And you know how tight we're starting to run maintenance cycles just to keep ships forward deployed, too. Just like you know we can't even activate the mutual defense provisions of the Alliance without a formal declaration. And Young's father and his cronies were totally willing to let the entire Star Kingdom go straight to hell to protect his worthless backside. That's beneath contempt, but it's also the way things are. So somebody on that court-martial board voted to convict on all of the non-capital charges, to at least get him out of the Service. But that same somebody—and, frankly, I have a few suspicions about who it might have been—also recognized that convicting him on the capital charges, getting him shot, would have driven his father and the Conservative Association even deeper into opposition. The

Progressives probably would have gone with them, and that could very well have—probably *would* have—brought down the Cromarty Government. It would certainly have delayed the declaration even longer, and it might even have forced a coalition government. One that could even have brought someone like *Janacek* back to the Admiralty. Just how do you think *that* would have affected the war?"

She looked around the table, and Henke cleared her throat. Honor raised an eyebrow at her, and the other captain shrugged.

"I can't fault a single point of your analysis," she said. "But I think it might not be a bad idea to add that in addition to the nepotism, cronyism, and complete and total corruption of the Conservative Association, there are those members of the House of Lords who still genuinely believe if we just stand back long enough, the Peeps will finish self-destructing and there won't be any need for a war."

"That's fair," Tankersley said. "Incredibly *stupid* of them, but a fair summation. And it's also fair to say some Peers, and even quite a few of New Kiev's Liberals in the Commons, simply can't bring themselves to give up their desperate hope that Pierre and his Committee of Public Safety truly do represent a genuine reform movement that will recognize the bankruptcy of its warmongering predecessors and embrace the cause of peace, justice, and interstellar amity."

"And I have some nice bottomland on Fenris I'd like to sell anybody stupid enough to genuinely believe that," Henke told her cousin tartly.

"I didn't say all of them who are *saying* it genuinely believe it, Mike," Tankersley said mildly. "I do think *most* of the ones saying they believe it truly do, mind you, probably because they have to. They live—or *want* to live—in a world where sweet reason will always triumph if we 'just give peace a chance.' It's the reason so many of them have fought our military buildup tooth and nail ever since King Roger's death, because 'someone has to be the voice of reason.' My God, some of them have been doing that for over half a century! You think someone dug into that deep a bunker can just abandon it simply because reality kicks them in the head?"

Despite his even tone, his expression was disgusted, and he shrugged.

"But my real point was that the justifications people like High

Ridge are giving—that the Peeps will simply implode if we leave them alone long enough—are bolstered by the 'give peace a chance' crowd, as well. Which gives the 'how do we save Pavel Young's worthless ass' cabal additional cover that their talking heads and the opposition 'faxes are playing up for all they're worth."

"And that's also one reason for the demonstrations." Honor nodded. "Oh, there aren't that many of them, and a few hundred— or even a few thousand—demonstrators represent only a teeny tiny percentage of the total electorate. But they can be a very visible and noisy teeny tiny percentage. Visible and noisy enough that they *seem* to represent a much larger chunk of voters than they actually do. And like Paul says, the ones still opposing the declaration aren't all in the Conservatives' pocket by a long chalk. In fact, darned near half of them are card-carrying Liberals—and even a few Progressives—who truly buy into that 'the Peeps will implode' theory. Quite a lot of them because they're genuine pacifists, horrified by the very notion of a war on this scale, and desperate to embrace *anything* that will avoid one." Her nostrils flared, and her eyes went bleak for a moment. "I know we all think they're wrong—and I think they're dangerous, as well—but a part of me wishes to God they were *right*... and that we had a single chance of dodging this pulser dart."

She sat silent for a moment, then inhaled deeply and shook herself.

"Of course, that only accounts for the demonstrators who *aren't* in the Conservatives' fold," she continued wryly. "According to a certain unofficial, unnamed source in Admiral Givens' office, at least half of the Conservative protesters waving Young's picture around outside Parliament are professional, paid demonstrators. But the other half aren't, and the fact that Young's father died in front of him while the verdict was being read bought him a lot of sympathy he doesn't deserve. And then there's the thorny little problem that with his father gone, he becomes Earl North Hollow, which makes him a member of the House of Lords, and his court-martial verdict doesn't do a thing to prevent that."

"And that makes this your fault, your problem, exactly how?" McKeon was a bit surprised by the amount of anger he heard in his own question.

"Well, for those who think I'm a loose warhead, it's *all* my fault!"

Honor surprised them all with a chuckle that sounded completely genuine, but then her expression sobered again.

"Right now, for better or worse, Young and I are the faces—the public...avatars—for the pro-declaration and anti-declaration crowds. I don't know about him, but I'd really rather not see the holo-posters with my face on them being waved around over clouds of old-fashioned teargas. That doesn't change the fact that it's happening, though." She grimaced. "And that means anything *I* can do to dial the temperature down, even a little, is completely worth doing."

"And you don't think letting the Opposition claim—tactfully, of course!"—Allison rolled her eyes—"that they've chased you clear out of Manticore won't embolden them? That they won't announce that the only reason you're leaving is because you're so furious that your unprovoked vendetta against the Young family has gone so poorly?"

"Mom, an act of *God* couldn't prevent some of them from claiming that! But when they do, Cromarty and his supporters can cut them off at the knees—tactfully, of course"—Honor actually grinned at her mother—"by pointing out that I'm also Steadholder Harrington. My ship's in the yard for repairs, I haven't taken any leave in the last couple of T-years, and I have legal obligations to the Star Kingdom's most visible ally—the ally in whose home star system we fought one of the critical opening battles of the war, I might add—*as* a steadholder. I'll be fulfilling those obligations—and I really will be, and you know it—if anyone wants to raise a stink over my departure. And, frankly, while it probably wouldn't have occurred to me under other circumstances, I darned well ought to have already been there and done that." She shook her head. "I took an oath, Mom, and it's time I stepped up and fulfilled it."

"Which is the only reason you're going at just this particular instant, of course." Allison's tone was far more sarcastic than any she normally employed with her daughter.

"No, it's not. But"—Honor smiled at her, much more gently—"that doesn't mean it isn't the reason I should have done this at least two T-years ago."

"Honor, are you attempting to convince me that you genuinely want to go to Grayson right now?" Allison asked skeptically.

"I'm telling you I don't genuinely *not* want to go to Grayson right now," Honor replied. "And, to be honest, one reason I *am* less than totally enthralled with the notion is that Paul can't come with me." She turned her head to smile warmly at Tankersley. "I'd a lot rather stay right here where I could keep an eye on him and his yard dogs—in a purely professional and platonic sort of way, you understand—while they patch up *Nike*'s holes and dents."

Her smile turned wicked and her eyes danced as Tankersley waved one hand in modest disclaimer.

"Unfortunately," she looked back at her mother, "*Hephaestus* and the Navy seem quite impressed with his capabilities and they won't let me stash him away in my luggage. And if they would," she added judiciously, "I'd probably get a lot less accomplished on Grayson, thanks to the distraction quotient."

"'*Distraction* quotient'?" Tankersley repeated in an offended tone.

"But a very *nice* distraction, Paul!" she reassured him earnestly.

"Hmpf!"

"Look at it this way," she said, unfolding her forearms to lay one hand on his shoulder as MacGuiness and the pair of second-class stewards mates he'd drafted for tonight's dinner party reentered the compartment, "if I'm gone for, say, two whole months, by the time I get back here I'll be in a mood to greet you very enthusiastically." She batted her eyelashes at him. "They do say every cloud has a silver lining, you know."

"I believe I've heard that somewhere," he said, smiling back at her, then looked in Allison's direction and arched one eyebrow as Doctor Harrington chortled.

"I think you'd better get your vitamins and your rest while she's gone, Paul!" Allison said. "She *is* half-Beowulfan, you know."

"Why, yes, now that you mention it," Paul replied, smiling broadly as the faintest trace of a blush brushed Honor's high cheekbones. "I *did* know that. Quite . . . exhausting sometimes, actually, isn't it?"

"Oh, tell me about it!" Alfred shook his head, his smile equally broad. "Tell me about it."

**Steadholder Hall**
**City of Austen**
**Sword Steading**
**and**
**Steadholder's Palace**
**City of Harrington**
**Harrington Steading**
**Planet Grayson**
**Yeltsin System**
**November 30, 1905 PD**
**[November 30, 4009 CE]**

ANDREW LA FOLLET STOOD AGAINST the rear wall of the enormous horseshoe-shaped chamber and hoped he looked less nervous than he felt. It was silly to feel so anxious, really, given how long he'd prepared and trained against this day.

He told himself that firmly. Very firmly.

Himself didn't listen.

His lips twitched very slightly at the thought, and then he stiffened as a harsh iron-on-iron clang echoed in the hall. He knew what that sound was, and he watched the Door Warden draw his sword as the huge, centimeters-thick panels swung slowly open in response to that summons.

They parted fully, and a single woman stood in the opening, flanked by the kneeling ranks of the Steadholders' Guard. She was tall—impossibly tall, for any Grayson woman—and she stood like a slender flame in a gown of white and a formal vest the same deep, rich shade as the green tunic LaFollet wore. The spired golden glory of the Star of Grayson glittered upon her breast in the light spilling through those portals, and the same light glowed in the green eyes of the treecat in her arms.

"Who petitions audience of the Protector?" the Door Warden demanded in formal challenge.

"I seek audience of no man." The soprano voice was clear and unwavering, with an accent never born of Grayson. "I come not to petition, but to claim admittance to the Conclave and be seated therein, as is my right."

"By what authority?" the Door Warden challenged, sword rising into a guard position, and she raised her head proudly.

"By my own authority, under God and the Law," she returned.

"Name yourself," the Warden commanded.

"I am Honor Stephanie Harrington, daughter of Alfred Harrington, come to claim of right my place as Steadholder Harrington," she replied, and the Warden stepped back a pace and lowered his sword.

"Then enter this place, that the Conclave of Steadholders may judge your fitness for the office you claim, as is its ancient right," he intoned.

LaFollet watched as she stepped forward in a swirl of skirts. The door boomed softly shut behind her, and the Door Warden went to one knee before the throne of Benjamin IX, Protector of Grayson, bowing across the jeweled Sword of State as he rested its tip on the stone floor.

"Your Grace, I present to you and to this Conclave Honor Stephanie Harrington, daughter of Alfred Harrington, who comes claiming a place among your steadholders," he intoned, and the Protector gazed at her for a long, still moment, then raised his eyes to the long rows of throne-like seats.

"Steadholders," his voice rose clear, "this woman claims right to a seat among you. Would any challenge her fitness so to do?"

LaFollet's nostrils flared. It was not the simple question of Grayson's normal formula, for this woman was the very first woman in the history of Grayson to claim Steading in her own right. It would take an extraordinarily brave or arrogant—or both—man to challenge that claim, but that didn't mean no one would.

Yet only silence answered, and the Protector nodded.

"Would any speak in her favor?" he asked quietly, and this time a rumbling "Aye" replied.

"Your claim is freely granted by your peers, Lady Harrington," the Protector declared with a smile. "Come now and take your place among them."

The massed steadholders stood as she climbed the stone steps to stand directly before the Protector. Two small velvet cushions had been placed before his throne, and she set her treecat carefully on one, then went to her knees on the other. More than one of the watching steadholders frowned as she knelt without the curtsy Grayson's formal etiquette demanded of its women, but no one spoke as the Door Warden went to one knee beside the throne to offer the Sword of State, hilt-first, to the Protector.

Benjamin accepted it, then extended its hilt to Lady Harrington, and she laid her hands upon it.

"Honor Stephanie Harrington," the Protector said quietly, "are you prepared, in the presence of the assembled Steadholders of Grayson, to swear fealty to the Protector and People of Grayson under the eyes of God and His Holy Church?"

"I am, Your Grace, yet I may do so only with two reservations." She withdrew her hands from the sword hilt. There was no refusal in her clear soprano, but she met the Protector's eyes levelly, steadily.

"It is your ancient and lawful right to state reservations to your oath," he said. "Yet it is also the right of this Conclave to reject those reservations and deny your place, should it find them offensive to it. Do you acknowledge that right?"

"I do, Your Grace."

"Then state your first reservation."

"As Your Grace knows, I am also a subject of the Star Kingdom of Manticore, a member of its peerage, and an officer in the Queen's Navy. As such, I am under obligations I cannot honorably disregard. Nor may I abandon the nation to which I was born or my oaths to my Queen to accept even a steadholder's high office, nor swear fealty to Grayson without reserving to myself the right and responsibility to meet and perform my duties to her."

The Protector looked over her head at the Conclave.

"My Lords, this seems to me a right and honorable declaration, but the judgment in such matters must be yours. Does any man here dispute this woman's right to hold steading on Grayson with this limitation?"

Silence answered, and the Protector turned back to Honor.

"And your second reservation is?"

"Your Grace, I am not a communant of the Church of Humanity

Unchained. I respect its doctrines and teachings, but I am not of your faith."

"I see." This time the Protector sounded grave, and LaFollet understood why perfectly. No steadholder not of the Church had ever held office, and now Benjamin looked at the white-haired man to his right.

"Reverend, this reservation touches upon the Church and so falls within your province. How say you?"

Reverend Julius Hanks, Grayson's senior religious leader, gazed back at him for a moment, then laid one hand on Lady Harrington's head.

"Lady Harrington, you say you are not of our Faith, but there are many ways to God." Someone hissed audibly, and LaFollet's eyes flashed with anger. But no one spoke, and the Reverend ignored the intrusion.

"Do you believe in God, my child?" he asked.

"I do, Reverend." Lady Harrington's reply was firm, unwavering.

"And do you serve Him to the best of your ability, as your heart gives you to understand His will for you?"

"I do."

"Will you, as steadholder, guard and protect the right of your people to worship God as their own hearts call them so to do?"

"I will."

"Will you respect and guard the sanctity of our Faith as you would your own?"

"I will."

The Reverend nodded—in satisfaction, not surprise—and turned back to the Protector.

"Your Grace, this woman is not of our Faith, yet she has so declared before us all, making no effort to pretend otherwise. More, she stands proven a good and godly woman, one who hazarded her own life and suffered grievous wounds to protect not only our Church but our world when we had no claim upon her. I say to you, and to the Conclave"—he turned to face the assembled steadholders, and his resonant voice, trained in twice a score of cathedrals, seemed to fill that vast chamber—"that God knows His own! The Church accepts this woman as its champion and defender, whatever the faith through which she may serve God's will in her own life."

Another, deeper silence answered, and the Reverend stepped back beside the throne.

"Your reservations have been noted and accepted by the lords secular and temporal of Grayson, Honor Stephanie Harrington," the Protector said, gazing down at her once more. "Do you swear now, before us all, that they constitute your sole reservations of heart and soul and mind?"

"I do so swear, Your Grace."

"Then I call upon you to swear fealty before your peers," the Protector said, and Lady Harrington placed her hands upon the sword once more.

"Do you, Honor Stephanie Harrington, daughter of Alfred Harrington, with the afore noted reservations, swear fealty to the Protector and People of Grayson?"

"I do."

Andrew LaFollet's spine straightened at the iron fidelity of that clear, unwavering soprano.

"Will you bear true service to the Protector and People of Grayson?"

"I will."

"Do you swear, before God and this Conclave, to honor, preserve, and protect the Constitution of Grayson, and to protect and guide your people, guarding them as your own children? Will you swear to nurture them in time of peace, lead them in time of war, and govern them always with justice tempered by mercy, as God shall give you the wisdom so to do?"

"I do so swear," Lady Harrington said softly, and Mayhew nodded.

"I accept your oath, Honor Stephanie Harrington. And as Protector of Grayson, I will answer fealty with fealty, protection with protection, justice with justice, and oath-breaking with vengeance, so help me God."

The Protector's right hand slid down to cover both of Lady Harrington's. Then he returned the sword to the Warden, and Reverend Hanks handed him a gleaming double-handful of golden glory in its place. Benjamin shook it out reverently, and Lady Harrington bowed her head for him as he hung the massive chain about her neck. The patriarch's key of a steadholder glittered below the Star of Grayson, and the Protector stood to take her hand in his own.

"Rise, then, Lady Harrington, Steadholder Harrington!" he said loudly, and Andrew LaFollet forgot discipline as his voice joined the roar of acclaim that rolled up against the crowded chamber's walls.

✦ ✦ ✦

"Ma'am?"

Honor Harrington turned from her conversation with Lady Bethany Clinkscales, Howard Clinkscales' senior wife.

"Yes, Mac?"

"Lord Clinkscales has arrived."

"And about time, too," Bethany said so tartly Honor chuckled. Clinkscales had sent her and his wives—Bethany, Rebecca, and Constance—ahead to her brand-new steading's palace while he dealt with the last few formalities. She'd offered to stay with him, but he'd only shaken his head.

"Trust me, My Lady, you'd be bored to tears," he said. "And to be totally honest, unless you've read my memos with a little more attention to the dreary formal details than I strongly suspect is the case, I expect you'd basically only be in the way." He'd grinned at her snort of amusement, then shrugged. "Go ahead, My Lady. It's a long flight back to Harrington, and I'll be along as soon as I can."

The armored air limo had delivered her from the shuttle pad to the palace an hour or so earlier, and Bethany and her sister wives had escorted her to her new office. It had been Clinkscales' office, and she supposed it still was, although a second desk had been moved into it.

One with her name on it.

"I think we have to cut him some slack, Bethany," she demurred now with a smile. "He's been handling all the details for the Steading ever since it was formally established. I don't suppose it's very surprising those details put a crimp in his schedule today, as well."

"When you've come to know my husband as well as I know him, My Lady, you'll realize that most of those 'crimps' in his schedule were inserted by him. Usually to suit his own nefarious purposes."

"I'm sure that's at least a *little* unfair." Honor's eyes twinkled as she tasted Bethany's loving exasperation.

"'Little' as in 'you'd need a microscope to see it,' you mean, My Lady?"

"Maybe not quite *that* little," Honor said around a spurt of laughter, then turned to face the office door as Howard Clinkscales stepped through it, still carrying his silver-headed regent's staff of office. She smiled as she saw him, but her eyebrows rose as she saw another dozen men at his heels, in the dark green tunics and lighter green trousers she'd chosen for the Harrington Steadholder's Guard. They followed him through the door, and a corner of her mind reflected that it was a good thing the office was so large as they fell into four neat ranks behind Clinkscales.

"Howard," she said.

"My Lady."

Clinkscales bowed from the waist, and the men behind him followed suit. Honor inclined her head to acknowledge the courtesy, but she felt more than a little awkward as she did. It would have been easier if she'd been in uniform, she thought, but she wasn't, and she had no idea how to curtsy properly in a gown. Besides, curtsying would have been the wrong response, since hers was the superior rank here in Harrington. On the other hand, there were no protocols—yet—for how a female steadholder properly acknowledged her subordinates. She hoped none of the guardsmen at Clinkscales' heels were offended by her "masculine" response, but if they were, they'd better start getting over it now.

"I realize I'm still learning the ropes," she continued, "but I can't help suspecting that I should have been taking care of whatever's kept you."

"Most of it was just collecting documents, My Lady." Clinkscales grimaced. "And, as I told you, it was also a boring process. I've shuffled all the paperwork off onto Arthur to keep an eye on for us. Tomorrow morning, though, you and I will have a marathon signing session to tidy up all the details. I'm sure," he added dryly, "it will be just as boring as collecting them was."

"I can barely wait." Honor's tone was equally dry. "Signing off on a new command's paperwork is bad enough. I suspect this will be worse."

"Oh, I think I can pretty much guarantee that," Clinkscales replied, and Honor chuckled. Then she waved gracefully at the guardsmen who'd followed him into the office.

"Why is it that I don't think you brought these gentlemen along just to protect you from my wrath when you warned me about that?"

"Because I'm not the one they're here to protect, My Lady," Clinkscales said, and Honor's eyes narrowed at his suddenly serious tone.

She gazed at him for a moment, then raised an eyebrow in silent question, and the tall, still-burly regent braced himself on his staff.

"Your Grace, I know how busy you've been. That said, I also... strongly suspect there are at least a few of your obligations you've used that busyness to put off. Unfortunately, you can't do that anymore."

He paused, and Honor cocked her head, tasting his fond exasperation and the underlying thread of seriousness that ran through it.

"And just which of those 'obligations' did you have in mind, Howard?"

"My Lady, Grayson law is very specific about certain of a steadholder's legal obligations. And one of those, as I've mentioned to you in more than one letter, is the requirement for any steadholder to be accompanied by his—or her—personal armsmen. As you may recall, I've suggested a time or two that it might be well for you to find time to visit Grayson so that we could take care of that minor detail."

"Howard, I'm a serving naval officer, and I've been looking after myself for forty T-years. I don't need—"

"Forgive me, My Lady," Clinkscales interrupted, "but that's not really the point. It's completely true that you're a naval officer with other valid requirements upon your time, and until today, those requirements trumped your obligations here on Grayson. But today you swore formal fealty and took your place as Harrington's Lady Steader. And that means the law can no longer look the other way and make concessions to relieve you of Steadholder Harrington's obligations."

He held her eyes, and an edge of shame went through her, because he had a point. She knew he did. She *had* used her naval duties to put off this moment, partly because she'd known that Clinkscales would do a better job of establishing the Steading than she ever could have done. But also because of its irrevocability. She admitted that to herself now. She'd put it off because returning to Grayson, swearing her oaths, formally accepting all of "Steadholder

Harrington's obligations," would force her own stubborn integrity and sense of duty to actually *shoulder* those obligations.

"Equally to the point," Clinkscales continued after a moment in a deliberately lighter tone, "while I'm perfectly prepared to concede how capably you've 'looked after' yourself in the past, I personally think it's time we added someone else to help with that little chore. Someone who might be there to lend a little assistance the next time, oh, you decide to take on an entire armed assassination team by yourself, let's say. That's definitely a factor in my thinking on this issue."

He gave her a very no-nonsense look as he reminded her of her and Nimitz's defense of Benjamin Mayhew and his family.

"But my personal feelings are also beside the point," he continued. "First, it's the law, and has been since the Civil War and the death of the Fifty-Three. And, second, allow me to point out that as of this morning, you are officially and legally Steadholder Harrington. That makes you a head of state, My Lady, and heads of state have responsibilities where the protection of the line of succession is concerned."

Honor opened her mouth, but his raised hand cut her off politely.

"My Lady, as you just pointed out, you're a naval officer, and as the Conclave recognized, your duties to your birth kingdom and your Queen predate your responsibilities to Grayson and your Key. I accept that, just as the Conclave did. And that means all of us accept that you may well be called to action yet again, where you'll be at risk of serious injury or death. But you have no heir, and this is a very new steading. That means it's . . . fragile, and if there's anything I or anyone else can do to minimize the chance of something happening to you and destroying that fragility, it's our responsibility to *do* it and your responsibility to *let* us do it."

He held her eyes steadily, and Honor tasted the steely core of his determination. And, she realized, more than a little unwillingly, he had a point. Just as the captain of a Queen's ship had no business leading ground attacks on something like Blackbird Base, a steadholder—any head of state—had no choice but to accept the protection of her own security service, at least when she was dirtside in her steadholder's role. Aboard ship or on active naval service, it might be different, but she *wasn't* aboard ship or on active service at the moment, was she?

"All right, Howard," she sighed. "I'm really not trying to be difficult or play hooky. It's just—"

"Just that you're still having trouble accepting that you're a steadholder, My Lady." Clinkscales shook his head. "I have hopes you'll figure that out before the Tester gathers me to His bosom, but to this point, I've been unable to convince the Austen City bookmakers to give me very good odds."

"I'm not *that* bad, Howard!" she protested with a gurgle of laughter.

"With infinite respect, My Lady, you're not 'that,' bad—you're worse."

Honor laughed out loud, then looked past him again at the twelve men who had followed him into her office. The one in the center of the front row wore the paired silver sword collar insignia of a major, and as he stood there, visored cap clasped under his left arm, she realized he looked familiar. She couldn't quite place—

Then she had it, and her almond eyes darkened as memory rose from the depths.

"Major LaFollet," she said quietly.

"My Lady." His heels clicked as he bowed again in acknowledgment.

"I hadn't realized you'd left Palace Security," she said.

"The Protector agreed to my transfer as soon as I requested it, My Lady."

"That's not precisely what I was getting at."

"My Lady, Allen died at your side." LaFollet met her gaze unflinchingly. "And you killed the man who killed him. And then you and Nimitz"—he twitched his head in the treecat's direction, never looking away from Honor—"went on to protect my Protector and his family from the men who'd come to murder them. Who almost killed you." He shook his head ever so slightly. "The day the Harrington Steading Guard was stood up, I knew where the Tester wanted me."

Nimitz made a soft sound from the corner of one of the office's desks, and Honor opened her arms without really thinking about it as he leapt lightly into them. Her bond to the 'cat and his empathic sense was still growing, still deepening, yet it was more than strong enough for her to taste LaFollet's iron sincerity.

And determination.

She closed her eyes for a moment, recalling that horrific dinner, the sonic disruptors, the blood, the terror, the sense of despair as she realized she and Nimitz were all that was left, and the agony of the disruptor bolt which had blinded her, destroyed the nerves for half her face, and hurled her paralyzed body to the floor. And as she looked at Andrew LaFollet, she saw again the blood-streaked face of the desperately determined lieutenant at the head of the Palace Security guardsmen who'd fought their way through everything the Maccabean traitors could throw in their path to reach their Protector.

The lieutenant who'd found his brother dead among the Mayhews' fallen protectors.

She'd seen him so briefly, over Benjamin's shoulder as the pistol of a fallen guardsmen in the Protector's hand killed the assassin who'd shot her, who'd been about to fire the follow-up kill shot. But she remembered every hideous detail of that night, and she'd met LaFollet again—briefly—at the small, private dinner to which Benjamin had invited her before her return to Manticore. He'd been a captain, then, she recalled, and a member of Benjamin's personal guard. The realization that he'd left a position like that to join Grayson's newest, poorest, most junior steadholder's guard...

"I can't speak for God, Major," she said, finally. "But I know *I* can't think of anyone I would rather have at the head of my own guardsmen."

He bent his head again, and she tasted the sober pleasure—the satisfaction—that flowed through him. Then she looked back at Clinkscales.

"So, Howard!" she said in a deliberately brighter tone. "Bearing in mind that I'm totally new to all of this liege lady and fealty business, how does this work?"

"My Lady, I know I sent you an organizational chart."

"Yes, you did," she acknowledged with an edge of true contrition. "And I put it in a file somewhere, I promise! But it came in about the time I was trying to get *Nike* into commission, and, well, one thing got in the way, and then *another* thing got in the way, and..."

"I see." Clinkscales gave her the kind of look tutors gave grammar school students who'd "lost their homework," and Honor smiled at him. Then he shook his head.

"Obviously, my work is cut out for me," he said dryly. His lips twitched at her smothered chuckle, but then he straightened his shoulders.

"At this moment, since the Steading has only a single city, no municipal police forces have been organized," he said. "For now, the Harrington Steadholder's Guard is charged with all police functions. In time, as additional municipalities grow and spread, their individual police forces will be responsible for enforcing local law while the Guard falls back to enforcing Steading law.

"As Steadholder Harrington, you command the entire Guard, which can be enlarged to whatever extent the Steading requires. The Mayhew Steadholder's Guard, for example, has a roster strength of over seven thousand. At the moment, the Harrington Guard is at only about four hundred."

Honored nodded, her expression serious, and even as she listened, she castigated herself for not having already paid more attention to Clinkscales' memos on this subject.

"Although you command the entire Guard, there are significant legal constraints on the orders you can give it. Once upon a time, every armsman in a steading's guard was answerable solely to its steadholder in his own person, but that was before the Civil War and Benjamin the Great's Constitution. Now, although a steading's police force is still known as the 'Steadholder's Guard,' there are strict constitutional limits on the orders a steadholder may legitimately give to its members. Within a steading's guard, however, a steadholder is entitled to a *personal* guard, a force of not more than fifty armsmen, which *is* answerable solely to him. Or to her. To whose armsmen he—or she—can legally give any order which doesn't violate the Constitution. And from whose armsmen the security detail Grayson law requires accompany him—or her—at all times is drawn. The oaths of the other armsmen in any steading guard are sworn first to the Constitution and only then to the steadholder they serve. The oaths of your *personal* armsmen are sworn solely to you."

Honor looked at him for a moment, then at the twelve men standing behind him. A part of her—a *large* part of her—shied away from the very notion that anyone might swear an oath which gave her such unbridled authority over them. If she understood

Clinkscales correctly, and she was fairly certain she did, what he was saying was that she could give those men *any order she chose*, and they would be duty bound to obey it. In one way, that was no different from the authority that came with her commission as a Queen's officer, but in another, it was totally different. As an officer of the Crown, she stood in a chain of command, of authority, which ran from the most junior passed midshipwoman all the way to the Queen herself. On Grayson—in Harrington—she *was* the Crown, and in an odd way, the notion of accepting "her" armsmens' personal oath of fealty drove that home as her own oath to Benjamin Mayhew had not.

"And there's no way I can get out of this, right?" she asked, only half-whimsically.

"No, My Lady. There's not."

Sympathy colored both Clinkscales' tone and the emotions she sensed from him, but that sympathy was unaccompanied by even the slightest hope that she might somehow evade taking on those oaths and the mutual responsibilities that went with them. The responsibilities which would be just as inflexible for her as for her armsmen-to-be. And which her own sense of duty would no more permit her to shirk than their sense of duty would permit them to shirk theirs.

"All right, then," she said quietly, meeting Major LaFollet's gray eyes. "If someone will tell me how we do this, we should be about it."

"Here, My Lady." Clinkscales passed her a handheld. She glanced down at its display and her eyes darkened as she read the terms of her personal armsmens' oath. Then she looked at the response required from her. It was just as clear, just as iron-ribbed, as she'd expected it to be, and she committed the formal words to memory even as she settled the responsibility that came with them into the bones of her soul.

"Are you ready, My Lady?" Clinkscales asked in a formal tone.

"I am," she replied, equally formally.

"Then hold out your hands, please. Palms uppermost."

She did, and Clinkscales stepped back and to the side.

"Major LaFollet," he said.

LaFollet braced to attention, passed his cap to the shorter, fair-haired armsman to his right, took two crisp steps forward, and went to one knee before her. He reached out, laying his own hands atop hers, palm-to-palm, and looked up at her with steady eyes.

"Before God, Maker and Tester of us all; before His Son, Who died to intercede for us all; and before the Holy Comforter, I, Andrew Enoch LaFollet, do swear allegiance and fealty to Lady Honor Harrington, Steadholder Harrington, without mental or moral reservation," he said, his voice as steady as those eyes. "I swear from this day, henceforth and forever, that I will be her true man, of heart, will, body, and sword, obedient to her word and to her will. I will stand before her in the Test of life, between her and those who would wreak her harm, and at her back in battle. I will do my utmost to discharge my obligations and duty to her, to her Key, and to her House, so long as I shall live, as God shall give me the ability and the wit so to do. I will fail not in this trust, though it cost me my life, and I submit myself to the judgment of the Steadholder and of God Himself for the fidelity with which I honor and discharge the obligations I now assume before Him and this company."

The words rolled through Honor, carried on the wave front of his emotions, the sincerity of that oath. This man knew precisely what he'd just sworn to do, and he'd meant every word of it. He truly would die before he failed that vow, and she felt the granite soul of Grayson within those words as they infused that same stony integrity into her own heart, her own soul.

"And I, Honor Stephanie Harrington, do accept your oath," she replied, her own voice equally steady, the sincerity etched equally deep into her bones. "You are my sword and my shield, and I will extend protection against all enemies, justice for justice, fidelity for fidelity, and punishment for oath-breaking. May God judge me and mine as He judges you and yours."

"So witness we all," Howard Clinkscales said softly, and a quiet tide of affirmations flowed from the armsmen behind LaFollet.

The major remained on one knee for a long, still moment. Then he stood and reclaimed his cap from his companion. But he didn't return to the formation he'd left. Instead, he stepped behind Honor and took his place at her right shoulder. A place, she sensed already, that he would never relinquish.

"Armsman Candless," he said, and the armsman who'd held his cap handed his own headgear to the man beside him. He went to a knee before Honor and extended his own hands to lay them atop hers.

"Before God, Maker and Tester of us all; before His Son, Who died to intercede for us all; and before the Holy Comforter," he began, his voice every iota as steady as LaFollet's had been, "I, James Alexander Candless, do swear allegiance and fealty to Lady Honor Harrington, Steadholder Harrington, without mental or moral reservation. I swear from this day, henceforth and forever, that I will be her true man, of heart, will, body, and sword, obedient to her word and to her will. I will—"

**HMS *Prince Adrian***
**Manticore Planetary Orbit**
**Manticore Binary System**
**December 7, 1905 PD**

"WHAT DO YOU THINK he's going to tell us, Skipper?"

"And what, exactly, makes you think I've added precognition to my many other talents, Lev?" Alistair McKeon asked just a tad testily.

"Because you're the *Skipper*, Skipper!" Commander Lev Carson, *Prince Adrian*'s executive officer, widened his blue-gray eyes. "They told me at the Island. 'Your skipper knows *everything*,' they said! Are you telling me they *lied*? Say it ain't so!"

"Just because we *know* everything doesn't mean we're supposed to *share* everything with the ignorant louts they assign us as XO's. You're supposed to be acquiring the experience—God help us all—to qualify as a cruiser captain someday yourself." McKeon shook his head. "I shudder to think of the apocalyptic consequences of giving you your own ship, you understand, but that doesn't absolve me of my responsibility to train you up for the role the best way I can, anyway. And, trust me, BuPers and the promotions board won't even consider promoting you to my own current, lordly status until you demonstrate that you, too, know everything."

"You know, it's perfectly okay to just say 'I don't know, Lev. What do *you* think he's going to tell us?'"

"That would hardly befit a lofty junior-grade captain such as myself when addressing a mere *commander*," McKeon said severely.

Carson chuckled, but then his expression sobered.

"Seriously, Skip. Do you have any idea what this"—he waved at the briefing room's bulkhead display, which currently showed only *Prince Adrian*'s wallpaper—"is all about?"

"Not a lot more than you do." McKeon shrugged. "I mean, obviously it's going to cover our operational stance, but until we get the damned declaration, we're all just pissing in our vac suits. So it'll probably be a bunch more of the same stuff. Not that I'm not positive the Earl would love to be giving us movement orders tomorrow!"

"Yeah." Carson scowled. "We're burning time, Skipper. It's gonna come home to bite us all in the ass before this is over."

"And precisely what makes you think that matters to cretins like North Hollow and High Ridge?" McKeon asked in a far bleaker tone.

Carson started a quick reply, then stopped himself. The commander knew much of that bleakness was his CO's own professional appreciation of just what the delay of a formal declaration was going to cost the Navy somewhere down the road. But a lot of it was considerably more personal. The entire ship's company knew about Alistair McKeon's deep friendship with Countess Harrington.

"Well," he began after a moment, "at least—"

A musical chime interrupted him, and the ship's wallpaper vanished from the bulkhead, replaced by a conference display centered on Captain Byron Hunter. A rectangle of smaller, individual windows surrounded the dark-haired captain. Most of those windows were filled by vice admirals or rear admirals and their chiefs of staff; the ones that weren't were all filled by commodores... except one.

That was the one that showed Alistair McKeon and Lev Carson.

"Good afternoon, ladies and gentlemen," Hunter said, nodding to the assembled squadron and division commanders on his own display. "Admiral White Haven will be with us shortly, but he's been delayed by a conference with the First Space Lord. And, no"—Hunter flashed a wry grin—"it's unfortunately *not* to get our sailing orders."

More than one of the assembled officers snorted—or chuckled— at that one, but it wasn't really all that humorous.

"In the meantime, though, the Admiral's asked me to go ahead with the background brief I was going to be presenting anyway," the captain continued. "So, without further ado, let's get to it."

McKeon sat a little straighter as White Haven's chief of staff touched a smart screen and brought up his own notes. McKeon hadn't really anticipated sitting in on briefings at this level, but that was before Commodore Erica Wilensky, Cruiser Division 33.2's designated CO, had "become unavailable." There were rumors that the *reason* she'd become unavailable was a conversation she'd had with Earl White Haven. Given that Wilensky was a second cousin of Pavel Young, with a reputation only marginally better than his had been, McKeon had little difficulty believing that. Any dictionary could have used Wilensky's picture to illustrate the definition of "corrupt, overbred, under-brained aristocrat," and she hadn't exactly covered herself with professional glory in the course of her naval career.

Hamish Alexander, on the other hand, was generally acknowledged as the best strategist and tactician currently in uniform, and he had remarkably little sympathy for marginally competent—at best—feather merchants. Worse, from Wilensky's perspective, very few members of the Star Kingdom's aristocracy could match the White Haven lineage, despite which—or possibly *because of* which—Alexander had exactly zero tolerance for anyone who used the accident of his or her birth as an excuse to sneer at those less nobly born.

Those factors would have been enough to produce a certain tension between him and Wilensky under any circumstances. The fact that she'd been even more vocal than most members of the Conservative Association in defending Pavel Young—and, by extension, condemning Honor Harrington—could only have made it worse. In fact, she was officially on record denouncing the Young court-martial, over which White Haven had presided, as a "hyper partisan witch hunt ordered at the highest levels of the current government for political reasons," which constituted a direct violation of the Fourth Article of War for any serving officer. The Judge Advocate General had let her off with only a slap on the wrist—solely, as everyone knew perfectly well, because the current political climate *was* "hyper-partisan," if not for precisely the reasons Wilensky claimed, and hammering her harder could only have made that worse. But the entire Navy knew about the White Haven temper, and a significant percentage of that Navy had heard the rumors that Honor was prominent among the outstanding junior officers to whom Hamish Alexander stood sponsor.

All of which made it . . . unlikely Commodore Wilensky would have found herself excessively welcome under his flag.

It was also why one Alistair McKeon, who didn't see eye-to-eye with her either, was delighted to not find himself under her orders.

And not just because it allowed him to step, however temporarily, into her slot as the Senior Officer in Command, Cruiser Division 33.2. He doubted a mere junior-grade captain would be allowed to retain that slot for long, but he was a full two months senior to Cristina Zaragoza, HMS *Cestus'* CO, and it was his until someone more senior turned up.

"First," Hunter began, "and as I've already said, we still haven't received anything remotely like movement orders. At the moment and—unfortunately—for the foreseeable future, it looks like we'll remain attached to Home Fleet. The Admiral's been assured—again—that if and when we ever get a formal declaration of war, Sixth Fleet will be formally stood up and we'll almost certainly be tasked to secure control of the Trevor's Star terminus. Obviously, like everything else, that's subject to change, and the longer the declaration's delayed, the more likely it becomes that change *will* intervene."

None of the faces on the display looked happy to hear that. None of them looked very surprised, either, McKeon noted glumly.

"At the moment, the Admiralty's forced to continue operating on an officially peacetime footing," Hunter continued. "What that means, in practical terms, is that we're mugging Peter to pay Paul. All of you know that without a formal declaration, Admiral Caparelli has only limited authority to commit forces to combat, but you may not be as fully aware that the same political factors which have delayed the declaration have stymied every request for additional, extraordinary funding, as well. Nor can the Admiralty legally mobilize any Reserve personnel or vessels without special—and specific—Parliamentary authorization . . . or that declaration we still don't have.

"That means we're restricted essentially to our active units as of Hancock and Second Yeltsin, minus those on the binnacle list with battle damage. We've recalled everything we can from Silesia, but we had very few capital ships in the Confederacy, so it hasn't added much depth to our wall-of-battle. And *that* means we're spread a lot thinner than anyone would like and that we're shorter on munitions than anyone would like. Even on our bare-bones operational tempo is running down spares and ammunition at an alarming rate, and between the damages from Hancock and Yeltsin, the captured prizes we're looking at adding to our own wall, and regular maintenance cycles, we're looking at significant serviceability issues and zero free yard space in which to address them.

"The good news, such as it is, that since we've accomplished virtually all of Riposte Gamma's immediate objectives, we'd have to basically stand down anyway until we get the declaration. We've run even essential maintenance dangerously short fighting a war on what they used to call a 'shoestring,' and the fact that we've been forced to suspend offensive operations will at least give us a chance to deal with some of our most critical repair needs. On the other hand, we've cut so deep that those maintenance issues won't go away anytime soon, even if we miraculously get a declaration and full funding tomorrow. And the fact that we're getting in at least some needed repairs is a very *limited* bright side to be looking upon, because while the Peeps are still in what you might call significant disarray, indications from ONI are that Pierre is steadily consolidating his power."

Hunter paused, then looked up from his notes to make eye contact with his listeners.

"At the risk of verging a bit too closely on Article Four, it's . . . unfortunate certain members of Parliament can't find their asses with both hands and approach radar," he said, and McKeon pursed mental lips in a silent whistle of surprise. Surprise not that Hunter felt that way, but that he was prepared to say so, even here.

Article Four prohibited conduct detrimental to the chain of command and national command authority. Among other things, it forbade a serving officer from publicly demonstrating contempt for his military or civilian superiors, which was where Commodore Wilensky had crossed the line by implying—hell, *stating*—that Young had been wrongfully court-martialed on the direct orders of someone in the Cromarty Government. Or, at least, of someone in the Navy's chain of command in order to curry favor with the Government.

Of course, Hunter had been careful to refer to *members of Parliament*, not to the institution of Parliament itself. It was a narrow distinction, but a real one. Yet while that fig leaf might protect him from legal or official consequences, it wouldn't do a thing to protect him against those members or their allies in the Service if word of it got back to them.

*Of course, he's* White Haven's *chief of staff,* McKeon reflected. *That means he's already on the shit list of anybody in the Janacek or North Hollow camps. And he's White Haven's* chief of staff, *not White Haven himself. So he could* probably *get away with a smack from Caparelli—or even just Cortez—whereas if* White Haven *said it, openly, at least…*

Somehow, though, he doubted Hunter would have said it if he hadn't known White Haven agreed with him.

"We had a golden opportunity," Hunter continued flatly. "Immediately after Hancock and Yeltsin, after the failure of the Parnell coup, the Peeps were in total disarray. We could've *walked* into at least a half dozen of their frontier systems. For that matter, we could've walked straight into *Trevor's Star!* But we weren't allowed to because those members of Parliament chose not to let us. And our people—*your* people—will pay the price in blood and lives when we're finally allowed to try to make up for that lost time."

Most of the heads on that display were nodding now, and Hunter shrugged.

"The good news—although I probably shouldn't be saying this, either—is that now that the Young court-martial is finally behind us, we may actually get that declaration sometime soon. We can hope, anyway. And in the meantime, the Admiral intends to continue preparing for that longed-for day."

He squared his shoulders and produced a smile that looked almost—almost—completely genuine.

"In pursuit of that goal," he continued briskly, "we'll be conducting a series of training simulations over the next few weeks. You'll receive a general outline of our plans immediately after this briefing. For now, while we're still awaiting the Admiral's arrival, let's look at some of the training elements he especially wants to stress.

"First, our own experience in Mendoza and Chelsea, as well as other reports from the front, have only reinforced the evidence from Hancock and Yeltsin that our edge in missile combat is even greater than we'd estimated it was, and there's no evidence that the Peeps have realized yet that we have even limited FTL communications ability. In keeping with the principle of playing to one's strengths, the Admiral's laid out a series of tactical training exercises that will examine ways in which we can best leverage those advantages.

"Accordingly, day after tomorrow, we'll fire up the simulators for a large-scale engagement based on the tactical records from Yeltsin. Vice Admiral Carmichael, you'll command the Aggressor Force. Vice Admiral Lemaitre, you'll command the Blue Force. For this exercise, Admiral White Haven will observe and umpire." Hunter smiled slightly. "I'm sure he'll be his normal gently compassionate and understanding self."

This time, the chuckles were outright laughter. Hamish Alexander was many things, including a charismatic commanding officer. Gently compassionate wasn't one of the qualities most widely associated with him, however.

"Having said that," the chief of staff went on after a moment, "the real purpose of this exercise is to build unit cohesion as well as develop tactical doctrine. Accordingly—"

**House of Lords**
**and**
**The Prime Minister's Residence**
**City of Landing**
**Planet of Manticore**
**Manticore Binary System**
**December 11, 1905 PD**

THE MAN WHO HAD BEEN Lord Pavel Young and was now the Eleventh Earl of North Hollow studied his mirrored appearance.

He didn't truly recognize the man in that antechamber mirror. Not yet.

He'd attended sessions of the House of Lords with his father, when he was much younger. And he'd attended as his father's proxy on a handful of occasions as an adult. But although he'd been the cadet holder of the North Hollow title as his father's heir, he'd never been seated in the House in his own right.

That was about to change, and the formal regalia of a new peer making his inaugural appearance was too ornate, too anachronistic, for his taste. Worse, the elaborate robes, embroidered with the North Hollow arms, were their own sort of uniform, and that reminded him entirely too painfully of the uniform which had been stripped from him in disgrace.

Anger rose like magma as he remembered the admiral reading the court-martial's sentence aloud, the assembled ranks of black and gold uniforms. As he remembered the junior-grade lieutenant who'd stripped away the badges of rank, the braid from his cuffs, the medal ribbons, the shoulder boards, the gold and scarlet Navy shoulder flash while the pitiless HD cameras recorded every instant of his shame, broadcast it throughout the entire Star Kingdom.

Oh, yes. He *remembered*. And the day would come, he promised himself yet again. The day when those who'd engineered that degradation paid dearly.

He made the fists which had clenched at his sides open, and his nostrils flared as he inhaled deeply. In too many ways, today was yet another opportunity for humiliation. His enemies, both political and naval, had to be waiting to pounce, waiting to dissect anything he said with merciless, partisan viciousness. He did have political allies, of course. Some because they, too, were members of the Conservative Association and shared his hatred of and contempt for the Cromarty Government and all its works. Others because they knew he'd come into possession of his father's secret files, with all the potentially embarrassing (or far, far worse) secrets the tenth earl had amassed in a lifetime spent playing the political game. But politics were a kabuki dance, in a lot of ways. Any reasonably competent analyst could unerringly predict how the partisans on each side would present and comment upon something like the speech he was about to make.

The speech he had no choice *but* to make, really. Any newly elevated peer was expected to make his maiden address before formally taking his seat. That expectation had the effective force of law under the unwritten portion of Star Kingdom's Constitution, although more than one new-minted peer's "speech" had been no more than a paragraph in length. But after the circumstances of his court-martial, his dishonorable discharge, and his father's death, he knew *he* couldn't get away with that sort of brevity. And he knew his enemies—his many and manifold enemies—must be salivating as they waited to pounce. No doubt most of them were gloating as they visualized what he must feel at this moment, waited for the inevitable grist for the mill of their unending persecution which his speech must provide them. After all, there was nothing he could say from the depth of his disgrace that couldn't be turned to that purpose, was there?

He understood that. And his lips curved unpleasantly as he contemplated what they were actually about to hear. The words might be bitter on his own tongue, but as far as *they* were concerned—

"Your pardon, Milord," a voice said behind him.

He turned to face the senior page who'd just entered the antechamber.

"Yes?"

"The House awaits you, Milord. May I escort you?"

"Of course."

The page turned to lead the way, and North Hollow drew another deep, focusing breath before he followed.

The House's chamber was unusually crowded for so late on a Friday afternoon. Many of the Star Kingdom's peers had pressing weekend engagements. They *always* had pressing weekend engagements, and the established practice of Parliament's upper house was to avoid scheduling anything important for a Friday. The minor inconvenience of Manticore's undeclared war with the People's Republic of Haven could scarcely be allowed to infringe upon that sacrosanct custom.

That was, in fact, one of the reasons North Hollow had requested a Friday time slot for his own maiden address. Not, as some might have expected, to turn it into a "stealth event" while so many of his enemies were away, but because it would give what he had to say an even greater surprise impact. And, of course, because it had permitted a greater degree of stage management.

Michael Janvier, the Baron of High Ridge and acknowledged leader of the Conservative Association, waited at the chamber's entrance to greet North Hollow and his guide. North Hollow's father had been one of High Ridge's closest allies, and their relations had been cordial . . . outwardly, at least. In fact, while they truly had shared political views and policies, High Ridge had never been allowed to forget the evidence the tenth earl had squirreled away in his secret files. The evidence that could have sent even a peer of the realm to prison for a long, long time, had it been whispered into the proper ear.

Now, High Ridge smiled warmly at the *eleventh* earl and turned to walk beside him to the Speaker's lectern. They climbed the low dais's steps side-by-side, and the Speaker beamed upon them—his smile even less sincere than High Ridge's had been—as they ascended the steps. Sergios Kappopoulos, the Baron of Eastlake, was a longtime member of the Duke of Cromarty's faction, and there was zero love lost between any of the Government's supporters and the Conservative Association at the best of times, far less today. But the false narrative of collegial affability had to be maintained, didn't it? North Hollow smiled back at Eastlake as he and High Ridge reached the top and he felt a twinge of pleasure at the way Eastlake's jaw tightened. But then the Speaker drew a breath and looked out across the chamber.

"My Lords and Ladies, the Chair recognizes the Baron of High Ridge," he said, and stepped aside to permit High Ridge to assume his place at the lectern.

"My Lords and Ladies," the baron said, "it is my great honor, and gives me considerable pleasure, to sponsor the maiden address of Her Majesty's newest peer. The son of a dear friend and colleague, a man who has already given decades of his life to the Star Kingdom's service, and a man who, I am certain, will as faithfully uphold his duties as a member of this House and a servant and steward of this Star Kingdom as even his father before him."

He paused, looking out across the chamber, then extended one hand toward North Hollow.

"My Lords and Ladies, the Eleventh Earl of North Hollow."

There was a spatter of applause. A spatter that grew suddenly louder, as several of the men and women in that chamber came to their feet. Quite a few of those men and women were among those who would normally have been elsewhere on a Friday afternoon, but High Ridge and the Conservative Association's whips had very quietly seen to it that they wouldn't be elsewhere on *this* Friday. Not when the HD cameras would have an opportunity to capture the sound of their applause—even their cheers, in a handful of cases— as a way to refute any claim that North Hollow had been snubbed by the bulk of the Star Kingdom's aristocracy.

North Hollow took High Ridge's place at the lectern, smiling out at those applauding peers, and the fact that he knew how many of them were there for the same reason High Ridge would never have dreamed of declining to sponsor today's speech only whetted that smile's keenness.

He waited until the "spontaneous greeting" had died away, then turned to the Speaker and High Ridge.

"I thank you for this opportunity to address the House, My Lord," he said gravely, bowing ever so slightly to the Speaker. "And you, for your gracious introduction, My Lord High Ridge," he added, bowing to the baron. Then he turned back to the waiting peers.

"My Lords and Ladies, I will not keep you long," he told them. "I've been told that brevity is the very soul of a maiden address, and until

I've been among you long enough to earn the right to a greater . . . loquacity, I will strive to bear that in mind."

A few chuckles ran around the chamber. One or two of them might even have been genuine.

"Nonetheless, there is one point upon which I have very strong views, and I believe for several reasons that this would be an appropriate time for me to share those views with this House."

Several of the peers who were *not* members of the Conservative Association grimaced, obviously anticipating what was coming next. Or what they *thought* was coming next, at any rate.

*Oh, yes, My Lords and Ladies*, he thought sardonically, watching those grimaces. *The day will come when I'll be free to say exactly what you* think *I'm going to say today. But that day isn't today.*

"My Lords and Ladies," he said somberly, "every man and woman in this Chamber is aware of events in the People's Republic of Haven, of the conflict even now raging across the frontiers of the Manticoran Alliance, and of the courageous men and women of our Navy and our Marines who are fighting and—too often—dying even as I stand here before you."

A stir rippled through his audience, and many of those who'd grimaced leaned forward in their seats, eyes suddenly narrowed.

"Just as all of us are aware of those events, we are aware of how my own naval service ended, and under what circumstances," he continued, and his tone was flatter than he'd intended. "I won't pretend I'm not bitter over that, nor will I pretend that I feel the verdict of my court-martial was either just or impartial. Having said that, I recognize, that *I* would feel that way, no matter how just my trial's outcome might have been, just as I recognize that none of you would expect me to formally 'acknowledge' a guilt I do not feel.

"But bitterness, anger, even a keen sense of injustice do not—*cannot*—excuse a peer of the realm's failure to discharge his responsibilities *to* the Realm. We are called to look past our own self-interest, our own grievances, when the fate of the Star Kingdom itself lies in the balance. And, My Lords and Ladies, this is such a time.

"The war against which we've been warned for so long is upon us." He swept the chamber with steady, bleak eyes. "For decades, since the accession of King Roger to the throne, we've prepared against this very day. We've built a Navy second to none in quality and fighting power. We've forged alliances fit to withstand the tempest of combat.

"We have drawn our line, declared that we will neither retreat nor falter."

He paused, let silence linger for a handful of breaths, then squared his shoulders with a solemn expression.

"There are many in this Chamber, and elsewhere in the Star Kingdom, who believe the tides of revolution and civil war sweeping the People's Republic mean it may be possible for us to avoid a head-on conflict we have dreaded and for which we have prepared for so long. And the truth is, that even I find that argument most tempting. Our quarrel, after all, was with the Legislaturalists, and they are gone, swept away—or being swept away—into the dustbin of history. One would hope the new regime would recognize the costs of the expansionist foreign policy the Legislaturalists pursued for so long. That the People's Republic's new leaders would renounce that expansionism, seek to compose the differences between us and live in peace with their interstellar neighbors.

"One would hope that, but it would be a grave, even fatal, error to *assume* it."

He paused once more, and he could almost taste the disbelief, the astonishment, flowing through the peers who hadn't been forewarned about his address.

"My Lords and Ladies, I understand how ugly, how brutal, how destructive war with the People's Republic would be," he resumed quietly. "I've seen that evidence firsthand. But the making of the war between us was not *our* doing, and much though I would prefer to allow a genuine renaissance, a genuine revolutionary zeal, to transform the People's Republic without further conflict, we *cannot* depend upon that outcome. Indeed, according to my own sources within the Navy, it is far more likely that 'Chairman Pierre' will seek to solidify domestic support by pointing at a foreign enemy: *us.*

"It's always possible I'm wrong about that. And it's always possible that those who call upon us to not throw away the opportunity, to hold our hand and 'give peace a chance,' are correct and my fears are wrong. But the truth is that we dare not wager the survival of the Star Kingdom, the freedom of Her Majesty's subjects, on the possibility that my fears are mistaken.

"I acknowledge that this is a grave decision, and one upon which any honorable man or woman must vote his or her own conscience. But I know how I intend to vote mine, and I call upon the members of this House to do the same. We've already lost months—over half an entire *T-year*—in which we might have taken the battle to the enemy, driven deep into the People's Republic, secured positions of strategic advantage ample to offset our inferiority in tonnage. We cannot get those months back, but it is *essential* that we squander no more of them. Every day we delay will cost the lives of more of our military personnel, cost more millions of dollars in damaged and destroyed starships, and deepen the danger in which our Star Kingdom stands.

"My Lords and Ladies of Manticore, I call upon you to join me in voting out a formal declaration of war against the People's Republic of Haven in order to permit our magnificent Navy to do what it was created to do and defend the people of this Realm against their enemies!"

✧   ✧   ✧

"God, I hate this," Lord William Alexander growled.

He sat in a private study which belonged to Allen Summervale, the Duke of Cromarty, and his comment had nothing to do with the twenty-six-year scotch in his glass. He wasn't even looking at that glass. Instead, his eyes were on the smart wall as the recorded HD played.

"How can you say that?" The Star Kingdom's Prime Minister sat behind his desk, watching the same smart wall, and his whiskey-smooth baritone was sardonic. "That's exactly what *you've* been saying for months now, Willie! You and Hamish both. Why aren't you *delighted* to hear somebody on the other side finally say the same thing?"

"I have a delicate stomach, Allen," Alexander replied. "If you don't want your carpet to need cleaning, you might want to reconsider that question."

Cromarty chuckled and sipped his own whiskey. Then he shook his head with a moderately apologetic expression.

"Sorry, Willie. I know exactly what you mean. But much as I know it galls you—hell, as much as it galls *me*!—this is exactly what we've needed from somebody—*anybody*—on the Conservative side of the aisle for months. It sticks in my craw to hear someone like North Hollow ape the role of 'statesman,' but none of High Ridge's other carrion-eaters were going to do it."

"Sooner or later one of them would've *had* to," Alexander countered, then raised his free hand with a grimace of acknowledgment. "But I take your point. Hell, I made the same point to Hamish earlier today." He rolled the blue eyes he shared with his older brother. "Trust me, you don't *even* want to hear his opinion of this particular 'statesman.'"

"Not only don't want to, don't need to." Cromarty snorted. "But I'll guarantee you he recognized how pivotal North Hollow's speech will probably be, didn't he?"

"Of course he did." Alexander sipped more whiskey. "But you know the chicken-shit bastard didn't give it because he gives a single good goddamn about the Navy or how many of our people are likely to get killed if this . . . this *quasi*-war stretches out much longer!"

"You think I was born yesterday?" Cromarty asked sourly. "He did it because he, or one of his father's advisors, has decent political instincts."

He took a deeper swallow of whiskey, as if to wash a bad taste out of his mouth, and Alexander grunted.

"Among other things, Burgundy's effort to expel him from the Lords because of his 'demonstrated lack of character' just got knocked on its head," he said.

"It was never really his *lack* of character the Duke objected to, Willie. It was the *nature* of his character. And simple fairness requires me to point out quite a few others among our fellow peers could legitimately face exclusion on that basis. Not in such extreme degree, perhaps, but still—"

He shrugged, and Alexander glared at him.

"Well, we can hardly support Burgundy's motion now that he's the only Opposition peer who's actually spoken in favor of the declaration, now can we?" the Chancellor observed acidly. "That's bad enough. I mean, let's be honest. Much as we both agree with Burgundy, the chance of his ever mustering the votes in North Hollow's case was . . . remote even before this. But in addition to that, this whole damned 'more in sorrow than in anger' bullshit is going to undercut the public's perception of his cowardice. We were never getting him out of the House, Allen, but at least we could have hoped to marginalize him, keep him politically gelded. Up until this afternoon, he was so toxic even High Ridge would have been forced to hold him at arm's length, deny him any official place at the Conservatives' table. The 'North Hollow Files' would've guaranteed him a place behind the scenes, but that's not remotely the same thing. Now they'll be able to reach out and *welcome* him!"

"I wouldn't go quite that far yet," Cromarty said. Alexander looked at him in disbelief, and the duke waved a hand. "I did say I wouldn't go that far *yet*," he pointed out. "There's still too much public disgust in the wake of his dishonorable discharge, but you're right. This *will* start eroding that, and you're also right that eventually—and sooner than either of us would like—they will be able to pull out a chair for him officially. And the bastard will sit down in it, and outwardly, he'll go right on supporting the war. Of course, whatever he may be saying for the cameras, you and I both know that behind the scenes he'll still be doing his damnedest to break our kneecaps, just because of how much he hates us. High Ridge is an arrogant pain in the ass and as politically corrupt as they come, but he's not motivated by the personal hatred North Hollow feels. Probably even more for you than for me, given how . . . frankly Hamish has expressed his opinions. Or the minor fact that Hamish was president of the court that cashiered him. He's never going to 'forgive and forget,' Willie, and coupled with his father's files and how much he hates all of us, he'll be far more dangerous in the long term than a simple corrupt political hack like High Ridge ever was."

"Damned right he will," Alexander growled. "And at least until we actually get the declaration, we have to keep our hands off him while he and his cronies and stooges work on repairing his public image."

"Oh, it's lots worse than that." Cromarty's expression was that of a man who'd just bitten into something rotten. "Tomorrow morning? Tomorrow morning I have to stand up and make a statement publicly *thanking* him for his 'thoughtful and patriotic' speech. The Government will have to *embrace* him, use him as our opening wedge into the opposition to the declaration. And all of High Ridge's cronies who have delayed it, who've finally started to realize just how bad a political corner they've painted themselves into, now that the tide of public opinion is turning against them, will do the same damned thing. 'If someone who was so brutally mistreated by the Cromarty Government can rise above the injustice he's suffered to so eloquently argue in favor of a formal declaration of war, then we have no choice but to do the same.'"

His eyes glittered angrily.

"I know I should be down on my knees thanking God he did it, praying that it will really make a difference, turn the corner on this thing. And I truly am grateful for it, Willie. But it's not only the first step in rehabilitating *him*; it's also the first step in letting High Ridge crawl back off the ledge and salvage his own political career. And I just can't convince myself that providing a way for High Ridge to walk won't turn out to be almost equally disastrous somewhere down the road."

**Earl North Hollow's Residence**
**City of Landing**
**Planet of Manticore**
**Manticore Binary System**
**February 28, 1906 PD**

"SO WE ANTICIPATE that the special funding resolution will be introduced in Thursday's session, Milord," Benton Toscarelli, Baron Montreau and Parliamentary Secretary for the Conservative Association, said. "I've already discussed this with Baron High Ridge, and he strongly believes you should join him in speaking for its support. Given how pivotal your address was in breaking the logjam on the declaration, I feel confident the entire caucus would agree with him."

"That's very kind of you and the Baron, Benton," Earl North Hollow replied. "I appreciate it very much. But the truth is that I'm still far too new to the House. For what it's worth, I'm of the opinion that the opportunity should be reserved for one of our more senior peers. In fact, I think *you'd* be an excellent choice."

"That's flattering, Milord, but—"

"Forgive me for interrupting, but I didn't make the suggestion to be flattering. Or, appropriate as it might have been, in appreciation for the kindness of the offer. I made it because it's a smart move from a political perspective."

Montreau closed his mouth. His eyebrows rose, and North Hollow looked around the half dozen men and women gathered in his townhouse's library.

Pavel Young's father had been an avid reader. Pavel had not, and he'd seldom graced that library with his presence when he was

133

younger. But he'd become a more frequent visitor since the tenth earl's death. Its gracefully furnished spaciousness made a much more appropriate backdrop for the meetings of a sober, serious-minded statesman than his much smaller—and much more efficient—office did. Which didn't even consider the sense of continuity it provided.

Dimitri Young had spent less time in the public eye than many of his fellow peers, but he'd scarcely been a complete stranger to the limelight. No politician could operate at his level without cultivating the proper media contacts and playing them skillfully at need, and Dimitri—who'd been almost as adept at that as he was at blackmail— had conducted the vast majority of his HD interviews from this very library. It had been one of his hallmarks, and his son Pavel, following his example, had already discovered what an elegant, quietly aristocratic backdrop it provided for the cameras. Not to mention the way his own use of it emphasized his position as his father's heir.

Yet that continuity for the public was the least of the library's attractions, in many ways, because it was also the sanctum to which his father had invited his political allies—although "summoned" might actually have been a more appropriate verb—when scheming was afoot. That meant it also underscored a rather different continuity for the political operatives with whom Pavel met here. This library was a reminder to them of everything else he'd inherited from his father, including Dimitri's well-honed political organization.

And, of course, his files.

"Let's be honest here, among ourselves," he continued now, leaning back in the armchair whose back just happened to be eight centimeters or so taller than any of the library's other chairs. "I understand why the Association took its original stance as a matter of principle." One or two eyelids flickered, but no one was impolite enough to snort out loud. "And I actually understand why the Liberals fought the declaration tooth and nail, right up to the final vote. But there's no point pretending we—the Opposition as a whole, I mean—didn't take damage in terms of public opinion along the way. God knows expecting the 'man in the street' to understand the finer nuances of diplomacy—or anything else, really—is an exercise in futility. Unfortunately, the electorate's beliefs and demands, however ill-informed and however changeable, are also inescapable factors in the Star Kingdom's political calculus."

He shook his head, his expression a careful mix of sober thoughtfulness and exasperation with the common herd's ignorant, unsophisticated, emotion-driven mood swings. Montreau and two or three others grimaced in agreement, and he shrugged.

"The House is supposed to be above the passions of the moment. The Constitution designed the peerage specifically to serve as a balance wheel against the tyranny of fleeting, changeable majorities in the Commons. But that doesn't mean we can *ignore* public opinion, especially when we stand in Opposition to the current government. In fact, if you'll forgive my frankness, the fact that the Association has no representation in the Commons, makes us even more vulnerable to marginalization in the hoi polloi's eyes because of how much easier it makes it to paint us as solely the party of self-interest and aristocratic privilege."

Heads nodded soberly, although none of them mentioned that the painting task was also made easier by the fact that the Conservative Association pretty much *was* solely the party of self-interest and aristocratic privilege.

"I also happen to know, from my sources," North Hollow let his eyes flick ever so briefly to the elegantly groomed red-haired woman seated to one side, "that several of New Kiev's senior supporters intend to speak *against* the funding resolution."

"Indeed, Milord?" Charlotte Mantooth, Baroness New Flushing, frowned, and her gray eyes narrowed slightly. "The Countess hasn't said anything to that effect."

"I'm sure that, as a loyal fellow member of the Opposition, Lady Marisa will get around to alerting us before Thursday." From North Hollow's tone one might have concluded that he expected nothing of the sort. "But I'm confident of my information."

Several of the others were frowning now. There was very little love lost between the Conservative Association and the Liberal Party, despite their current partnership in Opposition to the Cromarty Government. And much as the Association hated acknowledging it, New Kiev's Liberals were substantially the more powerful of the two. While the Association claimed roughly the same number of seats in the House of Lords, it had zero representation in the House of Commons. The Liberals, on the other hand, controlled the second-largest bloc of votes in the Commons. True, even they were considerably outstripped by the Centrists, who held a sixty-vote outright majority, but they still formed the closest thing Cromarty faced to an actual Opposition in the lower house. It also gave them a far broader support base than the Association could claim, and while they might be the Association's bitter ideological enemies, there were two points upon which they saw eye-to-eye: their equally bitter opposition to the Centrists and their peers' defense of the House of Lords' political dominance.

And, of course, of their own positions within that dominant house.

Those two points of agreement explained the alliance they'd forged to oppose the formal declaration of war against the People's Republic of Haven. But while both of them had supported their opposition with virtually identical sober, moral arguments, the truth was that they'd opposed it for rather different reasons. It would never have done for the Association to *admit* that its opposition stemmed far more from the need to protect one of its leaders' son from an outraged Royal Navy than from anything that remotely resembled an actual principle. The Liberal peers had always understood that aspect of their alliance, but the Association's decision to support the declaration once its true objective was accomplished had almost certainly been the death knell of a partnership both sides had always known could be only temporary.

The Liberals had yet to announce any decision to formally withdraw from that partnership, but they'd also refused to concede defeat on the declaration, and their impassioned, last-ditch opposition after North Hollow's maiden speech had drawn the battle out for yet another six T-weeks. They'd failed in the end, of course. Worse, from a political perspective, their losing battle had burned a lot more of that public support North Hollow had mentioned. The Liberal MPs who, unlike their aristocratic fellow Liberals in the Lords, were required to stand for election, had to be feeling the heat. Indeed, quite a few of those MPs had broken with the aristocratic wing of their party and crossed the aisle to side with the Government. That wasn't *quite* unprecedented in the Star Kingdom's political history, but it had happened no more than a handful of times over the T-centuries, and it said volumes about the bitterness of the Liberals' internal divide. Further resistance to the war could only make that worse, which undoubtedly explained New Flushing's skeptical surprise at the notion that any Liberal peer could be stupid enough to oppose the funding measure, the earl thought.

He looked back at the red-haired woman and raised a hand.

"Would you care to expand on that for Lady Charlotte, Georgia?" he invited.

"Of course, Milord," she replied, and everyone turned to look in her direction.

If the attention disconcerted her in any way, she showed no sign of it.

"As I'm sure all of you are aware, My Lords and Ladies," she said, "one of my responsibilities is to stay tapped into the undercurrents of both the Lords and the Commons on the Earl's behalf. And over the years, I've cultivated sources in quite a few unlikely places. According to several of those sources, including two senior Liberal peers, Lady Marisa is still trying to prevent any formal opposition to the funding resolution, but she won't succeed. I'm sure all of you are even better aware than I of how angry quite a few of the Liberal peers were when the Association chose to support the declaration. In fact, despite her public commitment to remaining in Opposition with the Association, Lady Marisa was pretty vocal about that 'betrayal' herself, at the time. I'm sure she still feels much the same way.

"But as Earl North Hollow just pointed out, the Liberals do have to worry about their representation in the Commons, and their MPs have made Lady Marisa fully aware of how strongly public opinion has turned in favor of the war. They've also made it *extremely* clear they don't want any of their peers continuing to oppose it because of the probable consequences at the ballot box. Nor are they the only ones aware of how this has damaged their support with their constituents. According to certain of my other contacts, there's actually been some discussion within the Cabinet about the desirability of calling a snap general election while support for Cromarty's war policy is so strong." Sakristos shrugged. "It's unlikely Cromarty would do that at the moment, since he's got an outright majority in the Commons already, but it's always possible he might, because if he did, the polling data all suggests the Liberals would lose ground, probably badly. Even if that doesn't happen, however, it's past time the Liberals started mending some fences with their voters.

"Lady Marisa is fully aware of that, and she's leaning on the holdouts just as hard as she can. Unfortunately, at least three of her peers don't see that as one of their priorities. Earl Dabney, Countess Winstainley, and Baron Silver Stone have all informed her they intend to speak against the resolution. She's still arguing with them, but you know those three as well as anyone, My Lords and Ladies. They have their heels firmly dug in. Do you really think she'll be able to change their minds between now and the vote?"

"No," New Flushing said, after a moment. "No, I don't, Ms. Sakristos. Not where those three are concerned. After all, before she could *change* their minds, someone would have to be able to *find* them, wouldn't they?"

Several people chuckled at that, and Georgia Sakristos allowed herself a small answering smile.

"We've all counted noses well enough to know the resolution will pass comfortably, whatever those three say about it," North Hollow said, recapturing his guests' attention. "And we also know that even though the Countess will gas on and on about how the members of her party must be allowed to 'vote their consciences' even when it's not the popular position, this will hurt the Liberals, at least in the short term."

Heads nodded, and he shrugged.

"Well, the other thing it's going to do is give us in the Association the opportunity to underscore our support *for* the war, now that we've been convinced as a matter of principle that it's our duty to do just that. Obviously, like the Liberals, we need to remain in *formal* opposition, if only to maintain our bargaining power for the future, but it's clearly our patriotic duty to cross the aisle on this *one* issue. In fact, I believe that's exactly how we ought to shape our speeches in the House. Of course"—he smiled thinly—"I see no need to mention that it will also give us considerably more leverage in future negotiations."

His guests returned his smile, and he shrugged.

"That's why I think you should be one of those who speak for us in this matter, Benton, since you were so eloquent in setting forth the basis for our initial *opposition* to the war." North Hollow smiled more gravely at Montreau. "I'm sure it would be extremely valuable to hear you speak with equal eloquence about the reasons our position has shifted and ... matured as additional information about events in the People's Republic, the growing tempo of confrontations, and the courageous sacrifices of our military men and women has become available."

Montreau nodded, and so did his fellows. After all, the baron truly was an unusually eloquent speaker. He was also a very facile one, with a well-developed ability to find deep and meaningful principle even in the most self-interested and calculating of positions.

"As for me," North Hollow continued, "I've already publicly stated my own reasons for supporting the declaration and, by extension, the special funding request. Obviously, the Navy's further expansion and wartime expenditures will require a more comprehensive, sustainable funding mechanism, and I'm sure we'll have the usual dogfights before we get the details for that settled. But this special measure should at least bridge some of the gap and repair much of the rundown in maintenance funds the Service incurred before the declaration was finally voted out.

"At the same time, however"—he allowed a carefully metered bitterness into his expression and voice—"there's no point pretending my relationship with the Navy, and especially the current Admiralty, is anything one might call remotely cordial. I believe my position on the declaration has improved the general public's view of me, but I could speak in favor of the funding resolution till I turned blue, and it would buy me, personally, very little in terms of improved relations with Admiralty House or the current Government. So rather than waste this opportunity on the newest member of the Association, especially when it wouldn't contribute anything to his own powerbase, we should use it to draw the sharpest possible contrast between our own, evolving position and the intractable, stubborn, dogmatic opposition of certain other members of the House. And for that we need an eloquent speaker with sufficient stature for the entire Star Kingdom to recognize him as an official spokesman for the entire Association. Don't you agree?"

"I don't know about Benton, but *I* certainly do!" New Flushing said with a smile. "And I'm sure I speak for all of us, Milord, when I say I deeply appreciate your willingness to stand aside in the interests of the Association—and of the Star Kingdom, of course—especially after the brutal way in which you've been treated by the Navy. And that I'm gratified by the insight your explanation demonstrates. It's the sort of analysis I might have anticipated out of your father, if you'll permit me to say so."

"Of course I'll 'permit you to say so'!" North Hollow's smile combined sadness and humor. "How could I not be pleased by a comparison to Father? He was one of the smartest, politically shrewdest men I ever knew. I only hope that, in time, *I* can contribute as much to the Association—and the Star Kingdom—as he did."

"I'm sure you will," New Flushing said. "In fact, I foresee a leading position for you in the very near future."

"Let's not get ahead of ourselves." North Hollow waved a graceful hand. "I'm still that newest member of the House, after all. Of course I hope to grow in both seniority and stature within the Association, but all things in their time! For now, I think my efforts and contributions will be most effective behind the scenes, in meetings like this. If only"—he allowed another of those carefully metered flashes of bitterness—"until the echoes of my court-martial have been allowed to die back down, at least."

"Of course," New Flushing murmured, and Montreau nodded soberly.

North Hollow nodded back, satisfied his true message had been passed. And that it would reach its intended recipient, as soon as Montreau could report back to Baron High Ridge.

No, Pavel Young didn't want the official position and authority within the Association which had been his father's. Not yet, at any rate. And everything he'd said about the considerations against giving him that stature tomorrow or the next day was true. But he fully intended to take a leading role "in meetings like this." Dimitri Young had been the Conservative Association's most powerful kingmaker, and *that* post Pavel intended to reclaim in the very near future. Indeed, he intended in the fullness of time—and rather sooner than Baron High Ridge might suspect—to aspire to an even higher position, once its current holder could be eased aside.

The true purpose of today's meeting had been to underscore his kingmaker status for the Association's senior leadership. And that was also why Georgia Sakristos had been present. Although almost every Manticoran politician knew about the "North Hollow Files," the true movers and shakers within the Conservative Association were aware that Sakristos had been Dimitri Young's senior intelligence operative, the woman who'd helped gather and update those files. And one of this meeting's points had been for her personal report to underscore that both of those lethal political weapons rested now in Pavel's hand.

*Of course*, he thought, *not even the "inner circle" knows* everything *Georgia did for Father, now do they?*

"Well, on that note," he said now, rising from his armchair, "I think we've probably covered everything we needed to discuss today. And, if you'll forgive me, there are a few other matters that require my attention."

"Of course!" Montreau said. The baron stood, joined by his fellows, and North Hollow ushered them personally and graciously to the townhouse's front door.

He smiled as he watched them climb into their vehicles and depart, although the smile disappeared as quickly as they did. Then he turned and walked back to the library.

Sakristos looked up from her handheld, her expression coolly attentive, as he reentered the spacious room.

He smiled and crossed to her. Then he cupped the side of her face in one palm, leaned forward, and put the tip of his tongue into her ear.

She sat very still, then reached up and covered the back of his hand with her own palm, leaning into it, and he smiled against her ear. Not because he thought she truly welcomed his caress, but because he knew she *didn't*. There was always an added spice to . . . *convincing* someone like Georgia, he thought.

He took his time making that point—for now, at least—before he straightened and walked back to his armchair again.

"I thought that went well," he said with a certain double-edged smirk as he seated himself once more.

"I think your message—*all* of your messages—got across, at any rate," she acknowledged with what was probably a double edge of her own.

"Good," he said. But then he leaned back in the chair and his smile faded.

"And that other matter?" he asked in a very different, far colder and harder, voice.

"If you're positive you really want to do this, I think I've found the next best thing to the perfect operative," she replied. "*Are* you positive?"

"And what could possibly make you think I'm not?" His voice had taken on an ugly edge and his eyes narrowed.

"It's one of my jobs to advise you," she said. "Not just figure out how to do what you need done, but to point out potential consequences of the things you decide need doing. And one of those consequences, frankly, is that if something happens—if *anything* happens—to Harrington at this point, attention will focus on you because of your history with her. I can probably—no, almost certainly—insulate you from the *legal* consequences of that attention, but the political consequences may be something else entirely."

"In the short term, maybe," he acknowledged. "In the long term, 'public opinion' will forget all about it as soon as some new, utterly absorbing event grabs the 'man in the street's' teeny-tiny attention span by its single-digit IQ. Even if that weren't true, I'm not some MP from Outer Backasswardborough who has to worry about elections, so fuck public opinion. And for anything I *do* need to worry about on the political front, I still have Father's files, don't I? Not to mention *you*?"

"That's probably true," she conceded.

After all, they both knew how potent a weapon the late earl's files truly were. Just as they both knew that the fact that *she* was an entry in them was what guaranteed Pavel would have *her* for as long as he wanted, as well.

In more ways than one.

"I just want to be sure you understand the possible ramifications before we move forward," she continued. "Yes, I can give you plausible deniability. No, I can't promise anyone will actually believe that."

"What makes you think I want anyone to disbelieve I had something to do with it?" he asked, and smiled as he saw what might be genuine surprise in her eyes. "Oh," he waved a hand, "I'd just as soon keep speculation about it off the boards, but we both know that's not going to happen. As you say, if *anything* happens to the bitch, a lot of people will automatically blame me for it. But the truth, Georgia? The truth is it won't break my heart at all if people like that bastard White Haven figure out who was really behind it. In fact, it won't break my heart if all the bastards who lined up behind him to stomp all over my career know *exactly* what happened. And the fact that they'll never be able to prove it—never be able to do one single, solitary damn thing about it—will only make that better!"

"All right," she said after a moment. "Understood. Doing it that way will make it a bit trickier, but it also means the operative I have in mind is probably even more suitable than I'd thought."

"Good! Then I'll leave it in your hands to arrange."

"I'm afraid it's not quite that simple," she said, and his eyes narrowed once again.

"Why not?"

"Because he'll insist on a face-to-face meeting."

"What?"

"Because he'll insist on a personal meeting to discuss exactly what you want done. It's the way he operates."

"I don't think so!" North Hollow half-snapped.

"Not meeting him isn't an option."

"Then *you* meet with him!"

"Oh, I will, Pavel," she replied. "I'll have to, if I'm going to set this up for you, so don't think there won't be plenty of my own skin in the game if it goes south. But there's no way I could convince him *I'm* the prime mover, and he'll insist on a face-to-face meeting with my principal, as well. And, to be honest, I'm sure he already knows who that is. No, not because I *told* him—yet," she continued calmly as North Hollow stiffened angrily. "I haven't even directly contacted him yet. But I won't have to tell him. One of the things that *make* him the right man for this job is how well tapped-in—and how smart—he is. People like Montreau and New Flushing aren't the only ones who know what I did for your father and, by extension, what I'm still doing for you. You might as well accept right now that the other people out there who do what I do know their fellow players—including me—and who most of us work for. And even if he didn't already know who I work for, as soon as I told him what you want and how you want it done, he'd realize there was only one person I could be representing. With all due respect, that's the flip side of the fact that you want her boosters to know who orchestrated what happens to her."

He glared at her for several seconds, then inhaled deeply.

"In that case, it sounds like he's *not* the ideal operative," he observed in an acid tone. "That whole 'plausible deniability' of yours goes straight out the window if he knows who hired him!"

"No, it doesn't. Not necessarily, at least."

"The instant somebody in authority squeezes him, he'll roll over," North Hollow shot back. "Of course the bitch's friends will know I set it all in motion! And do you honestly think for an instant that a Crown prosecutor wouldn't offer him the mother of all deals if it let Cromarty, White Haven, and their bastard buddies take *me* down?"

"First," she said in that same calm tone, "one of the reasons he's the perfect choice is that his preferred methodology doesn't give a prosecutor a leg to stand on." She smiled nastily. "The only illegal aspect of the entire operation will be the fact that he accepted payment for it. Absent evidence of that, no one will ever be able to touch him, which means—by extension—that they can never touch *you*, either. Admittedly, if the Crown could ever prove he was paid for it, *then* he could be prosecuted, but he's been handling assignments like this for a long time, and nobody's ever been able to prove anything of the sort. And, again with all due respect, I've been *paying* people like him for your father for a long time without leaving any fingerprints in inconvenient places.

"Second, though, the fact that he insists on knowing who's hired him is actually a pretty potent form of additional protection for you."

"How does letting him know who hired him 'protect' me?" he demanded skeptically.

"Because," she replied, "he operates that way with *all* of his clients, and every single one of them knows it. And that means that if there's ever even a hint he's about to turn the Crown's evidence on anyone, there'll be dozens of people—at least one or two of them pretty highly placed in the Outfit—lining up to make sure he's dead before he can add *them* to the list. So even if he wanted to tell the authorities who hired him and why—which, admittedly, he might, assuming they ever did manage to find evidence someone did—he'd be signing his own death warrant because of how many of his past clients have too much to lose if he ever started singing like a bird. After all, the Crown would hold out for every single thing they could squeeze out of him, and his client list couldn't let that happen."

North Hollow had opened his mouth to interrupt her. Now he closed it again, sitting back in his chair, his expression more thoughtful, and Sakristos smiled mentally behind her calmly attentive expression. She'd thought he'd like that. But—

"All right," he said. "I can understand the logic. I'm not sure I share it, though. And"—his eyes sharpened—"I'm confident someone with your expertise could find me someone else to do the job. Maybe someone less 'ideal,' but someone who understands the importance of anonymity."

"Yes, I can, if you insist. What I can't do is find someone else who checks off all the boxes on your to-do list the way this guy does."

"Meaning what?" he demanded suspiciously.

"Meaning," she said as she got out of her own chair, walked across, and settled into his lap, "that there's not a single person in the Star Kingdom better than this guy, especially"—she put her arms around his neck—"if you want to kick Cromarty and Alexander and White Haven and all the rest of them right in the teeth. If we let him do his job the way he always has, the blowback will spatter all over that sanctimonious bastard Cromarty. And the best part of all"—she nestled closer, leaning to nip gently at *his* earlobe—"is that there won't be a damn thing Cromarty or *anyone else* can do about it."

"And just why would that be?" North Hollow wrapped one arm around her while his other hand slid slowly up her thigh and under her skirt. "Not that I don't appreciate your efforts to entice me into agreeing," he added with a smirk, "but you have to admit that's a little hard to accept without a certain degree of reservation."

"Oh, I know that."

She leaned back to smile into his eyes as his hand crept still higher, and the fact that he knew just how . . . constrained that smile was only pleased him more. She knew that, and she hated it, but she made herself smile more deeply, then leaned forward again with a slow, lingering kiss. It lasted a long time, that kiss, before she pulled back again, at last.

"I know that," she murmured in his ear then. "But that's only because I haven't told you his last name yet."

**Chez Berthelsen**
**City of Landing**
**Planet of Manticore**
**March 5, 1906 PD**

CHEZ BERTHELSEN WAS RENOWNED for many things. One was the fact that it was the City of Landing's second-oldest continuously operating restaurant. Another was the peerless quality of its kitchens and the range of its menu, which didn't even mention its wine cellar and list of liqueurs. But yet another, and arguably the greatest, of the expensive restaurant's attractions, was its privacy.

Thorvald Berthelsen, Chez Berthelsen's founder, immigrated to the Star Kingdom of Manticore in 1640 PD, a bare half-T-century after the first transit of the Manticoran Wormhole Junction. He was less than thirty T-years old at the time, and his very first restaurant was a hole-in-the-wall delicatessen, known as Thorvald's Place, serving the steadily growing shipyard labor force of the Star Kingdom.

It was in that delicatessen that he met Siún O'Carolan, the daughter of a yard worker, who informed him in no uncertain terms that his corn chowder was substandard. At best. Thorvald asked her if she thought she could do better, and, when she assured him that she could, hired her on the spot. It was an inspired move, and not just because she brought her mother's chowder recipe with her. Her presence in the kitchen elevated Thorvald's Place to an entirely new level, and it became one of the most popular eateries on the barebone, rough-edged orbital platform which, in the fullness of time, was to become Hephaestus Station.

That delicatessen remained Thorvald's first love—well, after Siún *Berthelsen*, the mother of his children and the center of his life—until the day of his death. But (largely at Siún's urging) he opened a second, rather more upscale establishment in downtown Landing in 1649, near the newly built Landing Opera House. It was an inspired

147

location for attracting the upper crust of the upper crust, and Thorvald had promised that upper crust a *private* dining experience, free of interruption, disturbance, or inconvenient publicity.

There were those who thought that location and privacy guarantee explained his new restaurant's instant success. Thorvald knew better. *He* knew the true reason Chez Berthelsen thrived was who ruled its kitchen with an iron hand, and he threw himself into building it into the crown jewel of Landing's restaurant scene as a gift to the woman he loved.

But he never closed Thorvald's Place. He spent every Monday of his life there, with Siún by his side, sleeves rolled up and laughing in the kitchen and behind the counter, and that was where their five children learned the heart and soul—and joy—of the restaurateur's trade.

He lost Siún to a traffic accident in 1674.

She was in that air taxi only because she'd gone to meet one of their produce suppliers. It was an errand Thorvald had been supposed to run, but he'd been too busy with a staff meeting at the restaurant, so she'd gone in his place.

Thorvald was sixty-three that year. His and Siún's oldest son, Cathal, was thirty, and every time Thorvald walked into Chez Berthelsen, he remembered that meeting he'd been too busy to make. Remembered how Siún had died. So he handed Chez Berthelsen to Cathal and retired to Thorvald's Place and the memories of the young woman he'd met in its noisy, lively dining room and loved so very much.

Two T-centuries later, Chez Berthelsen was still there, still under Berthelsen family management, and still at the very head of every guide to Landing's five-star restaurants. But, like Landing City itself, times had changed in other ways. The Opera House had been demolished ninety T-years ago, and Chez Berthelsen's low-lying, four-story building nestled at the foot of the gigantic ceramacrete tower that stretched to the heavens where once the Opera House had stood. The three-hectare footprint of the restaurant's landscaped grounds, barely a kilometer from the Parliament Building itself, was worth an obscene amount, although the family would never have dreamed of selling it, and its clientele was even more stratospheric than it had ever been.

Yet there was another side to Chez Berthelsen, because Thorvald's policy of safeguarding his diners' privacy remained in force, and his descendants had incorporated the best technology, updated regularly, to ensure that it did. And because they had, quite a few of Chez Berthelsen's regular patrons ate there for reasons that had very little to do with the quality of its kitchens or the depth of its cellars. It was said that three quarters of Landing's political deals and half its business mergers had been sealed in one of Chez Berthelsen's private dining rooms. And it was rumored—no one could possibly prove it, of course—that those same dining rooms had hosted almost that many assignations between wealthy clients with . . . esoteric tastes and the courtesans who served them.

What was less often spoken of, although the Landing City Police Department was well-informed on the matter, was the way arrangements of questionable legality were also finalized at Chez Berthelsen. It was inevitable that a certain class of criminal would be attracted to such an environment, assuming the criminals in question could convince the maître d' to seat them (and that they behaved themselves, once they had). Far too many of the Star Kingdom's wealthiest and most powerful had a strong interest in maintaining Chez Berthelsen's confidentiality, for reasons which (of course) had nothing to do with criminal activity, for the minions of the law to surveil its clientele or intrude upon its precincts without a warrant.

And warrants to intrude upon Chez Berthelsen were difficult to come by.

Which was how the Earl of North Hollow found himself seated in the Cargill Room with Georgia Sakristos. The private dining room, which could seat parties of up to twenty in comfort, was scarcely inexpensive, even by the standards of his wealth, but he'd reserved the entire room and considered it money well spent. The food was as excellent as ever, his companion was astonishingly beautiful, and his hands could wander as widely as his heart desired. Not simply because the discreet staff would never dream of disturbing them unannounced, but also because the Cargill Room's privacy screening was impervious to every known form of eavesdropping.

That last point was very present in North Hollow's mind as he and Sakristos sat back in their chairs with after-dinner snifters of brandy and a side door opened.

The newcomer was slim and not especially tall, with fair hair and gray eyes, and he moved with a studied, almost predatory grace. He stopped, just inside the door, to survey the room, then crossed to the table and bowed.

"Milord," he said, then nodded rather more brusquely to Sakristos. "Georgia."

If he was disappointed—or surprised—to have arrived only after they'd finished supper, there was no sign of it in his tone or expression.

"Please," North Hollow invited. "Join us, Mr. Summervale."

"Thank you, Milord."

The new arrival settled into a chair across the table from the earl with that same feline grace, and North Hollow personally poured brandy into a third snifter and handed it to him. The newcomer took it in a manicured but remarkably sinewy hand, passed it under his nose, inhaling deeply, then sipped appreciatively.

"The Montresor '52," he said. "I salute your taste, Milord."

"I'm glad you approve." North Hollow set the bottle aside. "I'm afraid I can't offer you anything else. I've told the staff that Georgia and I will need a little . . . additional privacy tonight."

"Of course."

There might have been the slightest trace of condescension for the statement of the obvious in Summervale's voice, but North Hollow didn't much care.

"I believe Georgia's explained to you what I need done?" he said.

"She has." Summervale nodded.

"And the financial terms are acceptable?"

"They are." Summervale sipped more brandy. "And I suppose I might admit that there are certain fringe attractions to this assignment for me."

"I thought there might be." North Hollow grimaced. "I've always found the Duke a bit overly sanctimonious, shall we say, for my own tastes. I imagine it must be even worse having our esteemed Prime Minister for a cousin."

"Oh, it has its moments, Milord." Summervale bared his teeth. "Frankly, visualizing his reaction to what you've planned is one of them."

North Hollow smiled back at him.

"You understand that this needs to happen sometime soon?" he asked then. "My latest information is that her ship will be out of yard hands sometime in the next two or three T-months. I'm sure she plans to return from Yeltsin well before that to oversee the refit's final stages. It's important to me that her planned return be . . . expedited by unexpected news from home."

His expression might still have been called a smile, assuming Old Terran sharks had known how to smile.

"I believe that's feasible," Summervale said judiciously. "I've conducted some quiet reconnaissance, and I'm confident I can gain access, at any rate."

"Good!"

North Hollow took another, deeper sip—almost a gulp—of the expensive brandy, then looked at Summervale with glittering eyes.

"I would never dream of telling you how to do your own business, of course, Mister Summervale. One doesn't hire a specialist and then tell him how to do his job. But I really want the terms of the challenge, the reason for it, to hurt. I want her to know this was for *her*. I want her to know *she's* how you got to him. And the reason you did."

"Understood."

Summervale nodded serenely. North Hollow's requirements came as no surprise. Sakristos had already made the basic parameters clear enough. Besides, he was accustomed to requests very like that. People tended to engage his services only when it was personal—*very* personal—for them. Still, the passion in the earl's eyes was unusual, even in Summervale's line of work.

"I've already been thinking in that direction," he continued, sitting back and cradling the snifter in both hands. "And not simply because of what you've just said. The first part of this operation has to be presented carefully, in a fashion that makes it reasonable for me to issue the challenge, because, frankly, he *won't* challenge me." Summervale smiled thinly. "He doesn't approve of duels—that much I've already established—so I have to provoke him into provoking *me*, as it were. And in a way that discourages him from crying off once he's had time to think about it. I believe I've found a way to do that, and I'm sure the way in which I do it will get back to her. In fact, I'm rather counting on it."

"You are?"

"Oh, yes, Milord! It would be just a tad too obvious if I challenged both of them. So the trick is for the outcome of the first challenge to push her into challenging me. Especially since, as I understand it, you'd prefer the Ellington Protocol in her case?"

"Yes." North Hollow's calm tone was a poor match for the fire in his eyes. "Yes, definitely."

"Well, as long as I'm the challenged party, I can guarantee that, Milord. You do understand, though, that I won't be able to arrange that in *his* case?" Summervale grimaced. "Given his attitude, I'm afraid we can rely on his insisting on the Dreyfus Protocol."

"I know." North Hollow's nostrils flared. "I can't say I don't wish you *could* get him to agree to the Ellington. For more than one reason. I'm no expert with dueling pistols, of course, but forty meters . . . that's a *long* range for an antique like that."

"Don't worry, Milord. I realize it's a long range, but I train at it regularly. And after he takes his shot—and misses—I can take *my* time to do it right. Trust me, I can do the business with a single shot. Of course, you do understand that, to assure that, it will have to be immediately fatal? The attending medical staff is very good, I'm afraid."

"I can't have everything," North Hollow said. "I knew that going in. I won't pretend I wouldn't prefer something rather more . . . extended in his case, too. I have quite a few scores to settle with him, as well. But the truth is that he's more a means to an end in this case. As long"—his eyes stabbed Summervale across the table—"as you *do* 'do the business' with your single shot."

"Milord, I haven't been clumsy enough to miss my mark in years. I won't miss it this time."

North Hollow only looked at him, and Summervale shrugged.

"Milord, the way Georgia's arranged things, the funds will transfer only after the job is done. A third after the first duel; the balance after the second. If it should happen for some unimaginable reason that I do miss my mark, you'll owe me nothing."

"That's very reassuring, in a purely financial sense," North Hollow said. "But to be honest, the financial aspect of our agreement is its least important part for me."

"By the time I'm called in, Milord, that's almost always the case," Summervale said almost gently. "Believe me, I understand that. And

I might as well admit that in her case I have motives of my own which transcend your generous fee."

"You do?" North Hollow sounded surprised.

"Oh, yes," Summervale told him. "I have a bone of my own to pick with the Countess." North Hollow's eyes narrowed, and Summervale smiled slowly. "Don't worry, Milord. It's not something that will provide anyone with evidence that I have any personal motivation in this case. The truth is that even she doesn't know it, but she did me a significant disservice some years ago. So you might say this gives me the chance to kill two birds with one stone, as it were."

"I see." North Hollow gazed at him for another few seconds, then took another sip of brandy and set the empty snifter aside.

"I believe our business tonight is concluded, then, Mr. Summervale?"

"It is, Milord." Summervale emptied his own snifter, set it on the table, and stood. "I trust our departure times will be sufficiently staggered?"

"Oh, I think that can be arranged. After all, as I told our waiter, Georgia and I"—he smiled at Sakristos—"will need the room a bit longer.

"*Quite* a bit longer, actually."

"I DON'T THINK you're hearing everything Thomas and I are saying, Paul."

Alistair McKeon's eyes were bleak, his expression grim, as he looked across the private dining room's table at Paul Tankersley.

"I hear everything you've said, Alistair," Tankersley replied. "You and Tomas both. And I deeply appreciate how concerned both of you are. Hell, *I'm* concerned! But done is done. He's challenged me, and I accepted the challenge."

"Only because I was ninety seconds late to the party," Tomas Ramirez said bitterly. "If I'd gotten there even *two minutes* earlier—"

"He was already launched by then, Tomas. And I didn't have any reason to think—"

"That's only because I hadn't already warned you what it was like when he was still a Marine! And if I'd been there—"

"Oh, stop it!" Tankersley said sharply. "You couldn't have known what was coming any more than I did!"

"No, but I could damn well have stopped it when it did go down," Ramirez grated.

"After I broke his nose and took out one of his teeth?" Tankersley barked a laugh. "You really think he wouldn't have issued the challenge after that no matter *who'd* been there?"

"I *know* he wouldn't have, because he'd have been fucking unconscious on a stretcher. Or on his way to the station morgue! That's the problem, Paul. You pulled your damned punch!"

"I couldn't just kill him on the spot, no matter what he said."

"You didn't have to kill him; you only had to take him down and then walk away. You were too fucking *civilized!*"

155

Tomas Ramirez seldom used profanity or obscenities, but he was prepared to make an exception today. His voice was hammered iron, and Tankersley's eyes were hot as he half-glared at his friends. He opened his mouth again, but McKeon raised a pacific hand before he could speak.

"Look," he said, "Tomas may not be the most diplomatic soul in the galaxy, and you know—now—that he has his own, call it an *institutional* bone to pick with Summervale. And what that son of a bitch said about Honor makes this personal for all three of us. Especially for you. But the critical point here is that there's no way that bastard didn't know exactly what he was doing when he goaded you into punching him out. And that means it damned well didn't 'just happen.'"

"He doesn't even know me," Tankersley half-protested.

"And what the *fuck* does that have to do with it?" Ramirez demanded harshly. "That man's a professional duelist. Picking quarrels—goading people into attacking him so we can get them out on the dueling ground—is what he *does*."

"Then he should be in prison!"

"And he *would* be if the Crown could prove people paid him to shoot their enemies under cover of the law," Ramirez shot back. "But he's *good*, Paul. He's really, really good. And I'll guarantee you a gun like his doesn't come cheap. He's careful not to take on too many 'commissions' or space them close enough together to create probable cause for an investigation, so I'm damned sure hiring him costs a bundle each time he does take a job. And the way he got to you, the things he said about Dame Honor..." He shook his head. "There's only one person who could be behind this, and you know it."

"I know who you're talking about," Tankersley replied. "But to be honest, I find it hard to believe even he might think he'd get away with something like this. I have to admit the possibility, and God knows he's the most likely suspect, assuming this really is a put-up job. I just... I just have trouble wrapping my mind around how he could possibly expect this wouldn't lead straight back to him."

"I don't know Young—North Hollow—as well as you do," McKeon said. "I didn't ever find myself stuck as his XO, for which I'm more grateful than I could possibly say. But I've done a lot of poking around over the years since he tried to screw Honor over in Basilisk, and there's nothing—*nothing*, Paul!—that I'd put past that man. You probably know more about what happened between them at the Academy than I do, but I've dug up enough to make me want to put my boot right up his ass. And the other thing I know is that the man's a complete sociopath. Right up to the moment they cashiered him, he expected his old man to ride in and snatch him out of the fire yet again. For most people, what actually happened would probably constitute a rude awakening, but I'll guarantee you it hasn't in his case. Just like nothing that ever happened to him is *his* fault, he's absolutely convinced he can do whatever the hell he wants and get away with it. Hell, he's got *proof* of it, as far as he's concerned! The whole frigging Conservative Association—*and* the Liberal Party— ran cover for him."

"You may be right about that. No"—Tankersley shook his head— "scratch that. You *are* right. But that doesn't change the situation. I still laid hands on Summervale. Hell, if he'd wanted to, he could've pressed charges against me for attempted murder! Or did you two forget I hold a fifth-degree black belt in *coup de vitesse*? There's a reason my hands are legally considered deadly weapons, and the truth is, I came within a centimeter of putting him down as hard— and maybe even as permanently—as even you could wish Tomas. I was that angry."

His face was bleak, and Alistair McKeon felt his own smolder of rage. No one was repeating what Summervale had said about Honor. Not yet, anyway. But it was there, just waiting.

*"Tell me, Captain Tankersley—are you really that good a fuck? Are you so good she was willing to throw away her entire command to save you? Or was it just that she was that desperate to have someone— anyone—between her legs?"*

There was nothing the bastard could have said that could have hurt Honor worse. Except for the suggestion he'd *also* made that she'd held her course in Hancock, gotten thousands of additional Navy personnel killed, just because she refused to abandon the space station on which her lover was trapped.

"Instead of doing that, he issued the challenge," Tankersley continued. "And I'd accepted it before you got there to tell me about his reputation. But I'll be honest with you both—after the things he said about her, and the fact that he said them in a public place where

I know damned well some sick son of a bitch will repeat them to her even if no one dares to do it in print, I wouldn't have walked away from this even if I *could*."

His face clenched in anger, and McKeon reached across to grip his shoulder.

He was right, the captain thought, and as far as McKeon was concerned, that was the final proof of who was pulling the strings.

Only a tiny handful of people knew Honor Harrington as well as Alistair McKeon did. Any healthy human being would be disgusted by the things Denver Summervale had said about her, but only that tiny handful could understand how vulnerable to them she was. Because only that tiny handful had ever been allowed deep enough inside to recognize how completely she'd shut down that part of her life after her Academy experiences. How hard and how far she'd run to hide from even the possibility of risking a relationship after Pavel Young attempted to rape a first-year midshipwoman and then used his family name to attempt to destroy his intended victim.

That wasn't the only thing that had happened to her, either. McKeon knew that much, although he suspected the only person who might know the full truth was Michelle Henke. And now possibly Paul Tankersley. But Alistair McKeon knew enough. And he totally understood the rage—the fury—pulsing through Tankersley at this moment. Hell, he felt it himself!

And then there were the political ramifications.

"I understand how that's going to affect her, Paul," he said quietly. "I really do. And in your place, I'd want to put a bullet through the bastard myself. Don't think for a moment I wouldn't. But you need to think about what it will do to her if this son of a bitch kills you."

"Of course I've thought about it." Tankersley looked away, his voice harsh. "How could I *not* think about it? That's part of the problem." He looked back at McKeon. "I was stupid enough to let him goad me into doing something like this to *her*, too. My God, Alistair! Do you think I don't realize how she's going to react to this? Even if I walk away clean tomorrow morning, she'll know what happened. She'll know *how* it happened. And if I *don't* walk away—"

He broke off, and McKeon squeezed his shoulder again.

"All right, Paul. I understand—*we* understand. And the last thing you need is for us to get inside your head and mess with it at a moment like this. It's just . . . just that I want to be *sure* you know what you have to do tomorrow. That whatever it may be for you, this isn't any 'affair of honor' for him." His hand tightened with bruising force. "You need to take this bastard *down*."

"I know." Tankersley reached up and patted her hand on his shoulder. "I *know*, Alistair."

"Good."

McKeon sat back, reaching for his coffee cup, and Tankersley glanced down as his chrono chimed. He looked at it for a moment, then raised his eyes again with a crooked smile.

"For what I expect are obvious reasons, I need to get as much sleep tonight as I can. And that was a reminder that I'm having an early supper with my mom. I've got a shuttle to catch if I'm going to make it on time."

"Does she—?"

"No, and I'm damned well not telling her." Tankersley managed a more natural-looking smile. "There's no point worrying her when it'll be over in about fifteen hours, anyway. But I do want to spend some time with her."

"Of course you do." McKeon stood and held out his hand. "Tell her hello for me."

"I will." Tankersley gripped his hand, then looked at Ramirez. "Oh-four-hundred tomorrow, Tomas?"

"I'll be there."

"Good! And I'll see both of you at breakfast, after."

"I'll be there for that, too," Ramirez told him.

"Then I'd best be going. It always pisses Mom off when I'm late."

He nodded to his friends, and left, and McKeon settled back into his chair, looking across the table at Ramirez.

"He doesn't get it, Tomas," the captain said heavily. "God help me, I think he still doesn't get it. Not really."

"He gets it here." Ramirez tapped his temple. "He just doesn't get it on a gut level. Damn." The Marine shook his head, his eyes bitter. "He's just too good a man, Alistair."

"But he *knows* North Hollow." McKeon sounded like a man trying to convince himself of something. "He *has* to know North Hollow wants him dead, if only because the sick son of a bitch knows how losing him would just destroy Honor."

"Assuming it's really North Hollow," Ramirez said, then barked a wolf's laugh at McKeon's expression. "Of course it is! But like we've just been saying, there's no way in hell to *prove* it. And there's that tiny little corner somewhere down inside Paul that keeps whispering crap about 'innocent until proven guilty.' And there's that other tiny corner that thinks not even North Hollow could be stupid enough to think he could get away with outright murder."

"There's nothing North Hollow can't convince himself he can get away with."

"You know that. I know that. Hell, intellectually, *Paul* knows that!"

Silence fell. A brooding, unhappy silence.

"You think he's really up to this?" McKeon asked finally. "I'm not talking about guts. I don't think I know anybody any gutsier than Paul! And if it was any other kind of fight, I'd back him in a heartbeat. But this . . ."

"I don't know." Ramirez sighed. "You know Livitnikov pushed for the Ellington Protocol?"

"He did?" McKeon's eyes narrowed. "Paul never told me that."

"Well, he could hardly insist, since Paul was the challenged party. But he made it clear his principal would 'understand' if *Paul* chose to insist on it." Ramirez's lips twisted in disgust. "In a lot of ways, Livitnikov's as big a snake as Summervale."

McKeon nodded, his eyes worried, as he processed the new information.

Milorad Livitnikov was a Landing City attorney and financial advisor, with a reputation which was no more savory than it had to be. He'd represented quite a few professional criminals in his time, both in court and—if rumor was correct—in other, off-the-record fashion, as a go-between and broker of any number of illegal transactions. It was unusual, to say the least, to find him so much in the foreground, but he'd been Denver Summervale's friend—or his "associate," at least—for decades. They were semi-regular dinner companions, when they were both in town at the same time, so no one could prove Livitnikov hadn't "just happened" to be here, in the *Hephaestus* Dempsey's, at just the right moment for Summervale's "spontaneous" confrontation with Tankersley. In fact, the "friendly dinner" had been on Livitnikov's calendar for over a week, and he'd reserved a table at Dempsey's three days earlier. All purely coincidentally, of course.

Just like it "just happened" Livitnikov had acted as Summervale's second in a previous duel several T-years earlier. So it was totally understandable, when the quarrel with Tankersley just erupted out of nowhere, for Summervale to ask his oh-so-conveniently-present friend to act for him again. What could be more reasonable than that?

It all screamed setup, although no one could prove a thing. And if Ramirez was right about Livitnikov's pressure for the Ellington Protocol...

Dueling was legal in the Star Kingdom. Duels were frowned upon these days, and far less common than they'd once been, but the practice remained as an artifact of the Star Kingdom's earliest days, when concepts of justice had been ... simpler and more direct.

Manticore was scarcely unique among the galaxy's star nations in having once permitted legal duels. In fact, it was probable that at least half of them had allowed it, with or without benefit of a formal code duello, in their wilder and woolier days, and scores of them—like Manticore—still did. That didn't necessarily constitute a good reason it should *remain* legal, however. And the fact that it did didn't keep a great many people, including Alistair McKeon, from thinking that should have been changed long ago. On the other hand, he had to admit there'd been at least two occasions in his own life when he'd come within an eyelash of resorting to the practice himself. In fact, he was tempted every time he so much as thought about Pavel Young.

There were restrictions, of course. Serving officers couldn't challenge one another, for example, and debtors couldn't challenge their creditors, just as no party to a legal suit could challenge any of the other litigants. But for the most part, the practice was accepted, however grudgingly, by the Star Kingdom at large as part of its code of honor.

Most duels were fought because someone genuinely believed his or her honor had been impugned. It struck McKeon as a stupid way to go about resolving insults, and he'd never been particularly interested in the code duello's provisions until Tankersley was challenged. He'd done quite a bit of research since, and he'd discovered that the vast majority of them were fought under the Dreyfus Protocol. Under that protocol, each duelist had only a five-round magazine, and they were limited to the exchange of single shots at a range of forty meters, almost half the length of a standard soccer pitch. That was an extraordinarily long range for the archaic pistols of the dueling grounds, which meant that more often than not, neither party managed to hit the other with his or her first shot. More than that, the Master of the Field was charged with convincing both parties honor had been satisfied after each exchange, and *either* party— challenger or challenged—could declare that it had been. Even more importantly, perhaps, five rounds were all either side got, under any circumstances, and any duel *automatically* ended after the first exchange in which blood was drawn.

Because of those limitations, the Dreyfus Protocol practically never resulted in fatalities. It had happened, but that was almost always an accident neither combatant had desired . . . openly, at least. Honor required that the duelist stand his or her enemy's fire; it did not require that enemy's death, and that was what the Dreyfus Protocol was intended to accomplish.

But the Ellington Protocol was different, and there'd been pressure to ban it for decades, even among many who otherwise vociferously defended the practice of dueling. Under the Ellington Protocol, the range was only *twenty* meters, each duelist had a *ten*-round magazine, and each of them was free to fire without pause until his opponent went down or dropped his own weapon in surrender. It was, in fact, the protocol upon which someone who fully intended to kill his opponent insisted.

"Paul knows *Livitnikov* suggested the Ellington Protocol?" McKeon asked after a moment.

"He knows Livitnikov would have been *amenable* to it." Ramirez shrugged bitterly. "The man's a lawyer, Alistair, and one of the true bottom feeders, at that. He knows exactly how to weasel-word a sentence to make his point without saying anything you could nail him on in court. But he made it abundantly clear to me when Paul asked me to serve as his second. He never actually said it to *Paul*, of course. That's not how these things are done."

McKeon nodded again. From the moment a challenge was issued, all contact between the principals was prohibited. They communicated only through their seconds, and neither principal was a party to the actual conversation.

"I love the Star Kingdom," Ramirez said. "It took me and my family in when my father died and Trevor's Star went down. It's been good to us, we've done really well here, and I've always known Manticore was the only chance San Martin might ever be liberated from the Peeps. But if there's one thing about Manticore that never made sense to me, it's this whole dueling thing. It just seems so custom-designed for abuse! I *always* thought that, and now, with Paul—"

"And now with Paul, you've got *proof* it is," McKeon said bitterly. "But you told Paul about Livitnikov's attitude?"

"Of course I did! But Paul knows how pissed off I am, and he knows you and I both think this is a bought-and-paid-for setup, so I'm not positive he believed me. Oh"—the colonel waved one powerful hand—"he doesn't think I'm *inventing* things, but I think that 'civilized' part of him's half-convinced my own emotions might cause me to *misconstrue* Livitnikov's mealymouthed circumlocutions."

"What kind of Marine knows a word like 'circumlocutions'?" McKeon asked, and Ramirez chuckled sourly at the feeble bid to break the tension just a bit.

"I know. Doesn't mesh well with our hard-won reputation for simpleminded violence," he said.

"Agreed."

McKeon flashed a brief smile. Then his expression sobered again.

"But I don't like this at all," he said. "Not because it surprises me, but because of what it confirms."

"Confirms for you and me, anyway," Ramirez agreed.

"Damn." McKeon drummed his fingers on the tabletop.

A part of him was positive Tankersley had gone far farther than he was willing to admit in acknowledging—to himself—that Summervale was a hired gun, and that part wanted to rage at his friend for not withdrawing from the duel. There was no legal compulsion for him to actually meet Summervale. He could withdraw—legally—at any moment until they both stepped onto the field. If he did, he would be labeled a coward by all "right thinking" people, which would probably include at least some who might sit on future promotion boards. That was especially true given that, for whatever provocation, Tankersley had laid hands on Summervale in what—as he'd just pointed out himself—could have been classified as assault with a deadly weapon. A "man of honor" who had physically assaulted another was under much more powerful social pressure to meet the man he'd "wronged."

But that social pressure wasn't the real reason Tankersley would not—*could* not—withdraw. Not even the way Summervale's words would hurt Honor on a personal level was the *real* reason.

*Politics*, McKeon thought despairingly. *Why does it always have to be the goddamned* politics?! *Why can't the fucking vultures just leave her the hell* alone?!

It was obvious that Summervale's slurs had been designed as a multifaceted weapon, and in many ways, the potential political damage was just as deadly as the duel might prove to Tankersley, at least on the grand scale of things. So far, none of the Opposition scandal sheets or boards had repeated Summervale's despicable allegations, and they wouldn't while the duel remained unfought. If they did, Honor—or Tankersley—could sue for defamation and libel, and the Star Kingdom's libel laws had painful, very sharp teeth. Anyone who'd repeated the allegations would have to prove they were true (which, manifestly, no one could) or lose in court, and any jury would award astronomical damages to a peer of the realm, not to mention the way in which the verdict would nullify those allegations as a future political weapon.

But if Tankersley withdrew from the duel now, it would be taken as an admission that he'd chosen not to contest Summervale's accusations. That wouldn't *prove* they were true but it would extend a *presumption* that they were. In order to win a defamation or libel suit under those conditions, he and Honor would have to prove they were *false*, which they could no more prove legally than their opponents could prove the reverse.

Given the way she and Young remained rallying points for the Opposition and the pro-Government parties, respectively, the damage in the Star Kingdom would have been severe. What the political fallout for the Protectorate of Grayson's first female steadholder might be like...

Whether Tankersley lived or died, the fact that he'd faced Summervale at all would prevent that from happening.

And he knew it.

But if he died, the consequences for *Honor Harrington* would be catastrophic, no matter what else happened.

"I'm half inclined to get Paul on the com and have another go at him." McKeon shook his head. "He can't afford to screw around with this guy, Tomas! I already knew that much. But this—!"

"We've both taken our best shot," Ramirez said heavily. "And under most circumstances, I wouldn't be this worried. Like Paul says, practically nobody gets killed under the Dreyfus Protocol. Those antiques are hardly pulsers. They aren't going to just vaporize a limb or something even if they manage to hit each other at that range, and he'll only have to take one shot. Even assuming he's hit—unless he gets hit squarely in the head or something, which would take a *damned* good shot—the trauma team will be standing right there to stabilize him and rush him to the hospital."

"Sure. And Summervale just happens to *be* a 'damned good shot.' Which means that unless *Paul* hits *him* in the head—or somewhere else incapacitating—first, the chance of *his* getting hit there goes up like a missile!"

"Of course it does." Ramirez's expression was acid-etched iron. "And I've told him that, just like you have. And up here"—he tapped his temple again—"he gets it. But I don't know about here, Alistair." He thumped his chest. "Paul's one of the best men I know, but he's not Dame Honor." His eyes met McKeon's. "He just doesn't have that killer in his DNA."

**Landing Dueling Grounds**
**City of Landing**
**Planet of Manticore**
**Manticore Binary System**
**March 21, 1906 PD**

THE MORNING SUN SAT RED and heavy on the horizon, peeking out across Jason Bay between the water and a level roof of gray cloud.

The weather had been hot, even for Landing, for the past week or so, but the weather satellites—and those clouds—promised a break in the temperature and rain by late morning. The faintest breeze ruffled the trees as the ground car came to a halt outside the low, vine-grown wall, dew glittered across the smooth grass, and Paul Tankersley inhaled deeply as he opened the ground-car door and climbed out.

Tomas Ramirez followed him, and a Landing City Police lieutenant crossed the grass to meet them.

"Good morning, Captain Tankersley." The lieutenant wore a black brassard and carried a heavy, military-grade pulser in a holster at his hip. "I'm Lieutenant Carlson."

"Good morning, Lieutenant." Tankersley was actually a little surprised by how calm his own voice sounded.

"I'll be acting as Master of the Field today, Sir."

"I see." Tankersley nodded and looked around the quiet emptiness.

"Mister Summervale is already on the field, Sir."

The tiniest possible edge in Carlson's tone drew Tankersley's gaze back to him, and the naval officer's eyes narrowed ever so slightly. The lieutenant's expression was gravely professional, with the neutrality his morning's duties required of him, but there was something about his eyes. A flicker deep within them, coupled with that tiny edge, that told Paul Tankersley Lieutenant Carlson was fully aware of Denver Summervale's reputation.

"Then I suppose we shouldn't keep him waiting," he said, and glanced at the massive Marine colonel at his shoulder. "Tomas?"

✧ ✧ ✧

Tomas Ramirez followed Tankersley across the grass, the pistol box—borrowed from one of Tankersley's aristocratic relatives, its lid embossed with the arms of a cadet branch of the House of Winton—tucked under his right arm.

Ramirez had insisted Tankersley practice on *Nike*'s range with one of the heavy, deliberately anachronistic but still lethal ten-millimeter pistols inside that box. He was glad he had, although the experience had only confirmed what he'd already expected to discover. Unlike Marines, naval officers were required to qualify with small arms only every other T-year, and Tankersley had grown up on Manticore, as a city boy right here in Landing. Although he'd frequently fished the waters of Jason Bay, he'd never spent a day on a hunting field in his life, nor had he ever seen any reason to carry a weapon for personal protection or shown the least interest in competitive shooting. All of which meant his familiarity with even modern small arms, far less antiques like these, was minimal, to say the least. He was an adequate shot—for certain values of the term "adequate," at least—but he would never be able to match the polished proficiency of a professional like Summervale.

"He's going to be faster than you are, Paul," Ramirez had said somberly as they stood on the otherwise empty range while the fans cleared away the propellant fumes. "He's done this before—a lot of times. I wish we had longer to practice, but to be completely honest, I don't think it would make an enormous difference."

Tankersley had nodded, his expression sober.

"The one thing you absolutely have to be is *focused*," Ramirez had continued. "Unless you're a total idiot, you'll also be scared. I know we don't admit that, but you've seen combat. You know it's true. So you have to step onto that field with your fear already put away in a box somewhere, and you have to fill your mind with only one purpose: to get that pistol up as quickly as you can without jerking it around. You have to be quick, but you also have to be *controlled*, because it won't do you one bit of good to get off a shot if you jerk your gun hand and send it God knows where. So bring it up, find the sight picture, and squeeze. Those are the only three things in your brain. Don't pay any attention to what *he's* doing, because you can't affect or control that. Concentrate on what you *can* control. And whatever else you do, don't go into this thinking 'I only have to take one shot, so it won't really matter whether or not I hit him, because it'll all be over either way.'"

Tankersley's eyes had narrowed, and Ramirez had snorted.

"Of course you've thought about that! And in at least one respect, it's absolutely true. But this will be a matter of fractions of a second. That's how long it'll take. I think he's faster than you, and I know he's more practiced, but he's not *automatically* going to get off the first shot. And that's why you need to be totally focused on hitting him. On preempting his shot, if you possibly can. Not on not being hit yourself, not on 'it doesn't matter,' but on 'I am going to *kill* this son of a bitch.'"

He'd held Tankersley's gaze with his own, seeing the collision of understanding and rejection deep in his friend's eyes.

"I've told you this and told you this," he'd said. "I think this bastard's been hired to kill you. I think it's past time somebody killed *him.* And I would one hell of a lot rather piss on his grave than go to *your* funeral. Do you *read* me on this, Paul?"

"I read you, Tomas." Tankersley had nodded. "I read you."

Now Ramirez walked at Tankersley's shoulder and hoped he truly had.

✧ ✧ ✧

Denver Summervale stood waiting just outside the white wooden rail around the flat, smooth, immaculately groomed grass of the dueling ground itself. An LCPD sergeant stood behind him, and Milorad Livitnikov stood beside him, holding his own pistol box. Carlson led Tankersley and Ramirez onto the ground, then beckoned for Summervale and Livitnikov to join them.

"Mister Summervale, Captain Tankersley," the lieutenant said. "It is my first and foremost duty to urge a peaceful resolution of your differences, even at this late date. I ask you both now: can you not compose your quarrel?"

He looked back and forth between them, but neither man spoke, and he sighed.

"In that case, present your weapons."

Ramirez and Livitnikov opened their pistol cases, and Carlson chose one pistol at random from the pair in each case.

Ramirez and *Nike*'s armorer had personally stripped both of Tankersley's pistols, checked every part with painstaking care, cleaned and oiled them. He knew those weapons were in perfect working order, and he was confident the same was true for Summervale's, but still he watched like a hawk as Carlson examined both of his chosen pistols with skilled fingers. The lieutenant worked each action twice, then handed one to Tankersley and the other to Summervale and looked back at the seconds.

"Load, Gentlemen," he said, and watched as each of them loaded five gleaming rounds into a magazine. Ramirez snapped the final round into place and handed the magazine to Tankersley as Livitnikov did the same for Summervale.

"Load, Mister Summervale," Carlson said, and Summervale slid the magazine into place and slapped it once, with arrogant, practiced grace, to be sure it was seated securely.

"Load, Captain Tankersley," Carlson said and Tankersley inserted his own magazine. He didn't try to match Summervale's showmanship, but his fingers were steady as he pressed the magazine baseplate firmly to ensure it was locked in place.

"Take your places, Gentlemen," Carlson said.

Ramirez squeezed Tankersley's shoulder briefly, and the captain smiled at him, then turned and walked to the center of the field. He turned in place, facing south, as Summervale crossed to stand behind him, facing north, and Carlson took his own place at the side of the field.

"Mister Summervale, Captain Tankersley," he said, raising his voice to be clearly heard, "you may chamber."

Tankersley pulled back the slide, chambering a round.

"You have agreed to meet under the Dreyfus Protocol," Carlson said. "At the command of 'Walk,' you will each take twenty paces. At the command of 'Stop,' you will immediately stop and stand in place, awaiting my next command. Upon the command 'Turn,' you will turn, and each of you will fire one round and one round only. If neither is hit in the first exchange, you will each lower your weapon and stand in place once more until I have asked both parties if honor is satisfied. If both answers are in the negative, you will take two paces forward upon the command 'Walk.' You will then stand in place once more until the command 'Fire,' when you will once more fire one round and one round only. The procedure will repeat until one party declares honor is satisfied, until one of you is wounded, or until your magazines are empty. Should either of you violate the terms and procedures I have just explained, it will be my duty to stop you in any way that I can, up to and including the use of deadly force, and I *will* fulfill that duty. Do you understand what I have just said, Captain Tankersley?"

"I do," Tankersley replied.

"Do you understand what I have just said, Mister Summervale?" Carlson asked then, and there was an ever so slightly harder edge to his voice. Summervale heard it, and his lip curled, but he only nodded curtly.

"Very well," Carlson said, and drew his holstered pulser while Tankersley and Summervale stood back-to-back in the dew-slick grass. He waited a moment longer, letting the stillness settle into their bones like iron in the morning quiet.

"Walk," he said then, and watched them striding slowly and deliberately away from one another. He counted the paces silently, then raised his free hand.

"Stop," he said quietly, and the two men stood there, still facing away from one another, weapons ready. The morning held its breath around them like a living thing.

And then—

"Turn!" Lieutenant Carlson said and thunder shattered the stillness.

**HMS *Prince Adrian***
**HMSS *Hephaestus***
**Manticore Planetary orbit**
**Manticore Binary System**
**March 22, 1906 PD**

LIEUTENANT SCOTTY TREMAINE peered at the diagnostic readout on his handheld. He couldn't quite make out the tiny letters, and he blinked his eyes, trying to make them focus. They refused, and his mouth tightened angrily. He glared at the display, then hurled it back into the open toolbox at his elbow.

It hit with a clatter, and the youthful lieutenant clenched his fists for a moment, then scrubbed angrily at his eyes. He drew a deep breath, held it for a long, slow moment. Then he exhaled, and his shoulders slumped.

"Sorry about that, Horace," he said.

"Nothing to be sorry about, Sir," the powerfully built senior chief with the battered prizefighter's face replied, and Tremaine snorted harshly.

"Don't think Commander Yaytsev will be real happy if we go around breaking the equipment, though," he said.

"The Commander's not that kinda hardcase, Sir," Harkness said. "Runs a tight department, but he's not gonna chew your ass over a dropped handheld."

"I didn't *drop* it," Tremaine pointed out, and Harkness shrugged.

"Nope. But there's a lot of that going around," he said.

"Yeah." The single word came out in a gusty sigh, and Tremaine nodded heavily. "Yeah, I guess there is."

He drew another deep breath and leaned a shoulder against the bulkhead of the pinnace's electronics compartment while he ran one hand over his hair. He knew Harkness knew exactly why he'd had trouble reading the diagnostic, and he didn't really care. He and the senior chief had been through too much together to worry about trying to hide their emotions, especially when it was just the two of them. And they weren't the only people aboard *Prince Adrian* who were feeling those emotions just now.

Although it must be immeasurably worse aboard *Nike*, he thought. Among Captain Harrington's current crew, who'd watched the love growing between her and Paul Tankersley. Who knew that eventually the Captain would return to them and they would have to face her.

It wasn't their fault, any more than it was Tremaine's or Harkness'. And not one of them would feel they hadn't somehow failed her by not preventing it. It was illogical. It was unreasonable—even *stupid*—but all of them felt it.

"I talked to Gunny Babcock about it," Harkness said, and despite his lingering grief, Tremaine smiled ever so slightly.

Horace Harkness' relationship with Marines in general was a hate-hate affair. True, it had been quite some time since he'd faced a captain's mast for knocking the stuffing out of a Marine. But the list of bars he and various Marines had reduced to wreckage was legendary, and he and Sergeant Major Iris Babcock—"Gunny" Babcock, since that was the unofficial, and hence hallowed, title bestowed upon any warship's senior Marine noncom, regardless of his or her *official* rank—had a rather . . . fraught relationship. It was less strained than it might have been, since they'd served together under Captain Harrington in Yeltsin and both of them—like Tremaine himself—had been involved in the liberation of Blackbird Base and the surviving Manticoran POWs. Unfortunately, "less strained than it might have been" still left considerable room for improvement.

"And what did the Gunny have to say?" Tremaine asked, after a moment.

"She *hates* the son of a bitch." Harkness' voice was suddenly harsh, almost as cold as his eyes. "This isn't the first time the miserable piece of shit's killed somebody she cared about. Hell, I think the way she saw it coming only makes it worse for her! And the *Colonel*—!"

The senior chief clamped his jaw, and Tremaine nodded heavily.

He knew Colonel Ramirez almost as well as he knew Captain Harrington. Ramirez was a man of iron, everyone knew that. "And now with Paul, you've got *proof* it is," McKeon said bitterly. And Tremaine knew exactly how the bitterness of Ramirez's grief, his sense of failure, fanned the white heat of his rage. It wasn't his fault any more than it was anyone else's, but he'd been Tankersley's second. He'd been there on the field.

And he was the one who'd have to face the Captain and tell her how it had happened.

"I actually sat down with her over a beer," Harkness said in a voice that was much closer to normal, and Tremaine blinked.

"You had a *beer* with Gunny Babcock?" he repeated carefully.

"Well, yeah." Harkness looked a little embarrassed, but he met Tremaine's eyes steadily. "Seemed like the thing to do. And, for a Marine, I guess she's not that bad. For a *Marine,* of course."

"Oh, of course!" Tremaine nodded, careful about his expression, and grateful for the brief sparkle of amusement Harkness' semi-belligerent, defensive expression sent through him.

"Anyway," the senior chief went on, "thing is, I think she had to vent, and she couldn't do it with the other jarheads, so she had to settle for me." He shrugged. "Wasn't easy for her to open up even with me, really. Took a while. But she had a *lot* to say about Summervale, once I got her talking. More'n I expected, really." He shook his head, his face forgetting its duty to express disdain for all Marines. "She's hurting even worse than most of us, Sir. She actually..." He shook his head and half-glared at Tremaine. "I think she was right on the edge of *crying*, Sir."

His expression dared Tremaine to make anything of that, but the lieutenant only nodded. Harkness looked back at him for a moment, then shrugged.

"It's like she's seen this whole HD before, Sir. And she knows the bastard will just go right on doing this shit. It's what he *does*." He glared down into the toolbox, his eyes fiery. "It's like some kind of goddammed *curse*, Sir. It just keeps *happening* to the Captain! And there's not one fucking thing any of us—*any* of us—can do for her! Not this time."

Tremaine blinked again, this time on the same tears which had clouded the diagnostic. He reached out and squeezed Harkness' burly shoulder.

"I know, Chief," he said. "I *know*."

The surprising thing, he thought bitterly, was that Tankersley had actually hit Summervale. It had been only a shoulder wound, little more than a graze, but he was certain Summervale hadn't expected it. Not from a totally inexperienced opponent fighting his very first duel against a seasoned veteran of over a dozen encounters on "the field of honor."

Captain Tankersley had been completely outclassed in everything except courage and determination, but he'd actually gotten his shot off first, and it if had only been better placed...

Only it hadn't been. No doubt Summervale had been astonished that he'd been hit at all, but whatever else he might be, he was as cold and methodical as they came. He hadn't rushed his *own* shot, hadn't taken a chance on merely wounding *his* opponent. That wasn't the result Denver Summervale had been hired to assure, and the paid duelist—the paid *assassin*—had taken his time, ignored his own wound... and shot Paul Tankersley squarely in the head.

He hadn't even pretended he felt anything remotely like remorse, either. He'd only stood there, pistol still in his hand, looking down at Tankersley with a lip that was ever so slightly curled, while Livitnikov and the attending physician ripped his sleeve open to get at his own trivial wound.

And then he'd handed his weapon to Livitnikov with a haughty gaze, climbed into an air limo which had materialized out of nowhere, and simply disappeared.

"I'll kill him, Sir," Harkness snarled, scrubbing at tears of his own. "I'll kill the sorry-assed SOB with my own two hands. His fucking 'code of honor' won't help him when I catch him in a goddammed alley somewhere! Hell, the Gunny'll help me do it, and nobody'll *ever* find the body!"

"I didn't hear that." Tremaine's tone was just sharp enough to make Harkness look at him.

"I didn't hear that," Tremaine repeated, then. "And I'd better not hear about you and the Gunny deciding to go drinking dirtside together. It wouldn't break my heart if something fatal were to happen to Mister Summervale, but making it happen—much as I might approve of it—wouldn't be worth what it cost the two of you. And I'm not letting the bastard cost me any more people I care about. Do you read me on that?"

He held Harkness' eyes with his own, waiting, because Scotty Tremaine knew, far better than most, that Horace Harkness was capable of doing exactly what he'd just threatened to do. And between them, he and Iris Babcock almost certainly had the collection of talents—and contacts—to make it happen. But if they did, there was no way they could walk away clean. Too many knew how bitterly both of them hated Summervale.

Silence hovered, and then, finally, Harkness gave a jerky nod. It might not have looked like much to someone else, but Scotty Tremaine recognized a silently given word of honor when he saw it.

"Better," he said, and squeezed the senior chief's shoulder again. "Better."

He pulled the handheld back out of the toolbox and checked to be sure he hadn't damaged its display when he threw it down, then looked back at Harkness with a crooked smile compounded almost equally of humor and bitterness.

"Like I say, I won't be upset if—*when*—something happens to Summervale, Senior Chief," he said. "But you and Gunny Babcock don't have to make it happen."

Harkness raised an eyebrow at him, and Tremaine barked a short, harsh laugh.

"You and I both know it's going to happen, Horace," he said, with the certitude of a Delphic oracle. "I don't care where Summervale hides. It won't do him one damned bit of good, because you and I both know damned well the Captain's going to kill him as soon as she gets home."

**Bassingford Medical Center**
**City of Landing**
**Planet Manticore**
**Manticore Binary System**
**March 24, 1906**

ERNESTINE CORELL GRIMACED as her com pinged softly just as she was about to find exactly the right words for the memo on her display. She was sure she was about to. They were obviously right on the tip of her mental tongue.

*Yeah,* sure *they are, Ernie,* she thought. *I'm sure you can find* exactly *the right way to explain to Admiral Caparelli that the Admiral will be fit for duty anytime now without outright lying to him. Or pissing the Admiral off by telling the truth.*

Normally, she wouldn't have been too worried about Mark Sarnow's reaction to a more or less accurate summation of his condition, but he'd been in a really bad mood lately.

And her own mood didn't help matters, she acknowledged.

Part of the reason for Sarnow's short fuse and bitter frustration was simply that while regen worked for him, it didn't work as *well* as it worked for many others, which meant a longer convalescence before he could even begin rehab, far less get back on to a command deck. Battlecruiser Squadron 5 had been made back up to strength, including HMS *Cassandra,* which had finally rejoined her consorts after almost a solid year of repairs and working up exercises. *Nike* would be a while yet, since she'd begun her repairs so much later, but Rear Admiral Dame Guadalupe Moreno, BatCruRon 5's new CO, would take good care of it.

Sarnow knew that, just as he'd known he could never retain command after how badly he'd been hit. And he'd been promised his own superdreadnought squadron as soon as the medical types passed him as fit for duty, which was why he'd hung onto his surviving staff—with the exception of Joseph Cartwright, who'd been promoted to captain and given his own cruiser command. They'd have to replace him, as well as Casper Southman, who'd been killed by the same hit which had wounded Sarnow, and like a good chief of staff, Corell already had her eye on possible candidates. But given how much longer Sarnow might be stuck on the binnacle list, she couldn't justify pulling somebody onto the sidelines until they had a better fix on when the admiral would be returning to duty.

That was part of the reason for the usually even-keeled Sarnow's foul mood. It wasn't the reason he was snapping people's heads off, though . . . or the reason Ernestine Corell wanted to do the same thing. In fact, what she really wanted was to rip off one particular head, literally, not figuratively.

She closed her eyes in remembered pain as the com pinged a second time. She'd been in Sarnow's hospital room yesterday morning, going over a BuWeaps' analysis of the Battle of Hancock, when the news broke. It still didn't seem possible. Not really. Corell had never heard of Denver Summervale before his "run in" with Paul Tankersley in Dempsey's. She'd done a little digging at Sarnow's behest once news of Summervale's challenge got out, though, and she hadn't liked what they'd found. She'd passed what she'd turned up to Tomas Ramirez, and Ramirez had thanked her, although she'd realized from their conversation that he and Captain McKeon already knew far more about Summervale than she'd had time to disinter.

But whatever they'd known, it hadn't been enough to stop the duel. And now someone would have to tell Honor Harrington, one of the finest officers—and friends—Corell had ever known that the man she loved was dead. A corner of Corell's mind was deeply and profoundly grateful that that duty wouldn't fall to her. But what she felt most strongly—what she knew was driving Mark Sarnow's bitter anger—was the fact that *anyone* had to tell Honor.

The com pinged again, and Corell shook herself out of her dark mood and looked down, then frowned as the display blinked "Unidentified Caller" at her.

The frown deepened and her eyes narrowed as she realized the unknown caller had pinged her *civilian* com combination. That combination was known to very few people. Anyone to whom *she'd* given it was in her contacts list, and given the security protocols attached to her account because of her clearances, it should have been extraordinarily difficult for anyone to gain unauthorized access to it. So who—?

She tapped to accept the call.

"Yes?" she said without identifying herself. Under the circumstances, it was most likely simply a misdial, but it could be something a bit more problematical.

"Listen carefully, Captain Corell," a voice said.

It was clearly disguised yet it sounded indefinably female for some reason. That was Corell's first thought, but then the voice continued.

"I'm only going to say this once. I won't be repeating anything. I have information I think you'll find interesting. Yesterday morning—"

Someone rapped lightly on the door, and Mark Sarnow looked up from the book reader in his lap with an irritated expression. It wasn't time for his afternoon regen treatment, and he really didn't want to talk to anyone today. He'd already snapped at Ernie Corell twice, and he knew he'd have to make amends. Not because *she* expected it, but because it was what he expected of himself. Knowing that didn't make him one bit happier, which was why he'd tried—unsuccessfully—to bury himself in the novel on his reader.

He considered—briefly—simply refusing to acknowledge the knock. But that would be not simply petulant but childish, and so he cleared his throat, instead.

"Enter!" he called as pleasantly as he could.

The door to the office attached to the suite in Bassingford's senior officers' long-term treatment wing opened, and despite himself, he frowned as Corell stepped through it. He started to speak, then stopped.

One reason he regretted having snapped at her was that he knew her pain over Paul Tankersley's death was as deep as his own. They'd both come to know Honor Harrington and Tankersley well during their deployment to Hancock, and he knew Corell had been as pleased for them as he himself had been. Which explained why the two of them were irritable as a hexapuma with a bad tooth.

*Although* she *doesn't have the seniority to be an asshole to someone else over it like you do, does she, Mark?* he thought. But the thought was fleeting as her expression registered. Were those *tears* in her eyes?

"What is it, Ernie?" he asked quickly.

"I just . . . I just had a com call, Sir." Corell paused and drew a deep breath. "I . . . I don't know what to do about it."

Sarnow's green eyes narrowed. The Honorable Ernestine Corell was one of the most capable human beings he'd ever met. What in God's name—?

"About what, Ernie?"

"It came in on my civvy combination, Sir. I don't know who it was. All I got was 'unidentified caller.' That was enough to surprise me, given how closely held my combination is. And because it was on my civilian com, I couldn't get a recorder on it."

She paused again, and Sarnow nodded. The Star Kingdom's privacy laws were crystal clear and ironclad. Recording conversations on the Navy's official com channels was one thing, and happened on a routine basis, when verbal orders were being passed. Even then, the law required a clear audio alert that the conversation was being recorded. But recording a *civilian* conversation without the prior, recorded approval of both parties was a felony that carried a stiff sentence.

"Whoever it was," Corell said, "she said . . . Admiral, she said Summervale was *paid* to kill Paul!"

Sarnow stiffened in surprise. Not so much at the notion that Summervale had been paid, given what Corell had turned up on him before the duel, but at the fact that someone had gone to the trouble of finding his chief of staff's civilian combination to tell her that. He started to say just that, but Corell went on before he could.

"He was paid to kill Paul, but he's also been paid to kill *Honor*, Sir! And whoever hired him, wanted Paul killed *first*."

The tears he'd seen in her eyes broke free, trickling down her cheeks as she stared at him, and a bolt of savage pain went through him. The exquisite cruelty that could even contemplate such an action was breathtaking.

"You don't have any idea who the caller was?"

His voice came out flat, leached of emotion as he forced himself to focus.

"No, Sir. I don't. And whoever she was, she didn't tell me who hired him, either."

"So this was just some sick pervert calling to *gloat*?"

"No, Sir." Corell reached into her tunic pocket for a slip of paper. "She wouldn't tell me who hired him, assuming she knows. But she did give me this."

"Which is?"

"It's the address of a hunting lodge on Gryphon, Sir." Corell's voice was also flatter than it had been, but hers was the flatness of granite-boned anger. "According to her, it's owned through a legitimate front by the Outfit, and it's where Summervale is lying low while he waits for Honor to come home so he can kill her, too. She says the entire lodge is a 'safe house' for criminal types. The entire staff works for the Outfit, and there's a permanent guard force—at least twenty or thirty Outfit hoods, at any given moment—to provide security for its 'guests.' And probably to make sure they behave themselves while they're there, I imagine." She shook her head. "If there was ever any question about Summervale, there isn't now."

Mark Sarnow sat very still for a moment, considering what she'd said. The "Outfit" was the Star Kingdom's most powerful organized crime syndicate, and while it wasn't shy about using violent means to attain its goals, it normally shied away from anything as high profile as this obviously was. That meant Summervale—or whoever had hired him—had even more clout with the criminal element than he'd thought.

He pondered that, then nodded once and tapped the control panel, and his bed raised him into a fully upright seated position.

"Tell Doctor Chandler I'll need my life-support chair," he said.

"Sir, that's not a good—" Corell began, her expression distressed.

"I don't care whether or not it's a good idea." His voice was no longer flat. It could have been carved from the heart of a Gryphon glacier, and his eyes were colder still.

"Sir, your regen treatment will—"

"I'll just have today's treatment tomorrow, then." He managed a brief, razor-thin smile. "I'm sure we can make up the lost time. But for now, tell him I'll need my chair."

Corell started to protest again, but she knew that tone.

"Yes, Sir," she said instead. "Can I tell him where you'll be going in it?"

"I don't know yet." He gave her another of those icy smiles. "I expect you'll be the one telling *me*, because after you com Doctor

Chandler, I want you to find Captain McKeon. And then I want you to arrange a shuttle flight to wherever he is."

"Yes, Sir. May I ask exactly what it is you intend to do?"

"No one's getting away with doing this to Honor." She heard the grinding implacability of that Gryphon glacier in his voice. "That's for *damned* sure. But there's nothing *I* can do with this information. Not without legs."

"We *could* pass it on to the authorities, Sir."

"Where it would do no good at all. At best, it's hearsay. An anonymous caller who won't even identify himself? Who can't—or won't—say who hired Summervale?" Sarnow snorted harshly. "There's absolutely nothing in there that would constitute probable cause for any official investigation. And I'm pretty damned sure the person who gave you the information planned on that from the beginning. I don't know what he may be after. Maybe he just doesn't want to see someone get away with bought-and-paid-for murder. But assuming he's telling the truth, anything anyone's going to do has to be done quickly. And since *I* can't do it, all you and I can do is pass the information on to someone I know for damn sure *will* do something about it."

He held her eyes for a long moment. Then she nodded, and he nodded back.

"Screen Doctor Chandler," he repeated.

"Yes, Sir."

**Dempsey's Bar**
**HMSS *Hephaestus***
**Manticore Planetary Orbit**
**Manticore Binary System**
**March 27, 1906 PD**

"WHAT THE HELL IS GOING ON, Harkness?" Sergeant Major Iris Babcock growled.

"Say what?" Horace Harkness looked up from his beer in surprise. He'd been too deep in thought to notice her stalking across the bar toward his secluded corner.

"I asked what the hell is going on." Babcock glowered at him. "I know damned well *something* is, and I know damned well that you're involved with it. So spill."

Harkness gave her his very best "innocent as the new-fallen snow" expression. She snorted.

"Don't try that 'don't have a clue' bullshit on me, Harkness. I've known you too long for you to pull it off."

"So it wouldn't do me any good to tell you I really *don't* have a clue what you're talking about?"

"No."

The red-haired sergeant major looked at him, her expression implacable, and he grimaced. Somehow he hadn't anticipated this particular conversation. He should have. Nobody had told any of *Prince Adrian*'s Marines what was really up, but Gunny Babcock was at least as well tapped-in on the Marine side as he was on the Navy's. So even if she didn't know what was going on, she obviously knew— as she'd just so tactfully pointed out—that *something* was. And by cornering him on the civvy side of the station, she could push him for answers she might not have gotten—or wanted to ask for—in a shipboard setting.

"What makes you think that if something's going on, and it

obviously involves the jarheads, not us more cerebral Navy types, I'd know about it and you wouldn't?" he asked in the tone of a man sparring for time.

"Because Major Yestachenko suddenly doesn't know squat. Which strikes me as a little odd. And *then* I find out Lieutenant Tremaine just had a conversation with Major Hibson about volunteering you and him for Nike One. Which strikes me as even odder, given that I happen to know Colonel Ramirez happened to bring a pretty competent pinnace crew of his own across from *Nike*. That suggests that whatever's going on, Lieutenant Tremaine knows about it. And if *he* knows—"

She raised an eyebrow at the senior chief, and Harkness snorted mentally.

"If there was 'something going on,' and if Major Yestachenko didn't tell you about it, what makes you think *I'd* tell you about it, even if I knew anything. Which, of course," he added just a tad insincerely, "I don't."

Babcock glowered at him, but there was less wattage behind the glower than many people might have expected, given Harkness' legendary history with the Royal Manticoran Marines. True, he'd actually stayed out of any spectacular trouble for a couple of years now, but a single warm day did not a summer make. As surely as the sun would rise, eventually the shore patrol would be summoned to collect him and his Marine sparring partner—or *partners*—after yet another epic confrontation.

Some people probably thought that was because Harkness hated Marines. Babcock had thought that, actually, until the two of them served together under Dame Honor in Yeltsin. They'd been assigned to different ships, but they'd run into one another more than once, even before Blackbird, and she'd realized something about him.

He just liked to fight.

And he wasn't like a lot of other men—and women—she'd known, both in the Corps and in the Navy, who fought at the drop of a hat. He didn't fight because he was a bully, or destructive. In fact, those two qualities were the exact opposite of Horace Harkness. And it wasn't because of some inner demon of rage or because he hated discipline or truly had anything against the Corps, either. He just *liked* to fight, and when he did, he wanted someone who'd be a challenge, someone who was up to his weight. Well, and he didn't want to pick fights with someone in his own chain of command. So he picked Marines—the toughest readily available dance partners he could find. In its own way, she'd decided, that was almost a kind of compliment, although neither he nor the Royal Marines would admit it.

And then there was the *other* side of him. The one he worked so hard to keep other people from seeing.

Harkness hadn't been part of the landing force that broke into Blackbird Base, but Babcock had.

Colonel Ramirez—he'd been *Major* Ramirez at the time—had commanded the ground attack force, and Babcock had been right beside him when HMS *Fearless'* Marines fought their way into the Masadan Base's cellblocks and discovered what had happened to the Manticoran POWs. The murders. The torture. The rapes. Harkness hadn't been there for that, but Babcock was pretty sure Harkness had no idea she'd overheard him talking to Lieutenant Tremaine afterward.

Alistair McKeon had assigned Tremaine as Dame Honor's cutter pilot and he'd assigned himself as an additional bodyguard. Which meant he'd been there when *she* found out what the Masadans had done to her people. He'd seen the aftermath—the bodies, the brutalized survivors, the pools of blood—just like Babcock. He'd seen Ensign Jackson screaming as Dame Honor gathered her into her arms, heard Jackson's broken description of what she'd somehow managed to survive, what had been done to her and Lieutenant Commander Brigham, and he was only a kid. It had been bad enough for her; obviously, it had been worse for him. She'd realized that even at the time, before she'd learned how well he'd known Mercedes Brigham. When he'd seen what those bastards had done to *her* . . .

He'd held it together, though. He might be young, but he was one of the good ones. She'd realized that even before Blackbird, and what had happened there—especially if the stories about Dame Honor and the Masadan CO were true—only underscored that point. But afterward, when he'd had time to really think about it . . .

Babcock probably understood the relationship between Harkness and Tremaine better than a lot of other people did. And the fact that she did gave her a considerably higher opinion of the SCPO than she would have admitted even under torture. A Marine had to remember her tribal loyalties, after all. But nobody who'd heard Harkness talking Tremaine through his reaction to the horrific atrocities visited upon Manticoran personnel—upon people they'd both known and deeply respected, like Commander Brigham—could really think of him as a blunt instrument.

And then there was the evening he'd bought her a beer. Bought her *lots* of beers, really; enough that her recollection got a little hazy. But not hazy enough for her to forget the way he'd listened to her about Summervale. Not just about what he'd done to Captain Tankersley, but what he'd done to Lieutenant Thurston—*her* lieutenant—all those years before. He'd sat there, and he'd both known *how* to listen and recognized the times when to *just* listen.

No, he could be an unmitigated pain in the ass, he was insufferably determined to do things *his* way, and it was a lot easier for an officer to extract obedience and military courtesy than it was to earn his respect, but he *wasn't* a blunt instrument.

No matter how hard he worked at perfecting the image.

"Okay," she said, "cards on the table." She pulled out a chair, turned it around, dropped into it, braced her forearms on the top of the chairback, and leaned forward to face him across the table. "Whatever the hell you're involved in—and if Lieutenant Tremaine's involved, then I know damned well *you* are—it's got something to do with Dame Honor. With what happened to Captain Tankersley." Her expression was far grimmer than it had been, and her gray eyes bored into him across the table. "And according to a little birdie I know who works right here in Dempsey's, Admiral Sarnow dropped by when Captain McKeon invited Commander Venizelos and Colonel Ramirez to a beer after Summervale killed Captain Tankersley. And then, all of a sudden, two days later, we have this exercise on Gryphon. Pardon me if my naturally suspicious mind put all of that together, added in Lieutenant Tremaine's involvement, and came to the conclusion that the exercise in question stems from something the Admiral told the Captain and the Colonel. Which, given that he's supposed to be in Bassingford and that he snuck out without a single soul noticing and came all the way to *Hephaestus* to tell them whatever it was in *person*, suggests that this 'routine training exercise' everybody's so hot to organize is a consequence of that conversation they had."

Harkness' eyes flickered ever so slightly. That was the only flaw in his politely attentive innocent expression, but he knew Babcock had seen it. He'd always known she was sharp; clearly she was even sharper than he'd thought. And what the hell did he do now?

"Some random 'little birdie' just happened to tell you that? I think that constitutes what they call hearsay evidence, Gunny."

"My little birdie's right over there." Babcock jerked a thumb over her shoulder at the on-duty shift manager who'd just stepped through the swinging doors from the kitchens. "He's my second cousin. There's 'hearsay,' and then there's 'hearsay.' So, yeah, I'm pretty sure about my info."

"Well, *that* makes this difficult." Harkness grinned down into his beer, then took another swig and set the stein back on the table. "See, the thing is, Gunny, I don't officially know a thing more than you do."

"Officially," she repeated.

"Sure. You know how it works."

She nodded. Any senior noncommissioned officer "knew how it worked." Otherwise, they wouldn't *be* senior noncoms.

"It *does* have something to do with Dame Honor, doesn't it?" she asked in a quieter voice, and he sighed.

"Yeah." He shrugged. "I don't begin to have the full skinny myself. That's the truth. But, yeah. Near as I can figure it, the Admiral—or maybe Captain Corell—found out something about Summervale. Something he told the Skipper and Colonel Ramirez about. Now, if I had to guess, given that this training exercise was originally scheduled for week after next on Manticore, and it's been moved up to tomorrow on Gryphon—and that Captain McKeon and Commander Venizelos have volunteered *Prince Adrian* and *Apollo* to lift *Nike*'s pinnaces to Gryphon, since she's still in the shop—I'd have to say it's because there's someone on Gryphon the Colonel really, really wants to talk to."

He sipped more beer, then looked at her again.

"Wonder who *that* could be?"

**Pinnace Nike One**
**and**
**Roualeyn Lodge**
**Arduus Mountains**
**Planet Gryphon**
**Manticore Binary System**
**March 28, 1906 PD**

"NIKE FLIGHT, THIS IS NIKE TWO." Major Susan Hibson's voice was clear and composed in Iris Babcock's earbug. "Nike Two has lost track on Nike One and is assuming command until Nike One reestablishes contact. Two, clear."

The sergeant major smiled thinly. As a member of *Prince Adrian*'s Marine detachment, her skinsuit's com wasn't supposed to be plugged into the *Nike* com net. No doubt she should see about getting that glitch fixed as soon as she got back aboard ship. For the moment, she'd just have to make do, she told herself, and her smile broadened.

If her suspicions had required any confirmation, the captain's lack of surprise at Nike One's abrupt departure from her planned flight profile would have provided it. Not that she *had* required confirmation. Harkness had been a tougher nut than she'd expected. In fact, he'd been tough enough to crack that she'd been almost—*almost*—tempted to accept his protestations that he didn't really "know" anything for certain.

The fact that he'd disappeared into the pinnace's flight deck to join Lieutenant Tremaine just before Nike One separated from its borrowed slot in *Prince Adrian*'s boat bay suggested she would have been in error if she had. And the fact that Nike One had almost immediately veered away from the other six pinnaces involved in the drop exercise and shaped a course into the heart of an enormous storm system—the sort of storm system pinnaces on training exercises normally avoided like the plague—had been equally suggestive.

After all of that, Major Hibson's lack of surprise was really just icing on the cake. It did confirm that Hibson was in on whatever was about to happen, although Babcock supposed the official recording *might* cover the major's ass if this thing went as badly sideways as it had the potential to go. Not that Hibson's involvement was any great surprise to Babcock, either.

Despite all of that, the sergeant major had to admit that security on this had been pretty damned tight. She'd known François Ivashko, Ramirez's command sergeant major aboard *Nike*, for a lot of years, and Frankie hadn't said a word to her about it. They were going to have a little discussion about keeping secrets from old friends later, but for now, she'd chosen to let him get away with it, because as long as he didn't know she was sniffing around, he was unlikely to do anything about it. But he had to be fully in on it, and so did Lieutenant Karlal and the rest of the HQ Platoon's noncoms. The entire platoon was armed with stun rifles, not the laser-tag rifles and sidearms the rest of Ramirez's people carried, which—officially— was because the HQ Platoon was supposed to be the local quick-reaction opposition force, and the Colonel had decided that equipping it with stun rifles would make things more "interesting" for his invading Marines.

And if anyone in Karlal's platoon actually *believed* that, Babcock had some magic beans she'd like to sell them.

Not that any of them did. There was no way in hell the Colonel— and Ivashko—hadn't fully briefed the entire platoon on what was really going down. And she was positive they'd given every one of Karlal's people the chance to opt out, as well, given how totally off the books this entire operation was. Everyone involved had to know the consequences if it went sideways would be severe...and that obviously didn't matter one damned bit more to any of them than it mattered to Iris Babcock. Not where Denver Summervale and Captain Harrington were concerned.

That thought brought her to a rather more immediate set of potential consequences. It was time to face the music, especially if she didn't want to find herself confined to the pinnace with its regular flight crew when they reached their destination...whatever it was. Hopefully the Colonel wouldn't be *too* pissed, but there was only one way to find out about that.

She drew a deep breath and climbed out of the aft jump seat into which she'd slipped just before the hatch sealed. The second-class petty officer on the inboard end of the pinnace boarding tube had twitched in surprise as she went sailing past him down the tube. He'd actually opened his mouth as if to ask her what the hell she thought she was doing, but his IQ obviously exceeded his shoe size, because he'd shut it again just as quickly. And the pinnace's flight engineer had very carefully looked the other way as Babcock came through the pinnace hatch and disappeared into her little cubbyhole jump seat. From her expression, whatever happened to Babcock was the Marines' affair, and no skin off her nose or any other portion of her anatomy.

Speaking of which . . .

The sergeant major made her way up the central aisle as the pinnace began to buffet. Colonel Ramirez was looking down at his own display when she came to a stop at his shoulder, but then he must have caught sight of her in his peripheral vision, and his head turned toward her.

"Why aren't you strapped in, Mar—?"

He broke off, and his eyebrows knitted ominously as he recognized her. Anger sparked in his dark brown eyes for just a moment. Then he sighed and shook his head.

"Sar'major Babcock, would you mind telling me just what the *hell* you think you're doing here?"

Babcock popped to recruiting-poster sharp attention.

"Sir! The Sergeant Major respectfully reports that she seems to have become confused, Sir! I was under the impression this was one of *Prince Adrian*'s pinnaces, Colonel!"

"Won't wash, Gunny." Ramirez shook his head again. "*Prince Adrian* doesn't even have the Mark Thirty yet."

"Sir, I—"

"Hold it right there!"

Ramirez held up his right hand, forefinger raised in a "Silence, Marine" gesture, then turned to glare at François Ivashko. Ivashko looked genuinely surprised to see her, Babcock reflected—which either spoke well for her own stealthiness or poorly for his situational awareness—and he looked back at Ramirez more than a bit apprehensively.

"I don't suppose you happened to log Sar'major Babcock as an observer supernumerary, did you, Gunny?" Ramirez demanded sternly.

"Uh, no, Sir. But—"

"Well, in that case, get her logged now. I'm surprised at you, Gunny! You know how important the proper paperwork is. Now I'm going to have to clear this retroactively with Major Yestachenko and Captain McKeon!"

"Yes, Sir!" Ivashko grinned hugely. "Sorry, Sir. I guess I just dropped the ball, Sir."

"Don't let it happen again," Ramirez growled, then shook his raised forefinger under Babcock's nose. "As for *you*, Sar'major, get back in your seat. And stay where I can keep an eye on you to make sure you behave dirtside. Understood?"

"Aye, aye, Sir!"

✦　✦　✦

The Arduus Mountains were famous throughout the Manticore Binary System for their ski slopes, and almost equally famous for the regularity and severity of their blizzards. By their standards, tonight's weather wasn't actually all that bad.

That was a low bar, however, and touchdown was more energetic than even most rough field landings. Given the howling, sixty-kilometer-per-hour gale into which Nike One had flown, though, it wasn't bad at all. And RMN pinnaces were designed for rough landings. Nike One rocked drunkenly until Petty Officer Hudson, its pilot, brought up the ventral tractors and locked it down, but then it sat rock steady and the red lamp on the forward bulkhead turned green. The sharp "clacking" sound of seat harness releases filled the interior, and Babcock looked up as Lieutenant Tremaine emerged from the flight deck. Harkness was at his heels, and somehow the pair of Navy types had acquired stun rifles of their own.

"Sorry about that, Colonel." Tremaine shook his head. "I knew the nav systems were throwing potential fault signals, but I didn't think they'd pack up entirely."

He had not, Babcock noted, said that the navigation systems *had* packed up; only that he hadn't thought they would.

"It happens, Scotty," Colonel Ramirez said philosophically.

"Well, as we were heading in, I noticed some kind of hunting or ski lodge two or three klicks east of here, Sir. I'm sure they'd be able to give any poor, lost spacers who knocked on their front door a position fix."

"East, you say?" Ramirez cocked his head, then shrugged and turned to Lieutenant Karlal. "I guess we should go knock on that door, Gunnar," he said.

"Makes sense to me, Sir," Karlal replied.

✧ ✧ ✧

The trek from the pinnace to the hunting lodge was less than pleasant.

Officially, Babcock knew, Ramirez had moved his drop to Gryphon because he'd wanted a winter-weather exercise, and no one could deny he'd gotten it. The temperature was twenty degrees below zero . . . which the screaming wind converted to an effective minus forty degrees. A little thing like that was no problem for anyone in a Marine skinsuit or even the less rugged Navy skinnies Tremaine and Harkness wore, but meter-deep snow drifts, the solid sheets of fresh snow howling almost directly into their faces on that merciless wind, were something else entirely. Their skinsuits maintained a comfortable interior temperature and even wicked away and absorbed excess perspiration, but the sheer, exhausting exertion of slogging across mountain terrain under those conditions had to be experienced to be truly appreciated.

Not even the Marines' helmet systems see clearly through that howling snowfall, but the recon drones Sergeant Major Ivashko and First Sergeant McElroy had deployed were designed to operate under even worse conditions. They fed the Marines' tac displays from overhead as they bucketed through the gale, and Babcock frowned as the icons of human heat signatures appeared on her HUD. There were ten of them, five pairs spaced around the deliberately archaic-looking hunting lodge's perimeter, despite the weather.

Obviously, they had to be equipped with excellent cold-weather gear of their own, but as Babcock studied the display, she realized all of them were also huddled into the lee of whatever windbreaks they could find. The fact that they were there at all in this kind of weather said a lot about the paranoia of whoever had ordered them out to mind the perimeter, but they clearly weren't the most alert sentries in human history.

"Colonel," Lieutenant Karlal said over the com, "I don't want to sound suspicious or anything, but I've got to say that that looks like a security perimeter. Does it look that way to you, Sir?"

The youngster clearly had a future in holo drama. He'd managed to sound genuinely surprised.

"Now that you mention it, it does, Lieutenant," Ramirez replied. "What do the drones see, Gunny?"

"Actually, Sir, I think the Lieutenant has a point. Look at this." Ivashko threw a readout into Ramirez's—and Babcock's—HUDs. "Whoever these people are, they're not just standing around ass-deep in the snow, they're packing some serious hardware. I've got pulse rifles, sidearms, and even a pair of crew-served light tribarrels. That's one hell of a lot of firepower for a batch of civilians."

"I'd have to agree," Ramirez said. "That's the kind of firepower somebody who's actively *expecting* trouble deploys. Not too sure I want to just walk up to them, especially in this kind of visibility. It wouldn't surprise me if they didn't realize we were Marines at first, and if they're already proddy for some reason, that could be bad. Be messy if they decided to shoot first and ask questions later."

"Well, we do have the stun rifles, Sir," Ivashko pointed out helpfully. "Wouldn't hurt 'em, 'cept possibly for the headache when they come to. And it would make sure nobody on our side got accidentally shot."

"A valid observation, Gunny." Ramirez nodded inside his helmet. "Gunnar, I think Gunny Ivashko's onto something here. I'll take responsibility, of course."

"Aye, aye, Sir! First Sergeant, let's get our people deployed."

"Aye, aye, Sir," McElroy acknowledged and began giving orders of his own.

It seemed to take far longer than it should have, thanks to the way the deep snow and atrocious weather delayed things, but Karlal's people were good. Babcock stood at Ramirez's back, flanked by Harkness and Lieutenant Tremaine, watching her time display, and her HUD flashed the readiness alert in barely seven minutes.

"Position," Karlal confirmed quietly over the com a moment later.

"Take the shot," Ramirez said calmly.

"Execute!" Karlal said, and Babcock nodded in approval as every one of the sentries went down so close to simultaneously it was impossible to tell which one actually hit the snow first.

"Let's go make sure they didn't hurt themselves falling down," Ramirez said, and the Marines closed in on the downed guards.

"What do we do with 'em, Sir?" Sergeant Major Ivashko asked as he prodded one unconscious body with his toe.

"I'd like to let them freeze," Ramirez replied, "but that wouldn't be neighborly." He looked around, then pointed. "There's a storage shed over there, Gunny. Stack them in there out of the wind."

"Aye, Sir." Ivashko replied. "Coulter, you and Malthus have babysitter duty. Get these sleeping beauties tucked away."

"And remember to plug their weather gear's heaters into the power supply in the shed," Ramirez added. "Gotta keep them nice and toasty till we figure out what's going on here."

The pretense that *Nike*'s Marines had simply happened across the lodge became increasingly threadbare over the next few minutes. Since Babcock had chosen to tag along, Ramirez decided he might as well make use of her expertise, and he tasked her with locating and disabling the emergency landline while Ivashko and McElroy deployed the drones' jammers to take out the building's satellite uplink. It took less than four minutes, and then the platoon fell in around Ramirez while he parceled out the doors he wanted covered.

It was obvious from the precision of his directions that he was intimately familiar with the architecture of the hunting chalet across which his people had just happened to "stumble," and his Marines moved rapidly into position.

The colonel took the front entrance personally, and Babcock attached herself to his group. The colonel only glanced at her and shook his head with a resigned expression, then looked at Ivashko.

"It would appear that I'm stuck with Sar'major Babcock, Gunny," he said. "Why don't you go help Lieutenant Karlal on the north side while I keep my eye on her to be sure she stays out of trouble?"

"Aye, Sir," Ivashko said with a chuckle, and Ramirez looked at Tremaine and Harkness, who had also attached themselves to him.

"Navy personnel have no business in this sort of operation, Lieutenant," he said sternly.

"Of course not, Sir!"

"They aren't trained for breaching operations against potentially armed opposition where they might get hurt."

"No, Sir. They aren't," Tremaine agreed in an "and your point is?" sort of tone.

Ramirez glowered at him as the lieutenant gazed back with a politely attentive expression. Then the colonel exhaled gustily.

"All right, you can come. But you watch your ass in there, Scotty! Dame Honor will be really, really pissed if I let anything happen to you. *Harkness*"—he looked at the senior chief over Tremaine's head—"she could probably live without, but she's fond of *you*. So bear that in mind."

"Yes, Sir."

"Sar'major."

"Yes, Sir?"

"You've got my six. Try to stay between any potential trouble and our two enthusiasts here, please."

"Aye, aye, Sir."

Ramirez shook his head yet again, then turned back to the door and tried the latch gently. It was locked, and he shifted his stun gun to his right hand while his left pressed a small, flat box to the door.

A green LED blinked, the latch sprang, and Ramirez toed the door open. Somebody objected—loudly and profanely—as cold wind blasted through it.

Ramirez just squeezed the stunner's trigger and the complaint stopped abruptly.

"One down," he murmured over the com as he stepped through the door and across the man who'd objected.

"Make that two," Corporal Hansen said over the same circuit as Babcock followed the colonel through the door.

"Three," PFC Huan said.

"Four," McElroy said quietly a moment later.

Tremaine followed Babcock into the chalet's tastefully paneled interior while Harkness brought up the rear. All of the designated breaching teams were inside now, as well, advancing with quick, efficient stealth and taking out the chalet's inhabitants as they went.

As Captain Corell's mysterious informant had warned them, there were quite a few of those inhabitants. But however experienced at visiting violence upon others the Outfit leg-breakers might be, they weren't even in the same league as the Royal Marines, especially where things like situational awareness were concerned. Besides, it was the middle of the night. Most of those inhabitants who hadn't already been picked off as part of the exterior guard force were sound asleep, and gas grenades tossed through quietly opened bedroom doors wafted them gently into even deeper slumber.

They cleared the ground floor of the main building without triggering any alarms. That should have accounted for most of the staff, since the second and third floors were largely reserved for paying guests, and Ramirez led the way quietly up the central spiral stair while the rest of his Marines climbed stealthily up the emergency stairs, avoiding the lift shafts.

*So far so good*, Babcock told herself as they reached the second-floor landing, then shook her head quickly. Damn it, she *knew* better than to tempt fate that way. As sure as she decided everything was going—

"What the hell?!"

Babcock's helmet audio sensors picked up the voice from behind her, and she turned her head just as Harkness spun around to face the big, beefy thug who'd chosen that moment to emerge from the hallway bathroom. He was in shirtsleeves, the shirt in question was unsealed, and he needed a shave, but he obviously had some serious paranoia issues, since he'd taken his shoulder-holstered pulser into the head with him.

Now he reached for it even as he gawked at the intruders.

The newcomer was too close for Harkness to get the muzzle of his stun rifle around in time, so he brought its butt up in a flashing arc that landed on the other man's jaw... and sent him crashing to the floor.

"Aw, *shit!*" someone muttered as the impact shook the hall. And then other doors began to open as the lodge's "guests" roused.

Harkness dropped one of them with a quick shot. Lieutenant Tremaine stunned a third, but then a single pulser shot whined past him and skipped off Babcock's armored skinsuit. Colonel Ramirez took down three more—two men and the woman who'd fired—with a wide-angle shot, but Babcock found herself directly in front of another door when it jerked open.

The man and woman on the other side of that door had clearly been engaged in something besides sleep. Aside from the woman's briefs, they were neither clad nor armed, but they were wide awake, and the woman grabbed Babcock's stun rifle.

She pulled hard, and her eyes started to widen as Babcock let her. But then both of the sergeant major's feet left the floor. She pivoted on the weapon her adversary was kind enough to hold steady, and the other woman flew back with a gurgling grunt as two combat boots hit her in the belly. The impact flung her into her fellow, who opened his mouth to shout—just as Babcock touched the floor once more and her left elbow struck his skull like a hammer.

He went down without a sound, and Babcock stepped back, still holding her stunner, and shot the woman before she stopped whooping for breath.

It was over in a heartbeat, and the sergeant major glanced into the bedroom her victims had come from. There was no one else in it, so she stepped back and gave the man an insurance stun bolt of his own, then looked over her shoulder at Harkness.

"Next time, bring a goddamned drum and bugle band along!" she snarled over the com.

"Can it, Gunny!" Ramirez snapped. He stood still, running his skinsuit's external sound pickups up to max, then relaxed.

"No damage done, I think," he said, and did a quick count of the unconscious bodies littering the hallway.

"Twelve, repeat, total twelve down," he said over the com, then darted his own look at Harkness. From the senior chief's expression, he obviously expected something memorable. But the colonel only shook a finger at him and then turned back to his front.

"Let's try not to set off any more seismographs, people," he said over the general net.

✧　✧　✧

It took another five minutes to account for what should be every staff member and all of the "guests" in the second-floor bedrooms. The third floor's larger, more luxurious suites were reserved for VIP traffic, and Ramirez positioned his people to cover the access routes to the central staircase, then led Babcock, Ivashko, and Tremaine up the stairs.

Harkness wasn't invited, but somehow Babcock wasn't surprised to find him at her elbow as she brought up the rear.

They reached the landing and filtered quietly down a short hallway to suite 301. The door was closed, and this time Colonel Ramirez's magic box had no effect on the old-fashioned mechanical lock.

He shrugged and handed his stunner to Ivashko. It was no part of the plan to put this one to sleep, and he obviously had no intention of sharing the moment with anyone else.

He retreated to the edge of the landing, balanced for a moment, then took three running strides, slammed into the door, and went through the resultant rain of splinters like a boulder.

The man sleeping on its other side of that doorway reacted impossibly quickly, sliding one hand under his pillow even before his eyes had fully opened. Yet fast as he was, Ramirez reached him just as his fingers closed on the pulser's butt, and the colonel's hand fastened on the front of his expensive pajamas.

Tomas Ramirez had been born and bred on the planet of San Martin, one of the heaviest-gravity worlds humanity had settled. Its sea-level air pressure was high enough to produce near-toxic concentrations of carbon dioxide and nitrogen, and the colonel was built like a skimmer turbine with an attitude problem. The hand on Denver Summervale's pajamas yanked, and he flew out of bed like a missile. His gun hand hit a bedpost in passing; the pulser spun out of his grasp; and Ramirez released him at the top of his arc.

The duelist managed—barely—to get one arm up to protect his head before he smashed into the opposite wall. He bounced back, but even totally surprised from a sound sleep, he managed to land on his feet. He fell into a defensive stance, shaking his head to clear it, and Ramirez simply stood there, giving him time to recover.

Not, Babcock thought coldly, because he had the least interest in fair fights.

Summervale charged, and although he might make his living with the anachronistic firearms of the code duello, he clearly knew what he was doing with his hands, as well. Unfortunately, he was in pajamas, and a native of the planet Manticore, whose gravity was barely one percent higher than Old Terra's. Ramirez was in an armored skinsuit and *his* homeworld's gravity was almost twice that of humanity's birth world. The only reason Summervale got in even a single blow was because Tomas Ramirez wanted the opportunity, the pretext, to *hurt* him . . . and he did.

The colonel's right hand drove into Summervale's belly like a wrecking ball. The smaller man folded over it with a wailing grunt that ended in an explosive "crack" as Ramirez's left hand slammed into his face in a vicious, open-handed slap. And then Ramirez snatched him up, spun him like a toy, slammed him belly down over his own bed, jerked one wrist up behind him, and locked an arm of iron across his throat.

Summervale fought to break free, then screamed as Ramirez rammed a skinsuited knee into his spine.

"Now, now, Mister Summervale," he said softly. "None of that."

The killer whimpered in combined anguish and humiliation, and Ramirez glanced at Ivashko. The sergeant major laid a small recorder on the bed and switched it on.

"Do you recognize my voice, Mister Summervale?" Ramirez asked then. Summervale gritted his teeth, refusing to answer—then screamed again as those stone-crusher fingers twisted his wrist.

"I asked a question, Mister Summervale. It's not nice to ignore questions."

Summervale screamed a third time, twisting in agony. Then—

"Yes! *Yes!*"

"Good. Can you guess why I'm here?"

"F-Fuck you!" Summervale panted.

"Such language!" Ramirez shook his head reprovingly, and his voice was almost genial. "Especially when I'm just here to ask you a question."

He paused a heartbeat.

"Who paid you to kill Captain Tankersley, Summervale?"

There was no more humor in that cold, hard voice.

"Go to—hell, you—son of a bitch!"

"That's not nice," Ramirez said again. "I'm going to have to insist you tell me."

"Why—the fuck—should I? You'll just—kill me—when I do. So fuck you!"

"Mister Summervale, Mister Summervale!" Ramirez sighed. "The Captain would have my ass if *I* killed you. So just answer the question."

"Like hell!" Summervale panted.

"I think you should reconsider. I only said I wouldn't kill you, Mister Summervale," Ramirez whispered almost lovingly. "I never said I wouldn't *hurt* you."

**HMSS *Hephaestus***
**Manticore Planetary orbit**
**Manticore Binary System**
**April 4, 1906 PD**

"LADY HARRINGTON, would you care to comment on—"

Andrew LaFollet stepped in front of his Steadholder.

He and Corporal Simon Mattingly were the Steadholder's detail for the day, and, Like Jamie Candless, Mattingly was left-handed. That was why the two of them normally had the Steadholder's left while LaFollet had her right, and he'd been watching the cross corridor as she approached it. He'd seen the trio of reporters stepping out of it before she'd noticed them, and, as he'd anticipated, she'd stopped walking when they blocked her way, which had let him slide in front of her before any misguided sense of courtesy on her part might have stopped him.

Now he regarded them with the cold, measuring dispassion of a Grayson armsman. He didn't say a word, didn't move a hand toward his holstered pulser, didn't even scowl.

He didn't have to.

The center newsman reached up with one very careful hand and deactivated his shoulder-mounted camera. Then the three of them parted magically to clear the Steadholder's way.

She gave them a nod—far more courteous than they deserved, almost as if nothing at all had happened—and stepped past them, with Mattingly at her heels. LaFollet waited a moment, then gave them a far colder nod of his own and fell in two paces behind at her right elbow.

"That's not quite how things are done in the Star Kingdom, Andrew," she murmured, and he snorted.

"I know it isn't, My Lady. I spent some time viewing the garbage the Manties— Beg pardon, My Lady. I meant I viewed the *Manticoran* coverage of the Young court-martial."

He made no effort to disguise his opinion of that coverage, and the Steadholder's lips quirked. It was only the barest hint of a smile, but he was enormously relieved to see it.

"I didn't say I didn't appreciate your efforts," she said. "I only meant that you can't go around threatening newsies."

"Threaten, My Lady?" LaFollet gave her a wide-eyed look. "I never *threatened* anyone."

The Steadholder started to reply, then closed her mouth. She looked back at him for a moment, then shook her head and returned her attention to the space station corridor.

LaFollet spared a moment to glance at Mattingly with only the slightest hint of triumph, then returned his own attention to his systematic threat search as they continued down the passage to the personnel tube waiting to carry them still deeper into the enormous space station.

LaFollet stepped around the Steadholder again to enter the tube capsule first. She gave him a semi-resigned, exasperated look, but at least she stopped. That was progress.

After a quick but thorough inspection of its interior, he stepped back for her to enter. She gave him another look—rather like the ones his mothers had given a much younger LaFollet who'd been "obstreperous" in company—as she entered it and punched in their destination code. He only looked back blandly, and then, as the capsule doors closed and it began to move, allowed himself to relax— a bit—into his own thoughts while the capsule's icon moved across the bulkhead-mounted location display.

He almost wished the newsie had given him an excuse to discourage him and his companions a bit more proactively. Not that he'd expected them to. One of the many things he'd done in preparation for his current duties was to spend quite some time analyzing the differences between the Manticoran media and that of Grayson. He'd realized even before he'd studied them that there would inevitably be differences between the way in which Manticoran public figures interacted with one another, with their society, and with the media. Despite that, he'd been unprepared for the intrusiveness the Star Kingdom apparently took for granted. No Grayson reporter would have dared to waylay a steadholder in a public passage. For that matter, no Grayson newsfax or public board would have blasted out the story of Steadholder Harrington's relationship with Paul Tankersley—or, for that matter, with Pavel Young—the way the Manties had. It just wasn't done.

Fortunately, one of the first things a Grayson steadholder's personal armsmen learned was how to communicate in a nonverbal manner with the more loathsome specimens of humanity who crossed their steadholder's path. They might not need to do that with *Grayson* reporters, but the Manticoran subspecies was a different breed. Still, it would appear even *they* could learn—or at least recognize the path of courtesy—when suitably reasoned with. LaFollet was fairly sure Steadholder Harrington wouldn't approve of that sort of thing in the long term, but he didn't really care about that.

What he cared about was the Steadholder.

His lips tightened as he recalled the agony, the stunned loss, in her exotic brown eyes when Captain Henke gave her the news. The woman—the warrior—who'd faced a dozen assassins unarmed had swayed, unable for a long, terrible moment even to speak. And then she'd turned to Regent Clinkscales and begun giving orders in the dead, emotionless voice of a white-faced, dry-eyed automaton. She'd ignored the Regent's efforts to express his condolences, to comfort her. She'd only given those orders, and within six hours, they'd been aboard Captain Henke's ship and headed back to Manticore.

He suspected she hadn't even realized—then—that her personal armsmen were aboard.

He'd never imagined he might see her so . . . broken. So shattered. If any of the Graysons who'd whispered behind their hands about her "shameful affair" with Paul Tankersley had seen her, even they would have recognized the depth of the love they'd shared. And the fury of her armsmen as they learned the details of the duel in which he'd died had become a dark, savage flame on the day one of *Agni*'s Marines had finally told Jamie Candless what the miserable bastard had *said* to Tankersley to provoke it.

Captain Henke had settled them in *Agni*'s Marine quarters for the voyage. The captain had been surprised by their presence, but if she'd been tempted to object, Protector Benjamin's personal explanation of why they were there would have prevented it. Not that she had been. LaFollet was certain of that, and she'd made no objection at all to adding one of the Steadholder's armsmen to the Marine sentry she'd stationed outside the Steadholder's cabin hatch.

For two full days, the Steadholder hadn't even left her personal quarters. The only person who saw her, aside from her treecat companion, was Steward MacGuiness. No doubt there were Graysons who would be ostentatiously shocked by the mere notion of a male body servant for any woman, far less a steadholder. LaFollet wasn't. He'd seen the Steadholder and MacGuiness together on Grayson after she'd been wounded fighting for the lives of Protector Benjamin's family, long before the Protector created her steading. He understood the devotion—the love, really—between them, and he'd seen MacGuiness' desperate concern for the woman they both served.

He'd offered the steward as much support as he could, but for those first two days, there'd been nothing anyone could do. And then, on the third day, she'd emerged from her cabin.

Captain Henke had been there when she did. LaFollet didn't know what the two of them might have said to one another before they'd stepped out of the hatch, but he'd seen the concern in Henke's expression as the captain followed her into the passage.

He didn't think the Steadholder had. He didn't think she'd really *seen* much of anything, actually. Her uniform had been perfect, her grooming immaculate, but her eyes had been brown, frozen flint in a face that was gaunt with pain, and Nimitz had been hunched and silent on her shoulder, his tail hanging like a defeated army's banner. She'd simply started down the passageway, and she hadn't even noticed when LaFollet followed her.

He'd wondered where they were going, but only until the intra-ship car delivered them to *Agni*'s armory. The Marine armorer had snapped to attention behind the high counter as his CO and the Steadholder stepped out of the lift.

"Is the range clear, Sergeant?"

If glaciers could speak, one of them might have sounded like that soprano.

"Uh, yes, Milady. It is."

"Then issue me an automatic," she'd said in that same icy voice. "Ten millimeter."

The sergeant had looked past her at his captain, and LaFollet had understood the worry in his eyes. He'd spent almost half his own life in armories just like this one, and he would have flatly refused to issue a weapon to someone who spoke like that. Indeed, his own expression had tightened as he wavered on the very cusp of objecting. But he'd made himself stand silent, instead, and after the briefest of hesitations, Captain Henke had nodded ever so slightly to the sergeant.

The Marine had reached under the counter for a memo board and laid it in front of the Steadholder.

"Please fill out the requisition while I get it, Milady."

The Steadholder had started tapping keys as the sergeant turned toward the weapons storage, but her voice had stopped him.

"I need filled ten-round magazines," she'd said. "Ten of them. And four boxes of shells."

"I—" The sergeant had cut himself off. "Yes, Milady. Ten charged magazines and two hundred rounds in the box," he'd said.

The Steadholder had filled out the requisition slowly and methodically, then thumbprinted the scan pad and stood there, waiting, until the Marine returned.

"Here you are, Milady."

He'd laid the holstered pistol and two sets of ear-protectors, one of them adjusted to fit Nimitz's ears, on the counter, then placed an ammunition carrier beside them.

"Thank you."

The Steadholder had scooped up the pistol and attached its magnetic pad to her belt, then reached for the protectors with one hand and the ammunition with the other. LaFollet had stirred behind her, hovering once again on the brink of a protest. But before he could say a word, Captain Henke's hand had shot out and pinned the carrier to the counter.

The Steadholder had turned her head, looked at her, one eyebrow raised.

"Honor, I—"

Henke's voice had died, LaFollet had known what she'd wanted to say. What she couldn't find the words to say. The same thing *he'd* wanted to say.

"Don't worry, Mike." The Steadholder's mouth had moved in a cold, dead ghost of a smile. "Nimitz won't let me do that. Besides"—an edge of something hungry had crept into that frozen smile—"I have something more important to do."

Understanding had gone through LaFollet in that moment. Or perhaps it had been more of a revelation, the recognition of something he'd really known all along about the woman he'd sworn to serve, and he'd felt no surprise when the captain sighed and lifted her hand.

The Steadholder had picked up the ammunition carrier, settled its strap over her left shoulder, and looked at the armorer.

"Program the range, Sergeant," she'd said. "Standard Manticoran gravity on the plates. Set the range gate for twenty meters. Human targets."

And then she'd stepped through the firing range hatch.

LaFollet had stood outside the range, watching through the armorplast bulkhead as the Steadholder took her position. At least one of his concerns had been laid to rest as he watched her draw the heavy semiautomatic pistol, check the chamber, and lock the slide back. He'd never seen her handle a firearm before, not even one of the modern pulsers Grayson had been unable to afford before joining the Manticoran Alliance, far less an old-fashioned chemical-fueled weapon with equally old-fashioned iron sights, but she'd obviously known precisely what she was doing.

She'd laid out the magazines on the firing bench, then manipulated the joystick at her station to turn the holographic human target until it stood with one shoulder toward her, one arm raised in a one-handed shooting position. The firing range's physical depth was only ten meters, not the twenty she'd specified, but LaFollet had realized that the target had been downsized—and, he'd discovered later, the grav plates had been adjusted—to create a twenty-meter *apparent* range and bullet trajectory. And, as he'd watched, she'd raised the pistol . . . and put the entire magazine into the target's head. The entire group couldn't have spanned more than twelve centimeters.

Then she'd done it again. And again. Ten times, without a single shot that hadn't landed dead center. And as he'd watched, a sense of grim, cold satisfaction had filled his soul.

She'd reloaded the magazines methodically from the boxed ammunition, then done it again. And after she'd refilled them all for the second time, she'd gone back to the armorer for more ammunition, and then returned to the range. She'd spent the next best thing to eight hours on that range over the next two days, until they'd reached Manticore. After that first session, she'd shifted from a stationary target and reprogrammed the hologram to move—slowly at first, but with increasing speed—and still those unerring bullets had plunged through it again and again.

After the second trip to the range, she'd paused and raised an eyebrow at LaFollet as she returned the pistol to the armor.

"You have a question, Andrew."

It was a statement, not a question, he'd realized. And she'd been right. But how did he—?

"Actually, My Lady, I was just curious," he'd said after a moment. "A weapon like that"—he'd flipped his head in a nod at the pistol on the armor's counter—"would've been standard issue for any armsman before the Alliance. With holographic sights, but the basic platform would've been pretty much identical. The Star Kingdom's military hasn't used them for a long, long time, though. I've met quite a few Manticoran personnel who are pretty fair shots with one of *these*." He'd tapped the pulser holstered at his hip. "Not so much with one of those. They *really* don't like the recoil—or the muzzle blast—the first time they try one."

"They don't?"

There might actually have been a flicker of humor in those frozen brown eyes, and Lady Harrington had smiled ever so slightly. An Old Terran wolf might have smiled like that, and the humor was a cold, hard, *hungry* thing.

"No, My Lady. They don't," he'd said.

"My Uncle Jacques is from Beowulf," she'd said then. "He used to be a major in the Biological Survey Corps—don't let the name fool you; it's one of the best Special Forces organizations in the galaxy. I rather doubt Summervale knows about him, given how tight BSC's security is. And my dad may be a retired Navy doctor, but he was a Marine before that. And I grew up on Sphinx. You don't go into the bush on Sphinx without a gun, Andrew. So I learned to shoot before I was eleven, and you might say I had good teachers."

"With 'antiques' like that, My Lady?" he'd asked, nodding at the pistol again.

"That's where Uncle Jacques comes in." She'd smiled even more coldly. "He belongs to something called the Society for Creative Anachronisms. It's a bunch of hobbyists fascinated by the past. He gave me my favorite nitro-powder rifle—Daddy's always preferred pulse rifles—when I was twelve. And both of them made sure I understood handguns, too." Her smile had vanished. "I don't imagine either of them ever thought I'd need one for this."

"No, My Lady. I don't imagine they did, either," he'd said, and heard the grim approval in his own voice when he did.

The range was the only place she'd gone, and those frozen brown eyes had never thawed, but Andrew LaFollet had been satisfied. Not happy, only satisfied.

Now the capsule stopped. The door opened, and Mattingly stepped through it before the Steadholder. She shook her head but let him, and then LaFollet followed her out and down yet another passageway—this one a good twenty meters across and ten meters tall, with an island of greenery down its center—toward what looked for all the world like a pair of swinging doors under flowing golden letters that read simply DEMPSEY'S.

The Steadholder paused about two meters from them and drew a deep breath, then turned to her armsmen.

"All right, Andrew. Simon. I'm not going to have any problems with you two, am I?"

LaFollet gazed back at her. She hadn't specifically discussed what was about to happen with him, but he knew. Just as he knew the reason she'd left Nimitz in her quarters aboard *Nike*.

For that matter, he knew she would have preferred to leave him and Mattingly *with* Nimitz. In fact, it was obvious she truly hadn't yet fully internalized the requirements of Grayson law where steadholders' security details were concerned, and she'd tried to do just that. Fortunately, Regent Clinkscales had briefed Andrew LaFollet carefully against this very moment. Even better, in some ways, he'd spent hours picking James MacGuiness' brain on the best way to approach explaining the realities to her. MacGuiness probably knew her better than anyone outside her parents and Captain Henke, and he'd obviously approved of her armsmens' presence even before he'd learned of Captain Tankersley's death.

"Tell her it's her duty," he'd said with a sad smile. "That's the one argument she can never, ever ignore."

That was precisely what LaFollet had done, and when she'd pointed out that armed foreign nationals weren't permitted aboard Manticoran warships, he'd simply shown her his copy of the Star Kingdom's official response to Protector Benjamin's personal communication to its foreign secretary over a year ago in anticipation of this moment.

The one signed by Prime Minister Cromarty and countersigned by Queen Elizabeth herself. The one that officially recognized Lady Harrington as *Steadholder* Harrington, a foreign head of state who happened to share the same body with *Countess* Harrington, and specifically granted her armsmen the right to keep and bear arms in her presence, wherever she might be. And, for good measure, granted them diplomatic immunity, to boot.

That was the point at which she'd realized she truly was stuck with them, he thought as he looked back at her now.

"You're our Steadholder, My Lady," he said. "Your orders to us have the force of law. We don't like the idea of your risking yourself, but we won't interfere as long as this Summervale offers you no physical violence."

"I don't like qualifications from my subordinates, Andrew," she said, and his shoulders straightened in involuntary reflex. "I won't try to tell you your duty under normal circumstances, but when I tell you you will do nothing, *whatever* happens between Summervale and me, that's precisely what I mean. Is that understood?"

LaFollet felt his face go blank as, for the first time, he heard the unmistakable snap of command in her voice.

"Yes, My Lady. I understand," he said crisply, and the Steadholder nodded.

"Good," she said, then drew a deep breath. "In that case, gentlemen, let's be about it."

✦ ✦ ✦

She really shouldn't be here.

She knew that. She'd even told herself that. But sometimes Iris Babcock didn't listen to herself, and this was one of those times.

No one had told her what was likely to happen today, but it was a sorry excuse for a Marine noncom who couldn't figure out what was going on. She knew HMS *Agni* had returned from Grayson with Lady Harrington the day before, and she knew Lady Harrington. There was no question in her mind what the Countess intended to do, and there was really only one place she could do it. Babcock's cousin Malachi had confirmed that for her, and he'd also quietly reserved a corner table near the bar for her. Major Yestachenko had looked at her a bit oddly when she'd announced she had a personal errand to run aboard *Hephaestus*, if that was all right with the Major. She suspected Yestachenko had a pretty shrewd idea of what that "errand" was, but the Major was another of the good ones. He'd only suggested—a bit pointedly, true—that he expected her to "stay out of trouble."

Which she intended to do.

Probably.

Now she sat back, nursing a beer and watching the slim, fair-haired man at the bar. He'd been there for the last three hours, and according to Malachi, he'd been there for over five hours, yesterday.

*Nothing suspicious about that*, she thought with a snort.

"Now why did I expect I'd find you here, Gunny?"

She looked up with a start, and her eyes widened briefly.

"Harkness?" She produced a scowl. "What the hell are *you* doing here?"

"Really?" Horace Harkness said almost pityingly, then toe-hooked a chair out from under her table and sat down. "You think you're the only person tapped into the grapevine?" It was his turn to snort. "I wouldn't miss this for the frigging world, Gunny! Or maybe I should say I wouldn't miss this for the frigging world *either*?"

She glared at him for a moment.

"Okay, you caught me." She shrugged. "So sue me."

"Nah." Harkness raised a hand to catch the attention of one of Dempsey's real, live human waitstaff. "Couldn't do that without suing myself."

"What do you need, Senior Chief?" the waiter asked.

"A stein of Old Tillman, I think," Harkness replied. "Oh, and a side of fries. You need anything else, Gunny?"

"Actually," Babcock decided, "fries sound pretty good. Make that a double, Ken. And put it on my tab."

"You got it, Sergeant Major."

The waiter nodded and headed off, and Harkness grinned.

"That was right neighborly of you, Gunny!"

"Don't let it go to your head," Babcock said dryly. "Just remember, I get the family discount."

"Man, never thought of myself as a cheap da—" Harkness began, then paused in mid syllable as the double doors opened.

"Showtime, Gunny."

"Yeah," Babcock agreed, then twitched her head to her left. "Keep an eye on that big guy in the Hauptman shipsuit. He's had his eye on our friend at the bar as long as I have, and the son of a bitch is packing. I'm thinking our friend might have brought a little extra muscle along after his conversation with the Colonel."

"Shoulder holster on the left side?" Harkness nodded. "Noticed that while I was sneaking up on you."

"Observant bastard for a vacuum-sucker, aren't you just?"

"I try, Gunny. I try."

✧ ✧ ✧

Andrew LaFollet and Simon Mattingly followed the Steadholder through the swinging doors.

She paused long enough for a single, sweeping glance. It found the fair-haired man seated at the bar, his back to the doors, and she started across the restaurant with a steady, measured stride.

LaFollet and Mattingly held station behind her, and LaFollet's antennae tingled as a big, beefy fellow in a yellow shipsuit turned his head. The major didn't care for the way the Manty's eyes followed the Steadholder, but his weren't the only eyes following her. The man with his back to her looked as if he had not a care in the world, but his eyes were on the mirror behind the bar, focused on the Steadholder's reflection like lasers.

The Steadholder crossed the restaurant and stopped a meter behind him. LaFollet saw *her* eyes in the mirror, too, and then—

"Denver Summervale?" she said in a tone like a daggered icicle.

He sat for an instant, then turned, and Andrew LaFollet's palm itched as he curled a contemptuous lip at the Steadholder.

"Yes?" he sneered.

"I'm Honor Harrington," she said.

"Should that *mean* something to me?" he demanded in that same, sneering tone, but LaFollet saw something in his eyes that belied his finely honed scorn. Something that suggested this meeting wasn't developing exactly the way he'd planned. And then—

"Yes, it should," the Steadholder said. "After all, I'm the woman Earl North Hollow hired you to kill, Mister Summervale. Just as he hired you to kill Paul Tankersley."

She hadn't raised her voice, but it was a voice accustomed to command. It carried clearly, and disbelieving silence radiated outward across the crowded restaurant with stunning, lightning speed.

Summervale's disdainful expression vanished. He gaped at her, obviously dumbfounded, and LaFollet wondered just what the idiot had *expected* the Steadholder to say. In Summervale's defense, he'd never seen her ankle-deep in assassins' bodies, but a man with his record should have done his homework. Then again, perhaps that record of his was the reason he hadn't. LaFollet's research had turned up over a dozen duels Summervale had fought. He'd won all of them easily, and Lady Harrington had never fought even one. This was *his* game, not hers, and no doubt he'd expected her to approach him in a white-hot fury. For her to challenge *him*, put him in position to dictate the terms of their inevitable meeting. Clearly, he'd anticipated neither her ice-cold control not that she—that *anyone*—would dare to publicly denounce him as a paid killer . . . and name the man who'd hired him, as well. It was an understandable error, if not a forgivable one.

And it was also the last error he would ever make.

Andrew LaFollet was an armsman. He didn't like the thought of Lady Harrington exposing herself to risk, but what he felt in that moment was an overwhelming sense of grim, confident pride in his Steadholder.

Summervale simply sat there, thoughts obviously skittering like a ground car on ice as he tried to process what had just happened. There was no question in LaFollet's mind that the paid duelist had been waiting here, anticipating Lady Harrington's arrival, but his carefully planned scenario had just gone out the airlock. He no longer knew the script, and his brain was a beached fish, floundering on the sand, while he stared at her like a rabbit.

"We're all waiting, Mister Summervale," she said. "Aren't you a man of honor?" Her contempt cut like a lash. "No, of course you're not. You're a hired killer, aren't you, Mister Summervale? Scum like you doesn't challenge people unless the odds and money are both right, does it?"

"I—" Summervale began, then stopped, and LaFollet smiled thinly.

*Not working out the way you'd planned, is it, asshole?* the major thought coldly. *So* now *what do you do?*

Summervale clearly had no answer for that question. The accusation—the insult—Lady Harrington had just delivered left him no option. LaFollet understood that, too. Summervale had to realize as well as LaFollet what he had to do—what he had no option *but* to do—yet he seemed incapable of getting the words out.

"Very well, Mister Summervale," Lady Harrington said. "Let me help you."

She slapped him across the mouth.

Andrew LaFollet had seen Honor Harrington kill a man with her bare hands. He knew exactly what she *could* have done to Denver Summervale. But that slap—that open-hand blow, delivered by an arm reared in Sphinx's gravity—wasn't intended to kill. It was intended to do something far worse, and it landed precisely where she'd intended it to. Landed with all the contempt in the universe.

Summervale's head snapped back, his lips pulped, his mouth instantly bloody, and the Steadholder slapped him again, this time with the back of her hand. He staggered back, and she crowded in on him, pinning him against the bar, and slapped him again. And again. And *again*, forehand and backhand, full arm blows, each slap landing with an explosive *CRACK*, while every shocked eye in the crowded restaurant watched.

Summervale finally got a hand up, trying to grab her wrist, and she let him—for a moment. Then she broke his grip contemptuously and stepped back, watching him with brown-flint eyes.

"I—"

Summervale coughed, then dragged a handkerchief from his pocket as the blood drooled down his chin and across his shirt and tunic, and his eyes blazed with mingled shame, fury, hatred ... and fear.

The Steadholder only stood there, waiting, and he clutched the balled-up handkerchief in one hand and forced his shoulders to straighten. It was an almost pathetic gesture, LaFollet thought with cold pleasure.

"You're insane," he said finally. "I don't know you, and I've never met this Earl North Hollow! How *dare* you accuse me of being some—some sort of hired assassin! I don't know why you should want to force a quarrel on me, but no one can talk to me this way!"

"*I* can," Lady Harrington said coldly.

"Then I have no choice but to demand satisfaction!"

"Good."

For the first time, there was something in the Steadholder's voice besides contempt. There was hunger. There was *satisfaction*, and more than one of the restaurant's patrons shuddered as they heard it.

"Colonel Tomas Ramirez—I believe you know him?—will act as my second," she told him in that hexapuma voice. "He'll call on your friend—Livitnikov, isn't it? Or were you going to hire someone else this time?"

"I—" Summervale swallowed again, then drew a deep breath. "Mr. Livitnikov is, indeed, a friend of mine. I feel confident he'll act for me."

"I'm sure you do. No doubt you pay him enough." Lady Harrington's smile was a scalpel, and her eyes glittered. "Tell him to start studying the Ellington Protocol, Mister Summervale," she said.

He stood, staring at her, bloody mouth working, and she snorted contemptuously.

Then she turned away, nodded to LaFollet and Mattingly, and walked out of the restaurant's ringing silence without another word.

**Landing Dueling Grounds**
**City of Landing**
**Planet of Manticore**
**Manticore Binary System**
**April 5, 1906 PD**

"HERE SHE COMES," someone said, and Chris Scarborough looked up from his uni-link as the ground limo came to a halt.

The doors opened, and two men in green uniforms of obviously foreign cut climbed out into the early morning sunlight from either side. They turned their backs to the vehicle, sweeping the area visually, then stepped aside to clear the way for the limo's other passengers.

A brown-haired woman in black-and-gold Navy uniform and the white beret of a starship's commanding officer, climbed out next. She was tall—Scarborough knew she was actually a good five centimeters taller than *he* was—and broad shouldered, for a woman, but she looked almost petite beside the massive Marine colonel who followed her with the polished wooden pistol case under his arm.

"Took her long enough," someone else muttered.

Scarborough couldn't be certain who'd said it. There were too many possible candidates, given the crowd of journalists who'd gathered this morning. And the audience, he thought sourly, glaring down at the crowd of crass, gawking spectators who lined the landscaped walkway down one side of the dueling grounds to watch the drama which had obviously been provided for their entertainment.

Normally, duels were very private affairs, and most of the Star Kingdom's news community tried to ignore them as much as possible. A certain particularly loathsome subspecies of newsy went in exactly the opposite direction, pandering to the mob's voracious appetite for scandal and spectacle. And the opportunity to drag their betters through the mud of defamation and public censure when they met to settle an affair of honor, of course. But today, it was standing room only.

Whoever had pointed out Harrington's tardiness, though, he'd had a point, he thought sourly. But then he checked his chrono and grimaced.

Actually, she was almost precisely on time, he acknowledged, although Denver Summervale had been on the grounds for almost twenty minutes already. Of course, he usually was early for this sort of thing. Scarborough didn't approve of duels. No one did, after all. But the practice had always fascinated him, anyway, and he'd researched it with a sort of intrigued horror, which was why he knew that only two duelists in Manticoran history—both of them dead for over two centuries—had ever fought more of them than Denver Summervale. That was probably one reason Harrington's supporters— and at least some of the rest of the media, he acknowledged—were prepared to give any credence to the ridiculous accusations she'd supposedly made against Earl North Hollow. So far, Scarborough hadn't spoken to anyone who'd actually been there, so he didn't know for certain that she'd actually said what the rumors said she had. Yet even he had to concede that the number of duels on Summervale's record made it childishly simple to paint him as some sort of paid assassin. But if there'd been any truth at all to those long-standing rumors, he'd have been tried and convicted long ago.

Probably.

In his fairer moments, Scarborough also had to concede that privileged birth (or the protection of those who enjoyed that advantage) could provide cover for a host of sins. Even crimes, as long as there was no legal proof they'd been committed. He didn't like admitting that, and he tried to avoid doing so publicly, because the last thing he needed to do was to lend any support to the mob or to the crass sensationalist "journalists" who pandered to it. Like the fellow standing next to him at the moment, for example.

He glanced surreptitiously sideways at Bryant Hirsch as the auburn-haired man bent to adjust his camera. Hirsch—stringer for Minerva Prince and Patrick DuCain's syndicated *Into the Fire*—was old-fashioned in a lot of ways, and given how far back the Landing City Police had pushed the crowd of newsies this morning, he'd opted to use a tripod rather than rely on the camera's built-in stabilizers.

Now he straightened and adjusted the earbud from the shotgun mic mounted atop the camera.

Scarborough had his own directional microphone trained on the dueling grounds, but he saw no need to capture the video himself. He could rely on tech gnomes like Hirsch to take care of the dreary details. Besides, at least four of the newsies around him were on live feeds, which meant the Star Kingdom at large would see and hear every gory detail before he ever got around to recording his own opinion piece on the day's events. No, he wanted to hear—and record—what was actually said before he crafted his op-ed. The Star Kingdom's politics had become even more hyper-partisan since the outbreak of hostilities, and especially since the North Hollow court-martial, and as one of Manticore's senior political commentators, Scarborough fully understood the value of the well-chosen soundbite. And why it was so important to have the original sound in its entirety when someone inevitably accused one of selective editing or even outright fabrication.

Chris Scarborough had never *fabricated* a quote in his entire life. He was rather proud of that, as a matter of fact. But any journalist had to edit just to fit the material into his available screen time, didn't he? And *all* editing was ultimately "selective," wasn't it? One couldn't simply put in all of the raw, contextless audio, could one? The important thing was to prove that one had actually listened to the entire conversation before exercising that selective function. Besides, God knew there'd been plenty of out-of-context quotes from Harrington's supporters and the ravening hordes of Government hacks out for North Hollow's blood. As far as Chris Scarborough was concerned, it was past time somebody provided a little balance.

"She looks pretty damned determined to me," someone else said.

"Of course she does." Scarborough allowed only the faintest trace of a sneer into his reply; one must, after all, maintain one's obvious neutrality. "She's the one who pushed the entire thing. Which may not be the smartest thing she's ever done, really."

"You really think 'smart' had anything to do with her decision?" Hirsch asked skeptically, and Scarborough shrugged.

"Actually, I think this"—he waved at the dueling grounds as Harrington and her party walked toward the waiting Master of the Field—"is the exact opposite of *smart* on her part. Not given the way she obviously wants it to play out, anyway. After the way she physically attacked Summervale? In front of witnesses?" He shook his head. "There's no way she's walking off the field alive."

"Already have her dead and buried, do you?" Hirsch's lip curled. "Convenient for North Hollow if it works out that way, you think?"

"Only if you're foolish enough to give any credence to her ridiculous accusations—her *alleged* ridiculous accusations, at any rate—in the first place," Scarborough replied. "Even assuming she actually said what the wilder rumors say she said, I doubt anyone else is stupid enough to believe it. I mean, I'll grant that *she* might believe it, although I find even that difficult to credit. But given how long this vendetta of hers against the Earl's gone on, and how bitter it's been— and, I might add, the way she and her . . . patrons finally hounded the Earl out of the Service—it's not that great a stretch to accept that she genuinely thinks he's behind what happened to Tankersley."

"And you're sure he wasn't, of course."

"I can't *prove* it, but then it's always hard to prove a negative, isn't it?" Scarborough regarded Hirsch scornfully. "Assuming, like I say, that she actually said it in the first place. That's what she and the rest of the Earl's enemies are counting on, after all. How does he go about proving he *didn't* do something?"

"Especially when he probably did," Hirsch said flatly.

"That's preposterous!" Scarborough snapped. "And irresponsible as hell, out of a journalist, too!"

"Oh, I've seen how 'impartial' and 'evenhanded' *you* are, Chris!" Hirsch shot back. "Actually, now that I think about it, there's a certain similarity between you and Summervale." His eyes glittered, cold and hard. "I believe the appropriate term is 'hired gun.' And it pays pretty well, doesn't it?"

Scarborough opened his mouth quickly, then shut it again and glared at the other newsy, as angry at himself as at Hirsch for having allowed the cretin to get to him. Then he turned away, presenting a contemptuous back to the other newsy as Harrington reached the dueling grounds.

*It doesn't matter what* you *think is going on here, asshole*, he thought loudly in Hirsch's direction. *In about ten minutes, your precious Countess Harrington's going to be a statistic. Let's see how long her accusations against the Earl last after she's gone!*

He checked to be sure his uni-link's record function was engaged, then concentrated on his own audio feed as he watched the LCPD lieutenant greet her.

"Good morning, Lady Harrington. I'm Lieutenant Castellaño, LCPD. I will be serving as Master of the Field this morning."

"Lieutenant," Harrington replied, and Castellaño waved one hand at the crowd of people clustered around the field.

"Milady, I'm sorry about this," he said. "It's indecent, but I can't legally exclude them."

"The media?" Harrington asked.

"Yes, Milady. They're out in force, and those . . . *people* up there"— he jabbed a finger at the hilltop upon which Scarborough and the others stood—"have telephotos and shotgun mics to catch every word. They're treating this like some sort of circus, Milady."

"I see." Harrington gazed up at the hill for a moment, then touched the lieutenant's shoulder. "It's not your fault. As you say, we can't *exclude* them. I suppose the best we can hope for is a stray shot in their direction."

Scarborough's eyes narrowed in disgust at the utterly inappropriate joke. Disgust that turned into anger as Castellaño smiled.

"I suppose it is, Milady," he said. "Well, then. If you'd come with me, please?"

Scarborough fumed internally and made a mental note to include the incident in his article. It was one thing for someone like Harrington to joke about the possibility of a bystander's being wounded—even killed. It was a sad state of affairs even for *her*, of course. She was a Queen's officer, after all! But it was quite another, far worse dereliction when an official representative of the capital city's police did the same thing!

Harrington and her companions fell in behind Castellaño, following him toward the dueling grounds, but the lieutenant paused just outside the simple white rail around the dueling grounds proper.

"Excuse me, Milady," he said. "I was informed about your guardsmen, of course, but the law prohibits the presence of any armed supporters of either party at a meeting. If they wish to remain, they'll have to surrender their weapons."

"I understand, Lieutenant," Harrington replied, and turned to the green-uniformed men at her back.

"Andrew. Jamie," she said.

For a moment, Scarborough thought her bodyguards—*and what sort of idiot brings* bodyguards *to a damned* duel, *anyway?*—would refuse to surrender their pulsers, but then one of them drew his weapon from the holster and passed it to Castellaño. The other bodyguard followed suit a moment later and the lieutenant started to turn away, but—

"And now the other one, Andrew," Harrington said.

Scarborough's eyes widened, and he wished for a moment that he was looking through Hirsch's viewfinder. He would have loved to see the bodyguard's expression. Judging by his body language, he wasn't a happy fellow.

The man stood there for a moment, then his left hand flicked. A much smaller pulser popped out of a spring-loaded wrist holster and into his fingers, and he handed it to Castellaño, as well.

"I didn't know you knew about that, My Lady," he said.

"I know you didn't." She punched his shoulder lightly.

"Well, if you figured it out, someone else can. Now I'm going to have to find someplace else to hide it."

"I'm sure you'll think of something," she said as Castellaño took the weapons and a policewoman appeared magically at his side.

"Thank you, Milady," the lieutenant said, handing the weaponry to the policewoman, then waved toward the fenced off grass. "Are you ready, Milady?"

"I am," Harrington replied, and glanced at the enormous Marine with the pistol case. "All right, Tomas. Let's be about it," she said.

She, the Marine, and Castellaño stepped through the opening in one end of the rail that surrounded the grounds and headed for Summervale, his second, and the uniformed officer who'd accompanied them. Unlike Harrington's uniform, with its gleaming gold braid and rank insignia, Summervale wore the dark, subdued clothing of an experienced duelist, and his body language shouted his mingled anger and contempt as he watched her approach. The newcomers paused two meters from him, and Castellaño stepped to one side so that he could face them both.

"Mister Summervale, Lady Harrington. It is my first and foremost duty to urge a peaceful resolution of your differences, even at this late date. I ask you both now: can you not compose your quarrel?"

Harrington only looked at him, but Summervale's lip curled.

"Get on with it," he said. "I'm meeting someone for breakfast."

Castellaño's shoulders seemed to stiffen, but all he said was, "In that case, present your weapons."

The seconds opened their pistol cases, and the lieutenant chose two of the weapons, examined them carefully, checked their functionality, then handed one to each of the duelists.

"Load, gentlemen," he told the seconds, and watched each of them load ten rounds into a magazine, then hand it to his principal.

"Load, Mister Summervale," Castellaño said. He watched Summervale insert the magazine, then looked at Harrington.

"Load, Lady Harrington," he said, and waited while she did.

"Take your places," he said then, and Harrington and Summervale turned their backs to one another and walked to the white circles twenty meters apart on the dew-soaked grass. They stepped into the circles' centers and turned to face one another once more.

"Mister Summervale, Milady, you may chamber."

Scarborough heard the harsh, metallic sound clearly over his directional microphone as both duelists worked their anachronistic pistols' actions. He heard the voices around him as some of the newsies—especially the ones broadcasting a live feed—huddled over their hush mics, as well, but those voices only seemed to make the quiet morning even quieter, somehow.

"You have agreed to meet under the Ellington Protocol," Castellaño said, drawing his own pistol and removing a white handkerchief from his pocket. "When I drop my handkerchief, you will each raise your weapon and fire. Fire will continue until one of you falls or drops your weapon in token of surrender. Should either of those things happen, the other will cease fire immediately. If he or she fails to do so, it will be my duty to stop him or her in any way I can, up to and including the use of deadly force. Do you understand, Mister Summervale?"

He looked at Summervale, who nodded curtly. Then at Harrington.

"Lady Harrington?"

"Understood," she replied quietly.

"Take your positions," he said then.

Summervale turned his right side to Harrington, his arm straight down beside him, and Scarborough recognized the posture of the experienced duelist he was. Harrington's *inexperience*, on the other hand, showed as she stood facing him squarely, offering him the full width of her body as a target.

Tension crackled in the morning, and even the newsies around Scarborough fell silent, staring at the motionless tableau.

Then Castellaño's fingers opened, the brisk morning breeze frisked the handkerchief into the air, and Denver Summervale's hand rose. It came up smoothly, confidently, rising into the firing position with flashing speed—

And Harrington fired.

Scarborough's eyes flew wide in astonishment. She hadn't even moved! She'd just *stood* there! And then she'd fired—fired from the *hip*, at twenty meters!—and her bullet hit Summervale just below his rib cage.

Scarborough couldn't believe it. In fact, he *didn't* believe it ... until Harrington fired again, still from the hip, and her second round hammered home just above the first.

Summervale staggered. Even from the hilltop, Scarborough could almost taste the duelist's disbelief, his shock. His hand dipped, and a third shot cracked out. Crimson splashed his black tunic in huge, angry blots, and he looked down at the fresh wound, then back up at Harrington.

Her pistol was up, now, held in a two-handed grip, her brown eyes merciless, and he screamed, the sound born as much of fury as of agony, as a *fourth* shot smashed into him, less than a centimeter from the third.

Blood bubbled from his nostrils, his knees began to buckle, yet he still clung to his pistol. It was back at his side now, as he stared at her, but he was still on his feet. He *refused* to fall, and somehow— with an agonized effort Scarborough could feel even from where he stood—that pistol lifted slowly, grimly, as he fought to raise it.

Harrington only stood there. She watched him, her face expressionless, as he wavered for balance while that pistol rose. She *let* him raise it, let him bare his teeth at her in bitter determination. Waited until it was *almost* in firing position.

And then—*then*—she fired yet again, and the back of Denver Summervale's skull exploded.

✦   ✦   ✦

Chris Scarborough stood there, frozen, staring down at Denver Summervale's body, and felt his own shock ripple through the other newsies. Of all possible outcomes, this was the one he'd least expected! What did—

"Guess today didn't work out real well for Earl North Hollow after all, did it, Chris?" Hirsch said from beside him. Scarborough whipped his head around to glare at him, and the other newsy smiled nastily. "I mean, looks like Summervale wasn't quite up to the challenge—you should pardon the expression—this time around. How'll you spin *this* one for North Hollow and High Ridge? Inquiring minds want to know."

"Listen, you—" Scarborough began hotly, then made himself pause. He inhaled deeply, fighting for control.

"Obviously," he said after a moment, jabbing an index finger at the dueling ground, "that wasn't what I expected to see this morning. Somehow, I don't think *you* expected it, either, Bryant!"

"No," Hirsch acknowledged. "To be honest, I didn't. Not given Summervale's record. I can't say I'm *sorry* to see it, though. I've admired Lady Harrington for years, and Summervale was a prick who also happened to be a hired killer. Whether North Hollow hired him—this time—or not, he damned well had it coming, and you know it!"

"Oh? He *deserved* to be shot over and over again by a cold-blooded killer, even after it was obvious she'd beaten him? She shot him the first time before he even had his gun up—and then she shot him again and again and *again* when he was already almost certainly mortally wounded! *That's* the person you 'admire'?"

"Oh, give me a break!" Disgust flickered in Hirsch's eyes, liberally dusted with scorn. "You know as well as I do that Summervale killed at least eight people. Of course, those are the ones we *know* about— the ones he shot 'legally' right down there where he just died! But if your sources haven't told you about his connections with the Outfit, you're an even sorrier excuse for a newsy than I thought you were. Which, admittedly, would be hard. The man made his *living* killing people! And while you're waxing all sanctimonious over what a cold-blooded killer Lady Harrington is, what about *him*? Tankersley had already fired when Summervale stood right on that very field, took his time, and shot him squarely in the head. You think that bullet just *happened* to hit Tankersley in the head at forty frigging meters?! Give me a break! And unlike Tankersley, Summervale was completely free to shoot back at her when she did it. And he could have *stopped* her anytime he chose to. Go back and reread the Ellington Protocol, Chris. All he had to do was drop his weapon. But he didn't, did he? And that means every single shot she fired was legally justified."

"There's a huge difference between legally justified and *morally* justified!" Scarborough spat.

"That's an even bigger crock of shit," Hirsch said contemptuously. "There was no possible 'moral justification' in what Summervale did to Captain Tankersley. There's no question he deliberately provoked Tankersley, and the only reason I can think of for a hired duelist to provoke someone he'd never even met was to get him out on the dueling grounds where he could *legally* shoot him. But I didn't hear you whining about *that*, did I? And just between you and me, 'not for attribution,' I'm delighted—*delighted*, do you hear me?—by what happened here today. Tankersley's murder was *legal*, I'll give you that. But what Lady Harrington did today wasn't just 'legal.' She was here to execute—and I use that verb deliberately—*justice*!"

Scarborough glared at him, then turned and strode furiously down the hillside to the crowd gathering around Harrington. The horde of newsies were already shouting questions as she stepped off the dueling ground and handed her pistol back to the Marine, and the stampede of newsies crowded toward her, despite the police cordon's best efforts. They closed in, waving their microphones, and a couple got too close. Until, that was, one burly newsman ended up flat on the seat of his trousers, gasping for breath, after colliding with one of her bodyguard's elbows.

They backed off then—marginally—and she raised one hand. The gesture was almost regal, and it actually stopped the shouts, however briefly.

"I'm not taking any questions, ladies and gentlemen," she said then, in a voice cold as liquid helium, just as Scarborough arrived. "But I do have a short statement."

One of the newsies tried to shout another question anyway, but one of his fellows punched him none too gently in the shoulder and he chopped himself off.

"Denver Summervale killed someone I loved," she said coldly and clearly into the listening hush. "What's happened here today won't bring Paul Tankersley back to me. I know that. *Nothing* can bring him back, but I *can* seek justice from the man who had him murdered."

Scarborough's eyes widened. Surely she wasn't about to—?

The silence lingered for another long, still moment, floating on the morning breeze until one of the other newsies cleared her throat.

"But, Lady Harrington," she said in the careful tone of someone else who'd heard the rumors about what she'd said to Summervale in Dempsey's, "Captain Tankersley was killed in a duel, and you've just—"

"I know how he died." Harrington cut the speaker off, and her eyes were even colder than her voice. "But Summervale was hired—paid—to kill him."

*Jesus Christ*, Scarborough thought. *The woman's a frigging lunatic! She is going to say it again—and this time on Star Kingdom-wide HD!*

"I accuse," she said then, with icy deliberation, "the Earl of North Hollow of hiring Denver Summervale to kill not merely Paul Tankersley, but myself, as well." She paused, her thin smile a razor. "As soon as possible, I will so accuse the Earl in person," she said then. "Good day, ladies and gentlemen."

And then she turned, nodded to the Marine at her side, and walked away into the morning's quiet down the lane her bodyguards and the Landing City Police opened through the stunned, magically parting ranks of the Star Kingdom's press corps.

**HMSS *Hephaestus***
**Manticore Planetary Orbit**
**Manticore Binary System**
**April 9, 1906 PD**

"—AND THEN SHE SAID she'd shoot North Hollow, too!"

"And about goddamn time! Son of a bitch's had it coming for way too long, if you ask me!"

Brandy Bolgeo looked up from her work screen, eyebrows raised.

"Senior Chief Stúdlin," she said.

The dark-haired senior chief looked up quickly.

"Yes, Ma'am?"

"While I can't really quibble with your characterization, we're on the clock, Senior Chief," she pointed out with a moderate frown.

"Yes, Ma'am, and I didn't—"

"I said I couldn't quibble with your characterization, Martin." Brandy's frown segued into a tart smile. "Trust me, I don't. But we are sort of supposed to be concentrating on the job at the moment. True?"

"True, Ma'am," Stúdlin agreed, and glanced back at the second-class petty officer beside him. "We'll pick this up later, Josephine. Trust me!"

"Sure, Senior Chief," the PO said and gave Brandy a semi-apologetic smile of her own before she turned back to the display linked to the remote currently crawling through the destroyer *Incorruptible*'s fusion plant.

Brandy watched her for a moment, then turned back to her own display. As she'd said to Stúdlin, she couldn't fault a single thing the power systems noncom had said. And unlike quite a few people she'd encountered, including some in uniform, who damned well should've known better, she doubted neither the accuracy of Lady Harrington's accusations nor the inevitability of the consequences for North Hollow.

Her mouth twitched with distaste as her memory replayed North Hollow's response to Lady Harrington's dueling ground statement. He'd looked so...so *civilized*. And his voice had simply oozed sympathy for Lady Harrington.

"I'm certainly troubled by it," he'd said in response to a direct question when he appeared on Chris Scarborough's *Inside Sources* podcast. His father had been a frequent guest on the program, and the new earl had appeared on it even more regularly, as the political debacle over the declaration of war stretched out interminably. He obviously had what people still called "good chemistry" with the program's host, and it had been on display that day.

"I'm sure anyone would be, My Lord," Scarborough had said then, nodding sadly. "I mean, it's such an outrageous thing for a peer of the realm, even one who hasn't yet bothered to take her seat in the House, to throw at another on a broadcast she had to know would be seen by almost everyone in the Star Kingdom, eventually."

"Be fair, Chris," North Hollow had said. "Lady Harrington and I have a long history, and I don't want to get into all of the patently absurd things she's said about me upon occasion. There's no point. But having said that, anyone with a gram of human compassion has to sympathize with the pain she must be feeling at this moment. I've never approved of the practice of dueling. It's a relic of barbarism, frankly. There may be times when it's an appropriate response, given certain values for the adjective 'appropriate,' to personal insult or injury, but it's inherently vulnerable to abuse. And I think it's abundantly clear that Denver Summervale—who, I remind you, was cashiered by the Royal Marines for theft and accepting bribes—is— or, *was*, at any rate—a perfect example of the weaknesses of the system. No one can condone Captain Tankersley's physical assault on a chance-met stranger in a bar, regardless of anything Summervale might have said to him. By the same token, it's clear the Captain was provoked—deeply provoked—by Summervale. And it's also abundantly clear that, whatever his motives, Summervale deliberately *killed* Captain Tankersley after the Captain had fired without killing or even seriously wounding his opponent.

"How could a woman who loved a man as Lady Harrington clearly loved Captain Tankersley not see that final, deliberate, carefully aimed shot as anything but an act of thinly disguised murder? And, given what Summervale's rumored to have said to the Captain in their confrontation, how could Lady Harrington not believe that, for whatever reason, Summervale had deliberately targeted *both* of them? Obviously, she's dealt with Summervale himself, but equally clearly, Summervale's death can never assuage the depth of her pain, her loss. Grief for our loved ones doesn't just . . . go away, Chris! And if she genuinely believes—as I'm certain she does—that Summervale was, indeed, the paid killer, the hired duelist, she accused him of being, it's inevitable that she should proclaim, and quite probably honestly believe, that I must have been the one who hired him."

The earl had shaken his head, his expression sad.

"I'm sure I hardly need to say this, but she's mistaken. And while I deeply sympathize with her loss, her pain, I have no intention of continuing the senseless cycle of violence which has already claimed Captain Tankersley's—and, yes, Denver Summervale's—lives."

"I'm not certain I could be as sympathetic with her, in your place, my Lord," Scarborough said somberly.

"Oh, it's not always easy for me, either!" North Hollow acknowledged wryly. "It's not pleasant being accused of hiring a murderer, but, then again, I've become unhappily accustomed to being accused of things. Indeed, my attorneys have suggested to me that it would not be inappropriate to sue Lady Harrington over the clearly libelous allegations she's made against me, and a part of me is strongly tempted to do just that. But, as I say, I do understand why she might genuinely feel that way, and I've developed an aversion to judicial gladiatorial combat. It didn't"—he allowed himself a wintry smile—"work out very well for me the last time. And dragging this into the courts, rather than simply allowing it to die a natural death in the fullness of time, could serve neither me, the Countess, nor our current hyper-partisan political divides."

"I must say that I wish certain other participants in those 'hyper-partisan' divisions would show equal restraint, My Lord. But, that said, I also wanted to ask you for your opinion of Countess New Kiev's motion to increase funding for the Star Kingdom's gold star orphanages. I realize some of her critics are claiming it's simply a way to divert attention from the Liberal Party's continuing opposition to actually fighting the war, but I wondered if you—"

Brandy had wanted to vomit as she'd listened to North Hollow playing the role of responsible statesman. She known he was lying, of course; his lips had been moving. And she was privately sure her father was right about the real reason he wasn't suing. The last thing North Hollow could risk was the possibility that Lady Harrington had actual proof of her allegations!

But so far, at least, he'd managed to run between the raindrops, to at least some extent. His political allies' covering fire, which consisted of far less "sympathetic" denunciations of Lady Harrington as little more than a common murderess who had once again demonstrated her propensity for violence and her complete lack of self-control, helped in that regard. The newsies like Scarborough, who'd chosen to adopt the same "in sorrow, not in anger" attitude as North Hollow were subtler and even more damaging to her, though. And there was a segment of public opinion which found it impossible to believe any peer of the realm could have stooped to murder. Or, at least, that he could have done it without being caught at it. After all, if Lady Harrington had actual proof, the proper thing for her to do was to hand it to the Crown Prosecutors, not seek some sort of crazed vigilante justice of her own!

So as long as he continued to avoid her...

Brandy gave herself a shake.

*You just whacked* Stúdlin *for spending duty time on this*, she reminded herself. *Probably wouldn't be a bad idea if you didn't spend duty time wool-gathering on it, either, don't you think?*

She snorted and tapped her display for an update.

It felt good to be back in the saddle, so to speak, although she *did* wish *Timberwolf* would get herself home! In the meantime, the Navy had assigned her to TDY aboard *Hephaestus* once she'd completed her month of survivor's leave, and she had to admit that what they were doing made sense. The next best thing to a year had passed since she'd been wounded, and she'd needed this time to ease back into active duty. And given that *Timberwolf* was slated for overhaul as soon as she could return to the Manticore System, it really hadn't made sense to send an officer who needed some refresher time clear out to Grendelsbane to take over her engineering department. So, *Hephaestus* had assigned her to one of the enormous space station's yard modules, where she could spend her time overseeing repairs and standard servicing requirements on destroyers and light cruisers almost as old as *Timberwolf*.

She was actually a bit surprised by the way her current duties helped hold her impatience at bay. She needed the refresher time anyway, and getting her hand in on older systems could only be beneficial when it was time to take over her new slot.

Which, she reflected cheerfully, wasn't the same thing as not being impatient at all!

**Earl North Hollow's Residence**
**City of Landing**
**Planet of Manticore**
**Manticore Binary System**
**April 11, 1906 PD**

"NO." GEORGIA SAKRISTOS SHOOK her head and glared at Pavel Young, her eyes hard. "I'm telling you to drop it, Pavel. I don't know for sure what the answer is—not yet—but I know for damned sure *this* isn't!"

"I don't think you understand," Young said coldly. "I'm not debating this; I'm *telling* you this."

"No," she said flatly. "I won't."

"Aren't you forgetting something?" he asked nastily, and she shook her head again.

"You can hurt me, a lot. I know that. You know that. Hell, you could possibly even get me killed, just like you can 'convince me' to do all those other things you want." Her eyes were carven ice. "But it'll take you a while to figure out how to do it, because I'm the one you count on to do your . . . selective leaking. You don't have a clue how to rat me out to the Ballroom. Oh, I'm sure you could figure out a way, but you don't have one now. And you know what? I'll put up with one hell of a lot, Pavel. Even all those sex games of yours. But I won't do this. If you insist, then I'm out of here, and you do whatever the fuck you want with your father's files!"

Young's eyes widened at the flat, unyielding armorplast of her tone, and her expression was even more implacable than her voice. She meant it. She truly *meant* it, and he'd never expected that. Not with the threat he held over her head. Other people could go to prison for decades if he decanted the "North Hollow Files." Georgia would be lucky if she lived six T-months if he dropped her true identity into the right set of ears.

Surprise displaced fury, but only for a moment. Because the fury

237

was driven by fear—by terror, however little he wanted to admit it. On the other hand, she was right. Unmasking her to the people she'd betrayed all those years ago wouldn't be the easiest thing he'd ever done, especially given how little the people in question liked people like him. Worse, she knew where *all* the North Hollow bodies were buried—figuratively and literally. If he pushed her into fleeing, there was no reason she couldn't send the Crown Prosecutor's office a disastrous data packet of her own on her way out of town. So if she decided to run, to take her chances on her ability to disappear a second time, she might just succeed and completely destroy him in the process. And even if she didn't manage either of those things, he'd still lose one of the best "dirty tricks specialists" in the entire Star Kingdom. Not to mention one of the most . . . compliant bed partners he ever had.

His jaw clenched, yet even as he glared at her, a corner of his mind realized he'd take even more pleasure in compelling her into his bed after she'd thrown down her gage. There'd be a special, even sweeter savor to it.

None of which changed the fact that he *needed* her to do this.

"I can't let that bitch's accusations stand," he grated, "but I can't shut her mouth, either!"

He still couldn't really believe even *Harrington* had had the sheer gall to publicly accuse a peer of the realm of hiring a paid assassin. Not even in a private conversation, but in front of a slavering horde of newsies! It had been bad enough when she confronted Summervale with it, but this—!

He'd had his own operative in Dempsey's that afternoon, equipped with a buttonhole camera attached to his shipsuit. He'd wanted to savor the moment when the bitch challenged Summervale and consigned herself to the Ellington Protocol. He'd never, not for a single moment, expected what she'd actually done, and his blood had run cold as she named him as Summervale's employer and then drove *him* into challenging *her*.

He'd never seen that coming.

Fortunately, although there'd been plenty of witnesses, no one—except his own man—seemed to have actually recorded the confrontation. There'd been whispered rumors about what she'd said, but no *proof*, and no news service had wanted to risk what would happen to it under the Star Kingdom's libel laws if it reported such a politically explosive accusation *without* proof. He'd realized, even then, that Georgia had been right from the outset about the suspicion which must inevitably fall upon him, but at least he'd known the bitch would be dead within days, and he'd been prepared to ride out the rumors afterward. For that matter, like he'd told Georgia, he'd actually been pleased by the fact that Cromarty—and everybody else in the damned Government—would know he'd been behind it yet be unable to prove it.

But that had been then, and this was now. The effortless way she'd destroyed Summervale was bad enough. The fact that she was still alive was terrifying. Worse, he didn't know if she had anything like actual proof he'd hired the duelist or if she was simply assuming he'd been behind it, and that mattered. If he'd been positive she had no proof, he could simply have sued her for libel and been done with it. But if she *did* have evidence, even only circumstantial evidence, she could present it openly in a court of law in her defense, with catastrophic consequences.

Even that was secondary at the moment, though. The newsies had broadcast her allegations. They were out there, on the record, waiting. The bitch obviously intended to use them as the basis to challenge *him*. If he'd been able to sue, that wouldn't have mattered, since the Star Kingdom's law code specifically barred anyone from challenging someone who'd brought suit against him. But he couldn't risk finding out the hard way that she *did* have proof. He dared not take that chance, but if she'd been able to take down Summervale that way . . .

"How did she *do* it?" he demanded out loud now. "Where the fuck did she learn to *shoot* like that!"

"I don't know," Sakristos said. "And it's obvious *Summervale* didn't know, either."

Not that the duelist couldn't have known if he'd bothered to do his research, she thought. Unlike him, Sakristos had studied Harrington very carefully before she suggested Summervale as the solution to Pavel's problem, and her research tools were far better than most. Accessing the countess's public record hadn't been difficult, and she'd gotten access to Harrington's official personnel file, thanks to an Admiralty contact. More than that, though, she'd gone clear back to Harrington's childhood, long before she'd ever become a public figure, and discovered that young Honor Harrington had taken the Sphinx Forestry Service Youth League's Shelton Cup for pistol and rifle for two years in a row before she was thirteen. Sakristos had had no idea how current Harrington's firearms skills might be, but she'd hoped her capabilities would come as a surprise to Summervale.

Of course, not even she had dared to hope Harrington would be as proficient as she'd actually proved!

"Well, it looks like your brainstorm about hiring the 'perfect' man for the job just blew the hell up, didn't it?" Young said spitefully, and she glared at him again.

"You wanted her killed in a duel, Pavel," she said. "That was *your* idea, not mine. I warned you at the time that if *anything* happened to her, people would automatically suspect you. But if you wanted her dead, this was the most plausibly deniable way to do it, and Summervale was the best at what he did." She shrugged with a scowl. "Obviously, he wasn't good *enough*, but he was the best available."

"And now she's coming after *me*," Young snarled.

"If she can, yes." Sakristos nodded. "I don't know if she has any kind of evidence to support her allegations, of course," she lied, "but for God's sake, Pavel! If other people would have suspected you, just what the hell did you expect *her* to do?"

"Of course she 'suspects' me. Hell, she hates me enough she'd probably pin it on me even if she was positive I hadn't had a thing to do with it! But we've got to shut her up."

"Like you just said, we can't." Sakristos' patient tone was a deliberate goad.

"Yes, we can!"

"No," she said again. "Having her killed would be the worst thing you could possibly do. It was bad enough before, but after what she's said, nobody in the entire Star Kingdom would believe for an instant that you weren't behind it. Not now. And if she's killed anywhere except in a duel, the cops—and the Government, for that matter— will open the mother of all investigations. I don't think there's any way they can legally link you to Summervale, especially now that he's dead, but the instant you hire someone else, you create a fresh potential evidence chain pointing directly back at you. And

Cromarty and Alexander will move heaven and earth to find it. In my opinion, the odds are way too good that they *would* find it, too."

"I'll take my chances!"

"Not with my help." She shook her head. "I'm not brokering that one for you, Pavel. Not when it could come home to bite my ass right along with yours."

"But—"

"Listen to me," she interrupted. "*If* she has any sort of evidence, anything beyond her own suspicions, it obviously wasn't legally obtained. If it had been, she'd already have handed it to the authorities, and they'd have opened an investigation. And I'm way too well tapped-in for them to have done that without us hearing about it.

"That means the only way she can get to you is in another duel. It's pretty obvious that's exactly what she intends to do. What she said to the newsies was stage-setting. But she can't get you onto the dueling grounds unless she can challenge you, and she can't challenge you unless you give her the opportunity. The woman's a serving naval officer. I already know from the Admiralty that they're going to redeploy her ship in only another couple of months. That's how long you have to avoid her."

"And it will be obvious I'm *hiding* from her, damn it. You think that won't have repercussions? That it won't give Cromarty and his cronies more ammunition to use against me?"

"Like they need any more 'ammunition'!" Sakristos rolled her eyes. "If they could get to you, they'd've already done it. There's nothing new here, as far as they're concerned. As long as you can stay away from her until the Navy deploys her out of the home system, you'll be fine."

"Until she gets back to Manticore, you mean! What's to prevent her from challenging me *then*? I can't hide from the bitch forever!"

"She'll be going right back into a shooting war," Sakristos pointed out. "The Peeps may solve your problem for you, which would be perfect from your perspective. And if they don't, then once a little time's passed, it may be possible to arrange a suitable 'accident' for her when the finger won't automatically point at you. For that matter, I'd be a lot more willing to help arrange that accident farther down the road. If I can take my time, put the groundwork in place well ahead of time, maybe arrange it through a series of cutouts, then maybe—*maybe*—we could take her down without everyone screaming you had to be behind it. Lord knows the woman's made enough enemies who'd love to see her dead, from Klaus Hauptmann on down! I just need *time* to set it up, and I'm not going to help you put your neck into a noose by rushing things when my neck could be right beside yours."

She held Young's eyes levelly, refusing to back down.

Silence hovered between them for several long seconds. Then, finally, he shrugged angrily.

"All right," he half-snarled. "If that's the way you see it, that's the way you see it. But you better start that planning right now, Georgia!"

"Of course I will," she replied.

"Good." He checked his chrono. "I've got that a meeting with High Ridge and New Flushing in twenty minutes. We'll talk about this—and a few *other* things—when I get back."

"Understood."

She let him hear the bitterness in her tone, since both of them knew what those "other things" would involve, and she expected them to be thoroughly unpleasant. But she'd survived quite a lot of unpleasant things in her life, some of them even worse than the ones he demanded from her, and she could survive more of them if she had to. At least *he* only used the threat of having her murdered to compel her, not a neural whip.

She gave him a curt nod, then stood and strode out of his office.

She closed the door carefully behind her before she allowed herself to smile, and Pavel Young would not have liked that smile. Not that she had any intention of allowing him to see it.

For someone who believed he was so cunning, Pavel was remarkably stupid, she thought. Or, no, that wasn't really true. What he was was an arrogant narcissist, the sort of sociopath who lived in a universe populated not by other human beings, but only by himself and human-shaped *things* put there for his use and convenience. For him to do whatever he wished to with. And he was so busy thinking about all the things he could do with—or to—those things that it never occurred to him to worry about what they might do to *him* until something rubbed his nose in it. And his family's position of power and wealth, and his father's protection, had let him get away with that for his entire life.

Except for Honor Harrington. She'd refused to let him use her the way he'd used everyone else in his life, and that was the true reason he—and, to be fair, his father—had devoted so much time and effort to their efforts to destroy her. How *dared* she not lie down for him the way all those others had done? Obviously, she had to be *punished* for it!

*And how well has that worked out for you, Pavel?* she thought sardonically as she walked down the carpeted hallway.

The fact was that Georgia Sakristos approved of Honor Harrington. Or, at least, of the Sword of Damocles she represented for Pavel Young, at any rate. She'd expected Harrington to dispose of Denver Summervale, although she honestly hadn't anticipated that the countess would accomplish that phase of her own master plan quite so proficiently. It was true that her denunciation of Young as Summervale's employer might prove a tactical error on her part, since it had warned him of how she intended to kill him in his turn. As they said, forewarned was forearmed, even in Pavel's case. On the other hand, Sakristos had every intention of kneecapping any preventive measures Pavel might contemplate. And she had to admit that watching him squirm, watching the worm of terror devour him, was even more entertaining than she'd hoped. After what he'd done to her, the things he'd compelled her to endure since his father's death, she took a cold, vicious pleasure in his punishment.

Yet hurting him was secondary. A sweet elixir distilled of vengeance and satisfaction, but only a side effect of what she truly needed.

She reached her own office, closed the door behind her, and seated herself behind her desk, and her eyes were bleak and hard.

Dimitri Young had promised to delete *her* file from his records. In fact, she'd thought he had, until he died and Pavel gloatingly read her a synopsis of that file and wondered out loud what the Audubon Ballroom would do if they ever happened to find out what had become of the woman she'd once been.

Dimitri had never pressed any particularly onerous physical demands upon her, but that had been solely because of his age and infirmity. Neither of those things afflicted Pavel, and she'd quickly discovered that his demands were about as sick and degrading as they came. Unfortunately, she had no choice but to submit to them anyway, because what would happen to Elaine Komandorski, if the Ballroom's ex-genetic slave terrorists ever caught up with "Georgia Sakristos," was even worse.

*Far* worse.

Still, her first week as Pavel Young's "lover" had made one thing clear: either she had to run, taking her chance that she could evade the Ballroom once again . . . or he had to die. And the choice between those options had made itself when she realized he hadn't changed Dimitri's office security protocols.

That minor oversight might suggest she'd been wrong about whether or not he truly was stupid, she reflected, given the games he'd forced her to play. On the other hand, he might not be aware of all the nuances of the protocols his father had set up. That was the sort of "nuisance detail" he preferred to delegate to lesser beings, like her.

She knew he was aware that, as his chief of security, she had access to his father's files, but that access was limited. She could access files and she could add data, but only the system administrator—Pavel—could *delete* files. And, in the event of his death, the files and administrator authority would pass to his brother Stefan along with the title.

But what Pavel *didn't* realize was that in the interval between his own death and the probate of his will, Sakristos would serve as the credentialed administrator until those credentials transferred to Stefan. She'd managed to insert that little window of opportunity into Dimitri's security without his noticing when she'd set it up initially, and she ought to have used it when he died to make certain her file had been removed. But she'd thought—then—that the previous earl had kept his promise to delete it long since, so she'd seen no reason to risk Pavel's checking the access logs. It would have been bad enough that he might have realized she'd tampered with the files, but it would also have led him to her back door. At the very least, he would have slammed it shut, and she'd been able to visualize several even more unpleasant outcomes.

None of which had been as unpleasant as the ones she'd ended up with.

But once she'd realized Dimitri had lied to her, she'd known she'd have to see to the file's deletion herself. All she needed to do was to arrange Pavel's demise, then use her access before the database fell into Stefan's hands.

Hopefully, Countess Harrington was about to take care of that small task. Sakristos certainly intended to do everything she could to help Harrington, at any rate. It would provide the perfect solution to her problem, with no possible suspicion attaching to her, given the long-standing hatred between Harrington and Pavel Young.

And if the countess should fail, Sakristos could always fall back on Plan B, because whether she was willing to do it for *him* or not, Pavel was quite correct about Georgia Sakristos' ability to arrange a quiet murder or two at need.

And some things were definitely worth killing to escape.

**Chez Berthelsen**
**City of Landing**
**Planet of Manticore**
**Manticore Binary System**
**May 8, 1906**

THE EARL OF NORTH HOLLOW looked up from the remnants of a delicious meal he scarcely remembered tasting as the brown-haired, brown-eyed woman walked into the small, private dining room. Like everyone who could expect to get past Chez Berthelsen's portals, she was well dressed and well groomed—in her case, in a sleekly understated business suit whose elegance went well with the slim briefcase clasped under her left arm.

Her name was Marie-Claire Doisneau, and she looked like precisely what she was: a highly paid, highly skilled attorney who represented a significant number of the City of Landing's more prominent citizens.

Several of whom were also members of the organization known simply as "the Outfit."

Milorad Livitnikov hadn't wanted to help North Hollow locate her, but the earl had insisted, and when Livitnikov proved resistant, he'd pointed out that Honor Harrington wasn't known for moderation where her enemies were concerned. If she knew Summervale had been hired to kill Paul Tankersley, then presumably she also knew *Livitnikov* had been a paid accessory, which gave him and the earl a certain commonality of interest where she was concerned.

North Hollow had actually considered recruiting Livitnikov for the job, or at least using him to recruit others with the necessary skill set. In the end, Livitnikov's obvious nervousness where anything even remotely approaching Harrington's orbit was concerned had decided him against it. The man was too likely to screw up by the

247

numbers just because of how frightened of the bitch he was. Besides, his relationship with Summervale would make him an obvious suspect if something unfortunate were to happen to Harrington. Any investigators would have to look carefully in his direction, and there was no doubt in North Hollow's mind that Livitnikov would turn the Crown's evidence at the merest hint of an indictment.

But Livitnikov had possessed contacts with the Outfit. He might be unwilling to become involved personally, but he'd been prepared to quietly float North Hollow's interest to the proper set of ears. Which was what had brought Doisneau to this meeting...finally.

It had taken far longer than North Hollow had wanted, but as much as Georgia Sakristos' refusal to broker Harrington's murder infuriated him, he'd been forced to admit she had a point about where suspicion would focus if anything happened to the bitch. That suggested he should exercise extreme caution in any arrangements he made, including the caution that hid them from Sakristos, herself. He'd never anticipated that she'd dare to defy him, given his hold over her. And the truth was that any showdown between them might all too easily end in mutual destruction, given all she knew about the North Hollow bodies. Then there was the fact that however resistant she might be to having Harrington killed, it wasn't because of any qualms she might have arranging someone *else's* murder. She'd spent a long time building a successful, lucrative, and above all *safe* (as far as the Ballroom was concerned) identity here in the Star Kingdom. She wasn't about to give it up easily, and if he pushed her hard enough—or if she simply decided he was about do something that would bring the authorities down on her—she just might decide another tragic death in the Young family was in order and take her chances on what Stefan did with their father's files. So any arrangements he might make without her involvement also had to be made without her *knowledge*.

But whatever she thought, Pavel Young wanted the bitch dead, and he had no intention of waiting.

Over the past, endless weeks, he'd become a laughingstock. Oh, no one in his own circle was likely to say anything where he might hear of it. He had too many weapons with which to avenge himself on anyone that foolish! But behind his back, in their private clubs, or in the House of Lords cloakroom, the whispers were there. And however wary of his vengeance members of the Conservative Association or their allies might be, the Opposition newsfaxes and podcast commentators had no qualms at all about speculating breathlessly on what sort of evidence Harrington might possess, or how she intended to deal with him. The sensationalist scandal-mongering 'faxes that catered to the stupid Proles had lined up in droves to help the Opposition blast the bitch's allegations throughout the entire Infonet, as well. And then there were all the other bastards, who—secure in the knowledge that no homicidal maniac was hunting *them*—posted thread after thread on the boards to ridicule how perfectly he was emulating an Old Terran rabbit hiding deep in its burrow to avoid the fox outside it.

He'd become not simply an object of contempt among his equals, but a source of raucous amusement for the unwashed, ignorant mob.

He felt the pressure of his clenched jaw as Doisneau closed the door behind her and walked across to the table, and he forced his jaw muscles to relax.

It wasn't easy. The shame, the humiliation of knowing everyone in Landing, or at least everyone who *mattered*, knew how desperately he was hiding from the bitch burned like acid. He genuinely didn't know which was worse: the humiliation, or the terror. Or the added internal humiliation of knowing how terrified he truly was. The bitch was supposed to be *dead*. Instead, she turned his life into a living hell, and he was done tolerating it.

"Lord North Hollow," Doisneau said as she reached the table.

"Ms. Doisneau." He bobbed his head in acknowledgment and pointed at the facing chair. "Sit, please."

"Of course."

She settled into the chair and laid her briefcase on the table. Then she opened it, reached into it, and withdrew a compact electronic device. She set it on the table, tapped its touchscreen, and studied its display carefully for perhaps ten seconds before she looked back up with a faint smile.

"Chez Berthelsen has a well-deserved reputation for the quality of its security systems, but any conscientious attorney knows it's always best to be certain about these things, Milord. Especially when privileged information is discussed."

"Oh, I certainly agree." North Hollow poured wine into a pair of glasses and passed one across to his guest. She accepted it with a slightly broader smile, sipped, and then set the glass on the table before her.

"I imagine you know why I wanted to speak to you," the earl said, and she cocked her head.

"Under the circumstances, I imagine I do. It might be best for you to lay out your requirements clearly, however."

"My 'requirements' are simple. I want Harrington dead. I want her dead *now*, and I want her dead in a way that can't lead back to me."

"Well, that's certainly concise and to the point." Doisneau's dark eyes twinkled with what looked like genuine amusement.

"Believe me, if I thought there was another approach at the moment, I'd take it," he said bleakly. "Yes, I want her dead, and not just because of what she's saying about me and the way the 'faxes are carrying it. But no matter how careful I am, and no matter how good anyone you might help me contact may be, a lot of people will automatically blame me for anything that happens to her. That's why this has to be handled so discreetly."

"Oh, I'm *always* discreet, Milord."

"Good." North Hollow sipped wine moodily. "To be honest, I'd really prefer to engage your *courtroom* services and sue her for libel. Even if the case ultimately failed, the litigation would bar her from issuing any challenges before the Navy deploys her out of the system. But I can't risk it."

"Actually, and I provide this information free of any charge, Milord, suing her for libel would be a very, *very* bad idea."

"Oh?" North Hollow lowered his glass.

"As you're undoubtedly aware, my client list is extensive," she said. "Among my many clients is the Roualeyn Corporation. They own a château in the Arduus Mountains on Gryphon. A little over a month ago, Denver Summervale was a guest there, and during his stay, a Royal Navy pinnace supporting a Marine training exercise suffered a navigation systems failure and landed not far from the château. There was . . . some unpleasantness when the embarked Marines visited the château, ostensibly to seek directions." Her eyes met North Hollow's very levelly across the table. "While they were there, the senior officer present—a Colonel Ramirez, I believe—had a personal conversation with Mister Summervale."

The color drained from North Hollow's face.

"Speaking in a purely professional sense," she continued, "and based solely on my second- or thirdhand understanding of events, I feel confident Colonel Ramirez violated quite a few of the Star Kingdom's laws in the course of his interview with Mister Summervale. Unfortunately, for reasons I expect you can probably understand, the Roualeyn Corporation's management—and, frankly, Mister Summervale himself—had their own reasons for avoiding any scrutiny of his actions. One must assume, however, that the Colonel obtained whatever he'd come for, given that Mister Summervale was still alive when the Marines returned to their pinnace and departed."

"I see."

North Hollow's jaw clenched again, in fresh shame, as he heard the sick awareness in his own voice. So the bitch *did* have proof, or at least strongly suggestive evidence. Obviously, as Doisneau had just said, it had been illegally obtained, so she couldn't provide it to the Crown without at the very least exposing her toadies to the legal consequences their actions richly deserved. But if he sued her for libel, all her defense team had to do was to play a recording of any confession Summervale might have made. As long as she declined to file legal charges against him—or Summervale's estate, assuming he had one, declined to file charges against *her*—she couldn't be legally compelled to reveal how she'd obtained it. And, as long as analysis proved it was actually Summervale's voice, it would offer her all the legal defense against libel she would ever need, no matter how it had come into her hands.

"You may take my word for it, Milord, that the château's owners and their other business associates are less than happy about this entire episode," Doisneau continued. "By the same token, they have no desire to throw bad money after good by picking an open quarrel with someone who possesses the resources—and friends—Countess Harrington can command. None of them would shed any tears if something untoward were to befall her, however. Which, frankly, is the primary reason I'm here tonight." Her smile took on more than a hint of frost. "Believe me, if any of those business associates objected to my meeting you to discuss your needs, I would—regretfully, of course—have declined your gracious invitation."

"I see," he repeated in a rather different tone. "In that case, may I assume some of those associates of yours might be willing to make certain resources available to me?"

"Not out of their own organization, I'm afraid," she said. "Given Colonel Ramirez's intrusion into their affairs, the possibility is high that an investigation into Countess Harrington's sad fate—assuming, of course, that a sad fate were to overtake her—might lead back to them. After all, as you yourself are aware, suspicion would naturally, if unfairly, focus upon those who might have had a bone to pick with her. It's rather a case of mutual deterrence in that regard. As long as neither the Countess nor her friends draw my associates any more deeply into this unhappy affair, those associates will decline to become actively involved in its resolution."

North Hollow's lips tightened, and she shook her head at him.

"Don't despair, Milord. Their own organization is scarcely the only source for the capabilities you require. And while they must decline to become involved *themselves*, they have no objection to . . . facilitating conversations with unaffiliated individuals suitable to your needs. In this instance, I believe, it might be best to consider a blunt-instrument approach to your problem. One that eschews finesse in favor of extreme effectiveness."

"I certainly have no objection to that sort of approach," North Hollow said slowly. "May I ask why that seems the most advisable option to you, though?"

She sipped more wine with a thoughtful air, then lowered the glass again.

"Frankly," she said then, "it's because the individuals I have in mind, while undeniably effective, are definitely chainsaws, not scalpels. 'Finesse' isn't in their lexicon, I'm afraid, and they've always been a bit reckless. Or perhaps the word I want is *heedless*. Their notion of an assassination normally includes things like bombs or ambushes on public sidewalks with automatic weapons." Her lips twitched in distaste for such crudity. "Unfortunately, they seem unaware of, or at least unconcerned by, the long-term consequences of the collateral damage they leave in their wake . . . or of whom those consequences might splash on. To be honest, while some of my associates have engaged their services in the past, that heedlessness of theirs has made them more and more of a potential liability. Indeed, there's been some discussion about engineering their forcible retirement, and one or two of my associates have suggested that this might be an opportunity to kill multiple birds with a single stone."

"In what way?" he asked.

"Well, you have a problem which needs to be removed. My associates have a vested interest in assisting you, albeit indirectly, in its removal. Ideally, this should be done in a fashion which would prevent any unfortunate connections that might lead back to you or to my associates. Using a team of . . . problem removers who have no direct connection with my associates or with you would be an excellent first step in that direction. And if you were prepared to accept the financial burden of paying for their services, since they would no doubt insist upon receiving at least a portion of their fee in advance, my associates and I could guarantee that the actual arrangements were made by a third party with no direct connection to you or to them. In fact, it's quite probable that the third party in question would never actually exist, so any evidence leading back to their employer would hit a dead end, so to speak." She flashed him a smile. "And just to be certain that it did, my associates would also be amenable to . . . tidying up afterward. Using some of their own employees to guarantee that none of the individuals in question were ever available to assist in any investigations after the fact."

"I see," North Hollow said for a third time, and leaned back in his chair. "And assuming all of this proved feasible, how early an *execution* date, if you'll pardon the expression, might we anticipate?"

"That, I'm afraid, is a tactical question that lies outside my own area of expertise. My understanding, however, is that Countess Harrington is now accompanied by a security team of her own wherever she goes. More than that, her quarters are aboard her ship, even though it's still technically in dockyard hands, and getting to her there or aboard *Hephaestus* would be quite difficult. The good news is that she makes fairly frequent flying visits to Landing, especially to meet with her agent now that her prize money from Hancock has made her a wealthy woman. My sources suggest to me that some of those meetings have less to do with her business affairs and more to do with her own investigators' and agents' efforts to help her reach you to present her challenge. So we can be fairly certain her visits will eventually present a window of opportunity, and her Grayson bodyguards can scarcely be as well read in on threats here in the Star Kingdom as they might be back home in Yeltsin. The problem will be obtaining sufficient warning to take advantage of one of those windows, which suggests it will probably take some time."

"I hope you'll forgive me for observing that, from my perspective, it's a case of the sooner the better," he said.

"Oh, I quite understand that, Milord! And, should you desire to proceed in the fashion I've described, I can see to beginning to make arrangements tomorrow morning."

"What sort of funding will you require? And how do I provide it without its being traceable to me?"

That was the sort of thing Georgia would normally have taken care of for him. This time, unfortunately . . .

"I would think that perhaps a hundred thousand dollars would be in order, as a complete fee," Doisneau said thoughtfully. "Perhaps twenty percent of that would be in order as a down payment. Under ideal circumstances," she smiled coldly, "the remainder of their fee will never be required, of course."

"Of course," he agreed with an equally cold smile.

"I understand you're a betting man, Milord?"

"I've been known to make the occasional wager."

"On sports, I believe? Specifically, on soccer?"

"Yes." He nodded and cocked an eyebrow. "Why?"

"Because, Milord, if you were to contact this bookmaking agency"—she handed him an electronic business chip—"and place a twenty-thousand-dollar bet on the Clarkson Guerriers for this weekend's match against Uplands, I expect you could get very good odds."

"I expect I could!" North Hollow snorted. "The last time I looked, the betting was something like nine-to-one in Uplands' favor!"

"I'm sure it was. The object, however, would be for you to *lose* the bet. My associates have an understanding with this particular agency. When you lose your wager, the funds will disappear into an appropriately anonymous account from which the individuals whose services you require could be paid without any annoying little money trails leading back to my associates . . . or to you."

"Really?" North Hollow cocked his head and regarded her thoughtfully for a moment.

"Odd," he said then. "I feel a sudden urge to lay down a bet on the Guerriers. I'm not usually the sort to plunge at such unfavorable odds, but I have the strangest suspicion"—he bestowed an unpleasant smile upon her, feeling better than he had in weeks—"that *this* one will be money very well spent."

**HMSS *Hephaestus***
**Manticore Planetary Orbit**
**Manticore Binary System**
**May 21, 1906 PD**

BRANDY BOLGEO'S earbud beeped a priority attention tone, and she frowned as she tapped to accept the connection.

"Lieutenant Bolgeo," she said. Whoever had pinged her knew that already, but there were formalities to observe.

"Lieutenant, this is Commodore Allenby," a voice said, and Brandy's eyes narrowed. Allenby was *Hephaestus'* executive officer. Why was someone that monumentally high in the space station's food chain personally coming?

"Yes, Sir. What can I do for you?"

"Do you have someone down there you can turn the duty over to for a half hour or so?"

Narrowed eyes turned into a frown. It was barely ninety minutes till the end of her current watch, and she was up to her elbows figuratively speaking—in HMS *Trident*'s hydroponics power systems. She and Senior Chief Stúdlin were closing in on the infuriating glitch that had landed the tin can in the yard, and she hated to break off now. More to the point, though, this close to the end of her normal watch, what could be so urgent—or pressing, at least—for Commodore Allenby to be interrupting it?

"I do, Sir," she said a bit slowly. "My watch ends in about ninety minutes, though, Sir," she pointed out.

"I understand that. I really need to see you in person as soon as possible, though. So, if you can, I need you to hand over to someone else and report to my office."

"Of course, Sir. I can be there within ten or fifteen minutes."

"Thank you, Lieutenant. That will be fine. I'll see you then."

Brandy grimaced, trying to think of anything she might have

done that required intervention from on high, and especially intervention that couldn't wait another hour and a half. Nothing came to mind, though, and she pinged Joseph MacCann, the junior-grade lieutenant she was supposed to be mentoring.

"Yes, Ma'am?" he replied in her earbud from the other side of the repair bay, where he and Stúdlin were monitoring the output signals of the control circuits she'd been testing.

"Just got a call from on high, Joe," she said. "Dunno why, but the XO wants to see me. So looks like you're in charge until Lieutenant Commander Higman turns up."

"Uh, yes, Ma'am."

She heard the trepidation in his reply and smiled. Not all that long ago, *she'd* have sounded just as nervous as he did.

"The senior chief will keep you out of trouble, Joe," she assured him.

"Yes, Ma'am."

He sounded much more cheerful, and her smile deepened. She waited for a slow five-count and her smile turned wicked. Then—

"Just remember, though," she said in her sternest tone, "he's only a senior chief. *You're* the officer in charge now. So make sure you don't break anything while I'm gone!"

"Yes, Ma'am!" he said so quickly she could almost see him popping reflexively to attention.

She was still chuckling when she stepped into the lift car and tapped her destination code.

✧  ✧  ✧

"Lieutenant Bolgeo is here, Sir," Commodore Allenby's yeoman said into his hush mic. He listened for a moment, then looked back at Brandy.

"He's expecting you, Ma'am. Please, go on in."

He tapped the stud that opened the door to Allenby's office, and Brandy marched in and came to attention.

"Lieutenant Bolgeo reporting, Sir," she said.

"Stand easy, Lieutenant," Allenby said. The XO was a quiet, intense-looking redhead with a face that was naturally designed for smiling. There was no smile on it today, Brandy noted.

"In fact," he continued, "have a seat, Lieutenant."

"Thank you, Sir."

She settled into the indicated chair a bit tentatively. Despite her best effort, she knew there was an edge of apprehension in her expression, but she called it firmly to heel and cocked her head attentively.

"I wanted to see you in person, because there are some things that you just don't throw at good officers cold over the com, Lieutenant," Allenby said after a moment. "Especially not at officers who've already had the kind of war you've had." He raised a hand as he saw the alarm flicker in her eyes. "This is *not* an ass-chewing!" he said quickly. "In fact, we couldn't be happier with your performance here on *Hephaestus*. And I promise it's not bad news about your family." He shook his head. "Your dad's an old friend, though, and that's another reason I wanted to tell you this in person."

"Tell me what, Sir?" Brandy asked when he paused.

"It's about *Timberwolf*," Allenby said in a suddenly bleaker tone. "I hate like hell to have to tell you this, but she got hammered last month. We just found out. It sounds like the Peeps were probing the Grendelsbane perimeter, and her division got jumped by a light-cruiser squadron."

Brandy's face tightened, and he sighed.

"We don't have a complete report, but she got hit hard. Heavy casualties, I'm afraid. And the initial damage survey doesn't sound good. In fact"—he met her eyes levelly—"I don't think she's repairable. I could be wrong about that, but even if I'm not, the truth is that at her age they probably won't return her to service, anyway. Not in anything remotely like an immediate time frame, at least. It just wouldn't be cost-effective, given how strapped we are for yard space and personnel right now. Which means you won't be taking over her engineering department after all."

Brandy's stomach clenched. She'd never even seen *Timberwolf*, and yet in her own mind, the destroyer had already been "her" ship. Its complement had already been "her" people. And now this! First, *Cassandra*, and now *Timberwolf*...

"I'm sorry, Lieutenant," Allenby said compassionately. "I know how much an officer like you must have been looking forward to the new slot, the new challenges. But even though we haven't heard anything officially from BuPers yet, I'm pretty sure there's already a message somewhere in the queue telling you you won't be reporting aboard *Timberwolf*. I just wanted to make sure you heard it from a live human being first, before the new orders came at you with no warning."

"I appreciate that, Sir. A lot," Brandy said quietly, and she did.

"I know how disappointing it must be," Allenby said. "On the other hand, while it may be cold comfort just at the moment, I'm confident BuPers will find a new slot for you pretty damned quickly. God knows we're all running too hard to leave an officer of your ability sidelined any longer than we can help! And I know what you really want at a time like this is shipboard duty, not getting stuck in a repair yard somewhere. From what I've seen so far, I expect Admiral Cortez thinks that would be a better use of your time and services, too. In the meantime, though, I guarantee you *Hephaestus* will be glad to have you for as long as we get to keep you."

"Thank you, Sir."

It wasn't as if there were anything else she could've said, and she tried to put at least a little enthusiasm into her tone. From Allenby's expression, she'd been less than completely successful, but he only nodded.

"I think you can probably take the rest of your watch to process this, Lieutenant," he said. "And, again, I can't tell you how sorry I am."

"I understand, Sir. And thank you for telling me in person." She managed a smile. "I know you can't have enjoyed it."

"If our positions were reversed, Lieutenant, I'm sure you would have done the same thing. And probably not enjoyed it one bit more."

"Probably not, Sir. And I know you've got a lot of other things on your plate, so I especially appreciate your making time for this." Brandy inhaled deeply, then stood. "Permission to withdraw, Sir?"

"Permission granted, Lieutenant. And, if I may make a suggestion, I'd recommend screening your father. He's been there and done that a time or two, and right this minute, I can't think of a better person to talk this out with."

"Now that, Sir, is a very good suggestion, I think. Thank you."

She braced to attention again, briefly, then turned and walked out of the office.

**Brancusi Tower**
**and**
**Regiano's Restaurant**
**City of Landing**
**Planet of Manticore**
**Manticore Binary System**
**June 4, 1906**

ANDREW LA FOLLET STEPPED OUT of the air limo into the incredible midday heat. He'd known from his research that the City of Landing was far warmer than anything his own homeworld might have inflicted upon him, but it had been an intellectual sort of knowledge. Nothing in his experience had prepared him for the reality, and he wondered how Lady Harrington, whose homeworld was even cooler than Grayson, had put up with Manticore's sweltering heat during her studies at Saganami Island.

Or now, for that matter.

This was her fourth visit since she'd killed Denver Summervale, and those trips had made the man responsible for keeping her alive nervous. He'd become even more nervous with each, but at least he'd managed to enlist Commander Chandler, HMS *Nike*'s executive officer, in managing the Steadholder's shuttle flights. He didn't *think* the Steadholder had caught them at it, although he wasn't positive she hadn't. But until she said something about it, Commander Chandler was quietly omitting her—and her armsmen—from any passenger manifests submitted to Traffic Control. Those manifests weren't legally required, although it was customary to provide them, and LaFollet could at least hope that the commander's creative "oversight" made it more difficult for any unfriendly souls to predict the Steadholder's movements.

Given that the Earl of North Hollow had already paid for Lady Harrington's murder once, that struck Andrew LaFollet as a very good idea.

261

Now the major drew a deep breath of hot, early-afternoon Landing air, grateful for the cooling effect of his uniform's Manticoran smart fabric, and scanned the rooftop landing pad carefully. Passenger-list misdirection or no, anyone trying to monitor the Steadholder's whereabouts would be keeping an eye on the Brancusi Tower pad, given that the tower housed the business offices of Willard Neufsteiler, her Manticoran prize agent and financial manager.

Who, at the moment, was managing rather more than Lady Harrington's money. Which was why he was waiting to greet her this afternoon.

The major completed his examination of the landing pad, then moved forward to clear the Steadholder's way. She stepped out of the limo behind him, and he didn't need to actually see her expression to visualize the quizzical resignation in it. Not that he was particularly reassured by it. She might *think* she'd resigned herself to her armsmens' permanent presence in her life, but she was still far from developing the proper mindset. She seemed constitutionally incapable of understanding that keeping her alive was the most important thing in those armsmens' lives.

James Candless and Eddie Howard fell in behind her as Neufsteiler stepped forward to greet her.

"Milady," he said. He extended his hand, and the Steadholder nodded as she took it.

"Willard," she replied, and LaFollet saw something flicker in Neufsteiler's eyes.

The major recognized the Manticoran's dismay in that flicker. The Steadholder looked better than she had before the duel with Summervale, yet her brown eyes remained bleak, hard and dark with icy, focused purpose that held the pain at bay. Mostly, anyway.

LaFollet approved of Willard Neufsteiler, for several reasons. The banker's sorrow as he saw that bleakness yet again was one of them.

Now Neufsteiler led the way to a crystoplast-walled lift shaft that ran down the five-hundred-story tower's flank. He waved the Steadholder—and her armsmen—into the waiting capsule and punched a destination into the control panel, then turned to Lady Harrington and waved a hand at the sunlit city beyond the transparent wall as the capsule sped downward.

"It's such a lovely day that I thought we might meet in Regiano's," he said. "If that's all right with you, Dame Honor? I reserved an upper section to ensure privacy."

His tone was almost hopeful, and Lady Harrington cocked her head at him.

"That sounds fine, Willard," she said.

LaFollet had been afraid she'd say that.

"Excuse me, My Lady, but that's a security risk," he said. "We haven't had time to check out the restaurant."

"I think we can live with that, Andrew," she said, eyeing him a bit repressively, but he shook his head.

"My Lady, you've warned this North Hollow you're coming for him. It would solve his problem neatly if something happened to you first."

LaFollet saw Neufsteiler's blink of surprise from the corner of his eye, but he never looked away from the Steadholder. She held his gaze with her own for a couple of heartbeats, then her nostrils flared ever so slightly.

"The same idea had occurred to me," she acknowledged quietly, "but I don't plan on jumping at shadows. Besides, no one knew we were coming. Even the newsies missed us this time around."

"The fact that we *think* no one knows is no proof they don't, My Lady, and you're not exactly the hardest person to identify if someone sees you. Please, I'd feel much better if you stuck to your original schedule and met in Mr. Neufsteiler's offices."

"Dame Honor, if you think it would be better—" Neufsteiler began, but the Steadholder shook her head.

"I think it might be *safer*, Willard, but that doesn't necessarily make it better." She touched LaFollet's shoulder. "Major LaFollet is determined to keep me alive. We're still working on how much veto right that gives him—aren't we, Andrew?"

"I'm not asking for veto right, My Lady. All I want is a little commonsense caution."

"Which I'm willing to give you, within limits." She released his shoulder. "I know I'm a trial to you, Andrew, but I've spent my entire life going where I wanted without armed guards. I'm willing to admit I can't get away with that any longer, but there are limits to the precautions I'm willing to take."

LaFollet opened his mouth to argue, but then he looked into those eyes again and sighed.

"You're my Steadholder, My Lady," he said, instead of what he'd actually wanted to say. "If you want to go to a restaurant, we'll go, and I hope I'm worrying about nothing. But if anything *does* happen, I expect you to take *my* orders."

She gazed back down at him for a moment, and he let her see the stubbornness in his own eyes.

"All right, Andrew," she said finally. "If something happens, you're in charge. I'll even put up with your telling me 'I told you so.'"

"Thank you, My Lady. I hope you don't have to."

She twitched a small smile, patted his shoulder again, then looked back at Neufsteiler.

"In the meantime, Willard, where are we on our Grayson funds transfer?"

"We're doing fine, Milady," Neufsteiler said, "though I'm afraid the transaction was a bit more complicated than you apparently assumed. Since you're a Manticoran subject and your major financial holdings are here, you're technically subject to Manticoran corporate taxes even on out-system investments. There are ways around that, however, and—"

LaFollet tuned out the banker's explanation as the lift car continued to slide downward and he focused on just how *much* he hoped he wouldn't have to tell the Steadholder he'd told her so.

✧  ✧  ✧

Andrew LaFollet was an unhappy man as he stood behind the Steadholder's chair on one point of the triangular platform. Candless and Howard stood on the other two points, backs turned to him as they gazed out over Regiano's Restaurant, and he doubted they were any happier than he was.

The restaurant itself was pleasant enough, but it was also high-ceilinged, sprawling up and down a five-story atrium that reminded the major of a picture he'd seen from an ancient, pre-diaspora artist named Escher. It lacked the inverted perspective of the artwork, but its tables floated in midair, accessed by flights of steps that sprang from the restaurant floor or reached out from its walls with no apparent rhyme or reason. And without any visible means of support, either. The architecture wasn't what made LaFollet less than delighted, however. Indeed, under other circumstances, he would have thoroughly enjoyed the airy sense of spaciousness and the view of Landing's green belts through its crystoplast walls.

Under the current circumstances, he felt entirely too much like a target. Those walls were like a fishbowl, offering entirely too good a view into the restaurant from the outside. Worse, the table Neufsteiler had reserved was near the very top of the atrium, which provided a direct line of sight—or fire—to it and the people seated at it from almost any place in the entire restaurant. The only good thing, from LaFollet's perspective, was that those same sightlines made it an excellent lookout post, and he tried to focus on that instead of the Steadholder's refusal to take basic precautions.

She and Neufsteiler spent the meal discussing her various financial arrangements. When the servers cleared away the dishes, then vanished down the platform stairs, it was time for the real reason she'd come planetside.

"Well?" she asked quietly.

"You can't get to him, Milady," Neufsteiler replied, equally quietly. "He's holed up in his official residence, and he's only coming out to visit the Lords."

LaFollet listened to the conversation with only a corner of his attention, never interrupting his methodical eye-sweep of the restaurant. Lady Harrington's unhappiness with Neufsteiler's answer was obvious to him, though, and she gathered Nimitz into her lap as she considered it.

"Are you certain he's not coming out at all?" she asked finally.

"Positive." Neufsteiler leaned closer to her, his voice even lower. "We've gotten someone inside his staff, Milady. He's only a chauffeur, but he's in a position to see all their movement schedules."

"I've *got* to get to him," the Steadholder murmured. "There has to be some time—even if it's only for a few minutes—when I can catch him. All I need is long enough to issue the challenge, Willard." She frowned down into her wine glass. "If he's going to Parliament, then maybe what we need is someone inside that end of the pipeline. He's got to be moving around the building. If we can get hold of his schedule, then maybe—"

"Milady, I'll try, but the odds are mighty long. He *knows* you're hunting him, and he's got the advantage of being planetside all the time. Getting his schedule with enough advance warning for you to get down here and take advantage of it . . . ?" Neufsteiler shook his head.

Below them, three men entered the restaurant through the front entrance and paused just inside the foyer, scanning the tables, obviously looking for someone who'd already been seated. LaFollet's eyes touched them for a moment, then moved on as the maître d' started toward them.

"Well, we're already spending over eighty thousand a day on it," Neufsteiler said with a crooked smile. "A few more operatives won't pad the bill by *that* much."

"Good man. In that case, I think—"

Three more men came into the restaurant through the side entrance and looked casually around. One of them glanced up at the Steadholder's table for just a moment, then made eye contact with one of the three talking to the maître d'.

A lightning bolt shot through Andrew LaFollet, and his right hand flashed to his pulser as two of the new arrivals reached inside their unsealed jackets.

"*Down!*"

The fingers of his right hand closed on his pulser butt and his left hand flashed out and fastened on Lady Harrington's shoulder like a claw even as he barked out the single word.

Her surprise was obvious as he yanked her out of her chair. Her head started to turn in his direction, but he hurled her down—and under the table—with all his strength, then flung himself down on top of her. Nimitz exploded out of the high chair Regiano's staff had provided for him, and even through the ice-cold focus of his training, LaFollet felt a stab of fear as the newcomers' hands came out filled with weapons and the treecat bounded toward the stairs. If he started down those stairs in the face of that kind of firepower—

The Steadholder's hand shot out. Somehow, she got a grip on the 'cat and dragged him back, pinning him down, just as the snarling whine of a pulser filled the restaurant. Explosive darts tore up the stairs Nimitz would have used and shredded the end of the dining platform, and Willard Neufsteiler cried out as a jagged splinter drove into his back.

Candless grabbed the banker, jerking him out of the line of fire with one hand, and a pulser had appeared in his other hand. Lady Harrington tried to rise, reaching out toward Neufsteiler with her free hand even as she fought to keep Nimitz under control with the other.

"*No*, goddamn it!" LaFollet snarled.

He slammed her back down with an elbow even as his pulser tracked onto the killer who'd produced the sawed-off pulse rifle from under his jacket. He squeezed the trigger and hypersonic darts ripped through the would-be assassin in a spray of blood. The pulse rifle flew through the air as the gunman went down, and the screams began as the restaurant's other patrons realized what was happening.

Candless and Howard were up and firing, too, and LaFollet rolled off the Steadholder, coming up on one knee and laying his pulser barrel over his forearm for steadiness. More exploding darts ripped into the platform, and Eddie Howard grunted in anguish and went down even as Candless' fire took down a second assassin. LaFollet killed a third, then swore again as at least a dozen panicked diners surged for the exits and into his line of fire.

Candless managed to nail one more of the gunmen before the fugitives blocked his fire, and LaFollet came to his feet, trying to get a bead on the two survivors.

"*Shit!*" he snarled as they vanished into the surge of fleeing customers. He couldn't fire into that crowd, but that didn't mean *they* couldn't fire *out* of it.

"Stay *down*, My Lady!" he barked, as Lady Harrington started to push up to her knees. "There were at least two more of them! I think they're using the crowd for cover to get out of here, but if they try another shot—"

The Steadholder went flat again, still clutching Nimitz. But the 'cat's fury was ebbing—a bit, at least—and she released him cautiously. He leapt up onto the damaged table and crouched there, still hissing and ready to attack, but under control, and she turned to crawl toward Eddie Howard.

The armsman was down, trying to staunch the blood spurting from his thigh with one hand, and she whipped her belt purse out from under her tunic. She wrapped the strap around his leg, above the wound, and jerked the crude tourniquet tight. He sighed then and slumped sideways, dropping the pulser he'd clung to until unconsciousness took him. The Steadholder scooped up the fallen weapon and crawled over to the moaning Neufsteiler.

A raw-looking stump of wood, a centimeter across at the base, stuck out of his bloody shoulder, and she caught his head, turning it to look into his eyes. They were dark but clear, and she sighed in relief and patted his cheek.

"Hang on, Willard. Help's on its way," she said, and looked back up as the restaurant finished emptying and LaFollet lowered his pulser at last. He surveyed the carnage, the four ripped and torn bodies, and the spreading pools of blood, then looked down at her.

"I think we made it, My Lady." He went to one knee beside Howard, checking the tourniquet. "Good work with that belt, My Lady. We might have lost him without it."

"And it would've been my fault," she said quietly. LaFollet turned his head and she looked back at him levelly. "I should have listened to you."

"Well, to be perfectly honest, I didn't *really* think he'd try something this brazen myself," LaFollet admitted, and she nodded. Clearly, she had no more doubt who'd been behind it than he did. "I was just being cautious," he continued, "and, for that matter, you're right, My Lady. He couldn't have had them waiting for us, or they'd have tried sooner. In fact, it was seeing them come in together and how hard they were scanning the crowd that caught my attention." He shook his head. "He must've had them on standby, just waiting for someone to tell them where to find you. We were lucky, My Lady."

"No, Major. *I* was lucky; *you* were good. Very good, all of you. Remind me to think about raises all around when Willard's patched up."

LaFollet snorted. It wasn't much of a joke, but it was more than most people could have managed, and he waved an index finger at her.

"Don't worry about raises, My Lady," he said, as the first LCPD officers charged into the restaurant from the street with weapons ready. "We're all indecently rich by Grayson standards already. But the *next* time I give you some advice, promise to spend at least a few minutes considering that I might be right."

**House of Lords**
**City of Landing**
**Planet of Manticore**
**Manticore Binary System**
**June 7, 1906 PD**

"I DON'T KNOW if this was a good idea, Dad," Michelle Henke said quietly as she and her father climbed out of the air limo on the House of Lords landing apron. A command tapped into her father's uni-link sent the limo emblazoned with the Gold Peak coat of arms off to its assigned parking space, and he paused to straighten his tunic's lapels before he looked at her.

"Frankly, it's a *terrible* idea." Edward Anson Winton-Henke, the Earl of Gold Peak, was equally quiet. "And Allen's going to pitch three kinds of fit when he hears about it. Especially when he figures out what we—*I*—had to do with it." His lips twitched briefly. "I can live with that. It's where this is going to end for *her* that really worries me, sweetheart. In fact, it breaks my heart. But I couldn't tell her no when she asked me to help." He wrapped one arm around Michelle and smiled a crooked, bittersweet smile. "Got that problem with both my girls, really."

Michelle blinked suddenly misty eyes and nodded. Her parents had regarded Honor Harrington as a second daughter ever since she and Michelle had roomed together at Saganami Island. In all that time, Honor had never once presumed upon her connection with the Queen of Manticore's uncle or asked him for any sort of favor any more than she'd ever presumed upon the fact that Michelle Henke was Elizabeth's cousin . . . and that Michelle herself stood fourth in succession for the crown.

Today she'd finally asked, and the potential consequences terrified Michelle. Not for herself, but for the closest friend she'd ever had.

"God, I wish *someone* could tell her no! That someone could convince her that if she keeps this up—"

"She knows all that, Mike," her father interrupted. "Do you think for one second she *doesn't*? This is *Honor* we're talking about. She knows exactly what she's doing, and, frankly, I don't blame her one damned bit." Gold Peak's jaw clenched. "I've known the Youngs for decades. Dimitri Young was beneath contempt, and I've known Pavel was at least as bad as his father ever since that business with Honor at the Academy. But until he had Paul murdered, I hadn't even begun to realize how far beneath it he truly is."

Michelle's face tightened. She and Paul Tankersley were—had been—almost exactly the same age, and they'd always been close, but in many ways, Paul had been even closer to her father than to her. He'd been the younger son of her father's sister Frederica, and after Frederica's husband Roland's death, Edward Winton-Henke had taken over much of the father's role in Paul's life, as well. No wonder Paul's death had hit them all with such brutal force, even when they'd believed the duel had arisen spontaneously. They still weren't privy to Honor's evidence that it *hadn't* been a spontaneous quarrel, but none of them doubted that that evidence existed. She was obviously protecting someone, someone who'd gotten the proof for her, and that, too, was just like Honor Harrington. But now—

"And then, not content with having Paul killed, he sends gunmen with automatic weapons—*military grade* weapons—into a *public restaurant* to murder Honor when she calls him on it?!" Gold Peak continued. "Eleven casualties, Mike—*eleven*—and it's only God's own mercy all the dead were gunmen. And, from a political standpoint, at least, that none of the wounded were hit by Honor's Graysons."

Michelle nodded soberly. She'd known Pavel Young entirely too long, yet, like her father, even she had been stunned by *that* bit of insanity.

"I would've helped her even before Regiano's, if she'd asked," her father said bleakly. "After that?" His eyes were even bleaker than his voice and his lips worked as if he wanted to spit. "I knew she was right about him already. This only proves it. Well, proves that and also that—from everything *I* can see—he'll go right on trying to kill her through one proxy or another until he succeeds...unless she stops him. So now it's a total no-brainer for me."

"You're right," Michelle sighed. "About North Hollow, I mean. He *will* keep trying, no matter what. I used to think he was just a terminal narcissist with sociopathic tendencies. Now I think he's certifiably insane. No one with two working neurons thinks anyone but him was behind that Regiano's hit, and even he had to know that'd be the case before he ordered it. But he went ahead anyway." She shook her head. "I don't see how anyone who *wasn't* insane could've thought for a heartbeat he could get away with that in the long run! Even if the law can't touch him—yet; I'll guarantee you the Crown Prosecutor's already got a *ton* of investigators digging into the whole thing—if he had managed to kill her, it would only have been a matter of time before *someone* caught up with him for it! Howard Clinkscales would've hunted him to the ends of the galaxy, and he wouldn't have given a single solitary damn about 'due process,' either! For that matter, Benjamin Mayhew would've sent the Grayson *Army* after him and *dared* anyone to get in his way!"

"They'd have to get in line." Gold Peak snorted harshly. "I'll tell you God's honest truth, Mike. If Honor can't find a way to get to him and do the job, then I will *damned* well do it for her. In fact, that's what I should've told her instead of even mentioning the Coswell Protocol when she came to me. I tried to, actually. I even told her—*asked* her—to let *me* challenge the bastard, instead, because he was less likely to see me coming and hide from me." He shook his head, brown eyes dark. "She wasn't having it. And, God help me, I couldn't fight her on it."

"But if she does it this way—"

"Mike, she's out of time." Gold Peak's cold voice turned iron-hard. "She has to deal with him now, before he sends more killers after her and this time kills someone she loves. Someone *else* she loves, I mean. You and I both know that, but every goddammed politician in Landing is trying to stop her. Hell, the *Admiralty's* trying to stop her! You know as well as I do that the real reason BuShips is expediting *Nike's* repairs is so that White Haven and Caparelli can assign her to some out-system squadron and keep Honor away from North Hollow! For that matter, according to a couple of people who ought to know, White Haven actually *ordered* her not to meet North Hollow."

Michelle's eyes widened. Earl White Haven had tried to *order* Honor not to challenge North Hollow to a duel? That was—

"That would've been an illegal order, Dad!"

"And your point is?" Gold Peak snorted again. "Hamish Alexander's one of my best friends, Mike, but once he gets his teeth into something, God Himself can't talk him out of it! And he knows exactly what will happen to Honor's career if she kills a peer of the realm in a duel. Of course he tried to stop it . . . in his own inimitable, autocratic fashion. And when that didn't work, he put his head together with Caparelli. Oh, and just to gild the lily, Allen begged *Elizabeth* to order Honor off North Hollow! That was before Regiano's, of course. I suspect that after *that* little affair Hamish has probably changed his tune, but no one else has. Everybody who isn't trying to stop this because they see political disaster looming is trying to stop it because they're desperate to save Honor from herself. And I know up here"—he tapped his temple with an index finger—"that, in a lot of ways, I should be doing exactly the same thing."

"The Duke asked *Elizabeth* to order Honor not to challenge him?" Michelle asked.

"He did."

"Then when he finds out about this, what happens in the Cabinet?"

"You mean"—her father twitched a smile which, for all his anger, flickered with genuine amusement—"do I get replaced as Foreign Secretary?"

"Something like that, yes."

"I doubt it. For a lot of reasons. Including the fact that Allen knows as well as we do that Honor's absolutely right about North Hollow. If it ever comes out that I've helped her this way, I might have to step down because of the shitstorm the Opposition will raise, of course. And I won't be the only one the shit splatters on, either. But if that happens, it happens, and this time the political establishment and even Allen Summervale can piss up a rope, as far as I'm concerned. Besides, if he asked for my resignation, he'd have to explain to your cousin why he'd done it, and she's flat out refused to intervene. In fact, instead of saying a word to Honor about it, she ordered *Allen* to stay the hell out of her way!"

"She did?" It was a day for surprises, Michelle realized.

"Firmly, as a matter of fact. And not just because of how much she—hell, the entire Star Kingdom—owes Honor, either. I think it was—"

Gold Peak cut himself off with a curt headshake, then glanced at his chrono.

"We'd better get a move on. This is one maiden address I don't want to miss."

✦ ✦ ✦

Isaac McCallum looked up when the private lift shaft's door opened, and his eyebrows rose in astonished recognition as a tall woman stepped out of it into the House Chamber's vestibule, with an auburn-haired, green-uniformed man at her heels. That lift shaft bypassed all of the public entry points and security points, but only formally seated members of the House were authorized to use it, and although the newcomer wore formal red-and-black robes over the scarlet and gold of the Order of King Roger, she most definitely was not a seated member of the House. Which made her sudden appearance a matter of pressing professional interest to the man who was the House of Lords Sergeant-at-Arms.

She started across the vestibule toward the Chamber's open doors, but he stepped away from his own position just inside them and intercepted her on the threshold.

"Excuse me, Milady," he said, his expression polite but unyielding. "May I ask what brings you here?"

"I intend to address the House," she replied.

"I don't recall seeing you on the day's agenda, Milady," he observed.

"That's because I'm not on it."

"Then I'm afraid it will be impossible for you to—"

"I'm here under the Coswell Protocol, Mister McCallum," she said, and he closed his mouth with a snap. The Coswell Protocol? How the hell had she even *heard* of the Coswell Protocol? He didn't think it had been used more than twice—maybe three times—in the entire history of the Star Kingdom!

"Milady," he said after a brief pause, "how does the Coswell Protocol apply in this case?"

"Because I'm under orders to depart the Star Kingdom with my ship as soon as her repairs are completed, and supervising those repairs is eating up more and more of my time. That means it will be impossible for me to schedule my maiden address in the normal fashion. I happened to have some free time today, but that may well not be true again between now and my departure date. And, to be honest, Mister McCallum, it's long past time I took my seat in the Lords."

"But there are right ways and wrong ways to go about that, Milady. For that matter, there are right ways and wrong ways to invoke Coswell, and this—"

"I don't intend to stand here and debate with you." A snap of command crept into that crisp, Sphinxian voice, and it was much colder than it had been. "The same time constraints that have compelled me to be here today mean that, frankly, I don't have the time to waste. So either stand aside or else invite Baron Eastlake over here so I can . . . explain the situation to him."

She waved an impatient arm across the chamber at the Speaker, and McCallum's expression tightened. He glared at her for a moment, then tapped his personal com link.

"Yes?" a voice said in his earbud.

"I'm sorry to disturb you, Milord, but I think you'd better come over here. We have a . . . situation."

McCallum looked across the large chamber as the Speaker turned. They'd known one another a long time, and he half expected Eastlake to rip his head off for bothering him with some sort of routine matter. But then the Speaker must have recognized the intruder, because he stood up abruptly and strode across to them.

"How may I serve you, Milady?" he asked in a wary tone as he arrived.

"By giving me leave to address the House," she replied flatly, and something flickered in his eyes. Something that might have been a ghost of sympathy overlaid by a much stronger awareness of the potential disaster rising sharklike from the depths.

"I'm afraid that's out of the question today, Milady. I could put you on the agenda for early tomorrow afternoon, but that's absolutely the soonest—"

"Forgive me, Milord, but I'm afraid that won't work." Eastlake closed his mouth with an almost audible snap as she cut him off. "As I've explained to Mister McCallum, I'm under orders to expedite my ship's repairs and depart the system as soon as possible. And once I *do* depart, it may be months before I return. That means I simply don't have time to do this through the normal channels of protocol. And that, Milord, is why I'm here under the Coswell Protocol."

Eastlake's eyes widened. Who the hell had told her about the *Coswell Protocol*? He doubted more than ten percent—if that many—of the Peers even knew about that arcane bit of the House Rules. Its existence was buried in the archives—not even included in a new peer's initial briefing on the House's rules, for God's sake. Only a compulsive rules mechanic—or someone who'd decided on a deep dive into those archives—could possibly have told her about it. And how had she gotten access to the House Chamber without being stopped by Security at one of the public portals? Or without someone at least having warned McCallum she was on the way?!

His eyes narrowed again as suspicion struck. Just as only someone intimately familiar with the House of Lords' procedures and protocol would have known about the Coswell Protocol, only a seated member of the House could have given her the security access code for the peers' private lift shaft. Which, given her close friendship with Michelle Henke . . .

*Wonderful, Sergios*, he thought bitterly. *The Prime Minister wants her as far from North Hollow as we can get her, and the Queen's uncle is conniving to get her into the House when she knows he's here. It's got to be him, which means I'll be pissing him—and maybe the Queen herself—off if I try to stop it! But God only knows where it'll end if I don't stop it right here!*

Well, that wasn't entirely accurate. Only God might *know* where it would end, but Sergios Kappopoulos didn't need precognition to know its final outcome wouldn't be anything remotely good.

"Milady," he said, "the Coswell Protocol hasn't been used in at least fifty or sixty T-years!"

"Perhaps not. It's still a valid procedure under the House's Rules, isn't it?"

"Well, perhaps *technically*, but—"

"Then I'm afraid I must insist upon invoking it."

"Milady, with all due respect, if you can be here today, I feel confident you could coordinate a time properly with my office."

"Not in my judgment, Milord." Her voice was inflexible soprano steel.

"Then your judgment is questionable," Eastlake said sharply. "And this House has rules and procedures for a reason. It's neither proper nor seemly for someone to twist their clearly intended function for his or her personal convenience!"

"I regret that that's what you think I'm doing," she replied in that same coldly level tone of voice. "Despite which, I intend to invoke the protocol. Today."

"I think not!" he said, even more sharply as he sensed other peers rising, flowing toward the door as the confrontation attracted them.

"Milord Speaker," she said, "I've approached you as a peer of the realm and a serving officer of the Crown who, given the exigencies of the Service, has no option but to invoke the Coswell Protocol. Do you seriously intend to deny me that right?"

"I do!"

"In that case, Milord, I will be appearing on *Into the Fire* tonight to explain to Ms. Prince and Mister DuCain—and to their viewership—what happened here today. I will also publicly invite the Government—and you, specifically—to explain why my right as a peer of the realm and a naval officer was capriciously denied." Her ice-cold smile showed a white flash of tooth. "I rather doubt you *or* the Prime Minister will enjoy the questions that will undoubtedly provoke."

Eastlake flushed crimson as she put her pulser squarely to his head. The temptation to call her bluff flashed through him, but she only looked at him with those unflinching brown eyes, and he realized it *wasn't* a bluff. She'd do it. She truly would. It would be professional suicide for any naval officer, but no one could see those eyes and believe for one moment that she hadn't already decided that was an acceptable price. And if she added *that* to the fire . . .

*Damn it—damn it! She knows how hard everybody's fighting to avoid the three-ring disaster this is certain to turn into! And if I let her do this, Allen will have a fit. But not as big a one as if she really does go on the air. . . .*

More of the other peers were moving closer. Some of them stopped, and he heard the mutter and buzz of sudden, animated conversation behind him as they recognized the newcomer. This was sliding rapidly from bad to worse, he thought, and there wasn't one damned thing he could do about it.

"Very well!" he snapped finally, throwing up his hands in helpless, furious resignation. He glared at her a moment longer, then strode angrily back to his desk, seated himself, and banged his ceremonial gavel on the rest under its microphone.

"Be seated, My Lords and Ladies," his voice boomed, and the gavel fell again, so hard the handle snapped. "Be seated, My Lords and Ladies!"

Silence fell, and he cleared his throat.

"My Lords and Ladies, I crave your indulgence," he said harshly. "I apologize for this interruption of your deliberations, but under the rules of this House, I have no choice.

"I have just been reminded of a seldom used rule. It is *customary*"—he turned to glare at the newcomer, still standing beside the Sergeant-at-Arms—"for new peers to send decent notice to this House, and to be sponsored, before taking their place among us. Under certain circumstances, however, including the exigencies of the Queen's Service, new members may be delayed in taking their seats or, as I have just been reminded, may appear before us at a time convenient to them if their duty to the Crown will make it impossible for them to appear at one convenient to the House as a whole.

"That rule has just been invoked, My Lords and Ladies," he said heavily. "A member who wishes to make her maiden address to the House informs me this may be her last opportunity for some months due to the demands of the Service. As such, I have no choice but to permit this irregularity."

The buzz of conversation rose once again, louder even than before, as he waved a curt invitation to the woman standing in the doorway.

She crossed to stand before his desk, then turned to face the House. Her hands rose to draw back the cowl of the Knights of the Order of King Roger, and the Earl of North Hollow lunged up out of his seat with a strangled cry.

Honor Harrington smiled coldly up at him as he stood frozen, only his head moving, as it swiveled back and forth like a trapped animal's, and something cold and merciless flickered in her icy eyes. She let him stand for a long, agonizing moment, and then looked away, sweeping her gaze across the assembled nobles.

"My Lords and Ladies," she said finally, "I apologize to this House for the unseemly fashion in which I have interrupted its proceedings.

But, as the Speaker has said, my ship is under orders to depart Manticore as soon as her repairs and working-up period are completed. The demands of restoring a Queen's ship to full efficiency will be a heavy burden on my time, and, of course, my departure from the system will make it impossible for me to appear before you after my ship is once more ready for deployment."

She paused once again, and every man and woman there knew how the hunger at her core savored what must be ripping through Pavel Young in that moment.

"I cannot in good conscience leave Manticore, however, without discharging one of the gravest duties any peer owes to Her Majesty, this House, and the Realm as a whole," she said then. "Specifically, My Lords and Ladies, it is my duty to inform you that one of your members has, by his own actions, not only demonstrated that he is unfit to sit among you but made himself a reproach to and a slur upon the very honor of the Kingdom."

Her voice was calm, clear, but vengeful hunger flowed within it like an icy river.

"My Lords and Ladies, there is among you a man who has conspired at murder rather than face his enemies himself. A would-be rapist, a coward, and a man who hired a paid duelist to kill another. A man who sent armed thugs into a public restaurant only two days ago to murder someone else and failed in his purpose by the narrowest margin."

The spell was beginning to fray. Peers began to rise, their voices starting to sound in protest, but her soprano cut through the stir like a knife, and her eyes were fixed on Pavel Young.

"My Lords and Ladies, I accuse Pavel Young, Earl North Hollow, of murder and attempted murder. I accuse him of the callous and unforgivable abuse of power, of cowardice in the face of the enemy, of attempted rape, and of being unfit not simply for the high office he holds but for life itself. I call him coward and scum, beneath the contempt of honest and upright subjects of this Kingdom, whose honor is profaned by his mere presence among them, and I challenge him, before you all, to meet me upon the field of honor, there to pay once and for all for his acts!"

**Landing Dueling Grounds**
**City of Landing**
**Planet of Manticore**
**Manticore Binary System**
**June 9, 1906 PD**

AT LEAST THE RAIN had stopped.

The gusty wind, unfortunately, hadn't, and Chris Scarborough scowled as he pressed the button that folded his umbrella into a pocket-sized package and stowed it away. The wind had threatened to snatch it out of his hands more than once as he'd stood here, and quite a bit of the hard, driving rain had gotten in under its theoretical protection on the wings of that wind. And from the looks of the overcast, he might need it again all too soon, which was an unpleasant thought. Almost as unpleasant as contemplating the reason he was out here yet again.

He glared down at the field, where Countess Harrington and Colonel Ramirez stood waiting. They'd been there for over five minutes, although there was still no sign of Earl North Hollow. On the other hand, they'd been early. And despite Harrington's calm expression—all too clear through the telephoto lenses—the reason they'd been early was her eagerness. Her anticipation.

Her *hunger*.

He made himself look away from her, and his eyes swept the decidedly damp crowd of newsies about him. It was even bigger than the crowd which had gathered to witness her confrontation with Summervale. Of course it was. There'd been plenty of time for the sensationalists and scandal blogs to chum the water for this one. But the feeling vibrating around him was quite different from the last time. Then, Harrington had been the inexperienced tragic heroine, the grief-stricken, almost certain-to-die tyro confronting the deadly, experienced duelist who'd killed her lover. Today, she was no tyro, and not a soul in her watching audience expected *her* to die on that rain-soaked grass this day. But one thing hadn't changed, for she remained the avenging angel, out to destroy the man who'd orchestrated Paul Tankersley's death.

Assuming one actually believed that drivel, at any rate.

Scarborough glanced to his right, where Bryant Hirsch once again had his camera set up, and it was all he could do not to spit in disgust. Hirsch, obviously, *did* believe every word of it, and because he was only a cameraman and not an actual reporter, he was perfectly free to voice his personal opinion "not for attribution" at the drop of a hat. Which God knew he'd done! And because Scarborough had been forced to listen to him more than once, he understood exactly how the mental processes of the conspiracy theorists worked. And the worst of it, probably, was that Hirsch's convictions were absolutely honestly held.

He grimaced, but then he made himself draw a deep mental breath and acknowledge—little though he wanted to—that Hirsch's analysis of events since Harrington's return to the Star Kingdom wasn't as insane as Scarborough would have preferred. Oh, if Earl North Hollow had truly been behind Tankersley's death, and if Harrington truly had evidence of it, then certainly she would have presented it. Or that was what any rational, reasonable person who believed in the rule of law would have done, at any rate! If she had evidence that a peer of the realm had paid for someone's murder, then she also had an overwhelming responsibility to pass that evidence to the proper authorities for investigation and—if appropriate—prosecution. And if her evidence was valid, then undoubtedly North Hollow would have been convicted and punished. *Properly* punished, by the legal system, not by some crazed vigilante.

But she'd never attempted to do anything of the sort. Which suggested only three possibilities, really. First, that the evidence didn't exist. Second, that the evidence was merely suggestive, or illegally obtained and thus inadmissible, or both. Or, third, that she didn't *want* him prosecuted. Either because she was afraid the evidence she possessed—assuming it actually existed—was insufficient for a conviction... or else because she wanted to personally make sure the man she hated "paid for his crimes" in full, unlike the way he'd "escaped" the death penalty after his court-martial. It was always possible that even if he was convicted in a court of law North Hollow might escape with his life, and the fact that he would spend most of the rest of it—most of a prolong-lengthened life, at least a T-century—in prison obviously wasn't enough for her.

Chris Scarborough had seen a lot in his years as a newsy. He'd seen a lot of human passion, and a lot of human hatred. And because he had, he knew that even if Harrington truly had persuasive, legally obtained evidence, she would never present it, because she didn't want him prosecuted. She didn't *want* him disgraced and imprisoned. She wanted him dead. And even if he might have been sentenced to death by a court, she wanted him to die at *her* hands, after experiencing every gram of fear and humiliation she could possibly inflict upon him, and not in some impersonal, dispassionate, *dignified* judicial execution.

Most of the Star Kingdom had come to the conclusion that that was what she wanted, actually. And the repercussions of the way in which she'd challenged him, the way she'd perverted the House of Lords' procedures, bent and twisted them to suit her vengeful convenience, were only just beginning. Every Opposition figure had denounced her, and with damned good reason. She'd turned the highest legislative forum of the entire Star Kingdom into a gladiatorial arena where she could force a peer of the realm to accept her challenge for the express purpose of shooting him down like an animal. No wonder the Opposition was up in arms. Hell, even Prime Minister Cromarty had been forced to issue a statement decrying the confrontation! He'd stopped short of condemning her the way her behavior truly deserved, but more than enough of his own allies in the Lords were outraged by what she'd done. If he hadn't at least acknowledged and piously deplored the flagrant and barbaric fashion in which Harrington had perverted the House's rules he would have lost enough of the nonaligned peers to bring his government down.

So, yes, the wave of public condemnation, at least from those who could actually *think* about the implications of something like this, was still growing. In time, it would no doubt become a tsunami. Indeed, more than one voice was already calling for Harrington's permanent expulsion from the House of Lords—and Scarborough felt grimly confident that in time, those voices would prevail.

None of which could be much comfort to Earl North Hollow this wet, windy morning.

And not, Scarborough was forced to conclude, that *her* behavior, however barbaric, proved that her allegations against North Hollow truly were as false and insane as his own champions proclaimed.

Scarborough would have been much happier if he'd been certain in his own mind that the earl *hadn't* been involved in the shootout at Regiano's, for example, for several reasons. One was the fashion in which the assassination attempt provided at least partial cover for Harrington. After all, if someone had tried to have her murdered, how could she not be justified in challenging him to open and aboveboard combat? For that matter, who else would have wanted her dead? Or, at least, wanted her dead badly enough to have her killed in a public, upscale restaurant? Scarborough could think of quite a few individuals, mostly Opposition political figures, who would have shed zero tears over her death. Given the way she'd been used to bludgeon the antiwar party ever since that initial, disgraceful affair in the Yeltsin System when she'd physically *assaulted* Reginald Houseman, it would have been ridiculous to think they'd have felt any other way. But none of them would have resorted to hired hitmen.

And that was the sticking point for Scarborough when it came to North Hollow's possible guilt, as well. Because the truth was that he wasn't at all certain the Earl hadn't sent those killers. Not because he believed for a moment that North Hollow had paid Summervale to kill Tankersley and Harrington, but because Harrington obviously intended to kill *him*. She'd made that abundantly clear, and after what she'd done to Summervale, only a fool would have faced her on the "field of honor" willingly. So it was entirely too plausible that North Hollow or—more likely, in Scarborough's opinion—one of his supporters might have contracted her murder purely out of self-defense.

The very thought was nauseating, yet was it truly fair to blame North Hollow for it, even if he'd done it? The woman was a *killer*. She'd proved that repeatedly. And she'd launched herself at him like some sort of target-seeking missile. Of course he had to have considered any possible fashion in which he could protect himself!

That logic was what made it so easy for Harrington's supporters to sell her version of events, but—

"Here they come!" someone said, and Scarborough turned toward the entry gateway as Pavel Young and his brother Stefan walked through it.

"Doesn't look very happy, does he?" somebody said, and Scarborough turned his head to shoot an angry glare at the speaker, then looked back down at the field, watching the Earl approach Harrington and Ramirez. Of course he didn't look "happy"! And the idiot shooting his mouth off wouldn't have looked "happy" either, if *he'd* been the one walking out to meet the woman who'd coldly and deliberately executed Denver Summervale!

"Well, he didn't have to come, did he?" someone else replied. "He could've refused the challenge. For that matter, he *should* have, under the circumstances! Using the House of Lords as a way to issue a challenge to a duel? The woman's a lunatic!"

"If he didn't want to be challenged, he should have hired better shots when he tried to murder her!" a third voice shot back.

"Quiet, please!" Scarborough snapped, without turning his head this time. "I'm trying to listen to my earbud here."

The exchanges faded into silence, and he glared down at the field. A part of him agreed that North Hollow hadn't *had* to accept the challenge. He could have ignored it, especially given where and how it had been delivered, but there'd never been much chance of that. However justified he might have been, both in law and in custom, it would still have been the end of his political career, just as the court-martial had already cost him his naval career. It would also have made him a social pariah none of his political opponents would ever again so much as acknowledge. And for that matter, if Harrington had gone this far to drag him out into the open and kill him, who was to say she wouldn't respond to the Regiano's attack in kind and more effectively? Whether or not North Hollow had been behind that, *she* clearly thought he had. She was unlikely, to say the least, to let that lie, and that had to have been a factor in North Hollow's acceptance.

At least he'd been the challenged party, which meant they'd meet under the Dreyfus Protocol. She'd have only a single shot at him, at forty meters, where even someone with her shooting skills would be hard-pressed to guarantee a fatal hit. And assuming North Hollow survived the duel, he'd never have to accept another challenge from her. Not only that, but the same automatic assumption that he'd been the one who tried to have her killed would apply in reverse if anything happened to *him* afterward.

Given his unpalatable menu of options, meeting her here under the Dreyfus Protocol was probably the least bad one available to him. Unless he chose to spend the next T-century or so as a reclusive hermit after effectively admitting her charges were true by refusing to contest them on "the field of honor."

Scarborough watched the Earl and his brother follow the LCPD sergeant to where Harrington and Ramirez waited beside the Master of the Field. It was Lieutenant Castellaño again, Scarborough noticed. Was that just a matter of chance—of the rotation for the duty rolling around to him again? Or had he specifically requested it? Given his comments when Harrington met Summervale, Scarborough wouldn't have bet against the latter.

North Hollow came to a stop, facing Harrington, and Scarborough listened over his own directional microphone as Castellaño recited the formal, useless plea for reconciliation. Then the lieutenant examined and selected the pistols, and Ramirez and Stefan Young loaded the magazines and handed them to the principals.

"Load, Lady Harrington," Castellaño said, and Harrington slid the five-round magazine into the butt of her pistol.

"Load, Lord North Hollow," the lieutenant said then. North Hollow fumbled, almost dropping the magazine, as he obeyed the command, and even from his vantage point's distance, Scarborough saw him flush at his awkwardness.

Then the seconds stepped back.

"Take your places," Castellaño said, and the two of them stood back-to-back in the gusty morning.

"You've agreed to meet under the Dreyfus Protocol," he said. "At the command of 'Walk,' you will each take twenty paces. At the command of 'Stop,' you will immediately stop and stand in place, awaiting my next command. Upon the command 'Turn,' you will turn, and each of you will fire one round and one round only. If neither is hit in the first exchange, you will each lower your weapon and stand in place once more until I have asked both parties if honor is satisfied. If both answers are in the negative, you will take two paces forward upon the command 'Walk.' You will then stand in place once more until the command 'Fire,' when you will once more fire one round and one round only. The procedure will repeat until one party declares honor is satisfied, until one of you is wounded, or until your magazines are empty. Do you understand, Lord North Hollow?"

"I—" North Hollow paused, cleared his throat. "I do," he said.

"Lady Harrington?"

"Understood." Harrington's single-word response was low voiced but clear, almost calm.

"You may chamber," Castellaño said, and North Hollow flushed again as his fingers slipped on the pistol's slide. It took him two tries, but then he lowered the weapon once again.

"Walk," Castellaño commanded, and the duelists began walking slowly away from one another.

Scarborough felt his nerves coil even tighter as he counted those slow, steady paces, and he wondered what it must be like for North Hollow. Unlike Harrington, the Earl had never faced someone with a weapon in his hand. Fear—even terror—*had* to be working on him, the newsy thought. But at least he had to stand only one shot. Just one. And it was vanishingly rare for anyone to be killed under the Dreyfus Protocol. Of course, Paul Tankersley might have thought that, as well, Scarborough acknowledged. Not only that, unlike Tankersley's duel with Summervale, there was no question in anyone's mind that Harrington fully intended to kill North Hollow. And as she'd demonstrated against Summervale, she was lethally competent with the anachronistic pistols the two of them carried. So what—

"*Down!*"

The single, shouted word cut through the windy morning like the blade of an ax. It came out sharp, clear, incisive, and surprised heads flew up among the taut spectators, indignant eyes searching for whoever had shouted at a moment like this. It wasn't until later that Scarborough realized it had come from one of Harrington's bodyguards. But the countess obviously recognized it. Even as the newsies' eyes darted around, seeking its source, and even as Scarborough was only starting to wonder why whoever it was had shouted, she threw herself down, twisting to the right as she dove for the ground . . . and Pavel Young fired.

Scarborough's eyes flew wide in disbelief. North Hollow had turned suddenly, less than fifteen meters from Harrington, and the pistol in his hand bucked as he shot her in the back. The bullet exploded through her left shoulder in a spray of blood, and North Hollow fired again! But Harrington's dive carried her out of the path of the second bullet. Even as she hit the ground, North Hollow fired yet again. And again and again, shaking hand tracking her with every shot, clots of muddy sod flying as the bullets hit the ground beside her, emptying the entire magazine before she finished rolling.

Shouts of surprise erupted from the assembled newsies, yet they were only beginning as Harrington came back to her knees in a continuation of her dive that was so smooth, so controlled, it seemed almost planned. Blood soaked her uniform, pouring from the wound, and Scarborough couldn't imagine how she could move that quickly, that purposefully, with that bullet-shattered shoulder. Nor could he imagine how North Hollow had missed her with all of his follow-up shots at such a short range. Yet he obviously had, and a corner of Scarborough's eye saw Lieutenant Castellaño's pulser swinging toward the Earl. It tried to drag the newsy's attention fully back to North Hollow, but he couldn't—literally *couldn't*—look away from Harrington as her own pistol rose in a skilled, rock-steady hand.

When he looked at the imagery later, what would freeze Chris Scarborough's blood was the absolute calm of her expression. The dark, focused steadiness of those almond eyes, despite her pain, despite the shock she, too, must feel at North Hollow's appalling violation of the code duello. There was no sign of that pain, no trace of that shock, in her eyes that windy morning. There was only merciless, unyielding purpose.

But that was later. All he saw now was the pistol in her hand, firing even before Castellaño could. The chest of North Hollow's tunic was suddenly blotched in crimson, and he staggered. She fired again, and a third time, and each round hammered into him in a group barely five centimeters across.

And then Castellaño's pulser whined at last, but Pavel Young was already a dead man, and every watching eye knew it.

**HMS *Prince Adrian***
**Manticore Planetary Orbit**
**Manticore Binary System**
**June 14, 1906 PD**

BRANDY FLOATED DOWN the short tube from the shuttle lock, caught the grab bar at the inboard end, and swung herself through the interface from the tube's microgravity into the ship's standard single gravity.

*Don't trip*, she told herself sternly. *Don't trip!*

She'd actually seen a flag officer—only a commodore, perhaps, but still a flag officer—stumble over her own two feet and sprawl flat on her face boarding one of her subordinates' ships. It could happen to anyone, if she allowed her attention to wander, but the truth of that fact made it no less embarrassing for whoever's turn it was today. And at least the commodore had been a commodore, not the newest member of the ship's company reporting aboard for the very first time!

She landed neatly, just outside the decksole line that indicated the official, legal boundary between the ship and the rest of the universe, and the blond, snub-nosed ensign with the officer-of-the-deck brassard and a name tape that said "Nelson, Patricia," came to attention and saluted.

"Permission to come aboard?" Brandy requested as she returned the courtesy.

"Permission granted, Ma'am," Ensign Nelson replied.

"Lieutenant Bolgeo to join the ship's company," Brandy said then, extracting her order chip from her pocket.

The ensign took it, fitted it into her chip reader, examined the display briefly but thoroughly, then popped it back out and returned it.

"Welcome aboard, Ma'am," she said then. Her tone was courteous, but there was something about it.... A subtle note of tension, perhaps. "I believe the Captain is expecting you. Wait one, please."

She looked over her shoulder at the boat bay personnel, then whistled.

"Evans!"

"Yes, Ma'am?" a burly chief petty officer with a power-tech shoulder flash replied.

"Escort Lieutenant Bolgeo to the Captain's day cabin."

"Aye, aye, Ma'am!" Evans said, then looked at Brandy. "If the Lieutenant would follow me?"

"Lead the way, Chief."

It wasn't a long trip, especially for someone whose last shipboard assignment had been a battlecruiser, but it *seemed* much longer to Brandy. There were always a certain number of "opening-night" butterflies whenever one joined a new ship, and in her case, she was acutely aware that it was over fifteen months since she'd last held a shipboard assignment. At least her TDY aboard *Hephaestus* had provided enough hands-on time with the enormous station's engineering systems to get her feet back under her, but there was a distinct difference between running watches in a repair slip or space station fusion room and stepping into the assistant engineer's slot aboard a heavy cruiser.

They passed several other members of *Prince Adrian*'s company on the way, and despite her own nervous preoccupation, there was something...odd about them, Brandy thought. Almost an echo of whatever she'd seen in Nelson's eyes. It wasn't anything she could really put her finger on, but every ship had a personality. It could have a happy crew or an embittered one, although commanding officers and executive officers who let things get that bad tended to find themselves relieved of their duties. And it wasn't as if the people they passed seemed bitter, or angry, but from their expressions and body language, *Prince Adrian* was *not* a happy ship, and Brandy tried hard to avoid a feeling of dread.

The Marine sentry outside the captain's quarters came to attention as Brandy followed Evans up to him.

"Lieutenant Bolgeo," she said. "I believe I'm expected."

"Yes, Ma'am," the Marine said and tapped his earbud. "Lieutenant Bolgeo to see the Captain," he said, and the hatch slid open.

"Ma'am."

He indicated the open hatch, and Brandy looked at Evans.

"Thank you, PO," she said. "I expect we'll be seeing more of one another sometime soon."

"You're welcome, Ma'am." Evans braced briefly to attention, then headed back toward the boat bay as Brandy stepped through the hatch.

The cabin beyond it was moderately palatial. Smaller than a captain might have enjoyed aboard a capital ship, but enormously grander than the one a mere lieutenant would find herself assigned to. It was also comfortably arranged, with a scattering of holopics, a couple of pretty good old-fashioned watercolor landscape paintings, and bulkhead racks that held data folios and even some old-fashioned hardcopy books.

A tallish, broad-shouldered, powerfully built junior-grade captain, his brown hair just touched with silver at the temples, sat behind the desk in one corner. A sandy-haired lieutenant commander sat in another chair at the end of the desk, and Brandy crossed the carpet and came to attention.

"Lieutenant Bolgeo, Sir!" she said.

"Stand easy, Lieutenant," the captain told her with a crooked smile that looked somehow out of place. Although that might have been because there was no trace of it in his level gray eyes.

"Thank you, Captain McKeon," she replied, wondering what she might have done to provoke that somber, dark gaze. It was not, she thought uneasily, the sort of welcoming look a starship captain bestowed upon someone he was happy to see.

"This is Lev Carson, the XO," McKeon continued, waving one hand at the seated lieutenant commander. "I've buzzed Lieutenant Commander Yaytsev to tell him his new assistant's arrived aboard, but he's not actually in the ship right now. I believe he's trying to extort additional spares out of *Hephaestus*."

He paused, and Brandy nodded.

"Yes, Sir," she said.

"In his absence, I'd like to welcome you aboard *Prince Adrian*, and Commander Carson will take you down to Engineering and help you settle in."

He paused again, and Brandy nodded once more.

"I've read your file, Lieutenant," McKeon said then. "It's impressive. I know you've been on the binnacle list for a while after Hancock, but I've known Art McBain for a long time. Matter of fact"—he flashed another of those smiles that never seemed to touch his eyes—"I was the ATO in *Argonaut* when he made his snotty cruise. And what he had to say about you was even more impressive than your file. You might say you come highly recommended."

"Thank you, Sir." Brandy shrugged ever so slightly. "I'm glad Commander McBain gave me positive marks."

"And probably a bit surprised," McKeon said dryly, and snorted a chuckle as Brandy's eyebrows rose. "I said I've known him a long time, Lieutenant. And, just between you and me, he's pretty proud of that hard-ass image of his. The truth is, the people he rides hardest are the ones he expects the most out of. And from the way he talked about you, I'm pretty sure he rode *you* pretty damned hard before Hancock."

"Well, yes, Sir. I guess he did. But he was never unfair about it!"

"No, he wouldn't have been." McKeon nodded, then let his chair come fully upright and laid his palms on his desk.

"I'll hand you off to the XO now, Lieutenant. Hopefully, the Admiralty will formally stand up Sixth Fleet in the next week or so and finally let us go after the Peeps the way we should've done already. I think you'll have a few days to get your feet under you, first, though."

He nodded at Carson, and the lieutenant commander climbed out of his own chair.

"Yes, Sir. Thank you, Sir," Brandy said, coming back to attention.

"I've invited the ship's officers to dine with me tonight, Lieutenant. I'll see you again then."

"Yes, Sir." Brandy repeated.

"Until then."

McKeon nodded dismissal, and Brandy paused to allow Carson to lead the way back through the hatch and down the passage toward the central lift shaft.

"You really are a welcome addition, Lieutenant," Carson said after the cabin hatch had closed behind them. "It may not feel like it right this minute, but you are."

"Sir, I—" Brandy began, but Carson twitched an interrupting hand at her.

"Don't worry about it," he said. "And I'm not surprised if you're getting a less than cheerful vibration from our people right now. But you looked a tad nervous back there."

"I certainly didn't mean to, Sir," Brandy said a bit stiffly, feeling her cheekbones heat, and Carson shook his head.

"I said not to worry about it. Trust me, you were fine! And under normal circumstances, you'd probably be in a chair in the Skipper's cabin with a cup of coffee while he personally gave you the full 'welcome aboard' briefing. Which *I'm* about to give you, so don't worry about that, either. But I'm afraid you haven't picked the very best time to be coming aboard."

Brandy looked at him, raising puzzled eyebrows. What could he—?

And then she had it, and kicked herself for not realizing sooner what it had to be. She probably would have, if she hadn't been so preoccupied with moving into her new duty assignment. Captain Alistair McKeon's friendship with Honor Harrington was widely known, after all.

"Countess Harrington, Sir?" she asked quietly, and Carson nodded.

"Art said you were quick, Lieutenant."

"I should have remembered about him and the Countess."

"Maybe." Carson shrugged. "I don't know her as well as the Skipper does. In fact, I don't think we've ever met. But there are several members of the ship's company who *have* served with her before, and all of them think the world of her. That's the real reason I've mentioned this, because a couple of them are in Engineering. They're good people, Lieutenant, the best, but right now they're hurting, so they won't be *at* their best when you start settling in. Don't take it personally if they aren't. It really and truly doesn't have a single thing to do with you."

"Yes, Sir. Thank you for the heads-up."

"There's enough crap flying around for everybody right now, Lieutenant. I hope we'll be putting most of it behind us pretty quickly. And if we don't"—he turned his head and gave her a broad smile—"it'll be my job as XO to kick everybody in the butt until we do. Which, of course, I will do with the utmost tact and human kindness."

"Of course, Sir," Brandy agreed with a small smile of her own, and he chuckled as they reached the lift shaft and he punched their destination into the panel.

She stood with her hands folded behind her, watching the location display while she thought about what Carson had just said. No wonder McKeon's eyes had been so dark. God only knew where the fallout from Lady Harrington's duel would finally end, but two things were already clear.

The first of those things was that she'd become a political pariah. The Star Kingdom's peers had voted, by a substantial majority and with indecent haste, to expel her from the House of Lords. It had taken less than two days for Pavel Young's allies to demand—and be given—her political head. They couldn't touch her title, but they *could* refuse to allow her to take the seat to which that title entitled her. And they could turn the entire process into a political crucifixion while they did it. Peer after peer—not all of them Conservatives or Liberals—had taken to the floor to condemn her in the most scathing, bitter terms imaginable for the way in which she had "abused" and "misused," and "flouted" the rules of their own august chamber. And quite a few of them hadn't stopped there. Brandy literally hadn't believed her own ears when Baron High Ridge rose to condemn Lady Harrington for the "cold-blooded murder of an unarmed man."

The sheer gall of calling Earl North Hollow "unarmed" when the only reason the weapon in his hand was empty because he'd already fired every cartridge in it into the *back* of the woman High Ridge was accusing of murdering him had stunned Brandy. She'd stared at the HD, wondering what kind of diseased mind could throw that charge at Lady Harrington, and then her eyes had widened as a hard, angry rumble of *agreement* went up from the Conservative benches behind him. And not just the Conservatives. The growl—snarl, really—of approval had actually been even louder from the Liberals. After all, *they'd* been calling her a dangerous lunatic ever since the first and second battles of Yeltsin!

The Countess hadn't been completely without defenders, however. Baroness Medusa had risen with fire in her eyes and fury in her voice as she shredded High Ridge's accusation, and several others had spoken in Lady Harrington's defense, as well. But nothing could derail the juggernaut of her expulsion as unfit and unworthy of a seat in the Star Kingdom's senior legislative chamber.

But that was only the first consequence, and Brandy knew all of Lady Harrington's friends had to be waiting for the second, inevitable shoe. The political repercussions, the way in which the Opposition had demonized and vilified her, had to wash over into Admiralty House, as well. The minority of the Navy which supported the Opposition's interpretation of North Hollow's court-martial and condemned Lady Harrington as a loose warhead, had come out of the shadows like ravening near-weasels that smelled blood. They finally saw their chance to bring down the hammer, and the way in which her dismissal from the Lords had been politicized meant that this time it would be impossible for the Admiralty to ignore them. Rumor said Earl White Haven and Lady Harrington's other supporters were fighting a dogged rearguard in her defense, but this time they were going to lose. And that meant the *Navy* was going to lose one of its finest officers.

No wonder her friends aboard *Prince Adrian* were in a less than cheerful mood.

The lift car slowed, then stopped, and the doors opened outside the forward fusion room.

"And now, Lieutenant," Carson said, waving her out of the car, "allow me to introduce you to your new domain."

**HMSS _Hephaestus_**
**Manticore Planetary Orbit**
**Manticore Binary System**
**June 14, 1906 PD**

"SO, HOW'S YOUR NEW BOSS?" Tim Bolgeo asked across the table.

"Commander Yaytsev's gonna be tough, but he's fair, Dad," Brandy replied. "He reminds me a lot of Commander McBain, really. Different sense of humor, though. His is . . . dry. Really dry, actually." She snorted. "If I were a snotty aboard his ship, he'd send me looking for the particle flux monitoring system with a _totally_ straight face!"

"Did your training officer do that aboard _Montego_?" her father asked with a chuckle.

"Not Lieutenant Stuyvesant," Brandy said with an answering grin. "Senior Chief Tyler sure did, though!"

Her father's chuckle turned into a rolling laugh, and her mother shook her head at both of them.

"Could you at least hold it down to a dull roar, Timmy?" she asked tartly, although her own lips twitched as she did. "Remember we're in a public place!"

"I'm pretty sure they've heard people laugh in Dempsey's before. Assuming they could hear me anyway, over the background noise," Bolgeo told her with an unrepentant chuckle, and waved a hand at the well-populated tables around them.

He had a point, Brandy reflected. Like _Hephaestus_ itself, Dempsey's operated around the clock, but most of the station's "day" population synced its schedule to that of the City of Landing, so it was fortunate she'd reserved their table well in advance. It was approaching the peak of the dinner hour, the wait time for a table was creeping upward, and the restaurant area was crowded enough the seated diners' buzz of conversation actually made it difficult to hear the piped-in music.

"Oh, trust me," Linda Bolgeo said even more tartly. "People can hear the 'Bolgeo Bray' in the middle of a Gryphon thunderstorm!"

Her undutiful husband laughed again, harder than before, and Brandy shook her own head.

"Forget it, Mom. We're not changing him at this late date."

"Doesn't mean I have to give up the good fight," Linda replied.

"Oh, stop blackening my character!" Bolgeo said. "We're supposed to be celebrating Brandy's new ship, not picking on minor flaws in my otherwise impeccable social graces."

"I don't think 'impeccable' means exactly what you seem to think it means, Dad. But you're right. It is a celebration, so Mom and I will womanfully refrain from pointing out the many *major* flaws in your social graces and return to the topic at hand."

"Oh, thank you!" Bolgeo said soulfully. "And, on that topic, how's the rest of your department?"

"Pretty solid," Brandy said more seriously. "I don't know them as well as I knew my people aboard *Cassie*, of course. Not yet."

"You'll get over that pretty quick," her father told her, and his voice was more serious than it had been, as well. "Especially once they cut you loose from Home Fleet and *Prince Adrian* starts doing the kinds of things she *should* have been doing for the last six or seven T-months."

Brandy nodded and carefully didn't notice the shadow that flitted through her mother's eyes. It was official. Sixth Fleet, which included HMS *Prince Adrian*, would—finally—deploy forward the next day. No one knew—or not "officially," at least—exactly where they'd be deploying to. Scuttlebutt said they'd probably be basing out of Grendelsbane, or possibly the Madras System, but nobody had confirmed that for the ship's company yet. Brandy inclined toward the Madras destination, given that the Royal Navy's most pressing strategic objective at the moment had to be the Trevor's Star terminus of the Manticoran wormhole junction, but no one was interested in dropping casual information where Peep spies might hear about it. On the other hand, the fact that Sixth Fleet was Admiral White Haven's command pretty much guaranteed it would be committed to full-fledged offensive operations *somewhere* ASAP.

That was more than enough to explain the shadow in Linda Bolgeo's eyes.

"It's not going to be a picnic, Brandy," her father said very soberly.

He gave his wife an apologetic glance and reached across the table to take her hand, but his eyes went back to his daughter's face. "I know that, after Hancock, you understand that if anybody does, baby girl, but that's one reason I am so *pissed* with the Opposition. We should have been hitting the Peeps *months* ago, before this damned Committee of Public Safety got itself organized and their navy started getting its feet under it again."

"I know, Dad."

"I know you do, and if I were a more self-disciplined fellow, I'd keep my mouth shut instead of worrying you—and your mom—by talking about it. But I'm not, and I *am* pissed, and I know your mom is already worried about it. Because after Hancock, *we* understand what the costs can be, too. But it's also because everything I've ever heard about McKeon says he's one hell of a skipper. He's no slouch in a fight—he sure as hell proved that in Yeltsin!—and from everything I hear, he runs a taut ship, the kind that knows what it's doing when the shit hits the fan. The kind"—his eyes moved back to his wife's face and he squeezed her hand—"where people do their jobs and come home again even if the shit *does* hit the fan."

"Yeah, I'm pretty sure you're right about that, Dad. I can't say I've gotten to know him at this point—I've only been aboard a week! But that tracks with everything I've seen so far. And, like I say, the people in my shop seem really, really solid. If it falls in the crapper, we'll have good people to dig us back out of it again."

"Good!" Her father nodded vigorously, then released her mother's hand and patted it before he picked up his water glass again. "So I can take it you're happy with the new slot?"

"Mostly." Brandy frowned slightly and picked up her fork to play with. "I'm completely *satisfied*, I think, Dad, but 'happy' might be a bit too strong."

"Oh?" Bolgeo's frown was considerably deeper than hers had been. "Why?"

"It's just—" Brandy turned the fork in her hands, looking for the right words. "It's just that the *ship* isn't really happy right now."

"How surprising is that if everybody aboard knows you're headed for the front?" Linda Bolgeo's voice was ever so slightly edged with the anger—or the anxiety, at least—of a mother whose child was headed for the front right along with her ship.

"It's not that, Mom." Brandy gave a quick headshake. "Frankly, it's got more to do with *politics* than it does with fighting the war. And not just how darned long it took to get the declaration voted out!"

"Harrington, you mean," her father said, and she nodded.

"I don't mean one bit of disrespect for Captain McKeon, Dad, but that's a man who's really angry and really hurting right now. He works hard to keep it from showing, but I saw some of it the first day I went aboard, and I've seen more of it since. I don't think he even knows how to let something like that affect the way he does his duty, you understand. It's certainly not going to keep him from doing one bit less than the best job he absolutely can! Like I say, I've only been aboard about six days, and I've already seen more of him than I saw of Captain Quinlan in the first six *months* aboard the *Cassie*. I know *Prince Adrian*'s a lot smaller ship, but the real reason is that Captain McKeon makes a point of dining with his officers on a regular basis.

"The thing is, though, that everybody aboard knows how much he's hurting over this whole mess, and they *care* about him, Dad." She met her father's eyes. "So no matter how hard he tries to keep it from splashing on them or the fact that it's not affecting the way *he* does his job, I think it is affecting the way they do *theirs*. And it's even worse for some than it is for others. I was surprised to find out how many of *Prince Adrian*'s people have served under Countess Harrington. We've got at least six of them in Engineering alone! And all of them take this mess personally."

"*Most* of the Navy—the competent part of it, I mean—takes it 'personally,'" Bolgeo growled.

"I know, but it's worse for some than for others. Especially people like Lieutenant Tremaine, our boat bay officer. He was with Lady Harrington in Basilisk as a baby ensign—boat bay officer on the old *Fearless*, in fact—and he's taking it really hard. And Senior Chief Harkness—!"

She rolled her eyes, and her dad grunted.

"That'd be *Horace* Harkness?" he asked, and Brandy nodded. She didn't look at all surprised that her father had recognized the name, and he snorted when he saw her expression. "Yes, I used to get into trouble with him. 'Course, he got into plenty of trouble all on his own hook! Especially where Marines were involved."

"That certainly sounds like 'my' senior chief," Brandy acknowledged dryly. "Although, as far as I can tell so far, he hasn't had any fights with any of *Prince Adrian*'s Marines."

"He wouldn't have." Bolgeo shook his head. "He never did fight with any of 'his' Marines. Unless they had the bad taste to step up beside some *other* Marine in a bar somewhere. He'd make an exception in that case."

"Pining for the days of your misspent youth, are you, Timmy?" Linda asked sweetly. "I seem to remember at least once you caught a little brig time because *you* stepped up beside a petty officer named Harkness 'in a bar somewhere' and the two of you caused—refresh my memory, dear? Thirteen hundred dollars of damage, was it?"

"It was *fifteen* hundred dollars' worth of damage," her husband corrected, "and *we* didn't do the damage, the stupid *Marines* did the damage when Horace and I threw them—I mean, when they *fell* through the bar's front window."

"Oh my God," Brandy said. "I just hope he doesn't figure out I'm your daughter!"

"Horace?" Bolgeo laughed. "Trust me, baby girl, he *already* knows. He knows *everything* about his officers. But I promise he won't hold your DNA against you. And he's not the kind to brownnose or take advantage of an old friendship, either."

"Well, *that's* reassuring."

"Should be," her father said more seriously, "because he's one of the good ones. He'll look after you. You'll have to keep an eye on him where Marines are concerned if he gets shore leave—probably won't be that big a problem aboard *Prince Adrian*, especially with Iris Babcock as their gunny—but there's not a better missile tech or systems specialist in the entire Navy. And what he can do with cyber systems—!" He shook his head. "I'll guarantee you the only reason you've got him aboard a heavy cruiser is because of his discipline record. If he hadn't gotten himself busted as often as he did, he'd be at least a chief warrant aboard a battlecruiser somewhere by now. So take advantage of the fact that you've got him."

Brandy nodded. It was unusual for her father to give someone that strong an endorsement, and when he did, it was worth listening to.

She started to say something else, then paused as the server arrived with their orders. The large serving bowl of *spaghetti alla puttanesca* went onto the table, and their heads bent as her father murmured a quick blessing. Then her mother started serving their plates and they were too busy giving their food the focused attention Dempsey's kitchens deserved to worry any more about Horace Harkness.

✧  ✧  ✧

*That was good,* Brandy thought as she watched through the boarding tube's transparent wall while her parents made their way to the short-haul ferry back to Gryphon. *I wish Mom hadn't had to make the trip all the way to* Hephaestus *for just one meal, but she'd have killed me if I hadn't had dinner with both of them before I shipped out!*

She chuckled at the thought, but the chuckle faded a bit as she reflected on how long it might be before she had the chance to share a meal with her parents again. Or if she ever would, for that matter. Was this the last time she'd ever see them?

*Oh, stop that!* she scolded herself. *Dad would kick your butt if he knew you were thinking maudlin crap like that! Of course you'll see them again. And Mom will hop right back on the puddle jumper for Dempsey's the moment you dock at* Hephaestus *again! It's not that long a trip, after all.*

The Manticore Binary System was one of the vanishingly few star systems in which habitable worlds orbited multiple stellar components, and Brandy's homeworld was eleven light-hours from *Hephaestus.* That was why, despite the fact that everyone called them "puddle jumpers," the ferries that plied back and forth between Gryphon and Manticore or Sphinx were hyper-capable. While it would take the puddle jumper just under three hours to cover the roughly fifteen light-minutes from Manticore planetary orbit to the Manticore-A hyper limit, the hyper voyage to Manticore-B's hyper limit would take only half an hour. Of course, then they'd have to cover the distance from the Manticore-B limit to Gryphon at sublight speeds, which would add another three and a half hours. Although Gryphon was actually closer to Manticore-B's hyper limit than Manticore was to Manticore-A, the puddle jumper would arrive at the limit with a normal-space velocity of just about zero. It would have to accelerate for over an hour and a half, then decelerate just as long. Still, they'd be home in little more than seven hours, as opposed to the twenty-seven hours a normal-space trip would take.

Because the puddle-jumpers carried so much civilian traffic, their boarding tubes incorporated grav plates, which meant Tim and Linda were able to walk down the tube side-by-side. They held hands as they went, and Brandy's eyes softened as her mother leaned toward her father, resting her head against his shoulder. He released her hand, put his arm around her, and pressed a kiss to her hair as they moved out of Brandy's line of sight.

She stood a moment longer, looking after them with misty eyes, then inhaled deeply and headed away from the civilian docking facility toward the nearest Navy boat bay from which she could catch a shuttle to *Prince Adrian*'s parking orbit. A station as huge as *Hephaestus* had a lot more than one boat bay, for obvious reasons, and they were distributed around the platform to place them as conveniently as possible. "Conveniently as possible" wasn't remotely the same as "really, really conveniently," of course, she reminded herself.

Despite the hour, there was a lot of traffic along her route. There always was, she thought as she made her way down the passage, but at least it flowed fairly steadily. It shouldn't take long to reach the bay.

She reached a cross corridor, turned to her right, and both eyebrows rose as that steady flow halted abruptly. What in the—?

Her raised eyebrows lowered and her eyes widened as he realized why the men and women in front of her had stopped. For some of them, it was only because the people in front of *them* had, and those people looked as surprised—and confused—as Brandy had been. But most of the traffic hadn't simply stopped. No, most of those people had stopped, then stepped back with their shoulders to the bulkheads . . . and snapped to attention.

Outdoors, military courtesy required officers and enlisted to salute approaching superior officers. Indoors—or aboard ship or aboard a space station like *Hephaestus*—that was relaxed and only a courteous nod was required, since saluting indoors was proscribed. Even outdoors, however, the salute was a *walking* salute, because the Navy had better things for its personnel to do than stop dead every time they met a superior. And while Navy personnel were expected to make a hole for superiors in tight quarters, there was certainly no regulation which required shipboard personnel to completely clear a passage as broad as the ones in *Hephaestus*!

But the men and women in front of Brandy Bolgeo didn't seem to care about that, just at the moment, and she felt herself pop to attention, as well, as a tall woman walked down that magically cleared passageway toward her.

She wore a captain's uniform and carried her left arm in a sling. She was flanked by two green-uniformed armsmen, and a cream-and-gray treecat rode the shoulder of the master chief steward walking to her left. Pain and loss had left their marks in her expression, and the beret on her head was black, not the white beret of a starship's commander which had been taken from her. But she walked steadily, her head high and her shoulders back, and there was no surrender in those brown, almond eyes.

She seemed unaware of the way in which the path before her had been cleared, of the silent men and women who wore the Star Kingdom's uniform and who'd stopped, come to attention, to let her pass. But her treecat's head was raised, his ears pricked. His body language radiated his own awareness, his satisfaction, and her own eyes were suspiciously bright.

She was headed, Brandy realized, not toward a Navy boat bay, but toward the *civilian* bay her own parents had just left. Even that had been taken from her, Brandy realized. She was on half-pay, denied a command, told she was unnecessary—*unwanted*—at the very moment the Navy in which she had served for her entire adult life faced its sternest test.

And that Navy hadn't even provided her transport back to Grayson on one of the warships headed there.

Brandy stood at attention as Countess Harrington passed her, and the treecat turned his head, looked directly at her, as if he could read her thoughts, her awareness of how badly his person had been treated. She watched them go, walking into exile, and the bitter unfairness of it all suffused her. It was so *wrong*, after everything Lady Harrington had given, all the sacrifices she'd made—after so much had already been taken from her.

But there was no defeat in those shoulders, and as Lady Harrington disappeared from sight, Brandy Bolgeo realized there never would be. Not in *those* shoulders.

*The universe* can *kill her, if it tries hard enough*, she thought. *But beat* her? *Never!*

She stood for a moment, gazing down the passageway, then drew a deep breath, shook herself, and headed back toward the boat bay and the shuttle waiting to carry her to her own duty.

# Book Two

## HMS *Prince Adrian*
## In Hyper
## August 7, 1906 PD

BRANDY TIPPED BACK in her chair in her tiny cabin, nursing her coffee cup in both hands, and tried not to yawn while she waited. It wasn't that she was bored. In fact, "bored" was the last thing in the universe she was just now! It was just that it was the middle of the night for her, and her internal clock insisted she should be sound asleep. As *Prince Adrian*'s assistant engineer, she got the mid-watch, while Commander Yaytsev, as befitted his lordly seniority, got first watch and Lieutenant (JG) O'Brien got third watch . . . as befitted his lowly *lack* of seniority.

Brandy chuckled at the thought as she sipped more coffee and watched her display's bland wallpaper. At least Captain McKeon had authorized electronic attendance from quarters, if they weren't on watch. That helped a lot. And—

A musical tone chimed, the wallpaper on her display disappeared, and her screen was suddenly subdivided into four windows. One of them, larger than any of the other three, were occupied by the captain and Lieutenant Commander Chen. Chen was very much on the young side for a heavy cruiser's tactical officer. In fact, he was three or four T-years younger than Brandy. But he was also very good at his job, and Captain McKeon's status as CruDiv 33.2's senior-officer-in-command made him the de facto tac officer for the entire division. The captains and TOs of the division's other three ships occupied the display's other windows, but Brandy knew every other officer of the division was auditing, just as she was.

"Good morning, people," Captain McKeon said. "Captain Hunter has informed Admiral Nijenkamp that the entire fleet will carry out a simulated exercise of our plan of attack beginning at oh-nine-hundred tomorrow. The Admiral and Captain Bernardo have briefed all of the division COs on the ops plan, and Commander Chen will download the detailed file on our own part in the operation at the end of this conference. Before he does so, however, he'll present a general brief of the operational plan so that all of us are on the same page both for the simulation and when we actually go in."

Brandy nodded in approval. The RMN tradition was that ships' companies were kept informed. No one was going to compromise security by blabbing away, but the Navy assumed that a ship's company who knew what was going on, knew what was expected of them, were better prepared and motivated. Besides, they deserved to know what was at stake when they were committed to action, and good captains made certain they did. She'd been aboard *Prince Adrian* less than eight T-weeks, but she'd already decided that despite the fact that he had yet to make list, Captain McKeon wasn't one of the "good" captains. He was one of the *great* captains. She'd had plenty of good, even excellent, superiors in her career; none of them had been better than McKeon.

She suspected Earl White Haven felt the same, given McKeon's status as CruDiv 33.2's SOIC. It was true that all of the division's other skippers were also captains (JG), and that he was senior to all of them, but most flag officers would have thought long and hard before leaving someone yet to make list in tactical command of four of the Royal Navy's heavy cruisers. And if White Haven—or, for that matter, Sir Cyrus Nijenkamp, CruRon 33's CO—had possessed any doubts at all about Alistair McKeon, it would have been easy enough to swap *Prince Adrian* over to CruDiv 33.1 and replace her with a ship like Captain (SG) Dehnert's *Bellator*. That would have been no more than a routine housekeeping decision, under the circumstances, so Nijenkamp and White Haven obviously felt CruRon 33's "house" was just fine the way it was.

"Before Brian begins," McKeon continued, "let me say a few words about the situation as Fleet command sees it.

"Commander O'Hanlon's put together an analysis of everything ONI knows about our target, and—with the proviso that we can't know for sure till we get there—it all sounds pretty solid to me."

Brandy nodded. She'd known Commander Abdur Raheem O'Hanlon, Sixth Fleet's intelligence officer, since her Saganami Island days. He'd been two years ahead of her, and he'd mentored her in multidimensional math. He was undoubtedly one of the smartest people she'd ever met, and she hadn't been at all surprised when White Haven, who had an undeniable eye for talent, nabbed him for his staff.

"The one good thing about the delay in voting out the declaration," McKeon went on, "is that the Peeps have to have settled back onto their heels a bit in this region. There's been a lot of bickering back and forth around Grendelsbane, and we've pushed as aggressively as we could with our light forces to interdict their logistics, but we haven't hit them with a real offensive anywhere since Riposte Gamma wound down back in April. Specifically, they haven't seen squat out of us out this way, aside from a handful of long-range recon flybys and perimeter probes since January."

His expression made his opinion of that inactivity abundantly clear, Brandy thought.

"So the odds say we'll almost certainly have strategic surprise when we hit Samson. That surprise won't last all that long *after* we hit Samson, of course, and the truth is that Samson isn't what anyone would call a vital strategic objective. So I suspect some of you are wondering why the hell we're hitting it in the first place.

"Well, we're hitting it because it's one of the perimeter bases for the Peeps' defensive zone around Trevor's Star. Samson isn't officially part of the People's Republic, but the Samson System Republic's accepted 'associated' status. It didn't have much choice, after Haven overran Trevor's Star twenty-odd T-years ago, but it's still nominally independent. So while that means we have to be careful about hitting any innocent bystanders, it also means this is a liberation operation of sorts. We're not planning on hanging around, but it's not *too* unlikely they'll just leave President Turner and the Republic in peace afterward, because by the time *we* leave, there won't be any basing facilities to draw *them* back, either."

He bared his teeth in something too hungry to call a smile, and Brandy nodded soberly.

"It's possible we may be looking for basing facilities of our own here in the not-too-distant future, but for right now this is basically a hit-and-run sort of operation. A case of denying the Peeps operational depth and forcing them to reinforce their satellite bases if they don't want more of them punched out. Eventually, we'll have to stop bobbing and weaving around the perimeter and go after Trevor's Star itself, of course, and that's going to be messy."

His expression turned somber, and Brandy heard what he wasn't saying. It was going to be a lot messier than it had to have been, thanks to the delay imposed by the Opposition's delay of the declaration.

"Most importantly, though," McKeon continued after a moment, "this is the first true offensive since war was formally declared. The gloves are all the way off now. That makes us the opening shot in the real contest, people, and as Admiral White Haven and Captain Hunter put it in their briefing to Sir Cyrus and Captain Bernardo, it's up to us to begin the way we intend to continue. The Peeps got badly hurt in the opening phase, and we hurt them even worse in the course of Riposte Gamma, but now they've had months to get their wind back. It's our job to knock it right back out of them, starting in Samson in about three days."

He paused once more, looking steadily into the pickup through which dozens of other officers looked back at him. Then he nodded once, briskly.

"All right, then! Brian?"

"Of course, Sir," Lieutenant Commander Chen said rather more formally than usual. Then he, too, looked out of the display at all those listening officers.

"The attack plan's actually pretty simple," he said. "Those of us with sensitive stomachs won't like the preliminary very much, but it should be effective in attaining surprise. Unfortunately, the Peep base orbits Samson-4, a gas giant well outside the hyper limit. That makes it more vulnerable to a quick pounce, which is exactly what we intend to execute. It also means, though, that any ship with its hyper generator at readiness can hyper out before anyone engages it. On the other hand, no one's been poking around Samson in the last couple of months. With no sign of us to make them nervous—and damn all indication that we might get our thumbs out and actually take the war to them—they may well have elected to drop back to no more than standby readiness levels, or even lower, to avoid the wear on their hardware. We can't count on that, of course, but Fleet figures the odds are pretty heavily that they have.

"Obviously, given that—as the Captain just pointed out—this is our first operation after the formal declaration of war, we'd really like to hammer as many of their starships as possible, and that's what we intend to do. On the other hand, even if we can't—even if their mobile units *are* able to duck into hyper before we can take them out—their base facilities—the maintenance slips, the tank farm, the logistic nodes—can't. So even if every one of their ships get away, we'll still take out the entire base, and that's totally worth doing in its own right."

He paused, as if inviting a response. But no one spoke, and he gave a brief nod.

"All right, what we aren't going to be able to simulate tomorrow is the Alpha translation Admiral White Haven has in mind." He flashed a quick, evil grin. "We're going for a crash translation from the Delta bands."

Captain Cristina Zaragoza, HMS *Cestus'* CO, winced visibly, and Brandy didn't blame her. Nor did she like to think about what a four-band crash translation would do to *Prince Adrian's* hyper generator. It wouldn't present any safety threats to a well-found ship whose generator was in good repair, which *Prince Adrian's* was. It would, however, burn somewhere around two T-months of the generator's normal overhaul cycle in less than fifteen minutes.

That didn't even consider what that sort of sustained plunge through hyper space would do to the crews' stomachs. They'd hit each band's boundary at a maximum gradient, and a lot of people would be puking their guts out by the time they finished.

From Captain Zaragoza's expression, she expected to be one of them.

Brandy's stomach was less sensitive than many, but she still made a mental note to go easy on the pre-battle solid meal the Navy traditionally fed its people.

"Once we've made translation into n-space," Chen continued, "a lot will depend on how good our astrogation was. Either way, though, we'll be accelerating in-system at the wallers' maximum safe pod-towing compensator settings. The screen—that's us and Admiral Moreno's battlecruisers—will be well out in front of the wall-of-battle. We'll be Admiral White Haven's primary surveillance screen, and we'll deploy recon drones to supplement our shipboard sensors for relay to the wall. In addition, CruRon Thirty-Three and BatCruRon Five will have primary responsibility for the outer missile defense zone. Because of that—"

He went on speaking, laying out the operation's parameters clearly and concisely, and Brandy sipped coffee as she listened.

Unlike quite a few of Sixth Fleet's personnel, she'd seen combat. She knew how ugly it could be. But *this* time, the Navy would be attacking the *Peeps*, not the other way around, and she smiled vengefully as she contemplated that minor difference.

**Samson System**
**August 10, 1906 PD**

"OH, *SHIT!*"

It came out softly, almost furtively, but that didn't mean no one heard it.

"Ex*cuse* me, Citizen Senior Chief?" Citizen Lieutenant Barbier said sharply, and, despite herself, Citizen Senior Chief Geffroy rolled her eyes. Expressing exasperation with a superior officer could be unwise, in the current People's Republic, although she'd at least done it without ever looking away from her display.

And it wasn't as if she didn't have plenty of justification.

Citizen Lieutenant Barbier, who'd been Petty Officer 2/c Barbier before the Parnell Coup, had the sensor watch in *Orbit One*. Geffroy didn't much like the citizen lieutenant. There were a host of reasons for that, including how much less he knew than *she* did about the job she'd been doing while he was still cutting class, stealing uni-links, and mugging derelicts for fun in the towers of Nouveau Paris. Worse—and unlike some officers she could think of, like Citizen Commander Ancel, *Orbit One*'s XO—he was too busy upholding his shiny new authority to even *try* to learn anything from the experienced NCOs under his command—like one Citizen Senior Chief Geffroy—about the enormous number of things he was unable to distinguish from his own ass.

That would have been ample reason to despise him, but his revolutionary fervor was even worse. For her own part, Élisa Geffroy thought all the "citizen this-and-that" that had been forced upon the Navy was about as stupid as things came, but Barbier embraced it ardently as evidence of the Committee of Public Safety's determination to completely eradicate the trappings of the old, corrupt, Legislaturalist regime. Of course, the fact that the Committee of Public Safety's "New Order" was the only thing that

311

could conceivably have allowed a piece of work like him to attain officer's rank probably helped to account for his revolutionary ardor, as well. In many ways, though, the priggish prudishness he imposed upon his subordinates—at least in public; his own *private* vocabulary was rather different—was almost equally irritating. Ever since he'd discovered Lucille DeLisle, *Orbit One*'s people's commissioner, disapproved of "unprofessional language," he'd been constantly jumping "his" people for language DeLisle might find "inappropriate."

And making certain DeLisle knew he had, of course.

Getting reamed by the people's commissioner for something as trivial as an occasional obscenity was petty, frustrating, and stupid, but at least it was also far less dangerous than being called down for anything which might be construed as "recidivist" and attract the *serious* ire of the new Office of State Security. That didn't mean Barbier hadn't caused her more than enough grief, so she normally at least tried to stay on his good side. Or to *avoid* his bad side, anyway.

Just this minute, though, she had other things on her mind, and she ignored him as she brought the heel of her hand down on a large, illuminated button and an eardrum-shredding siren howled.

"What the *hell*, Senior Citizen Chief?!" Barbier demanded. "What the *fuck* d'you think you're do—?!"

Another alarm began to wail, and Barbier's mouth closed with a snap as the lurid icons of dozens of hyper footprints blossomed in the master plot.

✧  ✧  ✧

"Well, *this* isn't good," Captain Byron Hunter murmured over Earl White Haven's earbud. It was fortunate, a corner of White Haven's brain thought, that the chief of staff was on their private channel. At least no one else could hear him.

Not that he didn't have a point.

"Milord, I'm afraid—" someone else began.

"I see it, Wanda," White Haven interrupted, and Lieutenant Wanda Saldaña closed her mouth.

His tone had been calm, devoid of anger or reprimand, but his staff astrogator didn't look one bit happier. To be fair, there were a *lot* of unhappy people on *Queen Caitrin*'s flag bridge after their extended crash translation. Someone behind him continued to retch even now, and most of his personnel had made use of their sick bags as the nausea wrenched at them. That was quite enough to make most people thoroughly miserable, although translation had never bothered White Haven remotely as badly as others.

But Saldaña's tolerance was almost as good as her admiral's, and in her case, her unhappiness had far less to do with the mechanics of the translation than with its outcome. She was *very* good at her job, but her astrogation—normally as spot-on as anyone could have asked—had hiccuped this time, and at the worst possible moment.

Sixth Fleet's ops plan had called for it to enter normal-space on a course directly toward the Samson System's primary and thirteen light-minutes outside its 21.12 LM hyper limit. That would have put it 9,464,000 kilometers—about thirty light-seconds—from the Havenite fleet base, headed toward it. Saldaña had gotten their n-space base heading exactly right; unfortunately, that was of far less importance than the distance to their target, and White Haven's ships had reentered n-space *forty-two* light-seconds from their objective. That added over 3,000,000 kilometers to their range to target, and they'd shed well over ninety-nine percent of their base velocity in the course of their translation, which gave them a current normal-space base velocity of a grand and glorious 1,324 KPS.

It would take time to increase that speed, and *time* was something that might be in very limited supply.

If they had, indeed, caught the Peeps with cold hyper generators, it would be at least twenty-eight minutes before even something as small as a destroyer could hyper out. That was its best possible time, assuming an engineering crew poised and ready when the order came. Superdreadnoughts would need over thirty-four minutes, in the same circumstances, and given the maintenance demands of military-grade hyper generators and what holding them at readiness did to them, White Haven was relatively confident their generators *were* completely down.

He couldn't be *positive* of that, however, and even if their generators were down, he was much less confident about their impeller nodes. No ship could get underway under impeller-drive from a completely cold start in less than forty minutes. A competent engineering department could bring up a ship's wedge in little more than fifteen minutes, however, if her impeller rooms were at standby readiness, with their plasma conduits charged and the grav tuners spun up but not yet engaged. Holding beta nodes at standby for long periods of time stressed their components and burned through their operational lifespans, which required both more intensive (and better trained) maintenance and more frequent overhauls and replacement. That was why engineers hated doing it when they didn't have to. But even at standby, they suffered far less wear than a hyper generator did. For that matter, keeping just a trickle charge on an impeller room's plasma conduits cost only a tiny bit of power, caused only minimal wear on the system, and shaved about ten minutes off the activation cycler. So it was entirely possible they were powered, although it was unlikely they were fully active.

Assuming they did nothing more than keep the conduits fed, the aforesaid competent engineering staff could have a ship up and moving in a bit less than half an hour. A good staff could shave even more time off that—perhaps as much as four or five minutes, if they were *really* good and knew their systems well—whereas poorly trained or inexperienced engineers could take considerably longer. The People's Navy had always relied on officers and its never sufficiently abundant long-term NCOs to perform jobs the RMN, with the advantage of the Star Kingdom's better educational system, trusted to junior NCOs and noncommissioned spacers. Given ONI's assessment of how many experienced officers "the Parnell Purge" had cost the Havenites, these ships were far more likely to have poorly trained complements that couldn't begin to match his own people's performance. But if they had hot nodes, they could get underway far more quickly than he would prefer, and covering those extra 3,000,000 kilometers would cost him an additional 18.7 minutes.

If the Peeps got underway in the next fifteen minutes or so, they'd probably be able to completely screw over his ops plan. In the long run, they *couldn't* stay out of Sixth Fleet's missile envelope—not forever—if they were stuck in n-space. Low as Sixth Fleet's initial velocity was, it was still 1,300 KPS higher than the Peeps'. By the time White Haven's prey got their impellers online, even assuming they were all parked there at standby and set a new all-time galactic record, Sixth Fleet's velocity would be over 3,480 KPS, which would be ample overtake to run them down in normal-space eventually.

Except, of course, that they only had to stay away for an additional twenty or thirty minutes—long enough to get their hyper generators online and disappear into h-space forever.

He felt his staff's consternation and he totally understood the hunch of Wanda Saldaña's tight shoulders. She was a good, conscientious young officer, and she had to feel it even more keenly than anyone else.

"All right," he said calmly. "We're not quite where we wanted to be, but at least we're all here, and the formation looks really tight." Which it did, and which also owed a little something to Saldaña. "Get us underway, Wanda. And, Byron, poke Admiral Nijenkamp gently. We need those recon drones launched now."

Citizen Rear Admiral Carmella Secordo, commanding officer, Battle Squadron 43, came out of PNS *Véracité*'s flag bridge lift at a run three minutes after the alert signal reached her flagship. People's Commissioner Frouzan Hashemi was right behind her, and the flag bridge personnel popped to attention as they arrived.

"As you were!" Secordo snapped. "Get back on your consoles!"

Her staff, although calling it *her* staff was something of a stretch, with Hashemi perched like some carrion crow at her shoulder, turned hastily back to their tasks, and Secordo strode across to the master plot.

It wasn't any better than the preliminary report, she thought grimly. In fact, it was worse. Battle Squadron 43 was the primary heavy maneuver element—hell, the *only* maneuver element—assigned to Citizen Rear Admiral About's Samson System Command. Citizen Vice Admiral Costa's understrength Task Group 37 wasn't even supposed to be there; he was only waiting for the rest of Battle Squadron 107 to join up with him before he moved on to his own station in the Corrigan System. His presence had been a welcome—if temporary— addition to the SSDC's order of battle when he arrived, and he'd been here T-weeks longer than his original movement orders called for because of the endless delays in his remaining SDs' arrival. There'd been a *lot* of those delays over the last several T-months, and in the privacy of her own thoughts, Secordo had been very happy about this one. But there was no way in hell they could hope to beat off an attack this heavy, even with TG 37 in support.

CIC hadn't yet tagged any of the impeller wedges headed in-system with class IDs, but they didn't need to. From that formation, the Manties had brought at least three complete battle squadrons to the party—possibly four, depending on whether the lead group was a screen of battlecruisers or another dreadnought squadron. Costa had exactly four superdreadnoughts and six battlecruisers, with a single screening destroyer flotilla, and aside from the orbital bases' fixed defenses, Citizen Rear Admiral About had only Secordo's eight battleships and an understrength light cruiser squadron.

*We're toast*, she thought. *And that's assuming the damned Manties don't have any of their frigging pods on tow, which they certainly do.*

At least the icons of her own command had blinked from red to the amber of "Stations Manned," and as she watched, *Allégeance's* light code actually turned green, although she doubted that Citizen Captain Reed's ship really was completely cleared for action just yet.

"Anything from Command Central yet?" she asked.

"No, Ma—uh, Citizen Rear Admiral," her com officer replied.

Hashemi glared at the hapless citizen commander with dagger-sharp eyes, and Secordo bit her tongue—hard.

*Would it really hurt anything*, she wondered mordantly, *if someone slipped up and said "Ma'am" or "Sir" just once? Especially at a moment like this? It's only natural to revert to a lifetime's habits when the shit hits the fan, damn it!*

"Thank you, Charlotte," she said, instead of the comment she wanted to make. She'd found herself tending toward much greater familiarity with her subordinates than she might once have allowed herself, if only because using their given names was one way to avoid the Committee of Public Safety's comic opera "citizen whatever."

Besides, it wasn't so very long ago that Citizen Rear Admiral Secordo had been Lieutenant Commander Secordo, herself.

A display blinked to life at her elbow, and she looked down as Citizen Captain Kilian Ambros, *Véracité's* commanding officer, and People's Commissioner Milo Marchant, the battleship's political officer, appeared upon it.

"The ship is closed-up at battle stations, Citizen Rear Admiral," Ambros reported.

"Good," Secordo replied. "Engineering?"

"We're working on it, Citizen Rear Admiral. Best estimate right now is hot impellers in"—he looked down, obviously checking a time display—"thirty-six minutes."

*Bit of an overoptimistic estimate there, Kilian,* Secordo thought.

She very much doubted that Citizen Commander Shepherd, *Véracité*'s engineering officer, would be able to give her hot nodes in less than *forty-five* minutes. She'd be delighted to discover she was wrong, but there was no point pretending that was likely to happen. Nor was that Ambros' fault. He'd commanded *Véracité* for just over five T-months, and he'd spent that time drilling and training his people hard. But too much of that training had been in simulators, not hands-on with the actual hardware, and there were too many holes in the experienced chain of command he ought to have had. Many of the "citizen whatevers" promoted because of the post-purge People's Navy's desperate need for officers had the potential to become good officers—some of them *outstanding* officers—in time. But that was the rub. Even the best of them still needed time—a *lot* of time—to become proficient in their duties.

*And if the intelligence Hashemi's deigned to share with me is anywhere near accurate—which I wouldn't bet on, because I know it sure as hell isn't complete—the Manties are finally getting their act together. The only thing that's saved our asses this long has been that their politicos are at least as stupid as ours. But we've always known even they'd have to greenlight the resumption of offensive operations sometime, and it looks like "sometime" is now. Which means training time just ended. From now on, it's going to be a matter of how many of us survive long enough to learn just what the* fuck *we're doing.*

She'd rather hoped she'd be among those who had the time to truly master her new responsibilities. Too bad she wouldn't.

"Hyper generator?" she asked Ambros, and felt Hashemi stiffen beside her.

"Longer, Citizen Rear Admiral," the citizen captain said. "Best estimate right now is forty minutes."

"Stay on it."

"Of course, Citizen Rear Admiral."

Secordo turned from the display and almost ran into her people's commissioner. Unlike altogether too many people's commissioners, the dark-haired, dark-eyed Hashemi had at least served in the pre-coup navy. Unfortunately, she'd been only a third-class petty officer, despite almost seven T-years of service. That, as far as Secordo was concerned, was an eloquent comment on her . . . limited competency. Unfortunately, Hashemi was convinced it had been due solely to her Dolist origins. Worse, she was positive her lower-deck experience qualified her judgment in all things naval.

Which it manifestly did not.

Now Hashemi glared at Secordo, deliberately blocking the path to her command chair, and those dark eyes burned with suspicion.

"Hyper generator, Citizen Rear Admiral?" she said in icy tones.

"It's an obvious tactical question, Ma'am," Secordo replied. People's commissioners were the only people who got that honorific.

"At this point, hyper generators should be a secondary consideration—at best," Hashemi half-snapped.

*In other words, I'm being "defeatist" to even consider the possibility of trying to get some of my people out alive,* Secordo thought bitterly.

"Ma'am, hyper generators, like impeller wedges, are a critical component of our ships' maneuverability, and maneuverability is a critical component of our combat capability. Citizen Captain Ambros would be derelict in his duty if he *wasn't* trying to get the generator online, and I would fail in mine if I didn't ask him about it. For that matter, Citizen Commander Gwaltney"—she waved one hand at her ops officer—"would be equally derelict if he wasn't collecting the same information from every unit of the squadron. Without it, we can't project our maneuvering capabilities for combat, and since this is obviously an attack in force, we're definitely going to be fighting sometime very soon."

"I see." Hashemi's dark, narrowed eyes burned with cold suspicion, and Secordo made herself meet them levelly. What she really wanted to do was to point out to Hashemi how hopeless the situation was, if only to see just how far the other woman's revolutionary ardor went in the face of certain death. Unfortunately, Hashemi probably lacked the imagination—and she *certainly* lacked the naval experience, despite her vociferous insistence to the contrary and her authority to second-guess and countermand any order Secordo gave—to truly understand just what was about to happen.

Yet, at least.

"I suppose that makes sense," the people's commissioner said after a slow, tense pause. "So long as it's not a pretext for defeatism, at any rate."

"I assure you, Ma'am, that my people and I are prepared to do their duty, no matter what it is and no matter what it costs. It's why we're here."

Hashemi looked at her a moment longer, then nodded and moved aside, and Secordo crossed to her command chair and settled into it as Hashemi turned back to the master plot. The citizen rear admiral looked at the people's commissioner's back and allowed herself a cold, unseen smile. It was bitter, that smile. Bitter with the memory of the husband and young son back home in Nouveau Paris...and with the thought of what would happen to them in the name of "collective security" if anyone suspected for even a moment that their wife and mother *wasn't* "prepared to do her duty."

*I would've liked to see you grow up, Tommy,* she thought. *I really would've.*

She held those two beloved faces in her mind's eye for another moment, then glanced at the master plot's status board. All of the squadron's icons blinked angry red eyes at her now, and she drew a deep breath.

"Charlotte, inform Command Central the Squadron's weapons and active defensive systems are fully manned and ready. We'll advise them of the status of our impellers and hyper generator at ten-minute intervals."

Brandy Bolgeo sat back in her chair in *Prince Adrian*'s Damage Control Central. As the heavy cruiser's assistant engineer, that was her duty station. She only wished it didn't bring back memories of the Battle of Hancock and *Cassandra*'s DCC. Not that this battle was going to be the sort of desperate affair that one had been. She knew that.

Unfortunately, ships got damaged—even destroyed—even in battles their side won.

That was something else Hancock had taught her.

There wasn't really anything for her and her people to do, just at the moment, and, frankly, she would be simply delighted if things stayed that way. But because there wasn't, and because Captain McKeon believed in keeping his people in the loop, her earbud was tied into the feed from the bridge, and she frowned as she considered what she'd heard from Commander Alférez, *Prince Adrian*'s astrogator.

Brandy was an engineer, not an astrogator, but the Academy had forced her to study at least the rudiments of the astrogator's trade. Which meant she understood how hard it could be to hit a pinpoint n-space locus after a lengthy hyper voyage, and especially after a crash translation across so many bands. The truth was that Lieutenant Saldaña had done well to be off by only twelve light-seconds...although Brandy doubted anyone aboard *Queen Caitrin*—probably especially Saldaña—thought that right now.

But Sixth Fleet was underway now, accelerating ponderously in-system, and *Prince Adrian* and the rest of CruRon 33 were already well over a hundred thousand kilometers closer to the Peep naval base than the rest of the fleet. That meant very little for their onboard sensor systems, but they were responsible for Sixth Fleet's outer missile defense zone. A hundred thousand kilometers was barely two seconds' flight time for an incoming laserhead, but the gap was already growing. Unlike the wallers, or Admiral Moreno's battlecruisers, for that matter, CruRon 33 had no missile pods on tow. That gave it a maximum acceleration of 5.0 KPS$^2$, over twice the two hundred forty-five gravities a pod-laden superdreadnought could manage, and the velocity differential between *Prince Adrian* and her heavier consorts was increasing at 1.5 KPS every second as her squadron accelerated steadily away from the more ponderous dreadnoughts and superdreadnoughts. With that geometry, CruRon 33 could be as much as 1.3 million kilometers closer to the enemy than Sixth Fleet's wall-of-battle in only ten more minutes.

They wouldn't want to get *too* far ahead of the heavy mob lest they make themselves too inviting a target for Peep fire control to pass up, but anyone over there with a lick of sense would be focused on running away, not standing and fighting. Not against three-to-one odds in ships-of-the-wall and four-to-three odds in battlecruisers. There were also those battleships to factor in, but all eight of them combined massed no more than 35,000,000 tons. Even with them cranked in, the Peep mobile units massed barely thirty percent as much as Sixth Fleet.

Of course, Peep battleships were missile-heavy, which might go a little way toward improving the odds. Or would have, if the Peeps had possessed missile pods. Which they didn't...and which explained Sixth Fleet's lethargic acceleration. Each of White Haven's dreadnoughts had ten pods on tow. The superdreadnoughts had twelve, although the battlecruisers had only six each. That was over three hundred pods, each packed with ten of the Royal Manticoran Navy's missiles, and Peep missiles were perhaps sixty percent as good as the latest Manticoran hardware.

She had no idea how many launchers the three orbital bases might boast between them. It was at least remotely possible—although "remotely possible" actually meant "unlikely as hell," in a minor base like Samson—that they had enough to equalize the numerical odds. But orbital bases were immobile, unable to move or maneuver in any way, which, coupled with the fact that it was literally impossible to armor them the way heavy warships were armored, made them hideously vulnerable to missile attack.

It was not a winning position for the defenders, she thought.

Henri Costa, CO, Task Force 37 of the People's Navy, stared at the plot. The Samson Defense Force's passive arrays had finally pulled in enough light-speed data for PNS *Montressor*'s CIC to tag the crimson icons of the incoming hostiles with tentative class IDs. He watched them blink for a moment, then looked at the status boards for his command, and a ball of frozen helium settled into the pit of his stomach.

*We are so screwed*, he thought. *I knew I should've argued with Bozonnet, damn it!*

"What's happening, Citizen Vice Admiral?" People's Commissioner Aaron Bozonnet demanded.

"The Manties are attacking in strength, Sir." There was more bite in Costa's voice than was safe, but under the circumstances, that was a much lesser worry than it had been.

"What?" It was Bozonnet's turn to stare into the plot, although Costa knew how little ability to read its icons the people's commissioner truly possessed. "What do you mean, 'in strength'?"

"I mean that that's a minimum of three times our strength coming at us, Commissioner. I'm guessing they made translation farther out than they meant to, but that's not much help, since we can't maneuver."

"What? Why not?!"

Costa wheeled from the plot to stare at the people's commissioner in disbelief.

"Because," he said after a second or two, in a dangerously patient tone, "our impeller nodes were completely off-line at the moment they arrived. And so were our hyper generators."

"Well . . . well, get them *online!*" Bozonnet barked.

"That's exactly what we're trying to do, Sir. But we need time, and unless the Manties fuck up by the numbers, we don't have enough of it to go from cold nodes—which, I remind you, you insisted upon in order to save wear on the components—before those people"—he jerked a thumb at the plot—"are in range. And without an impeller wedge, sidewalls are useless. So aside from our counter-missiles and point defense, we're going to be mother naked when their missiles come in on us. *Sir.*"

Bozonnet swallowed hard, his eyes enormous, then wheeled back to the plot as if he could somehow change its iconography just by trying hard enough, and Costa turned from him to his ops officer.

"I know our commanders are already doing all they can, but remind them we need constant status reports. Those"—he twitched his head at the status boards—"can tell us how far along they are right now; I need a running update on how much time they think they might be able to shave off."

"Of course, Citizen Vice Admiral!" Citizen Captain Marlowe had been only a lieutenant seven T-months earlier—about the same time Costa had been a commander—and his face was pale. But his voice was commendably steady, and Costa touched him gently on the shoulder.

"And tell them for me," he added with a crooked smile, "that Engineering's safety protocols are officially relaxed today."

✧    ✧    ✧

"How bad is it, Hervé?" People's Commissioner Camille asked in a lowered tone, and Citizen Rear Admiral About looked at him.

"About as bad as it gets," he said, equally quietly, and Camille's jaw tightened.

"In that case, I'll just stay out of your way," he said, and About nodded before he turned back to his staff on *Orbit One*'s command deck.

In many ways, he knew, he'd been unreasonably fortunate to draw Jonathan Camille as his commissioner. Camille had possessed exactly zero naval experience when he was selected for his present duties. What he had possessed, in abundance, however, was revolutionary fervor and a commission in Internal Security with service as a "liaison" with the People's Army. His InSec rank hadn't been that high—About didn't know precisely what it had been, but a *high*-ranking officer in Oscar Saint-Just's security forces would have been assigned to a more prestigious base than Samson—and About had never been all that fond of InSec. But at least the man understood how a military chain of command had to work, and he'd tried hard to keep his thumb out of the soup.

The good news was that Camille had both understood that constant interference in About's orders could only engender confusion in his subordinates and recognized his own lack of experience where the Navy was concerned. The bad news was that he hadn't recognized the same thing in others, like that poisonous bitch Hashemi. About had suggested as firmly and tactfully as he could that Camille should overrule Hashemi on several points, including the readiness levels of the Samson System Defense Command's mobile units' impeller rooms and hyper generators. Unfortunately, Hashemi had used her *boundless* naval experience to convince Camille she knew what she was doing.

*And now that's all come home to roost*, About thought bitterly, because there was one other bit of bad news about having Camille for his people's commissioner. Jonathan Camille was a true man of principle, despite his InSec background. His support for the revolution went to the bone . . . and there wasn't a single gram of cowardice in the man's entire body.

Which meant the Samson Defense Command was about to fight gallantly to the death against impossible odds, and there wasn't one damned thing Hervé About could do about it.

✧ ✧ ✧

"Milord, we're getting better data from the drones," Commander Eccles said.

White Haven paused in his conversation with Captain Hunter and Commander O'Hanlon and turned to face Commander Eccles. He raised an eyebrow at her, and she grimaced.

"It's not a *lot* better, Sir," she said, "but the drones are close enough now to get emission signatures on at least some of their impeller nodes. It looks like their lighter units may be able to get underway in the next twenty-five minutes or so."

"Thank you, Laura," White Haven said, and looked back at his plot.

Sixth Fleet had been in normal-space for just over twelve minutes, accelerating at a steady 2.4 KPS². In that time, it had traveled almost 1,580,000 kilometers, and its velocity relative to the Peep base was up to 3,053 KPS.

"Ditch the pods, Milord?" Captain Hunter asked quietly, and White Haven snorted.

"No point," he replied, equally quietly. "They're not moving yet. Our overtake's already so great they can't possibly get away unless their generators come online and they hyper out on us."

"And if they *do* get their generators online, Milord?"

"Then we could lose their mobile units," White Haven conceded. "But we're going to want the pods against the orbital platforms, even if their starships manage to bug out on us, and I think we'll still get close enough for our shot before they can. Probably."

Hunter nodded, and White Haven twitched a brief smile. Passive sensors could pick up the gravitic distortion of impeller nodes ramping up to activation, but there was no way to do that for a hyper generator. All they had was their original guesstimate where that was concerned.

*We're not getting close enough for the engagement I had planned on*, he admitted. *Can't take the chance they will hyper out on us.*

The good news was that if the Peeps' generators had been at Standby levels, even their superdreadnoughts would have been hyper-ready by now. And, if they hadn't been at least at Standby, it was unlikely they'd been active at all. For that matter, if they'd had their impellers down, it was unlikely as hell they would have had their generators up, considering the relative maintenance costs. That meant a cold start, which gave him the thirty-seven-minute window, at least for their wallers, he'd hoped for. Probably, anyway.

Which was just fine, as far as it went, but—

*If the game were easy, anyone could win*, he thought with a grimace.

Unfortunately, it wasn't. His original plan—assuming they'd hit their hyper translation exactly—had been to accelerate for fifteen minutes, at which point he would have brought the platforms and the ships riding orbit with them 80,000 kilometers inside his powered missile envelope while the Peeps were still fifteen to seventeen minutes short of hypering out. Missile flight time would have been just under three minutes, which meant the first birds would have arrived on their targets eighteen minutes after Sixth Fleet broke the Alpha wall. And *that* would have meant the Peeps had to stand Sixth Fleet's fire for at least twelve minutes before they could escape. In that much time, he could not only have flushed his pods in a single enormous opening salvo but gotten in up to forty-eight follow-on broadside launches. Short of direct divine intervention, the Peeps could never have survived that deluge of fire.

But at this range, he had a far less favorable missile geometry. Instead of accelerating for fifteen minutes to reach attack range, he would have to accelerate for twenty-six, and even then, he'd still have to launch from almost 600,000 kilometers farther out than originally planned, with commensurately lower accuracy. But if he didn't fire by then, and if they were getting their generators online, missile flight times would mean they got away scot-free. Dropping the pods would buy him no more than a minute or so of engagement time, which would—possibly—give him time for four additional broadside salvos. But playing for that wasn't remotely worth giving up the saturation effect of his initial salvo . . . assuming he got to fire at the Peep starships at all before they disappeared.

*And if those bastards* do *get away, I guarantee the Opposition newsies won't pay much attention to what happens to their base facilities, now will they?* He shook his head with a wry chuckle. *Of course not! So I'll just have to see to it that they don't.*

✧   ✧   ✧

"Capacitors at seventy-seven percent!" Citizen Petty Officer Dombrosky called out.

"What's the charge gradient?" Citizen Lieutenant Mercier-Pascal demanded.

"Sixty-one percent, Citizen Lieutenant," Citizen Chief Aria replied.

Mercier-Pascal caught his lower lip between his teeth and glanced at the Engineering status board, then at the time display. Almost fourteen minutes had passed since the Manties were detected. According to the book, a fully trained engineering crew was supposed to need only ten minutes to fully charge the plasma capacitors, but Impeller Room Six *still* didn't have power to its beta nodes.

Mercier-Pascal's impeller room was scarcely alone in that, but all the others were at least closer than Impeller Six. That was sure to earn a reaming from Citizen Captain Philidor—or, at least, Citizen Commander Rust—which was more than bad enough. But until they had power on the impellers, *Montressor* was a sitting duck, and the Manties were rumbling steadily closer.

"Increase the gradient. Take it to seventy-five percent."

"Citizen Lieutenant, we're already eleven percent above Book levels," Citizen Chief Aria pointed out.

"I know that," Mercier-Pascal half-snapped. "But without a wedge, we can't even raise sidewalls, Citizen Chief! So which do you prefer? Taking a chance on blowing the capacitors, or sit around buck naked, waiting until we take a laserhead up the ass?"

Consuela Aria sucked her teeth for a moment. It was her job to remind Mercier-Pascal about little things like the potential to blow up the entire forward impeller ring, and the truth was that she didn't trust Mercier-Pascal's judgment. Or, no, that wasn't really fair. He seemed to have pretty decent judgment; it was *experience* he lacked.

Jumping the plasma flow that high before any of the nodes were actually online, actually drawing power, came under the heading of Really Risky. On the other hand, Mercier-Pascal had a point about sidewalls and laserheads.

"Aye, aye, Citizen Lieutenant," she said, and entered the command. "Plasma gradient seven-five percent."

✧　✧　✧

"Sir, I have active fire control emissions coming up across the board," Lieutenant Commander Chen said. "So far, the profile pretty much matches what our last reconnaissance probe showed, at least as far as the orbital bases, permanent installations, and battleships are concerned. Flag's designated the fixed installations as Bogey Alpha. The mobile units we already knew about are Bogey Beta, and they're calling the newcomers Bogey Gamma. Gamma looks like a light task force, about half a squadron of SDs, a half-dozen battlecruisers, and destroyer escorts. Based on active emissions, CIC estimates that all four of the wallers are *Duquesne*-class."

"And the small fry?" Alistair McKeon asked.

"Aside from the battleships, it looks like six *Tonnerre*-class battlecruisers, Sir. IDs on the light cruisers and destroyers are a lot more tentative. Looks like Bogey Beta's little guys"—the tac officer touched his display and a cluster of seven icons riding the same orbit around the gas giant as the battleships flashed on the plot—"are light cruisers, probably *Gardienne*-class. We have what might be a *Conquérante* down here in Gamma with the superdreadnoughts. Destroyers look like a mix of *Bastogne* and *Desforge* classes."

"Good." McKeon nodded. "Still no indication of active impeller wedges?"

"No, Sir. The drones are close enough to pick up emissions that indicate some of them are at least getting power to the nodes, but it'll be a while before they have any wedges online. It looks like we must've caught them with completely cold impeller rooms. If we hadn't, they'd be a lot further along by now. At present, CIC's best estimate is that we're still looking at a minimum of twenty-six minutes for the first beta node activation."

"Thank you, Brian."

McKeon nodded again and tipped back in his command chair, fingertips drumming lightly on the helmet racked on the chair's right armrest, while he projected the air of calm his people needed from him at the moment. And which was all he could *give* them at the moment, really.

*Prince Adrian*'s preparations were complete. Her entire crew was skinsuited, the air had been evacuated from her outer compartments, and every station was fully manned. She was as ready for battle as a ship could be.

And she also seemed very small and frail when he thought about things like *Duquesne*-class superdreadnoughts. They weren't the very latest Peep ships-of-the-wall—the *Haven*-class's design was a good twenty T-years younger—but they were still very capable platforms. Haven had always had a tendency to short its battleships on upgrades and refits, but their wallers' systems had been regularly updated, at least until the Parnell Coup, which meant the *Duquesnes* were about as dangerous as Peep ships got. The latest Manticoran *Gryphon*-class ships—none of which happened to be in Sixth Fleet's order of battle at the moment—were just over a million tons bigger, but the *Gryphons* had been designed before the current, far more lethal generation of missiles had become available to the RMN. Most of the additional tonnage had gone not into launchers and magazines, but into a much more powerful energy battery for what the designers had expected to be the decisive, close-range slugging match that would decide the outcome of a clash between walls-of-battle. In terms of missile launchers, there was very little to choose between the *Duquesnes*' armament and that of a *Gryphon*, and even the "smaller" Havenite ship was almost thirty times as massive as his own *Prince Adrian*.

He was rather more aware of that at the moment, since Rear Admiral Nijenkamp's cruisers were just over a million kilometers closer to the aforesaid *Duquesnes* than the rest of Sixth Fleet. Admiral White Haven's entire force had been accelerating for fifteen minutes now, and *Prince Adrian*'s base velocity was up to 5,823 KPS, 2,330 KPS higher than the lumbering ships-of-the-wall. In fact, it was just about time—

"Signal from *Circe*, Sir," Lieutenant McCloskey said, as if on cue, and McKeon grimaced wryly.

"What does Admiral Nijenkamp have to say, Andy?" he asked.

"The screen will reduce acceleration to zero and begin decelerating at two-five-zero gravities in"—McCloskey glanced at the chrono—"twenty-seven seconds, Sir."

"Very good. Please thank the Flag, with my respects, for the warning."

"Yes, Sir!"

McKeon looked back at the master plot. Sixth Fleet was still beyond powered missile range of its opponents, and that meant they were beyond *effective* range, as well. Given the nonexistent chance that missiles on a ballistic approach could penetrate modern missile defenses, there was no point sending in birds whose drives burned out before they reached attack range. Sixth Fleet's fire control could achieve solid targeting solutions, even launched from here, yet without the ability to maneuver, very few of them would get through to their intended victims.

But that would change once the opponents did reach powered missile range of one another, and at the moment, the screen was barely 600,000 kilometers inside the counter-missile envelope of Sixth Fleet's wall-of-battle. It would be approximately eight minutes before velocities equalized and the distance between them stopped increasing, even with the screen decelerating while the heavy ships maintained acceleration. At that point, the screen would be only about 200,000 kilometers inside the wallers' counter-missile envelope, which was far shallower than McKeon might have wished. But it would also put the screen's outer interception zone right on 3,000,000 kilometers from *Queen Caitrin* and her consorts, which would allow the defenders at least five additional counter-missile launches. CruRon 33 had too few launchers to take an enormous bite out of the incoming fire, but the longer engagement window would force the attack birds to spin up their penetration aides earlier and give the tac crews more priceless time to analyze the Peeps' penetration ECM for the waiting wallers. The downside was that if the Peeps were prepared to waste the limited number of missiles they were likely to get off before their destruction on the screen, things could get dicey. On the other hand, cruisers were much nimbler than lumbering ships-of-the-wall, and their massive consorts' defensive missile batteries would still offer devastating coverage against the laserheads' last 170,000 kilometers of flight.

*And it's not like those poor bastards will have very long to shoot at us, either,* McKeon thought grimly.

By the time velocities equalized, Sixth Fleet would be only four minutes from its projected launch point. After the ships-of-the-wall flushed their massive load of pods, their acceleration would increase by over a third, and the gap between them and the screen would close much more rapidly. But that same massive load of pods would have sent almost five thousand missiles into the Peeps' teeth.

Which was the reason those poor bastards wouldn't have long to shoot.

✧   ✧   ✧

The deck jerked against the soles of Citizen Vice Admiral Costa's feet.

He wheeled toward the display that linked his flag deck to *Montressor*'s bridge just in time to see Citizen Captain Philidor's head snap around to the structural schematic of the enormous superdreadnought. Whatever had sent that sharp, angry twitch through the deck had to have been massive to affect the seven-million-ton vessel, and Costa felt sickly certain of what he was about to hear.

He waited, forcing himself to remain silent despite his agonizing awareness of the seconds dragging past. The Manties had been in n-space for almost seventeen minutes now. They couldn't be far short of their launch point, and he hated every instant of lost time. But whatever he might feel, he couldn't begrudge Philidor the time to make certain of his facts before he reported.

Besides, *Montressor* was Philidor's ship, whatever the Committee of Public Safety might have decreed. Dealing with her needs—her *people's* needs—came even before keeping the task group commander informed.

"Sorry, Citizen Vice Admiral," Philidor said finally, turning back to the display with a grim, bitter expression. "Impeller Six just blew up. Impeller Five went with it—looks like a sympathetic detonation of the plasma capacitors. And Impeller Three and Seven took significant collateral damage when Five and Six's conduits breached."

"Do we know *how* significant yet?" Costa asked.

"For the moment, they're both completely down, but at least most of Three's people survived." Philidor's tone was tight, clipped. "Doesn't look like *anybody* got out of Six, and casualties in Five and Seven are 'heavy.'" He shrugged, his eyes bitter. "That's all they can tell me yet, Citizen Vice Admiral. Just 'heavy.'"

"Understood." Costa's jaw tightened. "Status on the rest of the starboard nodes?"

"The automatic cutouts threw when Six blew," Philidor said grimly. "The entire starboard ring is down. We're trying to override, but the automatics dumped the plasma. And"—his eyes were bleak—"Sidewall Two went up along with Six. Four doesn't look good, either. It's off-line now while we try to reroute power to it. Engineering says at least six minutes."

From the citizen captain's expression, that "six minutes" was probably more like six*teen* minutes, Costa thought, not that his engineers were going to admit anything of the sort.

He made himself pause a moment. Think before he spoke.

The news was even worse than he'd feared. Unlike a merchant ship's enormous, roomy impeller rooms, a warship subdivided the engineering spaces into individual, heavily bulkheaded and armored compartments. In *Montressor*'s case, there were twelve of them. From Philidor's report, a third of them—all serving the starboard beta nodes—had just taken catastrophic damage. Still worse, the *un*damaged—or, at least, *probably* undamaged—impeller rooms in her starboard impeller ring had vented their plasma capacitors. That meant a restart from completely "cold" nodes, even after Engineering managed to override the computers' safety protocols. And if Sidewall Two and Four were down as well . . .

"Do what you can, Josh," he said finally, and looked directly into his flag captain's eyes. "And start getting all nonessential personnel off the ship."

"Yes, Citizen Vice Admiral." Anguish flickered in Philidor's expression, but he nodded.

"Keep me informed," Costa finished with a nod of his own.

He turned from the display, then stopped abruptly as he found himself face-to-face with Aaron Bozonnet.

"I want the names of those traitors, Citizen Vice Admiral!" the people's commissioner snapped.

"Traitors?" Costa looked at him in disbelief.

"If this wasn't intentional sabotage, it was still somebody's responsibility to be certain it never happened," Bozonnet grated. "I want the names of those people, and I want them now!"

"Sir, assuming that anyone was actually responsible for what just happened"—*aside from* you, *you pompous, vindictive, pig-ignorant son of a bitch*—"they're dead now. It's a little late to start accusing them of anything."

"Those who fail the Revolution *will* pay the price," Bozonnet shot back. "And you know the Committee's policy in this matter as well as I do, Citizen Vice Admiral Costa! I advise you to remember that."

The unspoken words "collective responsibility" lay between them, like the poisonous stench of rotting fish, and Costa's eyes hardened.

"Sir," he bit each word off like a sliver of ice, "assuming either one of us is alive to write our after-action reports, I will be delighted to assist you in obtaining all relevant information. At the moment, however, I estimate that we're no more than ten or twelve minutes from the Manties' missile launch. I have other things to deal with just now. Excuse me."

He nodded curtly as Bozonnet gawked at him, then stepped around the people's commissioner. He crossed to his communications officer.

"General message to all task force COs."

"Yes, Citizen Vice Admiral?"

"On my authority, all units are to begin immediate evacuation of nonessential personnel. Anybody we don't need to actually fight the ships, goes. They are authorized to use all available life pods and small craft. I want them off in the next ten minutes—max."

"Citizen Vice Admiral!" Bozonnet barked from behind him. "That kind of defeatist—!"

"Shut the hell up!" Costa wheeled back to the people's commissioner. "You can put whatever you want in your damned report, assuming you're alive to make it, but I'm not getting anyone killed if I can keep them alive. We'll fight, Citizen Commissioner, but I'm stripping down to just the people we need to do that. That way at least some of our people—*my* people—may actually survive this clusterfuck!"

Bozonnet jerked back, his expression shocked, and Costa knew exactly what the other man's final report would say about his outburst. But he couldn't help it. Not anymore. *Montressor* could still move on just her after-impeller ring, even with her forward ring completely down—or could have, assuming they'd had time to get *it* up—but she'd been brutally lamed, and with Sidewall Two gone and Four off-line, she'd lost half her starboard sidewall, as well. Spreading her remaining capacity to cover the gap would weaken that sidewall catastrophically. Of course, the state of her sidewalls would be supremely unimportant if she couldn't get her impeller wedge up to protect her hull's unarmored top and bottom in time.

He glared at Bozonnet, saw the awareness of his own impending mortality finally dawning in the people's commissioner's eyes. Those eyes darted around the flag bridge, and he opened his mouth, only to pause as a harsh buzzer sounded over every earbug and speaker in the ship. Then—

"This is the Captain speaking." Philidor's voice was as hard and harsh as the buzzer had been, but it continued unflinchingly. "All Logistics, Support, Maintenance, Astrogation, Medical, Administrative,

Marines, and Engineering personnel not currently manning weapon systems or damage control are to evacuate the ship immediately. I say again, all personnel not currently manning weapons stations or damage control, lay to the nearest boat bay or life pod launch station at once. And"—that hard voice cracked for just a moment, then strengthened— "and may God go with you all."

Bozonnet froze. He looked at Costa again, eyes huge, then swallowed hard, turned, and started for the flag bridge hatch.

"Where are you going, Citizen Commissioner?"

Costa's voice crackled across the sudden silence. Com traffic continued to mutter in the background, but it seemed muted, distant, serving only to perfect the silence.

Bozonnet wheeled back to face the citizen vice admiral and the flag bridge's other uniformed men and women, and his mouth worked as every one of them looked back at him.

"I—" he began, then stopped, and Costa smiled thinly.

"I said we'd evacuate *nonessential* personnel, Sir," he said. "According to my instructions and the Committee of Public Safety's directives, people's commissioners are essential to our ships' operation. I'm sure someone who *isn't* essential can make use of your shuttle seat. I suggest you buckle back into your command chair."

Bozonnet swallowed, then darted a look over his shoulder at the two State Security troopers standing just inside the flag bridge hatch. Despite Philidor's evacuation order, they'd made no move to leave their stations. He started to open his mouth . . . until he saw the same cold disdain looking back from *their* eyes.

He looked around the flag bridge a moment longer. Then his shoulders hunched and he turned and walked silently back to his command chair.

✦ ✦ ✦

"Milord, sensors report what looks like an explosion aboard Gamma Three."

Admiral White Haven raised a hand, pausing his conversation with Captain Goldstein, and turned to Commander Eccles.

"Do we know what kind of explosion?" he asked, his eyes automatically seeking the icons of the force CIC had labeled Bogey Gamma. A crimson band pulsed around one of them. One of the superdreadnoughts, he noted.

"We can't absolutely confirm it, Milord, but it almost certainly has to be an impeller room. Probably more than just one, actually. Judging from the plasma vent, they may have lost the entire forward ring."

"Sounds like somebody over there doesn't know what he's doing," Captain Hunter said, and White Haven snorted harshly.

"They probably don't," he said. "Not if ONI's right. I think—"

"Excuse me, Milord."

"Yes, Laura?"

"I'm sorry to interrupt, Milord, but the drones are also picking up what look like escape pods from Gamma Three."

"They're abandoning ship?" White Haven's eyes narrowed. Had the damage been severe enough to actually threaten the ship? But Eccles shook her head.

"No, Milord. There aren't enough of them."

"What the hell are they—?" Captain Hunter began.

"Anything from the rest of Gamma?" White Haven asked Eccles.

"No," she began, then paused. "Yes, Milord!" she corrected herself and looked back at him, her eyes surprised. "We're getting life pods and at least some small craft from more of Gamma's heavy ships."

"How many?"

"Hard to say from this far out, Milord. At least till the pod transponders come up. Rough guess, maybe twenty percent of a *Duquesne*'s estimated pod load-out. I don't think it could be a lot higher, at any rate, although we *are* seeing more small craft. Looks like they may be launching all of those."

"I see."

White Haven nodded, then turned back to Captain Hunter and the display connecting him to Goldstein.

"Things are getting even uglier than I expected them to," he said grimly.

"Milord?" the flag captain quirked an eyebrow at him, and the earl snorted harshly.

"Somebody over there's just accepted that they can't fight us and survive," he said. "I'm as sure as I'm standing here that whoever it is, he just ordered his ships to strip down to essential personnel. He's getting as many of his people as he can out of our gunsights. And probably trying to get his small craft out for search and rescue after the missiles stop flying."

"Laura said there weren't enough life pods for that," Captain Hunter pointed out.

"No, there aren't. But that's why I said things are going to get even uglier. Whoever that is"—he jerked his head at the hostile icons in the master plot—"he's accepted that his ships can't survive . . . and he's going to fight anyway." He looked at his flag captain and chief of staff. "That's a hell of a different attitude from what we saw during Riposte Gamma."

"All he can hope to manage is to get even more of his people killed," Goldstein objected. Not to White Haven's analysis, but to the thinking that could have led to it.

"That's all he's going to manage *here*," White Haven said heavily, "but given the tonnage imbalance between us and the Peeps, attrition works for them, even at a steep differential. Every ship *we* lose will hurt us a hell of a lot more than every ship *they* lose hurts them. If what I think we're seeing here starts happening across the board, it'll be painful. Painful as hell."

"Launch point in eight minutes, Milord," Eccles said.

✦ ✦ ✦

"How much longer?" Jonathan Camille asked quietly, standing beside Citizen Rear Admiral About and watching the oncoming Manticoran icons sweep across the plot toward *Orbit One* and the rest of About's hideously outweighed command.

"I'd guess another minute," About replied, equally quietly. "Maybe two, but I wouldn't count on that."

Camille nodded. He absentmindedly blotted the drops of sweat from his forehead, and About pretended not to notice.

The Manties had been in-system for almost twenty-five minutes. Their velocity was up to over 5,000 KPS, and the range had fallen to 7,586,000 kilometers. From that geometry, Manticoran missiles had a powered range of almost 7,700,000 kilometers, so every unit of Sampson Defense Command was already inside their range basket. They wouldn't wait a lot longer, About knew. Not when they couldn't be positive none of the defending starships had been able to get their hyper generators spun up.

✦ ✦ ✦

"Launch point in fifteen seconds," Commander Eccles announced, and White Haven nodded.

It all came down to this, he thought.

Part of him—a big part—wanted to wait still longer, but some of the lighter Peep units—four destroyers and three of the light cruisers—had their wedges up now. It couldn't take very much longer for some of their larger consorts to follow suit, and he still couldn't know for certain about their hyper-generator status.

And even from this range, his missiles would take just under one hundred fifty seconds to reach their targets. Two and a half minutes in which some of those targets might yet escape into hyper.

"Ten seconds," Eccles said quietly. Then—

"Launch point!"

✧ ✧ ✧

"Dear sweet God," Citizen Senior Chief Geffroy whispered.

Her eyes darted to a computer display, watching the readout spin upward as the computers evaluated the stupendous tide of missile icons. That tsunami sped toward Sampson Defense Command and Task Force 37 like God's own curse, accelerating steadily at 441.3 KPS², and then—

"Tracking estimates minimum four thousand—I say again, four-zero-zero-zero—missiles inbound. Time of flight one-four-eight seconds," someone else announced with her voice.

✧ ✧ ✧

Henri Costa felt something almost like relief as the Manties finally fired.

He'd guessed the instant they arrived that they'd come with heavy loads of their accursed missile pods, and their heavy ships' leisurely acceleration had supported that initial assessment. Now the hideous rash of crimson icons racing toward his frail command confirmed it once and for all.

There was no way in the universe his ships, his men and women, could withstand that deluge. He knew that. But at least the agonizing wait was over now . . . or would be, in just over two minutes.

"All ships, Com," he said.

"Live mic," his communications officer replied quietly, and he faced his pickup.

"This is Cit—" He paused. "This is Vice Admiral Costa," he said. "I'm proud of all of you. It's been my honor to command you. And now, we have a job to do. God be with you all."

He looked into the pickup a heartbeat longer, then cut the circuit and settled back, distantly aware of the whimper coming from Bozonnet. Even now a corner of his brain reflected on how the Committee's watchdogs would have responded to that broadcast if they'd ever known about it. But the thought was distant, buried under his curiously serene calm. What mattered was that his *people* knew.

That he'd told them.

He fastened his shock frame as he prepared to face the missile storm at their side.

**HMS *Prince Adrian***
**Madras System**
**August 19, 1906 PD**

"SO ASIDE FROM YOUR CONCERNS with the node maintenance, the shuttles are in good shape, Scotty?"

"Yes, Ma'am," Scotty Tremaine replied. "Flight systems just passed their ninety-six-hour inspect-and-maintain cycle on everything but Shuttle Three—it's twelve hours off-cycle with the other birds, but we're going to short-check it to bring it on-calendar with the others next inspection—and Enviro checks green on all of them. Power systems on Shuttle Alpha and Marine Two are about due for I-and-M, but their diagnostics all look good, so I don't expect any surprises there. It's the nodes that worry us."

He and Senior Chief Harkness stood in Brandy Bolgeo's tiny alcove of an office, and she looked down at the memo board he'd handed her when they came in.

"We're not quite up to the book overhaul limit on any of them," she pointed out.

"No, Ma'am," Tremaine agreed. "But we're getting close, and the spares situation's not getting any better. When I realized how close we were, especially on the Alpha shuttle, I checked with Commander Tyson about availability."

Brandy nodded. Commander Richard Tyson was the Logistics Officer aboard HMS *Juan Navarro*, the superdreadnought-sized maintenance ship based in the Madras System as the core of Sixth Fleet's service squadron. They really should have had two of her, but there *weren't* a lot more of them, and the Navy was still playing catch-up on the lost time and seriously run-down maintenance stocks imposed by the formal declaration's long delay.

The *Johnny*, as she was known with varying degrees of fondness, was running at maximum capacity to keep up with Sixth Fleet's demands, especially with the repair of the light damage the superdreadnoughts *Kodiak Maximus* and *Paladin* had suffered in Sampson. The five laserhead hits scattered between the two of them had inflicted no significant harm on their heavily armored hulls, although the same damage would have been rather a different story for something as fragile as *Prince Adrian*. The most time-consuming repair was the replacement of two elements in *Paladin*'s Number Two Gravitic Array. But restoring the wallers fully to full capability took precedence over other, lesser chores, and more and more of what should have been "yard dog" maintenance had fallen on the shoulders of individual ships' engineering departments.

Engineering departments like *Prince Adrian*'s.

Technically, Lieutenant Tremaine shouldn't have gone directly to Tyson. He should have reported his concerns to Lieutenant O'Brien or Brandy, and Lieutenant Commander Yaytsev should have taken them up with Tyson. Going direct that way, especially on a pure information request, didn't violate any regulations or formal procedures, but it *was* frowned upon because of the way it could clutter the communication channels and requisition pipelines. The last thing they needed when everyone was so overworked were multiple or conflicting requests from different officers aboard the same ship. At the same time, it was the sort of initiative she'd come to expect out of Tremaine. She tapped the memo board, scrolling to the next page, and nodded mentally as she found exactly what she'd expected.

"They're that backed up?" she asked, looking back up from the neatly tabulated availability data Tremaine had assembled.

"For right now, yes, Ma'am. And, frankly, the Commander doesn't think it's going to get better anytime soon." Tremaine grimaced. "I think part of it's the construction programs, Ma'am. That and the refits."

Of course it was, Brandy thought. One of the first places the Admiralty had gone while it was busy robbing Peter to pay Paul was the new construction queue. Keeping ships they already had in service up and running—and provided with ordnance—was more important even than the ships currently under construction. So parts, personnel, and funds had all been diverted from the building slips to the maintenance of already operational units. And, in many ways, the initial successes of Riposte Gamma—not to mention the battles of Hancock, Yeltsin, and Seaford—had made an already bad problem even worse.

The Royal Manticoran Navy had captured almost forty Havenite ships-of-the-wall in undamaged or repairable condition before Admiral Caparelli had been forced to suspend operations. A dozen or so of them had been handed over to the Grayson Space Navy, which badly needed a solid core of wallers of its own. The rest had already become—or were still in the process of becoming—welcome reinforcements to the RMN's own wall-of-battle. Unfortunately, even the ones which had been almost entirely undamaged required significant refits to make them compatible with existing RMN units and practices. Most of them needed repairs—*major* repairs, in some cases—as well, however. That had actually made the delay between the end of Riposte Gamma and the formal declaration fortunate, in some ways, in that it had given the desperately overworked yard dogs time to get more of those prize vessels back into service under Manticoran colors.

Yet the effort which had gone into them had been still another diversion from the new construction programs, and it had eaten up still more of the Navy's maintenance resources without any special appropriation to replace them. All of which meant it was going to be quite some time—probably at least another T-year—before BuShips fully regained its balance.

And part of the trickle-down consequences of that was obvious in the spares manifest and projected delivery time fame Commander Tyson had shared with Tremaine.

"All right." She looked up from the memo board. "I'll take your report to Commander Yaytsev. I'm pretty sure he'll endorse your recommendation and we'll request enough spares to bring us fully back up to book inventory levels. But based on this"—she tapped the board—"we all know we're not going to get that."

"No, Ma'am, we're not," Tremaine agreed with a slight grimace, and Brandy moved her gaze to Harkness.

"May I safely assume you're keeping a sharp eye on the diagnostics, Senior Chief?"

"Yes, Ma'am," Harkness replied. "All my people are briefed in on the spares situation. We're doing everything we can to baby our systems along, and our techs are pretty damned good, you should pardon the expression. But no matter how good they are, the truth is that—like the Lieutenant says—we're going to start missing book mandatory replacement times in a couple of more T-months. Unless something changes, of course."

Brandy's grimace was less slight and considerably more sour than Tremaine's had been, but she nodded. She'd discovered, even in her relatively brief time aboard *Prince Adrian*, that Horace Harkness was every bit as competent as her father had predicted. And he'd been on his best behavior the entire time. In fact, she'd made a point out of consulting his service record, and it would appear Horace Harkness had reformed. The thought of a reformed Harkness was probably enough to boggle the mind of anyone who'd known the *old* Harkness, but there wasn't a sign of his fabled ability to circumvent the limitations of official regulations on things like games of chance and onboard intoxicants. For that matter, he hadn't had a single fight with a Marine in over three T-years, which was a new record for him.

Another thing she'd discovered about him was that even though he had to know whose daughter she was, he'd never once given any sign that he did. Still a bit rough around the edges, yes. Definitely. But probably one of the two or three toughest, most capable senior noncoms she'd ever met. If he said "his people" were on top of things, then they were on top of things. At least as well as they could be, given the spares situation.

"Ma'am," Tremaine said, "I understand why we're where we are on this stuff." He waved at the memo board on her desk. "And I get that we didn't have a choice. But do you have any better notion than we do of how long it's going to take to get fully back up to speed? Because, truth to tell, I don't have a clue, and some of our people in Flight Ops are asking me about it. Not just them, either. Gunny Babcock was in the shop bending the Senior Chief's ear about it yesterday."

"Babcock?" Brandy arched an eyebrow, then glanced at Harkness. "Senior Chief?"

"She wasn't bitc—complaining about it, Ma'am," Harkness replied. "She was just a little . . . concerned about long-term serviceability. Looking ahead, I mean."

"And is that an issue yet, Scotty?" Brandy asked, turning back to Tremaine.

"No, Ma'am. Not yet. But if you'll notice, the pinnaces' nodes are deeper into their life cycles than any of our other small craft. Mostly because they get more and harder use, of course. I think Major Yestachenko's cutting back a bit on training flights to stretch that. Nobody's told me that for sure, but the flight schedule's definitely lighter than it was. And I think the Gunny's worried about that."

"You mean you think Major *Yestachenko's* worried about it, and Sergeant Major Babcock, like the excellent NCO she is, is voicing *her* concerns to Harkness, so that he can voice them to you, so that *you* can voice them to *me*," Brandy said dryly.

"Well, actually, yes, Ma'am," Tremaine admitted. "Which doesn't mean she doesn't have a point."

"No, it doesn't." Brandy nodded, forbearing to mention just how well she and Iris Babcock knew one another. "In fact, that's exactly what both of you—all three of you—should be doing. Unfortunately, I can't tell you anything Commander Tyson hasn't told you already. I will say that my acquaintance with the Commander suggests that his numbers are pretty close to spot-on. That's about all I've got, though."

"About what I thought, Ma'am." Tremaine smiled crookedly. "It's just that—"

The com unit on Brandy's desk chimed, and she raised one finger at Tremaine.

"Hold that thought, Lieutenant," she said, and tapped the acceptance key.

The display lit, and Commander Carson looked out of it at her.

"Good afternoon, Sir," she said. "How may I help you?"

"The Captain needs to see you, Lieutenant," the XO said.

"Of course, Sir." Brandy hoped her sudden tickle of trepidation didn't show in her voice. "When would be convenient for him?"

"Now would be a good time, actually," Carson replied. "And, by the way, Lieutenant, you're not in any kind of hot water. Just in case you were worried about that. Which of course"—he smiled broadly— "no officer possessed of a sterling character such as your own could possibly have been."

"No, Sir. Of course not." Brandy allowed herself an answering smile, and he chuckled.

"In that case, please report to Captain McKeon's day cabin as soon as you can."

"Of course, Sir." Brandy glanced at her chrono. "I'm about done here at the moment, actually. I can be there in ten minutes, if that's convenient?"

"That would be just about perfect, actually. I'll tell him to expect you."

✦   ✦   ✦

"Lieutenant Bolgeo to see the Captain," Brandy told the Marine outside McKeon's cabin's hatch.

"Of course, Ma'am." The Marine braced briefly, then touched the com pad beside the hatch. "Lieutenant Bolgeo to see the Captain," he announced.

"Enter," a voice responded, and the hatch slid open. Brandy nodded to the sentry and stepped through it. She started to come to attention, but Captain McKeon waved a hand at her.

"Have a seat, Brandy," he invited instead, pointing at one of the chairs in front of his desk, then tapped his desk unit.

"Yes, Sir?" a voice said.

"I am in desperate need of coffee and two cups, Hiram."

"Sir, I gave you a fresh pot thirty minutes ago," Chief Steward Mate Brodzinski replied.

"And your point is? That was then, and this is now. Besides, Lieutenant Bolgeo is here, and I'm sure she needs a cup, too. That, by the way, is the *only* reason that I am disturbing you with my modest request."

"I'm sure it is," Brodzinski said dryly. "Three minutes, Sir."

"Well, if you *have* to take that long," McKeon said with a broad grin.

"I don't know, Sir. Might be more like *five*, now that I think about it."

"Just remember who signs your efficiency report, Hiram," McKeon chuckled, and released the key to sit back in his own chair as Brandy settled into hers.

"In case Commander Carson didn't already tell you this, Brandy, you're not here so that I can express any unhappiness with you. In fact, it's the other way around. I've been entirely satisfied with your performance aboard ship so far, and Commander Yaytsev gives you very high marks. Which, judging by the Department's performance, you fully deserve."

"Thank you, Sir."

A sense of satisfaction flowed through her. She'd already discovered that Alistair McKeon was one of those COs who believed encouragement of success was a better motivator than chewing out failures. By the same token, as far as she could tell he never offered false praise. His people had to *earn* his approval, and that made it even more satisfying—even more precious—when they got it.

"Obviously, all our departments are working hard," McKeon continued. "The truth is, though, Engineering's working hardest of all, and everybody else depends on Engineering. We were just about due for our next scheduled general overhaul when it all hit the fan in Hancock and Yeltsin. Obviously"—his tone was desert dry—"we missed it. And, trust me, I know exactly how tight margins have gotten on some of our systems."

Brandy nodded soberly, although she wondered where this was going.

"Riding herd on all of that, keeping all those balls in the air simultaneously, is not an easy chore," the captain said. "Commander Yaytsev's done an outstanding job, but there are limits in all things. The reason I mention this—"

He paused as the hatch to Chief Steward Mate's Brodzinski's pantry slid open and the steward emerged with a tray bearing a fresh carafe of coffee and two cups. He set his tray on the end of McKeon's desk, poured coffee into both cups, then lifted the lid on the small container of cream to check its level. Satisfied with what he saw, he replaced the lid, collected his tray, and left. All without a single word.

McKeon looked after him with a grin, then poured a hefty dollop of cream and dropped a single sugar cube into his cup. Brandy preferred hers black, and she'd already learned that Brodzinski brewed a superior cup of coffee.

She sipped appreciatively, waiting while McKeon stirred his cup, laid the spoon aside, and took a sip of his own. Then he looked back at her.

"The reason that I've mentioned just how hard Commander Yaytsev's job has been is that the Commander is leaving the ship."

Brandy sat straight up in her chair, eyes widening in surprise. This was the first she'd heard of anything like that, and there was something about Captain McKeon's eyes, a trace of . . . sorrow, perhaps, in them.

"May I ask why, Sir?"

"You may. I know you've met his wife, so you know she's also navy. You may not know, though, that Lieutenant Commander Yaysteva is a yard dog on *Vulcan*."

He paused, eyebrows raised, and Brandy nodded. HMSS *Vulcan* orbited Sphinx, not Manticore, but it was every bit as big—and busy—as *Hephaestus*.

"Actually, I did know that, Sir. She's worked with my dad on a couple of projects."

"Well, there was an accident aboard *Vulcan*," McKeon said heavily. "Just one of those things, especially with everyone pushing as hard as they are. It looks like one of the construction shuttle pilots misjudged his approach, but we'll never know for sure. He didn't make it, and the black box was unrecoverable."

Brandy's eyes widened. Navy small-craft flight recorders were engineered to survive under extreme circumstances. Any accident sufficient to destroy one of them had to have been a . . . significant event.

"The collision took out an entire construction bay assigned to *Dominion*, one of the new *Gryphon*-class ships," McKeon continued, as if to confirm her own thoughts. "Thirty-seven dead, nineteen injured, and just as bad, in many ways—although it's one hell of a lot less painful in human terms—*Dominion*'s completion date's been pushed back at least a couple of T-months. Probably more like three or four."

Brandy winced.

"Lieutenant Commander Yaysteva is among the injured." McKeon paused, made himself take a sip of coffee, then set the cup back down. "In fact, she's very *badly* injured. They didn't think she was going to make it for the first couple of days, and best estimate is that she'll be in regen and rehab for a minimum of seven or eight months. I think you've had a little experience of that of your own?"

"You might say that, Sir. And I'm really sorry to hear she's been hurt, but I can tell you from that 'experience' of mine that Bassingford does really, really good work."

"I know. But, the Yaystevs have three young children—the oldest is only about twelve—and they don't have a lot of family. So as soon as I heard what had happened, even before I told the Commander, I approved immediate compassionate leave for him to return to the Star Kingdom to see to his family."

Brandy nodded. Some skippers, especially given current circumstances, would have been less than willing to give up an engineering officer of Kirill Yaytsev's caliber unless BuPers twisted their arms hard. She wasn't at all surprised that McKeon wasn't one of them. That was her first thought. But then she realized the captain had settled farther back into his chair and was looking at her with one eyebrow raised. Now why—?

Then the coin dropped. Of course. If Yaytsev was leaving, obviously someone had to replace him, and it would probably take at least a couple of weeks to find someone under these circumstances. Until they *did*, Yaytsev's duties and responsibilities would fall upon one Brandy Bolgeo.

"I understand, Sir," she said. "And I'll do my best to fill his shoes until his replacement gets here."

"Well, that's the reason I wanted to speak to you," McKeon said.

"I beg your pardon, Sir?"

"About that replacement," the Captain amplified. "The way things look right now, there won't be one."

"Sir?" Brandy realized she was sitting very, very straight in her chair.

"I said there won't be one." McKeon shrugged. "I've spoken with both Captain Bernardo and Captain Hunter. They agree with me that Commander Yaytsev needs to be returned to the Star Kingdom as quickly as possible, under the circumstances. They told me, however, that it might be some weeks before they could find me a replacement for him."

He paused, one eyebrow arched.

"I'll certainly try to hold the fort until—" Brandy began, but his waved hand interrupted her.

"As I say, they told me it might be some weeks," he said. "And I told them that would be fine. That I can wait until they find me a new *assistant* engineer, because I'm fully satisfied with the *chief* engineer I already have. You."

Brandy's eyes flew wide. Chief engineer? At *her* age? After she'd been beached for so long? When she'd been aboard *Prince Adrian* for barely three months?!

"I appreciate that, Sir," she said, "but are you—?"

"Yes, I'm sure," he interrupted again. "I know you haven't been aboard long, but Kirill thinks the world of you. He didn't hesitate for an instant when I asked if you could take the slot. Which, I might add, only confirmed my own impression and my own inclination. I know you're junior for the position, and I'm sure putting you into it will raise some clerical-type eyebrows back at BuPers. For that matter, given what I just said about easy chores—or, rather, the *lack* of them—I'm not offering you any easy duty here, Lieutenant. On the other hand, I'm confident of your ability to hack it. And as long as you can, and as long as you do, the slot's yours. Fair?"

"More than fair, Sir," Brandy said firmly. "And I promise you'll get the best I've got."

"Never doubted it," McKeon said. "If I had, you wouldn't be getting the slot. So, Chief, I suppose you should be getting back to your shop."

"I guess I should, Sir. I need to talk to the Commander, anyway."

"He's aboard the flagship right now, arranging transportation. *Dandelion*'s pulling out for the home system in less than three hours, and I want him aboard her. So I'm not certain you'll have time for that talk."

"Yes, Sir."

Brandy hoped she sounded as confident as she wanted to. And the truth was that Yaytsev had seen to it that both she and Lieutenant O'Brien were fully up to speed on their department's operations. What she was less confident about was that she'd paid close enough attention to those briefings of his.

"I'm sure you'll do fine, Lieutenant," the captain told her, and there might have been ever so faint a trace of wickedness in the smile he gave her. "And, that said, I suppose I should let you go get started."

"Of course, Sir." Brandy inhaled deeply, set her cup on his desk, and stood. "Permission to withdraw, Sir?"

"Granted, Lieutenant Bolgeo." McKeon's smile was much broader now. "Let's be about it, Chief."

## Mathias System
## October 1, 1906 PD

"ALPHA TRANSLATION . . . now."

Lieutenant Saldaña's announcement wasn't actually necessary, Earl White Haven thought, given the ripple of nausea which always accompanied even the most gentle translation into normal-space. Despite which, SOP required his astrogator to announce it, anyway. Just in case anyone managed to not notice, he assumed.

"System primary bearing zero-zero-niner, zero-zero-seven." More than a trace of satisfaction colored Saldaña's professional tone as she made the follow-on announcement. "Range to hyper limit seven-zero light-minutes. Present n-space velocity one-four-four-five KPS."

"Very good!" White Haven said. "Begin acceleration."

"Aye, aye, Milord," Saldaña replied as her fingers flew across her panel. "Beginning acceleration . . . now."

"Lot calmer than Samson or Welladay, Milord," Captain Hunter observed with a crooked smile, standing at White Haven's shoulder.

"That's sort of the idea," the earl replied. "Well, that and keeping the bastards guessing."

Hunter nodded, and the two of them watched the plot as Sixth Fleet began its steady acceleration toward the Mathias System's G4 primary. From this range, it was only a tiny, barely brighter speck of light, and that, too, was part of the plan.

Mathias would be the third target Sixth Fleet had hit in less than three months since the Royal Manticoran Navy's resumption of offensive operations. Admiral Kuzak's Fourth Fleet had been almost equally busy on the far side of Trevor's Star, and White Haven hoped the Peeps were paying attention. Unlike Samson, which had been little more than a forward logistics base, or Welladay, which had provided basing facilities for only a pair of light-cruiser squadrons, Mathias was a significant fleet base. Still far smaller than the massive

Havenite base guarding Trevor's Star, but big enough to support major task forces. According to Commander O'Hanlon's latest intelligence summaries and scouting reports from ONI, there shouldn't have been any of those major task forces in-system at the moment, however, although he couldn't be certain of that. But it still represented a major node in Trevor's Star's outworks. One whose loss, hopefully, they'd be unable to ignore.

And if White Haven was especially lucky, those intelligence summaries and scouting reports were wrong. He'd *love* to catch two or three squadrons of Peep wallers in Mathias!

*Actually, I'd love to catch them just about* anywhere, *damn it!* he thought. *It was sheer luck we caught Costa in Sampson, and taking out four superdreadnoughts was a hell of a bonus prize, when all we expected was battleships. But I really don't like how damned coy their wall-of-battle's being. Especially not given the way their people are standing and fighting even when anybody must know they're completely screwed. We know they've got one hell of a wall hiding somewhere, but* where?

No one knew, and that bothered him.. It bothered him a lot, because what he wanted more than anything else in the universe was to whittle that wall down before it—and especially its officers—got any closer to properly trained. But where the hell *was* it? He frowned ferociously at his plot as his own ships-of-the-wall and their screening elements slowly built their vector toward Mathias, but the plot returned no answer to his burning question. Nor would it, until Sixth Fleet got a lot closer.

This time, he'd made his alpha translation much farther out than in his previous attacks. As Saldaña had announced, Sixth Fleet was seventy light-minutes from the system's hyper limit and over eighty-three from Smaragdenio, the system's only inhabited planet, which put it over ninety light-minutes from the system primary. In fact, only Pagovoyno, the system's outermost ice planet, lay astern of it.

It would have taken far more sensitive arrays than ONI's assessments gave the Mathias fleet base to detect such a gradual translation at such an enormous distance from Smaragdenio. Detecting impeller wedges covered by Manticoran stealth systems would be even harder—at least at this sort of range—so, if all went according to plan, no one would see him coming until it was much too late.

If all went according to plan.

"Deploy the drones," he said.

"Deploying drones, aye, aye, Milord," Commander Eccles replied, and the light codes of a half-dozen recon drones accelerated away from their motherships, spreading out before they settled down on a heading toward Mathias. Their acceleration rate was almost fifteen thousand gravities, sixty times that of Sixth Fleet's starships, but their impeller signatures were both tiny and enormously stealthy, and they'd accelerate for only fifteen minutes. At that point, their velocity relative to their destination would be 133,830 KPS, forty-five percent of lightspeed. They'd still be well over a light-hour from the hyper limit when their drives went dark, so they'd need another two and a half hours to reach it, but they'd also be effectively invisible to any waiting passive sensors.

He watched the plot for another few minutes, then straightened.

"I see it's about lunchtime," he said, "and I'm feeling peckish. Join me for lunch, Byron?"

"Of course, Milord," Captain Hunter replied in an equally casual tone, and White Haven looked at the slightly built, brown-haired young woman standing patiently and attentively at his elbow.

"Ping Captain Goldstein, Lori," he said. "Ask him, with my compliments, to join me and the chief of staff in my dining cabin."

"Of course, Milord," his flag lieutenant acknowledged.

"Thank you." White Haven nodded, then smiled slightly. "And you're invited, too," he told her. "I'm sure we'll be able to find something onerous for you to do."

"I don't doubt that for a moment, Milord," Lieutenant Barrera told him solemnly, and he snorted a chuckle before he and Hunter headed for the flag bridge hatch.

✦　✦　✦

"The Flag's reporting the first take from the RDs, Skipper," Lieutenant Commander Chen said. "Just got a relay from *Circe*."

"Ah?" Alistair McKeon swiveled his command chair toward the tac officer's station. "And what do we appear to have found?"

Slowed by the missile pods on tow behind all of its units— including CruRon 33, this time, but not the destroyers of DesFlot 17, which had been added to White Haven's order of battle only the month before—it had taken Sixth Fleet almost three and a half hours to build its velocity to 34,542 KPS. In that time, it had traveled only 242,915,000 kilometers, so range to the Mathias hyper limit was still over fifty-six light-minutes, but the speedier recon drones had crossed that limit over an hour earlier. Their superb passive sensors had examined the Mathias Fleet Base's platforms, orbiting Smaragdenio, in minute detail, then used tightly focused, directional com lasers to transmit their findings home to *Queen Caitrin*, whose equally tightly focused, and far shorter-ranged whisker lasers had shared that information with her subordinate flagships, like HMS *Circe*.

It had taken that light-speed data fifty-six minutes to reach Sixth Fleet, which was a little frustrating, given that the RMN, unlike any other navy, actually had an FTL com ability. *Its* drones could have transmitted that data in under fifty-two seconds if they'd been allowed to use it, but the FTL system was still in its infancy. Bandwidth remained very limited, so while transmission speed was faster than light, message *generation* speed was quite low. More to the point, the grav pulses the system used were impossible to conceal. So far as ONI knew, the Peeps didn't even suspect—yet—that the system existed, but eventually, if they kept picking up "random" grav pulses and started putting two and two together, they would. That being the case, standing orders were to deploy them only when it was absolutely essential. Which it wasn't here.

"Not as much as we'd hoped, I'm afraid," Chen said, studying his display as the results relayed from CruRon 33's flagship came up on it. He tapped in a command and threw the same data into the master plot. "Looks like they've reinforced with another squadron of battleships since our last flyby," he continued, "but no sign of any wallers."

"Damn it, Skipper!" Lev Carson muttered. "Where the hell *are* they?"

"So now we're back to the 'Your skipper knows *everything*,' are we?" McKeon shot back just a bit testily, then grimaced. "As a matter of fact, I *don't* know. But I have to agree with Admiral White Haven. The longer it takes us to find them, the more painful it'll be when we finally do."

"Exactly what I was thinking," Carson growled. "Damned inconsiderate Peep bastards just *have* to be difficult, don't they?"

McKeon snorted in sour amusement as he studied the neat columns of data.

According to the drones, the fleet base orbiting Smaragdenio was accompanied by eighteen battleships and a couple of dozen light cruisers and destroyers, but—as Chen had said—not a single ship-of-the-wall. That was unfortunate. Depriving the Peeps of eighteen more battleships would be eminently worthwhile, but they had almost four hundred of the damned things. In fact, they were the only first-line navy that was still building them, and not even they built them to use in fleet actions. They were area defense ships, cheap enough to build in significant numbers, then parcel out to cover the People's Republic's rear areas.

*And to suppress any local temptation toward independence*, he reminded himself sourly.

They'd be well worth removing from the Peep order of battle, but each of them were barely half the size of a superdreadnought and had maybe a quarter of the combat power. And he didn't like the fact that they were reinforcing a base like Mathias—scarcely vital to their survival, but significantly more important than someplace like Samson—with *battleships*, not wallers. If it was worth reinforcing at all, then they should have reinforced with something that might actually have made a difference. Clearly, they were saving those ships-of-the-wall for something more important. Like the defense of Trevor's Star itself.

*Well*, he consoled himself, *if we keep gnawing away at their perimeter long enough, they'll have to start peeling off some of the heavy mob, putting the damned wallers out where we can get at them. That's the plan, anyway.*

"Wonder about their impeller nodes," he said out loud, and Chen shrugged.

"Impossible to say till the birds get even closer, Sir. If I were a betting man, I'd say their drive-room capacitors are probably carrying a charge. *Mine* damned sure would be."

"There is that old saying about burned hands, isn't there?" McKeon observed.

"They did kind of get singed at Samson and Welladay, didn't they, Sir?" Chen replied with a grin.

"And they're going to get singed again in about"—Commander

Carson looked at the time display—"six hours. In fact"—he looked back at McKeon with a grim smile—"they're gonna get scorched right down to the *bone*, Skipper."

✦　✦　✦

"Crossing the limit in thirty seconds, Milord," Lieutenant Saldaña announced, and White Haven nodded.

Sixth Fleet had stopped accelerating fifty-two minutes ago. Their velocity was up to 70,640 KPS, a tad under twenty-five percent of lightspeed, but there was no longer an active impeller signature to give them away, every active sensor system was shut down, and their stealth fields were active. They couldn't avoid *some* electronic emissions, and the odds of detection increased steadily from this point, despite their cautious approach, but ideally, no one would see them for another forty minutes . . . the point at which he intended to demand their surrender.

From a purely cold-blooded tactical perspective, it would have been even better to continue all the way into powered missile range before giving away his presence. Unfortunately, if the Havenite battleships did have hot nodes—which they damned well should, after Samson and Welladay—they could raise their wedges in no more than fifteen to twenty minutes, depending on the proficiency of their engineering personnel. Worse, he would pass through his entire missile envelope in less than five minutes at his present velocity. That was time for only eight salvos from his internal launchers before they moved out of range. After that, it would take hours to decelerate to zero, then approach the planet once more, even using the Long Maneuver. And that, in turn, meant any mobile unit that hadn't been too cataclysmically damaged to move in that five-minute window would escape long before Sixth Fleet could do anything about it.

He'd give those Peep skippers one chance to save their people's lives. Experience in Samson and Welladay suggested their "people's commissioners" wouldn't allow them to accept it, despite the fact that there was no way under God's heaven those battleships could survive even a passing engagement against his wall-of-battle. He hated that, but not as much as he would have hated letting all those ships escape to kill other Manticorans in some future battle. He never doubted that the Peep propagandists would play up his "cold-blooded, cynical, impossible to meet" demands and ignore the fact that their commissioners had chosen to reject them, and he didn't like that, either. But his Star Kingdom hadn't started this war; the People's Republic of Haven had. So, yes, he would give those skippers a chance to at least try to save their people.

And if that chance was rejected, he would kill every single one of those ships without a moment's hesitation.

✦   ✦   ✦

"Shut that damned noise off!" Citizen Major General Jonathan Garrido barked.

The harsh, atonal howl which had summoned him to Mathias Alpha's command deck died, and he turned his glare to Citizen Colonel Spencer Blair, his operations officer, who'd beaten him to the command deck by perhaps fifteen seconds.

"How bad is it?"

"About as bad as it gets, Citizen Major General," Blair replied. "If we'd detected them sooner, maybe we could have done something about it, but at this point?" He shrugged, his expression bitter. "All we can do now is wait for the hammer."

"And why *didn't* we detect them sooner?" People's Commissioner Teymoori demanded.

"An excellent question," Garrido agreed. "Perhaps you'd care to answer it, Citizen Commander?" he added in a venomous tone, as he and Teymoori both turned to glare at the only naval officer on Garrido's staff.

*Because the Manties know what the hell they're doing and you idiots don't*, Citizen Commander Eligio Samper very carefully didn't say aloud. That sort of honesty could be fatal.

Citizen Rear Admiral Chelsea Simmons, who'd commanded the People's Navy base in Mathias until five months ago, had been relieved and called home for suspected "unreliability." Virtually her entire staff had been recalled along with her, "escorted" home to Nouveau Paris by a heavily armed detachment of State Security troopers.

No one in Mathias had heard a word from them—or about them—since, and Samper knew no one would.

That would have been bad enough, but the primary reason the Committee of Public Safety had doubted Simmons' reliability had been reports from Citizen Major General Garrido, who commanded the occupation and security forces making certain the Smaragdenio Republic remembered its place, and his people's commissioner. And since the Committee had no doubts at all about Garrido's devotion, it had seen no reason it shouldn't adopt his own modest suggestion and put him in direct command of the Mathias System's naval forces, as well. The fact that he knew exactly nothing about naval *warfare* hadn't dissuaded them for a moment when they gave him the slot.

And, in the process, put one Citizen Commander Samper into a job he wished to hell he'd been able to decline.

Now he turned to face Garrido and Teymoori squarely, his expression respectful.

"Citizen Major General, I'm sorry, but they must have made their alpha translation well beyond detection range."

"Really?" Teymoori asked in a biting tone. "And why are you so confident of that...convenient reason for System Tracking to have missed them, Citizen Commander?"

"I have to assume they're towing pods, Sir," Samper replied. "That would be in keeping with everything we've seen out of their tactics so far. Assuming they are, their maximum acceleration can't be much more than two hundred fifty gravities, but they're still coming in at almost seventy-one thousand kilometers per second. That suggests they must have accelerated for at least eight hours after making translation before they cut their impellers and went dark. There's no way to tell how long they've been coasting in ballistically, but I'd guess they probably arrived at least eighty or ninety light-minutes from Smaragdenio orbit. Our passive arrays simply aren't up to detecting a relatively gradual translation at that sort of range. We'd be hard put to hold and track even an active impeller wedge at anything much over forty-five light-minutes, even without Manticoran stealth systems to cover it. And once they went to silent running, even that disappeared, which left our passive sensors nothing to work with."

He kept his tone level, factual, and forbore to mention that even though this was the first they'd seen of the Manty starships, only a drooling idiot—which manifestly no Manty flag officer was—would have failed to send in an advanced screen of recon drones...which the passive arrays had *also* missed.

Garrido's jaw worked from side to side as he digested Samper's response. From his expression, he wanted to hold the citizen commander personally responsible for not somehow spotting the approaching Manticorans sooner.

"What about your active sensor systems?" Teymoori demanded, and Samper's own jaw clenched. "Why didn't *they* detect these... people sooner?"

"Because, People's Commissioner," the citizen commander said as soon as he was confident he had control of his tone, "they're still too far away for any active system to get a return off of them. This"— he waved his hand at the plot—"is driven solely by our *passive* sensors at the moment. And to be honest," he continued a bit daringly, "the fact that we've detected them at all was a lot more due to luck than anything else. Their wedges are down and their stealth systems are damping any electronic emissions, which gives even our passive arrays damn all to work with. We only found them because one of our optical platforms was looking in exactly the right direction when they occluded Pagovoyno, and that was what I can only call a very low-probability event."

Teymoori opened his mouth again, but Garrido raised his hand.

"I agree with you, Arnold, that it would have been much better to spot them sooner," he said, "but I think the Citizen Commander probably has a valid point."

Teymoori glowered at the citizen major general, but only for a moment. Very few of the People's Republic's current military officers would have dared to correct, far less contradict, their political watchdogs. Garrido had enough friends in sufficiently high places that Teymoori—who, to be fair, was generally on the same page with him, anyway—recognized the unwisdom of excessive zeal in his case.

"The important thing now is what we do about it," Garrido continued. "Spencer?"

"We've already alerted Citizen Rear Admiral Dietz and Citizen Rear Admiral Linton," the citizen colonel replied, "and the armed platforms are clearing for action. Offensive weapons systems should be online within the next ten minutes. On Citizen Commander Samper's recommendation, we're not bringing up our missile defense systems yet."

"Why not?" Teymoori pounced.

A flicker of irritation danced in Blair's eyes, Samper noted. Well, the citizen colonel might not be a naval officer, but even Marine officers understood the importance of emissions control.

It was a pity people's commissioners didn't.

The citizen commander started to open his mouth, but Blair spoke before he could.

"Because, Sir," the citizen colonel said, rather more frostily than he normally allowed himself to address Teymoori, "the instant we bring our defensive systems fully online, they'll activate their tracking and fire-control systems. Those are predominantly *active* systems, and the moment they start emitting, the Manties will know we've detected them. The longer we can keep them guessing, the better."

Teymoori flushed, but at least he had the good sense not to bite back at the citizen colonel. For the moment, anyway.

"What about the battleships, Citizen Commander?" Garrido's voice was at least marginally less belligerent, and Samper grimaced unhappily.

"The good news is that the Manties are sixteen minutes from attack range at their present velocity, and most of our ships *should* have time to get their wedges and sidewalls up before that, Citizen Major General." Best not to mention that fully proficient engineering personnel could have gotten *all* the battleships' wedges up from standby readiness with sixteen minutes' warning. "If they can, they'll be as combat ready as they could hope to be. But I'm afraid the truth is that it's not going to make a lot of difference. Not against this much firepower. There's always a certain degree of uncertainty relying on passive sensors, but if CIC's type estimates are accurate, we're looking at least twenty-four ships-of-the-wall, plus a screen of cruisers and battlecruisers and at least a dozen destroyers. Citizen Rear Admiral Dietz and Citizen Rear Admiral Linton only have eighteen battleships and nine light cruisers between them."

"Then they'll just have to do the best they can," Teymoori said sharply.

"Of course they will, Sir," Samper agreed. "And I'm sure they'll do the absolute best they can under the circumstances. I think it's probable these people will take losses of their own"—in fact, he doubted there was much chance in hell they would—"and as the Octagon's stressed, attrition works in our favor. But I'd be less than honest if I said there was any hope of our successfully defending the system."

Teymoori looked like a man who'd just tasted something rotten, but even he had to recognize the obvious truth of that statement.

✦ ✦ ✦

"We're coming up on the mark, Milord," Lieutenant Commander Groener said, and Hamish Alexander nodded at the com officer's reminder.

"Then I suppose we should go ahead and send it, Sean," he said.

"Aye, aye, Milord. Transmitting in . . . twenty seconds."

White Haven nodded again and tipped back in his command chair. He'd prerecorded the message Groener was about to transmit. In fact, he'd recorded it a second time, after reviewing the initial take, because he'd wanted to see it himself, be sure it said exactly what he wanted it to say, before he sent it on its way.

Sixth Fleet had been back in normal-space for just over nine and a half hours, now, and the system hyper limit lay 167,416,000 kilometers astern. The range to Smaragdenio orbit was still 3.9 light-minutes, but at his ships' current velocity, powered missile range was well over 19,600,000 kilometers, and they'd reach that range in only twelve more minutes. If the Peeps truly hadn't detected them yet, that would have been too little time for even Manticoran engineering crews to raise wedges.

"Transmitting now," Groener said, and White Haven's recorded message appeared on the repeater display deployed from his command chair.

"I am Admiral White Haven, Royal Manticoran Navy," his image said flatly, "and this message is to the commander of all Havenite forces in the Mathias System. The ships under my command will launch against your starships in twelve minutes from now. Your vessels cannot survive the missile exchange. I have no more desire to kill people than any other sane human being, however, so I offer you one opportunity to preserve your own people's lives. My recon drones have your ships and bases under continuous observation. You have five minutes from the receipt of this message to disable your starships by destroying their impeller rooms. Any ship which executes an emergency impeller room plasma dump and does not fire upon my command, will not be fired upon as we pass. Any ship which does *not* dump its plasma by the time my command has closed to within one hundred and sixty-seven thousand kilometers will be taken under fire and destroyed.

"The decision is yours . . . and the clock is ticking."

He gazed bleakly out of the display for four more seconds, and then it blanked.

"Here's hoping they're smart enough to do it, Milord," Byron Hunter said quietly, and White Haven shrugged.

"I know, and I'd like to think I'd be sane enough to do it, if the position was reversed. But truth to tell, I'm not sure I could swallow it, either. And I don't have these frigging 'people's commissioners' Abdur's been telling us about breathing down the back of my neck. Like you say, we can hope, but I honestly don't expect them to take the out."

Hunter nodded, and White Haven smiled grimly.

An emergency plasma dump wouldn't actually destroy any of the Peep battleships, but it *would* cripple their impeller rooms' plasma conduits. They'd be repairable—they were designed for emergency dumps in case of a catastrophic engineering failure—but those repairs would take months, even for a fully equipped repair yard, far less anything available in Mathias. And without impeller rooms, he wouldn't have to worry about their escaping before he could return to deal with them.

It was, as he'd told Hunter, the only sane option he'd left them, and as he watched the display, he found himself praying that they'd take it after all.

✧　✧　✧

". . . will be taken under fire and destroyed."

Citizen Major General Garrido's jaw ached from the pressure of his gritted teeth as he glared at the arrogant Manty aristocrat on his display. Then he turned his head and stabbed that same fiery glare at the split screen showing Citizen Rear Admiral Marika Dietz, Battle Squadron 71's commanding officer, and Citizen Rear Admiral Camila Linton, who commanded BatRon 113. The flag officers were flanked by their people's commissioners, of course.

"Well?" he snapped.

"He's right that our ships can't survive that much fire, Citizen Major General," Citizen Rear Admiral Dietz said from her flag deck aboard PNS *Martin Pelzer*. She was senior to Linton, which made her the tactical officer in command, and she met Garrido's glare levelly. "I'm not being defeatist. I'm just looking at the numbers. From past experience, they probably have at least three to four thousand missiles in their pods alone. Split the difference and call it thirty-six hundred for easy division. If they concentrate all of that on our battleships and distribute it evenly, that's two hundred laserheads per ship, and that doesn't even count their shipboard launchers." She shook her head. "I'm sorry, Citizen Major General, but that's the math, and no battleship ever built could survive that weight of fire."

"So you think we should accept his 'generous offer'?" Garrido demanded.

"I didn't say that," Dietz replied without even glancing at her own people's commissioner. "What I said is that we can't survive his fire. That doesn't mean we can't inflict damage in return."

From Citizen Rear Admiral Linton's expression, she wasn't in full agreement with her fellow citizen rear admiral, but she kept her mouth closed.

Garrido gave Dietz a choppy nod, but People's Commissioner Teymoori's eyes narrowed suddenly as a blizzard of icons appeared in the master plot, spreading away from the orbiting battleships. While he watched, the transponder beacons of escape pods began to flash.

"What are you doing, Citizen Rear Admiral?!" he snapped, and Dietz shrugged.

"I've given orders to evacuate all nonessential personnel, Sir," she said flatly. "They won't be needed to fight our ships, and I'd like to at least preserve them for the People's Republic's future service. Unless the Manties plan on permanently occupying Mathias, there are too many of our people in-system to haul all of them off as POWs, and there's ample life support aboard the platforms—or the planet, for that matter—to keep them alive until someone gets here to recover them."

"Who authorized that?!" Teymoori demanded.

"I did," Nicholas Riccardi, BatRon 71's people's commissioner said.

"What?!" Teymoori glared at Riccardi "I never—!"

It was clear Dietz's "defeatism" had infuriated him. Riccardi's endorsement of her decision only made it worse, but Garrido cut him off with another of those choppy nods.

"Makes sense, Citizen Rear Admiral," he acknowledged, and Teymoori closed his mouth with a snap, although his eyes blazed furiously.

"Thank you, Citizen Major General," Dietz said, and there was genuine gratitude in that unflinching tone.

"According to our readouts over here," Teymoori said sharply, "at least some of your ships' impellers are ready right now."

Dietz's nostrils flared. Unwisely, perhaps, but not surprisingly, Citizen Commander Samper thought. He'd often wondered what kind of mind it took to make a people's commissioner. Obviously, that included a steady diet of paranoia and suspicion, and Dietz's eyes glittered as she gazed out of the display at him.

"They are." She nodded. "But I'm not raising my wedges any sooner than I have to. And, no, Citizen Commissioner, it's not so I can vent the plasma at the last minute."

Teymoori's face twisted with fury, but Marika Dietz clearly didn't care about that any longer, and she moved those glittering eyes to Garrido.

"They can't know how long ago we detected them, Citizen Major General, so they can't know how far along our activation sequence is. At the moment, only four of our units are at full readiness to engage impellers, but several more are close enough they can probably raise wedges and sidewalls before any Manty missiles get here. I intend to wait until this White Haven launches. Hopefully, he won't know which of us can do that when he allocates his fire, and I want to give him as little time as possible to adjust that distribution once he does know which of us will be hardest to kill."

"Understood," Garrido said before Teymoori could respond. Then he turned to look at his people's commissioner himself.

"And now, Citizen Rear Admiral," he continued over his shoulder, gaze still locked with Teymoori's, "I'll get—we'll *all* get—out of your hair."

✧ ✧ ✧

"It looks like they're abandoning ship, Milord!" Commander Eccles announced. "We're picking up life-pod transponders, and the close-in drones show dozens of small-craft impeller wedges!"

She tapped a command into her console, using a corner of the main plot to zoom in on the orbiting battleships as the diamond dust icons spread outward from them. White Haven felt the hope rising from his staff, but he shook his own head regretfully.

"They're not abandoning ship," he said flatly.

"Maybe they didn't have hot nodes after all, Milord," Captain Hunter pointed out. "In that case, they couldn't vent the capacitors. So maybe they're just getting everyone they can out of harm's way and hoping we'll figure out they're abandoning ship and not blow them out of space anyway."

"Then they should have told us that's what they're doing." White Haven's voice was harsh, now, not flat. "Oh, I'm sure you're right in at least one respect, Byron—they *are* getting everyone they can out of harm's way. But it's the same thing we saw in Samson. Those"—he jabbed an index finger at the plot—"are their nonessential personnel."

"But if they can't vent the plasma," Hunter said, "then—"

"Then they should have told us that," White Haven repeated in a voice of cold iron. "We can't—and won't—take the chance that this is a bluff."

✦    ✦    ✦

"Evacuation complete, Citizen Rear Admiral," Citizen Captain Arias said in Marika Dietz's earbud, and she nodded to herself. It wasn't much, but at least she'd saved some of her people. Almost twenty percent of them, really.

"At least we got some of them out, Marika," People's Commissioner Riccardi said in her ear, too softly for anyone else to overhear. It was as if he'd read her mind, and she gave him a wan smile.

"As people's commissioners go, you're not too shabby, Nick," she said, equally softly, then cleared her throat.

"Good work, Cristóbal," she said in a louder voice. "Stand by to raise the wedge."

"Standing by, Citizen Rear Admiral," Arias acknowledged.

Dietz looked around her flag deck at some of the people she hadn't saved.

"Thank you all," she said simply.

✦    ✦    ✦

"Firing point in fifteen seconds."

Commander Eccles' quiet announcement seemed almost raucous against the hushed background of *Queen Caitrin*'s flag bridge. Tension had ratcheted steadily higher as the range dropped with no sign of venting plasma. Indeed, with no response of any sort to White Haven's demand . . . aside from those life pods and small craft.

He hadn't really expected there to be one.

"Proceed with launch," he replied.

"Launching in five . . . four . . . three . . . two . . . one . . . *launch!*"

✧   ✧   ✧

"Enemy launch!"

Citizen Commander Samper's head snapped up at the announcement, and his eyes darted to the plot. Unlike electronic emissions, gravitic signatures—or, rather, the "ripple effect" impellers generated along the Alpha bands—propagated at more than lightspeed. The incoming Manticorans were still almost twenty million kilometers, the better part of two light-minutes, from Smaragdenio, but the signatures of their incoming missiles appeared almost instantly on the display.

"Tracking estimates two-thousand-plus," *Mathias Alpha*'s tactical officer said harshly, and Samper closed his eyes for a moment. That was a smaller number than he'd expected, but not enough smaller.

*Be with them now, God*, he thought.

✧   ✧   ✧

"Return fire!" Citizen Rear Admiral Dietz grated.

✧   ✧   ✧

"The enemy has returned fire, Milord," Laura Eccles announced as the angry fireflies of Havenite missiles speckled *Queen Caitrin*'s plot.

"Oh, those poor damned bastards," Byron Hunter said quietly at White Haven's shoulder.

"Sometimes I hate my job," the earl replied. "This is like clubbing baby chicks."

"Not quite, Milord," Hunter replied. "These 'baby chicks' get to club back."

"I know."

White Haven's eyes never strayed from the plot as a second salvo spat from the doomed battleships' tubes. Then a third. The quiet background chatter increased in tempo and volume as Sixth Fleet's missile defenses began tracking the incoming fire.

"I know," he repeated harshly. "And that's why we've got no choice but to kill them, anyway. God *damn* the people who started this fucking catastrophe!"

✦ ✦ ✦

"Raise wedges *now*!" Citizen Rear Admiral Dietz barked, and impeller wedges snapped up almost instantly for twelve of the eighteen battleships under her command.

But only twelve. Six of them still weren't ready to engage . . . and now, she knew, they never would be.

✦ ✦ ✦

"Wedges coming up! One . . . five . . . nine—*twelve*, Milord!"

Whoever that was over there, he had battle-steel balls, White Haven thought ungrudgingly. Despite the tsunami of destruction rumbling down upon him, he'd timed it almost perfectly. Sixth Fleet's initial two-thousand-missile salvo was over two minutes downrange, barely forty seconds from impact. One of the downsides of the RMN's new missile pods was that they produced salvo densities which could all too easily overwhelm the firing ships' telemetry links. In many ways, that was a good problem to have, since those sorts of densities overwhelmed the defenders' ability to track and engage the threats, as well. But it also meant the attacker's fire control was too often less accurate than it might have been, because he simply lacked the links to update his missiles' penetration ECM or targeting queues. With truly massive salvos, it was a matter of assigning targets to the attack birds' relatively simpleminded onboard AIs, then sending them on their way without further communication. In this case, he'd deliberately limited his initial launch to something his wall-of-battle's fire control redundancy could handle, precisely because he'd wanted to retain a finer degree of control. Unfortunately, the Peeps' timing meant that first salvo was far enough downrange the control links had already been cut, so he couldn't retarget it to concentrate on the ships which had suddenly grown wedges and sidewalls after all.

But he'd taken advantage of those same control links to launch a second salvo from his remaining pods, eleven seconds after the first and made up to the same strength with his internal tubes. *Those* missiles were still under shipboard command.

"Tactical, redistribute the second wave. Assume the targets without wedges won't be there anymore."

"Aye, Milord. Retargeting now."

Sixth Fleet fired a total of four salvos, although the third and fourth, launched solely from shipboard tubes, were only half as heavy as the first two. There was no point firing more. Not unless White Haven wanted to target the orbital bases, as well, and he would vastly prefer to take those intact, if he could.

If he could.

✦　✦　✦

"Here it comes."

Marika Dietz didn't know which of her flag bridge officers had said that.

She never found out.

Battle Squadron 71 and Battle Squadron 113 had three minutes in which to fire. Their launchers' cycle time was twenty seconds, and there were forty-six tubes in each ship's broadside, so the defenders managed to launch nine salvos of their own, each over eight hundred strong, before the first Manticoran attack birds arrived.

The storm fronts of destruction crossed each other, but there was a vast difference between them. The Manticorans were firing capital ship missiles, with better targeting systems, much more capable EW and penetration systems, and far heavier laserheads with five percent more standoff range. Nor did it end there, because Sixth Fleet's antimissile defenses were both far deeper and far more capable than its Havenite counterparts', as well.

Marika Dietz's tactical officers were neither as experienced nor as well trained as the Royal Manticoran Navy's, but they fully understood the bleak menu of options available to them. That was why, at Dietz's direction, they'd targeted *all* their fire on just two of the Manticoran wallers.

✦　✦　✦

"Oh, shit!" Brian Chen snarled, even as his hands danced across his console. "They're concentrating everything—and I mean *everything*—on Admiral Triplett, Skipper!"

"All we can do is the best we can do," Alistair McKeon said, and Chen nodded.

CruRon 33 and BatCruRon 5 had the outer defense zone again,

and the twenty tin cans of Commodore Tyler Whitworth's Destroyer Flotilla 97 were a welcome addition to the missile screen. None of them offered that much individual firepower, but they provided a lot more platforms and telemetry links for counter-missile. Now the entire screen opened fire and incoming missiles vanished as intercepts blotted them away. More counter-missiles flashed past the advanced screen as the main wall brought its own defensive batteries to bear, and tension wrapped jagged jaws around McKeon's command deck.

"Standby to roll ship," he said in a taut voice.

*Prince Adrian*'s starboard point defense lasers began to fire as the range dropped. The incoming missiles' base velocity from launch was far lower than that of Sixth Fleet's birds, but the Manticoran's approach speed meant their *closing* velocity was identical, and they screamed in at forty-nine percent of lightspeed. The good news was that virtually none of them had been deliberately aimed at anything as insignificant as a heavy cruiser, far less a lowly destroyer. The bad news was that missiles that lost lock on their initial targets took whatever alternatives they could find.

"Roll ship now!" McKeon barked at the last possible moment.

*Prince Adrian* snapped up onto her side relative to the incoming missiles. McKeon had cut it too close for her to complete the maneuver before the laserheads reached attack range, but she didn't need a complete ninety-degree roll. Forty-five degrees was more than enough to bring the perimeter of her wedge up to block the Peeps' firing bearing. It also blocked her defensive fire, but McKeon had allowed for that. Given an inertial compensator and internal grav plates, impeller-drive ships were capable of incredible rotation rates in a snap roll. A superdreadnought would have taken at least two minutes to complete a ninety-degree roll; with less than a third the mass and seventy percent less beam, *Prince Adrian* could roll a full hundred and eighty degrees in only twelve seconds. That meant she could roll ship completely in the interval between Peep salvos, and the recon drones she'd deployed on tractors to beyond the perimeter of her wedge kept her plot fully updated while she rolled.

As she completed the one-hundred-eighty-degree roll to come fully inverted to her original position, her *port* defensive batteries knew exactly where to find the next wave of missiles and opened fire the instant they came on target.

The other ships of CruRon 33 spun with her, blotting away Havenite missiles with deadly precision. Whitworth's destroyers were even faster on the helm, and if Rear Admiral Moreno's battlecruisers were slower, they were still far nimbler than dreadnoughts or superdreadnoughts. Rather than complete rolls, they had to settle for thirty-degree arcs up and then back again. It wasn't as effective, but their close-in defenses were more powerful and their armor was far thicker.

Besides, none of those missiles had been aimed at them, either.

✦  ✦  ✦

"Impact in seven seconds!" Battle Squadron 17's ops officer announced harshly.

It wouldn't be an actual impact, of course. No one had relied on contact hits in a long time. But the term still served, and Dame Callie Chijimatsu, Baroness Triplett, braced in her command chair aboard HMS *Cycnus* for what she knew was coming.

*How the hell did we draw the lucky number?* a corner of her brain wondered bitterly. *There are three entire battle squadrons out here— why the hell pick on us?*

The screen had taken a huge bite out of the lead Havenite salvo. Sixth Fleet's carefully stacked wall had taken another, and the other squadrons' CM launchers continued to blaze away in BatRon 17's defense. But over three hundred missiles survived every counter-missile Sixth Fleet could throw at them, broke through to the inner defense zones, and hurled themselves against Admiral Triplett's dreadnoughts.

Their own point defense stabbed out under the calm, uncaring control of their tactical computers, and still more missiles died just short of the attack point. But then two hundred and seventeen laserheads detonated in a brimstone kaleidoscope, hurling bomb-pumped lasers like Ahab's harpoons, and *Cycnus'* seven-million-ton hull quivered as transfer energy blasted into her.

The dreadnought's sidewalls bent and twisted the incoming lasers and the anti-radiation fields inside the sidewalls degraded them. Besides, none of the incoming fire had originally been targeted upon her. Only a handful of the laserheads that reached attack range took her for their prey after losing their initial target locks, and her armor was up to the challenge. Despite the searing corona wrapped around

BatRon 17 as the nuclear detonations pumping those lasers detonated, Triplett's flagship took only superficial damage.

Her division mate, HMS *Hippogryph* was less fortunate. Unlike *Cyncnus*, she'd been singled out as one of Citizen Rear Admiral Dietz's priority targets. Less than twenty laserheads had targeted BatRon 17's flagship; over a hundred targeted *Hippogryph*, and half of them got through.

*Cyncnus*' sister ship bucked as that torrent of destruction hammered her. Her sidewalls blunted it—some. But nothing could have stopped it, and plating shattered under the merciless onslaught. Only her massive armor, and the fact that the battleships' laserheads were so much lighter than her own, saved her.

Not even that was enough to prevent brutal damage, and her defensive fire faltered as fire control arrays were blotted away and counter-missile tubes were reduced to twisted ruin. She staggered under the onslaught, and then the second salvo slammed home, ripping her wounded side like bomb-pumped chainsaws.

"Heavy damage to *Hippogryph*, Milady!" Triplett's ops officer said harshly. "They're concentrating on her and *Polyphemus*."

"Gutsy bastards," Triplett muttered. Whoever had ordered that fire plan must have known how unlikely she'd be to see how well it worked out, but Triplett had to admire the cold-blooded calculation behind it.

"Roll *Hippogryph* and *Polyphemus*!" she snapped. "Get them up on their sides and keep them there! And pull *Prince Edward* and *Thunderer* in tighter!"

"Aye, aye, Milady!"

✦   ✦   ✦

Admiral White Haven nodded in tight, bitter-eyed agreement as *Hippogryph* and *Polyphemus* rolled their broken, debris-shedding broadsides away from the enemy while their squadron mates pulled in close, interposing their own wedges against the incoming fire. Like Triplett, he recognized the icy logic behind the Peeps' targeting. But by the time the third incoming salvo reached the end of its run, there were no surviving Peep battleships to retarget its missiles . . . or any of those in the salvos behind it. That meant all of them continued to hurtle in on the two wounded dreadnoughts at the heart of Baroness Triplett's defensive formation, pounding remorselessly away at them.

But it also meant the defenders knew exactly who they were targeting, which at least doubled the effectiveness of their missile-defense firing solutions.

It was all over in three minutes. Three minutes in which HMS *Hippogryph* was knocked out of action for a minimum of seven months. *Polyphemus* was less badly damaged, but she'd be in yard hands for at least a couple of months herself... assuming anyone could find the yard space into which she could be put.

But in that same three minutes, eighteen Havenite battleships had been smashed into impotent, broken wreckage. Three of them had simply blown up; the other fifteen were in little better condition, and Hamish Alexander's mind flinched away from the scenes aboard those laser-threshed wrecks, where he knew men and women fought desperately to find and rescue trapped, wounded crewmates.

A handful of missiles—no more than a couple of hundred—had come from the Mathias fleet base's armed platforms, but they'd added very little to the carnage. Under the circumstances, White Haven hadn't taken them under fire in reply. There were far more human beings aboard those platforms, including several thousand civilian workers from Smaragdenio, who'd never asked to be part of this war. He had no desire to kill them if he didn't have to.

Two hundred and eighty-seven seconds after firing its first salvo, Sixth Fleet streaked across Smaragdenio orbit at 70,640 KPS, and the launchers fell silent on both sides. At that relative velocity, missiles simply couldn't overtake their targets, and White Haven inhaled deeply as he studied the plot.

Aside from a handful of light, inconsequential hits on three more of Vice Admiral Triplett's dreadnoughts, *Hippogryph* and *Polyphemus* were his only damaged units. Casualty reports hadn't yet come in, but he already knew they'd be bad enough to keep him awake for the next few nights. They were only a pinprick against the Peeps' losses, yet each of those pinpricks had had a name, people who loved that man or that woman.

People who would never see far too many of them again.

He stood looking into the plot for several seconds, then turned to Captain Hunter and Lieutenant Saldaña.

"Detach *Hippogryph* and *Polyphemus*, Byron. Have Whitworth peel off one of his divisions to ride herd on them. We'll send them back to rendezvous with the fleet train." He snorted harshly. "It's not like we'll need their firepower."

"Yes, Milord."

"While Byron sees to that, Wanda," White Haven continued, looking at Saldaña, "go ahead and prep for Sprinter."

"Of course, Milord."

✧  ✧  ✧

Citizen Commander Samper stood quietly to one side, watching Citizen Major General Garrido and People's Commissioner Teymoori with dark, bitter eyes.

*Mathias Alpha*'s command deck seethed with frantic activity as it tried to coordinate search and rescue. Every yard craft and tug Mathias could muster swarmed about the tangled wreckage which had been eighteen battleships and nine light cruisers only minutes before, looking frantically for survivors. It looked like there'd be more than Samper would have predicted, given the weight of fire they'd taken. Which wasn't to say there'd be a lot of them. At full complements, there'd been well over sixty-four thousand men and women aboard those sixteen battleships. The light cruisers which had died with them added "only" another twenty-seven hundred to the total.

Even with the "nonessential personnel" Dietz and Riccardi had managed to save, Samper doubted that more than a quarter of those sixty-six thousand human beings had survived, and what had all those deaths purchased?

Two damaged Manty dreadnoughts. Even if they'd killed every crewman and crewwoman aboard both of those ships—which they hadn't come close to accomplishing—Manticoran losses would have been less than fourteen percent of the People's Navy's.

*Attrition,* he thought bleakly, fighting the need to shout his fury at his superiors. *Attrition, hell! There's a point where "favorable rate of exchange" is frigging meaningless! And those bastards thought it was just fine. At least*—he smiled coldly—*they did as long as someone* else *did the dying on our side.*

From their expressions, they weren't so sold on the concept now.

In fairness, although "fair" was the last thing he wanted to be just at the moment, neither Garrido nor Teymoori had ever seen actual combat. Not naval combat, anyway. They'd only thought they understood what was coming. Now they'd seen it, witnessed the actual carnage, and they knew that same destruction could come even more easily to their unarmored orbital platforms.

"How much longer for search and rescue?" Garrido asked Citizen Colonel Blair, and Blair shrugged.

"It could take days, Citizen Major General. In fact, it *will* take days to be sure we've gotten everyone out of the wreckage."

Unlike Garrido, Blair had seen combat as an enlisted man, during the conquest of Trevor's Star and San Martin. He seemed less shaken than his commanding officer, and Samper thought he saw at least some of his own disgust in the Marine's eyes.

"How long to conclude *immediate* recovery operations?" Teymoori demanded. From his tone, Samper suspected the people's commissioner had seen the same thing in Blair's eyes.

"We can probably clear the life pods within four to six hours," the citizen colonel replied. "They're designed to make atmospheric entry on habitable planets, so they can set down on Smaragdenio independently if they have to. The small craft can dock with the bases and off-load anyone they've picked up. Collecting individual spacers who got out without pods will take considerably longer, and, frankly, they've got less time. Their vac suits don't have as much air as a life pod."

"So you're saying we'll be able to at least clear our fields of fire within, say, eight hours?" Garrido pressed.

"For certain values of 'clear,' at least, Citizen Major General," Samper offered. Garrido and Teymoori looked at him, and he shrugged. "Whatever we do about the life pods and small craft, the ship wreckage will still be there whenever the Manties come back. And, frankly, if they come back with blood in their eyes, they won't worry about not hitting ships they've already effectively destroyed. If they decide to treat our orbital bases to the same sort of bombardment, anything that gets in their way will be toast."

Teymoori gave him a dangerous glare, but Garrido nodded brusquely.

"Agreed," he said harshly. "But the best we can do is the best we can do." He inhaled deeply. "And at least it'll take them hours to get back here. Even without their pods, it'll take them—what, at least six, maybe seven hours?—just to kill that much velocity. Then they'll have to turn around and come all the way back, and they'll have to burn even more time decelerating if they want a zero/zero intercept with the planet!"

There were times, Samper reflected, when a little knowledge was a dangerous thing.

"I think your time estimate's likely to be a bit off, Citizen Major General," he said in his most tactful tone, watching the Manty fleet's vector in the master plot.

They weren't decelerating; they were *accelerating*.

Of course.

✧  ✧  ✧

"Sprinter executed, Milord," Lieutenant Saldaña reported, and White Haven nodded in acknowledgment.

Had he been able to eavesdrop upon Citizen Major General Garrido, the earl would have smiled broadly. And if he'd been privy to Citizen Commander Samper's thoughts, he would have smiled even more broadly.

Garrido was entirely correct about how long it would have taken Sixth Fleet to decelerate to zero. Killing its current velocity relative to Smaragdenio would, indeed, have taken the better part of six hours, during which it would have traveled over thirty-three light-minutes beyond its target.

What he'd overlooked was that it was only *twenty-nine* light-minutes to the hyper limit on the far side of the system.

Assuming Sixth Fleet simply continued at its current velocity, it would cross that limit in only *two* hours, and if it accelerated at the three hundred thirty-seven gravities it could attain now that it had jettisoned its pods, it would reach the farther limit in just over one hundred and four minutes.

That was exactly what Sprinter was designed to do . . . for reasons which would shortly become painfully obvious to Citizen Major General Garrido.

✧  ✧  ✧

"Are you sure about this, Citizen Commander?"

Under other circumstances, Eligio Samper would have taken considerable pleasure from the tentative note in Citizen Major General Garrido's voice. The system CO's arrogance was conspicuously absent at the moment. Under the circumstances which actually obtained, however, that was remarkably cold comfort.

"I'm afraid I am, Citizen Major General," he said. "And we'll know either way in about two or three more minutes."

Garrido looked at him, glanced at an ashen-faced Teymoori, then nodded and turned back to the plot.

The Manties were no longer concerned with stealthiness. Their impeller signatures blazed sharp and clear on *Mathias Alpha*'s gravitic arrays, and those signatures were FTL. At twenty-nine light-minutes, even FTL signatures took just over twenty-seven seconds to reach them, but that still allowed the base to track them in close to real-time. And in about two more minutes—

✧   ✧   ✧

"Hyper limit in two minutes, Milord," Wanda Saldaña said.

"Very good," White Haven acknowledged, sitting back in his command chair with a coffee cup clasped in both hands. He raised it and sipped as the time display ticked downward. Then—

"Hyper limit," Saldaña announced.

"Then I suppose it's time," White Haven replied. "Execute when ready."

"Executing now."

Saldaña tapped her console, and Sixth Fleet vanished into hyper.

The Royal Manticoran Navy called the maneuver White Haven had selected the "Long Maneuver," in honor of the long-ago tactical officer who had first devised it for the Royal Manticoran Navy. His brainchild wasn't unique to him. Most experienced navies were familiar with the concept, at least in theory. It simply wasn't something one could use very often, given that most naval combat occurred well inside a hyper limit. *Outside* a hyper limit, the weaker combatant normally disappeared into hyper space, avoiding battle as soon as it recognized the odds against it, which made any sort of combat that far from a system primary rare. Indeed, it practically never occurred unless someone had placed an especially valuable target—one valuable enough it *had* to be defended—in a distant asteroid belt or orbiting a gas giant outside its system hyper limit.

Under the proper circumstances, however, the Long Maneuver was extraordinarily useful.

Sixth Fleet translated upward into the lowest Alpha bands, carrying its prodigious velocity with it. And then, twenty seconds later, it translated straight back into normal-space.

Even that short a hop through hyper put it 113,250,000 kilometers beyond the limit when it translated back down again. But thanks to the translation's velocity bleed, its normal-space velocity was only 7,306 KPS, and at three hundred thirty-seven gravities of deceleration, that would reduce to zero relative to Smaragdenio in about thirty-six minutes. That would give its hyper generators ample time to recycle from standby to readiness, which would allow it to pop back up into hyper and micro-jump to the closest point to Smaragdenio outside the hyper limit in another twelve minutes. It would arrive with a normal-space velocity of approximately zero . . . 235,800,000 kilometers and barely four and a half hours flight time from a zero/zero intercept with the planet.

✦ ✦ ✦

"Well, at least we were close enough to detect *this* hyper footprint," Citizen Commander Samper said sourly to Citizen Colonel Blair.

The two of them stood side-by-side at the master tactical plot, watching the final stage of the debacle which had enveloped the Mathias System unfold before them as the Manties reappeared right on schedule, forty-nine minutes after they'd crossed the limit. They blinked back into normal-space, radiating the blue, forest-fire brilliance of a mass hyper transit, barely thirteen light-minutes from Smaragdenio. At the moment, they were headed away from their objective, but they were already decelerating, just as Samper—and, to be fair, Blair—had predicted. Neither of them was pleased by the confirmation of their prediction, and by this time, it would have been hard to determine which of them was more disgusted with their joint superiors.

"What do you think they're going to do?" Blair asked.

"Well, at the moment, they're decelerating to kill the last of their velocity away from us," Samper replied dryly. "After that, I'm pretty sure they'll head our way."

"I wasn't talking about the Manties," Blair said very quietly, and flicked his head minutely toward Garrido and Teymoori.

The citizen major general and his people's commissioner stood inside the crystoplast-walled booth around the secure communications terminal. It was specifically designed so that one outside it could hear anything said *inside* it—which was undoubtedly why they were there—but from their body language, they were not enjoying their current conversation.

Garrido's face was bleak, worried, clearly that of a man who felt the walls closing in. Teymoori's expression was harder to read. He *always* looked surly and two-thirds angry, as far as Samper could tell. Today, there was what looked an awful lot like an edge of terror in his eyes, as well, but fear only seemed to be making him even angrier. As the citizen commander watched, the people's commissioner's angry index finger jabbed the taller, stockier citizen major general in the chest.

"You want my honest opinion?" Samper asked, still gazing at their superiors, and his tone communicated far more than his words. Blair hesitated a moment, then nodded.

"Honestly, I hope that between the two of them they have enough sense to pour piss out of a boot, but I wouldn't bet anything on it. Especially in Teymoori's case," Samper said then, his eyes bitter but his expression carefully controlled. "You and I both know we're completely and totally screwed, Spencer. Those people have at least—*at least*—two or three hundred times our combat power. We've got eighty-six missile tubes spread across all our platforms. They've still got twenty-two wallers; each of them has a minimum of thirty-five launchers in *each broadside*; and there's no way in hell we could get a laserhead through the kind of point defense they've got. Hell! You saw what happened to Dietz's and Linton's salvos! They took out two of their wallers. Only two—and it's pretty damn clear they were only damaged. They sure as hell weren't destroyed! Now imagine what their defenses would do against salvos a tenth that heavy."

He turned away from Garrido and Teymoori, gazing bleakly at the lurid icons of the Manticoran fleet, instead, then shrugged ever so slightly.

"Mathias, Samson—almost all our prewar bases out here—were designed to support *offensive* operations. They were logistics nodes and staging points for us to use when we went after the Manty Alliance. They were never intended to stand off heavy *Manticoran* attacks—certainly not the way someplace like Duquesne Base or Trevor's Star is! The only reason this White Haven bothered with such a stealthy approach was to catch any mobile units in-system before they could hyper out. Which is exactly what he did. And he came loaded for bear because he couldn't know there wouldn't be wallers of our own here waiting for him. There's no way he needed that much firepower"—he flicked a finger at the plot—"to take out the base itself."

"And your point?" Blair's tone said he already knew the answer to his question, and Samper snorted.

"And my point is that the only sane option is to surrender before we get thousands of more people killed. Maybe—*maybe*—there was some point in not simply scuttling the battleships. They obviously got to at least a couple of his wallers, and people keep telling me how 'attrition' is supposed to work in our favor."

His eyes were even darker, more bitter, then before, and he inhaled deeply.

"It's funny, the people who keep telling me that aren't the ones who have to do the attritting. Not usually, anyway. This time, though, it'd be harder than hell for *anyone* to argue we could hope to inflict any worthwhile damage before the Manties blew us the hell out of space. And the citizen major general and the people's commissioner have had over two hours to think about that, let it settle in."

"So you think they'll surrender?" Blair asked even more quietly.

"I don't know. I honestly don't." Samper shook his head, speaking with more honesty—and far more openly—than he would have spoken under almost any other circumstances. "I think . . . I think Garrido might want to. Probably does, really. He's not the sharpest stylus in the box, and I think he really thought you and I were wrong about whether or not we could hold the system. But aside from being dumber than a box of rocks tactically, he isn't genuinely stupid, and he's not a fanatic. either. Teymoori, though . . . I think he actually believes all those horror stories Public Information's handing out about Manty atrocities and shooting their POWs. And I'm really afraid he *is* a fanatic. Or a true believer, anyway. Worse, I know damned well some of his State Sec goons are!"

✧ ✧ ✧

"Turnover in ten minutes, Milord."

White Haven looked up from the fresh, steaming cup of coffee the steward's mate had just provided him and nodded his thanks for Lieutenant Saldaña's reminder.

Sixth Fleet had accelerated toward Smaragdenio for just under two and a half hours. Its velocity was back up to 25,915, and it was coming up on the halfway point. He wondered what was going through the Peeps' minds as they watched their incoming nemesis rumble steadily nearer.

Nothing good, he hoped, sipping coffee.

✧ ✧ ✧

"We have an incoming transmission, Citizen Major General."

The com rating's voice was painfully diffident, and she flinched as Citizen Major General Garrido whipped around toward her.

"From the damned Manties, I presume?" he half-snapped.

"Uh, yes, Citizen Major General! I'm sorry. I should have been more speci—"

His waved hand cut her off in mid-word.

"Yes, you should've been more specific," he said, "but it's not like you didn't know I'd figure it out for myself, Citizen Corporal."

She looked at him, obviously uncertain where to go next in the wake of his half apology, and his mouth twitched in an unwilling, bitter half-smile. Then he glanced over his shoulder at Teymoori, and the people's commissioner glowered at him.

"Waited long enough, didn't they?" the citizen major general said.

"Obviously trying to let fear work on us," Teymoori replied harshly.

"Obviously," Garrido agreed.

The Manties had decelerated to rest relative to Smaragdenio, at a range of exactly 899,377 kilometers from *Mathias Alpha*, over twelve minutes ago. Their formation was immaculate, every targeting system was locked on the orbital platforms, yet they hadn't said a single word to anyone since their initial firing pass, and Garrido remembered a story he'd read once about a fellow named Damocles.

"Put it on my display, Citizen Corporal," he said.

"Yes, Citizen Major General!" the noncom replied, and Garrido's display lit with the same dark-haired, blue-eyed Manticoran he'd seen once before.

"What do you want?" the citizen major general said flatly.

"And you are?" the Manty inquired six seconds later.

"Citizen Major General Garrido," Garrido replied. "I repeat, what do you want?"

"Direct and to the point, I see," the Manty observed after another six seconds. "Good. I'll be equally direct.

"Several hours ago, I gave your battleships the opportunity to stand down. They didn't take it. I'm sure most of their crewmen and crewwomen are dead now. I regret that, but, frankly, that was your choice, not mine. So now I'm giving you the opportunity to make a *better* choice, and the fact that you haven't been stupid enough to fire on my ships—yet—gives me some hope that you may take advantage of it. This time, at least."

Those blue eyes bored into Garrido, and he felt himself flush angrily.

"I am beyond the effective range of any energy weapon your platforms may mount," the Manticoran continued, "and your missile batteries are too light to threaten my ships. I, on the other hand, can destroy every one of your orbital installations at any time of my choosing. I would prefer not to do that, since I have no more desire to kill people—especially civilian workers who have no voice in their employment conditions. Rather than risk my own personnel's lives, however, I'm prepared to do just that. So your choice, 'Citizen Major General,' is to surrender, now, unconditionally, or to refuse. And *if* you refuse, my missiles will destroy your armed platforms. Casualties aboard those platforms will be heavy, and no one can guarantee that other targets won't be hit as well, by mistake."

He paused for a moment—no doubt to let the unspoken threat to fire on the unarmed platforms as well sink in, Garrido thought. Then he shrugged.

"You have ten minutes to decide which option you'd prefer. If you haven't decided to surrender by the end of that time, I will open fire on your armed platforms. White Haven, clear."

The Manty vanished from Garrido's display, and the citizen major general glared at its blank surface angrily. Then he turned back to Teymoori.

"Well, none of *that* was a surprise, was it?" he growled.

Teymoori shook his head, and his eyes were barred windows in a stone wall.

"I don't see any option," Garrido continued. "I don't like it, but the bastard's right. We can't hurt him with anything we've got, Arnold."

Teymoori glared at him, and the Marine shrugged.

"This isn't like the battleships," he said. "They could at least hope to inflict a little damage before they went down. We can't. All *we* can do is get a lot of people killed, and I'm damned if I'll do that. I know you don't like it, but that's my decision."

"Decisions have consequences, Citizen Major General," Teymoori said coldly.

"I'm aware of that." Garrido's tone was even colder than his people's commissioner's, and he met Teymoori's eyes levelly.

His own wife and children were here in Mathias, although they'd been evacuated to the planetary surface along with as many civilian dependents as possible when the Manties were first detected. And he'd very quietly arranged for their planetary quarters to be guarded by Marines, not StateSec. He had other family back home in the Haven System, however, and he understood Teymoori's implication. But as Samper had observed to Blair, however blunt and unimaginative Jonathan Garrido might be, he wasn't insane. He'd just have to take his chances when it came to convincing Nouveau Paris and the Committee of Public Safety that he'd made the right decision.

He and Teymoori looked at one another for another tense heartbeat or two, then he looked back at the citizen corporal.

"Get him back again," he said.

"Yes, Citizen Major General!"

"You've made your decision?" Admiral White Haven asked when he reappeared on Garrido's display several seconds later.

"You haven't left me much choice," Garrido grated.

"I don't suppose I have," White Haven acknowledged. "To be clear, though, you surrender your command and the entire star system unconditionally?"

"Yes." The single word came out as if it cost Garrido physical pain, but his expression never wavered, and, six seconds later, White Haven nodded.

"Good. In that case, my heavy ships will remain exactly where they are. My cruisers will close with your platforms and their Marines will board them. Be advised that my Marines will be authorized and instructed to respond to any attack with deadly force, and that if any of your platforms should open fire on any of my units, we will destroy both that platform and any and all other armed platforms. Is all of that clearly understood, Citizen Major General? I don't think either one of us wants there to be any misunderstandings at this point."

"It's understood," Garrido got out.

"Good," White Haven said again, and this time there might have been just the faintest edge of sympathy in the word.

Of course, there might not have been, too, Garrido thought grimly.

"Prepare to receive my boarding parties shortly," the Manty said a moment later. "White Haven, clear."

◇  ◇  ◇

"Atten-hut!" Sergeant Major Babcock barked as Major Viktor Yestachenko strode into the briefing compartment just off HMS *Prince Adrian*'s Boat Bay One and the men and women in it popped to attention.

"As you were," he said, crossing to the small stage at the front of the compartment, and feet rustled as his assembled platoon leaders and their senior noncoms settled back into their chairs.

"All right," he said, turning to face them. "We're cleared to proceed, and Captain McKeon will launch pinnaces in about thirty-five minutes. All of us know basically what we're looking at here, but just to touch base once more—I wouldn't want any of you to think I didn't love you—our primary concern is *Mathias Gamma*. *Cestus* and *Princess Stephanie* have the other two armed platforms and Admiral Moreno's taking the command platform with *Nike* and Colonel Ramirez's people. This one is ours."

The holographic image of a gaunt, utilitarian orbital platform appeared, floating at his right elbow. A third of its substantial volume was clearly devoted to cargo handling and transshipment, but the rest was taken up by a dozen missile launchers, six laser point defense installations, and the sensors and tracking arrays to manage that firepower.

"It should be fairly simple," he continued, "but all of you know how I feel about relying on the verb 'should.' And I'm not all that much fonder of words like 'simple,' now that I think about it." He glowered at them, and someone chuckled. "Bearing that in mind, I don't want any chances taken. The Intelligence types tell us there shouldn't be more than a hundred and fifty or—outside—two hundred warm bodies over there. They're probably right, and the majority of those bodies are going to be Navy pukes. But the Intelligence types also tell me the Peeps have been steadily replacing their Marines with special security troops. We don't know that they've gotten around to doing that clear out here, but they'd started the process back in Samson. That was a lot smaller base than Mathias, so it's certainly possible they've already done it here, which could complicate things just a bit.

"Bethany"—he looked at Lieutenant Clark, Third Platoon's fair-haired, green-eyed CO—"your people will take point. We'll make entry at this boat bay"—the indicated boat bay flashed amber in the hologram—"and you'll secure the bay and its access passages and maintain control of them."

Clark nodded. She was the youngest of Yestachenko's platoon commanders, but her last assignment had been with a Raider battalion. She understood why her people would be Yestachenko's anchor.

"Jeremiah"—the major turned to Jeremiah Dimitrieas—"you and First Platoon will board as soon as Bethany gives us the all-clear, then pass your people through hers and proceed directly to Main Engineering to take over the power plant and Environmental."

Lieutenant Dimitrieas—a couple of years older than Clark and nine centimeters taller, with brown hair and eyes and a very dark complexion—nodded in turn, and Yestachenko turned to Lieutenant Gillespie, Third Platoon's CO. Gillespie, only a centimeter or so taller than Clark, was a fearsome-looking fellow who actually out-massed Dimitrieas, despite his lack of height. Although he was a native Sphinxian, he'd inherited that massive, fireplug physique—and also his blue hair and enhanced reflexes—from a genetic slave grandfather.

"Isaiah, you and Third Platoon will secure the command deck. And I want you to detach one squad to take physical control of the platform's computer core and, especially, it's fire control links, as well."

It was Gillespie's turn to nod, and Yestachenko paused to survey all three of them for a moment, then cleared his throat.

"Now, bearing in mind that we are all mere Marines, better suited by both training and inclination to breaking things or blowing them up than to anything *constructive*, Captain McKeon has reminded me that we're not supposed to touch anything. We'll simply hold the fort and provide security for the vacuumsuckers who, as the higher-minded, more intellectually capable sorts they so obviously are, will do the heavy intellectual lifting from that point."

There were more chuckles—and they were louder—and he smiled at them.

"The Gunny here"—he twitched his head in Babcock's direction—"has put together the best information/estimates we have on the platform's probable internal layout. The good news is that the Peeps build their frontier platforms, and especially their small-craft docking points, to standardized designs, and we've learned enough at places like Samson and Seaford to have a pretty good feel for them. The bad news is that this is the first time we've seen them graft weapon stations onto a logistics platform. So be aware that the layout you've loaded to your skinnies is more speculative than we'd like."

He paused until he got another set of nods, then shrugged.

"That's about it, except to remind all of you that at least some of these people are downright fanatical. Like I say, it looks like they're trying to replace their Marines with troopers from this new 'State Security' monster of theirs wherever they can. And according to some of our info from Samson and Welladay, State Security's been actively recruiting from pre-coup terrorist organizations, like the Citizens Rights Union. We haven't definitively confirmed that, but the intel types say the indications are strong, and if they *are* recruiting terrorist crazies, they won't think like Marines—even *Peep* Marines—would. That means watching your sixes every minute aboard that platform. Everybody got that, too?"

This time, the acknowledgments came back in a ripple of "Yes, Sirs," and he nodded in satisfaction.

"The Gunny will ride along with you, Bethany," he told Lieutenant Clark. "I'll be riding herd on you, Jeremiah." He grinned. "Won't that be fun?"

"Nothing my boys and girls could look forward to more, Sir," Lieutenant Dimitrieas assured him with enormous affability.

"In that case," Yestachenko said through the surf of chuckles, "why don't we get saddled up?"

✦   ✦   ✦

Iris Babcock stood in *Prince Adrian*'s forward boat bay, watching critically as Third Platoon boarded Marine Two. Lieutenant Clark might be young, but she knew her job, this wasn't her first boarding op, and Conrad Masters, her platoon sergeant, was a solid vet. Babcock wasn't worried about Third Platoon's people. Or not any more than she always worried about "her" Marines when they were about to go—potentially, at least—into harm's way.

It came with the job.

"Don't you go busting my bird, Gunny," a deep voice rumbled, and she looked over her shoulder at Horace Harkness. He stood in his Navy skinsuit, hands on hips, watching the Marines file aboard the pinnace.

"*Your* bird?" She raised an eyebrow. "Last time I looked, it belonged to the Corps. At least for this deployment."

"Nah, the Navy just lets you jarheads borrow 'em because you're too cheap to buy your own rides." Harkness grinned at her, and she shook her head.

"The thought that the Navy trusts someone of your limited attainments to look after *my* pinnace keeps me up at night, Harkness. You know that, don't you? I mean, every time I think about the fact that you can barely even *read* . . . !"

"Why they put so many pictures into the manuals," he told her with an even broader grin. Then his expression sobered a bit. "Seriously, Gunny. I've got a bad feeling. Kinda like an itch I can't scratch. And not about the bird."

"You getting paranoid in your decrepitude?" Babcock quipped, and he shook his head.

"Maybe. But something ain't right. These bastards got too reasonable too quick. I know—I know!" He waved one hand almost irritably. "They saw what happened to the battleships. What could happen to them. I got that. But—" He shook his head again. "Just an itch. Could be nothing. But you people watch your asses over there."

Babcock looked at him for a moment, then nodded.

"I'll have you know Marines always watch our asses," she said. "But I promise to be extra careful, just to make *you* happy."

"Good. And if I'm jumping at shadows, I'll stand you to a beer next time we're both off-duty together."

"I'll hold out for Old Tillman Premium!"

"Hell, I wouldn't expect anything *cheap* outta a jarhead drinking on the Navy's dime!"

✦ ✦ ✦

"Marine Two, you are cleared to dock."

The Marine coxswain looked over her shoulder at Lieutenant Clark, and Clark nodded.

"Flight Control, Marine Two acknowledges cleared to dock," the coxswain replied over her headset boom. "Docking now."

The pinnace drifted forward on reaction thrusters, nosing into the orbital platform's docking bay, and the boarding tube extended to greet it. The Havenite bay was smaller than its Manticoran counterpart would have been, and its boarding tubes used different pressure collars, but Marine Two's boarding hatches were designed to accept a wide range of collars. The flight engineer spent an extra handful of seconds assuring himself of a solid seal before he tapped a control and the green light blinked alive above the hatch.

"Good seal," he announced aloud, and Clark nodded to him, and then to Staff Sergeant Masters.

"Let's do this, Conrad," she said.

"Yes, Ma'am." Masters turned to the troop compartment. "All right, you people! Off your asses and on your feet!"

The waiting Marines came to their feet in their armored skinsuits, checking their gear one last time, and Sergeant Yolanda Higgins' Second Squad formed up at the hatch.

"Safeties off," Higgins said over her squad's com net, and green lights flickered to read on her heads-up display as her people's weapons went live.

"Second Squad, ready, LT," Higgins announced, and Clark nodded, then looked at the flight engineer.

"Crack the hatch, Chief."

"Aye, aye, Ma'am. Cracking the hatch."

The Navy petty officer tapped another command and the hatch snapped open. Higgins looked down the boarding tube's empty, well-lit bore, then nodded.

"Let's go, people," she said, and launched herself into the tube's microgravity.

She and the other twelve members of her squad soared down the tube like heavily armed birds. Higgins led the way out at the far end, catching the grab bar with her left hand while her right cradled her pulse rifle's pistol grip. She crossed the interface into the boat bay gallery's standard single gravity, landing with practiced ease, and stepped aside to clear the way for the rest of Second Squad.

"Fletcher, O'Toole, you've got the exit hatch," she said as the rest of the squad emerged behind her.

"On it, Sarge," Chet Fletcher acknowledged.

He and Jasmine O'Toole crossed to the hatch between the boat bay and the rest of the platform, and Higgins turned her attention to the half-dozen Havenite naval ratings manning the boat bay control center. The senior Peep—a second-class petty officer, from his insignia—turned to face her. His expression was unhappy, to say the least, but Higgins hadn't expected warm smiles and welcoming hugs.

"Higgins," she introduced herself.

"Rossignol," the petty officer responded with equal brevity.

Higgins nodded to him, then keyed her com.

"Skipper, Higgins," she said. "On the deck, and so far everything's green. You can send along the vacuumsuckers. I mean"—despite the gravity of the moment, she grinned—"the Navy control team."

"I knew *exactly* who you meant, Sergeant." Lieutenant Clark's tone was just a tad repressive, but Higgins' grin only grew broader. "On their way," Clark added, and Higgins turned back to the Peep.

"Our people are on their way to take over your stations— Rossignol, was it?" The PO nodded curtly. "Ask your people to step away from their controls, but don't go anywhere. In fact, I think you'd all better wait over there." She indicated an unoccupied corner of the spacious bay gallery. "Our people may have a few questions about your control setup."

"Got it." Rossignol waved his own work party away from their stations. "Into the corner, everybody. Leave your controls set where they are," he said, and the other five Peeps stepped back.

Higgins watched them go, then turned her attention back to the boarding tube as Ruben Mulder's squad emerged from it. Lieutenant Clark and Gunny Babcock were on Mulder's heels, and the lieutenant surveyed the boat bay thoughtfully while the quartet of naval ratings who'd accompanied her trotted across to the Peep control station.

The naval types studied the consoles carefully for a moment, and then the first-class petty officer in charge raised one hand, thumb extended.

"Marine One, Marine Three-One," Clark said over the com. "Boat bay secure, and our landing party has the controls."

"Three-One, Marine One copies," Yestachenko came back. "Proceed."

"Roger that, Marine One," she said, and waved at Masters. "Move 'em out, Conrad."

"You heard the LT," the staff sergeant said. "Move it, people!"

One of the enlisted spacers tapped a command and the gallery hatch slid open. Higgins stepped through it with the rest of her squad, weapons ready. The passage beyond ran almost fifty meters before it reached a bank of lift shafts. It was well lit, with a facing pair of airlock doors at its midpoint. A dozen armorplast viewpoints in the left-hand bulkhead showed the platform's hull stretching away into the distant blackness of space, and Higgins nodded. According to her schematic, the hatch in that bulkhead was an emergency small-craft docking point, while the one on the right gave lateral access to the orbital platform's second boat bay.

"Clear," she announced over the com and waved for Fletcher and O'Toole to take point.

The privates stepped around her and started down the passage, and she turned to look over her shoulder at the rest of her squad.

"Carver, I want you and Watson on our six," she said to the fire team with the light tribarrels. "I don't see any—"

The explosion took all of them by surprise.

Ten meters of the outboard bulkhead disappeared into a spray of shrapnel that blasted across the passage in a flat, lethal fan. Chet Fletcher and Jasmine O'Toole were in its direct path. Neither of them had an instant's warning . . . or a chance of surviving. Their icons turned instantly blood red on Higgins' HUD, and two more of her Marines blinked suddenly alternating red and amber as fragments of bulkhead slammed into their skinsuits. Unlike Navy skinsuits, Marine skinnies were armored, and only those armor appliqués saved Private McTavish and Private Guccione. McTavish was uninjured, and her skinny automatically sealed the two smallish, air-leaking rents shrapnel had torn. Guccione went down hard, both hands clutching at his right leg as his skinny's built-in tourniquets locked down on his deeply lacerated thigh.

Behind Higgins, the hatch through which the rest of her squad had just passed snapped shut, reacting automatically to the catastrophic hull breach, and the passage's air roared through the opening in a brief, violent gale.

"Bandit!" Clark barked over the all-hands net. "Marine-Three-One is Bandit! I say again, Bandit!"

Higgins heard her, but the sergeant was on one knee, pulse rifle up and covering the passage as the last of the air disappeared and McTavish dragged Guccione back behind her.

"All Marines this net," Yestachenko's voice came over the com. "Marine One. Marine-Three-One is Code Bandit. I repeat, Code Bandit. Rules of engagement Alpha are now in effect."

ROE Alpha was basically shoot first and worry about the details later. All of Yestachenko's Marines knew Admiral White Haven wanted to avoid unnecessary Peep casualties, but he'd made it abundantly clear where his priorities lay.

"Talk to me, Yolanda," Clark said over a private link, and Higgins grimaced.

"I've got nothing, Ma'am," she replied harshly. "Fletcher and O'Toole are gone, and Guccione's down. Looks like it was a shaped charge on the outboard side of the passage. No follow-up and no sign of other hostiles. We're zero-pressure on this side of the hatch."

"Figured. Hold one."

Bethany Clark inhaled deeply and turned her head to look at Iris Babcock. The sergeant major looked as bitter as Clark felt, but at that moment, the Gunny's decades of solid experience were a vast comfort to the lieutenant. There was no question who was in command, but Babcock would probably keep her from making any—any *more*, she corrected herself bitterly—mistakes.

"Porter," she said.

"Yo, LT," Sergeant Ludovico Porter replied.

"Take your squad EVA," Clark said. "I want a sweep of the rest of that passage's outboard side. We know there was at least one booby trap. Make sure there aren't any more, and watch your asses. I wouldn't put it past whoever this was to have covered her booby traps with direct fire."

"You got it, Ma'am," Porter acknowledged, and began waving his squad toward one of the gallery's auxiliary airlocks.

"You—Rossignol!" Clark snapped, and pointed at the deck one meter in front of her. "Get your sorry ass over here!"

Rossignol looked unhappier than ever, but he obeyed the command quickly, and she glared at him.

"What the fuck was that?" she demanded, jerking a thumb in the direction of the explosion.

"I don't have a clue," Rossignol told her. Sweat dotted the man's forehead, and he shook his head sharply as hard eyes bored into him like emerald augers. "Honest, I don't! The order was to stand down, and we did! That's all I know."

"Well, someone obviously didn't get the word." Bethany Clark's voice was icy. "So you just give me your best guess about who that 'someone' was and what else she may have arranged for us."

"Look, I didn't even know about *that*." Rossignol waved at the sealed hatch, and his tone was almost pleading. "How am I supposed to know what else someone crazy enough to pull that kind of shit might have done? If I had to guess, it was probably one of the StateSec types, and I'll be honest, God only knows what *they're* likely to try. And that's all I can tell you, I swear!"

Clark glared at him, but he only shook his head harder, his eyes desperate with his need for her to believe him, and she made herself step back from the white-hot edge of her rage when she realized *why* he was so desperate. Any sane human being would be frightened in his position, but this wasn't fear—this was *terror*. And the reason it was was that he knew exactly what StateSec would have done to him in Clark's place.

*Probably have just shot the poor bastard, then asked the next one in line if she had anything to say*, the Marine thought grimly.

A part of her wanted to do exactly that, herself. But it was a part she had no intention of listening to, and she jerked her head in a curt nod back toward the corner where the other Peeps huddled.

He half stumbled, clumsy in his haste to obey her, and she turned back to Babcock, then paused as Porter came up over the squad net.

"Mark One Eyeball doesn't see anything out here, LT," the sergeant said. "Except the hole where the first one went off, anyway. Electronic sniffers aren't picking anything up, either."

"What can you see about the explosion site itself?"

"Not a lot, Ma'am." Clark could imagine Porter's shrug. "Might be some blast residue, but from what I can see, Yolanda was right about the shaped charge. Looks like it was maybe a couple of meters long and half a meter wide. Got no idea how they could've gotten it into place, but I guess they did have plenty of time before we got back to them. If I had to guess, it was probably command detonated. Wouldn't want tripwires or infrared beams in a passage your own people might be using before the nasty Manties came along. Don't have a clue how they knew when to detonate, though. Lots of places they could've watched the outside of the passage from, but the inside—?"

"Surveillance systems," Babcock said grimly. She was tapped into the same conversation, and now she waved one hand at the visual pickups mounted at thirty-meter intervals across the compartment overhead. "If they've got this many in the gallery, there are damned sure more of them covering the passage, too. Somebody was tapped into them. Surprised whoever it was didn't wait until the rest of Higgins' people were farther into the blast zone, really."

From her expression, she didn't feel one bit better over those dead Marines than Bethany Clark did.

"Can you seal the hole, Ludovico?" the lieutenant asked.

"Negative, Ma'am," Porter replied "Not with anything we've got, anyway. The vacuumsuckers probably could. I mean, I'm *sure* they could, with the right gear, but I don't think *we* can with anything we've got."

"Okay." Clark nodded, then drew a deep breath. It was still her job to secure the platoon's entry and exit point, and she keyed her com again.

"Marine One, Marine Three-One."

"Go, Three-One," Yestachenko replied.

"Sir, I think we'd better shift laterally to Boat Bay Three. One of my squad leaders has eyeballs on the blast site, and he doesn't think we can seal it to repressurize this access way."

"Wait one," Yestachenko said, and Clark looked across at Babcock.

"Six of one, half a dozen of the other, Ma'am," Babcock said, answering the unasked question. "If we stick with this bay, we probably won't run into any more booby traps, but we'll have to lock everybody through to get to the lift shafts. Pretty nasty bottleneck, there. But if we shift axes, we may run our noses into another little surprise. In fact"—the sergeant major grimaced bitterly—"if I were doing this, that's exactly what would happen."

"Yeah, but now we know it's already happened once," Clark pointed out. "I'm thinking we take it slow and easy. And we put Porter on the outside of the tube to Bay Three to watch our flank going that way. And"—she looked back at the Peeps huddled in the corner—"I just had another thought. Rossignol!"

The Havenite PO's head popped up like a frightened Sphinxian chipmunk's, and she waved him back over with an impatient hand.

"Yes, Lieutenant?" he said cautiously.

"Surveillance system?" she asked, pointing at the overhead pickups Babcock had spotted and Rossignol nodded. In fact, he nodded so hard his uniform headgear almost fell off.

"Do your controls over there have access to it?"

"Yes, Ma'am!"

"Can you shut them down?"

"Uh, no, Ma'am. I can't," he said unhappily. "But I do know how to access the schematics for the entire bay," he added quickly. "We could probably isolate the camera systems that way!"

Clark considered him for a moment, then looked back to Babcock.

"Gunny, take him over to the Navy pukes. Have him show one of *them* how to access the schematics, then start looking for a way to kill the cameras. Hell, find a way to shut down their entire wired com net, if you can!"

"Yes, Ma'am!" Babcock smiled thinly, then nodded to Rossignol. "This way," she said crisply.

❖ ❖ ❖

"Pretty bad, was it?"

Babcock looked around the boat bay gallery and discovered Horace Harkness standing beside her, gazing through the armorplast at Marine Two. The pinnace rested in the forward bay's docking arms, once again, the boarding tube run out and sealed to its hatch while members of *Prince Adrian*'s engineering staff conducted routine post-flight maintenance. It had returned to the cruiser, along with the rest of *Prince Adrian*'s Marines—living and dead—almost four hours earlier. But Baker Company's hot-wash debrief had ended less than twenty minutes ago, and somehow, Babcock had found herself here, when where she really should have been was in her own berthing compartment, looking for a hot shower.

"Seen worse," she said. "Coulda lost a lot more people. And we got the job done. I don't know how much good it'll do, but we got the data dumps from all their computers and more samples of their hardware. And we blew the damned place up, after we evacced everybody. That's gotta count. And"—she shrugged—"like I say. I've seen worse."

"Yeah, and you've seen a hell of a lot better, too," Harkness replied. "Any idea who did it?"

"Oh, sure!" Babcock's crooked smile was bitter. "We've got all *kinds* of ideas who *might've* done it, but damn all evidence to pin it on anyone. My best guess? Some of the StateSec bastards on *Gamma*. There were more of 'em than anyone expected, and some of 'em are real pieces of work. I didn't really believe the Intelligence types when they said the Peeps were recruiting terrorists to be political cops, but I do now. It's crazy! And since they were the primary security force, they were the ones who should've *stopped* anyone from doing something like this. Which, you might have noticed, didn't happen."

"'Bout what I figured." Harkness shook his head. "That kinda crap always leaves a bad taste, but not a lot we can do about it, I guess. Unless we want to just shoot every one of the bastards on suspicion."

"Right about now, that would work for me."

"Not a good thought, Gunny." Harkness shook his head again. "Trust me, been there. Hell, *done* that, at least once. Didn't make me feel any better after."

"Maybe not," Babcock allowed. "But what really pisses me off is what Lieutenant Clark's doing to herself. She's kicking the shit out of herself for letting it happen."

Harkness opened his mouth, but she waved him brusquely to silence and continued.

"Oh, she knows it wasn't really her fault. Doesn't matter. Still blames herself. Hell, *I* told her it wasn't her fault—that it was *nobody's* fault—and that doesn't matter, either. She lost two of her people, Harkness. Two of *our* people. And Guccione's gonna be in the body shop for at least three weeks, even with quick-heal. So it doesn't matter that it wasn't her fault. She's not ready to hear that yet—not from anyone."

"Course she isn't," Harkness rumbled. "That's because she's one of the good ones. Learning how to let something like that go, that's not ever something you can really do. Not down inside, where it really matters. I remember the old *Fearless* in Basilisk. Hell, *Troubadour* and *Madrigal* in Yeltsin! You were there for those. You know what I'm talking about. Leaving all those people behind . . . that hurts, Gunny. And knowing it wasn't 'our fault' doesn't make it easier. Not for the good ones."

"Then she's just gonna have to get over it," Babcock said harshly. "This is gonna be a long war, Harkness. She's gonna lose more people before it's over. So she just damned well needs to learn to deal with it."

"Sounds like you're talking about more than just her," Harkness replied, and his voice was softer somehow. Babcock darted a look at him, and he shrugged.

"Sounds to me like Lieutenant Clark's not the only person who's not ready to hear it wasn't her fault."

Babcock stiffened as a bolt of pure fury went through her. She opened her mouth, ready to tell him where he could shove his amateur psychiatry, but then she stopped, because he only stood there. Stood there, gazing into her eyes, and she felt that gaze pin her. Felt it force her to face her own feelings . . . and to realize he was right.

"Yeah," she said after a a long, endless moment. "Yeah, you're right . . . damn you. It *is* always that way." She shook her head, gray eyes dark and suddenly sheened with a suspicious brightness. "Damn it, they're all so frigging *young*, Harkness! I'm supposed to look out for them."

"Sure you are. And you do. And sometimes, you can't. It happens, Gunny. You know that."

"Yeah, I do. And I'll get past it. I always do that, too."

"And a part of you *never* gets past it, Gunny," Harkness said quietly. "You know that, too."

They looked at each other for another minute or two, and then Babcock grinned crookedly.

"You know, for a worn-out old excuse for a vacuumsucker, you're not nearly so bad as people say, Harkness."

"Gee, spare my blushes! Dunno if I can handle all this effusive praise!"

"Hey, I didn't say you were worth a fart in a vac suit, Harkness! I just said you're not as bad as people *say* you are."

**Admiralty House**
**City of Landing**
**Planet Manticore**
**Manticore Binary System**
**October 9, 1906 PD**

"SO WHAT DO YOU THINK about White Haven's report?"

Thomas Caparelli tipped back in his chair, regarding Admiral Givens across his desk.

"What part of it?" Givens asked in return. "I'm not the best woman to ask for an analysis of his tactics, if that's what you meant."

"I think you can safely assume I wasn't asking you to critique his attack plan." Caparelli smiled crookedly. "I'm more interested in your reaction to what he brought back and to his conclusions about what's going on inside the People's Republic."

"Well, taking your points in order, he got a lot closer to a complete data dump from Mathias than we've gotten anywhere else, including Samson. How much good all that data's going to do us, I don't know. Unfortunately, Mathias wasn't exactly a strategic hotspot, so we didn't capture any copies of 'Our Secret Plan to Win the War and Destroy the Star Kingdom of Manticore in Ten Easy Steps.' She grimaced. "For that matter, we didn't capture anything significant about ship movement plans, either. Not outside the scheduled supply runs to Mathias, anyway.

"The hardware's a wash, too, I think. I don't think we picked up anything on that front that told us much more than we already had from Seaford, among other places. So from that side, there's not a lot to interest the folks in my shop."

She paused, and the First Space Lord smiled again.

"From that side?" he observed.

"Well, that brings me to your second point. And I have to say, he's offered a lot of confirmation of things we already thought we were seeing. In fact, when I look at his conclusions—well, his and

O'Hanlon's, really—I have to keep reminding myself to avoid confirmation bias. The two of them are saying so many of the same things that either we're all brilliant analysts or else we're all chasing the same wild hares."

"Ah?"

"I think it's obvious the Peeps' purges have hurt them even worse than we'd thought. Their performances at Samson and Welladay suggested that, but one of the things he did bring back from Mathias that we found really interesting were the service records on everyone assigned to the system." She shook her head. "Commander O'Hanlon made sure we had them, and he did a deep dive before they even got back to Madras. He sent both his conclusions and the raw data on to us, and he was right; there are a *lot* of senior Peep officers who were lieutenants, junior-grade lieutenants—even *enlisted spacers*—a year ago. That's already cost them, and his data dump suggests the problem's even broader than we'd thought it was. If we could have jumped on them the same way earlier, we could've—"

She cut herself off, nostrils flared angrily, and Caparelli snorted in harsh agreement with her unfinished thought.

So far, the war had gone well, in many ways. Manticore had captured and occupied a total of nineteen Peep star systems, including two major fleet bases, counting Seaford, and destroyed lesser bases and support stations in seven more, including Mathias. In the course of Riposte Gamma's operations, they'd destroyed twenty Peep ships-of-the-wall—seventeen superdreadnoughts and thirteen dreadnoughts—and sixty-seven battleships outright. In the same interval, they'd commissioned five new superdreadnoughts— all *Gryphon*-class ships—from their own construction programs and taken an additional twenty-six ex-Peep wallers into Manticoran service. Another eleven ex-Peep SDs, all captured by White Haven at Third Yeltsin, were being refitted to provide the Grayson Space Navy with a core of wallers of its own.

But aside from the four SDs White Haven had caught in Samson and two more Kuzak had picked off in Poicters, all of those wallers had been destroyed or captured *before* the eleven-month delay in the formal declaration stopped them short. If they'd been able to continue high-tempo operations while the Peeps were still in total disarray, they could have tripled that.

At least.

Of course, assuming that hadn't led to outright victory—which it most probably would have, in Caparelli's opinion—it would have created problems of its own. Welcome as the captured wallers might be, the prize ships imposed even more strain on their already buckling logistics. Thirteen of the RMN's prewar ships-of-the-wall were in yard hands—or queued up, waiting for yard space—with battle damage that would keep them sidelined for months under even the best of conditions. The prize ships were one of the reasons those damaged warships were waiting for yard slips, and the need to repair and refit fifty ships-of-the-wall—which represented over sixteen percent of the Navy's entire prewar wall-of-battle's strength—was a staggering burden. It came on top of all of the Navy's day-to-day maintenance and rebuilding needs, and, still worse in many ways, on the heels of how far down the Navy had run its maintenance cycles while it fought the non-war it couldn't get Parliament to declare.

*Adding nine percent to your battle fleet while taking the same ships away from the bad guys has to be a good thing, Tom,* Caparelli told himself. *So why do you feel like the guy clubbing pseudocrocs when all he wanted to do was drain the swamp?*

Possibly, he reflected dryly, it was because despite its atrocious losses, the Havenite wall-of-battle was still fourteen percent stronger than Manticore's augmented wall would be even after all fifty of those ships were restored to service. Haven's current margin of superiority was on the order of twenty percent, and that was in terms of hulls alone. The Star Kingdom's construction budgets had never been able to match the People's Navy ship-for-ship or, for that matter, to build enough ships to cover even their prewar deployment needs adequately. That was what had compelled Manticore to build a larger percentage of dreadnoughts rather than the pure *super*dreadnought battle fleet the RMN would vastly have preferred. A weak waller was infinitely better than *no* waller, and their need for platform numbers had forced them to accept the smaller, lighter ships, which was why forty percent of Manticore's prewar wall-of-battle had consisted of dreadnoughts, as opposed to less than eleven percent of the Peeps' wall.

Under the circumstances, getting those capital ships into service—or *back* into service, in the case of the damaged units—had to take absolute priority. He knew that, even though he hated to think about the implications for construction and overhaul schedules on their lighter units. Cruisers and destroyers were crucially important, but right this minute, not as much as ships-of-the-wall. They'd just have to wait their turns, and that meant too many of them weren't receiving critically needed overhauls.

Then there was the personnel problem. Havenite designs tended to be slightly more manpower intensive, class for class, and scaring up the trained bodies to crew the RMN's explosively expanding ship strengths was a nontrivial challenge. In fact, in many ways, the additional time the yards needed to restore the prizes to service was actually beneficial, since it would give Lucien Cortez and BuPers time to increase the size of their training programs to provide the crews to man them.

And just to fill Thomas Caparelli's cup to overflowing, entirely too much of the home system's skilled labor force was tied down in a massive expansion of the Navy's shipyards and repair facilities. Once those new yards were online—and the training programs had spun up—they'd solve virtually all of his current problems. Unfortunately, *bringing* them online could only make his current problems vastly worse in the short term. And, of course, he could count on the Peeps to do everything they could to increase *their* building programs, as well. None of their yards were as efficient as Manticore's. Best estimate was that the Star Kingdom had at least a twenty-percent edge in building speeds, and probably more. But the People's Republic had almost twice as many yards, and no one knew how rapidly—or how far—they could expand them. So it was highly probable their production rates would stay ahead of Manticore's even after the new crop of yards were completed.

All of which made White Haven's conclusions about these "people's commissioners" the Committee of Public Safety had introduced even more worrisome.

"We already knew Pierre was ruthless as hell," he said out loud. "That being the case, I guess we really shouldn't be too surprised by this new wrinkle."

"In retrospect, it was inevitable," Givens agreed. "Whatever they may say about 'the people's will' or any 'Legislaturalist coup attempts,' their Committee of Public Safety's a product of revolution and murder, not any sort of constitutional or representative political process. It has to be short on legitimacy, even in the eyes of some of its supporters, and who's most likely to do something about—likely to be *able* to do something about—restoring the 'legitimate' regime?"

She paused rhetorically, then shrugged.

"The military, that's who," she said, answering her own question. "And if what we *think* happened behind the scenes really happened, the military—and especially the People's Navy—were the ones most likely to figure out Parnell and the Octagon didn't have a damned thing to do with what happened to Harris and his Cabinet. So the senior officers, the ones most likely to want to restore the previous system, had to go. And that meant bringing up inexperienced, junior officers, a lot of whom were going to be in over their heads...and know they were. So how to encourage them to do their jobs or die trying while simultaneously *discouraging* any thoughts about regime change? Answer—first, create this new 'State Security' abortion to smash any potential recidivist collusion between the old intelligence and security organs, and then, second, recruit 'commissioners' to ride herd on their brand-new commodores and admirals. And because the commissioners will inevitably be so outnumbered by the military types they're supposed to keep an eye on, you give them a great big spiked club. You give them this...doctrine of 'collective responsibility.'"

Givens' hazel eyes showed her sick loathing for the concept, and she grimaced. But then she inhaled deeply and sat back in her own chair.

"It's sick, and it's disgusting, and I hate the very thought of it," she said flatly, "but that doesn't mean it won't work. At least in the short term. Who in her right mind will risk disobeying orders, even if following them is almost certainly going to get her killed, when her husband, her parents—her *children*—are all hostages at the mercy of something like this State Security? They may not be experienced, and there's no way they could be up to our people's level of training, but they're damned well going to *fight*. And they're going to fight *hard*."

"That's exactly what I'm afraid of, too," Caparelli said heavily. "And if you see that, and I see that, and a smart pain-in-the-ass like *White Haven* sees that, I doubt we're all wrong." He shook his head, his expression disgusted. "You and I have both beaten the same dead horse hard enough, but—*God*, I wish we could've hit these people even six months earlier!"

"It wasn't our idea, Sir. Doesn't make it feel any better or hurt any less, but it's not like we didn't tell anyone who'd listen what was coming."

"You ever hear the story of a lady named Cassandra?" Caparelli asked dryly, and Givens barked a laugh.

"All right." Caparelli let his chair come fully upright and planted his forearms on his desk. "White Haven's also right that we've got to get the Peep wall-of-battle to come out and fight before they finish training up all these new officers of theirs. In fact, I think he's also right that the reason they *aren't* coming out—yet, at least—is that someone back in Nouveau Paris has figured out how badly they need as much training time as they can get before they have to face us. They're working on that—hard—and that's the very reason we need to prune them back and *keep* them pruned back. Every additional month we give them will only cost us more dead and wounded in the end."

Givens nodded somberly, although even with Manticore's tech advantages, taking the war to someone who outnumbered the RMN so heavily was not a thought to induce a night of sound sleep.

"I think Sixth Fleet has to remain our main hammer," Caparelli continued. "White Haven's right that if we keep grinding away, keep eroding their prewar base structure, sooner or later they'll have to come out and fight. They can't just let us keep picking them off, if only because of how catastrophic that'll be for their people's morale, commissioners or no commissioners. So he's got the ball for now, and we have to trust him to take it downfield. But we've got to keep the center and fullbacks off of him while he does it. That means we need to reinforce Kuzak, and we probably need to pry another battle squadron or so loose for Hemphill down on the southern lobe, too. But all of that means coming up with the ships somewhere, and I only see one place."

"Sir, we have too many pickets of our own spread around to—"

"I know." Caparelli waved a hand. "I know! But we've got some of the same constraints the Peeps do. They can't afford to let us keep shooting bases out from under them—not indefinitely—but *we* can't afford to let them get in with a raiding squadron somewhere like Alazon. Not only would it be politically disastrous, but we have a moral responsibility to look out for our allies. So much as you and I would both love to reverse the 'penny-packet' tendency, we can't. And with so many of our lighter wallers tied down doing system security duty, there's only one other place to look for reinforcements."

"Admiral Webster will scream bloody murder, Sir."

"Probably." Caparelli nodded. "On the other hand, he used to be First Space Lord himself, so he'll understand when I explain. I'm more worried about the civilians' reaction to any notion of reducing Home Fleet, actually."

"Better you than me, Sir!"

"Your selflessness overwhelms me." Caparelli's tone was even drier than before. Then he drew a deep breath. "I think that's everything you and I needed to cover today. But do me a favor and shoot me an annotated copy of White Haven's report. Include O'Hanlon's analysis of their officer corps. Better include everything we've got on this State Security monstrosity—you may want to make that a separate briefing paper—and see if you can confirm whether or not they really are staffing it with ex-terrorists. I want the most detailed breakdown I can get in hand when I sit down with Baroness Morncreek, and I'll probably—or, since it's an intelligence matter, you'll probably—end up having to brief the Cabinet on it, too."

"The Cabinet?" Givens seemed less than enthralled by the notion, and he grinned sourly.

"To paraphrase something I heard someone say not so very long ago, 'better you than me,' Pat."

**HMS *Prince Adrian***
**Nightingale System**
**March 3, 1907 PD**

"COMING UP ON THE FIRING POINT, Skipper," Brian Chen said.

Alistair McKeon nodded and turned his command chair to watch the master plot as Sixth Fleet's wall-of-battle drove steadily deeper into the Nightingale System. Admiral White Haven's flagship had crossed the hyper limit almost two hours earlier and, assuming acceleration and deceleration had remained constant, could have entered orbit around Petrel, the system's inhabited planet, in another three and a half hours. But it hadn't worked out that way, because this time the defenders hadn't waited supinely for his attack.

They'd obviously been better prepared than any of Sixth Fleet's previous targets. In fact, they'd pulled their defending starships out of Petrel orbit sometime between the RMN's last recon and today's attack. From the look of things, they must have placed their defending force just over halfway between Petrel and the 21.12 LM Nightingale hyper limit, instead, to buy themselves extra reaction and maneuvering time.

It was clear they'd intended to stay between their base and any attacker, but their positioning had been off. It was easy enough to determine an attacker's most likely vector, since he'd cross the hyper limit as close to his objective as he could possibly get, yet they'd been out of position for a perfect intercept on a least-time course to Petrel. In one way, that had helped them, though; they'd been outside the cone White Haven's recon drones had swept, and their stealth systems had been good enough to hide their impeller signatures from Sixth Fleet's shipboard sensors at extended ranges if they accelerated slowly.

It was also obvious they'd detected Sixth Fleet's approach earlier than Samson or Mathias had, as well, since their velocity had been well over 10,000 KPS by the time Sixth Fleet detected them, despite an acceleration which couldn't have been much over sixty or seventy gravities. But they'd also been far enough off the least-time vector Lieutenant Saldaña had plotted that they'd been forced to increase acceleration to something their stealth field could no longer conceal if they wanted to intercept White Haven short of the planet. In fact, the reason they'd finally been detected at all was that they'd gone to three hundred gravities on a heading which would have crossed Sixth Fleet's track six light-minutes from the hyper limit, and roughly four light-minutes short of the planet.

That hadn't happened, however, because White Haven had reduced his wall's acceleration once he'd detected the Peeps' impeller signatures. He'd also turned away from a least-time course, sheering away from both the planet and the defending starships while he studied the situation.

And some studying had been in order, since they'd encountered not the two superdreadnought squadrons they'd anticipated, but four of them.

It was possible the additional battle squadrons had been there all along and Commodore Breton's drones had simply missed them when he'd reconned the system, but that was unlikely. Far more probably, White Haven's suspicion that they'd intended to reinforce Nightingale had been accurate and the newcomers had arrived between Breton's visit and Sixth Fleet's attack.

However they'd gotten there, Sixth Fleet suddenly found itself outnumbered four-to-three instead of outnumbering the defenders by three-to-two. Worse, all of the Peeps were superdreadnoughts, whereas sixteen of Sixth Fleet's twenty-four wallers were dreadnoughts. Admittedly, combat experience indicated Manticoran dreadnoughts were tactically more than equal to a Peep superdreadnought, but it was hard to know how much of that was inherent to the designs and hardware and how much was the result of unequal crew quality.

It looked like Sixth Fleet was about to answer that question, because rather than keep their distance, the Peep defenders—now labeled as Bogey One on *Prince Adrian*'s plot—seemed intent on forcing an engagement. Rather than taking the opportunity to see if Sixth Fleet's course change meant White Haven had decided to withdraw, Bogey One had actually increased acceleration. Its units were up to 330 G at this point, right on the eighty percent of military power which represented the People's Navy's normal maximum acceleration rate.

Since it was evident the Peeps wanted a fight this time, Sixth Fleet was prepared to give it one, and the missile pods on tow behind its ships offset much of Admiral White Haven's tonnage disadvantage. He was also outside Bogey One, closer to the hyper limit. Their vectors were converging, but once he fired his initial salvo, jettisoned the empty pods, and was able to resume his own maximum acceleration, he'd be well placed to hold the range open or even break clear back across the hyper limit.

Just at the moment, Alistair McKeon was happy the earl had ordered his screen to stay well clear of the scrum. His wall-of-battle was 29,801,000 kilometers, roughly a light-minute and a half, inside the hyper limit now, and its course change had turned it far enough away from Petrel to cut a chord across the hyper sphere. He'd further reduced acceleration to allow the Peeps to close, but his wall's velocity relative to the system primary was up to 26,829 KPS. Bogey One's present velocity was just over 18,000 KPS relative to Petrel, and the range between them had fallen to 14,275,500 kilometers.

If everyone involved maintained course, they would enter powered missile range—well over 10,000,000 kilometers, given their launch geometry—in about thirty seconds. Assuming they went right on maintaining course, their vectors would actually cross, with Sixth Fleet roughly 6,500,000 kilometers ahead of Bogey One, in approximately eleven minutes. Actually, 11.4 minutes at current acceleration rates, but once Sixth Fleet had emptied its pods, its current acceleration rate would climb by almost thirty-five percent.

At the moment, CruRon 33 and the rest of Sixth Fleet's screen was 7,000,000 kilometers on Sixth Fleet's starboard quarter, which placed Earl White Haven's wall almost directly between it and Bogey One. From that position, the screen would be unable to bolster Sixth Fleet's missile defenses against Bogey One, but these were wallers, not mere battleships. Their missiles were bigger, longer ranged, and carried far heavier laserheads than anything a battleship could cram into its magazines, and cruisers and battlecruisers had no business going toe-to-toe with that weight of metal if they could possibly avoid it. That was what their own navies' ships-of-the-wall were for, so White Haven had opted to clear the range and get the lighter units safely out of harm's way.

Now McKeon watched the final seconds tick away.

"Launching ... now," Chen announced as thousands upon thousands of missile impeller signatures spawned malignant fireflies across the plot.

Despite the numerical disparity, Sixth Fleet's three-thousand-plus salvo was almost three times heavier than the Peeps' opening fire. That much, McKeon had expected. But—

"Skipper!" Chen said. "The Peeps—"

"I see it," McKeon growled. "Looks like somebody over there's been studying the tac manual. Can we tell who the lucky prizewinner is?"

"Looks like BatRon Twenty-One," Chen said, and McKeon nodded unhappily.

Of course it was.

He watched the missiles streak across the display. More salvos followed—one every twenty seconds from the Peeps; one every eleven seconds from Sixth Fleet—and the Peep fire was far more effectively concentrated than anything they'd yet seen.

No, he told himself, not "concentrated;" the word he wanted was "directed." The doomed Peep battleships in Mathias had concentrated all their fire upon a handful of Sixth Fleet's ships, pouring in everything they could in the time they had. But this wasn't the desperate, despairing fire of those outnumbered and outweighed battleships. For the first time, Sixth Fleet faced the concentrated salvos of an even larger wall-of-battle, and as he watched, every bit of it rumbled down upon the superdreadnoughts of Battle Squadron 21— and completely ignored the dreadnoughts of White Haven's other two battle squadrons. Clearly, they recognized the most valuable prizes.

Sixth Fleet's initial, enormous salvo went in first. Counter-missiles raced to intercept the incoming birds. Decoys—not as good as their Manticoran counterparts, but still capable systems in properly trained hands—sang their siren songs, seeking to lure the laserheads astray. And as the surviving missiles steadied down on final approach, point-defense lasers stabbed out from the massive superdreadnoughts' flanks, ripping into them, shredding the wavefront of destruction.

White Haven had spread his fire over the three leading Peep squadrons, yet his salvo was so much larger—over three times the size of Bogey One's—that he'd actually put more birds on each of his targets. Despite everything Bogey One's defenses could do, scores of them broke through, ripping and tearing. Energy signatures fluctuated as impeller nodes and active fire control arrays were torn apart. Battle steel hulls shattered, and McKeon knew those bomb-pumped lasers were shattering men and women, as well.

But then it was Bogey One's turn. Even as Sixth Fleet pounded its enemies, the survivors of the first Havenite salvo broke past its own counter-missiles. It was Sixth Fleet's laser clusters' turn to spit coherent light, but the Peeps had chosen their target with malice aforethought. Battle Squadron 8 was too far astern, its point-defense lasers too short-ranged, to engage the incoming missiles. It was all up to BatRon 21 and BatRon 17, and they simply had too few clusters to stop that many missiles. Sheer weight of numbers swamped them, and the green lights of friendly ships flashed the spiteful sparkle of battle damage in *Prince Adrian*'s plot.

At 7,000,000 kilometers, it took twenty-three seconds for those damage codes to reach McKeon's display. Twenty-three seconds in which the *second* Havenite salvo came roaring in upon the same targets.

Of course, the next *two* Manticoran salvos had gone home in that same interval, he reminded himself, and damage codes sparked and flared about the crimson icons of hostile starships, as well. Those codes represented only the Combat Information Center's best estimate, which meant they lacked the certainty of the data coming to *Prince Adrian* directly from Sixth Fleet's wounded ships. Yet they were based on the data from recon drones barely two thousand kilometers clear of the Peep wall, and the plot was clear enough. Half a dozen of Sixth Fleet's wallers had been damaged, but most of that damage was relatively light, whereas three times that many Peeps had taken hits. At least two of them were badly damaged, indeed, judging from the way their salvos dwindled as launchers were ripped away, and McKeon waited for them to roll ship and turn away.

But they didn't do that, and his eyes narrowed as they continued to fire back, instead. Wounded, broken—yes, they were both of those, and their *defenses* weakened in lockstep with their offensive firepower. Their point defense was weaker, and from their emissions signatures, one of them had lost at least half the sidewall generators in her engaged broadside. Yet they never wavered. They maintained course, pounding away.

"Can't say I like this much, Skipper," Lev Carson said over McKeon's earbug from his own post in auxiliary control at the far end of *Prince Adrian*'s core hull. "This isn't Mathias, for God's sake!"

"No, it sure as hell isn't," McKeon grated, because Carson was clearly thinking exactly what he'd been thinking.

Citizen Rear Admiral Dietz and Citizen Rear Admiral Linton had been trapped in Mathias. They couldn't have avoided or evaded Sixth Fleet whatever they did. But Bogey One's units could have. Their wedges were up, their base velocity was two-thirds that of Sixth Fleet, and Sixth Fleet was outside them. They could break off, roll ship to hide their wounded sidewalls, and shelter behind the unbroken wall of their fellows while damage control worked frantically on repairs.

The fact that they were doing nothing of the sort was . . . worrisome.

"There, Skipper!" Lieutenant Commander Chen said. "That's one!"

"I see it," McKeon acknowledged as one of those crippled superdreadnoughts finally pulled out of Bogey One's wall and rolled to interpose the belly of its wedge. But he felt less exuberance than his tactical officer.

From CIC's estimates, that ship was a shambles, little more than a broken hulk that still had impellers. It hadn't fired a single shot in the last salvo before it rolled, but its wounded sisters never wavered, and they should have. By all rights, that wall should have been shedding ships by twos and threes as their damage mounted, and despite the disparity in numbers, it was being hit far harder than Sixth Fleet. By now, every Havenite spacer, commissioned or enlisted, had to know about the superiority of Manticore's missile technology. They had to know Sixth Fleet had every edge in a missile duel, and the fact that they were taking so much damage while so many of White Haven's capital ships were mere dreadnoughts must have driven home that proof of their tactical inferiority with brutal force. That *had* to have taken the heart out of them, yet they were coming in anyway, taking their losses in ships—and lives—and never flinching.

A pair of Peep superdreadnoughts slewed suddenly out of formation. Not to roll ship, but staggering aside as their wedges went down. One of them still had her after-impeller ring; the other was naked in the storm, and a torrent of missiles roared down upon her and ripped her apart.

Five seconds later, her wounded sister followed in the blinding glare of failing fusion bottles, yet *still* Bogey One's course never wavered, and Alistair McKeon knew why.

They *did* know how outclassed they were in a missile engagement. But they also knew they had a significant edge in numbers and tonnage, even with the losses they'd already suffered. The range between Bogey One and Sixth Fleet was little more than four million kilometers now, and they were trying to close all the way into energy range, force the devastating close engagement prewar theory had extolled as the decisive moment in a fight to the death between walls-of-battle.

*They're not going to get it*, he thought. *If they can turn away from us, then we can turn away from them, and now that we've dropped the pods, our acceleration's at least as good as theirs. White Haven will never let them get that close!*

Only . . .

The Peeps had to know that as well as McKeon did, and they were trying anyway, which made no sense. It would only allow Sixth Fleet to hurt them even worse before White Haven broke off. So why in God's name—

One of the plot's green lights suddenly flashed the red of critical damage as half a dozen Peep lasers blasted into HMS *King Michael*, and Alistair McKeon's jaw clenched as the superdreadnought's wedge faltered. But then it came back up again, and the 8.3-million-ton Leviathan continued to fire. McKeon relaxed slightly . . . then stiffened as the entire ship simply blew up, taking six thousand human beings into death with it.

He heard someone gasp, yet he never looked away from the plot as Sixth Fleet edged ever so slightly to starboard. White Haven wasn't breaking off, he knew. The Earl was simply holding the range, preventing Bogey One from closing.

The missile exchange redoubled. But the weight of fire favored Sixth Fleet ever more heavily as more and more Peep launchers fell silent, and another Havenite fell out of the wall, covering herself with her impeller wedge as best she could.

That was five of Bogey One's SDs out of action or destroyed outright, to only one of Sixth Fleet's, and the surviving Peeps were far more heavily damaged. At this rate, White Haven would have a decisive edge even in energy range, assuming the Peeps could get that close, and Bogey One's commander had to know that. So why was he still coming in this way? Nightingale was of only tertiary importance to the People's Republic. It certainly wasn't worth the destruction of a fleet Bogey One's size! And even if it had been, any sane tactician would settle for driving Sixth Fleet off rather than seeking a close engagement which had to be suicidal! It made no—

"New contact, Skipper!" Chen snapped, and McKeon's nostrils flared as a fresh rash of impeller signatures blazed suddenly in the plot.

"Designate this Bogey Two," Chen continued, dropping back into the disciplined chant of a tactical officer facing disaster. "Bearing zero-four-five, zero-three-niner. Range niner-two-million klicks. One-eight million from the fleet Flag. Estimate twenty-four—two-four—ships-of-the-wall."

McKeon slammed a fist on his command chair's armrest as understanding blazed through him. No wonder the Peeps had held their course so unflinchingly! Bogey One had known exactly where Bogey Two was, and it had drawn—or perhaps a better term would be "herded"—Sixth Fleet directly into the trap. Now the untouched superdreadnoughts of Bogey Two had pushed their own drives high enough to burn through their stealth fields to accelerate into battle, and on their current vectors, Bogey One and Bogey Two would cross Sixth Fleet's track in barely eight minutes.

At which point fifty ships-of-the-wall would pour a torrent of fire into Sixth Fleet's surviving twenty-three.

"Orders from the Flag, Sir!" Lieutenant McCloskey said suddenly. "The wall will alter to two-seven-zero, zero-zero-zero at maximum military power and roll ship against Bogey Two! The screen will alter to nine-zero-zero, zero-zero-zero at maximum military power and roll ship against Bogey Two!"

"Acknowledge!" McKeon snapped, and stabbed a look at Lieutenant Pamela Irvine, *Prince Adrian*'s astrogator.

"Punched in . . . now, Skipper," she said before he could speak, and he grunted approvingly.

"Execute order from *Nike*," McCloskey announced.

"Make it so!" McKeon ordered, and HMS *Prince Adrian* turned away from the enemy for the first time in her entire existence.

Even as the screen came hard to starboard and broke for the hyper limit at five hundred twelve gravities, Sixth Fleet's wall-of-battle broke in exactly the *opposite* direction, driving even deeper into the hyper sphere. Like the screen, White Haven's wallers had redlined their inertial compensators, running them with zero margin against failure. That invited catastrophic damage should one of those compensators fail, but it also brought their acceleration up to four hundred nine gravitics, and the earl was no longer attempting to avoid Bogey One.

Alistair McKeon watched his display, his jaw tight, as he realized what White Haven had done.

Bogey One had paid a hideous price to bait the Havenite trap, but Bogey Two had jumped the gun. Only by a very few minutes, perhaps, and probably only because Bogey One's damage had been even worse than their pre-battle planning had allowed for. McKeon could readily understand how that might work. How watching Bogey One being ripped apart must have torn at the very heart of Bogey Two's CO. And it wasn't as if he'd lit off his drives all that much sooner than the plan had undoubtedly allowed for.

But it was—it might be—just enough, Alistair McKeon thought, punching numbers into the auxiliary plot deployed from the base of his command chair. If he was right, if—

The vectors came together on his plot, and his jaw clenched even tighter.

It *was* enough, but only barely, and only because Admiral White Haven had responded almost instantly. Given the comparative accelerations and the geometry at the moment Bogey Two revealed itself, Sixth Fleet could evade it. It would still bring White Haven's wall into its extreme missile range, but it was "above" as well as "outside" Sixth Fleet, which meant Sixth Fleet could roll up on its side, presenting only the roofs of its impeller wedges to Bogey Two's fire. Some Havenite missiles would probably get through, find targets through the Manticorans' hidden sidewalls, but no more than a handful.

Yet there were prices for everything, McKeon thought grimly. The only course that would permit Sixth Fleet to evade Bogey Two would force it to cross *Bogey One's* track at a range of barely one light-second, and an attitude that shielded White Haven's wallers from Bogey Two's missiles would force it into a broadside exchange with Bogey One well inside energy range. It would be a passing engagement. Even if Bogey One altered to extend the energy envelope as much as possible, Sixth Fleet would be through it and out of range once again in barely twenty seconds, and once past Bogey One, it could interpose its wedges against both Havenite formations.

But those twenty seconds would be carved from the heart of Hell itself.

Alistair McKeon didn't know what the final losses were going to be, but he knew they would be horrendous.

And he knew the war had just changed.

**HMS *Prince Adrian***
**Madras System**
**April 11, 1907 PD**

A<small>LISTAIR</small> McKeon rapped his spoon against his water glass.

The ancient attention-claiming signal chimed musically through the buzz of conversation, and heads turned toward him. He gazed down the long table at the diminutive midshipwoman seated at its far end.

Midshipwoman Felicia O'Toole drew a barely perceptible deep breath, picked up her wine glass, and rose to her majestic hundred and sixty centimeters.

"Ladies and gentlemen," she raised her glass, "the Queen!"

"The Queen!" rumbled back in response as other glasses rose all around the table, and Brandy Bolgeo smiled as O'Toole settled back into her chair, her expression only slightly touched with relief.

The midshipwoman had just turned twenty-two, and she'd boarded *Prince Adrian*, along with fellow middies Bryant Atwater and Lawrence Shakoor, less than two weeks ago. Brandy remembered her own middy cruise, how terrified she'd secretly been that she'd somehow screw it up, despite all her hard work and preparation at the Academy. But at least—her smile faded—she hadn't had to worry about being killed in action before she was twenty-three.

"Thank you, Ms. O'Toole," Captain McKeon said gravely, then leaned back in his chair and regarded his guests with a thoughtful expression.

There were quite a few of them—Chief Brodzinski had been forced to use both extenders, and the lengthened table filled even his dining cabin almost completely—and he considered them gravely for a moment or two.

"Thank you all for coming," he said finally, and Brandy saw some of the others smile at the polite formula courtesy required. She'd sometimes wondered what would've happened to an officer who'd declined his CO's "invitation" to dinner. She was pretty confident the situation had never arisen, since a junior officer that stupid probably also forgot to breathe without being reminded.

"It's good to see you all here," the captain went on. "Most of us have been through a lot together by now, and the newcomers"—he smiled at O'Toole and Shakoor; Atwater had the bridge watch and had been unable to attend—"seem to be fitting in well. So far, at least, Which, of course, any middy had *better* do! Trust me, you two do not want to find out what happens to midshipmen who *don't* fit in."

Shakoor's gray eyes widened ever so slightly, but a reassuring chuckle rippled its way around the table, and O'Toole smiled back at the captain.

"As those of you who have been around a bit longer than our newcomers know," McKeon continued, "I try to dine with my officers on a fairly regular basis. It's a lesson I learned from probably the best starship captain I was ever privileged to serve under, and I commend it to all of you as your own careers progress. But tonight, as you may have noticed, the table is a bit more crowded, and that's because this is a special occasion. We're here tonight to say goodbye to someone who's served aboard *Prince Adrian* for well over two T-years. During that time, he's been a pillar of strength when we needed one, an outstanding mentor to his own subordinates, and one of the best examples of what it truly means to be one of Her Majesty's Royal Marines."

He picked up his glass again, raising it slightly, and nodded to Viktor Yestachenko.

"If I may be just a few days premature, Major?" he said, then looked at the other seated guests. "Ladies and gentlemen, will you join me in offering our well-deserved congratulations to *Colonel* Yestachenko?"

"Congratulations!"

The response filled the compartment, and Brandy realized she was on her feet—that *all* of them were on their feet, except Yestachenko. The Marine must have heard the sincerity in all those voices, because somehow the face that had always said whatever it was supposed to be saying seemed to have escaped his control. In fact, he reached up and wiped an eye as surreptitiously as possible.

"Speech!" Brian Chen said with a huge grin, and Lev Carson took up the chant. They even began clapping rhythmically, and Yestachenko lowered his hand and glared at them. But then McKeon raised his own hand, stilling the tumult.

"Let's not get *too* rowdy," he said with a smile. "We're all Queen's officers, if you'll recall. That means that a certain standard of behavior is required of us." He paused a beat. "Even those of us who happen to be Marines."

"Oh, thank you, Sir," Yestachenko said. "You've made me feel so much better."

"You're a Marine!" McKeon's smile segued into a grin. "Suck it up, Colonel!"

Laughter rumbled, and Yestachenko glowered at the entire compartment. It was a remarkably insincere glower, Brandy noticed.

"Well, as it happens, Marines, unlike mere naval types, always have contingency plans," he said. "My well-honed tactical instincts suggested the high probability of an unscrupulous ambush of this nature, and like any good Marine, I came prepared."

"That sounds vaguely ominous," McKeon observed, then shook his head. "I may regret this, but the floor is yours, Viktor."

"Thank you, Sir." There was less humor in Yestachenko's tone—and expression—as he stood and faced McKeon's assembled guests.

"The truth is that I'm genuinely torn," he said simply. "Obviously, I've always wanted a colonel's planets, but I never realized how much a part of me would hate giving *these* up." He touched the three golden pips of a major which adorned his collar. "I'm looking forward to the challenges, now that they've decided to trust me with an entire battalion, but a part of me—a *huge* part of me—will still be right here, with Baker Company. I'm going to miss everyone aboard this ship, but I'll especially miss you three." He looked across the table at his platoon commanders, who sat very straight under his eyes. "I haven't told you often enough how satisfied I've been with you and how enormously proud I've been *of* you," he told them. "I have never asked something of you and not gotten it, and believe me, I know how often and how far beyond the mere 'call of duty' you—*all* of our people—have gone for me.

"I know that you'll give the same loyalty, the same integrity, to Major Hendren when he reports aboard. In the meantime, of course, the Company will be in your hands, Isaiah." He looked directly into Lieutenant Gillespie's eyes. "Take care of it for me."

"I will, Sir," Gillespie promised, and Yestachenko nodded.

"Good!" He cleared his throat and nodded again. "Good."

He picked up his own glass, looked down into it for a moment, then raised it.

"Ladies and gentlemen—my *friends*—join me, please, in a toast."

Shoe soles scuffed and clothing rustled as everyone in the compartment rose, and he turned his head, sweeping his gaze over all of them.

"To the finest ship I have ever served in," he said. "To the finest crew I have ever served with. And to the finest body of Marines, I have ever commanded. May God hold you in His hands, preserve you from harm, and give you the victory every one of you absolutely deserves.

"Godspeed, *Prince Adrian*. Cool heads, strong hearts, stout ships, and damnation to the Peeps!"

✦ ✦ ✦

Much later, Brandy sat in front of her terminal in her much smaller cabin. At least as *Prince Adrian*'s senior engineer, she didn't have to share it with anyone, and she luxuriated in that sense of privacy as she recorded her letter to her parents.

"So we're all going to miss him," she said. "I can't tell you where he's going, of course, but I will say that it's no more than he deserves, and that I'm sure he'll do just as fantastic a job there as he's done here, and that's a pretty high bar to clear.

"And, to be honest, sad as we all were to see him go, I think we all really needed that dinner. That party. The chance to share our hearts and hopes with each other. It's been a tough couple of months."

She knew her expression and her tone were giving away more than she really wanted them to, but that was okay. They were her parents. They deserved the truth . . . and there was no point trying to fool them, anyway. Her dad was far too well tapped in to Navy channels to not know what had happened in Nightingale, what it meant. And the House of Winton had always leveled with its subjects. No one would give away any tactically or strategically critical information, but while Navy communiqués might occasionally omit information, conceal ship movements, they never lied. That had been Manticoran policy since Queen Adrienne's day.

And that meant her parents knew how brutally Sixth Fleet had been hammered.

She hit the pause icon and sat back, pinching the bridge of her nose as her eyes burned with unshed tears. They might be unshed now, but they'd flowed—oh yes, they'd flowed—before now.

Four ships. That was how many of Sixth Fleet's ships-of-the-wall had never left Nightingale. HMS *King Michael*, HMS *Hydra*, HMS *Prometheus*, and HMS *Thunderer*. *King Michael* and *Thunderer* had died in the missile exchange before Admiral White Haven turned toward Bogey One. The other two were simply torn apart in the indescribable violence of a point-blank energy exchange between ships-of-the-wall. Sixth Fleet's merciless missile fire had wreaked havoc with Bogey One before that, which was the only reason White Haven hadn't lost even more of his wall, and the final tally at the end of the battle had been a clear tactical victory for Manticore. Killing those four RMN ships-of-the-wall had cost Bogey One seventeen of its own, and all fifteen of its survivors were damaged, at least two of them almost certainly beyond repair.

But if only four of Sixth Fleet's wallers had been *destroyed*, six more had been removed from its order of battle by damage. As an engineer, Brandy doubted that *Kodiak Maximus* would be worth repairing, and HMS *Myrmidon* would need a minimum of eight months in the yard. HMS *Casey* and HMS *Vindicator* might need almost as long in the repair slips as *Myrmidon*, and all four of them were superdreadnoughts, not dreadnoughts. *Landing City* and *Hero* would probably need only a month or two, but between repair time and the personnel casualties they'd taken, neither of them would be returning to the battle anytime soon. In fact, it was likely *none* of them would be back in service before the end of the year, so they might as well have been destroyed right along with their dead sisters.

Taken altogether, that represented forty-two percent of Admiral White Haven's pre-Nightingale wall-of-battle, and under other circumstances, at least two more of his ships would have been sent home for repairs, as well. Instead, *Juan Navarro* had working parties aboard HMS *Hyperion* and *Victorious*—and half a dozen other ships—laboring with their own engineers and damage control teams to fix the damage which was too "light" to justify pulling them back for repairs. Like *Nike* after Hancock station, they were too desperately needed to be sent home until replacements were available.

Sixth Fleet was too vital to be left understrength, so those replacements—and reinforcements—were already in the pipeline. In fact, *Polyphemus* had returned to BatRon 17 only two days ago. Her reappearance after her damage in Mathias was a welcome shot in the arm, and it left Baroness Triplett's squadron only a single ship short. But it would take weeks—at least—to make up Sixth Fleet's other losses.

Intellectually, Brandy understood that the Peeps' losses in Nightingale had been far heavier than Sixth Fleet's. Abdur O'Hanlon's best estimate, based on Sixth Fleet's own sensor data and two cautious reconnaissance flights since the battle, was that the final ratio had been better than three-to-one in Manticore's favor. Thirty-two PRN wallers—over 229,900,000 tons of starship—had been destroyed or put out of action for months, compared to only ten Manticoran wallers with a combined tonnage of "only" 72,350,000 tons. But Sixth Fleet had also lost almost twenty-nine thousand men and women. She could hope the Peeps had rescued at least some survivors from the ships they'd lost, but even if they had, Havenite POW camps had been an ugly enough experience under the Legislaturalists. She didn't really want to think about the camps something like State Security would produce. And the truth was that losses aboard *King Michael* and *Thunderer*, at least, had to have been pretty much total.

All of that was bad enough, but in many ways, it was almost minor. Oh, the agony of lost friends was horrible for all of them, and she suspected it would get even worse once time eroded the anesthesia of shock. It had certainly been that way for *her* after Hancock. But what hurt even more, in a lot of ways, was less the number of ships the Peeps had destroyed, the number of people they'd killed, than the way they'd fought.

By any meterstick, Nightingale had been a tactical victory for Manticore. Outnumbered two-to-one and taken completely by surprise by Bogey Two, White Haven had not simply fought his way clear but inflicted far heavier losses than he'd sustained. Brandy was an engineer, not a tactician, but Janet Briscoe was a tac officer to her toenails, and as far she was concerned, Hamish Alexander had just proved he could walk across Jason Bay any time he chose. Sixth Fleet had trusted its commander before Nightingale; after it, it idolized him.

But, also by any meterstick, Nightingale had been a *strategic* victory for the People's Republic. For the first time, a Manticoran attack had been not simply stopped, but thrown back with heavy losses. And any Peep who looked at the tactical data from the battle would realize Sixth Fleet's escape—and "escape" was the only thing it could be called, Brandy knew—had been a matter of minutes. Possibly even seconds. *Any* hesitation on White Haven's part would have spelled disaster . . . and both sides knew it.

That same tactical data made it clear the People's Navy had a steep mountain still to climb before it became the RMN's equal in battle, but the losing side always learned more by losing than the winning side learned by winning. The Peeps were *going* to make up ground, and the days in which Manticoran strategists and tacticians could take their own Navy's superiority for granted had disappeared.

At least White Haven's screen had emerged from Nightingale unscathed. As he'd anticipated, Bogey Two's wallers had gone after the Manticoran wall-of-battle, hoping to at least help run down any cripples, rather than waste time pursuing ships whose acceleration they could never match. For now, most of those cruisers and destroyers would find themselves covering the fleet train and escorting convoys, not hunting down Peeps. For that matter, Sixth Fleet was pretty much anchored to Madras, covering it against a possible Havenite attack, until its losses could be made good.

It was . . . unlikely someone like Earl White Haven would stand around with his hands in his pockets. He understood the importance of maintaining as much momentum as possible, and unless Brandy missed her guess, that meant Sixth Fleet would continue its hit-and-run attacks, continue its efforts to prune back Havenite numbers. She suspected he'd approach the operation more cautiously than before, but she never doubted that he'd press the pace just as hard as he could.

In the meantime, however, reports from the home system made it dismayingly clear that the logistic logjam hadn't gotten any better. White Haven's cripples would make bad a hell of a lot worse, in that respect, and according to Janice, frontline commanders were even being cautioned about ammunition supplies. Not even the RMN, which had embraced the gospel of missiles over the old dogma of energy-range, had realized how heavy its missile expenditures would be in an actual shooting war. The less innovative Peeps almost certainly had smaller prewar stockpiles than Manticore, but that was remarkably cold comfort just at the moment. What Sixth Fleet and Bogey One had done to one another at close range in Nightingale only reemphasized Manticore's need to exploit its missile superiority. To stay clear of any Peep energy batteries, pound away from ranges where its pods and better laserheads gave it the clear edge. But it took a *lot* of missiles—even with RMN capital ship laserheads—to kill a superdreadnought. And according to Janice, the Fleet had burned through over three T-years of peacetime missile production in substantially less than one year of active operations.

*We can't keep this pace up*, she thought, staring at the frozen display in front of her. *We just can't. Sooner or later, we have to stop and regroup. We know it, and I'm pretty sure whoever had the... intestinal fortitude to put together something like their battle plan in Nightingale has to know it, too. And I guess it's worth running risks where things like maintenance and overhaul cycles are concerned if we can keep pushing at least a little longer. Push them back a little farther, buy ourselves a little more defensive depth. But Adrian's already in the red for at least a quarter of her systems. There's a limit to how long my people can keep them up and running.*

Her jaw tightened, but then she shook herself.

Sitting around worrying wouldn't solve a thing, and it wasn't like she was the only engineer worrying about her ship! If misery loved company, she was one of a multitude of well-loved people.

She snorted, lips twitching with sour amusement at the thought, then cleared her throat and tapped the icon to resume recording.

"It's been rough," she told her parents, "but I hear there's a lot of that going around, and the ship and I are in good hands with Earl White Haven. The people out here love him. *Man*, do they love him! And with damned good reason. He's the best. He really, truly is. So don't worry about us too much.

"In the meantime, there seems to be a glitch in our communications traffic. Somehow the last info packet from home overlooked the soccer scores. And it happens that your daughter has placed a small wager with her executive officer on who's taking the Simpson Cup this year. So, if you could see about getting those numbers out here, I would appreciate it. The last I heard, the Jaguars had dropped all the way back to third place in Gryphon Central. I *do* hope you're going to tell me that's not the case, because if you don't—"

**HMS *Prince Adrian***
**Madras System**
**April 17, 1907 PD**

THE COM CHIMED.

The sound wasn't very loud, but Brandy Bolgeo's head popped up quickly, and an impartial observer might have described her expression as "relieved" as the attention request pulled her—oh, regretfully, of course!—out of her unending sea of paperwork.

She hit the acceptance key, then hid a frown as her caller's face appeared.

"Lieutenant Bolgeo," she identified herself. Regs required that, although her name and rank already appeared across the bottom of the other officer's screen.

"Major Hendren," her caller, equally a slave to regulations, replied, and she nodded, although she had no idea why he might be screening her. In fact, unlike Viktor Yestachenko, Clint Hendren held the rank of captain, which meant he and Brandy were equal in rank, although she was sure she was senior to him, thanks to time in grade. He was, however, properly referred to as "Major Hendren" aboard ship because a warship could have only one "Captain," and could afford no confusion about who was intended when *that* title was used. Because of that, Marine captains received the "courtesy promotion" to major. It had no effect on their actual ranks, although Brandy had known a couple of Marines who hadn't seemed to grasp that point. She didn't really know Hendren yet—been aboard less than three days—but he seemed a pleasant enough sort.

"How can I help you, Major?" she asked.

"Well, as it happens, there's a small problem." Hendren smiled, but something in his tone sounded a warning, and she didn't much care for the way he paused. Clearly he wanted to draw a response from her.

So she smiled back and simply cocked her head invitingly.

His lips seemed to thin ever so slightly.

"I've just come from Boat Bay Two," he said. "Both of my pinnaces are off-line. I need them back."

Brandy bit down—hard—on her immediate, instinctive response.

"I'm sure you do, Major," she said instead. "I'm assuming, since you screened me, that it's a maintenance issue. If so, I assure you my people will have you back up as quickly as possible."

"At the moment, *my* people can't do their jobs," Hendren replied. "They won't be able to until we get the birds back."

"I'm aware of that." Brandy's expression showed just a bit too much tooth to be called a smile. "And you'll get them back, as soon as possible."

"I'd feel more confident of that if I hadn't just come from the boat bay and an . . . interesting conversation I had there." Hendren's voice was cool, but his eyes had hardened.

"What sort of 'conversation'?"

"One which makes me wonder just how much priority my birds actually have," he said flatly. Brandy's eyes flared with true anger, but he continued before she could respond. "I initially spoke to Chief Harkness about it. His response was . . . less than satisfactory, so I screened Lieutenant Tremaine to express my concerns. He seemed unimpressed. Which is why I'm contacting you directly."

"In what way was *Senior* Chief Petty Officer Harkness' response unsatisfactory?" Brandy asked coldly, and watched the Marine's expression tighten at her pointed correction of Harkness' rank.

"He basically told me to wait my turn." Hendren's voice was equally cold. "I told him that was unsatisfactory, and he said that was too bad, because there wasn't anything he could—or, apparently, *would*—do about it. Since he seemed intransigent, I asked to speak to Lieutenant Tremaine. He *is* the boat bay officer, I believe. But when I expressed my concerns to him, he told me he had no intention of overriding Harkness. I believe the term he actually used was 'second guessing.'"

"And did Senior Chief Petty Officer Harkness tell you what had occasioned the delay?"

"He said my people 'broke the birds' by overstressing the impeller nodes in our last training exercise, and that he'd had no choice but to down-check both of them until he had time to run full diagnostics. Despite the fact that both of them showed green boards when we recovered to the bay after the exercise."

"Senior Chief Harkness is one of the most experienced small-craft flight engineers in the entire Navy," Brandy said coldly. "He's certainly the most experienced one aboard *Prince Adrian*. If he down-checked your pinnaces because he's concerned about their nodes, I'm not at all surprised Lieutenant Tremaine declined to override him. I would have done the same."

Hendren's eyes narrowed.

"And would you have done that without even asking to see the evidence for his concern, Lieutenant?"

"When a petty officer with a quarter T-century's experience tells me he's 'concerned,' I tend to assume he has a reason." A small voice in the back of Brandy's brain told her she wasn't pouring any water on the fire, but at the moment, she didn't much care.

"So you wouldn't have?"

"I would have waited for his write-up of the problem. It may surprise you, Major, but *Navy* personnel can actually read and write."

*Not good, Brandy,* that little voice said more loudly. *Your mama taught you better than this!*

Which was true, she thought. Her *father*, on the other hand . . .

"I'm not surprised Navy personnel can read and write," Hendren said. His voice was still cold, but lava smoked in its depths. "I may, however, have some slight reservations about what some Navy personnel will *choose* to write."

"Which means what, precisely?"

"Which means, Lieutenant, that I've read Harkness' jacket. The man should be in the stockade, in my considered opinion. He's a walking discipline disaster, and he's never made any secret of his opinion of Her Majesty's Marines."

"Are you implying that Senior Chief Harkness is fabricating his concern?"

Brandy's eyes blazed, and her right hand clenched into a serviceable fist just outside her com's field of view.

"I'm *saying* that this petty officer has a problem with discipline, doesn't like Marines, and was rather vague in his explanation to me. And that his immediate superior—who, I see, has served aboard the same ship with him almost continuously for the last five T-years—didn't even call him in for a more comprehensive explanation. So, no, I'm not implying that he's 'fabricating his concern'; I'm simply observing that he hasn't given me any cause to believe he isn't."

"Let me explain some things to you, *Major*." Brandy's tone could have frozen helium, and the "courtesy" part of Hendren's courtesy promotion seemed sadly absent. "First, the operations of my department are my concern, not yours. Second, I have never known Senior Chief Harkness to be less than fully professional where his shipboard duties are concerned. Third, Lieutenant Tremaine is one of the most competent young officers with whom I've ever had the pleasure of working, and—as you've just pointed out, as a matter of fact—he's known Senior Chief Harkness far longer—and better—than you possibly could on the basis of less than one *week* aboard this ship. I am not prepared to entertain aspersions against either of them."

She held his angry gaze with one just as angry, then inhaled.

"And, fourth," she said then, her tone marginally less steely, "this ship has been on continuous operations for well over a T-year, with no opportunity for comprehensive maintenance. For your information, we're eighteen T-months overdue for general overhaul, and one of our reactors and about a third of our gravitics were scheduled for replacement at that time. We are well past mandatory replacement times on both. My people, including Senior Chief Harkness and Lieutenant Tremaine, although the Lieutenant isn't actually in my chain of command, are working double watches just to keep *Prince Adrian*'s systems online. And while you may find this difficult to believe, Major, little things like—oh, I don't know, Fusion Two and Life Support One, let's say—take precedence. Senior Chief Harkness is short of his assigned personnel by almost thirty percent. That means he—and I—have to prioritize his time."

Hendren's jaw clenched.

"I assure you that he will provide me with a full explanation of his concerns no later than end of watch," she continued. "I will review that explanation exactly as I review all reports from my people. And if, as I do not for one instant expect, I discover that he's allowed his . . . fractious past with the Royal Marine Corps to affect his thinking, I will deal with that. But that is my affair, not yours."

Hendren started to open his mouth, and Brandy raised one hand, index finger extended.

"I advise you to let go of this until and unless there's some evidence—beyond your obvious personal dislike for what you *think* you know about Senior Chief Harkness—that he has, in fact, allowed his own feelings to affect the performance of his duty. At this moment, there isn't any. You are, of course, free to take your concerns up the chain to the XO or Captain McKeon, if you wish. I think it would be... unwise of you to do anything of the sort, particularly in the Captain's case, unless you have substantially more evidence of misconduct than you have so far shared with me."

The captain clamped his jaw again. Then, finally, he nodded curtly.

"You're probably right," he said. "And you're certainly right that the operations of your department are your affair—and responsibility—not mine. So I'll leave this with you." *At least for now,* his tone added. "Please inform me of when I can have my pinnaces back as soon as you have that information."

"Of course, Major."

"Hendren, clear," the Marine said, and her display blanked.

✧　✧　✧

"That's not exactly what I told him, Ma'am," Horace Harkness said.

"Well, it's obviously what he *heard*. So what did you say to him?"

Brandy raised her eyebrows and SCPO Harkness scratched his chin thoughtfully.

"I did tell him his birds would have to wait for their place in the queue," he said. "He didn't seem real happy to hear that. In fact, he told me it was 'not acceptable.' So I told him I was sorry if it made problems for his people, but that *my* people had way too much on their plates for me to make any promises about adjusting priorities without clearing it with Mr. Tremaine, at least. And probably with Lieutenant O'Brien or you. That's when he screened Mr. Tremaine, I think."

"So you never told him it was 'too bad' he wanted them back?"

"No, Ma'am." Harkness shook his head, then grimaced. "Not too sure that wasn't the way he *took* it, though. I wasn't trying to pick any fights, but I kinda had the feeling he expected me to."

"No, really?" Brandy widened her eyes at him. "How do you suppose he could possibly have leapt to a conclusion like that?"

"Ma'am, for whatever it's worth, you know I've never taken shortcuts or rearranged schedules just to spite the jarheads. May have been *tempted* a time or two, but I'd never do that. If nothing else, it'd give them too big a club to beat me with." Something that was almost but not quite a smile flickered in his eyes. "Besides, I don't pick fights with officers. Not even *Marine* officers."

And that, Brandy reflected, was true. In fact, Horace Harkness never actually *picked* fights at all. Instead, he'd perfected what her father called the art of "interpersonal judo" designed to suck even veteran Marines into taking the first swing, and he'd used it well over the course of his career. After the last twenty-odd T-years, his role as the innocent victim of Marine combativeness might have worn a tad thin, but even granting that, he'd never, so far as Brandy knew, lipped off to a Marine officer or even offered one of them what the Service still called "silent insubordination."

"It would appear Major Hendren is unaware of your sterling self-restraint in that regard," she said.

"Yes, Ma'am. I sorta noticed." Harkness grimaced again. "I really tried to avoid stepping on his toes, but I think he takes his people's readiness states seriously. I don't blame him for that, and he's right, Ma'am. Till we get these birds back up, they can't do their jobs, either. Gunny Babcock and I have already had that discussion."

Brandy snorted. She had no doubt at all that Babcock had "discussed" the state of the Marines' pinnaces with Harkness.

Loudly.

"All right, let's leave that for the moment," she said now. "He told me both pinnaces show green boards."

"Far as the birds' flight engineers' boards go, they do." Harkness nodded. "But I'm looking at the boat bay diagnostics and service flags, and they're edging into amber on four of Marine One's nodes and two on Marine Two."

"Only 'edging,' though?" Brandy asked thoughtfully.

The flight engineer's station aboard the pinnaces monitored current hardware states and functionality. Each time the pinnace recovered to the boat bay, however, *Prince Adrian*'s computers used the umbilical connections to generate a significantly more sophisticated analysis than its onboard systems allowed. Those same monitoring shipboard computers maintained a detailed, continuously updated history of every system aboard the pinnace, plotting trendlines over time and checking all of them against the "Book"-specified parameters for mandatory service.

Of course, the Book parameters incorporated a hefty safety margin. A point, she suspected, of which Major Hendren was aware.

"Yes, Ma'am. Edging. Right this minute, the computer's showing us a range between ten and forty-three percent into the Book's Service Immediately margin on the nodes I'm worried about. And, yes, the Major asked the same question. Wanted to know why I was pulling the birds off flight status when they hadn't actually reached the mandatory service point."

"And you told him—?"

"I told him we're taking maintenance histories and warning lights real seriously right now, on account of how overdue at the yard we are. For that matter, I told him we're having issues with spares. Ma'am, I'm showing warnings on six of his nodes, and we're down to *eleven* certified replacement nodes. That's it, for *all* our birds, not just the pinnaces, and we don't know when—or if—we're getting more of 'em. Some things we can print ourselves; all-up node modules, we can't." He shrugged. "To be honest, I think the Major's probably right that the ones I'm worried about wouldn't blow tomorrow, and none of them look like they'd produce the kind of catastrophic failure that could take down one of the birds completely. But if one of 'em *does* blow, you know we'll have at least some collateral damage, plus we're gonna have to write that node completely off and slap in one of our eleven replacements."

"So what you really want to do is a teardown inspection and service-as-needed? Not a complete replacement?"

"Yes, Ma'am." Harkness looked a bit surprised. "Why would we do a replacement before we even looked?"

"The Major said you told him his people 'broke the birds.' That suggests something a little more serious than 'edging into amber' on the diagnostics."

"Ma'am, what I said was the *flight crew* might've broken the birds. I specifically said 'might've,' and I never said the jarheads had broken anything."

Brandy frowned. *Prince Adrian*'s naval personnel provided the pilots and flight crew for all of her small craft. That included the pinnaces, although the Marines regarded those pinnaces as their personal property. Not without reason, from an operational viewpoint. What the pinnaces actually did, how they operated and—specifically—how hard they maneuvered while they did it, was determined by the Marines, and Marines had a reputation for being hard on their toys because of their aggressive training. As a consequence, there was a certain traditional tension between the Marines and their Navy "chauffeurs." Had Hendren thought Harkness was trying to blame the maintenance down-check on systems abuse resulting from the Marines'—which, since he was the senior Marine, would mean *his*—unreasonable demands on the Navy flight crews?

"What's the bottom line here on downtime?" she asked.

"My people still have two node replacements on the Number Three shuttle, and we've got that inertial compensator problem on the Number Two bird."

"I know." Brandy grimaced.

As Harkness had just pointed out, the spare parts issue had forced *Prince Adrian*'s engineering staff to begin rebuilding and refurbishing components that would normally have been returned to depot for repair or reclamation (whichever seemed the simplest) and replaced with depot-certified components from her onboard stores. That tied up not only personnel and workspace, but also printer capacity in the cruiser's machine shops, which further slowed both repairs and replacements. And, as Harkness had *also* just pointed out, Brandy's department was responsible for keeping *all* of *Prince Adrian*'s small craft up and running, not just the pinnaces, and with Shuttle Two and Three down, the cruiser had only a single shuttle currently available.

"We can probably put the Three bird back online by the end of the next watch," he said. "Two'll take longer. Problem's not all that bad, but we can't just fix it in place. We'll have to open her up to get at the compensator, and we don't have the working space to do that until we get Three out of the way."

"And if we pull people off either of those to concentrate on the pinnaces, both shuttles stay down longer than that."

"Yes, Ma'am."

"Much as I hate it, I think we'll have to do that, anyway. Or some of it, at least." Brandy didn't much like that thought. Especially if Hendren was going to take it as some sort of capitulation on her part. But they really did need at least one of the pinnaces back as soon as they could get it.

"Some of it, Ma'am?" From his expression, Harkness wasn't especially eager to hear what he suspected was coming.

"I agree we can't take avoidable chances on losing any more nodes than we have to, but the Major's right that his people need their birds back. So, what we'll have to do, I think, is put Marine Two back on limited flight status. They can have her in the event of an emergency, but we'll restrict her power levels to minimize stress on those iffy nodes. Then we'll prioritize getting Shuttle Three back up, but move the inspection of Marine One up in the queue, before the compensator teardown on Shuttle Two. As soon as we can clear Marine One's return to full flight status, we pull Two off and keep her there until we've had time to get Shuttle Two back up."

"We can do that, Ma'am. Switching teams back and forth is gonna slow us down, though."

"I know. It'll take longer for each bird, but not a lot, and this way the Marines at least get half their capability back. I doubt Major Hendren—or the Captain, for that matter—will be happy about having *only* half their pinnaces available, but the best we can do is the best we can do. I'll screen Lieutenant O'Brien and Lieutenant Tremaine to make it official, but you can go ahead and give your people a heads-up now."

**HMS *Prince Adrian***
**Madras System**
**April 19, 1907 PD**

"EXCUSE ME, LIEUTENANT. Do you have a minute?"

Brandy Bolgeo didn't reply, but she did pause, then turned to look up at Major Hendren with an arched eyebrow. The Marine had quickened his pace to make it into the intra-ship lift car before the door closed, and his expression was ... odd.

It was the first time they'd physically crossed paths since Hendren's complaint about Harkness and Tremaine, and she'd been just as happy about that, thank you very much. Unfortunately, they were both on Captain McKeon's guest list for tonight's dinner. This would be the first time Brandy and Hendren had been invited at the same time.

She hadn't been looking forward to it.

Now the far taller Marine looked back down at her as the lift car began to move, and she thought she saw his lips tighten a bit at her nonresponse to his conversational gambit.

That was nice.

"Look," he said, after a moment, "mostly I just want to apologize for having been a dick."

Brandy's eyes widened slightly, and her lips twitched.

"I ... ah, don't think I would have applied exactly that term," she said.

"I actually cleaned it up a bit. Filed off a few Marine-style adjectives and adverbs." Hendren shrugged. "I was pissed off, I was worried about readiness states, and I'm very much the new kid on the block in *Prince Adrian*. None of which is an excuse. An explanation, maybe, but not an excuse. I hadn't realized just how behind the ship is on her maintenance schedule, or how overworked your department was. Again, an explanation and not an excuse."

"Not to mention the fact that you were predisposed to think the worst about Senior Chief Harkness, too," Brandy suggested, and he grimaced.

"Yeah, I was," he admitted. "I admit I shouldn't have been, without personal firsthand experience, but you have to admit he has a . . . checkered record, to say the least, where Marines are concerned."

"That's probably fair," she acknowledged. "Most of that's because he just likes to fight and figures it's better to pick fights with somebody from outside his own ship. But despite his rep as a discipline problem, he hasn't shown much evidence of that aboard his last few ships. And there's never been a more qualified or *professionally* disciplined spacer in the entire Navy."

"You may be interested to know that someone else told me basically the same thing about him."

"Really? Who?"

"Gunny Babcock." Hendren rolled his eyes slightly. "Sort of pinned my ears back with that infinite 'You really *are* dumb as a rock, aren't you, *Sir*' courtesy only senior NCOs have truly mastered."

Brandy surprised herself with a snort of laughter. Partly because she understood exactly what Hendren was talking about, but also because she could just picture Babcock doing exactly that. Partly because she and Harkness had learned to work smoothly together, but even more because she knew how much the cruiser's senior Marine did *not* want to get on the wrong side of the ship's company. And, despite what Hendren had correctly described as a "checkered" career, in more ways than one, Horace Harkness was immensely popular with his crewmates.

Well, maybe not so much with the ship's *Marine* detachment, but he couldn't have everything.

"Anyway," Hendren continued, "I did want to apologize, and I also wanted to thank you for working with us to keep at least one pinnace available."

"And did you read Senior Chief Harkness' post-inspection report on Pinnace One's impeller nodes?" Brandy pushed with gentle malice.

"Yes," Hendren sighed. "And he was right. It's not really my area, but the Gunny pointed out to me that we'd have lost two of those nodes, almost for sure, if we'd had to go to max acceleration for any sustained period."

"Well"—Brandy's tone relented a bit—"I have to say I'm glad we didn't. We managed a rebuild on both of them, too, which was huge from our spares perspective." She shook her head. "We're babying so many systems that really need overhaul right now that it's not even funny."

"I know...now." Hendren nodded soberly. "I had no idea how bad things were getting out here before they rotated me out from Manticore, though."

"I understand why we're still pushing," Brandy said, watching the display as the lift car slowed to a halt. "I'm not in favor of giving the Peeps any more time to recover than we can help, either, and I know that means running maintenance margins thinner than the Book requires. For that matter, at least some of that's probably inevitable under wartime conditions, even without the ops tempo we're maintaining. But it really is getting out of hand."

"Well," Hendren said, nodding her through the opening lift doors before he followed, "I do have a better feel for the situation now. And, in the interest of non-dick-like behavior, I promise I'll do my best not to make it any worse next time around."

"That strikes me as a very good idea," Brandy told him with a small smile.

**HMS *Prince Adrian***
**Madras System**
**May 15, 1907 PD**

BRANDY'S UNI-LINK PINGED.

She glanced down and frowned at the caller ID, then looked at Oliver O'Brien and Felicia O'Toole. The three of them stood in Impeller Room 12's plasma conduit monitoring station, where the midshipwoman had been somewhat nervously displaying her proficiency.

The better Brandy got to know O'Toole, the more she approved of the tiny midshipwoman. She was smart, competent, and not one bit afraid of getting her hands dirty. For that matter, she gave a very good impersonation of a sponge around the ships' senior NCOs. Her ability to soak up the benefit of their experience was outstanding, and she had the gift, the knack for taking advice and accepting instruction without ever forgetting who was senior to whom in the chain of command.

If she had a fault—and it was a minor one—it was the anxiety she apparently felt when one of her own superiors, and especially Brandy, evaluated her proficiency. It never adversely affected her performance, so far as Brandy could tell, and it wasn't as if she were breaking out in any cold sweats. In fact, it didn't even seem to stem from any qualms about her own capabilities. It was more as if she didn't want to let her superiors down. Didn't want to give them less than the very best performance possible.

Truth be told, Brandy could think of very few "problems" she would rather have with one of her middies. And she had to admit she'd been very much like that on her own snotty cruise. Maybe that explained why she wished O'Toole would ease up on herself just a bit?

She brushed that thought aside and grimaced at her companions.

"I'm afraid I have to take this one," she said. "Felicia, what I've seen so far today absolutely rates a four-oh evaluation. I'll let you and Lieutenant O'Brien continue this, but drop by my office when you've finished. I think we should expand your duties a bit. I'm thinking maybe we slot you in as Reactor Officer for first watch."

O'Toole's eyes widened slightly, and Brandy saw O'Brien smiling at her across the middy's head. First watch was Brandy's watch, which meant she'd be available to backstop O'Toole if anything happened. And CPO Evans was the senior noncom of the watch. The burly chief was the next best thing to thirty centimeters taller than O'Toole, probably weighed twice as much, and was half again her age, all of which made him a reassuringly solid presence. More importantly, after Horace Harkness, he was probably the best power tech in the ship. Although Brandy hadn't realized it the day she reported aboard, he was also a fellow native of Gryphon. Not that she'd been all that surprised when she found out, given the number of career noncoms Gryphon provided to both the Navy and the Marines. He'd keep an eagle eye on the midshipwoman, so unobtrusively she probably wouldn't even notice, and he was exactly the sort of noncom O'Toole clearly knew to listen to.

"Yes, Ma'am," the middy said after a moment, and Brandy smiled. Then she nodded to the other two, stepped out of the compartment, and found a quiet corner of the impeller room. It wasn't hard; Impeller 12 was running only a skeleton watch, with *Prince Adrian* riding planetary orbit and no more than a trickle charge on her plasma conduits.

That was good. Brandy rather expected this was one com conversation no one needed to overhear.

She parked herself in a corner, her back to the bulkhead, and keyed the com function on her tablet.

"Major Hendren," she told it, then waited.

Despite his effort to overcome her initial negative impression of him, she wasn't looking forward to this. The Marine boarding exercise Baker Company had conducted that morning had gone very, very well . . . right up to the moment Marine Two's fusion bottle shut the hell down, anyway.

There'd been no time yet for Brandy to get into the nuts and bolts, but at least the fusion plant had vented to space the way it was supposed to when a bottle failed. There'd been no casualties, but Marine Two had returned to her boat bay under tow, with no impeller wedge, and in an actual operation, that could have been fatal. So—

Clint Hendren's face appeared on her tablet.

Somewhat to her surprise, he wasn't actively frowning.

Yet, at least.

"Major Hendren," she said affably. "How can I help you?"

"I'm sure you've heard about Marine Two's little ... misadventure this morning, Lieutenant?" he replied.

"I have." Brandy nodded. "I'm afraid I haven't had time to dig into the actual situation just yet. That was on my list for this afternoon."

"I'm not surprised you haven't gotten to it yet." Hendren shrugged. "I know how busy you are, and it's not exactly a galaxy-shattering event. Not on an exercise, anyway."

His tone was so reasonable Brandy had to order her eyes not to narrow.

"The real reason I wanted to talk to you about it," he continued, "is to tell you that any qualms I might have had about Senior Chief Harkness are now a thing of the past."

"Really?" Brandy's eyebrows arched, and he snorted.

"I'm not quite ready to adopt him into the Corps just yet," he said dryly. "But he was absolutely on the spot the instant Marine Two reported its problem."

"That sounds like the Senior Chief."

"It does, now that I've gotten to know him better." Hendren nodded. "I didn't really expect him and Lieutenant Tremaine to personally come to collect us, though."

"Excuse me?"

"You didn't know?" Hendren chuckled. "Tremaine took Shuttle One out to tow us home, and Harkness locked aboard Marine Two to monitor the fusion plant personally. He was running diagnostics before we even got back to the ship!"

"That really does sound like the Senior Chief," Brandy said with a smile.

"Yeah, and from what he's saying, we should have the bird back up within forty-five hours or so. Nothing actually *broke*, but one of the regulators threw a fault signal and the bottle went into emergency shutdown. He says it looks more like a sensor failure than an actual fault in the bottle."

"That's good news."

"I agree, but you should've heard Gunny Babcock." Hendren grinned. "She beat him back aboard in Marine One, and she was waiting when the Two bird recovered to the bay. Wanted to know what a 'drooling Navy idiot' who couldn't even seal his own shoes 'was doing aboard *her* pinnace.' And why he hadn't already fixed the problem, if he was such a hotshot. And, by the way, how long did he plan to take, because she wasn't getting any younger and she'd really like the bird back before she hit retirement age."

"Oh, Lord!" Brandy surprised herself with a chuckle as her imagination conjured up the scene.

"Don't worry, he gave as good as he got," Hendren assured her with an even broader grin. "Something about Marines too stupid to read the manual—if it wasn't written in crayon in ten-centimeter letters—who couldn't be expected to understand how to operate equipment any more sophisticated than clubs and brass knuckles. And something else about sergeant majors who thought the best way to fix molycircs was to beat on them with a five-kilo hammer. And would she please get her unqualified ass out of the way of the *Navy* people who—unlike certain sergeant majors he could have named but wouldn't—actually *were* capable of finding their asses with both hands and approach radar."

"And should I assume everyone in the bay was listening to this with suitable appreciation?" Brandy asked, although it was difficult to get it out through her chuckles.

"Oh, of course they were!" Hendren rolled his eyes. "How often do both clans have the opportunity to watch their tribal elders smite one another hip and thigh without actual bloodshed?"

"Would be interesting to watch those two on the training mat actually," Brandy said in a thoughtful tone. "Gunny Babcock's one of the best at coup de vitesse. I've watched her workouts a couple of times, and I think she was actually a senior instructor at Saganami Island a few T-years back. But Harkness must out-mass her by— what? thirty percent?—and from everything I hear, he's one heck of an old-fashioned bruiser."

"So far, we have at least been spared any blood on the deck plates,"

Hendren replied. "And, fascinating as the match would no doubt be, I'd prefer to keep it that way."

"So would I," Brandy agreed.

"Anyway," Hendren shrugged, "I just wanted to screen you with the good news that it's a minor glitch, and to tell you that Her Majesty's Marines are suitably appreciative of your department's services. We'll try not to impose upon them any more than we have to."

"I appreciate that, Major. Thank you."

"De nada." He shrugged again, then smiled. "Hendren, clear," he said, and her tablet blanked.

## HMS *Prince Adrian*
## Madras System
## June 9, 1907 PD

"AND I HOPE THEY'RE NOT MAKING a horrible mistake," Honor Harrington said from Alastair McKeon's display. "I have to admit, I had my own doubts." She looked straight out of the display, as if she were looking directly into his eyes. "I've been in a . . . really bad place since the duel, Alistair. I think for a while there I didn't really even *want* to come back from it."

McKeon's eyes prickled. He knew how few people in the universe Honor Harrington would ever have made that admission to, and the fact that she'd made it to him filled him with almost as much pride as pain. He didn't blame her for not wanting to "come back from it." How else could she have felt after everything an uncaring universe and the vilest specimens of humanity in it had done to her?

But she had come back. And he'd always known she would. No matter how badly wounded she might have been, she simply didn't know how to quit. The universe could kill her. If it didn't, then no matter what it *did* do to her, she would crawl up off her knees and tear out that universe's throat with her bare hands.

Now she sat back from her pickup, letting him see the treecat sprawled across the back of her chair and the enormous, luxuriously furnished flag cabin in which she sat. And the blue uniform of a Grayson admiral she wore.

"I'd always hoped to make flag in the *Manticoran* Navy," she said now. "These days, I'm not sure there's much chance of that. But High Admiral Matthews was right. They need my experience, Alastair, so I couldn't tell him no. Although"—her firm mouth twitched slightly—"I never expected to find myself with Alfredo Yu as my very first flag captain! Trust me, that one's taking some getting used to. But both Mercedes and Nimitz insist that he's the right man for the job, so I'm trying to convince myself."

Nimitz raised his head, looking over her shoulder, and yawned complacently at the mention of his name. Honor glanced back at him, then turned back to the camera. She twitched another smile, but it faded quickly.

"I have to say that some of the news we're getting here in Yeltsin doesn't exactly enthrall me. We've heard about Nightingale." Her eyes darkened. "Thanks to my newfound elevation, I get to see a lot more of the intel than even in Hancock. So I know how wicked it was. I don't need to tell you how relieved I was that *Prince Adrian* didn't get caught in the gears.

"I was especially struck by what ONI had to say about Esther McQueen, though." She shook her head. "I'd never heard of her before the coup, but everything ONI's heard since is bad news. I don't think she's Earl White Haven's equal, but she may be the closest to it the Peeps have, so you people watch your backsides out there."

Her nostrils flared, and she ran graceful fingers across braided brown hair that was longer than McKeon had ever before seen on her.

"I've got to wrap this up, because if I don't, I'll miss the mail packet, and I still owe Mom and Dad at least a brief note. But before I do go, I just want you to know how much you mean to me. You've been one of my rocks ever since Basilisk, Alastair, and never more than you and Tomas were after Paul's death. Whenever I think about a Pavel Young or the carrion eaters like him, I remember you. I remember integrity. I remember duty. I remember the man who's become my friend. So you take care of yourself. And you take care of the other people out there who mean so much to me. Scotty, Harkness, Babcock—all of them. You're not God. You can't *promise* me you'll all come home again. If anyone in the entire galaxy knows that, *I* do! But the universe has taken away enough people I care about, so you do your darndest to not be another of them, got it?"

She flashed him a brief smile. It still wasn't the smile he remembered, but that one was hidden in there somewhere. He knew it. He saw the humor, the affection . . . the lingering pain. But she was back on her feet, he thought. Back on balance, ready to do the things only she could do and eager to be back about it.

"Goodbye, Alastair," she said. "Be safe, my friend."

The display blanked, and McKeon drew a deep, deep breath. He sat gazing at its blankness for several moments, then climbed out of his chair, crossed his own day cabin, and turned that gaze out the armorplast viewport at Chembrambakam, the Madras System's inhabited planet. Technically, that viewport was a chink in *Prince Adrian*'s armor, but McKeon was just fine with that. It was a very, very small target, and it was above the cruiser's side armor, well outside the core hull. If anything managed to get through *Prince Adrian*'s sidewalls and target a viewport that was less than a meter wide, then "chinks in her armor" would probably be the least of his ship's problems. And the view could sometimes be spectacular.

At the moment, *Prince Adrian* rode in one of the outermost parking orbits, and Sixth Fleet's wallers were sharply silhouetted against the planet's blue-and-white marble. They looked impressive, and they were, but it was difficult to avoid bitterness as he thought about how much more impressive they might have looked without the losses at Nightingale. The lingering logjam of the Star Kingdom's logistics.

He thought about what Honor had said, and especially about Esther McQueen. Honor probably did have far better intel access these days than the commander of a mere division of heavy cruisers, but he'd heard the name before. McQueen was a rising star amongst the Peeps, and he wished to hell that she didn't so amply deserve the reputation she was building.

If ONI was right—and Commander O'Hanlon and Captain Hunter were pretty sure it was—then McQueen had commanded Bogey One in Nightingale. It was a pity they hadn't managed to kill her, but he had to wonder how she felt about Citizen Vice Admiral Jorgensen. She'd done her part, holding her course with an iron determination McKeon could only admire, even in a Peep. And if Jorgensen hadn't jumped the gun—and if Earl White Haven hadn't had the reflexes of a treecat—it would've worked.

Even with Jorgensen's premature movement, McQueen had ripped hell out of Sixth Fleet's wall. He didn't want to think about what she could accomplish with a few more months of prep time!

ONI was far from sure—intelligence was always more of a guessing game than anyone wanted to admit, especially in wartime— but according to their analysts, McQueen was probably the one who'd come up with the Nightingale defensive plan. And there were some indications she might be taking over the Trevor's Star command shortly. He hoped not. At the moment, he would far rather have her off doing something—*anything*—else.

He thought about that for another few moments, then squared his shoulders, turned and marched resolutely back toward his desk terminal and the waiting megabytes of paperwork.

A part of him would rather have faced incoming Peep missiles.

**HMS *Prince Adrian***
**Madras System**
**June 16, 1907 PD**

THE OFFICERS SEATED around the briefing room table stood as Alistair McKeon strode through the hatch. He crossed briskly to his own place, then nodded a bit brusquely.

"Sit. Sit!"

They settled back into their chairs, and he looked around the compartment.

"It's official," he said. "Admiral White Haven's sending a task group to Slocum. Rear Admiral Steigert will command it, and CruRon Thirty-Three's drawn the short straw as BatDiv One-Seven-Two primary screening element. That means us."

"I thought they were finally going to cut us loose for overhaul, Skipper," Lev Carson said, and Brandy nodded mentally. Her relationship with Major Hendren might have improved significantly over the two T-months since he'd joined the ship, but the cruiser's maintenance problems had only worsened...a lot. Her people had been fighting a losing battle for months, even before that; now, the situation was snowballing, and too many of her "repairs" were little more than slapdash emergency band aids. They *worked*, and she was proud of her people's ingenuity in *making* them work, but there was no way she could regard any of them as truly reliable. They *needed* that overhaul, and the sad truth was that, bad as their state had become, it was still worse for other ships. In fact, CruRon 33 was well short of its assigned strength because serviceability states for four of its units—*Prince Charles, Princess Adele, Prince Karl,* and *Cestus*—had become so bad, Admiral White Haven had been forced to send them home for repairs despite the home star systems' enormous logjam.

Their departure had reduced CruDiv 33.2 to only *Prince Adrian* and *Princess Stephanie*, and *Prince Adrian* wasn't in much better shape than *they'd* been. In fact, there were times she wished her people were just a bit less good at their job. Just enough that she could tell Captain McKeon—and he could honestly tell fleet command—that *Prince Adrian* was no longer mission capable. A return to the Manticore Binary System and a few boring months waiting for yard space in a parking orbit had a certain appeal at the moment.

"I raised that point with Admiral Steigert," McKeon replied to Carson's question with an affable smile that was perhaps one micron thick. "Actually, I told her that despite our Engineer's daily miracles"—he nodded down the table's length at Brandy—"we're way past any sane reliability margins. In fact, I told her we're starting to push basic ship safety into the red. Her exact response was 'There's a lot of that going around just now, Captain.'" His jaw tightened for a second, then he shrugged. "In fairness, I don't think she's a lot happier about it than we are."

"She can't be any *un*happier, Sir," the XO said.

"I agree." McKeon nodded. "Which is no slam on you, Brandy." He looked at his engineer again. "When I said 'daily miracles,' I meant it."

Brandy nodded back, grateful for the acknowledgment, and he returned his attention to the rest of his officers.

"I know none of you are happy to hear this," he continued, "but there really is a method to the madness. The Peeps are still badly short of experienced officers, but they still have a lot more hulls than we do, and the officers situation's getting better from their perspective, unfortunately. The good news is that they don't seem to have a lot more Esther McQueens tucked away—yet, at least—so it'll be a while before their bench is really deep enough to go toe-to-toe with us.

"That *is* changing, however, and from our recon probes, someone—most probably McQueen—seems to've convinced them to rationalize their deployment patterns pretty brutally. They appear to be concentrating heavily to cover Duquesne Base in Barnett and Trevor's Star. Well, of course they are, since those are the obvious anchors for their defense in this area, and because of our losses and their concentration, we're in no position to launch full bore attacks against either of them. At the same time, however, we need to keep pushing. We need to keep them reacting, make them worry about all the places we *might* go until we *can* go after the hard targets. And what we especially *don't* need is to give someone like this McQueen a big enough respite to start thinking about spoiling attacks against us before we get more of our wall deployed forward. If she starts trying to do to us what we were doing to the Peeps before Nightingale, she might just have the hulls to hurt us badly."

He paused, looking around the compartment, while he let that sink in, then shrugged.

"It's not all doom and gloom, though. I know all of us took getting *Polyphemus* back as a good sign, and that's what it was. Within the next three to four months, Admiral White Haven will be substantially reinforced from the wallers finally coming out of the yards. We're talking *battle squadrons*, people, not individual ships. But until then, we need to keep the Peeps looking over their shoulders, which is what this op is all about.

"Slocum's sort of like a reprise of Samson," he continued. "There's nothing there except the gas refineries, and that means it's probably lightly picketed, if at all. Intelligence thinks they're unlikely to have diverted a lot of combat power to cover what's basically a useful but not vital support facility for Barnett. Sure, they'd prefer to hold onto the system and the refinery complex, but they can live without either of them if they have to, and they need everybody they have to cover Duquesne and Trevor's Star. If they have to choose someplace to skimp, it does make sense to pick Slocum."

Brandy considered that. She was neither an astrogator nor a tac officer, but she knew the Peeps had established their base in the Slocum System, ten or twelve T-years before the shooting started, to take advantage of its three gas giants. Slocum's atmospheric extraction ships and refineries had been intended to provide the bulk of the reactor mass and thruster fuel for Duquesne Base, the enormous forward base they'd built in the Barnett System. Duquesne itself had been built primarily as a jumping-off point and logistics support base for their long-planned attack on the Manticoran Alliance. It had lost much its offensive value in the wake of the Peeps' initial disasters, but it had become the linchpin of the Trevor's Star defenses, instead. And Captain McKeon was right. If she'd been the

Peeps and she'd had to leave a star system uncovered, she'd pick one like Slocum rather than one like Barnett, too.

McKeon tapped the controls at his end of the table and brought up a holographic star map above it. The Slocum System blinked alternating amber and white, but so did three other star systems, stretched in a line from the Owens System through Mylar and Slocum to Gualt. Together, they formed an arc that stretched three quarters of the way around the Barnett System.

"Welcome to Operation Mangonel, people. Just hitting Slocum probably wouldn't get the Peeps' attention. In fact, Commander O'Hanlon and Commander Eccles are both pretty much convinced it wouldn't get McQueen's, if she's the one calling the shots." He shook his head. "So, Earl White Haven and Captain Hunter came up with Mangonel. Hopefully not even a McQueen would be able to ignore us when we hit four star systems almost simultaneously. Admiral Kuzak will be responsible for Owens and Mylar. Sixth Fleet will have Slocum and Gualt. Because Gualt is so much deeper into Peep space—and because at last reports the Peeps had at least one battle squadron stationed there—Admiral White Haven and most of Sixth Fleet will be responsible for taking it out. To be totally honest, Slocum is pretty small beer compared to the other systems on Mangonel's list, but taken together, they'll hopefully convince the Peeps that Barnett is our primary objective, at least for the moment. And that, in turn, will—hopefully—convince them to concentrate more of their available wall to defend it, because every ship they have in Barnett is one more they *won't* have at Trevor's Star."

He paused again, then cleared his throat.

"Anyway," the captain continued, "they'll be sending us; BatDiv Three-Oh-Three, minus one ship; and a destroyer division or two to hit Slocum. We'll take a look, and if Intelligence is wrong and they've got a picket too strong to take, we back off and settle for jumping around the hyper-limit perimeter like fleas on a griddle. At the very least, we should be able to make them nervous. But we'll also take along half a dozen tankers from the Fleet Train. If the system's not held more heavily than ONI expects and we can pull it off, Admiral Steigert figures there's no reason all that nice reactor mass the Peeps are busy refining couldn't fuel *our* ships, instead."

He smiled with genuine humor for the first time, and two or three of the officers around the briefing room table chuckled. Then he shrugged.

"It's more likely they'll blow the tank farm as soon as they see us, but we might get lucky. And Intelligence wants the base's computers. They don't expect us to find anything earth shattering, but we got a lot of useful information from Mathias, so it's probably worth trying to do the same thing at Slocum."

"It's always worth *trying*, Skipper," Carson agreed. "Of course, they're just as likely to scrub the files as blow the tank farm."

"I didn't say anyone really expects us to get our hands on their files, Lev. But, like you say, they'd like us to try. We'll see if we can hack our way in while we're there, and one of our mission objectives is to haul their servers home with us for the forensics people back in Manticore. That's going to be your people's job, Clint." He nodded at Hendren. "We'll be putting you aboard their main platform. And I'm sending Brandy along as senior officer onboard and to keep the lights on and bird-dog the computers for Anderson."

He twitched his head at Anderson McCloskey. *Prince Adrian*'s com officer was an excellent cyberneticist, as well, and he nodded back to McKeon. Then the captain looked at Lieutenant Commander Chen.

"In some ways, I'd prefer to send you, Brian," he said. "Truth be told, I think you're a naturally more devious and suspicious soul than young Anderson, better suited for dealing with the wicked Peeps if they try to hide stuff. But if anything hits the fan, I want you closer to home running Tactical, just in case. And let's face it, Anderson's better with computers than you are. In fact, just about *anybody's* better with computers than you are, now that I think about it."

"I'm crushed, Skipper. *Crushed!*" Chen protested.

"And if you understood anything more subtle than a pointed rock when it comes to breaking into an enemy database, I might have let you go anyway," McKeon replied dryly. "I said you were more suspicious than Anderson. I didn't say you were *smarter*."

McCloskey buffed his fingernails on his tunic, then blew on them complacently, and Chen grinned.

"Okay." McKeon let his chair come fully upright and plugged in a data chip, and a file header appeared in the briefing room holo display. "We need to go over the rough—at this point, *very* rough—ops plan, but I did manage to get one promise out of Admiral Steigert."

They all looked at him, and he shrugged.

"We're not the only unit of the Slocum task group who's overdue for a date in the yards. In fact, everybody they've picked for this little shindig is almost as overdue as we are, people. Assuming we manage to steal the Peeps' reactor mass, we'll send the tankers back to the fleet with the destroyers. Then the rest of the task group—including *Prince Adrian*—will continue straight home to the Star Kingdom." Brandy's eyes brightened, and McKeon smiled at her. "I understand the *Hephaestus* yard dogs can hardly wait to see us!"

*Sigismund Alpha*
**Slocum System**
**July 27, 1907 PD**

"YOU'RE KIDDING."

"No, Citizen Commissioner. Citizen Captain Rummo just confirmed it."

"He's *positive* it's not Citizen Commodore Androcles?"

"That's what he says, Citizen Commissioner."

"Oh, shit."

People's Commissioner Danielle Barthet glared at Porthos Radeckis. She knew it wasn't his fault, but he was the only person available to glare at. Even he wasn't close enough for her to do it in person, and all he could see was her com's personal wallpaper, anyway, since he'd just woken her up less than two hours after she'd gotten to bed. At the moment, he wore the crimson tunic and black trousers of the Office of State Security while she wore nothing at all.

Her current bed partner had started yanking his trousers on the moment the com jangled and she sat up in bed. Now she jerked her head at the sleeping cabin hatch, and he vanished through it, carrying his boots in one hand and the rest of his uniform in the other.

The hatch closed behind him, and she ran her fingers through her short-cropped blond hair while she tried to kick her brain fully awake.

"How bad?" she asked after several seconds.

"Rummo doesn't have definite numbers or classes yet." Radeckis shrugged unhappily. "His people picked up their hyper footprint about fifteen minutes ago. He says they're sixteen light-minutes from the primary—about seven from us—which is why he's sure it's not Androcles. There's been plenty of time for an arrival ID from her to reach us. As far as numbers are concerned, we don't have first-line sensor capability." That, Barthet reflected bitterly, was a colossal understatement. "But he says his people have identified at least three

453

dreadnoughts or superdreadnoughts, five cruisers, and nine destroyers or light cruisers. So far."

Barthet's jaw tightened.

So much for its being Androcles. She didn't know exactly how powerful the citizen commodore's task group was supposed to be, but she did know its heaviest unit was supposed to be a battleship.

*Damn it. I told* them we needed to reinforce the system pickets! *We're too exposed out here! But did anyone listen? Not until it was too frigging late!*

"What does he mean 'so far'?" she demanded.

"He says they're picking up five impeller wedges that could be additional dreadnoughts." Barthet flinched, but Radeckis wasn't finished. "As I say, he said they *could* be dreadnoughts, but at the moment he's inclined, based on their formation, to think they're tankers, instead."

Barthet puffed her lips, then nodded grudgingly. That actually made sense, even if it didn't make Slocum's situation any better. The entire existing "Slocum System Defense Force" consisted of exactly six destroyers, which might—*might*—have been capable of scratching a single ship-of-the-wall's paint.

On a good day.

"So they figure they can steal our reactor mass, do they?" she growled.

"That's what it sounds like, Citizen Commissioner."

"Well, we'll see about that!"

Barthet glanced at the time display.

"How long for them to reach us?"

"They're still over a hundred and twenty million klicks from the platforms." Radeckis glanced down to consult his notes. "Current velocity is about thirteen hundred KPS, and they're pulling two hundred fifty gravities. That puts them just under four hours—three hours and forty-seven minutes, to be exact—from a zero-zero with *Sigismund*."

"Wonderful." Barthet inhaled sharply. "All right. Go ahead and activate Omega. And tell Rummo I'll be speaking to him as soon as I get dressed."

"Of course, Citizen Commissioner," Radeckis replied, and Barthet killed the circuit with a furious finger stab.

Radeckis' response had been just a little too toneless for her taste, but that wasn't surprising, given how little Omega appealed to him. Fortunately, he also knew better than to argue.

Unlike Barthet, Citizen Captain Porthos Radeckis had a lengthy history in the People's Republic's security forces. In fact, he'd been an Internal Security sergeant before the Legislaturalist coup attempt. That, however, was scarcely a ringing endorsement in Barthet's opinion.

Oscar Saint-Just's Office of Internal Security might have been instrumental in defeating the coup attempt, yet however quickly and effectively InSec had responded after the traitors' initial attack, no one had seen it coming in time to *stop* it.

That was what had prompted the fundamental consolidation and reorganization of the People's Republic's entire security apparatus. And Saint-Just's decisive response to the coup had made him the only real candidate to command the newly created Office of State Security when the Committee of Public Safety folded Internal Security, the Mental Hygiene Police, and half a dozen other, smaller security services together.

After their leadership positions had been purged of Legislaturalists, of course.

Radeckis had come over to StateSec from InSec. Barthet hadn't. She'd been a member of Cordelia Ransom's Citizens' Rights Union, the proscribed action arm of the Citizens' Rights Party. In fact, she'd been one of the CRU "terrorists" people like Saint-Just had hunted for decades, while Radeckis had been one of the InSec thugs who'd done the hunting. That created a certain...tension in their relationship. And, frankly, she distrusted his commitment to the new regime trying to clean up the Legislaturalists' mess. In particular, he was far too prone to defer to Citizen Captain Rummo.

Barthet's own relationship with Rummo was less than congenial. Two T-years ago, Citizen Captain Rummo had been *Lieutenant* Rummo. He hadn't been a Legislaturalist himself, or he wouldn't still be in uniform, but anyone who'd been commissioned before the coup bore watching. That was Danielle Barthet's job. And part of that job was keeping him aware that he continued to serve only on her sufferance.

She stood and reached for her own uniform.

✧    ✧    ✧

"With all due respect, I think that's a bad idea," Citizen Captain Abelin Rummo said.

"Does that mean you intend to protest the Citizen Commissioner's orders, Citizen Captain?" Porthos Radeckis asked him.

"It means I think those orders should be . . . carefully considered," Rummo replied. His tone was respectful but unflinching, and Radeckis gave him points for intestinal fortitude. Arguing with Danielle Barthet wasn't the best tactical decision a man could make, though. Radeckis knew he should shut down this entire conversation quickly, but—

"Why?" he asked.

"I don't have any objection to destroying the tank farms or the refining platforms, to prevent them from falling into Manty hands, Citizen Captain," Rummo said. "If we're going to do that, though, we should do it immediately. Or at least as soon as they formally demand our surrender. What the Citizen Commissioner is proposing could very well be interpreted as a violation of the Deneb Accords."

"I understand your concerns," Radeckis said after a moment. In fact, Rummo's "concerns" were a close mirror of Radeckis' own reservations. "But as far as not immediately destroying the storage and refining facilities is concerned, the Citizen Commissioner is basically playing for time. Citizen Commodore Androcles was already supposed to be here, and the Manties will be pinned down here for at least a couple of days, if they really intend to transfer all that reactor mass to their tankers. If Androcles turns up in the next, say, twenty-four hours, she may be able to drive them off without what they came for."

Rummo's eyes rolled ever so slightly, but he kept his mouth shut. He and Radeckis both knew how unlikely it was that any picket force the People's Navy might have scraped up for a hole-in-the-wall system like Slocum would have a chance in hell to "drive off" three dreadnoughts. It *was* remotely possible. So was the possibility that the system primary would go nova in the next twenty minutes. In the real world, the People's Republic was going to lose the storage tanks *and* the refinery platforms, one way or the other. That being the case, Rummo was exactly right, in Radeckis' opinion. They ought to blow all of them immediately.

And they sure as hell *shouldn't* blow them with Manticoran tankers docked to them. If they did that, if they killed the crews of those ships, the Manties would be fully justified under interstellar law in destroying every habitat platform in the system... without evacuating the Havenite personnel. Radeckis had pointed that out to Barthet when the people's commissioner first hatched Omega, only to be told that she had no intention of waiting *that* long. *Obviously,* the tank farm would have to be destroyed before the Manties actually docked to it!

But Radeckis had enjoyed more access to InSec's pre-coup files on Barthet than the people's commissioner might realize, and based on her CRU cell's taste for spectacular, mass-casualty events, he didn't trust the ex-terrorist's assurance about exactly when she intended to blow up the storage facility any more than Rummo did. Nor did he care for Barthet's decision for the system's SS personnel to "go to ground." He didn't object in the least to her decision against trying to defend the platforms when the Manties arrived. It seemed unlikely the Royal Manticoran Marines aboard those incoming warships would find it difficult to deal with little more than three hundred StateSec troopers, after all. And he wouldn't have had a problem with just stripping off his uniform and disappearing into the two-thousand-strong Slocum workforce. Unfortunately, that wasn't what Barthet had in mind.

"As I say, I appreciate the reason for your concerns," he said, "but we both have our orders, Citizen Captain. Don't we?"

He held Rummo's eyes with his very best bleak, InSec gaze, and the naval officer inhaled deeply. His wife, two kids, three brothers, and parents lived in Nouveau Paris. Which meant he wasn't about to do a single thing that could point StateSec at the people he loved.

"Yes, we do," he said, and Radeckis nodded.

"The Citizen Commissioner will join you in Command One shortly," he said.

## Slocum System
## June 27, 1907 PD

"THERE THEY GO, Skipper."

Lieutenant Commander Chen sounded a bit disgusted, but not surprised, and Alistair McKeon grunted in acknowledgment. He didn't blame the Peep destroyers one bit. They would have been hopelessly outclassed just by TG 16.3's own destroyers. Against Steigert's dreadnoughts, they might have lasted five minutes. On a good day.

"Smartest thing they could've done," he said, gazing at the large-scale plot, where the icons of the destroyers' impeller wedges had just crossed the hyper limit. Five of them had disappeared into hyper as soon as they could, but one remained behind.

"There wasn't a damned thing they could have done to stop us," he continued. "So they leave one tin can to keep an eye on us and the others haul ass to spread the word."

"Think they're likely to bring back friends, Sir?" Chen asked.

"I doubt it." McKeon shrugged. "It's unlikely they have anyone close enough to get back here before we finish up and head for home. That was one of the reasons we got Slocum and the rest of Sixth Fleet got Gualt. And if they did have someone close enough, the smart move would've been to send a single courier to call them in while the rest of the picket hung around and kept an eye on us." He shook his head. "No, I'm not going to make any ironclad assumptions that there *isn't* somebody close enough, but this looks more like spreading the word as broadly as possible."

"At least that's how they'll write it up for their reports," Lev Carson observed dryly from McKeon's com. The XO was once again in AuxCon with the backup bridge group. "Given the new management's 'collective responsibility' crap, *I'd* make damned sure I covered my ass against any hint of cowardice or 'defeatism.'"

"So would I," McKeon acknowledged. "But the truth is, it's the best thing they could do, anyway. And—"

"Excuse me, Skipper," Lieutenant McCloskey said.

"Yes?" McKeon looked at him.

"Admiral Steigert's on the com for you, Sir."

"Thank you."

McKeon touched the acceptance key and Rear Admiral Jožefa Steigert replaced Commander Carson on his display.

"Ma'am," he said.

"They've surrendered." Steigert snorted. "Surprise, surprise!"

"Actually, I *am* a little surprised they didn't blow the tank farm first, Ma'am."

"So am I," Steigert acknowledged. "Especially given how fond of shooting people the 'Committee of Public Safety' seems to be. Of course, that could cut both ways. If you don't blow the tanks to keep them from falling into the hands of those nasty Manties, you're likely to get hammered—or shot—for lack of revolutionary zeal. But if you blow them in time to prevent that, you're probably just as likely to get hammered—or shot—for defeatism."

"I can see that, Ma'am. But if it was me, I'd have pushed the button."

"Well, Citizen Captain Rummo apparently doesn't see it that way."

"Citizen Captain?" McKeon repeated. "Not 'People's Commissioner'?"

"Regular Navy officer." Steigert shrugged. "Maybe they just hadn't gotten around to assigning a 'commissioner' way out here yet."

"Maybe." McKeon nodded, but he also frowned. Admittedly, the Slocum System was scarcely a critically important installation, but the Committee of Public Safety had made a point of assigning their 'people's commissioners' to every single hyper-capable unit of the People's Navy. And there'd been commissioners in every other system Sixth Fleet had hit after the formal declaration.

"It seems odd to me, too," Steigert said. "And just between you and me, Alister, I'm not a big fan of 'odd.' Tell your people to watch their asses when they go aboard the main platform."

"Oh, I will, Ma'am. I will."

✧  ✧  ✧

"Marine One is docking now, Ma'am. We're number two, behind Major Hendren."

"Thank you, Scotty," Brandy said. Lieutenant Tremaine was

technically too senior for a mere shuttle pilot, but she hadn't been surprised to find him when she boarded the shuttle. After all, as *Prince Adrian*'s flight operations officer, *he* got to make the cockpit assignments.

That no doubt also explained why SCPO Harkness was Shuttle One's current flight engineer, as well.

She smiled at the thought and leaned forward in her seat, craning her neck to watch Marine One settle into the docking buffers in the orbital platform's Boat Bay One.

Like most industrial platforms, *Sigismund Alpha*'s design was bare-bones, practical, and as devoid of aesthetic value as it was possible to be. The main platform was an untidy aggregation of habitat modules, hydroponics sections, and cargo platforms, gleaming in the reflected light of Sigismund, otherwise known as Slocum III.

Slocum was unusual for an F8 star in its possession of three exceptionally massive gas giants. Sigismund, the largest of the trio (and the only one which had actually been named), was about ten times as massive as the Sol System's Jupiter, just short of "brown dwarf" territory. It wasn't significantly larger than Jupiter, only denser and more massive, but it supported two separate refinery platforms—*Sigismund Beta* and *Gamma*—and a bountiful flotilla of atmospheric mining ships.

The refineries and storage tanks were well separated from *Sigismund Alpha*, probably as a safety precaution in case of industrial accidents. They were actually a bit larger than Brandy had anticipated, too. It looked like at least two or three times the storage capacity she'd expected. If those tanks were full, TG 16.3 should have brought more tankers.

Her lips twitched at the thought as she watched the boarding tube run out to Marine One and pictured Hendren and his Marines swinging through it to the *Sigismund Alpha* boat bay gallery. Over the last few months, she and Hendren had even gotten as far as using one another's first names, occasionally. She suspected he still cherished a few reservations about Harkness, but given Harkness' record, she couldn't fault that. If she'd been a Marine, *she* would have had reservations about him! And whatever the Marine's other faults might be, at least he had a lively sense of humor. Brandy could forgive a lot in someone who knew how to laugh at himself.

His obvious competence was another mark in his favor. In Brandy's experience, Marines in general had something of a fetish about training, but Clint Hendren took it to an even higher level than most. His people spent a *lot* of time in small craft and EVA exercises. *And* in fully geared-up shipboard exercises, tasked both to defend and to seize the ship. In fact, the time they spent practicing boarding and SAR exercises put enough wear on "his" pinnaces to eat up a disproportionate amount of Brandy's severely overtaxed service and maintenance time. On the other hand, once he'd become aware—one might have said *painfully* aware, given their initial contact—of how overworked her people were, he'd assigned six of his Marines to help with the load. It wasn't the same as having additional trained Navy ratings, but all six of them had extensive experience with Engineering as damage control team leaders, and they'd proven extremely useful.

She wasn't about to let him completely off the hook for the way he'd put his foot into his mouth that first time. Or, at least, she wasn't about to admit it to him, anyway. But he'd made some long strides toward rehabilitating himself in her eyes. And he—and the rest of his Marines, of course—were a very reassuring presence when she found herself going aboard a platform inhabited by the next best thing to two thousand Peeps.

"Bay secure, Ma'am," Tremaine announced, and the shuttle quivered as its thrusters engaged. "Initiating docking sequence now."

✧  ✧  ✧

Brandy followed Major Hendren down the final passage to *Sigismund Alpha*'s command deck. As the senior officer present, she was technically in command, and where engineering issues and her party of ratings were concerned, she was just fine with that. But she didn't know a damned thing about boarding a hostile orbital platform, and she was delighted to leave the details of securing that platform up to the Marine.

Like the rest of her Navy personnel, she wore a standard-issue skinsuit, but Hendren's Marines—aside from his single platoon in battle armor—wore Marine-issue armored skinnies. At the moment, the major was watching the system schematic displayed on his helmet's HUD as he and Brandy moved at the center of a five-Marine diamond formation, and all of the Marines in question carried unslung M32 pulse rifles. At least no one in her immediate vicinity had unlimbered a tribarrel or a plasma rifle, she thought dryly.

*Oh, stop that!* she told herself. *They're doing their jobs, and they're doing them damned well, and you know it.*

She did. In fact, what she felt most at the moment was impressed... and reassured. She was an engineer, not a tac officer, and sure as hell not a *Marine*! She carried the mandatory sidearm, and she'd qualified with it, as required. She was fairly certain she could at least not shoot her own foot off. Anything more was... problematical. So it was a good thing people who understood such things were along to keep her out of trouble.

*And the fact that this is so far outside your comfort zone is one reason you're feeling nervous enough to make snitty remarks, if only to yourself,* she thought. *And I hadn't realized how damned big this place was, either!*

In fact, compared to something like *Hephaestus* or *Vulcan* back home, *Sigismund Alpha* was tiny. Compared to *Prince Adrian*, it was huge, as was probably only to be expected of an orbital platform which housed a workforce closing in on three thousand. In addition to the environmental sections, there were engineering and maintenance spaces, docking racks for workboats and remote repair and maintenance drones, and God only knew what else, all located with the sprawling contempt for concentration microgravity made possible.

In addition to the boat bay, designed to allow the transfer of personnel in a shirtsleeve environment, which was located in its own module and covered now by one squad of Lieutenant Dimitrieas' First Platoon, there were five docking platforms arranged to service *Sigismund Alpha*'s extensive cargo modules.

First was the only battle-armored platoon of the short company of *Prince Adrian*'s Marine detachment, and its second squad was distributed covering those cargo docks. The modules they served were *much* larger than Brandy had anticipated, but their size had made sense when she discovered that all of the system's spare parts and support equipment were warehoused aboard *Sigismund Alpha*, rather than distributed to the refineries and tank farm. In addition, the Peeps had been building a second refinery—and additional tank farms—in orbit around Slocum IV. Most of the materials support for *that* was passing through *Sigismund Alpha*, as well, and its cargo space had been expanded accordingly. All of those docking platforms had to be covered, though, which had sucked away more of Hendren's battle armor than Brandy might have preferred. On the other hand, battle armor was bulky, and most of *Sigismund Alpha*'s internal passages were too narrow for it to pass through readily.

Dimitrieas' third and final squad had been broken up into four two-person fire teams, rather than the standard three-person sections, and detailed to cover the platform's central lift shafts. The shaft access compartments were much wider than the connecting passages, which made them a more comfortable fit for battle-armored Marines. And a Marine in battle armor was a very untempting target if anyone felt fractious. If Hendren had to hang somebody out on his or her own—and he did, given the number of points that had to be covered—it made sense to use his best-protected, best-armed personnel.

Lieutenant Gillespie's Second Platoon had been tasked for *internal* security. He and his first squad had headed for Power One, located in *Sigismund Alpha*'s central engineering section, along with Oliver O'Brien and Felicia O'Toole, to secure the platform's reactors. His second squad had already accompanied Scotty Tremaine and Horace Harkness to secure Life Support Central, and third squad was on its way to the command deck along with Hendren, Anderson McCloskey, and, of course, Brandy herself.

Bethany Clark and Third Platoon were still aboard *Prince Adrian*, skinsuited and ready to go in the second pinnace in case they were needed.

"Marine One, Marine Two-One," Gillespie's voice came over Brandy's earbug.

"One," Hendren acknowledged. "Go, Two."

"We're in Power Central, Sir," Gillespie reported. "The Peep power crew chief is walking Lieutenant O'Brien through the control panels now. From the Lieutenant's expression, I think he's getting the straight skinny."

"Copy your arrival," Hendren said. "Any sign of security types?"

"No, Sir." Gillespie didn't sound entirely happy about that, Brandy noticed. "Haven't seen hide nor hair of them."

"Understood. Stay on your toes, Isaiah."

"Wilco that, Sir! Two-One, clear."

Brandy couldn't see the captain's expression, but from the set of his shoulders, she was willing to bet he was frowning. She picked up her own pace until she was walking beside him, and he glanced down at her.

He *was* frowning, she saw. It wasn't all that *much* of a frown, but still...

"Yes?" he cocked his helmeted head.

"I hadn't really thought about the fact that we haven't seen any of their security personnel," she said quietly. "That seems...a little strange to me."

"Only a little?" Hendren snorted. "Everything we've seen about the Peeps since the Harris assassination says they've been beefing up their security forces, not just aboard warships but for every other imaginable base and outpost. Given this place's size, they ought to have at least a couple of platoons of StateSec goons to ride herd on everybody's political reliability."

"Apparently, Rummo doesn't have one," Brandy said.

"He doesn't?" the Marine sounded surprised.

"Nope. Surprised me, too, Clint. I would have expected their 'commissioner' to be hovering in the background when Citizen Captain Rummo surrendered, but there was no sign of one."

"There wasn't?" Hendren frowned. "I didn't see any of the com traffic," he added. "I should have figured something was odd when Captain McKeon told me Rummo would be the one surrendering the platform to us." His frown deepened.

"Do you think they're planning something?" Brandy was pleased her voice sounded so level, but she felt her eyes flit around the passage, and their escort no longer seemed quite so ostentatious.

"I think they'd be incredibly stupid if they were," Hendren replied grimly. "Unfortunately, nobody issues any guarantees that the people on the other side *won't* be incredibly stupid. So far the platform maps they've provided seem to be a hundred percent accurate, and Rummo's boat bay people and now Engineering seem to be cooperating exactly the way he promised they would. So he sure looks like someone who's minding his manners, but I don't know..." He shook his head. "It's just like I've got this itch I can't scratch."

"Lieutenant Bolgeo?" another voice said in her earbug, and she raised one hand at Hendren, index finger extended in a "hold that thought" gesture.

"Yes, Scotty?"

"The Senior Chief and I are in Life Support Central, Ma'am."

"Any problems?"

"No, Ma'am, but it's a little weird. Life Support was unmanned when we got here. Not a soul in sight."

"Really?" She glanced back up at Hendren. "Scotty says Life Support was unmanned when he got there."

The Marine nodded.

"We're a little concerned over the fact that we haven't seen any of the base's security personnel yet," she told Tremaine. "May be nothing, but keep your eyes open."

"Gunny Babcock's already watching our backs, Ma'am. But we'll keep our own eyes on things, too."

"Good. Back to you later."

"How unusual would it be for that station to be unmanned?" Hendren asked after a brief, thoughtful pause.

"That's hard to say. It would depend on a lot of factors, including how sophisticated the control links from Command Central are and how short on personnel they are." Brandy shrugged. "On a Manticoran platform this size, everything—Power, Environmental, all of it—would be controlled from the command deck, so there wouldn't *have* to be any operators physically on station. Not for routine ops, at least. But we'd have at least someone physically monitoring on-site, just in case. Even today, the human eye and brain are still about the best safety and servicing system around. And the Peeps tend to be more manpower intensive than we are, because their system reliability's lower."

"So there ought to have been someone on Life Support?"

"I'd say yes. Probably." She grimaced. "I have no idea how their purges have affected personnel here in Slocum, though. A lot of their people in Mathias weren't what anyone might have called the sharpest styluses in the box, and Slocum's a much lower priority system than Mathias was. And given how much poorer than ours their serviceability is, I'd expect an experienced command crew to have duty watches on all the critical stations, if only for redundancy."

"An *experienced* command crew," Hendren repeated.

"Yes. But whatever they've done to their officer corps, they have hung onto the bulk of their long-term noncommissioned," she said. "As I understand it, their career noncoms have always been the real backbone of their maintenance and operational personnel. So I'm pretty sure if it was left up to *them*, they'd have had a Life Support duty watch up and running. If they don't, then presumably it's because their officers told them not to."

"Which indicates either sloppiness...or maybe that that itch of mine has a certain justification."

"I'd prefer sloppiness," Brandy said.

"So would I, Brandy."

They turned the final corner and found themselves outside the open hatch of Command Central. The first Peep Marine they'd seen stood outside the hatch. His sleeve bore the chevrons of a sergeant, and the pistol holster at his hip was conspicuously empty.

He came to attention as they saw him, although he didn't salute.

"Sergeant—I mean, Citizen Sergeant Lloyd Bigby," he said.

Hendren looked him over.

"First one of those uniforms I've seen since we came aboard, Citizen Sergeant," he said, after a moment.

"Aren't many of them around, Major. I've only got twenty-seven people, all told." Bigby shook his head. "We're basically just traffic cops."

"And there's none of those—what? State Security types—around?"

"You see any?" Bigby shook his head again.

Hendren frowned, but then he shrugged and stepped past the citizen sergeant major onto the spacious command deck.

A tall, brown haired officer in PRN uniform awaited them.

"Citizen Captain Rummo?"

"I am."

"Major Clint Hendren, Royal Marines. And this"—he indicated Brandy—"is Lieutenant Bolgeo. She's now in command of *Sigismund Able*."

"I understand." Rummo gestured around the command deck. Only a third or so of its stations were manned by the obviously skeleton bridge watch. "My people will show your people anything you need them to, Lieutenant."

"I appreciate that, Citizen Captain," Brandy replied.

"Before you do that, Citizen Captain," Hendren said, "I'm a little puzzled. You seem pretty lightly staffed, and we're getting similar reports from Life Support and Fusion One."

"And you're surprised?" Rummo shook his head. "Major, everybody aboard this platform—hell, everybody in Havenite uniform—is doing his damnedest to keep his head down. And to be brutally honest, no one wants to be accused of collaborating with your people after you finish your business here and withdraw."

"Including you, Citizen Captain?"

"*Especially* me, Major. Unfortunately, this comes with my job description, under the circumstances. Although"—he showed his teeth in something that certainly wasn't a smile—"you can bet I'm not going to 'collaborate' with you one damned bit more than I have to. My people will show you the basic hardware, but that's it. All you get." He looked Hendren in the eye. "I have family back in Nouveau Paris. Almost all of us do."

"Understood." Hendren nodded, then stepped back, positioning himself at Brandy's shoulder, and she nodded to Rummo.

"And now, Citizen Captain," she said, "please be good enough to walk me and my people through your command-and-control systems."

"Of course, Lieutenant."

✦  ✦  ✦

"I don't think Hendren's a happy camper right now, Skipper," Lev Carson said.

"And I don't think I blame him." McKeon's tone was a bit absent, but his eyes were sharp as he gazed into the main navigation display. "He's right that they seem awful light on security personnel over there. Twenty-eight Marines? None of them State Security, and the senior's a *sergeant*? With the next best thing to three thousand people to ride herd on?"

He shook his head.

"Should we put some more people onto the platform to back him up?"

"Who?" McKeon snorted and waved at the display. "All we've got is Clark's platoon, and nobody else is close enough to peel off any more Marines." He shook his head again, and Carson nodded.

The Slocum System housed a significantly larger Havenite presence than ONI had allowed for. The People's Republic had begun ramping up for its attack on the Manticoran Alliance well before

Hancock Station or Third Grayson, and it looked like Slocum's expansion had been part of that ramping-up process.

The system's current refining capacity was at least three times the intelligence types' projection. *Sigismund Alpha* was twenty percent bigger than their prewar data had suggested, and in addition to the two refineries riding Sigismund's orbit with it, an entire secondary complex—including two more dedicated refinery platforms and their own fuel-holding tanks—had been built in Slocum IV's orbit, eight and a half light-minutes farther from the primary. It wasn't complete yet—it seemed likely the intent had been to build a complete clone of *Sigismund Alpha*—but the first few modules of an additional personnel habitat had been parked around Slocum IV. For the moment, only construction workers and a skeleton force, barely large enough to operate the refineries, actually lived aboard them, and the bare-bones habitat was obviously regarded as a hardship post. The prewar planners had clearly concentrated on increasing the system's refinery capacity first, with comfortable housing for its increased workforce second on their priorities list. Or even third.

Given all of that, the refinery workers cycled between Slocum IV and Sigismund on a monthly basis. The construction workers didn't have the same opportunity, but they at least got to visit *Sigismund Alpha*'s "bright lights" occasionally.

The system's increased infrastructure made StateSec's curious absence even more puzzling, since it was clear Slocum had been more important to the People's Navy than ONI had assumed. It also meant Rear Admiral Steigert's task group had a broader volume to cover.

At the moment, Slocum IV lay almost sixteen light-minutes from Sigismund. Unlike Sigismund, it was also outside the system primary's hyper limit, but both superjovians were large enough to generate hyper limits of their own that were nearly five light-minutes deep. Steigert had opted to move her abbreviated wall-of-battle—all three dreadnoughts of it—to a solar orbit just outside the stellar hyper limit and about midway between Sigismund and Slocum IV. From that position, she could move to either of them in the unlikely event that the People's Navy should put in an appearance. Her destroyers were deployed to scouting positions, scattered around the system periphery, and she'd retained CruDiv 33.2, HMS *Magician* and HMS *Bellator*, with her dreadnoughts. HMS *Princess Stephanie*,

*Prince Adrian*'s sister ship and partner in CruDiv 33.1, had been assigned to ride herd on the Slocum IV facilities.

That left *Prince Adrian* all alone, keeping an eye on *Sigismund Alpha*. And that, in turn, meant that only Major Hendren's Marine detachment was available. Two of his three platoons were already deployed aboard the platform. Lieutenant Clark's forty-four Marines were the only reserve Hendren—and McKeon—had.

"I'd feel better if Brandy had all of Clint's people over there," the captain said, looking back down into the display again. "But Lieutenant Clark's our only mobile response force. I can't afford to send her over and get her tied down. Besides, all we have right now is Clint's 'itchiness.'" He chuckled harshly. "Not the most detailed threat assessment we've ever had, is it?"

"No, it isn't," Carson said after a moment, and grimaced. "The thing is, he's not the only one feeling a bit itchy just now, is he, Skip?"

"No. No, Lev, he's not. Not at all."

✧ ✧ ✧

Danielle Barthet swore softly, but with feeling, as she watched her displays.

She knew Citizen Captain Radeckis had thought she was paranoid, at best, when she insisted on fitting up their current hideaway in Cargo Seven. Actually, he'd probably thought it was her "terrorist" instincts coming to the fore, not that she'd cared about that.

She didn't trust the regular armed forces. For that matter, she didn't trust Citizen Sergeant Bigby and his Marines' loyalty to the Committee. She didn't really expect any recidivists to try something, but she'd also had no desire to be caught napping if that happened anyway. So she'd created her hidey-hole, with discreet taps into *Sigismund Alpha*'s internal com and surveillance systems. One of her own techs had established standalone links to the system's surveillance platforms and communications buoys without mentioning it to Citizen Captain Rummo or his personnel, as well, and all of them were tied into the three enormous crates in Cargo Seven's lowest tier of containers which had been fitted up as an emergency barracks and armory.

Her foresight had served her well when it came time to disappear, but at the moment, "disappearing" was all she'd been able to do.

"Two of their tankers are heading for the farm, Citizen Commissioner."

"I see it!" she snapped at the hapless citizen corporal manning the link to the survey platforms. She tightened her jaw for a moment, then turned her glare on Radeckis.

"I should wait till they connect to the tanks, then below the entire fucking farm!" she snarled.

"Ma'am," Radeckis began in a careful tone, "if you do that when they're moored to the tanks, it'll be—"

"A violation of the Deneb Accords. I know that." Barthet's hands fisted at her sides. "It's all a pile of steaming shit."

"I agree," Radeckis said, with less than complete honesty. "But that's the standard the Manties will be operating under."

"Oh, yeah? They're going to blow *Sigismund Alpha* out of space with their own frigging Marines onboard?"

"I don't know, Ma'am. All I know is that if they did, they'd claim they were justified under interstellar law." *And we'd all still be dead*, he very carefully did not say aloud.

"I know. I know!"

Barthet took a quick, angry turn around her cramped command center.

Half the troopers of Radeckis' StateSec company were concentrated here in Cargo Seven. The other two platoons were distributed between two additional hiding spots. Their concealment wasn't as good, but she'd managed to edit the schematics in *Sigismund Alpha*'s computers to delete the compartments in which they were stationed, so the Manties' electronic maps didn't show them. The bad news was that if something started the Manties seriously looking for them, they'd be far easier to find than her command center.

The good news was that she had the Manties vastly outnumbered. There were less than a hundred of them onboard, and they were scattered out in vulnerable packets. She was confident she could take them all, especially with the advantage of surprise, but what then?

She growled deep in her throat and her pacing redoubled.

✦ ✦ ✦

Porthos Radeckis watched Barthet striding around the compartment, and his eyes were unhappy. He had no choice about taking her orders, since his only alternative would have been a pulser dart, either from her or from a StateSec firing squad when her report reached Nouveau Paris. And, like everyone else in Slocum, he had "hostages to fortune" back home. He might've taken a chance for himself, but...

*All you can do is say "Yes, Ma'am, yes, Ma'am, three bags full, Ma'am" and try your damnedest to keep her from doing something outstandingly stupid,* he told himself, and knew it was true.

But he would have been far happier if she hadn't been one of the CRU's terrorists. The kind of terrorist who thought in terms of hostage-taking and "bargaining from a position of strength." He strongly suspected she'd already have tried something very like that if not for those Manty warships out there. In fact, it was probably what she'd had in mind from the beginning. But at least even she wasn't stupid enough to think she could face down ships-of-the-wall with pulsers and plasma rifles.

So far, at least.

✦ ✦ ✦

"Hyper footprint!"

Alistair McKeon wheeled toward Tactical.

"Multiple footprints," the sensor tech continued. "Range five-point-five-six light-minutes."

Brian Chen stood at the petty officer's shoulder, leaning forward to look at her display, and his eyes narrowed. He watched for another moment, then turned to McKeon.

"Hard to be certain from here, Skip, but it looks like a half-dozen battleships, with escorts."

"I see." McKeon folded his hands behind his back and turned to the master display as CIC updated it. It would take a while for anything more than the newcomers' impeller signatures to reach their light-speed sensors, and the data codes beside the bloodred icons strobed to indicate uncertainty about their classes and tonnages, and he waited as patiently as possible.

Some of them began to steady as CIC's confidence in its FTL data extrapolation solidified, but it took over five minutes before *all* of them steadied. They burned in the plot then, and his lips tightened as he looked at the junior-grade lieutenant sitting in for Anderson McCloskey at Communications.

"Get me Lieutenant Bolgeo and Major Hendren, Lieutenant Horne."

✦ ✦ ✦

"It'll be a few minutes yet before Admiral Steigert can confirm our numbers, given the com lag, but CIC's confidence is high," Captain McKeon's voice said in Brandy's earbug. She looked across at Clint Hendren as he listened to the same transmission. "We're looking at six battleships, five cruisers, and six destroyers. They were headed in-system, but they've cut their acceleration, at the moment. I suppose"—his tone turned very dry—"they may have spotted Admiral Steigert's dreadnoughts."

Brandy snorted. Her pulse might have been beating just a bit faster, and she felt an odd emptiness in her midsection, but she understood why the Peeps might feel a tad cautious. Steigert's *Bellerophon*-class dreadnoughts massed just under seven million tons apiece, whereas a Peep *Triumphant*-class battleship massed only about 4.5 million. That gave the newcomers a six-million-ton advantage, but each of their ships was more lightly armed, more lightly armored, with weaker sidewalls, fewer counter-missiles, less point defense, and weaker electronic countermeasures.

And no missile pods.

"If they have any sense, they'll admit they got here too late and write the trip off as a bad idea," Captain McKeon continued. "Unfortunately, we can't guarantee that's going to happen. So for right now, you need to sit tight while we find out what they're going to do. For now, I'm moving *Prince Adrian* a little farther away from the platform. I don't expect them to start chucking missiles in this direction, especially from a range like that, but they might, and I don't have the liveliest possible faith in their missiles' onboard tracking."

"Understood, Sir." Brandy was pleased her voice sounded steadier than it felt.

❖ ❖ ❖

"It's *got* to be Androcles!" People's Commissioner Barthet hissed triumphantly, eyes burning as she stared at the repeater display. It was too small to show a great deal of detail, but Radeckis felt unhappily certain she was right.

"Probably, Ma'am," he said, and she darted a withering look over her shoulder before she returned her attention to the display.

"Plug me into the com buoy," she said.

❖ ❖ ❖

"It's a pity we were too late, Citizen Commissioner," Ingunn Androcles said as CIC updated her flagship's tactical plot.

PNS *Splendor* and the other five battleships of Androcles' understrength Battle Squadron 217 coasted ballistically toward the system primary at a mere 1,410 KPS. That was the velocity they'd attained before her light-speed sensors detected the Manticoran dreadnoughts and their escorts at a three-light-minute range, just outside the Slocum hyper limit and almost directly between them and the primary. The Manties' superior stealth systems had hidden the dreadnoughts low-powered impeller wedges. Fortunately, Androcles had known about their systems superiority, which was why she'd sent a trio of recon drones ahead of her. One of them had spotted the Manties optically and pointed them out to her more powerful shipboard sensors.

It had taken a little longer to detect the pair of heavy cruisers deployed to cover Sigismund and Slocum IV, but she'd known they— or *some* Manty ships, at least—had to be there.

"What do you mean, 'too late,' Citizen Commodore?" People's Commissioner Andre Simpson's voice was frosty.

Androcles' lips tightened. She made herself study the display for another handful of seconds—until she was certain she had her expression under control—and then turned attentively to her political watchdog.

"Citizen Commissioner," she said in a calm, respectful tone, "I'm afraid it's obvious the Manties have already secured control of both *Sigismund Alpha* and Slocum IV."

"And?" Simpson frowned at her. "Your ships have more Marines than they could possibly have landed from a pair of cruisers. They'll have no choice but to surrender when you threaten to board."

"That would be true, Sir, if we could take control of the planetary orbital space." She chose not to mention that Manty dreadnoughts carried *far* larger Marine detachments than their cruisers did. It would have been less than tactful and *might* have sounded "defeatist." It also didn't matter, however. "Unfortunately, we can't do that with three ships-of-the-wall hovering in the background."

"Then engage them," Simpson said coldly. "You have twice that many battleships!"

"Each of which has perhaps a third of the combat value of one of their dreadnoughts, Sir." Androcles folded her hands tightly together behind her back. Had Simpson learned *nothing* from what had happened in places with names like Samson? "They have heavier broadsides, more active defenses, and much thicker armor than we do, Citizen Commissioner."

"Those are *Bellerophon*-class, correct?"

"That's CIC's identification, yes, Sir." Androcles kept her voice level, but her heart sank as she saw the triumphant glitter in Simpson's eyes.

"Well, I took the time to find them in the Intelligence database," the people's commissioner said, tapping his uni-link. "According to that, each of them mounts a broadside of thirty-three missiles. So they have a total of ninety-three in a single salvo, whereas your six battleships, with thirty launchers per broadside, have a salvo strength of a *hundred and eighty*. That gives us an edge of seventy-five missiles, Citizen Commodore—an advantage in 'throw weight' of over eighty percent!"

Androcles bit her tongue, but it was hard not to speak.

Two T-years ago, Citizen Commodore Ingunn Androcles had been *Commander* Ingunn Androcles, who'd never commanded anything bigger than a destroyer.

It was amazing how much difference two years could make.

Personally, she'd never bought the evidence that Admiral Parnell had had a single thing to do with the coup attempt. Of course, she'd also known that saying anything of the sort would have bought her a one-way ticket to a prison camp . . . or a firing squad. Unfortunately, she was also the daughter of Dolists and a prewar member of the Citizens Rights Party. That had made her one of the handful of "reliable" officers in the Committee of Public Safety's eyes following the "Parnell Coup."

At first, the prospect of accelerated promotion had been seductive. But that had been before she found herself pushed up first to battleship command, and then to command of an entire battleship division. No one in the entire galaxy could be more aware than she of how completely unqualified she was to command a single capital ship, even one as small as a battleship, but saying "no" to promotion just wasn't possible in the current People's Republic. Things hadn't gotten any better when they assigned Simpson as her people's commissioner. His fervor for the Committee of Public Safety was matched only by his utter and complete lack of naval experience. He was probably the only person in BatRon 217's senior command even less qualified than she was, but he didn't seem to realize that. As far as she could tell, he honestly believed that looking up ship data in an electronic file qualified him to make tactical decisions. That was bad enough. The fact that his position as her official keeper put him in a position to *dictate* tactical decisions was far, far worse.

And then she'd found herself senior officer in command—under Simpson's beady, distrustful eye, of course—of a barely understrength battleship *squadron* . . . and escorts. But at least they'd only ordered her to picket a backwater star system, guarding a strictly secondary base. She'd actually been looking forward to having time—hopefully weeks, or even months of it—to spend exercising her command, her command staff, and herself. Maybe they'd actually have long enough to become reasonably proficient at their jobs.

And now this.

"It's true we have a large numerical advantage, Sir. In shipboard launchers, at least," she made herself acknowledge. "They also have fifty percent more—and substantially more *powerful*—energy weapons than *Splendor*."

Simpson's eyes narrowed, but she continued in the same measured, reasonable tone.

"Admittedly, the difference in energy armament wouldn't be a factor in a missile engagement, and we'd have the maneuver advantage. We wouldn't have to enter energy range, unless we chose to. But their missiles are also larger than ours, with more powerful laserheads. That means each hit will do more damage, which offsets some of our numerical advantage in launchers. If you'll recall, NavInt also estimates that their missiles are more accurate than ours, which means they'll score a higher percentage of hits, as well." She kept her expression gravely respectful. "The fact that their armored protection is substantially superior to ours, and that they have much stronger active defenses, further degrades our numerical advantage. And I must also point out that we don't know if they've deployed missile pods."

She watched his eyes, saw them flicker ever so slightly, and allowed herself a cautious glimmer of hope.

"Pods may be good for only a single salvo, Citizen Commissioner," she said, "but each of them mounts ten box launchers. That means three of them would equal a *Triumphant*'s entire broadside. And the missiles they fire are even heavier and more powerful than the Manties' standard capital ship missiles."

Simpson looked unhappy, but he also nodded slowly, and she let that glimmer burn a little brighter.

"Those are, unfortunately, reasonable points, Citizen Commodore," he said. "I still think that we should—"

"Excuse me, Citizen Commissioner. Citizen Commodore."

Androcles turned her head and raised one eyebrow at Citizen Lieutenant Hatcher, her communications officer.

"Yes, Ed?"

"I apologize for interrupting, but we've just received a message. It's a burst transmission from Citizen Commissioner Barthet."

◊　✧　✧

"The Peeps are actually maneuvering to engage, Skipper," Lieutenant Commander Chen said.

"You're kidding." Alistair McKeon held up one hand, pausing his com conversation with Commander Carson.

"No, Sir. They've just started accelerating toward Admiral Steigert. Five-Three-Zero gravities."

McKeon looked at the master plot, and his frown deepened as he realized Chen was right. The Havenite battleships were accelerating toward Battle Division 17.2. That was either remarkably gutsy or remarkably stupid.

Or both.

At the moment, they were still three light-minutes from Rear Admiral Steigert. Effective missile range against a maneuvering target was only about 6.8 million kilometers, so they'd have to close the gap by at least two light-minutes before they could engage, which would take thirty-four minutes at their current acceleration.

The question was why they were doing something so . . . unwise.

Of course, if the Peeps could close to missile range and launch at half-power settings, they'd be inside Steigert's reaction cycle when they did. Flight time would be only three minutes, a minute and a half less than her minimum time to hyper out. But only their first salvo could reach Steigert's ships before they vanished into hyper, and initial salvos were notoriously less accurate than follow-up launches. So unless she chose to stand and fight, they were unlikely to inflict any significant damage. And if she *did* choose to stand and fight, a missile duel between six battleships and three dreadnoughts, each with eight missile pods on tow, would be a very unpleasant experience for the Peeps. Unless...

"You know," he said slowly, "there may just be a method to their madness. They may hope that if they close to the very edge of the missile envelope, they'll get inside the Admiral's hyper cycle. They might be figuring on launching and then immediately translating out themselves, on the theory that even blind fire would score *some* damage. And if they could entice her into flushing the pods *before* they hypered out..."

"Not going to happen, Skip," Chen objected. "The Admiral's too smart for that."

"Yeah." McKeon nodded. "But they can't know that unless they try, now can they? And if she doesn't bite, all they really lose is a little time and, maybe, the missiles they flung at her hoping to draw a response." He shrugged. "Makes sense to at least see if they can convince her to do something dumb, doesn't it?"

✧  ✧  ✧

"We sure about this, Citizen Lieutenant?"

Citizen Sergeant Jean-Luc Demaret's voice was very, very quiet, almost inaudible in Citizen Lieutenant Désiré Fresnel's ear. He and the citizen lieutenant crouched side-by-side, just inside the innocuous panel that concealed access to what had once been a storage compartment for maintenance spares.

"I thought the Citizen Captain was pretty clear, Citizen Sergeant," Fresnel replied in an equally low voice, turning her head to look at him. "Was there some part of it you didn't understand?"

Demaret looked back at her levelly, and her nostrils flared.

They wore armored skinsuits, like everyone else in the compartment, but their helmet visors were raised so they could speak to each other without using their coms. There were several reasons for that, including the fact that they'd been ordered to keep transmissions to a minimum as a security measure. The chance of the Manties detecting such low-powered, short-range transmissions from inside a shielded compartment was essentially nonexistent, but

Citizen Commissioner Barthet had decided her Omega contingency posts had to be linked for wired communications anyway. Demaret thought that was a bit excessive, but neither he nor his citizen lieutenant had objected to avoiding their coms just in case. Especially since all com traffic was automatically recorded. It would be unwise to say anything for the record that might suggest a lack of fervor, especially in the face of imminent combat operations.

And neither of them wanted to involve the platoon's forty other troopers in the conversation.

"I'm just thinking it might be better to wait a little longer, Citizen Lieutenant," the citizen sergeant said after a moment. "Once we pop the hatch, it's gonna be kinda hard to disappear again, if we need to."

"I understand that." Fresnel's voice was still low, but her *tone* was much sharper. "But if we're going to be in position when the ball drops, we need to start moving before it does."

"That's assuming the ball *does* drop, Citizen Lieutenant. If it doesn't, then—"

Demaret shrugged and Fresnel half-glared at him. Mostly, he suspected, because she agreed with what he was saying.

Unfortunately, their hide was inconveniently placed relative to their assigned objective. They knew where the Manties were; the problem was that they had to cover over thirty meters just to reach the lift shaft, which they would then have to take one deck down to reach their target. And when they got there, the Manties would have a clear field of fire down an arrow-straight twenty-five-meter approach corridor. Trying to cover that distance against the fire of modern weapons in the hands of Royal Manticoran Marines would be a losing proposition.

Conversely, they could head forty meters in the opposite direction, crack the hatch on a service access shaft, and come directly at Life Support Central through the shaft. The problem there was the shaft's dimensions. They'd have to stack on the ladder between decks, and they'd be able to come at the Manties only one at a time through the hatch at its other end.

Neither proposition was attractive, but Demaret understood Fresnel's thinking. If the order to execute the attack came through— and Citizen Captain Radeckis had made it pretty clear Citizen Commissioner Barthet was *going* to give it—the less distance they had to cover before the Manties could react, the better. Especially since they would be only one of multiple attacks, any one of which could jump the gun and alert the Manties before the other attacks rolled in.

But, of course, the same thing could happen if one of the attack forces—like, say, their own—was spotted moving into position early.

The whole plan was way too complex, Demaret thought in disgust. Especially for something that was basically an improvisation. And even more especially given the presence of Manty ships-of-the-wall. Citizen Captain Radeckis had been just a little vague for his taste on exactly how those capital ships would be neutralized.

"Look, Jean-Luc," Fresnel said, "I don't think this is a great idea, either. I think it's just the best of the crappy ones available to us. And because you're the citizen sergeant and I'm the citizen *lieutenant*, I'm the one who has to make the call on how we do it."

"Yes, Citizen Lieutenant." Demaret nodded. One thing about Fresnel, she never waffled. That made up for a lot.

✧ ✧ ✧

"Marine Four, Marine Two-One. Coms check."

"Marine Two-One, Marine Four," Iris Babcock replied. "Read you five-by-five, Lieutenant Gillespie."

"Good to know, Gunny," Isaiah Gillespie said dryly. "Your voice is always such a comfort to me."

"What I'm here for, LT," Sergeant Major Babcock replied with a grin. Gillespie was one of her favorite junior officers, although she would never have admitted it, even under torture.

"Marine Four, Marine One-One," another voice said in her earbug as Jeremiah Dimitrieas checked in. "Coms check."

"One-One, Marine Four reads five-by-five."

"Five-by-five this end, too, Gunny. One-One, clear."

"Still good, Gunny?"

Babcock looked over her shoulder and smiled at Lieutenant Tremaine. He, too, had always been one of her favorite junior officers, even if he was Navy, and despite the fact that he'd come equipped with Horace Harkness. That had definitely not been an entry in the plus column the first time they met.

"Yes, Sir." She shrugged slightly. "Everything on the green, as far as I can tell. What about the Navy's end?"

"Well, that's an interesting question," Tremaine said. He and Horace Harkness sat in comfortable chairs at Life Support Central's primary board, watching the displays, but the lieutenant had plugged a smaller display into the station-to-ship net *Prince Adrian* had established so he could watch a tiny version of the cruiser's main plot. "Off the top of my head, though, this looks like a losing proposition for the Peeps."

The Peep battleships had been accelerating for just under an hour. They'd traveled almost 3.85 million kilometers, and their velocity relative to Battle Division 17.2 was up to 5,329 KPS. That was still less than halfway to any possible launch point, but they certainly looked like they meant business.

"I'm just fine with idiots running the show on the other side, Sir," Babcock said. She moved up to stand between him and Harkness, where she could see the same display. "Matter of fact, I prefer it."

"Me, too," Harkness said, but there was something a little odd about his tone, and she looked down at him with a raised eyebrow.

"Few months ago, I'd'a been assuming they were idiots," the senior chief said. "After Nightingale, not so much. I mean, maybe this guy *is* gonna screw the pooch, but maybe he's not, too. Maybe there's something going on we just don't know about. Yet."

"Point." Babcock nodded. "But you don't think that's what's happening here, right?"

"I dunno." Harkness grimaced. "Sure doesn't look like it, but I think that might be part of my problem. This is so goddamned dumb part of me keeps thinking there has to be a trick. Something we're just not seeing. And if there is, it's really gonna suck if we walk in all fat, dumb, and happy."

"Actually, it's not completely pointless," Tremaine said. "I've run the generator cycle times. If they start their translation clock and launch their first salvo the instant they enter powered-missile range of the Admiral, they can get off nine broadsides before they hyper out. That'd be a total of two hundred and seventy birds per battleship, and she's got five of 'em, so call it thirteen hundred total. That's a lot of missiles."

"Yes, sir." Harkness nodded. "But in that same window, Admiral Steigert could get off *ten* salvos. That's three hundred per ship just from her internal launchers, so call it nine hundred there, plus whatever pods she's got deployed. And her point defense and ECM's a *hell* of a lot better than anything the Peeps have!"

"Yes, they are. But if the Peeps time it just right, they'll translate out about seventeen seconds before their fire reaches BatDiv Three-Oh-Three . . . or Admiral Steigert's fire reaches *them*. And it'll take the *Bellerophons* a minute and a half longer to translate." Tremaine shook his head. "Even if Admiral Steigert starts her translation clock the instant they enter range, she'll have to take four of their salvos and they won't have to take *any* of hers. They'll lose the control links to even the first salvo early, so their accuracy will suck vacuum, but even blind fire's likely to score *some* hits, and they wouldn't take any from us."

Harkness and Babcock looked at him.

"Gee, thanks, Lieutenant," the Marine said after a moment. "And here I thought this vacuum head"—she twitched a sideways nod at Harkness—"knew what he was talking about. For once."

"Yeah, thanks for making me look so bad in front of the Gunny, Sir," Harkness added with a grin.

"Well," Tremaine said in a rallying sort of tone, "all of that assumes the Peeps are as smart as me, and we all know how unlikely *that* is!" He smiled as both noncoms chuckled. "And it *also* assumes Admiral Steigert wasn't smart enough to work out the same math *I* just did. And frankly"—his smile turned into something much colder and harder—"that's one hell of a lot less likely."

✦  ✦  ✦

Citizen Commodore Androcles tipped back in her command chair, elbows on the armrests, her raised hands folded while she tapped her chin with her index fingers.

*God, this is stupid*, she thought. *Oh, I suppose it* might *work, if that Manty over there is as stupid as my own damned "people's commissioners." What are the odds of having three people* that *stupid in a single star system, though?*

She didn't know, but they had to be pretty low.

It wouldn't be the first time since the Parnell Coup that she'd seen lives thrown away by incompetent amateurs so utterly clueless they thought they were brilliant. It was just the first time she'd been cast for a starring role in the debacle.

At least the ops plan she'd sold to Simpson, coupled with her battleships' higher acceleration rate and lower generator cycle times, meant it wasn't outright suicidal on *her* part.

She just didn't like to think about how many people were likely to die aboard *Sigismund Alpha* in the next hour or so.

The tankers which had been in company with the Manty dreadnoughts had disappeared into hyper, which was wise of them. Manty fleet train units carried at least rudimentary point defense and ECM, but no one would ever mistake them for regular warships. They had no business anywhere missiles might be flying, and they could always come back once the dust settled.

She watched the plot while the kilometers fell astern and wondered what the Manty admiral thought she and her ships were doing.

She hid a frown of disgust behind a carefully attentive expression. The burst transmission from Barthet had come at the worst possible moment. She'd had Simpson *almost* convinced, and then Barthet had chimed in.

The entire idea was ludicrous. Even assuming Barthet's StateSec goons could take *Sigismund Alpha* away from what sounded like at least two complete platoons of Royal Manticoran Marines, it would accomplish exactly nothing unless Androcles' own command was able to at least drive off those Manty dreadnoughts. First, there was no way in hell she would have backed StateSec against Manty Marines. StateSec was a bunch of head-bashing goons, and Manticoran Marines would eat them for breakfast. Second, there was equally no way in hell her battleships were going to defeat three *Bellerophon*-class dreadnoughts. She knew that; Citizen Captain Taylor, *Splendor's* CO, knew that; and she was pretty sure that if Citizen Captain Rummo had known what was going on, *he* would have known that. Unfortunately, none of them could tell Barthet and Simpson to shove it up their asses.

They'd received three more burst transmissions from Barthet. Obviously, they couldn't reply without the Manties wondering just who her ships were talking to. That only made things worse, since she couldn't ask any questions whose answers might have convinced Simpson Barthet was a frigging lunatic. She'd wanted to point out that there was no reason the Manty admiral couldn't simply blow away the system's infrastructure and leave, if Androcles made herself too annoying. It wouldn't take a lot of missiles. In fact, it would take about one per orbital platform, since they couldn't dodge and had exactly zero in the way of point defense. The range wouldn't matter under those circumstances, either. Unfortunately, the other people's commissioner had actually convinced him her people could retake *Sigismund Alpha*, which would turn the Manty boarders into human shields—hostages—against that sort of parting shot. The three tankers which had already moored to the tank farm would do the same thing for the refineries. The Manties couldn't take the platforms out with missiles without destroying their own ships . . . and if the tankers tried to disengage, *Barthet* would blow the tanks and destroy them before they could.

*I wonder how much of it is that* Simpson's *afraid of being made an example for "defeatism" if he doesn't go along with her?*

The thought made Androcles feel a trace—a very, very *tiny* trace—of sympathy for her StateSec keeper. Technically, he was senior to Danielle Barthet, but that wouldn't save him if somebody back in Nouveau Paris decided he'd shown too little élan in the People's service.

✦　✦　✦

Citizen Corporal Gwen Lawrence eased her way cautiously along the maintenance access trunk. It was a tight fit with the plasma carbine slung from her shoulder, and she wished she'd been able to armor-up properly. But Havenite battle armor was bulky. In fact, it was slightly bulkier than the Manty equivalent. There was no way she and the five troopers behind her could have squeezed their armor into a space this small. And those same constricted quarters were why she had a plasma carbine instead of a plasma *rifle*.

That made her just a bit nervous about what she was supposed to do when the balloon went up, because the Manty she was supposed to take out *was* in battle armor.

*Won't matter if you surprise the bastard*, she told herself firmly.

By this time, the Manties had to be convinced they had the situation under control. If any of *Sigismund Alpha*'s personnel had dared to cross the people's commissioner, the Manties would have torn *Sigismund Alpha* apart until they found the State Security hideouts. So unless something went wrong in a big way, she should have surprise, and not even Manticoran battle armor could handle a direct hit from a plasma carbine.

Probably.

✦　✦　✦

"Whoa," Corporal Montoya murmured. "What do we have here?"

"What'cha got, Timmy?" Corporal Handley, his teammate, asked over the com from her position on the far side of the central lift core.

"Don't know," Montoya replied. "Probably nothing, but the Gamma block motion sensors say there's movement."

"What kind of movement?" Handley's voice was sharper in Montoya's earbug.

"*Movement* movement," Montoya said. "That's all I've got so far. Hold one while I check."

"Roger."

✧   ✧   ✧

Lawrence swore under her breath. She'd meant to ease the access hatch no more than a centimeter or so, just enough to slip the camera snake through and take a look, but poor maintenance had caught up with her. Instead of swinging smoothly, one of the hinges had stuck and refused to move. She'd been forced to apply more muscle than she'd wanted to, and when the hinge finally gave, she'd lost her grip.

She'd just leaned out into the corridor, reaching to recapture it and pull it shut once more when something made her glance up.

She never had a chance to figure out what that "something" might have been.

✧   ✧   ✧

"All Marines this net, Marine One-Delta-Three. Bandit. Repeat, Bandit!"

Clint Hendren twitched as Corporal Montoya's voice came over his earbug. A sudden strobing icon on his display showed him Montoya's position, three decks down from Command Central.

"One-Delta-Three has engaged," Montoya continued. "Bandit down. Repeat, one Bandit down. In armored skinny with plasma rifle. StateSec—I repeat, *State Security*—insignia!"

The high, shrill whine of a tribarrel on full auto came over the com. Montoya's visor must be up for him to hear that, a corner of Hendren's brain thought.

"*Multiple* bandits!" Montoya said. "I have multiple bandits! Looks like they're using a service conduit!"

"All Marines this net, Marine One," Hendren cut in. "Case Hotel. Repeat, Hotel. The ball is in play!"

✧   ✧   ✧

"Oh, shit!" Citizen Captain Radeckis snarled as Citizen Corporal Lawrence's icon turned crimson on his master display. An instant later, three other icons from her six-trooper squad did the same thing.

That display showed the central portion of *Sigismund Alpha*, all of its corridors and access routes, plus lift shafts, blast doors, and emergency airlocks. He didn't know what had gone wrong, but it was way too early.

"What is it? What happened?!" Barthet demanded.

"I don't know. I just lost four of my people."

"To the Manties?"

"I don't know what else could've happened." Radeckis glared at the display. "But the bastards know we're here now!"

"Tell your people to attack!" Barthet snapped.

"They're not in position!" Radeckis protested, but it was pure reflex. At least two teams from Citizen Lieutenant Castaneda's platoon were already moving on their own. "Half my people just began moving two minutes ago," he said. "They're still at least ten minutes from their jump-off points!"

"We don't *have* ten minutes! Tell them—*now*." Barthet glared at him, then turned to the com tech. "Burst transmission to Citizen Commodore Androcles and People's Commissioner Simpson!"

✦ ✦ ✦

"Oh, shit, Ma'am—I mean Citizen Lieutenant!" Citizen Sergeant Demaret looked up at Citizen Lieutenant Fresnel. "It's a go—*now*!"

"What?!" Fresnel stared at him. "Why? What happened?"

"No idea." Demaret unslung his pulse rifle with one hand while he closed his visor with the other. "But whatever it is, it's not good."

Fresnel barked a harsh laugh of agreement and reached for her own rifle.

"All right, people! Let's hit these bastards!"

Demaret kicked the concealing panel aside. It clattered across the passage floor, and the citizen sergeant vaulted over it. The rest of Fresnel's platoon, minus the six troopers she'd sent off to the access shaft, followed him, and boots pounded the deck as they charged for the lift shaft.

✦ ✦ ✦

"All Marines this net, Marine One. Case Hotel. Repeat, H—"

That was all Private Callie Owens, Manticoran Marine Corps, had time to hear before the plasma charge struck her squarely in the back. Not even her battle armor could take that kind of damage. She was dead before she hit the deck.

Corporal Trent Mehta was still turning in her direction when the trio of StateSec troopers—all of them in battle armor, in this case—came up the passage at him.

"Bandits! Marine One-Echo-Two! Engagi—"

His heavy tribarrel whined, and two of the Havenites went down.

The third StateSec trooper's plasma rifle blew straight through his breastplate.

✦ ✦ ✦

"Case Hotel!" Sergeant Major Babcock snapped. "Meadors, Brownback, Tremblay—on the door!"

She and Sergeant Quan had walked Quan's squad through their contingency plans as soon they arrived in Life Support Central, and First Section knew exactly what it was supposed to do. Private Liam Meadors tossed a pair of remote sensors into the passageway, rolling one of them each direction, then went prone at the base of the open hatch. Privates Brownback and Tremblay knelt on either side of him, covering the access passage in both directions. Lance Corporal Drinkman, First Section's grenadier, stood to Tremblay's left, his back against the wall, grenade launcher muzzle raised, waiting for one of the riflemen to call on his support, and Private Stuart, the section's plasma gunner, cradled his long, heavy weapon to Brownback's right.

The squad's second section spread out on either side of the door, ready to reinforce or replace casualties.

"Well, *this* ain't good," Horace Harkness muttered.

"Y'*think*?" Babcock snarled at him, and both of them looked at Tremaine.

"For now, we just hold what we've got," he told them.

✦ ✦ ✦

Two more of Jeremiah Dimitrieas' teams went off the net as abruptly as Corporal Mehta's, and access to *Sigismund Alpha*'s central lift shafts on Decks Five and Seven went with them. The two-Marine team on Deck Six tossed a grenade into the outboard shaft to disable it and settled into its preselected position to cover the *inboard* shaft. Nobody would be getting off on their floor, which meant no one could come at Power One that way.

The team watching Cargo Dock Two found itself under sudden attack by skinsuited StateSec plasma gunners who'd overridden the automatic alarms on two of the emergency airlocks to come at them from behind. One of the Manticorans died almost instantly. Her teammate bellied down behind a moored cargo sled and returned fire desperately.

The teams on the other cargo docks, alerted in time, were waiting when Citizen Captain Radeckis' troopers came at them.

As it happened, even Ingunn Androcles' more pessimistic assessment of the relative lethality of the Office of State Security and the Royal Manticoran Marine Corps had been wildly optimistic.

✦ ✦ ✦

Brandy watched Clint Hendren respond to the sudden, unexpected onslaught. His voice was sharp, tense, but if there was anything remotely like panic in it, she couldn't hear it. And while she was the officer in command, she was far too smart to joggle his elbow at a moment like this. So she stalked across the spacious compartment to Citizen Captain Rummo instead.

The Havenite platform commander and the half dozen of his personnel present in Command Central knelt at one end of the compartment now, hands clasped on their heads under the angry, watchful eyes of two Marines. She stopped in front of Rummo, glaring down at him.

"No StateSec, was it?" She half-spat the words.

"I never said that," Rummo replied, meeting her furious gaze levelly. "And neither did Citizen Sergeant Bigby." He twitched his head at the Marine sergeant kneeling beside him. "We just never said there *were* any State Security people on the platform. And I told you when you came aboard that no one could afford to be accused of collaborating with you people." He shrugged. "I figure worst thing that happens here is you shoot me. If I'd told you there were StateSec troopers on this platform, they'd have shot my entire family. So you tell me, Lieutenant. What would *you* have done?"

"How many of them are there?" Brandy demanded.

"You've got everything you're getting from me, Lieutenant." Rummo's eyes never wavered. "If that's not enough, you'd best go ahead and shoot now."

She glared at him, sorely tempted to do just that, then made herself turn away. Hendren looked up as she stalked back across the deck to him like an angry treecat.

"Well, the good news is Jeremiah's got the boat bay locked down and they aren't getting into it," the Marine said.

"And why do I think that if there's good news, there has to be *bad* news, too?" Brandy asked.

"Because he's not getting back aboard the platform anytime soon." Hendren grimaced. "They've got too much firepower in the access passages. And he's lost over half his dispersed teams. He's sending PO Brixton and the pinnace out to do what they can to support his people on the cargo docks, but he can't afford to send any of his own people along with them. So at least until Beth can get here from the ship, they're on their own. Those I've got left."

Brandy heard the pain in his voice and laid a hand on his forearm.

"It looks like something went wrong with their timing, though," the Marine continued in a deliberately brisk tone. "They shouldn't have hit the boat bay in isolation that way. This whole thing is really, really stupid, but I'm guessing they thought they'd have the advantage of surprise. Except that *this*"—he waved around the control room—"should have been their priority target, the very first thing they hit." He shook his head. "It looks to me like they were still getting to their jump-off positions when Montoya spotted them, although I don't know what kind of tactical genius might've thought they could get into position *without* somebody being spotted. Or what they think Rear Admiral Steigert will do if they manage to pull this off, either. But"—he inhaled sharply—"that's not our problem. Kicking their asses is."

"I can get behind that," Brandy said, and he flashed her a tight smile.

"They haven't hit Life Support yet, and I don't think they can get to Power One past Jeremiah's people on Deck Six. Plus O'Brien has Wright's squad for cover even if they get that far. But I imagine *we'll* be seeing them sometime soon."

He showed his teeth, then turned to Lance Corporal Fitzhugh and waved at Command Central's hatch.

"Go, Ezra," he said, and the lance corporal snatched up a heavy rucksack and headed for the access passage with Private Chornovil.

Brandy raised an eyebrow, then stepped to the hatch and leaned out, watching as Fitzhugh dove into the rucksack and tossed Chornovil half a dozen fourteen-centimeter discs. They were about four centimeters thick.

"You've got the inboard side," he said.

"Gotcha," Chornovil said, and headed toward the central lift shafts.

Fitzhugh watched her go, then turned and trotted in the opposite direction.

✧ ✧ ✧

"Movement on sensor one!" Sergeant Major Babcock announced without looking up from the handheld display.

"Got it, Gunny," Colin Brownback replied, shouldering his pulse rifle as the lift shaft doors slid open. They were slower than usual, their motion uneven. "They're using the shaft but not the lift cars," he said. "Looks like they're opening the shaft doors by hand."

"*Some* brains on the other side, anyway. Damn it," Corporal Drinkman muttered.

The doors opened fully, and something—*several* somethings, actually—sailed through them, obviously thrown by people still below deck level in the shaft.

"Grenades!" Brownback's voice was sharp, and the Marines pressed themselves more firmly against the bulkheads.

The grenades bounced down the passage. Some of them, at least, were flash-bangs and erupted in blinding bursts of light and concussive shock. The searing flash was disorienting—or would have been if anyone had been looking at them—but the thunderous concussions had little effect on Marines in armored skinsuits. Others were aerosol grenades, and a blinding "smoke," designed to be opaque to thermal sensors and laser sights, filled the passage.

✧ ✧ ✧

"*Go!*" Citizen Lieutenant Fresnel barked, and her first squad flung themselves over the lip of the lift shaft door. They hit the deck prone and rolled toward the passage's bulkheads before they came up on one knee, rifles and fléchette guns ready.

Fresnel hadn't liked using obscurants. She was supposed to take the Manties alive, and blind fire with automatic weapons wasn't conducive to accomplishing her mission objective. On the other hand, charging straight down that passage *without* covering smoke—and fire—would only get her people killed, which would also prevent her from accomplishing that. If that cost her a few dead Manties on the way in . . .

Citizen Commissioner Barthet would just have to settle for the best she could do.

"Position!" Citizen Corporal Danacek announced over the com.

"Second Squad!" Fresnel said.

Citizen Corporal Pasteur's squad rolled over the lift shaft lip, formed into an assault stick, and went forward in a crouching run. They were careful to stay in the exact center of the broad passage, tracking down the lane defined by the red lines projected onto their HUDs, while Danacek's riflemen sent pulser darts cracking past them to either side.

✦   ✦   ✦

"Now!" Iris Babcock said, still never looking up from the display.

The Peeps' covering smoke had blinded her Marines' thermal sights, but while the sensor remotes Brownback had deployed utilized the visual spectrum, when they could, they were also equipped with audio sensors. It wasn't as good as direct vision would have been, because the sound of the Peeps' boots generated a less than perfectly differentiated moving blob on her display which prevented her from picking out individual targets.

But she didn't really need to.

Meadors and Brownback swung into firing position while the supersonic darts of the Peeps' suppressive fire crackled past them. They sent their own darts howling back in reply, firing on full automatic and sweeping their muzzles across the passage. The suppressive fire ebbed abruptly, and Drinkman stepped out into the passage just long enough to send a three-round burst of antipersonnel grenades into the Peeps' faces.

Three or four darts became screaming ricochets, bouncing from the grenadier's armored skinny, and he swore unhappily as he ducked back into cover.

"Fuckers winged me!"

There was more indignation than pain in his voice, and he held up his right forearm, examining the ugly rip through the skinsuit's tough fabric. It had just caught the outside of his arm on its way through, and blood welled through the torn skinny. If it had struck him even half a centimeter to his left, he would probably have lost the arm.

"Well, next time don't stand in the middle of the fire zone unless the Gunny or I damn well *tell* you to!" Platoon Sergeant Quan snarled as he grabbed the injured arm and sprayed a bandage over the wound. "Frigging *enthusiast*."

"Hey, Sarge, I was only—"

"Shut it, Drinkman!"

✧	✧	✧

"Movement, Skipper," Private MacGregor announced. "Got movement on both sensors."

"Figures." Clint Hendren glanced at Brandy and shook his head, then returned his attention to the minicomp in his hands. "Told you we'd be high on the list."

"Wonderful." Brandy glanced down, checking the power and ammunition readings on her pulser . . . and visually confirming that she'd remembered to switch off the safety. "Sometimes being popular really sucks."

"One way to look at it." The Marine actually chuckled. "Don't know how 'popular' we'll be in the next two minutes or so, though."

"Suits me just fine," Brandy said grimly.

"Just do me a favor and don't shoot any of *our* people," he replied, never looking away from the minicomp. "Wouldn't want to say anything unflattering about Navy marksmanship, but—"

She could actually *hear* the shrug in his voice.

"You are so going to pay for that one, *Major*," she promised.

"I can hardly wait."

He sounded a bit absent that time, like a man concentrating on something else.

✧	✧	✧

Citizen Lieutenant Arsenault and Citizen Sergeant Brunel had worked carefully on their timing. The citizen lieutenant had gotten Fourth Platoon's troopers into position at both ends of the Command Central's access passageway by using the maintenance crawlways rather than the lift shafts, and he was confident—well, *pretty* confident—no one had seen them coming.

But spotted or not, he could be positive the Manties knew he was coming, damn it. When he found out who'd fucked up the timing on this, he'd—

*Time enough, Jared. Time enough for that later. For now, get your head in the damned game.*

They'd be waiting. That meant he was about to lose people. Probably a *lot* of them.

He knew that. He'd accepted it. But he was determined to lose as few of them as possible, and *that* meant getting in as quickly as he could.

Now his assault teams raced down the passage, staying close to the sides, moving as fast as they could behind a rolling, bouncing barrage of smoke and flash-bangs.

✧   ✧   ✧

"Fire in the hole!" Hendren announced as the thunder of Arsenault's covering grenades vibrated the bulkheads.

His fingertip came down, and four of the dozen directional mines Ezra Fitzhugh and Beth Chornovil had planted detonated. They'd been mag-locked to facing bulkheads in pairs, positioned to interlock their fire to maximum effect.

Their lethal cyclones of antipersonnel fléchettes sizzled across the passage in a dispersal pattern six meters wide, and the sensor remotes thoughtfully placed to cover the passage—coupled with Citizen Lieutenant Arsenault's meticulous coordination and planning—allowed Clint Hendren to time the detonations perfectly.

Twenty-three members of Fourth Platoon, Able Company, 43rd Battalion, Office of State Security, survived the explosions. Citizen Lieutenant Jared Arsenault and Citizen Sergeant Frederica Brunel were not among them.

✧   ✧   ✧

Citizen Corporal Harrelson snarled as the plasma bolt hit Citizen Private Jacobs and the incandescent fury amputated the citizen private's left arm. No one could hear someone scream through his battle armor's helmet . . . unless they happened to be on the com at the instant they were hit.

Like Jacobs.

Harrelson heard the citizen private's shriek of agony, and the bubbling wails that followed only too well. In fact, he couldn't hear anything else, and he wanted to scream at Jacobs to shut the hell up, or at least get off the tac frequencies.

He tried to see where the shot had come from without poking his own helmet up too high. They'd already lost three troopers—Jacobs made four—to the single Manty crouched behind the cargo sled. In fact, the single Manty left from *any* of the cargo docks guard posts.

There wasn't much left of that sled now, not after all the plasma fire and grenades Harrelson's section had poured into it, but there was obviously still enough, and he'd taken down both of Harrelson's drones before they got a fix on him. Damn it, where *was* the sorry-assed son of a bitch? He had to be up there somewhere!

Jacobs' wailing sobs faded into silence, and Harrelson tried not to feel grateful as the com net cleared.

"Tobias," he said into the silence, "flank left. Try to get around behind—"

HMS *Prince Adrian*'s Marine One pinnace rose silently over *Sigismund Alpha*'s curved flank.

Harrelson had a sliver of time to see it before its nose-mounted pulsers ripped him apart.

✦ ✦ ✦

"They're what?" Citizen Commodore Androcles looked at Andre Simpson.

"They're attacking now," Simpson repeated. "Something gave them away. They had to go immediately—*now*!"

"No, Citizen Commissioner," Androcles said. "They aren't attacking *now*; they attacked eight and a half minutes ago."

Simpson's jaw tightened, and Androcles managed to not roll her eyes. Even a people's commissioner should know enough to allow for transmission lag.

"Anything else from them yet?" the citizen commodore asked, turning to Citizen Lieutenant Hatcher.

"No, Citizen Commodore," the com officer replied, watching Simpson from the corner of one eye. "Not yet."

"Thank you."

Androcles looked at the plot. Her battleships were just under eighteen minutes short of her planned launch point. Closing velocity was up to 14,008 KPS and the range to the Manty wallers was down to 28,292,800 KM, but her powered missile range from that geometry was only 9,360,000.

The idiot people's commissioner—the idiot commissioner aboard *Sigismund Alpha*, that was, not the one aboard *Splendor*—had been *supposed* to hold her attack until Androcles was in position, because *both* idiot commissioners had expected the "simultaneous" attacks to break the Manties' morale when Barthet made her demands. The fact that the ships-of-the-wall wouldn't know anything was happening aboard *Sigismund Alpha* until eight minutes after it did had obviously escaped their attention.

*But it doesn't really matter,* she told herself. *Whatever Simpson and Barthet may have thought, nothing you do out here is going to affect what happens in Sigismund orbit. And you're not planning on hanging around long enough for anything that happens* there *to affect you, either.*

✦  ✦  ✦

"*Shit!*"

Désiré Fresnel pressed closer to the lift shaft wall as the grenades bounced off the yawning void's rear bulkhead. They caromed back toward the front of the shaft, hit the wall less than a meter above the outthrust flange under which she sheltered, rebounded, and detonated. Lethal fragments erupted from the explosions, ricocheting from the bulkheads like deadly, sizzling rain, and someone screamed over the com.

"Citizen Lieutenant—*Skipper*, we *have* to move!" Citizen Sergeant Demaret said, but she shook her head.

Inside, she knew Demaret was right. Her frontal attack, exactly the sort of frontal attack taught by the instructors responsible for training StateSec just as they had InSec, had been a disaster. She'd lost damned near half her platoon when she obligingly turned the passage into a kill zone.

*And that's the difference between busting terrorists or "subversives" and going up against the fucking Manty Marines,* she thought bitterly. *They weren't worried about what we were going to do to them; they were too focused on what* they *were going to do to* us. *Do to my people!*

The suppressive fire should have kept their heads down. The smoke and flash-bangs should have blinded and disoriented them. Even allowing for the protection of their skinsuits, they should have at least flinched! That was what her terrorist-hunting instructors had told her, anyway. But they hadn't, and they'd cut her first two squads to pieces. And now that frigging grenadier was dropping his grenades right into the lift shaft, and she couldn't even get to the doors to close them.

The bastard was firing blind. Fresnel had personally caught—and destroyed—two of the remotes the Manties had tried to roll into the shaft with Fourth Platoon, and Citizen Private Garrett had batted a third back down the passage with the butt of his pulse rifle. But they couldn't keep that up forever, and when the bastards finally got one of the damned things past them—

"Not yet," she grated back, staring at the moving icons on her head visor's HUD. "Ten more seconds, Jean-Luc!"

Another three-round burst of grenades scorched into the lift shaft, and she pressed her helmet against the bulkhead as they plummeted past her people and exploded somewhere below.

✧　✧　✧

"I need a remote in that shaft, Meadors," Sergeant Major Babcock said pointedly, never looking away from her handheld.

"I'm working on it, Gunny," Liam Meadors replied. "I don't know how the bastards are spotting them. Should've brought some Mark Sevens!"

"I'll make a note of that." Babcock's tone was sour, and despite the moment's tension, Horace Harkness grinned at Lieutenant Tremaine and rolled his eyes.

Tremaine shook his head reprovingly, but not without a smile of his own. The Mark Seven was designed for battlefield deployment in both airfoil and counter-grav modes. It also had a deployed wingspan of over two meters, which made it . . . contraindicated for deployment in close quarters. What they really needed was something between that and the vastly smaller Mark Three remotes Private Meadors was trying to lob into the lift shaft. The Mark Three was actually designed for static deployment. It came without airfoils *or* counter-grav, and while it was very stealthy once it was deployed, it wasn't very hard to see if someone tried to toss one past you.

"We've only got five more, Gunny," Sergeant Quan pointed out. "At the rate Liam's using 'em up—"

"Hey!" Meadors protested.

"Just saying, Liam. Just saying."

Quan chuckled and moved closer to Babcock to look over her shoulder at the display.

"Point," Babcock agreed.

✧　✧　✧

"Position!"

Citizen Corporal Dumont's voice sounded sharply in Citizen Lieutenant Fresnel's earbug.

"Go—Go!" Fresnel barked back.

✧　✧　✧

"Okay, Meadors," Babcock said. "You can try two more. Then we keep the rest in reserve. Hell"—she scowled—"we've got the passage covered, and Drinkman may already have nailed 'em all and we just don't know it yet. But until I'm sure—"

✧　✧　✧

Simon Dumont pressed the button, the breaching charge blew, and he rolled through the sudden opening with his pulse rifle already in position.

He'd been nervous about drilling the tiny hole in the service crawlway's bulkhead, but the Manties hadn't noticed, and he'd gotten the even tinier camera through it without being spotted. Despite his need for frantic haste, he'd spent several seconds studying the Manties, nailing down their positions in his mind and patching the same feed to the other five troopers of his section. They could make entry only one at a time, and they damned well needed to know where the bad guys were before they did it.

The odds for the first man in the stick sucked. Dumont knew that, but he also knew he was the best man for the job. And the time he'd spent studying Manty rank insignia had paid off.

He knew exactly where the senior Marine was. If he could take the bastard out before they realized what was happening...

✧　✧　✧

"*Iris!*"

Iris Babcock's head jerked up.

She was never certain later if it was the "CRACK!" of the breaching charge, the fist of overpressure, or the sound of her own name that did it. They all came so close together, in one shattering instant.

The handheld seemed to fall in slow motion, like an accident in microgravity, as she dropped it. Her right hand found the pistol grip of her M32 with the clean precision of almost thirty T-years' experience, and she spun toward the explosion from behind her, knees flexing into a firing crouch. But she was moving slowly—*so slowly.*

*Too slow,* something said in her brain. *Too slow this time, Iris!*

And then the shoulder slammed into her, smashing her to the deck, and she realized whose voice had shouted her name.

✧   ✧   ✧

*What the fu—?*

It was a damned *Navy* puke. That was the last person Dumont had worried about!

The sheer surprise of it distracted him. Only for an instant, less than an eyeblink in the heart of eternity, but in that tiny sliver of time, the petty officer launched himself, slammed into Dumont's target, and knocked the Marine out of the line of fire even as Dumont squeezed the trigger.

The three-round burst missed its intended mark. Dumont started to snarl as he brought the muzzle around, and that was when he discovered the other thing the Navy puke had accomplished.

✧   ✧   ✧

"*No!*"

Babcock heard herself scream as the darts meant for her ripped through Horace Harkness in a spray of blood.

The pulser in his right hand whined with lethal precision in the same heartbeat, and then he hit the deck with a horrible, limp looseness.

"*No!*" she cried again as she came up on one knee and her M32 rose. She had the opening now, and her fire ripped into it as the second StateSec trooper started through.

It was strange, a corner of her brain noticed as she tracked onto the third Peep in the stick. There was something wrong with her eyes.

✧   ✧   ✧

"No good, Citizen Lieutenant."

The voice in Fresnel's earbug was faint and fading. She couldn't even identify it.

"Tried," it said. "Sorry...tried. But we're all...dea—"

It stopped, and she blinked burning eyes.

"Time to go, Jean-Luc," she heard herself say. "Pull 'em back. We're leaving."

"But, Citizen Lieutenant—"

"No more," she said harshly. "No fucking more of my people. Not today."

✧  ✧  ✧

"Horace!" Sergeant Major Babcock ripped at Horace Harkness' skinsuit. "Don't you die! Don't you *die* on me, you miserable goddammed vacuumsucker! Don't you *dare*, goddamn you!"

She could hardly see through her tears, but she recognized the second set of hands as Scotty Tremaine went to his knees on the other side of Harkness' motionless body.

Navy skinsuits were designed to remove in panels in the case of catastrophic wounds, and Tremaine peeled away the chest section while Babcock ripped open the torn and shredded upper arm. It wasn't a Marine skinny, with armor appliqués, but it was a combat skinsuit, and it had slowed the pulser darts.

Slowed, but not stopped, and Babcock's jaw tightened as she saw the wreckage in their wake.

The left arm was . . . gone. Just gone. Two of the darts had hit it, and the upper of the two, ten centimeters below the shoulder, had simply destroyed the humerus. Nothing remained but bloody rags of flesh, and only the automatic tourniquet the skinsuit had applied just below the armpit had kept him from bleeding out already.

But the other wound, the one in his chest—

"Missed the heart," she heard Tremaine say. "Hit the lung, though."

His hands moved quickly, competently, spraying coagulant into the sucking wound, spraying a bandage to protect it, and his voice was calm. Impossibly calm. *Hatefully* calm, like an echo of *her* voice too many times before, kneeling over too many wounded, broken bodies. Keeping her head together. Doing her job. So why—

"I've got this, Gunny," the lieutenant said softly. She looked up, saw his eyes through his visor, realized she wasn't the only one crying.

"I've got this," he repeated. "See to your people."

✧  ✧  ✧

"Breaching . . . *now*!" the voice in Clint Hendren's earbug said, and fresh icons blinked on his display as Bethany Clark's First Squad blew its way through the platform's skin and dropped in behind the StateSec troopers besieging Boat Bay One.

Third Platoon had been armed up and Marine One had been spotted for launch, just in case, when all hell broke loose aboard *Sigismund Alpha*. Unfortunately, *Prince Adrian* had also been over a quarter million kilometers from the platform. Even at 4.4 KPS², the flight had eaten up eight minutes. But she was here now. Her second and third squads had already made entry through the cargo docks, and Hendren smiled thinly.

"Marine Three-One, Marine One," he said now. "Secure the boat bay, then take out the bastards on Deck Two. We're heading for the central lift shafts now. Meet us there."

"Marine One, Three-One copies. Secure the Bay, meet you at the lifts."

"And now," Captain Clint Hendren said coldly, "we have some StateSec ass to kick."

✧   ✧   ✧

"It's over, Citizen Commissioner," Citizen Captain Radeckis said quietly.

He stood behind Danielle Barthet, watching the displays.

Fresnel's brutally truncated platoon had fallen back to its original hide with less than a third of its starting personnel, but at least she was still alive. Fourth Platoon was still at almost half strength, but it had lost both its CO and its platoon sergeant. Its remnants had tried to hold the passage outside Command Central, but they'd been badly shaken and only too aware of how outclassed they were. When the Manties counterattacked out of the control room, a single squad had gone through Fourth like shit through a goose.

Second Platoon was down by a third and falling back from its abortive attempt to break through to Power One through the service access ways. Only Third Platoon, which had been tasked as Omega's reserve, remained intact, and it couldn't take the vengeful Manties long to track it down now that they knew it was here.

"No," Barthet said flatly.

"Citizen Commissioner, they *tried*," Radeckis said as gently as he could. "But—"

"It's not over!" Barthet shouted. She punched her com officer in the shoulder. "Tell Citizen Commodore Androcles we've failed to secure complete control of the platform, but that I remain confident of the final outcome."

The com officer hesitated for just a moment, and she punched him again—harder.

"Send it!" she snapped.

"Yes, Citizen Commissioner!" he said, and she turned back to Radeckis.

"The bastards haven't won yet," she said flatly. "We've still got the whip hand, as long as Androcles is out there!"

"Citizen Commissioner, she's got *battleships*, against dreadnoughts," Radeckis replied, trying to get through to her. "And for all we know, the Manties have deployed more of those damned *pods* of theirs. I'm afraid we can't count on her driving them off."

"No?"

Barthet's eyes glittered, and she smiled. It was an odd, frightening, cold-eyed sort of smile, and something tightened inside Porthos Radeckis. She looked at him for a moment, then turned back to the com officer.

"Contact the Manties," she told him. "Tell them I demand the standdown of all their personnel aboard *Sigismund Alpha*. And arm the destruct circuit for Tank Farm Two. If they're not willing to see reason, we'll just blow one of their tankers to hell and see how they—"

Her head exploded, spraying blood, bone, and tissue across the control panel. The com officer lurched to his feet, retching, as the corpse hit the deck and the blood pooled.

"I don't think so, Citizen Commissioner," Radeckis said, and synthetics whispered as he holstered his pulser. He looked down at the sudden corpse for a moment, then back up at the gagging com officer.

"Stop puking, wipe that crap off the com, and contact the Manties. I'll be damned if I get any more of our people killed for that bitch."

✧ ✧ ✧

"Well, I'm afraid that's pretty much that, Citizen Commissioner," Ingunn Androcles said.

Her battle squadron was not quite seven minutes from her planned launch point as she looked across her flag bridge at Andre Simpson.

"Nonsense!" Simpson shot back. "Citizen Commissioner Barthet's first rush may have failed, but she hasn't given up yet!"

"With all due respect, Citizen Commissioner, it doesn't matter." Androcles shook her head. "The Manties have more than enough Marines to take *Sigismund Alpha* back. They'd have enough combat strength to do that even if she hadn't lost a single soul."

"But if she threatens to—"

"Citizen Commissioner, if the situation was reversed—if you were in the Manties' position—would *you* let a threat like that stop you from doing your duty?"

Androcles held the people's commissioner's eye until Simpson's gaze fell. He shook his head.

"Of course you wouldn't," she said quietly. "And neither will the Manties. I just pray People's Commissioner Barthet's wise enough to not go through with destroying any of their ships. So far, they'll probably be willing to let her people surrender. But if she kills more of them when it's obvious she can't win . . ."

"And if we succeed in defeating the Manty navy?" Simpson asked.

"Well, in that case, the position *would* be reversed, wouldn't it?" she said and looked past him to her ops officer.

✧   ✧   ✧

"Still coming, Ma'am," Commander Powell said, and Jožefa Steigert nodded.

"The question, of course, is how long they'll *continue* coming." Her tone was almost whimsical.

"I'm not worried," Powell replied, and Steigert chuckled. A bottle of thirty-year Glenfiddich rested on the outcome of her bet with the chief of staff.

"A man of confidence, I see. You hang onto that, Adrian. I'm going to enjoy drinking your whiskey."

She watched the display for another two minutes, lips pursed, then looked at Commander Politidis.

"Send the launch code," she said.

✧   ✧   ✧

Citizen Commodore Androcles settled deeper into her command chair as the time display on PNS *Splendor*'s flag deck ticked downward.

It hadn't been easy to sell Simpson on the path of simple tactical sanity, but she'd managed it. Probably because he wasn't really suicidal.

"Launch point in fifteen seconds, Citizen Commodore," her tac officer announced.

"Astrogation, start the hyper clock in five seconds," she said.

"Aye, aye, Citizen Commodore," her staff astrogator acknowledged. "Five, four, three, two, one, Mark."

"Coming up on launch point," the tac officer said.

"Engage as specified," she said levelly.

✧  ✧  ✧

As it happened, Scotty Tremaine's analysis of Citizen Commodore Androcles' tactical options had been spot-on. He'd deduced exactly what she intended to do, and Admiral Steigert and Commander Politidis had made the same calculation, which wouldn't have surprised Androcles. The options were simple enough, just as it was painfully obvious that five battleships didn't want to engage three dreadnoughts.

The fact that she'd accelerated straight at them for over an hour, building a vector from which it would have been impossible to avoid close action in n-space, was another giveaway that she had no intention of *remaining* in n-space. But it didn't really matter that they'd figured it out.

Except for one tiny detail of which she'd been unaware.

The first broadside erupted from her ships, streaming straight for the Manties. She'd have time for eight more launches, but even if the Manties launched right this instant, their birds would still be over a million kilometers short of *Splendor* when she and her consorts banished into hyper.

"Missile launch!" Tactical barked, and Androcles nodded to herself. Of course they were launching. It was only to be—

"Missile launch at fifteen-point-six light-seconds!"

Androcles jerked upright in her command chair. That had to be wrong!

"Confirm range!" she barked.

"Confirmed, Citizen Commodore," the tac officer replied. Then swallowed hard. "Second launch detected! Time-of-flight one-zero-two seconds!"

Androcles felt the blood drain out of her face.

"*Third* launch!"

"What is it?!" People's Commissioner Simpson demanded. "What's happening, Citizen Commodore?!"

"The Manties have mousetrapped us," she said, almost absently, never looking away from the plot. Her own broadsides ripped out at twenty-second intervals, but the Manticoran salvos were launching every *ten* seconds.

"Mousetrapped?!" Simpson repeated.

"Yes. I wondered why they didn't come out to meet us. I even considered that they might have more of those damned missile pods than they had tractors, so they couldn't tow them along. But"—she smiled with no humor at all—"it didn't occur to me that they might have already deployed them half a light-minute between them and the hyper limit. Right where someone like us would sail straight into them."

"My God," Simpson whispered, his own face white as he stared at serried waves of crimson icons streaking across the plot. "*Do* something, Citizen Commodore!"

"There's nothing we *can* do," she said calmly as a fourth massive launch blossomed.

*And this is how* professionals *do it*, a corner of her mind thought as the uncaring computers updated the display.

There were a hundred and forty missiles in each of those waves. According to NavInt, the Manties' new pods had ten box launchers each. So that was fourteen pods per salvo. But if they'd had that many pods deployed, they could have fired even bigger broadsides. So why—?

*Control links*, she thought. *Thirty-three tubes in a* Bellerophon's *broadside. And—what? Eight, in a* Prince Consort's. *So assume a twenty-percent fire control redundancy and that would be about right. And ten-second intervals.*

Ten seconds. Just long enough for them to cut the control links to each salvo and update the targeting for the *next* one before it hit.

*Four salvos, five targets. That's—what? Hundred and twelve per battleship? I wonder how they allocated them?*

Thirty-three seconds later, she found out.

**HMS *Prince Adrian***
**Manticore Binary System**
**August 19, 1907 PD**

"Well, fancy meeting you here, Lieutenant. I mean, Lieutenant *Commander*," Clint Hendren said as he stepped into the lift car. He checked the destination on the control panel, nodded, and stood back with his hands clasped behind him.

"Yes," Lieutenant Commander Brandy Bolgeo said brightly. "I am your superior officer now, aren't I?"

"No, you're *senior* to me," he replied. "I, after all, am a Marine . . . Ma'am."

Brandy laughed.

They'd come a long way from that first unpleasant encounter, she thought. A long way. And too many of his Marines hadn't completed the journey with them. But they'd done their jobs. By *God*, they'd done their jobs.

The laughter faded from her eyes as she thought about all the people they'd lost. Nineteen of *Prince Adrian*'s Marines had died, and three more had been wounded, two almost as seriously as Horace Harkness. That was a sixteen percent casualty rate, but they'd have lost a hell of a lot more without Clint and Gunny Babcock.

"Actually," he said, leaning closer to her ear with a confidential tone, "a little birdie from BuPers just whispered in my ear, too."

"Oh? Really?" She looked at him.

"Yep. They're moving me when *Adrian* finally goes into the yard, of course."

"Of course."

She grimaced.

Rear Admiral Steigert's task group had arrived home two T-weeks ago, and they should all have been in yard hands by now. HMS *Memnon* and *Cyncnus* had both taken damage in what had been dubbed the Battle of Slocum, although their casualties had been thankfully light...unlike the Peeps. None of their battleships had lived to make it into hyper, and their personnel losses had been massive. Citizen Commodore Androcles had been among them, and Brandy had found herself wondering what the Peeps' final thoughts had been when she realized what she'd sailed straight into.

But the dreadnoughts' damages had required surveys, and that had backed up everything behind them, and somehow, *Prince Adrian* had lost her slot in the queue in the process. Still, BuShips had rescheduled her, in the end, and Captain McKeon would hand her over to the yard dogs—finally—in ten days. Brandy was glad. The ship needed it—she *deserved* it—and it was damned well time she got it. Yet even that had a downside. Given the current operational tempo, the one thing Alistair McKeon could completely count upon was that his tight-knit, experienced ship's company was about to be mercilessly raided and broken up for other assignments.

Brandy herself already had orders to a brand-new *Star Knight*-class heavy cruiser. HMS *Conjurer* wouldn't commission for another five T-months, though, which would at least give her time to tuck *Prince Adrian* away in HMSS *Hephaestus'* capable hands and hand off to her replacement.

And at least they'd gotten those three extra T-weeks first, she thought.

"And where are they moving you *to*?" she asked.

"Camp Edward," Clint said.

"Training duties?" Brandy stared at him, knowing how much he'd hate an assignment like that.

"Sort of." He smiled broadly. "Actually, I'll be standing up a new battalion. And the next time you see me, that 'major' won't be a courtesy promotion anymore."

"That's wonderful, Clint!" She reached out and squeezed his upper arm. "And you damned well deserve it!"

"We tried, anyway," he said in a softer tone, and she squeezed his arm again, then released it as the lift car came to a halt.

The doors slid open and they walked down the short passage toward *Prince Adrian*'s sick bay.

"And I'm telling you, Doc," an exasperated voice said, "I've got better things to do than lie around here. And I sure don't need a transfer to Bassingford!"

"Senior Chief—" Surgeon Lieutenant Ansari began.

"Will you please shut the hell up?" another voice demanded. "I swear to God. Even for a Navy puke! Do the words 'vaporized lung' mean *anything* to you? What the hell do you use for *brains*, Harkness?"

"Oh, that's rich, coming from a *Marine*." The first voice was less forceful than its norm, but it rose gamely to the challenge. "On the other hand, guess it's not too surprising you don't know what *anybody* uses for brains. Not that many of them going around in Marine Country!"

"At least our senior NCOs don't have *negative* IQs. How the hell d'you find your way around that boat bay every day without cutting your *other* arm off?"

Brandy stifled a chuckle, her eyes laughing up at Clint as they entered the ward. Surgeon Lieutenant Evelyn Ansari stood to one side with folded arms and a resigned expression. Horace Harkness—unshaven, one arm missing, his battered prizefighter's face more than a little gaunt, but very much a going concern—sat up in one of the sick bay beds while Sergeant Major Babcock stood at that bed's foot, hands on hips, glaring at him.

"Unlike *some* people, *I* know how to do my job," he retorted.

"Oh, yeah? Then how come you're the one in the body shop?" Babcock demanded, but her voice had softened, and there was an odd light in the gray eyes which had smitten generations of Marines with terror.

"Oh, I dunno." Harkness' voice was softer, too, and the corners of his mouth twitched. "Just seemed like the thing to do. Probly because I've been hanging around with too many Marines. Sort of thing a jarhead would do, now that I think about it."

Brandy shook her head. For some reason, Iris Babcock had been spending a lot of time in sick bay on the trip back to Manticore. She'd checked in conscientiously on her three wounded Marines, each time she visited. But somehow, inexplicably, she always ended up *here*, giving Harkness grief.

Harkness turned his head as they entered the ward.

"Oh. Good to see you, Ma'am—Major."

Babcock turned and came to attention.

"Sir. Ma'am," she said.

"Gunny," Clint answered for both of them, then looked at Harkness. "My God," he said. "If I'd realized what a useless, idle layabout you were that first day, I'd've really given you grief, Harkness!"

"Don't know if you want to admit that kinda prejudice with the Lieutenant standing right there, and all, Sir." Harkness grinned, reaching out with his remaining hand, and Clint shook it firmly.

"No lieutenants here, Senior Chief." He nodded at Brandy. "Just found out on the way down. Somebody's a lieutenant *commander*."

"Outstanding!" Harkness held out his hand again, and Brandy gripped it firmly.

"To what do I owe the pleasure?" the senior chief continued, looking back and forth between the visitors.

"Just thought I'd tell you that in addition to your wound stripe, you'll probably be picking up a Navy Star," Brandy said. "*I* told them you lacked the sterling character for that sort of recognition, but the Major here and the Gunny sort of insisted. So—"

She shrugged, and Harkness' eyes widened ever so briefly. Then they narrowed and darted to Babcock.

"You already know about this?" he demanded suspiciously.

"Who? Me? Recommend an award for somebody so stupid he couldn't even get out of the way of a batch of pulser darts?" Babcock shook her head, her eyes bright. "Must have me confused with somebody else, Spacer."

"Yeah, sure I do." His voice had softened, and he smiled at Babcock.

"Well, anyway, just wanted to let you know," Brandy said. "And to mention that by the time you get done regenerating and finish PT, *Conjurer* will be in service. *Competent* boat bay chiefs seem scarce just now, but I suppose I could make do with you, instead. Somehow."

"I think I'd like that, Ma'am. Unless"—he looked at Babcock again—"something else comes up in the meantime."

"Just keep it in mind, Senior Chief." Brandy patted his good shoulder and looked at Clint. "Guess I'm about done here. How about you, Major?"

"Actually, I was just looking for the Gunny," Clint replied.

"Yes, Sir?"

"When you're through here, Gunny, we've got some equipment

inventories to beat into submission." He rolled his eyes. "I can hardly wait for BuSup to start going over the paperwork."

"Oh, wonderful . . . Sir." Babcock rolled her own eyes. "I'll be along in—fifteen minutes sound about right, Sir?"

"That'll be fine, Gunny."

Clint nodded and waved for Brandy to precede him back toward the lift shafts. She gave Harkness another nod, then smiled at Babcock and led the way out of the ward.

"Couldn't get out of the way, huh?" they heard Harkness behind them. "Listen, at least I don't fall over my own two feet the way *some* people do. Not naming any names, but—"

The closing hatch cut off his voice, and Clint shook his head.

"I don't think the galaxy is ready for this," he said.

"Ready for what?" Brandy asked innocently.

"Babcock and Harkness." He shook his head again. "You know, Gunnery Sergeant Water and Senior Chief Oil? I mean, *listen* to them! There's not a single Marine anywhere in the Star Kingdom who'd believe what you and I just heard. Not *one*! Well, not outside *Prince Adrian*, anyway."

"You can't possibly be suggesting that there's anything going on between the two of them," Brandy said severely. "That would be a betrayal of . . . of *generations* of spacers and jarheads! The heart attacks would come fast and quick in the chiefs' messes. And I hate to think how your weaker, frailer Marines would handle such a seismic shock!"

"You're right. You're *right*!" Clint pursed his lips. "I don't know what I was thinking. Obviously all nonsense. Besides, it'd never work. A Marine and a navy puke? A travesty of nature!"

"Absolutely." Brandy nodded firmly as they stepped into the lift car. The door closed and she tucked one hand lightly into his elbow. "Unthinkable. A perversion of all that's right and good."

"Precisely what I was thinking."

He looked down at her, and she smiled.

"Well, now that we've got that settled, Major . . . buy a girl a cup of coffee?"

# Author's Note

As established Honorverse readers will have noted, this book takes another look at a critical period in Honor Harrington's life and the history of the Star Kingdom of Manticore's conflict with the People's Republic of Haven. In fact, it is the first volume of what we will be calling The Expanded Honorverse series: novels dealing with earlier periods in Honor's life and, for that matter, her parents' lives. There are quite a few back story corners I've always wanted to paint in.

There were several reasons I wrote it, not least the fact that I've promised people for many years that they would someday see the courtship of Sir Horace Harkness, PMV, and Sergeant Major Babcock. In addition, however, I wanted to expand the story of Lieutenant Bolgeo and Captain Hendren from the novella "Travesty of Nature" and—very badly—wanted to add her father and mother to the tale. Tim Bolgeo was one of the finest men I ever knew and one of the best friends I ever had. I hope that somewhere on the other side he's laughing hard at what I've done to him here.

In addition to those considerations, I wanted to revisit Honor's assumption of her steadholder's duties—and her loss of Paul Tankersley—from a different perspective and different viewpoints. And to underscore just how critical the months of operational time the RMN lost due to the delay of the declaration of war truly were. Without that delay, it is highly probable (I speak here as the author, you understand), that the Pierre Regime would have been toppled and the PRH defeated within the first year of fighting. To quote Clausewitz, "It is even better to act quickly and err than to hesitate until the time of action is past." The TRMN would have been unlikely to err significantly in its operations, but it was certainly delayed until the time for quick, decisive action had passed.

And, while I was at it, I took the opportunity to correct the way the Ellington and Dreyfuss protocols were laid out in *Field of Dishonor*. As I'd initially constructed them, the Ellington Protocol began at forty meters' range, the opponents advanced five paces between each exchange of shots (to a final range of twenty meters), and the duel ended only when one participant was hit or the *challenger* declared honor had been satisfied. That is, even dropping one's weapon in token of surrender didn't oblige one's opponent to stop shooting. The Dreyfus Protocol called for all shots to be exchanged at forty meters, with either party allowed to declare honor had been satisfied at any point after the first shot. When I decided I wanted Honor to fire from the hip, rather than simply surprising Summervale by hitting him with her very first aimed shot from forty meters, I revised them—in my head and in my notes—to the ones which appear in *this* book. Unfortunately, I failed to execute the change cleanly in the final manuscript, so we sort of fell between stools. I've taken this opportunity to fix that, too.

Mostly, though, I wanted the opportunity to go back and visit some of my favorite characters from Honor's world—most of whom, alas, are dead by the end of *Uncompromising Honor*—because of how much I missed them.

I hope you've enjoyed the chance to visit them again with me.